The critics praise

ADEL

unf

TELL NO MAN

"This is a highly entertaining novel with swift narrative pace, a good love story and well-realized characters, including the most fascinating heroine I've encountered in recent fiction."

—Louise Cassels, *Sacramento Bee*

"Anyone who reveals the ending to another human soul should have his reading privileges taken away from him for the next five years."

—Ruth C. Ikerman, *Los Angeles Times*

"Incredible, impossible, but strangely convincing —and I hasten to add, an achievement in literary craftsmanship . . . moves always toward the final climax that is the most startling in modern fiction."

—Dr. Daniel A. Poling, *Christian Herald*

"It's a simple story. All great stories are simple. . . . But, ah, the telling of it! The crisp, clean, reportorial style. The good, gutty plotting. And above all, the tough and tender characterizations. . . . A GREAT BOOK."

—Maxey Brooks, *Houston Post*

The byline ADELA ROGERS ST. JOHNS is known to millions of Americans who have read the author's work in magazine serials and more than two hundred short stories. Her first full-length book, Final Verdict, was published in 1962. In that bestseller, Mrs. St. Johns gives an account of her famous lawyer father's life. In her newspaper days, Mrs. St. Johns was a feature writer for the Hearst newspapers; she covered almost every big story of the mid-twentieth century and she also won acceptance on the traditional man's beat—the sports world. Mrs. St. Johns has also written for the movies.

Other Outstanding Novels in SIGNET Editions

THE LIBERATION OF LORD BYRON JONES *by Jesse Hill Ford*

The powerful bestselling novel portraying the drama behind racial conflict in a small Southern town. "A remarkable achievement"—*New York Times*. (#Q3043—95¢)

THE RECTOR OF JUSTIN *by Louis Auchincloss*

The brilliant novel portraying the controversial headmaster of a New England boy's school—a man larger than life, looked upon by some as a god, by others as the greatest of sinners. A best seller. (#T2719—75¢)

INVISIBLE MAN *by Ralph Ellison*

A novel of extraordinary power about a desperate man's search for his identity. Winner of the National Book Award. (#Q2722—95¢)

STERN *by Bruce Jay Friedman*

An incisive first novel, both funny and sad, about an introspective man who becomes obsessed with the fact that he is Jewish. (#P2349—60¢)

Adela Rogers St. Johns

TELL NO MAN

A SIGNET BOOK

Published by
THE NEW AMERICAN LIBRARY

This is an authorized reprint of a hardcover edition published by Doubleday & Company, Inc.

FOURTH PRINTING

The following page constitutes an extension of this copyright page.

Grateful acknowledgment is made to the following for copyrighted material:

BRANDT & BRANDT
Lines from "John Brown's Body" in *Selected Works of Stephen Vincent Benét*. Published by Holt, Rinehart & Winston, Inc. Copyright 1927, 1928 by Stephen Vincent Benét. Copyright © 1955 by Rosemary Carr Benét. Reprinted by permission.

HARCOURT, BRACE & WORLD, INC.
Lines from "The Rock" in *Collected Poems 1909–1962*, by T. S. Eliot. Copyright 1936 by Harcourt, Brace & World, Inc.; copyright © 1963, 1964 by T. S. Eliot. Reprinted by permission of Harcourt, Brace & World, Inc. and Faber & Faber Ltd.

NORMA MILLAY ELLIS
Lines from "The First Fig" and "To Jesus on His Birthday," from *Collected Poems* of Edna St. Vincent Millay. Harper & Row, Publishers. Copyright 1922, 1928, 1950, 1955 by Edna St. Vincent Millay and Norma Millay Ellis. Reprinted by permission.

HARPER & ROW, PUBLISHERS
Excerpts from *Divine Milieu* and *Letters of a Traveler*, by Pierre Teilhard de Chardin. Reprinted by permission.

THE MACMILLAN COMPANY
Excerpts from *The Great Divorce,* by C. S. Lewis. Reprinted by permission of The Macmillan Company and Geoffrey Bles Ltd.

MILLS MUSIC CO.
Lines from "Joan of Arc, They Are Calling You," by Alfred Bryan and Willie Weston. Copyright 1917 by Mills Music, Inc. Copyright renewed 1945. Reprinted by permission.

RANDOM HOUSE, INC.
Excerpts from *God Speaks,* by Charles Peguy, translated by Julian Green. Reprinted by permission.

ROBBINS MUSIC CORP.
Lines from "Don't Sit under the Apple Tree with Anyone Else but Me," by Lew Brown, Charlie Tobias, and Sam H. Stept. © Copyright 1942 Robbins Music Corporation, New York, N.Y. Reprinted by permission.

CHARLES SCRIBNER'S SONS
Lines from "Richard Cory," by Edwin Arlington Robinson. Reprinted by permission of Charles Scribner's Sons from *The Children of the Night,* by Edwin Arlington Robinson. (Charles Scribner's Sons, 1897.)

STEIN & DAY
Lines from *Kennedy,* by Mollie Kazan. Reprinted by permission.

SIGNET BOOKS are published by
The New American Library, Inc.,
1301 Avenue of the Americas, New York, New York 10019

PRINTED IN THE UNITED STATES OF AMERICA

I offer this tale of a young man named Hank Gavin to those greatest of all storytellers, the sportswriters who for some brief shining hours admitted me to their company.

Ring Lardner	Damon Runyon
Paul Gallico	Quentin Reynolds
Grantland Rice	Mark Kelly
Bill Corum	Harry Salsinger
Dink Templeton	Joe Williams
Arch Ward	Warren Brown

They knew all about the forty days in the wilderness. And the temptations. When felled by Fate or the double cross, as all were at one time or another, they got up off the floor without squawking and went on when they couldn't, which Dempsey calls the mark of the champion. I pray that they, some of them already in that Tavern at the end of the road where Runyon always said we'd meet again, will love Hank Gavin. I think he's their kind of guy and this is their kind of story, though it has nothing to do with sports. These were *men* who understood all kinds of men and most women. Tough of soul, gay of humor, fond of laughter but not immune to tears, kind of heart, witty of tongue, picturesque of speech, elegant of dress, knowing the grace of gratitude for life. Many had trouble with churches as such. For they were hard-boiled and skeptical. But I know they *prayed* in their struggles, triumphs, and disasters, for I was *there*. They loved and believed in Christ as the Man, a Man of God and their brother. I hope they may find this book not too unworthy of their genius and guts, and of all they taught me. I've done my best to write it with the integrity and simplicity which they beat into my head in press boxes from Madison Square Garden to the Coliseum, from the Polo Grounds to Forest Hills, from Churchill Downs to that Augusta golf course where Bobby Jones won the Grand Slam. I accept them as my severest critics by right because I am so proud to remember them as my best friends.

TELL
NO MAN

Book ONE

1

This is a true story.

As you will see, it is incumbent upon me to tell it as a novel.

I have therefore put into direct narrative things which I knew only long afterward, from separate recollections or records. I have given chronological sequence to crises and trivia, wit and woe, triumph and catastrophe. Whatever imagination has allowed me to make my living as a teller of tales has been used to fill in conversations, round out characters, employ hindsight for the reader's benefit and spotlight value. Pour people, places, times, circumstances, and backgrounds into the test tube of trained imagination, the result will be as trustworthy as any obtained in a laboratory, for I am convinced that inspired imagination, and I pray some measure has been given me for this task, is the gateway to reality.

Biographers of the stature of Catherine Drinker Bowen state that they use this method. Irving Stone, who has expanded the biographical novel into our favorite historical reading, explained to me that he believes the truth of his structure to be inevitable, if he is able to find a percentage of facts, dates, letters, lists, bills, records on which to build.

I do not conceive it to be necessary that the leading character in such a novel or biography be a famous personage, or that the scene be in some unfamiliar past. If I am right about the young man I have chosen to call Hank Gavin, this fiction-biography may contribute to history. In a few centuries, or years at our accelerated pace, if Gavin jarred the big boys of the hierarchy, if as he himself said his single, individual experiment was a success, other generations may show as much interest in what manner of man he was as we have shown in Martin Luther or Martin de Porres. A highflying, young American, the potential importance of his life to date seems to me more vital and exciting than many of the politicians, generals, poets, painters, and moneymen whose careers have rated millions of words.

Of course the rash gamble Hank Gavin took is that stuff of which melodrama is made. And I must tell it without benefit of togas, helmets, camels, or walls to fall off of, not as a costume play to believe which makes no demands on our credulity, but as a reality of our own day, time, household, and city, wearing a business suit and originals by Mainbocher and requiring of us not less than everything.

Nothing could stop Hank Gavin from trying what Chesterton said had never been tried.

A wisecrack, a sneer, an attack upon social, sexual, or intellectual vanity sometimes distorts a man's visions and these young Gavin had to meet head on. Usually, the world around him found it amusing to be brightly skeptical or kindly tolerant about almost everything. Like circus acrobats, its members rode gaily—and expertly, with one foot on the intellectual famine of the black horse in Revelation, the other on the red horse of those passions audibly possible to back-fence cats. But the moment came when his wife, she who had been Mellie Cheyne, said to him *Hank, you have to be kidding,* and this was the springboard for the attack in which they abandoned their policy of *neither hot nor cold* and attacked him with no holds barred.

Mellie was more or less my goddaughter. To her mother, my old friend Evadne D'Harcourt Cheyne, I had pointed out it wasn't fair to appoint a godmother who would be in a wheel-chair if not in her coffin by the time the child required godmothering, but this Vadne insisted was ridiculous since what with *shots* everybody was now going to live to be a hundred. I am glad I wasn't able to talk her out of it, for by the time Mellie and I drove home alone from the country club that Sunday afternoon we were on terms of communication closer than is usually possible between members of different generations. I didn't, in the beginning, know

Hank as well, though during the engagement we had gone out a couple of times to see the Chicago Cubs play, and nine innings of that can often make you better acquainted than nine years of hit or miss social meetings.

As for the other members of the cast, my tenure on Chicago papers at the time of the Leopold-Loeb case, the Roosevelt third-term convention and other news stories, plus my love for the Windy City as the real center of *America* enabled me to be more than just audience. Moreover, people unpack to a writer secrets withheld in the confessional. This remains a mystery to me, but I know it to be a fact. Whether each one feels that what he has endured or experienced is such exceptional material that it would be a crime to withhold, whether they find you more sympathetic than a friend who perhaps already knows and may have formed an opinion, or whether they are impelled by the discovery that you will *listen,* I don't know. It is impossible to bore a dedicated writer who knows that all humanity is a field of stories, and this flattery stimulates and removes all barriers. Whatever the reason, throughout the unfolding of the extraordinary story of Hank Gavin and Mellie Cheyne I was told things by the principals and the chorus, as conversation, gossip, scandalmongering, inspiration, glorification, and intense concern mounted to a fever pitch not apparent in a thousand and one years.

After our long, sterile diet of snake pits and manure piles that never admitted to grow roses we long for hope. For light. And you cannot let the darkness out, you have to let the light in. If you are reading this book now, it means I was able to convince my publishers that like a candle it might throw its beam far and *far*. For it is not the book I had contracted to write at this time.

My obsession with the story of Hank Gavin and his wife began specifically one day when I was sitting on the sand in front of a beach house on the coast of California which I have managed to keep as home for my family through the ups and downs, the go-here-go-there of a professional writer's life. I began to think about my goddaughter Mellie in some continuity. Perhaps some bosomy young creature parading her bikini nakedness against all good taste and cold economics—since a girl with one brain cell working should know that nudity can be made sacred, exclusive, or expensive instead of free-for-all, made me remember Mellie Cheyne in two pieces of a chic bathing suit, designed to protect both her privacy and her provocativeness. I thought I'd never seen a girl on this fairly fashionable beach with the style in a bathing suit of Mellie Cheyne.

Meditating upon Mellie, who had style about everything, I tried to foresee the end, which had then not transpired.

What *was* the word for Mellie?

A taxi driver, watching her walk away from us and vanish in the revolving doors of the Ambassador East, nodded emphatically and said, "Now there's a dame with *class.*"

A word I dislike, can't define, and yet no amount of book research nor discussions from beatniks to college presidents has given me one better than his. Thoroughbred? Society editors who write whole sections about those who have it, like young Mrs. Henry Angus Gavin *née* Melanie Cheyne, refer to them as The Elegants or sometimes The Arrogants. One of them at least has had her picture on the cover of *Time.* I know that to see Mellie was to know that she had a right to be entered for Kentucky's Run for the Roses. It wasn't that Mellie always wore the right clothes. The clothes she wore were right because she wore them. She could never be left out of anything because if she wasn't there it didn't happen. My grandmother had a jingle, it went *Politeness is to do and say, The kindest thing in the kindest way.* Mellie Gavin had a warm and casual kindness, an easy courtesy as remote as indifference. But there was an active ingredient. She did things for people. *Noblesse oblige,* I daresay, though I never heard her use such words. Prospective voters on her precinct worker's list found her as amiable and unaffected as a duchess bringing broth and she treated the great Narcissa Thorne herself with exactly the same naturalness. Mellie didn't have to prove anything, she felt no need to establish equality nor break the ice, since she never considered the possibility of either existing.

As I sat that later day, drowsing in the hot California sunshine, there crashed upon me a full memory sequence from the night Mellie Cheyne made her debut, as did all girls who were lucky enough to be invited and whose fathers could afford the staggering fee of the world-famous Passavant Hospital Cotillion. I had come on for this and I had total recall, as they say, of Mellie's honest *oh-dear-what-the-hell-now* expression when she saw Sheila Quaglino. Now the Social Register to those who are IN is merely a supplementary telephone directory, to those who are still OUT and want in it becomes Mount Ne Plus Ultra. In some unfortunate self-dramatization or defiance, being shoved by her father, the Quaglino girl had arrived at the cotillion point of her climb into the Social Register done up in a dress of shocking pink velvet cut almost to her belly button in front and her coccyx behind.

A hurricane of consternation swept backstage that night

when the committee which presented the cotillion to make money for the hospital glimpsed this unprecedented social error. *I told you we shouldn't have her,* Eleanor Smith hissed. To this Mrs. Charles Isaiah Martin, chairman of the selection board, said plaintively that her husband had said they daren't NOT have Sheila Quaglino. NOT with her father being so *rich* and having a finger in every *pie* in Illinois and prone to take an entire *jaw* for a *tooth.*

So there Sheila was, her body upholstered like a chrome sofa and no one with a glimmer of what to do. Except Mellie. Girl-to-girl, as it were, her face screwed into a ferocious scowl, Mellie said, "What in the world are you made up for, Sheila my pet. We're supposed to be virgins, remember? You have to have a white dress somewhere." Defiantly Sheila said, "I loathe white, I'll wear what I please—if I have it's in Winnetka," and Mellie said, *"Oh Nuts.* If you appear in what you've got on they'll put you on a bun with mustard and pickles." Her grin was sheer exasperation when she said to Mrs. Martin, "Aunt Lizzie, keep them playing 'March, March on Down the Field' or 'Hail to the Chief' or something, I've got a white dress Sheila can wear—" So Sheila, whose father could have bought and sold Dior and probably would if Dior showed signs of mismanagement, came down the famous cotillion stairs in a borrowed gown. Probably she was too overwrought to notice that in spite of its immortal Mainbocher lines the gown was a good deal worn. For it had been almost as difficult to raise Mellie's ten-thousand-dollar ante as demanded by the cotillion as it had been to get Sheila IN at all. Naturally that was a lot less than individual debuts had cost in the good old days and holding a charity ball salved the consciences of the rich and quieted the criticism of any in poverty nearby. But Francis Cheyne, the best bridge player at the Chicago Club, had lost every finesse he'd made with the diminished fortune his father had left him. His father had bid grand slams in all the wrong real estate so that now the entry fee for the Cotillion Stakes, Fillies Only, had presented a problem. As Mellie's mother said, without meaning it, we are the New Poor. To me, when we were alone, she said *Mellie can marry anybody.* Not that her mother felt Mellie should marry *for* money but it didn't occur to her that she would *want* to marry anyone *without* it.

It was characteristic of Mellie, I noted that evening, that she did not embarrass Sheila by paying any further attention to her. For very sound reasons Sheila had as many partners as she needed, almost as many as Mellie who was the belle of the ball, as we used to say, and obviously the Debutante of the Season.

In California sunshine, some years later, when I was thinking of Hank and Mellie Gavin miles away from Chicago by then but only a little way from me down the Coast, I remembered that as I pondered their incredible place and position, with pain and panic and slightly hysterical amusement, I saw in my mind's eye a series of Mellies. At ten, Mellie fighting her way home from Latin School, chin out against the wind. In her gray-and-white Chanel nurse's aid uniform, bending over a bed at the Children's Hospital with the authoritative calm of a good nanny. At the season's biggest wedding, the bishop himself officiating, when she married the catch of the town, young Henry Angus Gavin didn't have money exactly but he was making it. In time he would inherit his grandmother's pile. At her wedding I discovered for the first time that Mellie wasn't actually a beauty. At least not of the udder and adenoid school now become popular. The exquisitely simple wedding gown fell in elegance over her small, pointed breasts, her mouth was closed in firm and tender lines which turned up at the corners with a joke she was keeping secret. Not a beauty. Who needs it? Mellie would doubtless have said.

With this clear before me, I went back to find out the exact point where I must begin my story.

Probably when Mellie Gavin and I drove back to her house from the country club. Her eyes were thoughtful, then, very cool, I saw that there was a fire behind them. Could it have come as such a complete surprise to her as she indicated that day? She must have known Hank as a young man of reckless extremes, of driving impulses. A fighter. *You should have seen the silly bastard in Korea,* his best friend, Colin Rowe, had said to me soon after they got back.

Also in those early days, I was confronted in my own mind by the *WHY*.

Why Hank Gavin?

Why a swaggeringly successful young super-salesman from Chicago of all places?

Why Mellie Cheyne?

Débutante extraordinaire.

Why these two?

As Mellie herself said on first contact, *You have to be kidding!*

As I gave myself to write this book in spite of anything, I saw that I was in the grip of a high-pressure compulsion personal to me.

All my life, a life sometimes desperate, driven, worldly,

defeated, repentant, magnificent, filled with fun and love as it had been from the day my grandfather with holy simplicity read to me from that book called The Acts of the Apostles, I had been invaded by a passion for, an overpowering excitement about, a painful, always hopeless yearning toward what came to Paul on the Road to Damascus. As he, still Saul of Tarsus, led his followers to institute a St. Valentine's Day Massacre against the uncircumcised cult of a false Messiah. Saul the Avenger, Young Saul whose hands were red with the blood of those who believed in a carpenter —a laborer—from Nazareth whose name was Jesus. Saul who had ordered the stoning of his boyhood chum, Stephen, a fate beside which being mowed down with machine gun bullets is merciful indeed. A Jew of family and fortune, culture and position, Saul was also a Roman citizen and this made him a member of the Syndicate, the Establishment. When he set about exterminating this new sect called the Nazarenes, it was with premeditation as cold-blooded as Murder, Inc.

Yet to him, there and then, as the camels made their way within the circle of hills along the road to Damascus, a light shone for all to see. Such, they told afterward, as had never been seen before. A voice spoke with such love and hope as no voice has spoken to us since. So that the cruelty of Saul's being was melted. His known world, with its fabulous riches and dreadful poverty, its Roman might and fatal Jewish rebellion, its sensuous pleasures and insane ambitions, perverted sex and strange gods and unceasing wars, its tides of hatred and revenge vanished away. He was blind to it. As he knelt swaying in the dust he could see only the shining figure that was made of light itself; when this was gone to Saul all was darkness, for compared to that light what the world of human senses called light was darkness.

Why that dark and dangerous young man Saul, who had witnessed the Crucifixion from afar and indifferently despised the other young Man, ignominiously hanging on the felon's tree?

For years I had tried to assure myself I couldn't hope for it to happen here. Or now. Not in our enlightened century, our scientific age, our age of intellectualism and education. A myth. We must call it one of the many myths. Or dramatic license, like the ghost of Hamlet's father. Or an illusion.

Miracles yesterday. Miracles tomorrow. No miracles today.

Perhaps this is why I was selected to be the one to whom Hank Gavin told his story of light. An additional reason why I must tell it, without phonying it up with costumes into a Biblical charade. Certainly Hank Gavin was not, like Paul, *hot*—he was cool, noted for a sense of humor, and as custom decreed he took nothing too seriously. He wasn't *dark*, his hair was straw and he was always tanned from the golf course, but to begin with he had been fair and ruddy. *Dangerous?* Hard to say. Combat in Korea, body-contact sport on the football field, and what big city streets today are without blood and danger at all hours? Some people found it difficult to believe in Hank Gavin. Some people have difficulty believing a thing or saying they believe it. I have difficulty not believing and now I must say it. How can you not believe, having seen so much that was unbelievable come to pass before your eyes?

The painters, singers, poets—they have always managed to believe.

. . . Upon our so sore loss, shall shine the traffic of Jacob's ladder, pitched betwixt Heaven and Charing Cross . . . and lo, Christ walking on the water, not of Gennesareth but Thames— From a poet, from the past, from far other lands, not next door. . . . *Not Gennesareth but Lake Michigan . . . not Bethlehem but Winnetka . . . not Jerusalem but Beach City, California*— He's got to be kidding!

Saul-Paul? We know *him*. Hustle him out of Damascus, over the wall in a basket, shoo him into the desert. Peter who saw his Lord face-to-face will never agree that a man who only saw him later in a vision has the same power over all the power of the enemy. James will undermine and try to destroy since The Holy One came not to the Gentiles of all the world but only to followers of The Law, members of the hierarchy.

Hank? Forcrisake, we know *Hank*. Hustle him out of the lunatic fringes of the Pacific Ocean. Shoo him into the oblivion and confusion of a beach town. The dean will tolerantly laugh him to scorn with intellectual deadly doubt of his or any other vision and the Reverend I'm-so-glad-the-boys-call-me-Jack Knowles will mock him, saying with bland sufferance come come old boy we don't advocate any of this Cloud Nine nonsense in this knowledgeable age, do we?

One more thing I must add to this prologue.

Now that I find myself compelled to tell this story, no hold can be barred. This is the law of the literary jungle. I have changed names, altered some locations, invented scenes and dialogues. That is as far as I am prepared to go to protect the true story, the real characters. I am not only privileged but duty-bound to put down all I know, calculated, deduced, or was told from whatever source. To repeat some words, describe some scenes just as they were, since they cannot be replaced. To uncover, to use every secret circumstance or combination.

Every writer is without what others may call honor save that one honor, to tell the story as well as he can. Once he has accepted the assignment, no favor can be granted to his dearest friend.

Only the story itself can be honored.

I apologize to no one, not to the real Vadne Cheyne, my old school chum, not to the real Steve Retzlaff, who found out the hard way, nor to any of the bishops, no, not even to Sybil Rowe.

When Sybil Rowe told me what she knew of why her husband Colin jumped out the window that fine day, she spoke in confidence. Now I know that his suicide was a black guilt that tore Hank Gavin's heart open so that he could fall on his knees. So whether Sybil claimed the seal of the confessional can make no difference to me now. I need it. It is a piece of the truth without which I may not be able to make you believe the truth.

2

Chicago. In the spring of the year.

When I arrived at my hotel after taping Chicago's favorite TV program, the Kup Show, my phone was ringing. I was pleased to find that as usual Vadne Cheyne and I picked up where we'd left off months before. Her question sounded like the end of another conversation.

"Do you want to go to church in the morning, darling?" she said.

"It depends," I said, having found by long experimentation that churches as such can have on me the opposite effect from what is intended.

"We've got a new rector," Vadne said. "Quite hypnotic. Then we could go on to the country club for brunch, you'd see everyone in a swoop. Even Francis has a permanent bridge foursome every Sunday."

I'd known Evadne D'Harcourt before she married Francis Cheyne. I'd always been fond of her. In some ways a stupid woman, she had absorbed by osmosis a good deal of worldly wisdom and she had some intuitive feel about people. By her standards, she lived a good life. As long as a woman lived under the same roof with a man, whether he kept it over her head or she over his, she also kept her mouth shut about his faults or failures. This was difficult for Vadne who was by nature a prattler. During the years of Chicago's most fantastic growth, any man with the Cheyne name could have restored the family opulence. If to this opportunity Francis was at once superior and inadequate, nobody heard of it from his wife. Or his daughter Melanie, though I think they both knew it was his pride that kept him from entering the hot competition. Evadne had been a butterfly beauty, and after her marriage she had come up with a definite gift. There are people who can raise money for charity, political campaigns, Olympic teams, new wings on old buildings or new buildings, for scholarships and grants. Faintly ironic it seemed to me that Vadne Cheyne, so often skimping for cash on those aristocratic social heights where she had been born and married and dwelt, could come out of Joe Quaglino's office with fifty thousand dollars for a Protestant hospital, or call on a leading industrialist and get a check for her Republican candidate equal to the one he'd given the Democrats. Society, the one with the capital S which still rates more pages in the daily papers than sports or finance or editorial opinion, has been completely revolutionized on the basis of good works. So that east or west no ball can be danced, no luncheon enjoyed, no dinner nor theater opening attended unless in the end it benefits a Cause. This talent of Mrs. Cheyne's increased their social power more than the loss of wealth had hurt it.

This is important because it was against this particular background, in this special milieu, by these perennial standards that Melanie Cheyne had been brought up. Even the rich who are poor speak a language all their own, the first-of-the-month terror is never quite real to them, and *this* Melanie had inherited both from the Cheynes and the D'Harcourts. Her mother's way of life wasn't superimposed, it was in the very stream of her blue blood. When she had served the required time emptying bedpans as a nurse's aid, automatically she would be put on the Junior Board of the Children's Hospital. Service was a tradition and Melanie accepted it without thought. True, Evadne D'Harcourt Cheyne was kind. Kindness was in voice, smile, hands, courtesy. She made the most of what we used to call the *nouveau riche,* the social climber with gold, quite ruthlessly for her own purposes and the good of the needy. Vadne would say vaguely of a former night club singer who had married onto the fringes of the IN circle that she'd be perfect on the Food Committee of the Casino, *I mean we really have to do something about the menus,* Vadne would say. So the night club singer on the Food Committee would dig up her old friends in the restaurant business who knew that success can come only to the man who knows how to buy food, and suggest new dishes to brighten up the monotony of the menus. This did not mean that Vadne Cheyne was unaware of or disregarded class distinctions. There they were, weren't they? One couldn't change them. A squirrel had a bushy tail and a mouse didn't, a leopard had spots and a fox didn't. There was a *difference.* So that it would be years before the night club singer, who adored her, ventured to call her Vadne instead of Mrs. Cheyne.

Running a hospital, a medical school, a congressional battle in the Ninth, a horse show for the Boy's Athletic League came naturally to Mellie Cheyne when she became Mrs. Henry Angus Gavin. So likewise did the assumption of that *difference.*

All this sort of flitted through my head on the phone that

Saturday when I had just arrived in Chicago, as Vadne said the children were clamoring to see me, which I hoped was more than a pleasant fiction—the children being my goddaughter and her husband Hank. Vadne added that they probably wouldn't be at church since Mellie usually rode with Joe Quaglino's paper chase or whatever and Hank played golf but they'd be at the club by the time we got there. So I said I'd see her in church.

One is apt to call moments of ESP by the less far-out word of hunch or feminine intuition. Whatever it was I am sure now, without hindsight, that I began to be aware of a tension about Hank and Mellie that Sunday before I saw them at the country club. When I did see them I was startled by what I felt under the merry and accustomed glitter, a hint of violence. Violence? I said to myself. Surely not. Of course it was always easy to imagine any of the Young Marrieds, as they have been so unfortunately catalogued, having a row of words, a snappy difference of opinion and if they'd been drinking a sort of brawl, but violence as I knew it should be outside their circle. Yet my nose for news, which had sometimes sent me back to the seventeenth hole to watch Gene Sarazen or down into the cellar to find The Voice of a political convention now gave me notice that if I didn't know these people so *well* I'd phone the desk to stand by.

Then it occurred to me that after all suicide was violence. In essence, it was murder—taking a human life.

And I was face to face with Sybil, Colin Rowe's bitter young widow.

On the whole, I felt little change of atmosphere, set, caste, purpose, or conversation as Vadne and I moved from the church to the club.

The tall, pointed cathedral windows of the club's main lounge were of clear glass. The effect of rose, green, deep blue, and gold came from the beauty of nature spread outside them instead of the rose and crimson stained in Assisi hundreds of years ago. But the impression was much the same. Only-one-cocktail-so-far-before-brunch voices were a rippling buzz mingling with hi-fi or Magnavox, which, in honor no doubt of Sunday, was playing Brahms. The giant chandeliers suspended from the vaulted ceiling and the wall brackets with ivory electric candles were softly alight. In the circulating, flowing throng the men wore dark suits, sometimes striped trousers and cutaways, often golfing togs or tennis shorts, and the women were chic and stately in print dresses for church, in bright silk suits and small feathered or flowered hats, here and there girls in riding breeches and polished boots or jodhpurs. To add the final familiar touch, raised a step or two on the stairs leading up to the dining room I could see the spectacular white-before-he-was-thirty head of the new rector, Dr. John Hamilton V. Knowles, D.D. They call me Jack, I'm glad to say, he told me almost at once with a fine, frank, free smile.

After a bit, of course, as Vadne and I stood in one of the bow windows, the gorgeous colors no longer blended. I could see clearly the rolling lawns, the velvet greens, the freshest blue of the spring sky above stately new-clad trees, and the scarlet panes turned out to be a hedge of rhododendrons almost as beautiful as those to which I was accustomed in Golden Gate Park. What had suggested an altar was only now a small stone bridge over a ripple of silver water, and the kneeling figure turned out to be a man lining up a putt. Nevertheless, the transition had been painless for everybody, no doubt.

We were, Vadne and I, a little outside the main throng of guests. People came over to say hello, they were kind enough to be glad to see me back, the Kup Show had been marvelous to which I was able to reply quite truthfully that this was due to Kup himself, but all the time I was looking for the children. Sheila Quaglino, she who had once worn shocking pink velvet to the Passavant Cotillion, came by, she was just back from Paris. Dodo Kenyon, just back from Phoenix where she usually spent the winter, and Bootsie and Bobbie Hart, just back from Florida, and Janie Kiplinger who shrieked at me that she was just back from Tahiti, would I lunch with her one day? Peering about I saw Al Patton, that eminent legal light just back from Washington, where he had, as usual, been needling the Attorney General, and the president of a nearby university just back from Greece and Joe Quaglino, black patch over one eye probably just back from a hit-and-run foray with Captain Kidd or Long John Silver. A waving white glove caught my eyes. It belonged to Katie Ogilvie Gavin, Hank's grandmother, in emerald taffeta with a sable stole against spring drafts. A bossy old skinflint was Katie, everybody put up with her because she was entertaining and unpredictable as a cage full of monkeys. After they came over from Scotland, she'd seen her husband working in his shirtsleeves as the grain ships came up to the docks along the lakefront and she said her grandson, the present Henry Angus Gavin, was the spitting image of him.

All this time I felt that tightening of the viscera called apprehension, a warning which seems to me no more remarkable from one set of brain cells to another than one set of TV tubes to another. As people began to drift toward food in the dining room, Vadne said, "There she is. How do you think she looks? I tell her when your collarbones stick out you're too thin but she says she's the skinny type." And I saw Mellie Gavin silhouetted against a cream-washed panel and a tremor in my nerves yelled a warning, nor was it any use telling myself that these premonitions or commands to *attend* didn't make sense, for over the years they had.

She was wearing jodhpurs of a brick-brown over highly polished shoes, and a tight tailored yellow shirt with a button-down collar and a narrow orange tie. Her hair was brushed straight back from her forehead and came out from behind her ears in gay little waves; it was dark and shining and had been combed and groomed and probably washed under the shower since she'd slept in it. I knew that she was the product of all that can be done to enhance a woman's charms, and she had achieved a clear simplicity, a fresh naturalness, with no sign of makeup or design.

Bending over her, David Kenyon looked so lost and enchanted, and Vadne and I arrived at the same thought, as no doubt did many others, seeing those two together again and that expression on David's face.

"I never thought it was really an *affair,*" Vadne said, "I mean she was so *young,* of course they grow up early now—still—"

I'd interviewed Dave Kenyon once or twice for my paper, and I found I was still wondering what it was actually like for you yourself, as a human being, to have too much of everything. Too much money to know you had it, so simply existed at that altitude of money; there couldn't be that kind of money in dollars and cents as I knew them. Too much prestige, too much brain power, and looks that could be cartooned only in terms of the man of distinction. Nor did he show any age other than *distinguished,* though I knew he couldn't be under fifty.

Everybody in this room, everybody with a Florida-Arizona, Acapulco, Honolulu, Côte D'Azur tan as well as those who'd had to stay home for some reason, knew there had been something between David Kenyon and Mellie Cheyne when she was *the* debutante of the year a while back and *what* had been a major topic of conversation at the time. At that time the astonishment was that Dave Kenyon's roving eye had been captivated by someone of his own class, this having not happened since he married Dorothea McKelland. A string of movie stars and starlets, career girls of one kind or another, actresses, night club entertainers and once a ballet *première danseuse* had kept Chicago agog, entertained, and indulgent. In whatever he did, David Kenyon had style and the utter disregard for public opinion which always makes it lie down and roll over. However, Mellie Cheyne was something else again, for this time perhaps Dodo, his wife, wouldn't be able *not to see it,* in her own circle, under her own nose.

"Dodo told me once," Vadne said in my ear, "that she was Mrs. David Kenyon and proposed to die with her boots on. Not about Mellie—before that, I think it was about that movie girl, Ya-Ya or Yo-Yo or something, who never washes her neck." She waited, but I had nothing to say. "Of course it would be different with Mellie—he *adored* her—in a way it was flattering." I said *in a way,* and Vadne went on, "Just the same I've always been sure there wasn't anything wrong—"

Vadne was mistaken.

As is often the case, Mellie had been glad to unburden to me what she couldn't bring herself to discuss with her parent. It may be that this is one of the things godmothers should be for.

She had been David Kenyon's mistress and she used the word to me with a small, qualified smile, as though to apologize for using a *two*-syllable where a *one*-syllable word would have done as well.

What was more, she had intended to marry him.

From the age of four, when she had rid herself of a stern and rockbound English nanny the Cheynes had imported, by the expedient of refusing to eat, Mellie had achieved her own way in most things. She saw no reason why she shouldn't be able to make an honest woman of herself by becoming Mrs. David Kenyon.

At seventeen she had entered into a romance with the youngest scion of the Speed family. Her first experience of the throbbing, driving, and unexpected sex reaction to the touch of lips and pressure of bodies, from which her fastidiousness had guarded her before, caused her to act with high-handed generosity, and like more normal, *compos mentis* females she assumed this to be love. Up to then she had never seen clinkers and ashes, so that when this hot fire was put out by utter incongruity of moods and tenses and painful discrepancy of mental equipment, and left something of a peculiarly repulsive kind, Mellie decided that love was just another of those Santa Claus fables, mostly hankey-pankey and hokey-pokey. She spent some dark hours examining the marriages she had known including that of her father and mother. Having found herself that passion was an insufficient reason for spending the rest of your life with a man whom you disliked, she decided to let her head rule her heart. To marry as did her friends in France (she had spent two years in school in Switzerland) for advantage, family, and fortune, for the life she preferred and the power she would enjoy which money would give her.

At a given moment, Mellie was quite sure she could unseat Mrs. Kenyon. No one had told her that it wasn't the first but the second time a girl went to bed with the man that determined her hold; perhaps like the Creole Josephine who became Empress of the French, Mellie had been born with this ancient clairvoyance, and she felt very sure of herself.

Here I inject what came to me at another time from the man in the case, he to whom the papers often referred as a multimillionaire.

David Kenyon fell in love with her. I had no doubt of that as he talked.

Through satiety, through passing of years, through a growing sense of repetition, he was beginning when he met her to find women a bore and sex a little dull.

"My grandmother used to say there's no sauce like hunger," Dave Kenyon said to me with a shrug. He was talking to me then because he wanted very much to know what the situation was between Mellie and her husband Hank Gavin and I suppose he felt it necessary to explain his interest. "When I first fell in love with Mellie, I had no appetite. Sex had always been to me one of the pleasures, neither a need nor a neurosis. Lack of desire had disturbed me, it is then a man is aware that death will come when it will come."

Mellie had given him back more than his youth, much more.

If youth but knew, if age but could. To this peak, this fusion, his love for Mellie Cheyne had brought him.

He had seen her first—really seen her, he said—one day when she brought her horse back into the stable out at Joe Quaglino's farm. He made it plain that he had fallen in love at first sight and that he was at that exact moment sure that it was for the last time. In his prime at forty-five, he was ripe for danger and unbridled emotional momentum, but he was afraid they weren't going to happen and then he fell in love as he had with Dorothea McKelland over twenty years before, only now he was a man at the height of all his powers, all his knowledge.

And he had felt sure that she loved him. In full force, in response, so that the circle of love was complete as it must be and is on only such rare occasions. His experienced love-making, his care, his romantic and beautiful approach, had wakened in Mellie the natural, healthy sex impulses which the ravages and fumbling awkwardness of her boy lover had caused to recoil.

For Dave Kenyon, the love affair was a return to Paradise.

More. Much more. For Mellie had one gift which Dodo had always lacked. Like all women who have really enchanted men to their enslavement, she had a touch of the clown. They were gay together, and this was *sauce piquant* and *tartare* and gave the final zest for a man who had, as the saying goes, been around.

Followed a few months of trips on his yacht. Meetings in New York where good Chicagoans go for their amours. Luncheons and dinners at out-of-the-way places. Finally, time in his magnificent big city apartment when Dodo was in Bangkok or Madrid. Even as his madness mounted, David Kenyon was not able to believe himself invisible as lovers often do. By the weight of his advertising and the power of his millions he had managed to keep their names out of the columns though he knew quite well that every paper in town had pictures to illustrate the story of this trio, if it ever broke, already to go. They both knew that they were the talk of the town and the man wasn't sure whether Mellie had allowed him to compromise her as part of a plan or whether she loved him so much she didn't care. By this time, it made no difference to him anyway.

Her mother and his wife moved about the same time. In force. This brought about the fireworks.

One day Melanie said casually enough that she was going to spend the summer on the Riviera. At that, David Kenyon had been overcome with sheer panic and final certainty. At the idea of being without her for months he was staring into a cold and dismal void, or the oasis in the desert had turned out to be a mirage.

"I can't live without you," he said, "don't go."

Her head tilted back and her eyes crinkled at the corners, her face looked as it did when it lay back against his shoulder, rewarding him with her radiant smile. "I have to go," she said. "Someone has loaned Mama a *villa*. With all the servants. Of course the Riviera isn't really nice any more, but the swimming is divine. We can't be together all the time, you know." This had about it a very young practicality.

"I want us to be," David Kenyon said.

"Then you'll have to do something about it."

"Will you marry me?" he said.

"Ask me when you're free to make a deal," she said, and began to giggle. She held onto him, utterly limp and warm against him, nuzzling into his neck, kissing him and letting him kiss her. "I do rather adore you at that," she said.

So for the first and only time he had asked Dorothea for a divorce.

She had stared at him, her face gone gray-white. Then she said, "Let me think it over. I take it you want to marry Melanie Cheyne."

"Yes," he said.

"I'm no dog in the manger," Dodo Kenyon said. "Is she willing?"

"I think she—will be, if I'm free," he said. And was amazed and a little shocked to find that he could not think of Dodo at all, he could only think of Mellie and that satisfied smile of reward she sometimes gave him.

At about that same time, it seemed, Mellie's mother had at last found courage to give tongue. "I mean," she said, "your father is *really* upset."

"He won't be," Mellie had said.

Chicago, knowing as places and people do things by a communication older than backfences or radio all that was going on, now waited for news that in exchange for X millions of dollars Dodo Kenyon would soon take off for Florida or Las Vegas. Thereafter David Kenyon would marry Melanie Cheyne in Paris or Istanbul or Rio de Janeiro. All this was exciting, dramatic, and personal; opinions varied as to Dodo's surrender, with or without her boots on, David's middle-aged moronity, but unanimous in approval of little Mellie Cheyne's *bringing it off*.

The only difficulty was that Dodo didn't go to any of the divorce capitals and the reason was this—and as Mellie told me a bigger puzzlement to her than anyone else.

On a snowy, blowy night around ten o'clock, Dorothea Kenyon, nodding to the elevator operator, came up to the top floor of the fine old hotel where her husband had his town *pied-à-terre*. The Kenyons had a house of majestic proportions in Lake Forest where Dodo could hang her Picassos and Renoirs and set up her modernistic sculpture, another one in Scottsdale, another on a ranch in Wyoming, and still another in London. And of course Dodo traveled so much she really didn't need a Chicago town house. So David had taken the top floor of this hotel, no longer really fashionable, redecorated it, installed his own private elevator, and it was understood that this was exclusively his. Mrs. Kenyon of course had a key, but when she turned it that night, slightly surprised to find the lock hadn't been changed, it was the first time she had used it in years.

Mellie was there, as Mrs. Kenyon had known before she came.

She had expected something more Rabelaisian or O'Haraesque than her husband and his girl friend (Dodo's word) sitting across a card table intent on a cut puzzle. However, they were dressed *for* bed and appeared to have just come *from* it or about to go *to* it. When, as Mellie told me the story, I asked her how she felt and she said she was damned annoyed. Dodo had accepted the rules and played by them for years. Mellie thought it gauche and vulgar and unsporting to break them thus, without notice. Why *me?* Mellie thought. After her first experience no one could expect her to enter into marriage without a prenuptial flight. Her relationship to David she regarded as an *engagement,* an agreement to purchase if the goods lived up to the promises, or what the late Judge Ben Lindsey offered as Companionate Marriage, a testing time not to be official until there was a child. Mellie had neither a guilty conscience nor a sense of *faux pas,* such as using the wrong fork.

She saw Mrs. Kenyon first and sat quite still, holding a piece of the puzzle she took to be the end of George Washington's wig crossing the Delaware. She put it carefully into place before she stood up. Over Chinese pajamas from Hong Kong she wore a tie-silk dressing gown by Lanvin, much too large for her, and as David turned to follow her gaze she found her body betraying her brain. To her surprise, it wasn't her heartbeat nor her breath, it was her knees wobbling bonelessly. For one moment, generations of ancestresses were stronger than her modern philosophy of hedonism and she put her hand flat on top of her head as though to hold her hair on—or down. But as she lit a cigarette her hands were steady so she decided to call it a draw. David was saying something, something a good deal like what she had said about abiding by the amendments they'd made to the laws of God and man, but she didn't really hear him, she was concentrated on his wife.

Apparently Dodo didn't hear him either, for when she spoke it was directly to the girl. Her voice was breathtakingly level and painfully controlled. She said, "If you will say to me now that you love him, I will give him to you."

"I don't think you have any right—" Mellie began.

"Oh yes," David Kenyon's wife said, "oh yes. You know I do. Whether you know it yet or not, he has to have it, he can't live without it, he takes a lot of it. He doesn't know it either but it's the rock under his life. I—do. I always have. I can give him up to a woman who loves him—you see that?"

Mellie saw Dodo Kenyon then, for the first time. For this my-whole-life-depends-on-it personal appearance, she wore a suit of deep orange under a knee-length sable coat, the lines of her body were slim and svelte, on her perfectly groomed head she wore a chic hat of brown satin trimmed with an orange polka-dot veil. A nominee once more for the list of best-dressed women.

Mellie observed all these things.

What she saw was Dodo Kenyon's hands.

To live in a world where more than ever in history the values were distorted in favor of youth, that was animalistic. And often unfortunate. Hands showing the first faint signs of *age* could forever lose their hold so that all else was forgotten. A younger body, a girl's hands fresh as buds could undo years of devotion and loyalty and care.

Her eyes met the older woman's.

So nothing had ever meant anything to Dodo Kenyon except the man who now wanted what she had been twenty years ago and could never be again, not with all the cosmetics and salons and attention. All the other things—was it possible that they had already been corrupted by moths and covered with dust?

There was a fundamental rule here, unchangeable, incontestable. Her mind worked slowly around to it. Bullying betrays an ignoble mind, Dodo is outmatched, her hands are frail and mine are young and strong, she's giving away too many years to make it a fair fight.

Two fundamental rules.

If you will say to me that you love him—

"Hell with it," Mellie said and started toward the bedroom. Dave moved in front of her. He sounded as though somebody had a cord around his neck and was slowly strangling him; it was a frantic protest, not a word.

In a quick movement, Mellie flanked him. She said, "I'm sorry, Dave." Quite seriously she said it. No no, mustn't be *serious*. This is farce, bedroom farce. Tragedy, as everybody knew, couldn't occur in such a setting as this, tragedy could no longer be *Hamlet* nor *Macbeth* nor *King Lear* nor *Romeo and Juliet* unless you transferred it to the *West Side*. Tenements—the poor—the dissatisfied—only to them could tragedy happen. How could Dodo Kenyon be a tragic figure in a sable coat and that hat, no matter what her eyes and her hands said? What the hell did she *want?* Remember, this is comedy, drawing room comedy, keep the dialogue light and bright between the husband and wife and the other girl. If they *laugh,* nobody will notice the rules or the commandment, and President Kennedy's assassination was tragic only because he loved the poor and they loved him.

She put up the index finger of her left hand and shook it at David.

"Wars are won on the playing fields of Eton, old boy," she said, "mustn't let our side down." In the door, her back to them, she said, "Don't worry, Dodo. He'll get over it—"

David Kenyon, bending over Mellie on this morning at the Onewansa Country Club several years later, conveyed to me that she might have been wrong. He didn't look to me as though he'd gotten over it given half a chance.

"Would you have approved of a divorce and Mellie marrying him?" I said, and Vadne's mouth fell open and then said, "Be our age, lamb. I am a mother and Francis is my husband all these years. David Kenyon is so very rich you would hardly be able to afford to disapprove of marrying him, would you?"

"Dorothea's always been a good friend of yours," I said.

"I always say if a woman can't hold her husband it's her fault," Vadne said airily. "And to repeat myself, friendship at that price comes too high."

I admitted this. Yet, I'd lived as many years as she had and been around more, and somewhere in my inner being I *believed* that come a day when in whatever guise we hear the cry *à la lanterne* friendship will command a damn sight more than money. I believe that. I had a moment of wishing my godchild's mother believed it also, a hunch that so did Francis Cheyne.

"We were lucky," Vadne said complacently, "you know Hank Gavin was *the* catch—I mean he's young and good-looking and no *trouble,* not as much money of course but still—every girl in Chicago was *after* him—and it's always better when they're in love, isn't it? Not that you can always marry just for love, can you?"

"You did," I said and she gave me a funny look. "I mean," she said, "that Mellie is a girl who needs money, she's been brought up to need it, it's a hard habit to break and Hank's father—it's not in the Kenyon class—but still—and his earnings, Francis says it's fabulous that a man so young and I suppose you could call it inexperienced can make that much a year. Katie—his grandmother—says easy come easy go—and I admit they *spend* it but mostly on their house and a good deal of that they could get out. But you know Katie. She's a miser. I let Mellie have the petit point chairs—it's a darling house, you'll adore it—and of course she has the

Sevres, the pink—and I gave her some of the D'Harcourt chairs and the spinet—"

While she talked my eyes strayed on David Kenyon, and I thought that maybe that was just his usual batting stance and I didn't think it was seeing him with Mellie that made my nerve ends stand up like a jackrabbit's ears when he hears a low rattle in the nearby cactus patch.

Just then I saw Hank, and I thought that while I might, as sometimes happened, be making up half of this, there was half of that that I wasn't. He was standing with two women, and the crowd had begun to eddy and swirl, the noise had increased cocktail by cocktail, and now it was composed of squeals—*Sweetie pie, I thought you'd gone to India*—and of shouts—*You listen to me, buddy, you just let me tell you something boy, if the governor has any idea* —higher and higher above the music which you will remember was Brahms instead of Bongo-Bongo because it was Sunday. A hat like a ladies' room lampshade moved and I saw that one of the women was Sybil Rowe, whose husband had shocked rough and ready Chicago by his mysterious suicide, must have been neurotic, the older men said, what the hell was the matter with him, had everything, didn't he? A wife like Syb, they were going to make him a vice president in June, they'd just brought back a Mercedes-Benz from Frankfurt, he was shooting in the low seventies—what'd he *want,* for Chrisake? Was there an undercurrent of resentment because they still missed that wit and glitter which Colin had carried through the Chicago Club like a Fourth of July sparkler? For which they had loved to have him around *in spite of*. The younger men felt none of it was as simple as it used to be. Trite and banal to say this since he got back from Korea, for of course the older men had been at Omaha Beach and some of them at Belleau Wood but that was a long time ago, they'd forgotten Pusan and Pyongyang. Of course a *window*—messy—*très* messy—still, as Dorothy Parker had remarked, razors pain you and rivers are damp—still, *jumping*—probably a good psychoanalyst could have helped him. They found out that Colin had been to a hundred-dollar-an-hour psychiatrist, that had to be the best. "They monkeyed around with his poor soul, all right," Hank was to tell me. "If he needed a final shove that was probably it."

Colin's widow, standing there beside Hank, looked to me as though she stayed awake nights trying to figure *why*. Walking the floor. Saying to herself *What did I do, what didn't I do, what was he thinking when he stood looking down and decided to leave me, to die and leave me of his own free will?*—well, even an about-to-be-vice president of anything cannot go jumping out windows without headlines, and after taking a look at his books, and finding them okay, these hinted at bad news about an old war wound from Korea, but being a newspaperwoman I knew by the way the stories were written that this was pure invention.

I saw Hank Gavin put a big hand on Syb Rowe's arm and turn her toward us, and then for the first time I noticed the girl clinging to his other arm. She would have resented this tardiness on my part. Everything about her shrieked for attention. She'd made herself the kind of blonde gentlemen are supposed to prefer, all bosoms and bottom.

To Vadne I said, "Who's the blonde girl with Hank?" and after a quick look Vadne said, "You remember her—that's Toodie Goodrich, you knew her father," and I said, "She's really lovely, why is she done up like that?" and Vadne said, "Being married—a man being married—they don't pay much attention any more. Hank doesn't know there's another girl on earth."

"And Mellie?" I said.

All vagueness vanished and Vadne said, "They're both—that's what makes it so wonderful, isn't it?"

David Kenyon's wife, a lady of quality in a white Italian silk suit and a ruby blouse, a ruby clip pinning back the white hat over her hair, had joined her husband and young Mrs. Gavin. I had begun to think of another time when that triangle had been joined, and then Mellie became conscious of my gaze and with a little cry she broke through the field in a rush and came and put her arms around me and her young cheek aginst mine. She said, "I didn't know you were here, why didn't you holler, what have you been up to?" Then lower, so that only I could hear, "You'll never believe it. I know, you've seen everything but this one you'll never believe. I give you two million guesses." Her little gasp of laughter was *shrill*. Mellie—being shrill? My ESP messages had been right then, they were coming through strongly now, but they were in some kind of code. I didn't get it yet. I saw that behind Mellie's dark eyes there was a fire, I thought it was a golden flame of anger, maybe not, maybe it was fear or determination or trying to see something just out of range.

Not the blonde. Too obvious, too blatant. Still, adoration is heady, it is an aphrodisiac anesthesia, in this age of speed and speed and speed the cheap and easy may appeal momentarily, there is no *time* to storm the heights of the unattainable, or return to the cave. The cave where our ancestors were safe from bombs and knew not atoms and where maybe now they wished they had stayed.

Surely not Hank Gavin. Both he and Mellie were, by nature, competitors. I am not going to try here to make you more than passingly acquainted with Hank Gavin. I only came to know him myself as time passed. There has to be a whole chapter—maybe two—given to what he told me some days later as we walked along the lakefront and sat at a small table in the off-hour emptiness of the International Club at the Drake. As he came to greet me that Sunday morning and even in the following discussion which my friend Al Patton precipitated, he was still to me simply Mellie's husband, a rangy, husky guy, with dangerous shoulders and a flat stomach and small waist and I thought he must have a good barber, his sandy-tow hair was thick and as a kid must have grown in all directions with a dozen cowlicks, but now it was a thick pelt worn in rather a dashing crest like a young lion. His eyebrows didn't match it, they were too dark, they all but met over his eyes and his eyes were—gray—gray-green—yellow-gray-green—and the tanned skin was tight with youth and top condition over a craggy bone structure that bespoke his Scotch ancestry.

I dislike charm. Let me say I am allergic to charm. I have seen so much of it. It is fun if you can afford it, but sometimes you find the price too high. Yet somehow I felt—it was the first thing about Mellie's husband that I did feel—that Hank Gavin's charm was without guile, without effort, had no technique. This is rare indeed. Even Churchill and FDR and Jack Kennedy knew about their charm, knew how to use it and when to turn it on how far. Charm has probably changed empires more drastically than Cleopatra's nose and of course any young man who was Chicago's leading *salesman* had to have some of it. He was one of Chicago's favorite sons, a typical, top-ranking, free-wheeling, big-dealing high-on-the-hog young businessman.

That much I knew already. Hank's boss, Stu Margolis, head of the international brokerage house for which Hank worked, told me that Hank was Chicago's leading investment counselor at the level calling for actual *selling*. Moreover, Mr. Margolis told me, the charm was backed up by *I'm the boy who can tell you everything about the stocks and bonds I sell you,* management, equipment, personnel, from U. S. Steel to wheat to a cosmetic firm listed on the Board for the first time.

To be trusted, Hank Gavin was.

All this had to have its part when it came to selling Christ the tiger.

3

At first I thought I might leave out this scene about the angels.

Two things decided me to put it in. A recall so vivid that it must have been as unusual as it seemed. Second, in a way it triggered so much that followed, for it was actually the first time Hank had come out in the open. There has to be some explanation for Al Patton's behavior, unpredictable as we all knew that Irishman to be. In view of what happened to Hank, it seems to me it must have been *meant*.

In the club's lofty dining room long tables were set in an alcove and we helped ourselves from steaming dishes to nine different kinds of eggs, creamed chipped beef, chicken à la king and finnan haddie. Platters of cold meat and salads and bowls heaped with fruit were brilliant and appetizing, the linen and dishes and silver glittered pleasantly. All seemed well with the world.

Vadne Cheyne had managed to get the big round table in the corresponding alcove, we were separated from the main room by an arch and heavy drapes, we could hear each other speak. Which was a good thing for, as it turned out, none of us would ever be quite the same again. The light from the tall windows that gave on the terrace was bright. I had one of those trained reconnaissance moments such as sometimes came in the press box at a World Series or an Army-Navy game, it wasn't any longer the team, the Giants or the Yankees, each man was a unit, and you could tell whether they were going to have a best or a bad day. Now in the circle at the table I saw each face as though it peered from a porthole. Monty Berkowitz, publisher of a big newspaper, as black and white as his own front pages. Al Patton, as wickedly mischievous as James Joyce, who I am sure is chortling throughout eternity at what I, as an Irishman myself, believe to be the most stupendous hoax ever put over on the intellectual highbrows and bigwigs of the world. Joe Quaglino had joined Al and me, and down at the end sat Katie Ogilvie Gavin, her red wig as unashamed as that first Queen Elizabeth's, her seagull eye fastened upon her grandson in a fine attempt to conceal the idolatry she felt. I was glad to know she felt that way about Mellie's husband. Not even a grandson could fool Katie all the time. Sybil Rowe's bright mask slipped from time to time and showed the ravages of festering grief, for it is grief that festers, not sorrow. And there was Dr. Hamilton Browne, shining with the warm, sincere benevolence which a true money-raiser must have so benevolence will reflect back to him, and naturally today moneyraising is the chief talent required of a college president. His wife was a large and impressive and Monty Berkowitz was small and quiet. Across from me the new young rector, Dr. John H. V. Knowles, and beside him Mellie, quite at her ease. Hank stopped behind her and dropped a kiss on top of her head and she looked up at him and the corners of her eyes wrinkled. Evidently he asked her a question without words, waited for an answer, and didn't get it; it was an evasion on her part of whatever lay between them.

So much in love.

About that I was surer than ever that Vadne was right.

I also realized that Al Patton was in that stylized state of inebriation which he attained over week-ends. Of him it was possible to use that old-fashioned phrase that he could drink like a gentleman and did. Never wobbled in gait or speech nor repeated himself and there was no hostility in him, the man who in business hours was the mainstay of clients in fifty states. Only he often let his fancy prance like a leprechaun when he was free of them and their needs.

Halfway through brunch he made one of his most sensational surprisals and I felt its impact on Hank and Mellie in their indirect disagreement to follow. Though for the life of me I couldn't see what it was about.

Up to the moment Al rose conversation had proceeded according to precedent. The bang-bang of his knife-handle brought silence, his words caught and held them in it.

"My friends," he said, and his high-pitched voice had tremendous authority, "I've been listening to the talk around here about the sex life of some not very good movie stars and inaccurate predictions about flights to the moon and tales about how to raise money and chitchat about fashions and frivolity and cabbages and kings especially Prince Philip and I'm disgusted. I say you might as well be yakking about why the sea is boiling hot and whether pigs have wings."

The rudeness I knew was deliberate, and while I expected some loud kidding, some give-as-good-as-they-got, instead the table sat perfectly quiet, hypnotized by the round-and-round of the champagne in the glasses, that old pirate Quaglino having insisted that champagne was the only thing a civilized man could drink with breakfast. I noted with alarm that Al Patton was weaving a little, whether with glee over his mischief-making or whether for once he had misjudged his capacity I couldn't tell.

"We've got enough brains and brawn, genius and connections, know-how and know-about at this table," Al Patton said, "to take control of this country if we were so-minded and instead of all this piddling bumfuss we ought to be talking about something important. That's what you read they used to do in those country houses in England and the salons in Paris and the groves of Greece."

"Or the swimming pools of Rome," Dave Kenyon said.

"I expect around the swimming pools of Rome they were talking about who is sleeping with who and of what sex, just as we'll probably be any minute. That's why taking a look around at who we've got here, I decided we ought to do better. Hell, with the money, power, education, press, church, and state around this table we ought to be doing more than shout about who can hit a piece of gutta-percha the farthest. We've got women here could have changed the map of empire all right, we've been everywhere, to visit Nasser in Egypt and De Gaulle in France and Wallace in Birmingham, and ole Dirksen in Washington where we put him, I say when even one man puts his shoulder to the wheel it can make a difference."

"Some relaxation is necessary," Dr. Browne said with pedagogic mildness.

"I guess our proportion of relaxation's not to be sneezed at," Al Patton told him, "so I have decided we're going to talk about something important and worthwhile."

"And who is going to decide what is important and worthwhile?" Sybil Rowe said.

"I am, sweetheart," Al Patton said, "so everybody drink up and I'll tell you." Wary now, watching him, they drank. "The last time this good lady on my right and I were together," Al said, "we had an illuminating conversation I've never forgotten." I came out of my speculative absorption to note with horror that *I* was the good lady on his right and tried frantically to remember *what* we had talked about eighteen months before when I had dined at his house with several other writers. Like all lawyers, Al Patton wanted to write. I didn't need to remember for Al was telling us in ringing hoots. "We talked about *angels,*" he said and landed a free-swinging blow between my shoulder blades. "Paul Gallico was there, and Harlan Ware and Allen Drury, that right? and you were talking about a story Philip Wylie had written about an angel some pilots found on a Pacific island, a dead angel, wishing you'd thought of it. Anyhow, we got to talking about angels, didn't we?" I nodded. I remembered now, but that had been a different group, we had been talking from the literary standpoint entirely. We were people who can and could and must believe beyond what they can see or they wouldn't dare to *write*—or paint—or compose music.

"Nothing more important than angels," Al Patton said, "I've had a nudge or two and I expect if they're honest so has everybody at this table. It's amazing what you find folks feel and think once they loosen up a bit, a man you've thought of as pretty crass and shallow in the pan and playing practical jokes—seems he's hungry to hear about somebody who saw an angel dead or alive. That's been my experience. Now I'm a believer in angels myself—"

From halfway down the table his wife said, "Oh *Al*—you *really* are impossible, *all* the Irish are impossible, actually it's the Scotch who've run the British Empire for years—" Katie Gavin said Hear Hear like a tin whistle and Monty Berkowitz hollered out, "And don't forget Disraeli" and Al shut them up with a furious look and I heard Dodo Kenyon laugh and saw Hank Gavin give Mellie his wife a hot glance of question which she ignored.

"NOW," Al Patton said, "probably a lot of you believe in angels and maybe you've even had experiences with them only you're shy about coming out with it, everybody is that's why we're going to talk about angels which we need a lot worse than these bloody *psychoanalysts* around here, and you'll all have a chance to speak up and we'll start with the lady on my right, she believes in angels, now you go ahead and tell 'em, sweetheart."

Beaming, he sat down. I heard Joe Quaglino say *sonofabitch* and Mrs. Browne mumble to her husband about *the proper place* while I was sending up a frantic appeal—*take no thought what ye shall say*—and there came back the one word *Mons*. Embarrassment which had been trickling between my shoulder blades disappeared. Storytelling is my business, if the *story* is *good* enough sometimes I can switch to audio without disaster. To a collection of expressions from Syb Rowe's white rage to David Kenyon's nonchalant amusement to the Reverend Mrs. Knowles' isn't-this-in-rather-bad-taste to Joe Quaglino's bull challenge and Dr. Browne's academic tolerance, I began the saga of the angels of Mons as I remembered it.

Of that time, longer ago than seems possible to us who lived through a war when we had believed civilization had outgrown war, when the world's fate was at stake on the blood-stained fields of France, of the days when great gray-green hordes of German barbarians poured across the sacred neutral of little Belgium, of how Papa Joffre, God rest his soul, and his poilus and a few British regulars held the line at Mons long enough to allow the army to reform and the general to call up the taxi drivers of Paris, so that the Allies a few days later could win the Battle of the Marne. Hindsight by the military experts agreed that though it took four more years, the First World War was won for the Allies at the Marne, at *Mons* where their poor armies held for that vital third down.

How? *How?* Soon after the day itself whispers began. One soldier to another in the shallow trenches. In the rear, to officers and chaplains when the troops were pulled out for a few hours' rest. At the end of the war, confidences to families, questions to priests, exchanges between veterans in bull sessions recounting their Iliad and it went something like this: Their line was worse than paper thin there, they were praying for the would-to-God-reserves to come up, but soon enough they knew there were no reserves, slaughter and holocaust and defeat were sure as death before them. Then—they glanced at each other as they spoke of this—then they saw the Germans, singly, in platoons, in their new tanks, hit the one-man-thin defenses, hit the empty spaces yards—kilometers—wide and bounce back as though they'd hit Gibraltar itself. They couldn't believe their eyes but they had seen the Germans drop their bayonets and run—run *backwards.* Some of the men, in questions, in half-sentences, finally in eager torrent, said they had seen angels and archangels fill up the thin red line of heroes. A few—strangely enough many of these were English—had seen Joan herself, the Maid of Orleans, carrying the fleur-de-lis and fighting for France again not far from where she had crowned her dauphin King. Who could or would believe this fairy tale? The French people did, those who heard it, they had always believed in La Pucelle. Oddly enough, soon some pundits and authorities who knew about these things were *puzzled* and said so. How is it, they said, that British Tommies, the most skeptical of all men, who had never in all their cockney lives *heard* of Joan of Arc, could describe with accurate detail the specially built armor worn by the Maid in the fifteenth century? And the design she herself had created for the banner she always carried to lead her armies? Had to be amazing that these men from Bow Bells knew particulars, and in some instances could repeat in ancient French dialect, of which they knew not one word, what Joan had shouted to them as she beckoned them forward behind the golden lilies. Of course there had to be a logical, sensible explanation but at the moment nobody came up with it. Ah well, Joan of Arc had always been a stumbling block to the historian; the playwright like Shaw or the creative biographer like V. Sackville West or Anatole France did better.

From my elbow, with a roar like the bull of Bashan, Al Patton let his asleep-in-the-deep bass roll forth, keeping time with his knife. He had the Irishman's memory for old ditties, and the alcove echoed and a few curious heads popped through the curtains. He sang with gusto—

Joan of Arc, Joan of Arc,
Can your eyes, from the skies
See the foe?
Can you see the drooping fleur-de-lis,
Do you *dum-do-dum* of Normandy?
Joan of Arc, Joan of Arc,
Let your spirit guide us through.
Come lead your France to vic-tor-eeee,
Joan of Arc, we are *calling* you.

It had been a big First World War hit, at the end some of us were giving out with a word or two, such as fleur-de-lis, even the youngsters were humming.

Playfully, Dr. Browne said, "I care not who writes my country's laws if I may write its songs," and from far down the table where he had been very quiet, Hank Gavin's boss, Stu Margolis, always so quiet, said, "Well right now it seems to be the new nations of Africa, doesn't it?"

"Now," Al Patton took charge once more, "maybe you and the moguls in the Pentagon wouldn't think much of calling *Joan of Arc,* but somebody did and the clincher is—go on, go on," he said to me.

I said that while they agreed a man didn't always think too clearly when he was fighting for his life, covered with mud and blood and sweat, he could see and hear and a mass of evidence about the angels of Mons had accumulated.

The most difficult evidence to combat, however, as Papa Joffre said, was that there was no other—no military—no logical—no sound explanation for the Battle of Mons. There never had been. The authorities agreed that there still wasn't.

A palpable silence followed, keyed-up, partly hostile, partly throbbing with man's millions-of-years-old desire to believe. Monty Berkowitz was scowling at me in a familiar city editor are-you-sure-of-your-facts fashion, and Stu Margolis' wife, who was an alcoholic though we had all agreed to ignore this, beginning with Stu, clapped her hands and said something incoherent before she filled her glass again, getting some of it in Stu's lap. He always sat beside her.

Came, to break the silence, a tinkle of laughter. Every head turned. Mellie Gavin finished lighting a cigarette, she dropped the still-flaming match into an ashtray, she gave me her small, qualified smile and with loving tolerance she said, "Dear godmama, what a pretty story. Now tell the one about Goldilocks and the Three Bears."

I could have smacked her. Nor was I alone in this. Her husband was staring at her in red anger. Looking at him with fellow feeling I noticed how much weight he had lost, and I saw that he was changed, though I did not know how, nor how much. This was a radical alteration of something, of some kind, and my first clue to the nature of the chasm that was opening between these two who loved each other so much.

Before either of us had time to move, a quiet voice invaded us.

If Francis Cheyne knew that his daughter had been insolent and arrogant enough to be ill-mannered, he skipped it. So low and true that he might have been speaking to himself we had to *listen,* and as he spoke for the first time in ages, I remembered that Francis Cheyne had been with the AAF in the Second World War, not as a pilot, but at some liaison job with the RAF in London. He said, "Some months after the war, I was at a banquet honoring Air Chief Marshal Lord Hugh Dowding. The King was there, and the P.M. and a lot of brass. By that time the man who had commanded the RAF in the Battle of Britain was out of uniform. He had on an antique dinner jacket and I recall that his spine was stiff as a ramrod and when he left he put on an old gray topper. Anyway, we cheered him like madmen, nobody knew better than we did how right Churchill was when he said never had so many owed so much to so few—he said it again that night. And the Air Chief Marshal had been chief of those few. At first he looked annoyed as though the whole business was a social and military error. Then as the cheers kept rocketing, he held up his hand and they lifted him up onto the table and you never heard such quiet. I suppose it's the same story. Please realize that it was told by the man who planned every move of the strategy of that flying show that saved England when she stood alone to save a free world. This was the man who was always there, who—the men always told us—never slept, who talked over and over with the FEW he had. He told us that night that *angels* had flown the planes for pilots already dead. When they came down the crew told him their pilot had been hit by the first burst, but the plane kept on flying and fighting, and sometimes they saw a figure at the controls and none of them were startled by this—by this time they were beyond human limits anyhow."

Dodo Kenyon said in a conversational tone that she'd seen a picture where Spencer Tracy got killed and came back to fly a plane for—Van Johnson she thought it was—but of course that was just a *movie*. Francis Cheyne waited courteously, then he said, "The Air Chief Marshal wrote a book about it, *Many Mansions*, it was called. He told—all the stories. It was published, I saw it myself, then it sort of disappeared, and I've never been able to get hold of a copy since."

Around me I could feel the desire-to-believe coming up in a wave and meeting a wave of disgusted skepticism. A crash made us all jump. Sybil Rowe had dropped her glass, or thrown it. "The old man must have been gaga," she said, and plainly it was worse for her if they *could* come back and her husband hadn't. But Francis Cheyne answered her softly enough. He said, "I suppose sending the few boys up day after day and so many not coming back—quite possible it drove him over the line. Ground officers had a bad time. On the other hand that night after he'd put on his gray topper and gone home, the rest of us sat up till dawn, men who *knew* about these things, and as Papa Joffre said of Mons, there just wasn't any way to explain how the RAF, outnumbered by planes so much better and outgunned 100 to 1, how they won the Battle of Britain—even now, with hindsight and information, nobody can figure that one."

Mellie began to say sweetly, "Daddy, lovey, you're *wonderful* and men like Ulysses and Baron Munchausen always had tales to tell when they got back from the wars, darling, but—" Her voice was young and hard and edged with the you-can't-kid-us-any-more skepticism. She spoke so loudly it surprised me and though her expression was light, forced I thought, and I had never seen Mellie force anything before. Monty Berkowitz broke through with his from-behind-the-city-desk authority which is as effective as a top sergeant's and he said, "More people than you'd believe write to the paper about angels. Guardian angels, mostly. Usually they don't sign their names—moral cowards like a lot of folks. All right, admitting a percentage of letters to the editor are written by nuts, some aren't. Anyhow, here's one for Mellie that didn't happen in any goddam war, it happened right here in Chicago. I get a letter one day from a woman says she is confined to a wheelchair and all her neighbors and *friends*, such as they were, she said, told her she ought to have her old dog put out of the way. He was half blind, she couldn't take him out any more, not to put too fine a point on it he smelled some, and it would be for his own good. But she wrote that they'd been together a long time and she didn't think if *he* was the one to decide he'd have her put out of the way though she was in this wheelchair and couldn't take him for his walk any more. But they had her where she was about going to have to give in and do him dirt and then she'd be without the only *companion* she had. Just then an angel arrived though whether it was her guardian angel or the dog's—his name was Whitey—she wasn't sure. She couldn't see him herself, but all of a sudden the damn dog would wake up, and he'd look up and start wagging his tail with a thump and then he'd get real frisky and pretty soon the door would open and off the dog would trot. After twenty minutes, half an hour, back he'd come, wagging his tail. Well—" Monty Berkowitz stopped to glare at us, "when you've seen as much as I have, anyhow I sent a reporter who wasn't doing anything out there. He saw Whitey all right. The neighbors had seen him taking his walk and they were surprised he could cross the street without getting hit —one woman said he waited for the light but my man wasn't going to fall for that, anyhow he got one little girl who said he raced around the park playing and once she said she saw a stick sail through the air but you know how kids are and her mother told my reporter her favorite program was *Topper*— Of course my boy didn't see any angels, but he did say he saw a half-blind dog that pranced through *traffic,* he said it was all goddam peculiar—"

Everybody laughed.

"Of course I never believe anything," Monty said. "But it made a pretty good little feature."

Probably it was all this conversation, but right then something goddam peculiar, as Monty put it, was taking place with me. I could see all the people around our table clearly, they were beautiful and colorful and glittering, I knew they were *real,* but I had a sense that they were in a different dimension. Some more, some less. Some darker—much darker —and I wondered what dimension it was. Only two of them were in the lighter, higher dimension, the one William James and Ouspenshy and Buck called Cosmic Consciousness. The dimension in which I longed to be some day. Of all people, Monty Berkowitz and to my astonishment Hank Gavin. *Hank?* Al Patton was walking toward it, moving toward it, I should say, and I patted his arm because he'd had the moral courage to start this conversational gambit that might give us a chance to see, to believe *something,* to stir people up, out of the apathy of Laodicea.

Then Joe Quaglino came out of the kaleidoscope shouting. Joe Quaglino could shout when he felt like it. He shouted, "What's all this what's all this—" and I thought *now* we'll get the same moneyman's twentieth-century American viewpoint, by one of its most successful apostles. I heard, "—I gave up childish things like a man has to, but when I was eight I had a guardian angel and everybody did only they're too pigheaded and conceited to say so and while I'm not going for any of this we've been hearing around here today exactly, it's probably because we're too pigheaded and conceited as I said to pay any attention. When I want to do what I want to do, you can bet I think I'm smarter than any angel that wants to disagree with me. They want you to give up something probably every time and then you can *bet* I having eyes see not and ears I hear not like all the rest of you."

With a suave, smooth, friendly amusement, David Kenyon said, "Joe, old boy, could I ask whether your guardian angel had wings, such as the soldiers saw on the dead one Philip Wylie wrote they found on the island, or do you simply mean a man's better self or what your psychiatrist might call his humanistic impulses?"

"I don't have any truck with psychiatrists," Joe Quaglino shouted, "I had a couple at one of my plants and when I talked with them I always had to look to be sure the guards had locked the door on 'em—that's how they struck me anyhow. Whatever angels are, don't you forget, Dave, that every time they'll leave ninety and nine self-righteous bastards like you and go after one lost sheep like me maybe." So, I thought, Joe Quaglino had been brought up where they sang *There were ninety and nine, which safely lay, In the shadow of the fold, But one was out in the hills away, Far off from the gates of gold.* It sang in my head, nevertheless I felt myself getting slightly hysterical at the picture of the Pirate with his black patch as a lost sheep. So I stared hard at Mrs. Browne who like many academic wives looked rather like a sheep, and at Stu Margolis' wife who was talking to herself.

Beside me, I felt Hank Gavin listening with painful concentration, tightening up like a steel spring, but when he spoke it wasn't to Mellie, so amused and contemptuous of these antics, blowing small, perfect, blue-gray smoke rings around her head. "Jack," he said, and Jack Knowles smiled at him cheerfully. They were about the same age, mid-thirties, they faced each other from the same kind of schools and families. "You're a priest—" Hank Gavin said, and the word sounded strange, as a matter of fact the Reverend John Knowles was a priest but it is not a Protestant word. I felt that tingle of apprehension again and looked at Monty Berkowitz to see whether he felt it, too, and he did, but for the moment Jack Knowles took it very much in stride. He had a big, friendly, much-practiced smile meant to put one and all at their ease, he used it now as he said pleasantly, "I'm a minister of the gospel, Hank, if that'll do."

With an effort, Hank returned the smile. He said, "Isn't it about time we heard from you, buddy? This is your *business*. Angels and ministers of grace defend it. Out in Korea we had a chaplain, I'm not likely to forget him, he was a Jew who'd been converted to Christianity and he saw angels both ways, God's thoughts passing to man without wings or in the front lines turning the bullets at—with wings."

"That's a convenient way to look at it," Jack Knowles said, the smile growing wider.

"What about you?" Hank Gavin said. "Seems to me you ought to be counted on this subject of angels, wings or no wings. You've got a vote here, buddy. How about you?"

Now there was complete and utter silence. Even the growing noise from the other room seemed to have receded. Jack Knowles looked directly at the man asking the questions. Plain to see, young Knowles had been born to the purple and probably gaiters. I wondered whether if as an undergraduate at one of the old and honored universities he'd been forced to make a choice between the postgraduate drama school and the famous theological seminary.

In the warmest possibly way Dr. Knowles said, "You'll forgive me, Hank—and you, Al?—if I say this doesn't seem to me quite the time or place for this discussion. It's our position that arguments on religious subjects are seldom either wise or safe. Emily Post said the two topics always to be avoided in mixed groups were religion and politics. They do so often seem to bring out the worst, don't they? Not long ago, one of the really great minds in the church in an article—I don't think I dare pretend to quote it exactly but it made such an impression on me that I can give you a good deal of it almost verbatim. He said something about the fact that scientific explanations today exist side by side with expressions of religious faith. He pointed out, so *wisely*, that religious affirmations about the mystery and *meaning* of human selfhood and human history contain a substantial part of our sense of humanity—emphasized, as it were, in Western culture as one of our dearest achievements. And this achievement, as he said, is of course imperiled by our technocratic preoccupations, and, since this is an important contribution, one hopes that an open and pluralistic culture will tend to purify the culture by freedom in which all versions of the truth are criticized and assessed and with this I fully agree, as I'm sure you do. But not, I think, on an occasion like this when perhaps we're neither in the mood nor the surroundings to make the best of it."

"Reverend," said Katie Ogilvie Gavin's old treble from the foot of the table, "you'll now allow me a very old lady's privilege of making a nuisance of herself. For what this has to do with the subject under discussion, which was angels, or what you're talking about I cannot come by."

Without taking his eyes off Jack Knowles, Hank Gavin said, "Take it easy, Granny, we'll get back to you." Then to Reverend Knowles, who had turned to bow in her direction, "Are you saying we mustn't bring the church into the market places or angels into the country club to sit down at table with publicans and sinners—like me?"

"That's not quite fair, is it?" Jack Knowles said strongly. "You must not misinterpret me. We try to speak in the language of our day—"

"Sure sure," Hank said, "pluralism and technocracy and Western culture, but even if the seed is sowed now by a machine, it has to be the same seed—isn't there a simple language the same today and yesterday and tomorrow?"

"Certainly," Knowles said, "but if we can't meet the intellectual test of our contemporaries, if we can't speak to them man to man at the level of today's enormous advancement in scientific expediency, what hope have we?"

"And if we can what hope have *they?*" Hank Gavin said and somebody gasped loud enough for all to hear. "Wasn't it supposed to be spoken by the roadside everywhere, on hillsides, in fishing boats, at meat in the Pharisee's house, at the beach, in the desert?"

You could have heard a match scratch.

Something new had entered the smoky, crowded room. I glanced around the table, every face had reacted to it, some with anger, resistance, speculation—some with hope. Hope? It seemed to me there was more *hope* than anything.

What we need is hope.

Who had said that? Timothy to Paul? Paul to Timothy?

I found myself amazed that the young man I thought I knew as my goddaughter's husband was willing to shove his blue chips into the middle of the table in this kind of an argument before an audience which included his boss and several of his most important and most cherished customers.

There was also his wife and through the smoke and smell of champagne I saw that Mellie's face was drained white.

At this point Dr. Knowles re-entered the fray. Patiently, brightly, he said, "I wonder if that's for us, in a different age, so many utterly different situations and conditions and problems—"

"Onesimus was a runaway slave," Hank Gavin said, "a black man and the Romans in Jerusalem were anti-Semitic it seems like, and the union of the silversmiths in Ephesus whose trade was to make statues of Diana gave Paul the most trouble, and the five thousand didn't have enough to eat, and Barabbas was leader of an underground rebellion and some of them were beatniks, and Paul's grandfather booted him out for not going to *his* church, and there was a woman taken in adultery and a man born blind. Why are the problems so different?"

Around Rev. Knowles' aristocratic nose I noticed a suggestion of pinching and I glanced again at Monty Berkowitz to see whether he thought the bigger, richer smile was the one that means a fighter has really been hurt. He knew it wasn't —and so did I, because Jack Knowles said gravely, "I was thinking as I drove here this morning, in fact I said to my wife, I must make myself more available to all of you. I must persuade you to come and talk these matters over with me at the proper time and in the proper place. Come any time, Hank, you've obviously been doing some unguided and undirected reading, I'm glad you're interested, I'll be glad to help you. We need men like you, and now I can see that the ladies think we should enjoy this fine day, and being together with our friends and see if we can figure out if the White Sox are going to be as good as they look, though as an old-time fan I must admit I resent their doing it without Nellie Fox."

In a sharp and profane whisper I heard Al Patton saying to himself, "The silly sonofabitch dropped the ball, they always do, why do they? Maybe it's a dead hand," and I said, "He didn't drop it, he threw it away, I think it's a matter of policy."

A sharp tug at my sleeve startled me. Mellie was standing there, her wash leather gauntlets in her hand, her round cap under her arm, she said to her husband in a husky voice, "Behave yourself, buster," and to me, "He's going to play some more golf, let's you and me get out of here while I still can, how about *that?*"

4

Through the soft, green spring woods, past the few remaining farms, by the well-cared-for estates, the open foreign sports car let the wind blow upon us. Sweet scents of new-mown hay and fresh-cut grass and lilacs and broom filled the air. Mellie drove too fast, she always did, I was always sure she wasn't looking at the other cars, but we slid in and out and from lane to lane without wasting a hairsbreadth. She was the best woman driver I had ever ridden with and if her attention did not seem to be on her driving neither did she give any sign that she knew I was sitting far down on my spine there beside her. Once or twice I glanced at her profile and found it arrogant and remote. Suddenly, as often before, the outsize violences of Chicago hit me. No other city, not even Naples, seemed to me to have such shocking contrasts, the whole thing was splashed as though on a giant canvas with a brush as passionate and frenzied, as malevolent and beautiful and naked and hung with jewels and brocaded velvets, as chaste and as lewd, all by a brush as dynamic as Gauguin's. There was the lake, free, wild, molten gold under the setting sun. It could have been the setting for Cleopatra's barge yet instead a long pedestrian string of flats laden with coal smudged the horizon. There on my right was the fringe of apartment houses and mansions new and old, towering in stone and glass and brick beyond conception in luxury, and a spit and a holler back slums of unimaginable filth and poverty, city jungles, though now the private citizens and private industry were tearing all this apart in an urban renewal project bigger than the building of Rome. Shoulder to shoulder, the Loop and some of the finest museums in the nation. There had been Al Capone and Johnny Torrio, the best brain the underworld ever had, and Bathhouse John and Hinky-Dink. At the same time men who built, McCormick and Deering and Patterson and Swift and the Fields. If there had been Big Jim Colesimo's there had been the Chicago Opera and the Symphony, where once an old lady had said to me, "My husband gave me these very seats when we came back from our honeymoon sixty years ago," and if there had been a St. Valentine's Day Massacre, there had been the greatest newspaper editor I'd ever known, one Walter Howey, and men like Ben Hecht and Charlie MacArthur to write about it.

Mellie picked up speed dangerously, cut in front of a bus, the driver of the truck in the lane beside us who'd slowed down to let her by of necessity, leaned out and yelled in uninhibited fury, "Lady, I can't think of anybody's funeral I'd rather go to than yours if you go *alone*—" and then he stared, and a grin came through the thunderstorm and he said, "Oh it's *you*. Look, for Chrisake will you be a little careful please?" I said he seemed to know her, and Mellie said, "I think he has a little girl at the Children's Hospital," and I said: "Okay, we've had our coincidence for the day, haven't we?"

Without looking at me, she said, "Does Hank suggest to you a young man who has blown his roof?"

I said, "Far otherwise. He must be a strong and reasonably sane man to have gained the position he has in this town. It's not easy to impress. I like him more and more. I liked very much what he did today."

Then she turned to stare at me, horns began to honk from behind, on both sides, she picked up speed, we wove and slid through the heavy Sunday traffic.

I knew I couldn't hear the motor of the big sports car, yet way down deep an engine was warming up, it sounded the way trains used to when I was a little girl and my father and I traveled on them.

The same prickle I always had when a story was beginning to break big.

The house the young Gavins had bought was half a block back from the lake, built of dark red-brown stone with a pitched tile roof. I had been eager to see it. Little enough chance I got on this occasion. A tall, narrow house, on the left side of the entrance hall I had a glimpse of a room with cream walls and on the one facing the arched doorway a modern picture in startling colors to which I took an instant dislike. I was surprised to find anything of the avant-garde in Mellie's house. As far as I knew, she had no reason to feel defiant. On the right hand a silver green glimmered and the crystal of a chandelier. When we had climbed the narrow, straight stairs I felt at home. For here was a grown-up version of the third floor sitting room belonging to Melanie Cheyne at the family home in Lake Forest.

Mellie said, "Let me get out of this gear, please," and went away.

Two children's chairs, the backs in petit point of Mother Goose rhymes. A corner cabinet of priceless pieces of family silver, over the fireplace a superb reproduction of Van Gogh's Skylark, these were old friends. I picked up some books from the marquetry table that had belonged to Melanie's nth great-grandmother, she who according to tradition had gone smiling to the guillotine with a rose in her teeth. A couple of novels that didn't matter and one that did, very much, Richard Kim's *The Martyred*. A new life of Keats. A paperback of a Josephine Tey mystery and, to my astonishment, de Chardin's *Phenomenon of Man,* showing signs of wear and tear. Opening it, I saw that it was much underlined and annotated in the margins. It must be Hank who was so immersed in this book which I believed might be a turning point of our civilization and century. As I browsed among Mellie's books, I realized how often I judge men and women by the books they read, by those in even a small library that show signs of real use, by the paperbacks they keep. Those of us who *read* must speak the language of our books, their words and thoughts must be in our brain cells and memory stream-of-consciousness as Rowse says the Bible and the Book of Common Prayer were in Shakespeare's and that there is hardly a page that does not show their influence. We often could not find words to exchange feeling, to express beauty, to convey anything without the books we have made part of ourselves, as all musicians have made Mozart and Beethoven part of their very breath, even the most modern of them. Hank and Mellie, for instance, had been brought up on *Wind in the Willows, Alice in Wonderland, The Wizard of Oz,* and then *Romeo and Juliet* and *A Midsummer Night's Dream,* they had a common speech with each other. And now that I saw the de Chardin book, open and so heavily marked, I could tell what trend Hank's mind must be taking and how deep this must be, that he was sold on this declaration of one of the great scientists for Christ, again and yet again for Christ as Jesus taught him in the New Testament. I was filled with a glow of gratitude for all the spiritual experience and enrichment of all the great minds and loving souls down through the years and for the testimony of such men as Sir James Jeans and Eddington and Millikan and Einstein as well as the saints and for all the sinners who had found God and glory and told us about it. How poor must we be without the books of the world—there lies our real treasure, it may be.

Upon this thinking of mine, Mellie came back.

She had changed into a long, plain cotton housecoat the yellow of daffodils, and knotted a scarf around her hair so that the high cheekbones and lovely markings of the temples showed, but I saw also for the first time the deep blue shadows under her eyes. When she stopped to give me a sudden hug, I felt that her whole body was trembling. Shoving me into the biggest chair she said, "You have to be sitting down for this one, lovey," and went and perched opposite me in the middle of a high-backed sofa.

Her laughter, coming off a deep sigh, sounded all right. She said, "It occurs to me that I am making a fool of myself to take this seriously. Boys will be boys and it's better than taking to drink—nonetheless it's been upsetting. And that's making a molehill out of a mountain! I suppose I might have guessed that after Yale and Korea, selling stocks and bonds, because that's what it amounts to *really* even if you're the ace and make more money than anybody, can be a bloody awful bore part of the time but I honestly thought Hank liked it. Anyway I'd give you forty-two guesses what Hank now says has happened to him."

"I'm a bad guesser," I said.

"He has been converted to God and Christianity, by Jesus Christ himself, the way he tells it," she said. "None of these gradual intellectual conviction processes—the *works,* as far as I can make out."

She kept staring at me. "It's been going on a long time," I said slowly, "so they tell us."

"Oh—with crackpots and lame-brains and paranoiacs," Mellie said, "or malcontents that can't cope or—forgive me, sweetie—old ladies that are through living. Or pipsqueaks that can't make a living anywhere else or hollow pomposities like that *ass* Jack Knowles was quoting from at lunch."

"What about the angels—" I began.

"It's all very well for Al Patton and Joe—but none of them are going off to an island to *look* for a dead angel or a live one either," Mellie said and began to laugh again.

"Well," I said, "it can't do Hank any harm."

"Wait," she said, "you haven't heard the half of it. He wants to go and be a minister—a *preacher*—can you believe it?"

This time I was stunned. Yet way down within me, much deeper than thought, something said *There!* As though a gong struck or a bell tolled. I knew this was the big story that had given me the prickles. I said the first words that came to me, "You mean a real minister in a *church,* like Dr. Knowles or the bishop?"

Mellie roared. "You heard him today on that bunch," she said. "No, no, none of that Tillich-Niebuhr Western culture crap. Our Henry Angus thinks he's the second coming of St. Paul to the Chicagoans or the Phoenicians or Ye Men of Palm Beach—believe it or not."

This time her laugh sounded deep and honest and joyous as though she'd convinced herself of something. She was laughing at herself now, her eyes all wrinkled up, and she said, "Oh, what a fool am I. Honestly. I ought to know my Hank by this time, the lad's an extremist and always was and a practical joker besides. He has to be kidding, doesn't he?"

Paul? St. Paul on the road to Damascus? We *know* Paul.

Hank Gavin? For Chrisake, we *know* Hank.

He has to be kidding.

Doesn't he?

5

At the door, Mellie said, "Do let me get you a taxi, lovey," and put her arm through mine. "I wish you wouldn't *go*. There's lots more—"

I said, "I have to think over what you've already said before I can make sense of any more. After just so much talk I have to try to figure out what it means."

"If anything," Mellie said.

"Oh—" I said, "it means something. Only I don't know just what."

"Nor do I," Mellie said. "Nor do I. Such an odd sort of thing for Hank to come up with. Drink or drugs or other women or wanting to run a bookshop in Tucson, Arizona, or a sheep ranch—you do think he has to be kidding, don't you?"

"No," I said, "no. I knew a young man once who left a prosperous hardware store in Nashville, Tennessee, and a wife and four children and went to Paris to learn to paint. In fact I own one of his pictures."

"Oh, that!" Mellie said. "That's different, men are always doing that. Ask Somerset Maugham."

"You mean wanting to be a painter is more acceptable to Western culture than wanting to be a preacher?" I said.

"Don't be a cat, sweetie," Mellie said and followed me down the steps and stood on the curb signaling for a cab. "You will try to see Hank?"

"No I won't," I said. "One of the few things I've learned is that you can only do anything, good or bad, if someone comes to you."

"Well," Mellie said as a taxi swung out of State Street and slowed down for me, "I shall continue to ignore the whole thing."

"I doubt if you'll be able to do that," I said, "a thing like this doesn't just go away."

She didn't answer me. She stared at me with eyes that were too bright and very dark, still taking it for granted that she was mistress of all she surveyed. I felt that awful pang of pity for the young, who are being taught either that the world will lie down and roll over for them or that it may blow up tonight. So slight and frail and young and arrogant, defying the lightning, I was sure that Mellie Cheyne Gavin had never opened the book of that hard-pressed boil-ridden old Indian-fighter Job. Nor read Jehovah's question *Answer me now, if thou knowest, who shut up the sea with doors?* It seemed to me painful that so many of them had to go out into today's deadlocks and dilemmas and disasters with nothing but a puny little worldly education, without strength of character or discipline or the sword of the spirit in their hands.

The taxi moved away and we waved.

Against the clear twilight, the street lamps had come on, still pale as candles. Now the evening air came straight off the lake and had the clean pure scent of water. Soul and body were refreshed by it. Here and there windows at the street level were squares of light, figures moved, I felt my usual profound curiosity to know the stories of all of them, the unexpected passions, the grand nobilities, the murder and merriment. I thought that I knew the foundation of the story unfolding behind the windows of the young Gavins' expensive, elegant, tall and narrow house, a story that none of the curious walking by it, peeping in, whispering about, would believe. The tall apartment buildings were checkerboards of light and dark, orange or silver and ebony. As we slid up in front of the Drake, and I went up to my rooms, like the White Queen in *Alice,* I kept saying to myself *important—unimportant. Important—unimportant. True or false, true or false.* In my box had been a message to call Mrs. Katie Gavin as soon as I came in. I felt it could wait. I had more important things to do. My score made no sense. And there were too many facts and fancies undetermined in the middle, small things, but who could ever be sure which were small and which big? Later it turned out that quite small and unimportant things had changed lives and that what was important about the dog-in-the-night was, as Sherlock Holmes saw immediately, that he *didn't* bark. A negative was what had been important.

My first clue in all this had been Mellie's startling identification of the angels of Mons with Goldilocks and the Three Bears.

Three Bears.

Second, Hank's open challenge to Just-Call-Me-Jack Knowles.

To these I now added what Hank Gavin had or had not told his wife concerning what she called his "conversion."

Next, the stand Mellie told me she proposed to take in case he wasn't kidding.

When I was a reporter and used to cover court cases, I

could put down Q. and A. in my head when it went too fast for my pencil. My father had taught me this and once more I was grateful for it. I sat down with only one small desk lamp on and began to review slowly and thoughtfully what Mellie had told me. How she had told it.

I felt sure first of all that he had been feeling his way as he told her of his—enlightenment? his "conversion," and that when she laughed at him—*who wouldn't,* Mellie had said, *you had to laugh or send for the men in the white coats, didn't you?*—that laughter had sent him back into his shell. Probably he was still amazed and so it hadn't been made at all clear to his young wife, only one word kept coming strong and clear—the word *light.*

"Yet to that very day, hour, and minute," Mellie said, "I give you my word we'd never so much as discussed religion. Between us. Oh, sometimes in a group, not as bad as that awful asininity about angels, but somebody would give tongue about agnosticism, or becoming a Zen Buddhist, or the philosophy of Western civilization, or Colin would do an imitation of Billy Graham balancing the Bible on one finger and there'd be a dingdong as to whether he was sincere—Graham, not Colin—and of course Lulu Steele became a Catholic, very spectacular, and once or twice in some political seesaw it would come up that the Communists believed in man, not God, whereas it said right on our golden calf In God We Trust. Colin raved against the church, he said ours was a glorified *club* that never faced anything, but Colin only did it to annoy. Hank and I went to church when the bishop preached his farewell sermon, such an old duck and such a phony, he told David he'd marry us if Dodo got a divorce which is certainly Gog and Magog or whatever they call 'em, and of course we went to functions, weddings, and baptisms—"

"Why haven't you and Hank any children?" I said.

"Give us time," Mellie said. "You have a right to the first five years to yourselves. You're only young once. I don't suppose you stay that much in love, do you?"

"For better or for worse, it changes," I said.

"Once I start, I want four in a row," Mellie said, "they have such fun. I was an only child and that's rough. It's odd, Colin of all people wanted kids, they tried but nothing came of it."

"You two and Colin and Sybil were a young married foursome, weren't you?" I said. "Colin was Hank's closest friend?"

Mellie said, "Oh yes he *was*!" and then sat silent, obviously she wasn't going to have any part of Colin or anything he might have had to do with this.

In this tight little silence it came over me that while Sybil his wife hadn't known what Colin was thinking when he stood there in the window, his best friend had. Through several wars, big and little, I had seen men drawn together, moved, changed, affected to themselves and each other forever by some moment, some shared longest day or hour. Once a young Marine lieutenant had told me of a night sitting around the fire with a colonel he'd never seen before. Of how the faces of his men—snuffies, he called them—had struck him all of a heap. Those funny-faced kids sitting around making bum jokes, by tomorrow night this time one of them at least wouldn't be there, he wouldn't be *anywhere* except in a letter he himself would have to write to the kid's folks, and maybe that *one* might someday have written a great poem or invented a cure for the common cold or a way to inspire teachers—and his eyes had met the colonel's and knew they shared a rage, a blindingly deadly rage against our statesmen and politicians and leaders who weren't *smart* enough with all their power to keep our *boys* from being torn loose from their homes and families and work to be killed out there and what the hell for? The young Marine said he and the colonel were closer then than any other friend he'd ever had in his life and they *stayed* that way, they still were. ..

The war in Korea wasn't supposed to amount to much, still it was life-and-death, which made the difference between bull-fighting and tennis.

Hank Gavin and Colin Rowe had been there together.

Colin Rowe, because of this, would always be part of Hank's story. Mellie would never like it.

"You know," Mellie said finally, "there wasn't one single, damn, lousy syllable about any of this religion bit to warn anybody. Not a *hint*. No staring off into space, no hearing voices, no quaver in his larynx. As far as I know, he slept like a baby, like a normal, healthy, hard-working, hard-playing guy which he was, I swear he was. You do know he's a truly great *salesman*, don't you?"

"They don't call them salesmen any more," I said.

"If anybody used those crash methods you used to read about, All-American halfbacks from Yale roaring through the line, they'd be fired forthwith," she said with glee. "People trust Hank's judgment, that's his secret. That's what makes this whole thing so fantastic. Out of nowhere he just came in and said, Look, honey, listen, baby, he said, in the same *trustworthy* way, with the same *enthusiasm*, I have seen a light and I may have to do something about it. The laborers are few."

"That's all he said?"

Her shoulders moved restlessly. "Just about. I said something like, Are you trying to be amusing, and he sort of blinked—and until this morning with all that flumdoodle about angels he hasn't mentioned it since. So I've continued to ignore it. This morning—the way he *talked*—I can't figure it. Do you think he's just bored?"

"What about before he married you?" I said.

Mellie shoved back the scarf that bound her hair. It gave the impression of trying to free her thinking apparatus. "Katie's religious," she said, and laughed, "if it doesn't cost her anything. You know Katie, she's terrific and I dote on her but she's a miser. The idea of her grandson giving up a fifty-thousand-dollar-a-year job to go out and sit in the heather like the Converters or whoever they were in Scotland would send her over the edge, Hank thinks she's funnier than Jackie Gleason, but I'm not sure how much influence she has, though it might be quite a lot at that, they're a *family*, the Gavins and the Ogilvies, if you know what I mean. If you're asking did he ever see things I wouldn't think so. Yale isn't exactly Princeton, is it? They get a bit woolly there. As far as I can find out he never had any epileptic fits like Savonarola or Vivekananda and he wasn't constipated like Martin Luther. He played an ordinary college brand of football. He was graduated *cum laude* though he'd deny it with his last breath. He has a temper that explodes and I sometimes think he's franker than he need be to prove he takes orders from no man, but mostly he's a sweet guy. If it won't shock you, lovey, he's a remarkably successful husband, I didn't have any *idea*—of course fumbling around in back seats and I was never in love with Dave Kenyon and *that* is what it's all about actually—Hank's wonderful."

"I take it your sex life is natural, happy, and an act of love," I said. "You're fortunate."

"I know," she said, and grinned at me wickedly. The young are so naïve. Then she said more cheerfully, "I expect the whole thing's a popoff. Like when he decides to play bridge by the Italian system or some such and bids one club without any to ask his partner to lead hearts against a no trump—he loves to hear his partner scream. Or he gets very drunk, drunker than anybody you ever saw, and goes off on a binge on a barge. The Comptons—he handles their account—have barges and barges. Godmama darling, he takes his work very very seriously, my Hank does." Her eyes opened wide; they were dark and troubled. "He has clients putting their children through college on their dividends, and *funds* for foundations and insurance companies, and pensions and old people who hope to live out their time independent of any serpent-toothed children. What happens to them if he leaves them flat to be a missionary to the Mau Maus or to Selma, Alabama? Why should Hank give up all that he's got?" she said.

"What did he mean *he might have to do something about it?*" I said. "What would be the steps, what happens next?"

"That," Mellie said, "I don't know."

At a small buffet made from an early American maple sink, she made herself a drink. She was too courteous to offer me one since she knew I didn't. While she was doing this I thought how little I knew about the structure of the Protestant Church or the mechanics by which a man of thirty-seven or thirty-eight offered himself to become a laborer therein. Would he join the Salvation Army or go on the sawdust trail with Billy Graham? When these conversions came to Catholics it was simple and direct, once they'd been proven. And it wasn't for some time that I discovered how large a percentage of the men in theological seminaries, of that Tower of Babel which is called Protestantism, had given up work and success in other fields. Lawyers, mechanics, insurance brokers, policemen, baseball players, scientists. On that Sunday afternoon at the Gavins I knew nothing of this.

As soon as Mellie was back in her seat I said, "It would be tough on you."

"On *me?*" Mellie said.

"You're his wife," I said.

"I am indeed," Mellie said, "and—I'm sorry, sweetie, but it's best to be honest. I don't believe in God, not even under any of the phony names like a Higher Power or Western Culture or Mind over Matter, or the Philosophy of Science or the New Phallic Worship or Come Up and See Me Sometime. Churches are whited sepulchers or social clubs at various levels and if my guy wants to enter into any such preposterous humbug you'll have a Gay Divorcée on your hands."

"You can't divorce a man because he decides he believes in God," I said.

"Oh yes I can," Mellie said, "if he makes a move that means I have to be part of it."

Shock held me silent. It had flashed through my mind that Mellie Cheyne Gavin wasn't cut out to be a minister's wife. But that she would resist to the point of divorce I couldn't believe.

"You're married to him," I said.

"I am indeed," said Mellie, swirling the drink in her glass. "You must see yourself that I wouldn't have dreamed of marrying him if he'd been a parson."

"Are you sure?" I said. "If you love him—"

"I wouldn't have loved him," Mellie said, "any more than if he'd weighed four hundred pounds. I can't bear preachers."

"But you did—you are *married* to him," I said. "It would be a breach of the better-or-worse contract—"

"That's the church's contract, not mine," Mellie said. "Hank knew what ours was. The law doesn't uphold that contract you're talking about. And it's a breach of mine and a fraud in the eyes of the law. I knew a girl in Washington who had her marriage annulled because the man told her he was an explorer and had been to the South Pole with Byrd and all the time it turned out he was a dentist in East Orange, New Jersey. If a man marries me on my knowledge and acceptance that he is a successful young businessman in a city I know and love and that he can support me as I expect my husband to do, of which he is well aware, and then he wants to become a sword-swallower in a circus at seventy-six dollars a week and make me go on the road with the circus, any court in the country will say he has breached our contract and free me from it—that's for sure."

"A most unfortunate analogy," I said.

"They seem equally dimwitted to me," she said.

She put her feet on the coffee table, her chin on her knees, and stared at me. Pain communicated itself. Underneath this defiance I felt a tumult going on, a troubling of the waters. Convinced though *she said* she was that this was a psychological explosion or a moon madness, but knowing Hank she had to face a very strong possibility that it was for real. She had recognized the strong strain of Scotch mysticism in him—though she didn't call it by that name—and so now her heart went cold with terror. For as she talked I felt how much she loved him, all she knew of love or had ever known of it was here. The first fine careless rapture, the capture, the wedding, the honeymoon had mounted over several years into a flame of possessed and possessing love.

Then slowly her eyes narrowed, and her lower lip swelled out, and I had never seen a look more blatantly, lustfully triumphant than the one she gave me. The same no doubt that Josephine gave Napoleon when he came back to her bed after the Italian victories and she reduced him from conquering hero to a puling vassal helpless with tormented desire. It occurred to me frequently that Mellie might be a little like Josephine, who became Empress of the French by charm and wit alone. Mellie had the same dark curls which she kept as smooth and straight as she could, the same wide dark eyes under rather ragged arched dark brows, the chaste mouth of amorous promise. Utterly feminine, both of them, in ages where women sat under the guillotine or had been lured into the competition of the market place. A woman of feminine charm would have untold advantages at such times in history.

"He won't do anything," Mellie said, and lighted a cigarette and blew small, deliberate blue-gray rings around herself. "I won't let him. I just thought of that."

"Men with a real urge—" I said, "maybe you can't stop him."

"Oh yes I can," Mellie said.

I got up then. After all, until I knew what had really happened to Hank Gavin and whether he had any intention of doing anything about it there were many things it would be unwise to say. So far, this was all pretty academic except for Hank's offense against Jack Knowles in the matter of angels. This I couldn't forget. His words had power, to repeat themselves to me as I drove home in the taxi. *You mean we mustn't take the church into the market place?* His face had hardened as the discussion went on, it wasn't the face of a young man indifferent to spiritual forces or needs or possibilities.

A fighting face, I thought.

I wondered what Jesus of Nazareth had looked like when he overturned the tables of the moneychangers in the temple.

At this point I picked up the telephone and called Hank's grandmother.

The moment Katie Gavin answered I knew she was sitting comfortably in bed, propped up by many pillows, that she heard better by phone than ear to ear, and that long conversations by phone were something the old shared with the young, in fragmentary and often pointless conversational exchange that went on for hours with no beginning nor middle nor end. The old are often too weary, disinclined for the dangers and difficulties of transportation, so that they prefer to gabble by phone and the young are confined by certain rules and the remnants of authority with the same result. Katie, I could tell, was ready and willing to spend the rest of the evening on the phone.

"Do you know what's going on with Hank and Mellie?" she demanded, Katie never being one to beat around the bush.

"I'm not sure," I said.

"There's no monkey business with either of them, though when they married I had my doubts," Katie said. "Hank had been tumbling girls since he was twelve and has been ever since and you know about Mellie and that middle-aged lecher, Dave Kenyon. But they're in love, it's beautiful to see, I was like that when Matthew Angus asked me to leave home and come to a pagan land though I knew we'd find gold in the streets I couldn't have done it did I not love him, we came steerage, and we were on our way to the Promised Land but we carried it with us, too, and it makes my heart ache to think there'd be anything amiss with Hank and Mellie. I weep with joy to look at them, and tears don't come easy to the old."

"You raised him," I said. "What kind of a little boy was he?"

"A runaway," Katie said. "More days than not I'd look up and there'd be a policeman bringing him back from the other side of town. With a bloody nose or a black eye most likely. Oh, he's an Ogilvie and fight they will. Always asking questions, he was, once they wouldn't allow him back in the Sunday School because he asked the teacher who it was he was supposed to be praying to, he wasn't, he said, at all satisfied with what they told him about God." Her chuckle sounded like a steam engine on a grade. "If you want the truth, he was a little devil as what right-minded boy is not and he could take care of himself with his fists like his grandfather and his father before him."

"Did he keep on asking about who he was praying to?" I said.

A clear cold pause ensued. Not just an ordinary pause where someone lit a cigarette, for all cigarette smokers must light one immediately when they begin to talk on the phone. This was a moment of careful thought.

"Is that what this is all about?" Katie Ogilvie said.

"What?" I said.

"You know I'm psychic," Katie said. "The Scotch are. The Queen Mother's psychic, did you know that? My grandmother —Meg Ogilvie—could see the past and the future. Don't tell me that's what Hank is being sought after by." The expression was new to me but I understood it. "His uncle Angus heard a voice saying leave your nets and follow me," Katie went on, "not that he'd any nets worth speaking of to leave which seems often enough to be the case. It'd be a terrible thing if Hank was to regard himself as called, stubborn as he is, *that* I know. And them as is called is not always chosen. Nor is it for him to decide to give up all when it's only a tithing that's required of us. Maybe somebody to finance the *works* is what Our Lord requires most right now."

"Do you believe that?" I said.

The pause was longer. "Come to lunch tomorrow," Katie said, "this'll take a bit of thinking."

"And praying?" I said.

"We'd be better off if there wasn't so much difference between the two," Katie said tartly and hung up.

I sat down and found the chapters in *Acts of the Apostles, about St. Paul.*

I would go to Katie's tomorrow and see if I could find out anything more about Hank Gavin because I found that I had been taken over by an extraordinary degree of suspense.

Perhaps she couldn't tell me much but I must go and see.

There I met Hank Gavin and when we left he asked me if I minded walking partway along the lake. He said he had to talk to somebody who wasn't personally involved.

"I can't even talk to myself any more," he said quietly.

6

Katie's apartment was in an old building with lofty ceilings. Its huge rooms were so overcrowded you had to do some broken-field running to get through. Much of the furniture looked as though it had been bought soon after the first Henry Angus Gavin struck it rich. Mellie had told me that Katie never threw away anything, so now I had a slightly eerie sensation of being hemmed in by closets full of the winter coats and party dresses Katie Ogilvie Gavin couldn't bear to part with. In her chair by the window, red wig sparkling, the impression was of an unconquerable, domineering old lady and yet somehow I felt a tremor within. As to where she would stand if her prize grandson made any move out of the rich and successful brokerage field into religion, crackpot fringe or legitimate, no lead reached me.

To this moment I don't know whether she had asked Hank to come in for lunch, but since coincidence must be anathema to authors I must assume that she did. Before he arrived, we ate sparingly, she discussed the coming summer theater season, the price of white fish today as against the time of her arrival in Chicago, and the loose morals of the younger social set. "I try to keep up with the times," she said. "I can't get used to people hopping in and out of bed with each other, as though they were playing post office. Stupid, I call it." This brought her to the real object of her invitation to me.

"It's not money," she said, "I've looked into that." And I knew she was rich enough and active enough in the financial world of investments to find out anything she wanted to know. "That house—it's an extravagance but all Chicago real estate will come around in the end. They live up their income and aren't building up their principal, I doubt if his own portfolio's any heavier than it was two years ago. Well, they're young and she's a girl needs money to make the best of herself and her life, she's aristocracy while we're only Johnny-come-latelies, some day he'll have the little I've been able to scrape and save, though I'll tie it up so he can't fritter it away. I was watching him and at my age I can see around corners and don't you forget it, and when he was speaking to that young preacher Knowles I saw a streak of the Ogilvies—he's more Ogilvie than Gavin—and many of them have been called. D'you figure Hank's got any such notion?"

"Isn't that something you ought to ask him?" I said.

"Come now," Katie said, "these young things don't know much and that's the truth and you and I have seen the same thing going on for generations. Oh, they change the words and the music and the clothes, and maybe airplanes for horses and television did-you-bring-your-music parties and better teeth and toilets and sticking needles in your bottom, but that don't alter anything to speak of. My grandmother used to say everything's changed and nothing's different. Let's not you and me stand on etiquette when it may be we can help those two young ones, for seeing them together is the last great joy I'm likely to have."

"What I know isn't very sound," I said.

"Still if there was nothing to it you'd say so without all this waltz-me-around-again-Willie," Katie said. She was back in the window and I felt her brooding. "If Hank's got a bee in his bonnet—it'll take some getting it out."

"You'd be against it?" I said.

"I'm for every man minding his own business and serving in the place where Providence has seen fit to put him," Katie said, "and you'll note that it says many are called but few are *chosen*."

"Well," I said, "if he's not chosen we have nothing to speculate about."

Upon that the doorbell rang and an exclamation of real pleasure came from the antique maid, "It's fine to see you, Mr. Henry, your grandmother's looking forward to it."

With interest, I watched Hank enter this atmosphere that was part of his youth for I had always thought of him as Mellie's husband, never as Katie's grandson, nor as a persuasive Scotch business-salesman. Though I had come to realize that this is the Era of Salesmanship, dedicated to it from Jack Kennedy as President to Girl Scout cookies or pets on television.

My surprise now was to see how mobile the lean, tanned young face was, the wide sensitive mouth, the quick eyebrows, the eyes that were the light, clear gray with no blue at all but some topaz yellow, the kind of eyes that most easily grow luminous. He had a short nose and a long upper lip and a terrier jaw. For some reason I remembered an early-days flight to Seattle to cover a kidnaping when we had lost our beam and were low on gas and between jittery prayers I was asking myself how the hell I got up there in the first place and playing an old game as to whom I'd like best to have with me right that minute. The man I chose had been both a racing driver and one of the world's greatest fighter pilots in a war long, long ago, and to my surprise I realized that this tall lanky young man before me now had the same kind of eyes, they both had that weatherbeaten look which has nothing to do with weather. They both had a sort of dauntless aspect that would make them your choice for the man beside you in a tight spot.

Suppose Hank Gavin *had* been called to something?

Suppose in time he was *chosen?*

Would that old lady whose craggy face I could see over the young man's shoulder refuse him sanction and attempt to exercise that unforgettable authority which had been hers in the crucial years before he was seven? If he interfered with her greed for gold, and the triumphant hope of founding an aristocratic Gavin-Cheyne clan, now that he had married into Chicago aristocracy, could she terrify him with no-night-light threats from the past in which they had been interlocked? If his experience of conversion, whatever it had been, led him outside her stern, narrow creed would she put the curse of the clan of which she was master upon him?

Cursed shalt thou be in the city and cursed shalt thou be in the fields. Cursed shalt thou be when thou comest in and when thou goest out because of the evil of thy doings whereby thou hast forsaken me.

With that curse his aged grandfather had blasted Saul of Tarsus, who had become Paul, and whether either he or Hank's grandmother had any clear idea who the *me* was or whether they identified it with themselves, how could anyone tell?

Katie's eyes over her grandson's head as he bent to kiss her forehead were empty and cold as a seagull's, they seemed as she had said to see sideways around corners. I knew now that she would defeat him if she could and my blood ran cold for this was something I had not bargained for, the demand of the very old for their own way, the conflict between the hundreds of different doctrines and interpretations, their confidence that they know best what is right for coming generations.

These would array Katie against any move out of Chicago on his part. I saw that even now as the ice melted and I saw the pleasure and gratification the old feel when the young pay them kindness and attention.

They were pleased with each other, fond of each other, tied together by a shared past.

Two formidable women as far apart as the poles to be reckoned with by Hank Gavin.

There was some fast and familiar conversation. She rallied him about the maneuver by which he had brought all the business of the new and youngest president of a big oil company into his firm. She used her adder's tongue on a young executive she didn't like and Hank said he was a good fellow and would have been okay if his father hadn't interfered when the guy wanted to be a college professor. Ah—his grandmother said—some, like his father, never had to prove anything, by the time the fruits are there it's too late to tell.

Time to go. Time to go. Hank felt it, and so did I. Somehow on a wave of good cheer and fast talk we swept out and Katie and the antique maid were waving at us as we went.

On the sidewalk, Hank paused and said, "Shall I take you somewhere?" and I said I'd like to walk. This disconcerted him. Chicago isn't as bad as Beverly Hills where the police pick you up if you walk a block, but it remains to them a matter of astonishment that you should want to. Hank's laughter struck me as breathless and uncertain, and he said, "Could I walk along with you?" and we turned toward the lake. He didn't break the silence, so we strolled along comfortably enough, though I could not take this as a casual happenstance. With delight I breathed in the air that seemed for the moment without a single trace of the vast and terrible and magnificent city behind me; the lake was so close I felt as though we were on the deck of a ship far out at sea. I thought that people who live where they can see water are always different, faith is easier for them in a way.

Hank said, "Mellie told me she'd talked to you. Did you form an opinion?"

"Like Sherlock Holmes," I said, "I haven't enough facts for deduction."

We had walked half a block before he said, "You may not regard them as facts." His forehead was tormented with new lines and I knew he was at a moment and mood of communication. As quietly as I could, I said, "Truth and facts aren't always the same. I've had some expert experience at sifting one from the other."

"You have influence with Mellie," he said.

"I doubt it," I said. "Are you figuring to need influence?"

"That's a bad word—a wrong word," he said. "Some other viewpoint than hers or mine. Besides, if I don't tell someone I'll burst. I don't know you well enough to be embarrassed and you don't know me well enough to keep checking what you know about me against what I *say* so I won't tie up in a knot—"

He's thinking *why me?* I decided. Why has this happened to Hank Gavin?

"Monty Berkowitz told me that the art of reporting is partly to put yourself in the other fellow's place," Hank said, "and as a writer the—the unusual—even the impossible—isn't so strange and incredible to you, is it?"

I said it wasn't, and this time the pause was a block long. He walked now as though he'd started around the world and hoped to be back for dinner, as though he couldn't and wouldn't be stopped, he had the long easy stride of the athlete or the mountain climber. I was neither, I had difficulty in keeping up with Hank, even in the walking shoes which I wore. I wanted to be unobtrusive, a presence which would listen so quietly that he could hear himself and know what his adventure sounded like put into words. At a light he slowed down and said with an irresistible appeal, "I don't know where to begin."

"At the beginning?" I said tritely.

"How do you know where it is?" he said. He put his hand under my elbow as we crossed the street and I thought what a funny place this was to begin this conversation, but then it nearly always is, things like this never get said on purpose. I saw that I had ceased to exist for him. "Churchill talks about the beginning of the end," he said to himself. "Do I start with war? Our war that wasn't a war in Korea that nobody really knew what it was about, so vague and disorganized and the little brown men on both sides looked alike, and we were always surprised as hell when somebody got *killed*. We'd expected them to get up, the way a man who'd been knocked out on the football field would do. But then—they looked awfully dead. I'd never seen a dead man before and neither had Colin. I got used to it but he never did, especially when they splattered. His reactions were unusual a lot of the time and on this he was filled with a burning resentment I never saw the like of. Nobody wants to talk about this bloody little police action, nobody wants to talk too much about any war, if they pretend it never happened maybe it won't again, maybe there isn't any such thing, I'm sick of it myself, but it has to be put in a little bit as part of the beginning, I *think*." I could hear the deep breath he drew. "I've talked to men who were in the big one, the Second World War, and *they* say a combat soldier, one who was at Iwo or the Siegfried Line, he's different from all other men. Well, even if it was a stinking little ole war

Colin and I were combat soldiers. If I say that much, will it do?"

As we walked, on our right was a fringe of grass and a couple of trees, under them two or three benches facing the lake. Hank steered to one of them and I was glad to sit down. My heart had begun an actual curious physical beat and I didn't recognize it, or maybe I was afraid to hope. Here it was as necessary as it had ever been in my life to be a good reporter, without prejudice or leaning one way or the other, with the eye of a trained newspaperman for faults and exaggerations and impossibilities and contradictions, not letting anyone give themselves too much the best of it, which naturally everybody does. News is news and it is necessary to make it as sharp and clear as possible and put in the color only when it is a real part of the story. Yet in spite of anything I could tell myself, my heart had begun to burn within me and I remembered that at the angel brunch I had thought what we needed most was hope. Also, I faced some amazement. Naturally, I have had to be a fair judge of speaking voices, in courtrooms, jails, interviews, and press conferences. Since radio and television became so large a part of our Free Press voices and whether they can make people believe what they say, or persuade them to think this way or that, or convince them of something have become a deciding factor in our lives. Not just orators any more, nor preachers nor politicians but newsmen and baseball players and executives and old soldiers and panels of housewives—all these are America Singing now whether we have a Walt Whitman to hear or not.

Hank Gavin had a hard, extremely masculine young voice with a Middle Western twang. Behind it was a kind of ring that covered laughter and irony and desperation and bewilderment and then impact and glory.

The bench wasn't any too comfortable but he didn't seem to notice, he pulled out a pipe and lighted it without any of the affectations, his thoughts felt far away and once or twice he ran his hand through his hair so that it stood up like a stubble of wheat, and I was falling under the spell of his silence. A man who can keep a thought-filled and active silence for more than two minutes can hold anyone for two hours.

"Before Korea," he said, "my life had been average normal, in that class and state where I was born. My mother died when I was little and it's no use saying I was heartbroken, you can't exactly miss what you've never had, and I don't understand things well enough to know whether it would have made a difference if I'd had her instead of Katie.

I want to tell you some of this because it doesn't seem to me *usual*, I had everything I wanted on earth, I had a good time, I had a fair record except I got bounced out of one school for—well, I socked one of the masters and we needn't go into that. I had ambition, but it didn't keep me awake nights. I was popular enough, I had the usual girls and got drunk the usual number of times, I had fun, as they say now. We took it all pretty much for granted, Colin and I didn't call it by any such fancy name as an earthly paradise.

"When I read Salinger's *Catcher in the Rye* I thought it was the greatest book I'd read about a boy in our times but—I'd never had anything as—emotional as that in my own life. It was all run-of-the-mill except for one thing.

"In my junior year at Yale I took a course in comparative religions from a man named Daladier. He'd been born in India and educated at Oxford and then at the University of Calcutta, but for some reason he wasn't one of those hotshots who get written up in the magazines and his classes weren't crowded with panting undergraduates. Maybe it was his personality. He was a quiet little man, rather bald, he liked his liquor, and he impressed me because I felt he could see beyond the pat answers if I came up with an idea myself. Most of my professors had written books because a prof is only as important as his books and Daladier hadn't any, though I did find out—later—that he had done some translations from Oriental languages which were well-regarded abroad. Anyhow, his classes fitted into my schedule and it was a sort of pipe course and to tell you the truth I had a sneaking interest in the subject. Did you ever read a book called *Kim?*"

I said I'd been brought up largely on Kipling and had read and reread *Kim* to all my children and grandchilren.

He came back from his steady contemplation of the past to look at me and nod. Evidently it made it easier that I knew *Kim*.

"I don't suppose it's regarded as a deep book," he said, "I suppose it's a popular novel or adventure story. But it was the book that affected me more than any other I read when I was a kid. I wanted to be Kim more than I wanted to be Rogers Hornsby or Pepper Martin. I wanted to go down the Grand Trunk Road as the chela of the Red Lama of Tibet. I wanted to go to Mr. Lurgen's and learn to memorize the jewels on the tray and I tried it sometimes on my grandmother's that were on her dressing table. I wanted to help my lama to find the River of the Arrow and to meet the Babu carrying his little parasol and have a letter with a number after it like R 17. Above all, I wanted to hear the lama chant of the Wheel—*just is the Wheel, swerving not a hair,* to hear him chant the Blessings, to *know*—to meet—a Holy One. One I knew to be Holy. Remember how Kim used to say I am Kim—Kim—Kim—Kim? I tried to do that. Sometimes I said I am Hank—Hank—Hank, who am I? They called Kim Little Friend of All the World—does this seem to make any sense at all to you? I was an ordinary kid—eleven—twelve—growing up in Chicago and going to gangster movies and getting my ear chewed off once in a neighborhood gang war—and all the time after the lights went out I was the lama's chela and went forth with his begging bowl and came back to hear him say *Learn,* chela. Do you believe all this?"

I said, "I once read *Kim* to a ten-year-old grandson and it wouldn't have kept him quiet for three postoperative days if *he* hadn't believed it."

I couldn't tell whether he heard me or not; he seemed to be pursuing a path far from me. Finally he said, "I'm almost sure it was because of *Kim* that I took Dr. Daladier's course in comparative religions. I thought he might explain to me more about the Wheel—and the eightfold path of Buddha. And all the other things in *Kim*."

"Did he?" I asked.

A smile that had pain in it came over his face. He said, "Oh yes—but he made a Christian out of me, as it were. He was very concerned about what he always called the Teaching and the Teacher. He said it was strange that all the great teachers the world had ever known were in the fields of religion and philosophy and that most of the teachings were the same. But he thought Jesus of Nazareth was by far the best of the teachers of all time. Impersonally, he based all this on the fact that as a teacher Jesus didn't handpick or screen students, he taught anybody who'd listen. He said he must have been a teaching genius, whether we followed the Word as he taught it or not, the Way had survived everything intact. Second, given his basic premise that as son of God God's active grace was always available to all, he proved it right then and there on lepers and lunatics as much as the Wrights proved at Kitty Hawk that man can fly. Daladier said that Jesus would have been right among 'em at Kitty Hawk, he'd probably have walked the whole way to *see* this and when the prof got on how far Jesus could walk in a day he made the Kennedy brothers look like pikers. A mountain climber, a fisherman of great catches, Daladier painted him as nothing like the *ghastly* consumptive skeleton Mellie and I saw hanging on a cross all over Europe. He said, too, there had always been queer and incomprehensible explosions of the *practical* teachings of Jesus. St. Francis had been one, probably Luther, and Mary Baker Eddy and Joseph Smith and his Book of Mormon, and Mahatma Gandhi, *of course,* he said, as soon as the rebellion was over organization and take-it-easy-brother and Gog and Magog swallowed it up because it is very tough indeed to *go and do likewise*—remember at this time I was an undergraduate and my training was to retain what the professor said. I was bowled over by these names in the same list, and here was a prof in comparative religions including Gandhi, who was a Hindu, and Mrs. Eddy, whom I'd been taught was a fraud to say the least, and Joseph Smith whose follower Brigham Young was covered with bloody feuds in Utah and had as many wives as Solomon—that's one reason probably I remember it all so well. However I expect I'd have forgotten Daladier and this kind of talk if it hadn't been for what happened one night after a bull session Colin and I had with him."

There was a remembering sound in his voice. He jumped up, restlessly, and walked around the bench, back and forth, for a couple of minutes. He needed to stretch his legs, also he was trying to tune in on all the recall he could get. Finally, he stopped and stood in front of me, looking way over my head, one hand in his pocket, the other, with his pipe cold in it, free for gestures.

"It was around two in the morning when Colin and I came out of Daladier's. It was an—unusual night. It made you understand that there is such a thing as starlight, brighter than pitch dark, not as bright as the moon, a glow of its own. I want you to understand that until I fell in love with Mellie I wasn't romantically inclined at all. I don't insist I was an altogether clod, but poetry and starlight and the perfume of spring flowers couldn't spark any power of imagination to *create* something beyond what was actually *there.* I wasn't susceptible—I want to make that clear if anything is.

"Just before we left Daladier had been talking about the Essenes, whom he called the White Brotherhood. He told us they were a group of mystics who lived in a monastery in India and his theory was that Jesus had spent part of the missing years, between the time he was left behind in the Temple when he was twelve and the beginning of his ministry and teaching at thirty, with the Essenes. He said a number of independent scholars had come to this conclusion and I *think* he said something in the Dead Sea Scrolls could be interpreted to confirm this. All this was way over my head but—I can't explain except that he talked about it the way you would about whether Roger Maris' breaking Babe Ruth's home run record was legitimate or not—as though it happened yesterday and was part of our everyday lives. Up to that time the only things I knew about God and religion came from Katie, and God was a cross between Captain Hook and Tom Sawyer's aunt, and none of it had anything to do with me personally."

He sat down in a sort of knees-giving-way-under-him fashion, turned sideways on the bench to face me, his eyes now intent upon me. He said, "You knew Colin, didn't you?"

"I'd met him," I said, "I remember him well."

"He's pretty hard to forget," Hank said. For that moment, Colin was *there* with us, how I'm not prepared to say, but I *felt* him *there*.

"Colin was sore because he said he'd tried to make Daladier come out with whatever it was he *knew* about the Essenes, he thought it was something important, he said Daladier was one of those seekers who couldn't go *back* now and didn't have the guts to go forward and that way, Colin said airily, lie alcohol and sleeping pills and the state of that man shall be worse than the first."

Hank paused and shut his eyes and put both hands over them. When he dropped them he said quietly, "I have to be careful here. I don't want to put in anything I've learned later or figured out by hindsight and I know I was excited by something, the way the professor had talked I'd felt a new kind of excitement.

"Well—anyhow—the prof lived a ways out, in a cheaper neighborhood, we had quite a walk ahead of us. My mind, such as it was at the time, was going over what the old man had said about mystics. I had to ask him what he meant by the word, and he said something like mystics were those who had spiritual intuition and consciousness and could through what he called meditation and contemplation—find a—find themselves in the *Presence* of God. He quoted some of their writings and experiences—did you ever hear of Juliana of Norwich or Jacob Boehme—all right, but remember up to that moment I never had and it seemed to me this was double-talk but just the same I couldn't get it out of my brain track. I was just going to ask Colin a couple of questions when he began to sing and I realized he was loaded. He and the old boy had been drinking drink for drink and Colin got drunk like a wave that went up and up and you never noticed except to think how—I don't know—how sparkling he was, and then it crashed. I'm not one to believe that old *in vino veritas*—when I get drunk all I want to do is fight—but I do know the demons we have finally got control of bust *loose*—" He broke off and a frown tightened his forehead and he said, "You want to hear all this?"

"More than I can tell you," I said.

"Well—all right," he said. "When Colin was plastered he had to *do* things. I was satisfied to sock a cop but Colin had whimsical notions. He used to say he could see himself in several other incarnations and they were all—anyhow, he said he wanted another drink, *I don't want to waste this beautiful wassail I have so carefully acquired,* he said, *let's go and harass some pure-souled professors like that monumental poop who's dean of this revered institute of learning.* He hooted and then he said, *Let's wrap him up in his winter drawers and take him to Lulu's and see if the girls can prove he's still alive and fornicating.*

"Don't get the idea I was against pranks. There are a few on my record. But I wasn't about to get us both booted out after nearly three years' work because Colin had a skinful. Daladier's wasn't a place I enjoyed drinking. I thought it was disgusting and—contradictory for a man who talked the way he did to sit there and soak up booze until he was incoherent —so I was cold sober. Besides I was still trying to concentrate on what the prof had said. But Colin didn't care where he drank. So I said No, let's not go to the Dean's, you're not as funny as you think you are, old boy. And he wasn't—but this was such a—such a *loving* guy. I guess what you'd call a blithe spirit."

Colin—*Colin,* who had jumped out a window?

Then I saw that Hank Gavin was weeping.

Sitting there on a bench just off the walk that ran parallel to the lakefront, in the early afternoon sunshine. The tears were running down his face and I could hear the long breaths he was drawing, trying to control the sobs. To say it hurt to watch him since he was a man to whom weeping came hard is to say the truth and yet—as I watched I was uplifted by it. He wasn't weeping only for his lost friend. He *cared,* he cared with all his being about something, and I didn't yet know what it was.

"You have to understand," Hank said, "I loved the crazy bastard. All this talk-talk about homos—poor devils—has got the thing so smirched up a man's afraid to mention the finest thing that can happen in his life—even finer than the love of man and woman because it's *without* that fire—lots of men friends have loved each other ever since Damon and Pythias—anyhow, I loved this mad guy. Most times I could handle him, except one night in Korea—but this night in New Haven he was *looping* like I'd never seen him, way out of control. There was a sort of—violence—I don't know whether I can make you feel it or set the scene the way it was—"

"Look here," I said, "you're supposed to be the best salesman in a city of salesmen, you can speak articulately—do stop apologizing."

He managed a smile. "All right," he said. He had taken out a fine white handkerchief and, without trying to hide it, blotted away the tears. His tone was quiet and unemotional when he said, "It was an ordinary street, with some of the famous elms sort of dying at the top. The houses on both sides were old, dark, only a window or two upstairs showed lights. Somewhere in the distance I could hear a shriek of tires and brakes. I knew this street well, one family were friends of mine, their son was a class ahead of me—I even saw his car parked in front. The street lamps weren't too bright, the globes shone in small circles, and then the darkness lay between them. It made a nice pattern and I kept looking up at them, the circles of light and the darkness and in one of the dark spaces I could see a bright star—

"I'd like to—to *impress* on you how plain and clear and ordinary and familiar all this was to me. As much—as simple—as if I'd been pacing up and down my own room with my Greek grammar—"

"Greek?" I said, I couldn't help it.

"Don't ask me why," Hank said. "On impulse, I'm not bad at languages if I swat. Did you ever—you know anything about Aramaic?" I nodded and he said, "There's a man—that comes much later, though.

"As we walked along I kept talking to Colin, because by then he was giving me the business and that look he had on always scared me. Like a free-wheeling locomotive going downgrade without any brakes—and he was carrying on about me being the wet blanket and the good brother which naturally is something nobody wishes to be. *I've got me a real tankful of high octane this time*—and the way he said it reminded me that Colin had been in one of his black moods, dark and pessimistic and everything was no good—he got them—and when he came out he came with a bang. You read about boys going to parties and tearing down the chandeliers, Colin and I weren't much more than boys at that, and I knew Colin was capable of any crazy stunt and if he did it *again* he'd probably go to jail, and he was on borrowed time already. Now here—some of this is hindsight possibly—but I had a cold, sinking feeling in my stomach.

Call it fear or premonition—I don't know. I tried reason and he said *Hell with that, chum. I'm going to Lulu's by myself, she's got a new girl, Chinese, and I may take her to Bridgeport and marry her. I'm certainly not going to marry any of those belles were up here for the Prom—I* knew, I *knew* I tell you, that I mustn't let this guy go haywire right then, I knew it, I put my hand on his shoulder and he shook it off and I thought of tackling him but I knew he'd yell like a hyena, I was a lot bigger, but he was tricky and fast and drunks are all over you like a swarm of bees and I didn't know what the hell to *do.*

"Just at that exact moment I found myself walking down a dusty road, with Colin beside me, I could smell the dust and the sage and sand and dawn light, it's no use trying to explain, I can just *tell* you. I knew I'd never been there before—remember I'd only had one bottle of beer—anyhow, now the road we were walking along wasn't—it wasn't only space and place that were different. It was *time,* too. The houses were gone, there was space all around us, I'd been so conscious of the light of the lamps and the dark between and the one bright star and now, unexpectedly and without any passage of time as we know it, it was all light around us. Oddly, this didn't surprise me. I began to—to forget where we had been, where we really were—and I couldn't tell whether it was dawn or twilight, the one thing I was sure about was that it was *light* and in this light Colin and I were now walking, I felt we could *see,* that we were simply seeing what was *there,* just beyond our usual way of seeing. I had for that brief space a conviction of power, a powerful conviction I mean, that always beyond what I saw every day in New Haven, at Professor Daladier's or in my Greek class or at Lulu's or walking down a plain ordinary street it was possible to extend the range of our *seeing,* as a —a television does, which it does, actually, doesn't it? You are sitting in a room and then by electronics we once knew nothing about you can see and hear to the other side of the globe. Time has been eliminated and space as well. That's now an everyday extension of having *eyes*—but what was taking place when I walked along that dusty road we were going somewhere on, was more than that. It was seeing what existed—I expect now I would say in the spirit or something, anyway around us all the time in another dimension—and having eyes we—we do not *see!* It's difficult to explain but I understood it perfectly. It seemed quite natural to me. The light—I can only—I can only say it wasn't just visible to my eyes, it was part of me as I was part of it, I felt as though I could keep moving in it and it in me forever, and

I felt *comforted*—I didn't really know the word consolation then, but I think that's what it was. The light consoled me the way a fire warms you. How long this lasted—as near as I could test it was probably not more than seconds—but I knew it was the most important thing that had ever happened to me. The light itself was important and the experience—I didn't know what to make of it or whether I'd gone crazy but that much I did understand.

"When I looked at Colin, he was walking along beside me, perfectly sober. The—the road—the dusty road and the light—they were gone and we were walking along the street under the lamps and I could see my friend's car parked there, and Colin was sober. I couldn't even smell anything. He was smiling at me, he had a smile that pulled people to him, after he was—dead, people would say to me that they remembered his smile. I remember it the way he had it on that night and he was talking in a sort of wistful, quizzical tone, and I can even remember the words. He was saying that probably some time we would understand why shoemakers like Jacob Boehme and a drug clerk like Keats and a third-rate actor like Shakespeare and a carpenter—a highly educated man like *Paul*—"

I interrupted him there. "He said Paul?" I asked and Hank said, "Oh yes, he said Paul all right." I had a moment of things adding up, of glorious satisfaction, I have no idea whether any theologian would agree, but I have always thought that Jesus spoke to Paul that day on the Road to Damascus because he saw that Paul *cared* enough about his God to try to wipe out those whom he believed to be blasphemers against Him. He couldn't have been wronger, but he *cared*, about God, and that stream of caring could be used—redirected, it was alive, whereas apathy and inertia, neither hot nor cold, good-humored tolerance of any and all differences, would remain forever in limbo.

"Well," Hank went on after the moment of silence in which I had connected all this up somehow, "Daladier had a lot of interest in Paul. And just about as Colin got to him and said sometime maybe we'd understand why all these men had been able to venture into new dimensions—we turned into our own street and he yawned and said *Bed bed bed—I can hardly keep my eyes open*—and we went upstairs and went to bed."

"Did he know—about the light or the change?" I said.

"No," Hank said, "I didn't want to ask him exactly how he got sober from being roaring drunk in about three seconds—the truth is I felt like a fool. My mind was popping with questions and I went and got a book by Juliana of Norwich—and Meister Eckhart but I don't think I ever *read* them. You get busy. One thing—he didn't know he'd been swacked the night before—he didn't so much as remember anything about the dean or Lula's. I edged around that. So —I didn't tell him, I didn't know how.

"I wish to God I had. It might have made the difference." He stood up and in a tight, hard voice said, "Let's get out of here."

7

We began to walk the blocks toward my hotel, the lake still there on our left hand. The two of us, our steps slower and slower, were conducting an inquest on the still incredible suicide of Colin Rowe.

The crucial moment begins at the cradle, the culmination of a long series of important events, failures, decisions, you-go-your-way-and-I'll-go-mine, the timing of when a man met certain people, books he read, music he heard, little things of no importance. In my marrow, I knew I had not yet heard what Hank Gavin with passionate urgency wanted to tell me. The short, happy-unhappy life of Colin Rowe was leading us to it inevitably. During his silence, broken only by sentences that burst from him and added a bit here, a piece there, to the picture of Colin, I reviewed what evidence I had.

From these things, from later witnesses, I can here put a lot of it together in one production. Stu Margolis, for instance, the last man to whom Colin had spoken on that fatal day, memory of which still started a shock within those built-to-be-shockproof walls of the Chicago Club, admitted Colin's charm and at the same time that he had always disliked him. From his exalted position and his own strength of character, developed in the unbroken, bland front he presented in utterly ignoring his wife's tragic alcoholism there beside him, he had always ruled the friendship as a danger to his boy, Hank Gavin. After the suicide, scandal at the least was to be expected. Circle after circle, Sybil enclosed her own truths within them, she had loved Colin desperately, and her failure—*I had to be a failure or he wouldn't have done it*—haunted her by day and by night. Once in New York I met a man named Potocki who had been at Yale with Hank and Colin. Too bad, Potocki said to me, too bad he didn't stick it even if he had to live in an attic, to go on with his song-writing, he had talent. *Talent!* I had thought then of something Gracie Allen had said to me. *Lots of people have talent, can they wrap it up*, that's the question. As Potocki told it, Colin couldn't, he didn't have the stamina, the discipline, the ability to work which, no matter what the dissipation or temperament or nonsense, must be there to bring talent into production. Birth is attended by labor and without it any talent remains an unlaid egg. Nobody in Chicago had mentioned Colin's song-writing. Whether he had concealed it successfully or whether nobody took it seriously, I'm not sure.

As we swung off the drive in a lovely circle toward the tall buildings, Hank said loudly and unexpectedly, "There's a poem reminded me so much of Colin I memorized it. It's the only poem I know by heart." Then in a voice of hopeless sincerity, against the horns and roar of traffic, he began to recite, very badly—

Whenever Richard Cory went down town,
We people on the pavement looked at him;
He was a gentleman from sole to crown,
Clean favored, and imperially slim.

And he was always quietly arrayed.
And he was always human when he talked;
But still he fluttered pulses when he said,
"Good morning," and he glittered when he walked.

And he was rich—yes richer than a king—
And admirably schooled in every grace;
In fine, we thought that he was everything
To make us wish that we were in his place.

So on we worked, and waited for the light,
And went without the meat, and cursed the bread;
And Richard Cory, one calm summer night,
Went home and put a bullet through his head.

"Poets—that was Robinson, wasn't it—or Benét—anyhow poets are allowed to say things like that," Hank said. "In prose you can't *say* a man glittered when he walked, but Colin *did*, that's why I memorized it."

As I absorbed it, through the days at Yale up to the war in Korea Colin's activities had ranged farther and farther in search of excitement. He had, I thought, begun with our inborn desire for happiness—and beauty. Stronger than most, poor child. But the world in which he existed was geared to seeking excitement as a synonym for happiness, thinking of happiness and joy in terms of excitement, speed, high pressure, blood, guts, passion, *thrills*, the devil and danger, never as serenity, as bright images in a garden, as peace and quiet and beauty. Its music, its dances, its sports, its painting, more and more were intended it seemed to me to arouse nerve-hunger, stepped-up vibration, until soon even excitement became excitation which is a horrid thing indeed. But excitement cannot be smoked in regular doses, the pill put in the pipe has to be more and more frequently increased, doesn't it? A boy of Colin's sensitivity, his lovely swift responses, would beat his wings against the best of rules, and he would follow not the bluebird, so seldom seen now, but the *ignus fatuus,* fata morgána, the illusion instead of the reality. And soon freedom to sin would seem a natural part of the over-all rebellion, not that he or any of the rest of his generation would permit anything they did to be called by so obsolete and mildewed a word or hypothesis as *sin.* Psychiatry had furnished him a new vocabulary that never *bit* morally, nor in fact recognized moral or spiritual values. In the circles where he glittered, humor alone was the alibi, the *esprit*, and primary skill. *Always leave them laughing* was the theme song. My heart felt loaded with sorrow as I got a sort of picture of this bright-haired gay youth coming back to the world he found after he had seen death on the battlefield. Humor was the missing link. Regard the monkey, my friends, always so full of amusing and whimsical tricks. The jolly animal without conscience or responsibility—the Bandar-Log who are not recognized even in the Jungle. Flippancy was the only possible *glittering* attitude in which Colin could walk and with laughter, with a sense of humor, singing a song, he walked gaily toward that open window when life no longer seemed worth living and the last smoke of the pipe had no kick left. This happens oftener than autopsies or investigations record as the Reason For—

I wished I had known Colin. I wished somebody had known him in time.

For as he talked Hank showed heartbreakingly that much of this had been invisible to him, and the rest he had forgiven and alibied and tried to get the best of. "There was so much *good* in him," he kept saying, "you don't have any idea how much good there was in him. He appreciated beauty—I mean really appreciated it, it *moved* him, he *knew* about poetry and music—" and his anguished words would fade out. Then after a pause he said, "He was *sorry* for Sybil. If he hadn't been engaged to her before we went to Korea, it's a cinch he'd never have looked her up when we got back. She was a secretary in an automobile agency where Colin worked after he got back from New York, finding out he couldn't sell, I guess, and her folks had a little farm somewhere in Iowa and they cut up like maniacs. They warned her he was nothing but a skirt-chaser and a playboy but somehow the announcement of their engagement came off about dawn at a farewell celebration we had the night before we took off—the one *after* the one at the Ambassador East. Well—she wrote him every day, letters mean a lot, you know that, and she said her folks said she'd just be humiliated and he'd leave her for everybody to laugh at for a fool, but she trusted him absolutely. I saw those letters. They had him hooked all right. He never could bear to see anybody humiliated. He was sorry for her, doesn't that mean anything to you? There were plenty cooler heads and more callous operators around, if they'd been in a jam like that they wouldn't have given her a tumble if she met them at the pier. The truth is Colin wasn't hard enough to play the game the way he—tried to. Another thing. He thought her father and mother being poor and having had to struggle, he thought that would make her understand and ready to go along if he wanted to take another crack at starving in Tin Pan Alley. As a matter of fact, it'd be the girl from the Castle itself, like Mellie, who'd follow a man if he decided to take the low road."

"You think Mellie would follow you?" I said.

His look expressed absolute sincerity if ever I saw it, and my job has depended often enough on my being right when I committed my paper to a man's sincerity. His grin meant he was visualizing her, and he said, "She may squawk some; she won't want to leave the festivals and high jinks, but when she knows I'M going somewhere she'll come along."

In a flashback, I saw Mellie's face with the Josephine-after-the-Alps look and felt a chill, slight but unmistakable, in my blood stream.

Adding up everything, it is plain that as soon as she was Mrs. Colin Rowe the former Sybil Heidecker took the high road in a hurry. Watching through a hole in the fence she knew that the way to social success, to being asked to small luncheons at the Casino, or going to the Theater-in-the-Round as a lark with half a dozen IN young marrieds, was within her talents and powers. Her talent, like Vadne Cheyne's, was considerable. Unlike Colin, she had staying power. She knew what work was, she'd gone to the office every day at nine and *stayed* until five or six or whatever hour the boss required. She'd never been able to escape to Mexico City for some sleep. Syb Rowe, good-looking in a rangy, career-girl sort of way, had studied carefully how to dress and above all how *not* to dress, and she was lucky in having a good ear, so that she soon acquired the cadence and speed and ever-changing exaggerated off-key IN vocabulary, lack of which betrays quickest. Before long she had acquired an enviable reputation for finishing any job anybody gave her.

Let Sybil do it.

Get Sybil Rowe to take it on. A bit of a bore, she's so absolutely vicious about being functional and efficient. But *quite* marvelous, actually.

Before long, by systematic attention to duty, restless vitality, and the habit of work, young Mrs. Colin Rowe was a No. 1 gal.

"I think she thought this was what Colin wanted," Hank said, "because all he did was laugh at her. It—it hypnotized him. Like she was a liontamer."

Before a couple of years had passed, starting from Colin's position within the social highest echelon, she headed half a dozen big committees and that sin by which some of the angels fell had her in its grip.

"Ever occur to you that this takes *dough*?" Hank asked me as we turned our backs on the lake. "Lots of it. All Colin knew about the magic of money was how to spend it if he had it and how to do without if he didn't. Pretty soon, Syb had to entertain, and hold rallies, and give political luncheons and hostess charity teas and she always got left holding the bag for some of it, everybody always does. Big shots were on her lists and big shots are softened for the kill at big dinners with other big shots present and if the one that's putting the bee on 'em is intimate with THE Mrs. Martin and Mrs. Francis Cheyne and Mrs. David Kenyon and Mrs. Solomon Potter it helped."

And by now, the young Rowes and the young Gavins weren't in their glittering reckless-all-is-forgiven twenties any more.

The turning point of the critical thirties, the decisive part of the ball game, had been reached.

At the time they were married, Colin was the first advertising and public relations director of a big outfit that had never had such things before. He was good at it, he had a feel, a flair, and it was all new to business and industry. Moving up to better and bigger brackets, young Rowe was about to be made Vice President-in-charge of PR and the young Rowes would have been an integral part of the scene I had witnessed on that Sunday morning at the country club. Although Colin was absent in the body he certainly seemed to be present in the spirit, and in the conversation around and about the table pretty often.

Like an honest researcher, Hank went back carefully, looking for determining factors, for the specific truth.

Just as we came up in front of the entrance to the Drake, he stopped and said, "I let him jump out the window."

"That's morbid, my friend," I said.

"No no," Hank said, shaking his head, "no. It's willy-nilly whether I like it or not, as inevitable and irrevocable as the Ides of March.

"Look. I did my best. Right?

"My best wasn't good enough. A man comes to that sometime, somewhere. His best isn't good enough, so either he settles for his best is the best he can do, and it won't ever be good enough. *Or* he tries to find or develop a best that *is* good enough, by God."

People passed us, the wind had turned chilly—or was it the wind? I shivered and Hank noticed it and said, "Let's go up to the International Club, shall we, and have a drink or a cup of coffee, it ought to be practically empty about now. Have you time? Can you—I'd like to finish this now I've *started*."

"So would I," I said.

8

The International Club at the Drake is big, low-ceilinged, and paneled in oak like the dining room of an English country house. The tables, large enough to eat on and talk across, are covered with red-and-white checked tablecloths, giving it somehow the air of a respectable tavern where Dr. Johnson might have talked, the silver is old and heavy, and from wall brackets and swinging lamps of copper comes light bright enough so you can see what you have on your plate and with whom you are lunching. People who aren't interested in either of these like to coagulate around touch-me tables and since this is the fashion and saves the restaurateur rent, no one has the courage to turn any light upon it and all accept its obvious inconveniences and shoddy glut of sardines in a can without open protest. However, the International is a warm, friendly, well-bred room for people who want comradeship, conversation, and something to eat that doesn't have to be hidden in Stygian gloom. The maître d' is expert and friendly without indicating that his nod of recognition is your ticket to social and civic standing and when we sat at a *window* there was a window there, through which you could see the lovely spring sunshine and the narrow busy street one floor below. Only a few people were lingering over late luncheons, four women from the suburbs though what it was that told you this I don't know, unless it was the chessy-cat smile with which they lingered over their brandy enjoying the last moment and drop of it all, two men, heads close, were talking contracts with, it appeared, a good many points unsettled between them, in one corner a couple of not-too-young lovers, it was easy to tell that, lunching here in the light because obviously it was a place where none of their friends or neighbors ever came, about them was an illicit air, this was not the first time they had met where no one knew them and now they had an air of sadness, of abandoned hope, about them. Two men sat at the bar, without lunch, they would still be there at dinnertime. The headwaiter had bowed to us and the waiter said, "Hello, Mr. Gavin, how's everything?" and hovered while I ordered coffee and Hank asked for beer. When it came he poured it carefully, steadily, and sat looking at its foam subside before he spoke.

"Syb had gone to New York with Toodie Goodrich to buy cuff links or candlesticks or confer with the editor of *Life* about a party—I don't know. Mellie was in Scottsdale with her father and mother for the weekend. Colin and I had dinner and he said he wanted to talk to me, so we went to his apartment. He still had a grand piano, though Sybil told Mellie he hardly ever played any more. She had sense enough to let that worry her but not brains enough to do anything about it. Too busy—no no, that's wrong, her best wasn't good enough either. The piano was in the big living room, Syb had done it all avant-garde or whatever and it was about as cozy as a gymnasium. Anyhow, Colin sort of drifted over to the piano and began to play. Something I'd never heard before. There is a lot of music I've never heard, if I tried to place it then I would have thought it was Chopin or a real early piece of Mozart's like the one he wrote to pay his plumber's bill, poor little devil. In a poem I read once—I only memorized one line of this one—it said, *My heart is like a singing bird,* it came over me maybe this could be that song. A man still singing with his heart breaking—probably that's sentimental hindsight—music does get to me more than all this *painting* everybody in Chicago is so nuts about."

"Few art patrons care to gamble on music or writing," I said. "With painting, there is always the chance that some day they may sell it for a lot more than they paid for it."

When I spoke, Hank seemed to listen intently. I don't think he heard me. It seemed to give him a breather, a moment he needed.

"I asked Colin," Hank began again, "what he was playing and he smiled at me over his shoulder and said he intended to call it the song of Van Gogh's skylark and that hit me. You know how Mellie loves that picture—it's her favorite.

"I seem to be making an awful lot of this—you'll see why— Well, Colin had been writing songs all his life as you know, they still sing a couple of them at Yale when there are no ladies present, but this song filled me up with—is anguish a good word? It's the first time I ever used it, that's for sure. I have to tell you I was worried, though I—it never entered my head why I ought to be *that* worried. Everybody was always telling me that Colin had me bamboozled, but—did it ever occur to you that people fall in love in a lot of different *ways?* I knew a boy once that fell in love with a woman old enough to be his *mother*—he didn't have one. And an old man can fall in love with a young one to be the son he never had but always prayed for. I've seen that, too. These goddam psychiatrists try to foul it up, but it's simple the way I've seen it. I never had a brother and I'd fallen in—in what Emerson calls friendship love (we were strong on Emerson at Yale) with Colin to be my kid brother when we were in *grammar* school. I took the obligation of that seriously, and if they want to drum me out of the regiment for that I'll go out in the desert and eat cactus with the camels.

"All of a sudden, Colin rolled a couple of chords and jumped up and began walking back and forth like a tiger. I'd seen him walk up and down from Lawrenceville to Skull and Bones to Hill 1110 in Korea, it meant he had something in his gizzard that was bothering him and I couldn't figure what it was!"

No written word can reproduce the pain in his voice. In my life I have heard a good deal of pain, from cancer, to losing a child, to treachery from someone you love, and I recognize it when I hear it. This was now beyond anything but unadorned truth and Hank told it with pain.

"Colin had what looked like a rich, full life, and it was *empty*. He was staring into a void. He was living the way he didn't want to live and he knew it. He didn't like things the way they were and he couldn't see any way to change them.

"By the time he got through telling me this," Hank Gavin said, twisting the glass in his hand and watching the beer swirl round and round, "he looked like the picture of an explorer taken by the relief party when it arrived in the spring and it—Colin was—a *fun* guy. The chaplain used to say sometimes that the way he laughed when things were tough was a—a form of prayer. *Faith*, the chaplain said. All the laugh was gone when he stood there with his head on one side waiting for what I was going to say."

Somewhere in here—I never understood this part of it very well—Colin had been careless with some of his firm's money. Spent it recklessly, as near as I could make out.

The scene took shape before my eyes, the words and music sounded in my ears. The big, *moderne* room of the young Rowes' apartment, as cozy as a gymnasium, the grand piano open. The two young men, Colin glittering like a pinwheel on its last spin, head tilted, tiptoe to escape the coming blow yet all the time sure Big Brother would try to save him. And Hank Gavin, his face furrowed with an *I'masonofabitch* fury, taking long breaths, his eyes blazing over the *mess* Colin was in. The dialogue must have gone something like this:

Hank. *Now you've given all those stuffed bastards a stick to beat your head in, you bloody fool.*

Colin. *So? I've done it before and I'll do it again—*

Hank. *Look, young Colin, you've been the life of the party and the wit of Michigan Avenue long enough, you're too goddam old to play Peter Pan.*

Colin. *Ah yes, but the prodigal son always gets the ring on his finger and the best robe, don't forget that. Sometimes, buddy, I think you've got too much of the elder brother in you—remember that sulky oaf who stood outside the door and didn't want to let the poor prodigal in?*

Hank. *Never mind the comedy. Where did Sybil think you got all that lovely money?*

Colin. *With your brilliant help, or the stock market, where else?*

Hank. *Jesus. They still believe that. Why didn't you say a daily double at the track, it's easier.*

Then the tempo changed. Colin, swift, light, haggard, came over and put a hand on Hank's shoulder, the way he'd done on the high school football team (he'd been too light for football at Yale so he'd captained the fencing team) or when they took their snuffies on a night patrol in Seoul, or when Colin was his best man. It was almost part of a ritual, a plea for help—an offer to help.

Colin. *Hank Gavin, young Mr. Chicago, that's you, hey, buddy? You're a big strong man and I'm a new instant dessert, but I know you better than anybody, right? You're kidding yourself, buddy, and that's the sin against the Holy Ghost. Remember one night the chaplain said the only thing that mattered was how far away from God you were, and what kept you there whether it was rolling in the hay with some loop-the-loop whore, or not having compassion for somebody because you didn't like him was of no importance. Remember he told us settling for an earthly paradise without knowing who gave it to you could be as far from his God as sleeping it off in a gutter? Remember that? Remember he said how rough it was for some long-toothed, wall-eyed, pot-bellied camel with a solid gold hoodah trimmed in diamonds to get through that narrow narrow little gate they call The Eye of the Needle into the kingdom of heaven? Okay, I wasn't the first man over the top any time and you were. Always. One thing I want you to remember and you may be going to have some rough times remembering all by yourself. I may have been trying to kid that old man of the sea, my boss. And that cold-storage eskimo, Joe Quaglino who thinks I don't know he owns the silly agency. Or that one-dimensional female I'm married to, she wants what a lot of women want, if they didn't why would a society leader with a face like a prune be one of the women to get their picture on the cover of Time? Maybe I kept on trying to kid the wife of my bosom that I was a big shot. But I quit kidding myself a ways back, Mr. Chicago.*

You're still kidding yourself and you've got your big, double-barreled ass squeezed so tight in the Eye of the Needle your rectum's bleeding and it may take you another incarnation or two to get it out if you're not careful.

They both began to laugh. They belonged to the cult of insult, the school of using the opposite word, the light word in reverse English, a pugnacious contrariety.

"This is familiar," Hank had said. "*You're* in a goddam jam so you give *me* hell."

The laughter almost healed them. But—for the first time, not entirely.

"I could fix up his trouble all right that time," Hank told me, "but it left him there, staring into a vacuum. Where do we go from here, boys, where do we go from here? He—you could say he leaped into that vacuum, couldn't you? There's one more thing, we never told anybody. A lot of questions came up about whether he left a note. They agreed he hadn't. But—I got it in the mail, the next day at the office."

He'd burned it. But he couldn't forget it. It said: *There isn't any privacy left any more. I'm a man needs privacy. They talk about too little too late, what I say is too much too soon. That's what's wrong with me. I haven't got any hunger any more, buddy, and without hunger you perish. It's all flat and phony. Jesus we invent ways to kill an afternoon, I heard one of those bright and shining game-show announcers say that the other day. We've only got such a little time here, and now we have to invent methods to murder it like the Mad Hatter. Pass it, use it, fill it with flapdoodle and fornication, have fun, but let's not kill it, buddy, shall we? Phony challenges, new frontiers, who the hell cares whether we get to the moon? Hang in there, bud. A choice between jumping out a window or doing a reasonably honest job of finding out whether there is a god. The god the chaplain prayed to is dead. The choice there is. I took the low road and you take the high road. You know everything I can't write here, huh?*

Empty, silent, the big dining room had withdrawn around us.

This time there were no tears.

I wished there could be.

"On the way through the lounge Colin stopped and put his hand on my shoulder," Hank said. "Did you ever see a man after he jumped?"

No use trying to stop him now. "When I was a police reporter," I said. "It didn't mean anything. He was a stranger." But—I knew what he meant all right.

Did Paul *see* Stephen. I must look it up in *Acts*. Nineteen hundred years. What did it matter? Paul never forgot all his life that *he* ordered Stephen stoned. In Rome, in Thessalonica, in Philippi, always he took with him that sadness of the heart. That was why he was so kind to Timothy, with his women and liquor, to stupid, well-meaning Titus, to Barnabas, who left him, to the Negro Onesimus. Because of Stephen.

Hank Gavin's voice, stronger now, new, driving, said, "I had to tell you about Colin, you see that? My best wasn't good enough, my human love wasn't good enough, it almost never is, my intelligence wasn't enough, there is no healing power in intelligence, is there? Colin was beyond it. It was Colin who said *You're kidding yourself, buddy, and that's the sin against the Holy Ghost*. Not a big sin, I know now what *that* is. But it's *a* sin against the Holy Ghost all right. Maybe it was partly Colin who plugged me into the light."

After a moment, he made a sign across the room to the waiter, who brought him another bottle of beer. He poured it and drank thirstily. "I never talked so much before in my life," he said, "makes a man dry." He looked around and said, "We've got the place to ourselves, looks like, if you want to hear more."

9

For several months after Colin's death, Hank Gavin lived three lives.

One, his normal, exterior existence, the how-you-been? Yes-I-can-handle-it-golfing-dining-out more often than usual, a little bridge here and business meetings there.

Two, was the adjustment of Mellie and Sybil and all their friends and most especially himself to Colin's absence, to *missing* Colin, to his bizarre and disturbing suicide.

And the third, a growing inner alertness, a nudging and prodding and signaling, which came in the form of questions he'd never asked himself or anybody else before, of *ideas* in clean-cut sentences within his consciousness that did not seem to be his own yet were by no means to be called *voices* or anything like that, sometimes they turned out to be quotes from centuries of teachers, thinkers, men of God, philosophers from Socrates to Spinoza to Santayana, none of these to be expected by a busy, up-and-at-'em young businessman. Many, he felt, began back in Professor Daladier's study, continued into and out of the experience with Colin as they walked down a street in New Haven one spring night.

In the International Club, by this time the middle of the afternoon had arrived, that brief pause between the day's occupations and the cocktail hour. The ladies had picked up their shopping bags and departed for Outer Suburbia. Only the one-for-the-road boys were still clinging to the bar, with the bartender dozing on his stool, perhaps overcome by the fumes. Even the traffic on the street below had slacked to an occasional car, a spasmodic toot.We seemed isolated in the middle of the great city.

More intensely, Hank began to deal with these lives of his; he knew that whatever had come to him couldn't have arrived overnight.

With and to him, Mellie was tender and kind. All her hard, young contempt was for Colin. Consoling Hank in his sorrow, sympathetic to his loss, she was nevertheless coldly impatient, deadly hostile to his self-condemnation.

"Morbid," Mellie said, "Colin was determined to come to a sticky end. You know that. In New York now I under-

stand if a character gets on a ledge the populace turns thumbs down. They yell Jump, you muttonhead. That may be barbaric, on the other hand, my own precious husband, people that get out on ledges ought to be allowed to choose, it's their life. Who needs them?"

Behind her as she talked one night up in the sitting room he remembered how he saw the skylark in her favorite picture tossing just above her head, and he heard again the bird's song that was like a man's own heart. Oddly enough, he also understood Mellie, her point of view was one side of his own thought. The mockery of weakness, the derision for failure, the Jesus-what's-wrong-with-the-guy annoyance at anyone who couldn't *cope,* the increasing complicating of the gloriously simple, the scoffing at the uselessness of suicide, the waste, this entered into his own summing-up. "A man has a right to lay down his own life," Mellie had said, "how can he arrange that it's just his own life? How about Sybil, and you—and me since *you* is *me*—how about us? He's squirreled us up plenty. And for what? If there is anything after this, which I don't believe for a moment, Colin's taken himself along with himself, hasn't he? This getting to the moon, I know it's a national occupational therapy, but if we get there we'll take our own ways with us, won't we?"

Ironically, or so Hank Gavin saw it, his work which had been growing like a cornfield, began to harvest. He had brought in all the investment business of a big insurance company, in Detroit he'd advised about the investment of a labor pension fund and it had been turned over to him, he'd presided over a new stock issue with imagination and integrity. Naturally, in all of these he had to consult with the Boss, so that he and Margolis spent a lot of hours alone together. More than usual.

The matter of Stu Margolis had nothing to do with Colin, directly at least though the suicide actually may have increased his torments.

As it turned out, in the secret chamber of his own soul, under the inspired touch of comedy and behind the unstoppable fullback quality of his success, Stu Margolis twenty-four hours a day faced the stubborn desperate fact of his wife's alcoholism, about which for years all Chicago had been concerned. Not just social Chicago. In that bracket, hostesses had long been obliged to determine whom to seat on the other side of her at dinner parties since no matter what Stu always brought her and still always sat beside her. In her cups, Natalie Margolis was apt to wander into dives, black and white and mixed, and Stu, frantic with worry, would get a discreet call, or an equally discreet cop would bring her home. How Stu had *stood* it, the sleepless nights, the racking terror, was hard to understand. Why he stood it and how he managed in public to ignore it with a bland and seeming blindness, nobody knew, and not even the bishop had ever dared find out or offer solutions.

Hank was not apt to forget the day Stu unburdened to him in an echoing, empty, dusky office after they'd concluded a ticklish deal for Joe Quaglino. Nothing but seeing it with his own eyes could have made Hank Gavin believe that the Boss, the V.P., the big guy, could show him such a boiling cauldron of fear and pain and shame and heartbreak. Oh, it had all the tragedy-comedy, serio-hilario-hysterio pathos and melodrama of *drunks*. Here was King Lear quarreling with the blasts he'd brought down upon his graying head, he had turned over his kingdom not to an ungrateful child but to a gin-guzzling wife. And she was, always had been, always would be *the one woman* to him. Hank's inner eye presented him with a picture of Natalie as he had last sat next to her at dinner—I'll put Hank next to her, he's a doll really, he won't mind and anyhow she's his boss's wife—and she had dribbled down her Balmain front and her comments on the other guests would have scorched a slut on Rush Street. Stu had gone on kidding Bill Wrigley across the white and glittering table, trying to persuade him to come in on a new sports arena, with a roof, where the Cubs and the White Sox and the Bears could all play.

Then, noticing me, as a human being and not a try-out audience or pseudo-confessor, Hank said, "Look, are you hungry or anything? How about a sandwich or a piece of pastry or another cup of coffee? I—I still don't understand—why me? I couldn't figure Stu at all. I work for him, I'm twenty years younger than he is, we'd spent a couple of weeks in the woods once, but Stu never talked to anybody about his private affairs. Now—this is a great guy, make no mistake. A *good man*. You haven't any idea what he does for people. If I could tell you about Arnold Cohn's son—and the way he's kept things steady on the Board of Trade a dozen times and saved the farms, and yet there he was, I *saw* him, being burned at the stake. Not for a few hours, like Joan of Arc, for years on end. She got plastered on their honeymoon twenty-two years ago, she's never drawn a sober breath since, and he's never drawn a—a happy one, a peaceful one."

"What has he done for her," I said, having myself spent a long term in this particular antechamber of hell.

"Everything," Hank said, "doctors, priests, psychiatrists, though the honest ones tell him no top man in that field ever claimed to be able to help an alcoholic. That one you can *have*. AA—Alcoholics Anonymous—he called them, gave them carte blanche, said to rent a house and get their best people, he'd pay any price, and pretty soon a humpty-dumpty little fellow, very bald he said, showed up and said Mrs. Margolis would have to take the First Step herself, whatever that meant. Stu found out pronto the whole thing was a religious shennanigan that had to do, the Humpty Dumpty told him this straight out, with what he called a Higher Power or God-as-we-understand-Him, and of course the first step was to turn her will over to Him and ask help, and this wasn't much good as Natalie wouldn't admit to anyone that she needed help and Stu had never admitted it himself before."

"AA isn't exactly *religious,*" I said, somewhat tartly. "It's a spiritual program, it says only your cooperation with God's power can defeat the devil when he puts on the form of alcoholism or John Barleycorn. And I have reason to know that's true."

He stared at me. Then he smiled, he said, "I found out one peculiar thing. May be some help to me sometime. While he was talking and I was trying to understand how he could still be in love with this—this woman I'd sat next to that night at dinner, I kept hurting to think of his having to go home with her or to her, and then I knew he never saw her, this woman, at all. I—I had a sort of sight of her *through* what she was now, and I could see Stu's wife as she was when he married her. I'd had this happen a couple of times on big deals with—men, heads of companies, sharks like Joe Quaglino, I got a sight of them as though I was seeing *through*—and it was sometimes a kind of strange, wistful, desperate fellow—like the kid he'd been when he went fishing with angleworms. That may sound far out, but it had *happened* a couple of times and—I'd made the pitch to—to *that* fellow and it worked. So I saw Natalie Margolis' face through that bloated flesh and the bleary eyes the way she looked when she was Mellie's age, and I knew Stu still saw her that way no matter—he had been in love with her all his life and he always would be and take care of her the best he could. He couldn't bring himself to—to humiliate her to her face."

"The best thing—" I began.

"Any of our bests," Hank said angrily, furiously. "My best, your best, Stu's best, human best. All right, I offered him my best and all it was was just sympathy and that's about as—oh, it's *all right,* he was grateful for it, he was glad he'd found somebody he could talk to, sure—but it was about as potent as a stuffed crocodile."

"It's more than that," I said. "I have come to value kindness more than anything else. You and Mellie were kind to him—and to her."

"Mellie—" Hank said, "Mellie said women drunks were all *whores de combat,* they started drinking the fourth martini with one hand and stopped using deodorants with the other and the smell was a return to the cave. She said trying to reform drunks reminded her of St. Teresa and her little brother starting out to convert the Turks, which she'd read about somewhere. Just the same Mellie gave it the old college try, she asked Natalie to come up and help her at the Children's Hospital but Natalie never showed up. Mellie took her to lunch—you know Mellie does get along with people, all kinds—but by the time Natalie had drunk her lunch she couldn't remember who Mellie *was* and told the maid she thought Mellie was a Communist spy—Mellie said the Turks would be easier but she did her best. Don't we all."

During this period, the dead weight was Sybil Rowe.

Sybil was sick with guilt and self-condemnation, yet it forked off into passionate denunciations of Colin. *How could he do this to me?* she would say and then she'd shriek damnation upon him, *leaving me to face it all alone,* she'd say. "I was a good wife to him, Hank, you know that," she would say, and begin to cry again, "I know you never liked me much and thought it was a mistake for him to marry me, but he owed me a lot, didn't he? Didn't he? I never looked at another guy and you may not think so but I had my chances. I was loyal and I worked hard and I never drank and I kept a lovely home for him and had all the right people for him—look what I did for the hospital, would they have that new wing if it wasn't for me? You know better. What kind of a God could do this to me?"

Slowly, she hardened. She got back into harness, and drove everybody and herself with ruthless concentration. And all the time the whys and the wherefores haunted her and she was a widow and lived alone and loathed it. She had loved Colin and now some nights she hated him and bit her pillow and called him yellow and a quitter and a snob.

Of one thing she was sure. There was no God. In this, Hank couldn't help her though once again he did his best.

About that time, Hank told me, he began to read again. Not much, not study as he understood it, but some. He remembered Daladier had talked about certain books on Zen, and certain mystic philosophers, and it had stirred his interest then. He wrote to ask for a list, but Daladier was dead, whoever had taken his classes was too busy to bother, so he got hold of Huxley's *Perennial Philosophy* and the man at his bookstore recommended one or two books including a couple by C. S. Lewis and finally read Thomas Kelly's *Testament of Devotion.* That enchanted him but none of it took hold, as it were. Then it came back to him that Daladier had said Jesus Christ was the greatest teacher who ever lived and that the Way as he taught it was still there for all to read and find, so he got out a pocket New Testament his grandmother had given him years ago and began to read. Of course he had never *read* it before. Not to say *read* it. By osmosis as all English-speaking people know Shakespeare, he knew some of it, the stories, the quotes, the phrases that are part of the English-American heritage. But to read it—no.

Now he found himself caught by some of the characters, parables were good stories, he had a feeling that there was much more to all this than he'd had any idea. He wished desperately that he had someone to talk it all over with. He *had* to see the chaplain. The chaplain named Ike Freiberg who wore the cross of Christ on his collar and had been with them at Pusan and all the way north to the Yalu. In and out of Seoul, which had once been the biggest city in the world and was now a battleground. Captain Freiberg had been with them the day they saw a bomb splatter those little brown children all over the street and on the walls of the buildings, those children who had been children one minute and bloody flesh and bomb fragments the next. Colin had kept being sick for two days and Hank Gavin had gone burning berserk and killed four or five men he wasn't even sure which side they were on, how the hell could you *tell* whether those little brown men were North or South Korea or Viet Nam or the men who had bombed those children or their fathers and brothers, forchrisake.

When he finally caught up with him, he found Captain Freiberg was somewhere—Africa or China or Viet Nam or Berlin—so the best Hank could do was write.

Very carefully, Hank took a fine brown wallet out of his pocket. Very carefully, he took a letter in an Army Air Mail envelope out of the wallet. He passed it to me, watching me all the time very carefully, to see that I didn't spill coffee on it or anything.

The letter had been typed on a broken-down portable by a man in a hurry to get what he had to say on paper for somebody who needed it and couldn't have cared less about the typography or how it looked as long as it could be *read*. The paper was cheap gray-white and in some places the words blurred but it was quite easy to understand.

Dear Hank; Sorry about Colin. Don8t worry about him, that8s not your business any more. None of this is important, hank. The nature nametime or number of material things or whether people have colds or leprosy or jump out windows or make a million dollars or get elected this is not what is to considered. These are all phases of the same thing and some are a little more comfortable than others. Not many people know or believe this Hank but it's true. What you must now face Hank is that you cannot give to others what you have not got yourself. You see that, buddy? The Master, the only one who ever said the whole thing right, spoke about giving a cup of cold water in His name.You get it? Now the cup has to have cold water in it, it wouldn't do anything for anybody if it was empty, would it? it would be no use offering an empty cup even if it was gold and diamonds and pearls.This would not keep a man from dieing of thirst.It is not even enough to have cold water in the cup, though this is better than nothing and if it is the best you can do is acceptable. For a while.But The Master said Give them a cup of cold water <u>In</u> <u>My</u> <u>Name</u>. How about that? Give in the name of Love, the Love of Christ for his brothers. Other wise they will only thrist again and be around every few minutes for another cup, huh? In His Name, it is the water of eternal life, it is the healing wine of love, and he will never thirst again. You get that, buddy? It doesn't make much difference in a ball game does it how good a citizen the man is or how educated or honest, let's say, if he can't <u>hit</u>, as far as the ballgame is concerned, studying to be a minister has not interefered with Bobby Richardson's <u>hitting</u> for the Yanks, in fact the last time I saw a Sports Page he was leading the team. So he must be doing both of them In His Name-maybe.Work out your own salvation, Our Lord said, with fearndtrembling. In other words, no matter how scared you are and you can be, this is no journey for a man without guts, this following In His Steps.Who's tried it. that8ll show you.They talk big, who does it? Though you have all the wisdom like some I could name but they are Christ too just like Salinger's Fat Lady—remember her?—but they have all education and intellect and they are NOTHING.Who do they help? Though I have all faith so that I can remove mountains—hell, derricks and bulldozers can remove mountains, like those poor garbage collectors the psychiatrists they can diagnose and move a mountain and what have you got? A hole in your head, buddy.Unless you know where to move it and have the Love that heals the hole, you are NOTHING. You have to have love and if you think _you_ can love your brother much less your enemy, take a look at yourself. Only the Christ can do that for you, My son, it is impossivle for an emptysack to stand uprgith. Hank you8ve got to gain a point of view. Without it you are an empty sack. No matter how your heart aches to give, if your own sack is empty you can't fill any stockings, buddy, any more than some poor woman without a dime can fill her kids stockings. You have to let Him fill your sack, buddy. Look Remember the day after we landed and started for Inchon? In those big, empty, dirty box cars? You and I and Colin were in one car, jolting along from nowhere to nowhere and I don8t think one of my kidneys has ever got back in the right place, we were jolting along through plains and fields no houses nopeople, and it got dark where we were out there in the middle of nowhere. The train kept stopping and one time all og a sudden out of the dark and the middle of nowhere all those kids showed up. Remember? I bet you do and so does Colin. They were panhandling coming as close to the train as they could get, begging and whining and pleading for food, poor little devils and they looked like they could sure use it, they were the first starving kids you and Colin had ever seen. All pinched-and anyhow out of the kindness of your hearts you and Colin made a great mistake. You picked out the littlist and the hungriest like picked baby chicks and you handed them some food, good food, quite a lot of it. Remember what happened, buddy? The bigger kids, the 13-14 year old boys, began beating up on the little fellows to get the food away from them, it looked like they'd beat them to death, and maybe they did, we didn't know, did we? because right then the train got going again, you see, you musn't give gifts unless you can give the Christ with them to protect them. Not in dangerous spots. You have to give The Word-accompanied by the Holy Spirit-it'll take care of itself, but you have to know it is The Word. We all give by grace. It can't be any other way. Get a point of view, buddy. Ask for it. Seek it. I shall pray for you, my dear son. Yours in Christ.Ike Freiberg. Keepintouch if you want to. Ike.

As I finished the letter, Hank reached for it. Very carefully, he refolded it and put it back in his wallet. I saw how worn the creases were, and it was easy to believe that he'd gotten out of his sleepless bed many a night and gone downstairs and paced up and down, reading it over again. In twentieth-century style it was by way of being an Epistle To. He found that he had kept so much more of what the chaplain had said, one time and another, in his heart that some of it was already habitual to his thinking. It was *there*. It was part now of what a man *is* and seeks beneath all the worldly living.

How long it had taken me to read, how long we sat silent after he put it away, I have no idea. My heart had begun to beat noticeably more quickly. Part of my thought was that perhaps the chaplain was unorthodox, but I wasn't quite sure how much I knew about Orthodoxy.

As Paul, an apostle of Jesus Christ had written to Timothy, his own son in the faith.

As Peter, an apostle of the Lord Jesus Christ, had written to the strangers scattered throughout Pontus, Galatia, Cappadocia, Asia, and Bithynia.

As James, a servant of God, had written to the twelve tribes scattered abroad.

As John, the older, had written unto the elect lady and her children.

Why not?

Here was Ike, an apostle surely of his Lord Jesus Christ, writing from some land as foreign as Cappadocia or Bithynia, to his own son in the faith, Hank Gavin. The Word was to be spoken to all the world in continuity and in perpetuity and it was always *to be with power.*

Hank Gavin had gone on this traditional barge trip with considerable reluctance and chiefly because Stu Margolis had asked him to. He wasn't, he said, in the mood, he'd been on 'em before.

The so-called barge belonged to a steel company and was used by the president and the brass for inspection trips and entertaining. It was fitted up with extravagant luxury and for some reason no one had ever been able to explain gave a sense of going off on a long long trip to the South Seas or the North Pole or the Mediterranean, detached from Chicago, Illinois. No yacht or steamer had ever duplicated this get-away-from-it-all atmosphere and invitations to week-ends abroad were much sought.

"This needs Stephen Vincent Benét or Salinger to tell it," Hank said, "to speak the language of today and yet bring with it all the truth and impact of tying the past into the present. I am still—afraid. I didn't succeed in selling Mellie. All she did was explode with laughter and give me that I-won't-buy-any-of-it-you-have-to-be-kidding look. If I can't *sell* it, that means I better not go forth into all the world to tell the good news. It means I have maybe been called to believe myself—but I have not been *chosen.*"

He took that deep breath I was beginning to recognize as an interlude for the 'cello or the French horn in a symphony. His eyes had begun to burn more gold than green or gray and when he spoke it was plain he had transposed the key. The prelude was over, this was to the the first clear, simple statement of the theme.

"The bar-cabin on the barge was big and roomy and beautiful, but after midnight it was stuffy and crowded. Comes that time when everybody starts talking at once and shouting at each other and hollering with laughter, having a big time, I enjoyed it for a while but I wasn't drinking at all, I didn't exactly know why, I'm a moody drinker, and so I went out on deck to get some air and a little quiet. Up front, there was a space entirely cut off by the kitchen and the crew, and of course the big salon had air conditioning so all the doors and windows were closed tight. Wherever we were on the lake, no lights showed along the shore and I could see nothing behind us but the wake of the big dark barge moving like a prehistoric creature of the deep.

"The night was leaden, the air full of dampness that wasn't quite fog. Had to be that the sky and the stars were still there, but you couldn't have proved it by me. It couldn't have been darker or clammier in the belly of the whale.

"I wasn't trying to pray, I just wanted to be alone. Whatever it was that kept nudging me, I hadn't found out any more about how to pray than I'd been taught in Katie's Sunday School or I'd heard since at church on Sunday. Nobody expected it to be *answered*. My insides had stayed twisted about the boy in Somerset Maugham's book, *Of Human Bondage*. He was praying that God would heal his club foot and his uncle the rector told him maybe God would if He was feeling so disposed that particular day and felt the poor little bastard was worthy of it. I knew by now the kid had been praying to the wrong God, there wasn't any such Monster as his uncle the rector told him about, this was the myth, I knew that, and I knew the only time I'd ever contacted prayer that *expected* to be answered and was addressed to God Who was able and willing and that sometimes did answer like that night in Pan Mun San—" He stopped and headed back to Pan Mun San, but whatever he relived there for the next few minutes he wasn't prepared to share with me. "Or sometimes," he said, "when I'd gone into a Catholic church and seen the old women going to Communion at early Mass.

"What you keep, after the myths are destroyed—what you can't bear to let go no matter how much you scoff—that's *there*. That's *you*. Every man has some of these, if you ask me. When I *read* the gospels after the chaplain's letter came, I was knocked silly by what Jesus had to say about it. I knew I had to *ask* to believe, then I had to ask believing it was worth a try and not naming the answer. I had to seek. Somehow I had gained a feeling that this desire to seek was prayer. From what Katie had taught me, I had an idea that most Protestant churches were against giving a man much *help*. No beauty, no candles to suggest *light* and praying hands, no things to start a chain of prayer, no music—neither the majesty of Handel nor the stirring marches and hymns of Gilbert and Sullivan.

"Certainly I didn't have any humbug of any kind as I sat there that night, in that tepid porridge that turned in my lungs gray as a dirty sponge. So I tried to do what I'd done on exams and on the football field just before the whistle blew in a big game. I tried to empty my mind. In the exams, I used to sweep out all the details and mistakes and junk and leave it so the question could trigger the answer. The question and answer are one, come down to it. On the football field, you have to get rid of your nerves and that terrible sense of *time,* now is the time, this is *the* Saturday afternoon, and it's too fast to think, most of the time, you have to leave it clear to react, you've been practicing to react for years. So I sat there in the blackness, trying to empty my mind of all the wisecracks, the doubts, the frozen assets and dead doctrines and personal guilts and separation. I wanted to be able to see and hear if there was anything to see or hear.

"The minute I got it empty, all the devils in hell rushed in.

"First thing that came shouting at me was common sense. Be sensible, Gavin. All you need is to get out of this miserable town, when it isn't fog or damp or rain or snow or sleet, it's humidity or wind or blizzards or thunderstorms. What you need to keep you from getting neurotic about religion or something and ending up on the Couch for chrisake is to go somewhere where there's some sunshine. I felt such an unbearable longing for sunshine I thought I'd sell my soul for a day, an hour, in a place I knew near Palm Springs. If Mellie and I could live there in the sun and bake all this chill out of the marrow of my bones, then all this creaking crackpot nonsense about God, or that time at Yale when we were ambling down a street at night and I saw a light and Colin was drunk and then not drunk, all this stuff fit for old women and guys that couldn't hold any other kind of a job, would dissolve. End of winter, end of summer, half the time in between everybody in Chicago felt that way, probably in New York and Seattle and Dallas, Texas, everybody was thinking about the weather and looking for snow or sun or some special kind of weather to ski in or swim in, that was a real sales job, that was; so people who could afford it never stayed anywhere, we had become a nation of gadabouts darting around like waterbugs. Seeking the unattainable Garden of Paradise that we got tossed out of.

"At that point, the bile came up in my mouth, I could taste the gall. The devils were jumping around and yelping questions. Make God answer these if there is a God and He can. Why did Colin have to die like that? Couldn't God have done something to save him? Maybe God, if there is a God, wasn't able to do anything for him. One of Christ's twelve disciples committed suicide, didn't he? The one named Judas. God didn't do anything about him, either. Did He? Those kids in Korea, oh God weren't they Your children, too, what did they ever do to You? Why do You make it so tough to find You? And a two-bit phony like Jack Knowles up in Your pulpit telling me what to do, he couldn't sell A.T.&T. at two dollars a share.

"It was all the way it is when you dial in a television set. First there is no sound but a hum. No picture, the screen is flat, moving gray, then it's full of moving things, dots and lines, black and white or color if you have a color set, some of it geometric and some in waves that make you seasick, and you decide there'll never be a voice or a tune or a picture—that's the way it seemed to me and I felt—goddam *alone*—

"I don't know *when* the light began."

At this point I wished I could put Hank into a robe, a white robe, or a flowing cloth of gold, or a graceful tunic or even bright silver armor.

It's hard to sell this in a business suit.

Even such a simple gray suit as Hank Gavin's, with a white shirt and a bright, striped tie.

It is hard to try to sell this in a business suit in Chicago—or for that matter in Milwaukee or Hartford or Los Angeles.

Then as I looked at Hank Gavin I saw that he was clothed in a new, very young dignity. Younger than his years.

"I've got to use words here that aren't familiar to me," he said, "they may sound strange and—stiff. Unnatural, maybe. I have to do the best I can.

"A radiance began to glow on the water. *That's not metaphorical,* it's a fact in my life.

"Out of those leaden skies, a star melted the mist, the surface of the water was lighted up, *my* world was filled with light. Compared to that night in New Haven, it was a million watts to one, but I knew it was the same light.

"Sit right there where you are—try to imagine all the light and all the kinds of light you've ever seen. Or the most beautiful. Maybe on the ocean, or some hills you love, there were beautiful hills in Korea, and the light there is northern and very bright, clearer than any other light I have ever seen. Or moonlight on the Bay, crossing from San Francisco to Oakland on a boat.

"Okay, take your best shot.

"I'm trying to tell you there is light beyond and beyond, so much farther beyond—no words, I have no words at all! I had one instant just at first of saying Watch it, Hank, *watch it* and then I was in it. Just as it had done away with the blackness and damp air outside, the darkness and despair and *hopelessness* and all the bitter questions *inside* me were gone. I was—*new*. The *joy*—I can't tell you—the joy was as much beyond any joy I'd ever dreamed could be as the *light* was beyond and *more* than any light I'd ever seen. I can only tell you they were as bright as music and it was greater than the sky we knew—and yet it was small enough to fit me and for me to have it."

He still looked younger, but before my eyes I saw his face change. The lines deepened and it seemed to me that the bones were defined and the eyes were luminous, they were *golden* and full of light.

He could not go on for a moment, he smiled at me, then quite low he said, "That was the coming of the light.

"Then—the light began to take form. To take—shape. It's a—a kind of weak, silly comparison, but as you see the silver come on your television set when it's tuned in, it's alive with light and then there is a picture at last out of the light from far away, so now I saw made of light the form of—at first I wasn't sure—it was an angel of light—and then I *knew*."

Now it seemed to me that there were tears on his face, that I knew he was touching a memory that made him shine with some brightness from another country.

"My heart—turned within me, there was enough joy in that moment to do away with all the fears and sorrows in the Universe—*love* flowed from him as real and *warm* as the light—and it was—it was as though I'd *leaped* to throw myself at his feet, only I didn't because I couldn't bear to give up a second of—of *looking*.

"For that one second I knew how he can be everywhere at once, a little like the picture on television can be on *all* the sets in every town across the whole country—and I knew if we found the light and it led us to him we could leap into his presence and there is no darkness at all."

The pause was long, the big young man opposite me there at the table seemed to brood over what he had called back into being. But it was a joyful brooding. A—a memory of something blissful. The big room, the ordinary circumstances, the business suit, the glass of beer—I dared not call it ecstasy but I knew that it was.

"I think I went to sleep after that," Hank said simply. "When I woke it was morning, the gray mist had thickened to fog, and the rising sun was only a glare. I was hungry. And that started my common sense talking to me a mile a minute. I always wake up hungry. So I was Hank Gavin waking up with an empty stomach thinking about ham and eggs. What was all this hallucination? I said to myself *You've been hallucinating, old boy*. I knew that word all right, a lot of people I know go to psychiatrists mostly because they haven't any place else to go any more. Or, I told myself, you were crocked to the eyeballs, but that didn't seem possible when I hadn't had anything to drink. Or I'd had a—a dream?

I sat up and stared back at the glare and pretty soon behind us I could sort of see the barges sunk down deep in the steel-gray water. I remembered about Kim and I said to myself I am Hank Gavin, I am Hank Gavin, I am an ordinary young man in Chicago, Illinois, in the United States of America in the last half of our scientific Twentieth Century of Progress and I said Hank, if you go around telling people you have been converted, or enlightened, or illuminated, or walking to Emmaus, they will send you to a loony bin. I thought about different people—Mellie first, of course, And then Stu Margolis, that gallant gent. And my grandmother Katie. Yet all the time I never once for one single second doubted what I had seen and felt in the night. And you know something? You'd be *surprised* if you knew how many people have had —oh, moments—a ray of light—a—not a voice, probably just as well not, too, but a thought in their minds calling to them that wasn't part of their own thinking, if you can figure that out. Only I know, too, that they're afraid to say anything about it. Even ministers in churches aren't encouraged to tell anybody if they felt the Presence—if you do, then you have to do something about it.

"So common sense or no common sense or hallucinations or whatever, that cold gray dawn out there on a coal barge—my heart was high. It was singing like a bird. I knew I had been *chosen*. *He'd* chosen me."

In the long silence that followed, Hank stared out the window. Finally, he looked back at me. He was smiling, but in his eyes was a question. *The* question.

I said, "Could this have been a dream? Sometimes if you desire something a great deal you—invent it? You said the question and the answer have to be one unity, actually. This —this experience—could be what your imagination created in answer to your question—?"

It didn't sound very sensible but it was the best I could do and Hank smiled at me even more cheerfully. Gaily, would probably be his word for it.

"All right," he said, "let's say Mozart *dreamed* the music he composed, so far far beyond any music that had ever been composed before that it was a new world altogether. Nobody had ever heard such music, had they? So he dreamed it or imagined it, he wrote it, didn't he? He created it, didn't he? Who cares where he got it? Not in this world, for sure. Suppose Jules Verne wrote about underwater ships twenty thousand leagues down in the sea, I read that when I was a kid, nobody believed it, it was a fantasy, but it was true all the time, wasn't it? If you'd been blind and then for half an hour you saw, and then you were blind again or could only tell the difference between light and dark, could anybody convince you you hadn't *seen* light? And how could you in darkness *imagine* light if it didn't exist somewhere? If you did, you create light. That's good enough. I'm—a broker. In Chicago, Jacob Boehme was a shoemaker, Peter was a fisherman, Mary Baker Eddy was a bedridden old lady, Bernadette was a slum child with asthma. George Foxe was a nobody, St. Martin de Porres was a poor little Negro bastard—

"Do you understand what it means to *know* a thing?

"Could you make Glenn believe he didn't orbit and see the earth in the universe? If you'd told that to the Pilgrims they'd have burned you for a witch. Or stoned you, the way they stoned Paul when he told them what he'd *seen* on the road to Damascus. He kept telling it, though, even in Imperial Rome where they were pretty well satisfied with their own gods at the time. Could you make Benjamin Franklin say there hadn't been any electricity?"

He stopped and met my eyes squarely. "Do you believe any of this?" he said.

I had to get my breath. A ridiculous thing came to me, who can control thoughts in a big moment? The words took over my mind, written by a man named Thurber, about a man named Ross. *He sometimes threatened to quit, he was at least threatened with being fired, but he kept on going like a bullet-torn battle flag, and nobody captured his colors and nobody silenced his drums.*

I said, "I believe you."

"Mellie didn't," he said. "You know what she said when I told her—some of it?" His eyes began to twinkle. "*A likely story*. That's what *she* said."

All of a sudden he was overcome with laughter, his eyes were blazing with the delight he felt in her, in her honesty. I felt the full impact of his love for her and of what *fun* his companionship must be. His *zest* was real and exciting. Mellie would love that, she loved life herself.

People had begun to flock as usual into the International Room for cocktails, for early dinner before a movie or a ball game or theater-in-the-round. Somebody yelled *Hi, Hank* and he flipped a hand in reply. I saw an old lady who had once taken me to the Cosmopolitan Club, but couldn't remember her name. Now Joe Quaglino was at the bar, I kept my eyes away from him for fear it would draw him to turn and look at us, and join us; it would never occur to Joe that he wasn't wanted, or for that matter would he care if it did.

I said, "In a way, it would be better for you if I was more of a skeptic, a cynic not so eager to believe. But—my grandfather used to have—he used to talk with his Lord, Jesus

Christ. When I was little, I believed that and every word in *Pilgrim's Progress*. My grandfather thought a good many more people did than we—heard about. So I—have been eager to believe again. What are you going to do?"

"It says Go and do likewise. Probably I had better start to find out what likewise means. The chaplain always said the teaching of Jesus was—fairly specific. And he said we—we ought to at least try to believe he meant what he said—Jesus, I mean."

It took him a couple of minutes to light his pipe. Through the smoke, as fragrant as a wood-burning fire, he glanced around the room. He was already estimating potential clients, realizing that *Christianity likewise* would have to be sold to *people*. All kinds of people. With all kinds of troubles. The works of the flesh which are these: adultery, fornication, uncleanness, lasciviousness (The Flesh and the Fiends for instance), idolatry, witchcraft, hatred, envyings, murders, drunkenness, and such like. No no, things hadn't changed much. In his steps a man would find the same problems. Right here in this room; and the fruit of the spirit in his steps was Joy—but it was hard to tell whether Hank Gavin knew much about the Holy Spirit just yet.

He said and sounded surprised, "The point is, these people don't love evil. You know that. They've been sold a bill of goods. No one has made them hope in the power of God's works, and that this power can be called on today in Mississippi or Mozambique—or hurricanes and wars."

"How are you going about it?" I said.

"I don't quite know," he said. "I suppose what I say is *so much for my will, now show me yours*. I told Mellie—it seems to me now I must work inside the church devoted to his teachings. I wish I could go out along the Grand Trunk Road with a lama the way Kim did. Or start off into unexplored territory the way Paul did. But if I put on a robe and sandals and took a begging bowl all I'd do is end in jail. In his church must be a bond of common faith of some kind. I want to find out what they've done with his commandments. Anyhow people do turn to a church, go into it if only to get married or buried or baptized as they say. I think I can sell *inside* better than any other way. Mellie and I—"

I didn't hear the rest of what he said.

Mellie's voice took over. *You'll have a gay divorcée on your hands—he won't do it—I won't let him*—then my own *Maybe you can't stop him* and Mellie's again with the Josephine expression on her face *Oh yes I can.*

Breach of contract breach of contract breach of contract

Over and over it rolled in my ears.

Nobody had silenced Mellie's drums, either. Not so far.

The twinkle was still in Hank Gavin's eyes. I could estimate now the enormous virility and male vanity of the young man opposite me, why as Vadne had told me, all the girls in Chicago had been after him. Oh yes, this was a *man,* more of one than most. It had no more occurred to him that Mellie could resist or refuse him than it had occurred to Chanticleer that Pereletote would fail to come when he stood tiptoe and flapped his wings or the sun to rise when he crowed.

10

About a week after this, to me, amazing experience with Hank Gavin, I went to meet Vadne Cheyne at what she ingenuously called "my hospital." It was midmorning and every table at the small coffee shop on the first floor was filled with nurses in uniform, young men in white coats, old and older men in dark suits and office workers in skirts and blouses of gay colors. The loudspeaker droned frequently with its *Dr. Walker please Dr. Ralph Walker—Dr. Mandelbaum, Dr. Mandelbaum telephone please for Dr. Mandelbaum*—nobody paid any attention. A waitress in starched blue brought us remarkably bad coffee, nobody except me paid any attention to this, either, they were long gone in the resignation with which most of us accept these failures.

Sybil Rowe sat beside Vadne. She was gaining weight, and I assumed that like many unhappy people one of her only occupational recesses from pain was eating. Next to me I found a dear old friend, when I first knew her she had been a beauty and a successful actress, she had married a medical genius and devoted her life to his well-being; no change of time nor scene could rob Paula Branch of the art of speaking lines, presenting pictures, and *seeing* other people more clearly than the rest of us. I noticed that though her ears might have been occupied with Sybil's sharp presentation of some plans for a coming benefit, Paula's eyes were oftenest upon Melanie Gavin, who sat beside her mother, looking chic and polished in a white suit worn over a thin, turtle-neck pullover of vivid red and white stripes going round and round. Once or twice she nodded in the wrong places and when Sybil asked her a question wrinkled up her face without answering. Paula lifted questioning eyebrows at me. Indication of how many eyebrows were beginning to go up in that same inquiry around the young Gavins. The best I could do for Paula was a shrug to which she said too low for anyone else to hear, "She's a very strong girl, our Melanie. They often need help the most. If I can ever—will you sort of let her know I'm on her side? Whatever it is."

At that moment, unexpectedly, I found that I was able to see that Mellie had a side, and to understand it. *Breach of contract* was, to her, a fact and a drum call to arms. There was no calm, dishonorable, vile submission in Melanie. I saw, too, that in the circle in which she had lived all her life, in that place where the young Gavins lived, even to Paula who didn't know what it was about, public opinion and private support would be on Mellie's side, willy-nilly. Once they had found out what Mellie's side was I hesitated to contemplate the probable reaction.

As we gathered up gloves and bags Mellie said, "I'm going to pick up Hank—want to come and have lunch with us?"

Vadne and I had planned to go on to the Art Institute but she gave me a kick which left a slight bruise on my ankle, so I said, "I'd like that."

The hospital was near the lake, there was a wind so violent you had to push against it to make any progress, we got to the parking lot and into the car and Mellie said, "Katie told me you and Hank left there together the other day, he didn't mention it but I asked him and he said you had a long talk. He's being very merry and bright and *cagey* these days. He's up to something but I'm not quite sure what. He says he gave you the works—what did you think of it?"

The long low car leaped into the stream of traffic, the wind hit in a Valkyrian shriek, I refused to compete with it, and Mellie turned and gave me a direct glance of command, I shouted, *"The wind,"* and she lifted one shoulder. Much as I loved Chicago I wished for a moment that all of it wasn't so violent, so in motion, I felt I was being plunged into storm and stress, and had an impulse to turn tail and run. Mellie pulled over into the protection of a building, slid to a stop in front of a No Parking sign, and nodded to the doorman who waved back. It was quieter, I could hear her plainly when she said, "Well? What about it?"

I said I felt sure that Hank had had an authentic spiritual experience.

"What the hell does that mean?" Mellie said darkly.

For some reason, plus the nervous fury of the wind, this annoyed me. I said, "It's not entirely unknown, many people do. I suppose, quite simply, it means that Hank was reached by the power of God, Who needs laborers in these days. Why not? Why should we be beyond His direct love and care? Don't you forget that however materialistic we may seem in this country, we are actually the greatest idealists on earth and always have been. *Lafayette, we are here.* We can probably believe a man has a call—is *chosen*—"

In an icy whisper, Mellie said a word I have begun to accept as part of the paucity of the present-day vocabulary. I said, "That's neither true nor explanatory, is it?" and she laughed.

She tried to light a cigarette in the gusts that blew by us, and when she had finally succeeded, she said in a steady, clear, young voice, "I'm sorry I used a naughty word. But—you listened to Hank for *hours,* listen to me a couple of minutes, huh? To me, all this is balderdash, to be polite about it. If he had come home and told me he had just been to the Land of Oz and seen the wizard it couldn't be more childish and fantastical. Whether you can agree or not, will you try to believe that's the way it looks to me? Nothing I've ever seen or felt or heard has ever given me the slightest impression that there *is* what you and Hank imply when you use the word God. There are two sides, etc., etc., etc.—mine is I've not only seen no evidence nor heard any valid testimony or evidence, my whole life says the opposite. All that about *angels,* for instance. Do you know what that does to me?"

"Not exactly," I said, "I knew you weren't sympathetic."

"It embarrasses the hell out of me, lovey," Mellie said. "I tried to be fair, I read some of the books that chaplain—I'd like to meet him in a dark alley—recommended to Hank. To me, they're indecent and slightly obscene escape mechanism."

"Does it seem strange to you that most of the great minds, though they sometimes use different languages, agree about this? Plato and Pythagoras and Augustine and Emerson—"

"Also, most of them thought the world was flat," Mellie said.

I said, "I often have trouble myself, with that one. Beatrice Lillie sent me a Christmas card once with a picture of the earth as flat and if you just go on driving down this street—you have to *believe* somebody, don't you? It works as though it was round, doesn't it? But if you just take what you see and feel actually you're going to—"

"These visionaries, they're too subtle for me," Mellie said. "Let's leave that. Suppose Hank wants to believe in God—he'll have trouble believing in Jack Knowles, let me tell you—and I don't. So he's a Democrat and I'm a Republican. And he roots for the Giants because of Willie Mays and I root for the Cubs when I think about it. We can—manage. People who—love each other don't have to agree about everything. It makes it more exciting, you have more to talk about sometimes if you're on opposite sides. But—if he proposes to *do* something—have you given a thought to what this might bring about in *my* life? Do you think I was cut out to be a minister's wife? Or a poor man's wife for that matter?"

"No," I said, "and—while I understand Hank's experience I do see that for you—"

"But he likes it," she cried out, "he liked making money and living the kind of life we do. It's—all he ever wanted.

He hasn't ever been one of those dreamy occult characters. Can't you see that if a man like Hank Gavin starts behaving like a—convert of Billy Graham's and—what mama calls hits the sawdust trail, it has to be neurotic? It's *sick*."

"I can't buy that," I said, "I think it's solid—and some very sound and intelligent people believe that Billy Graham is a man of God. I do myself, whether or not I approve all his methods. His sheep hear his voice. Mellie, can't you see at all that *without* God, we are lost? There is fear and emptiness and misery and—"

"Sure sure," Mellie said, "I know. The lepers and the prostitutes and the lunatics and the blind all came to Jesus. As it happens we're not any of those things. We've got it made. And if we haven't, why did this God you talk about set it up the way it's going?"

"I don't think he did," I said. "A lot of people are seeking an answer. To believe only possibilities would have left us in the cave, wouldn't it? I happen to know that some of the boys who washed out at Cal Tech, where they had dedicated themselves to science, have gone to the divinity schools."

"A lot easier," Mellie said. "I'm not sure all those boys know what they're doing, either. They get sold a bill of goods. The old myths or the new? Space ships and super-rabbit from the time they can first look at television. Who knows?"

"Television itself," I said, "no matter what's *on* it sometimes—to *see* the Kennedy funeral—"

"It looked great, didn't it?" Mellie said. "I always liked to see Jack and Jackie and the children coming out of church. Why not? And if you tell me Colonel Glenn prayed while he was orbiting all I can say is what did he have to lose? He probably carried a rabbit's foot, too."

She glanced at her watch and started the engine and we took off. If we'd soared above traffic it wouldn't have surprised me much. My mind was busy with the new practical problem she had presented.

Did a minister's wife have to believe in God?

Was it indeed a breach of contract to ask Melanie Cheyne to—go along with whatever it was that her husband was planning to do and I knew he was planning to do something. Something drastic, unequivocal, absolute.

"You'll be doing him a service," Mellie said, "if you try to convince him that I am immovably fixed in my little plush-lined rut and that to get me out of it would be difficult to the point of impossibility. I haven't had any angelic visitants, but I have just as much right to my opinion and my reading of the contract as he has." We pulled up in front of the building where Hank had his offices and she said,

"Go up, will you, sweetie? I can't park here." The glimmer in her eyes—I couldn't tell whether it was laughter or tears or both. The wind had blown her hair from its brushed bright sleekness, the curls were dancing, she took one hand off the wheel to press them down. "You are in the middle, aren't you," she said, "and we can shoot at you from both sides. Look, don't think I'm not sorry for him. This Jesus obsession is *the* worst. Hank's got a book called *The Way of the Pilgrim,* he got it because Salinger writes about it, and you are supposed to say the Jesus prayer twelve thousand times *a day*. This prayer has seven words—*Lord Jesus Christ have mercy on me*—that's it! I tried it. There are eighty-six thousand seconds in twenty-four hours and if it takes seven seconds to say the Jesus prayer once it'd take eighty-four thousand seconds to say it twelve thousand times and that leaves you two thousand seconds to go to the bathroom! It's nuts, Godmama, isn't it?"

"I don't suppose he meant it quite that literally," I said. "In the same book it says that a continual yearning of the human spirit toward God is ceaseless prayer. It's too simple just to say something is *nuts*."

A cop loomed upon us, I left her to it, or him to her, more probably.

Hank had someone at his desk in deep conversation. As I stood a little hesitant I heard a faint *Pssst!* and looking around I saw Stu Margolis' head peeping out a crack in the door to his private office. He jerked it back, and I said, "Will you let me know when Mr. Gavin is ready? Mr. Margolis wants to see me."

In the handsome, stately office where much of the western business of the stock exchange and Board of Trade took place, Stu offered me a cigarette and when I said no he waved me to a chair. He said, "Hank's been in here telling me he wants to resign. He must be crazy. He's got a deal cooking right now—you realize he's pretty damn near a great salesman?"

"What makes him that?" I said.

Stu gave me a quick look. "Well, he's a fine, pleasant, well-balanced, likable fellow but—there's two things, really. He's got a mind for absorbing facts and figures and a memory like an IBM machine. He can answer all the questions—and you'd be surprised the kind of questions clients can think up and he has more knowledge and information and he can remember how many shingles they put on the new roof of a company whose stock he's trying to sell when they put up a new factory in 1957."

"A memory works several ways," I said. "He seems to remember a lot that took place in Korea."

"I went through a fair-sized war myself," Stu said, "and it's my theory that war leaves a man where it found him. The weaklings and the self-indulgent ones that could never have coped with life anyway—they can't cope with it any more than they'd have been able to without a war. It's like any other tough test of a man's character and nerves. Colin Rowe would probably have jumped out a window anyhow, he was just plain no good. You know what Hank's got on his mind exactly?"

He had the kind of shrewd, penetrating eyes that always surprise you in such a warm, guileless, innocent face. He wanted to pump me if possible without spreading Hank's aberration around more than could be helped. Obviously, he loved the boy as though Hank were his son, instead of the flaming disappointment of the one he had. He said suddenly, "I'd have sworn Hank had his feet on the ground, by God I would, on the ground." And for some reason I began to hear hymns and spirituals they'd sung at a camp meeting I'd gone to a long long time ago with my grandfather, who was riding the circuit then in Arizona. About *oh them golden slippers, climbing up the golden stairs*—something like that—music started in my head, and a choir began to lift its voice in *Steal away, steal away, steal away to Jesus, Steal away, steal away home*. Softly softly that was and then the great fine shouting began *My Lord He calls me, He calls me by thunder, The trumpet sounds within-a-my soul, I ain't got long to stay here*. Came the whippoorwill song, the whippoorwill music, so loud in my ears—*dump-diddle-dump*—I thought Stu must hear it, too, *Whippoorwill*, then with a big hurrah of laughter *And hell's broke loose, Hell's broke loose in Georgia* and Illinois and don't you know when the thunder rolls and the trumpet sounds you can't stop a man any more than you can stop a tornado? Not from the days of Moses to the days of Paul to the days of Junipero Serra, to the days of John Brown and Abe Lincoln of Illinois—old Mr. Chicago, I'm a-warnin' you—

I said, "You remember any of the old revival hymns? My, they were grand."

He gave me a look of such surprise that I thought it was as well for me, and for Hank, that Mr. Stuart Margolis, V.P., couldn't read or hear my mind, yet I had a longing to tell him about it, they had to begin to face it, they couldn't contain this anywhere, not in Georgia nor Illinois nor Pennsylvania where William Penn had shouted it and the Mennonites still do, I wanted to warn him and something said he'd listen and understand, he must be so very lonely living there with the wreck of the woman he loved, the corpse of the one woman tied around his neck like an albatross. That wasn't my business, it came over me with a conviction that this was *Hank's business.*

"—point is that people trust him," Stu Margolis was saying, "that's the other reason, they trust him."

I said, "Why don't you do likewise?" and when he stared at me, "How do any of us know? Are we doing so well we can afford to—turn aside? Now I think I'd better pry Hank loose. Mellie's waiting, there wasn't any place to park and she's not a patient young woman."

At the sound of Mellie's name, Stu Margolis' whole being relaxed. The worry that had tightened his face let go. He said, "There now. I don't know what I'm carrying on about. She'll keep him in line. That's quite a girl."

As I went across to Hank's office I saw Toodie Goodrich coming out. She gave me a perfectly graceless grin and said, "He takes care of my investments. And so far that's all the good it's done me."

As we went down in the elevator I said to Hank, "Toodie—she reminds me somehow of Potiphar's wife."

He swung to look at me and said, "Who was Potiphar's wife?"

"If I were you," I said, "I'd look her up. It's Genesis—somewhere around the thirty-ninth or fortieth chapter, as I remember it. You may meet up with her."

Our luncheon at the new French restaurant which was IN at the moment was without incident. Everybody knew everybody. Katie was there with old lady Savonard and I thought she looked a little peaked.

There was an undercurrent between Hank and Mellie. They were gay, I felt the oneness of happily married people, the small gestures, the shared understanding, the jokes without words, the vitality of a man and woman who are a complete unit. Nothing in the world is as strong. Nevertheless, on this day the boat was rocking and Mellie jammed the tiller before she'd had a second martini. She had a gesture of putting her hand, palm down, on top of her head that was supposed to indicate deep thought. Then, she engaged her husband with a grin that was pure imp. "Try," she said, "go ahead and try. Think of one good Christian reason why he should have married her, *if* she had been a penniless waif."

Hank Gavin followed her eyes across to where Jack Knowles' wife sat. Surely with all her money somebody should have told her that pink made her skin look as though it had been antiqued. Gently, he said, "Honey, until an IBM machine catches up with it nobody will ever know why lots of people marry lots of other people. Right now I expect whispers are running all over the place trying to figure why I married you. You didn't even have money." He put his hand over hers, and said, "Honey, often—*he* is badly served. We can't go by that."

"I can," Mellie said. "It's always the top guy's fault if his secretary is rude and his assistant is a dope. The way I see it."

He was enjoying a steak, which one wasn't supposed to order at Maxim's, before he got around to say to her, "Do you know who Potiphar's wife was?"

"Certainly I know who Potiphar's wife was," Mellie said. "How uneducated can you be? Her husband was the head man and she had tea-for-two with Joseph. The one with the coat of many colors. But he was a good guy and spurned her Come-lie-with-me invitations because her husband trusted him and she got even by hollering rape. And her husband believed her and slung him in the hoosegow, which goes to prove that he might as well have had a little fun while he was about it. I read a novel about it once when I was in school and I always thought she must look like Sophia Loren, Egyptian ointment and perfume and no bath." She blinked at him and said, "Why do you want to know about her—Potiphar's wife, I mean, not Sophia."

"A young man ought to be warned," he said.

Over the espresso, she said, "You had another letter from your friend the chaplain. He's getting to be quite a correspondent. What did he have to say this time?"

"It's very odd," Hank said. "Here he is, a Reformed Jew who has been converted to Christ and now he writes me a long letter about a Catholic saint."

"Which one?" Mellie said.

"Bernadette," Hank told her.

"I adored *The Song of—*" Mellie said. "Pure enchantment. The classic myth of the little shepherdess who sees a beautiful lady, very much à la mode, and by a touch of her wand produces a magic spring."

"Cap Freiberg had been to Lourdes," Hank said. "What amazed him, he said, was not the miracles of those who were healed, convincing as they are, but the utterly incredible joy and peace of those who weren't. As though it couldn't matter less. And he doesn't think—" he broke off.

"It continues to seem odd that if the Lady *was* the Blessed Virgin she should have chosen a girl who was not very bright, let's face it," Mellie said, "and had asthma and lice, wasn't it? Why do you suppose she chose to appear to Bernadette in that filthy hole?"

"Cap Freiberg says the Blessed Virgin didn't appear to Bernadette."

"Ah?" said Mellie. "Then he doesn't go for the canonization?"

"He says the Blessed Virgin didn't appear to Bernadette. Bernadette could *see* her," Hank said.

"There's a difference?" Mellie said.

"Oh yes—" Hank said. "Oh yes!"

For a minute or two I didn't see it. When I did, I had to look at Hank Gavin more closely. Of course it confirmed all his own experiences. And as I met Hank's eyes I couldn't help wondering how it was possible that Mellie, who loved him, could fail to see the light in them. Or the way her husband's face was molding into new lines. Above all the incandescence in the yellow-gray eyes.

The next day I went back to California and locked myself in with some work. From that time for several months I only heard rarely from Vadne or Mellie and only once from Hank.

Vadne wrote that everything seemed serene, the children had been in the country with the Pattons for a week or two, now Mellie was planning to go to Paris to shop, and Hank was going on a trip somewhere. Hank had been away a lot lately, no one seemed to know quite where, Stu Margolis said the change was good for him, he'd been sticking too close to his work—Stu's wife was much worse, she'd fallen down and blacked both her eyes, quite awful.

Mellie called twice to see how I was and to tell me not to worry, as far as she could tell all that nonsense had blown over. Though something odd was going on about the mail. Not the chaplain, she said. "I'd read them, without a qualm, but he keeps them locked up. I know they're not from another woman, they're too long. What do you think he's up to?"

One brief note came from Hank, postmarked Princeton, New Jersey.

In a couple of lines it said that there was more to this than met the eye, though what *this* was he failed to explain. "I have met one saint," he wrote, "several moneychangers, a couple of High Priests, and a lot of well-meaning folks. Now that I know what I'm going to do I've been trying to break it gently to Mellie. I can't put the showdown off much longer. Pray for me. Yours in Christ, Hank."

Book TWO

1

In the months that rolled by, the issue was not joined between Hank and Mellie Gavin. No decisive move was made concerning his position with the firm. Without allowing herself to be angered or frightened into open warfare, which at this stage she was sure was a tactical error, Mellie used every means and methods of pleasantry, enjoyable living, and loving seduction she knew or could invent to pull her husband back from whatever cliff she honestly believed he was hanging on. Back into the rich, wide, busy and exciting world where Mellie Gavin knew they had a past, present, and foreseeable future. Once or twice she contemplated getting pregnant but she felt sure this would arouse all Hank's Scotch stubbornness, he would say Very Well, bring the baby with us. Thus not altering the choice in any way.

On the telephone she said to me, "He's coming around nicely. I've heard very little of it. He's been galloping around on business. Right now he's in Minnesota, isn't that where the Minnesota Mining & Manufacturing Company has its headquarters?"

I said it was, but didn't add that in that state there was a small theological school of some kind where a young professor from his own university was teaching rebellious renewal of the total commitment of Christians to the literal Christ teaching and the eventual coming of the Holy Spirit.

Katie, Mellie told me, thought it was probably an inner conflict between the Ogilvie second sight and the Gavin common sense. And Katie, too, was in favor of watchful waiting and pampering enticement to which she contributed her widow's mite of moneymoneymoney. Now and to come. In Katie's long experience the young man with great possessions may have turned away from the Way sorrowful, but turn away he did.

Paula Branch, who had an admiration for Mellie, wrote me that she had been surprised to see Mellie lunching with Jack Knowles' wife Judith, a young woman whom Mellie had never paid the slightest attention to even before she married the new rector. The rumor of Hank's conversion had started shortly after that morning when Al Patton led us to discuss angels, and had grown steadily, and with her nose for drama Paula wondered if Mellie was doing a bit of research. Not that I can see her in the role, Paula scribbled, but even if she was, there couldn't be a worse example. Yet why else lunch with her?

About this time, Mellie went to see the bishop.

Frail, gentle, a little absentminded, Mellie found him in the garden of his small country estate, which suggested a cloister, a gentle withdrawal from the world by a contemplative priest. Certainly the bishop belonged to that school which regarded the Army, the Navy, Statesmanship, and the Church as the only possible careers for gentlemen, and his eloquence and ecclesiastical charm had lifted him to the top. Now, in the safe and pleasant twilight of his life, he was perfect casting and the members of that church where he was now *emeritus* were honored by an invitation to call upon him and hear once more his melodious voice and enjoy the deposit of literature and the arts which surrounded him within and without. He was delighted to see young Mrs. Gavin who, in spotless white slacks and immaculate white shirt, hair held back by a bright yellow band against the heat that existed even here, gave him what she remembered of the little knick-curtsy she had been taught by an English nanny. Nor did she slouch and there couldn't be a more delightful addition to his garden. It made him wonder what it would have been if Gertrude hadn't died twenty years ago. Not that she had resembled Mellie Gavin, more like the bishop's wife in Trollope's classic

Barchester Towers, still she had understood church politics perfectly, she had advanced his career.

Up to the second cup of tea the conversation was witty and worldly, then the bishop said, "How is your good husband?" and young Mrs. Gavin said, "I thought you might know better than I do. Hasn't he been to see you?"

The bishop put down his cup and studied her. He had been too long the equivalent of confessor-psychiatrist to a large flock not to read real concern under the spirited approach.

"No," he said, "no. Tell me about it, Melanie."

As far as she knew it, as she herself saw it, Mellie told him.

"Then you aren't at all sure what his intentions—his plans—are?"

Mellie's hand was entirely steady as she lighted a cigarette. Watching her, the bishop thought that *memorable* was a good word to describe her. A man would be unable to forget her if he moved on. As, to be frank, he himself had so soon forgotten Gertrude. "Not," Hank's wife said, "in practical terms. Not what, if this—continues—he could or would expect to do. But I'm pretty sure he's up to something," and she flashed him a brilliant, conspiratorial smile. "That's one reason I came to you. What—could it be? I think he's investigating—and I know so little of the structure, the ways and means, of the—the church that I haven't the foggiest. My ignorance is—if you don't mind my putting it this way—beginning to bug me. If he's toying with the idea of giving up his profession and his coming partnership and that state into which it appears to me—and his grandmother—he has actually been called—what *are* the steps? Does he have a tryout and then get sent to the minors for a season? Katie says there are theological *schools* or seminaries or something."

The bishop's mild gaze had clouded. He said, "My child, are you a believing Christian?"

Mellie was unembarrassed. Truth was required of you, and come to that she was by no means sure that the bishop himself was one. He had indubitably been born a nice guy and a gentleman and the silver tea service in front of him had been in his family for generations, but as for putting out his hand and touching a leper, somehow this she couldn't see. She said, "No, not really. Nothing particularly against the Christian faith. I daresay it's as good as any. You'll forgive me, lamb, I was born without faith in myths."

"I have just been rereading the New Testament," the bishop said rather absently. "It *is* the greatest story ever told, you know. Much better reading than its commentaries and contemporary rewrites. The story of this young carpenter—"

He seemed to have forgotten her and Mellie said, sweetly, "I've always wondered why they made him look so *unlike* a carpenter. Such a shame. Probably great art, but is it anything to make us want to know what philosophy he lived by? Do you believe he actually looked like that—?"

The bishop said, "Perhaps some of the fine contemporary portraits would be more to your taste."

"I haven't any taste really," Mellie said, "about religion. You'll forgive me? And—what about Hank, dear dear Bishop? Do you believe this call business? I went to see Dr. Wilderstein the other day, he thinks psychiatry would help him if I could get him to go."

"What would you term the nature of the psychiatric disturbance?"

Mellie's eyes were steady and her voice was strong. "I'm afraid it seems to me more or less an hallucination, darling. He thinks he *saw* Jesus. At first I thought he was kidding, it's rather beyond that. Why *Hank?* If I ever knew a perfectly normal—"

"That brings us to the semantic discussion of what *is* normal, doesn't it?" said the bishop who at the proper moment was fond of semantic games, "and of course among the wood shavings and the fishing nets—however, I am myself inclined to regard these visionary conversions with some doubts. Perhaps not quite hallucinations, but some form of emotional instability, surely. Self-dramatization, sometimes, or a desire for the center of the stage. My experience has been that they peter out. They haven't the intellectual foundation for the long pull. Yet I suppose we must consider Paul—on the road to Damascus—"

"And dear Joan of Arc," Mellie said with a small chortle. "It's all rather a long time ago, isn't it? I don't wish to go into that dull bit about the twentieth century—look, lamb, how would Hank go about this—Would he present himself at one of these seminaries and would they accept him if he told them about this—*call,* or even if he just told them he wants to be a minister?"

The bishop said slowly, "I expect so. He's a graduate of one of our great universities, isn't he? He did graduate?"

"Oh yes," Mellie said, "and though both he and Colin concealed it as though it was a police record, it was with honors."

"As far as you know did he have any undergraduate classes in religion?"

"Something about comparative ones," Mellie said. "He has

some books on Buddhism, classical and Zen, and the Essenes and Lao Tse and some Aramaic—is that what I mean?"

"It is the language in which Jesus spoke," the bishop said. "Then what you have come to me for is to see what the actual steps would be, assuming that his desire to serve takes him into the church?"

"I always believe in going to the top," said Mellie with a twinkle.

"I should say he would be able to convince a seminary that he has been called—or moved—toward the ministry. Moreover, he would be a large fish. He is by no means a failure in his own world, as a good many are, I fear. His position civically and socially and financially—"

"But of course *financially,*" Mellie said lightly, "he hasn't a dime except his salary. Unless Katie wants to make him an allowance and when I mentioned this she smashed a lamp with her cane, purely by accident I'm sure. Civically, socially, professionally, yes. Financially, no. We belong to the salaried class."

"I see," the bishop said. "However, isn't he what I have heard called a sure-sell young man?"

"So I understand," Mellie said amiably.

"Then I am sure that some none too careful nor perhaps too scrupulous head of some seminary—there are a great many, you know, small and large—will take him in," the bishop said.

"Why do you say not too careful or scrupulous?"

"I would feel myself," the bishop said, choosing his words with care, "that his vocation should be most carefully tested, most carefully. Sometimes one of these inspirational afflates—or is it afflata—inspirational blasts, let us say, can be merely a psychic trauma or a form of schizophrenia or even a functional disintegration. A sense of guilt, a depression regarding the state of many people in the world, and I have noted that it is commoner with the returned soldier than others. There has been a psychic shock, of course, I saw this as far back as 1917–18. Or such an impetus may lose its force soon in the ebb and flow of accustomed existence. Or lack of stimulation. Or some slight disappointment with those he encounters *within* the apparatus of the church itself. As Paul once said to the Athenians we also are but men with like passions, but the illuminated convert wishes to find somewhere to place his garlands. As I say, I would hope that those he consults, if that is what he is doing, will be both wise and patient in dealing with him."

"So he finds one that will take him because he's Henry

Angus Gavin and he does look rather nice, doesn't he? Then what?" said Mellie. "How long would he have to do whatever it is?"

"He would enter, doubtless," the bishop said, "and then there are various courses and lengths—a three-years' course probably—"

"Three years!" Mellie said, and shoved her hair back from her face, ignoring the band. "Well, that's a comfort. You mean it would be three years before he could take his final vows and he'd be a college student again—or as good as?"

"In a way," the bishop said, "there must be a period of preparation and—probation. However—"

"However what, Bishop darling?" Mellie said.

"There are shortcuts, if a man knows how to arrange them," the bishop said. "By means of extra work, night classes, summer sessions, a heavy load academically—"

"Academically?" Mellie said.

"Yes yes—" the bishop said, "history and intensive Bible courses even today, I think, and sacred music, and the use of the theater and a great deal of psychology and sermons and all. But if a man is anxious for field work—for pastoral duty—"

"And that is?" Mellie said.

"To become part of the work of a parish," the bishop said, "to preach and—and run a church and the congregation. So many men now prefer the executive or administrative or teaching side of the ministry that the need for laborers in the fields is grave. A brilliant young man like your husband with experience in handling people—in selling—as we now use the term so all-embracingly—who has presence and poise and knows his way around *and* has a sufficient academic background to begin with, he might be sent to a church as an assistant pastor quite soon, if this is his choice. He could do the last part of the work needed to give him the necessary credentials, as a doctor does his interneship in the field. There are also, I have been told, already in existence or in process specially designed courses and even campuses or schools for the older professional- and businessmen who are called to the ministry after a life in those fields and who are older and have had more training than the undergraduate who moves directly from the university into the postgraduate work in theology."

"It all sounds very well organized," Mellie said politely, "but again—by the way how *many* kinds of churches are there?"

Mischief touched the bishop's smile for one moment.

"Don't tell anybody," he said, "but I haven't known for years. Hundreds, I should say."

"All considered—orthodox?" Mellie said.

"Oh yes," the bishop said, "within the framework of the Protestant church."

"But—aren't there others?" Mellie said. "Not Methodists or Baptists or Presbyterians or Lutherans—how many of those are there?" The bishop continued to shake his head. "You will think me woefully ignorant, but can you—how does one tell the difference?"

The bishop, smiling still, poured himself another cup of tea and finding it cold, shoved it away. He said, "Melanie, a lot of it would seem absurd and even wicked to an agnostic like yourself. Yet, appalling as I find some of them, trivial and ridiculous as the differences in doctrine or creed or observance may be, I have come to wonder whether or not they all have had a purpose. They at least do away with the sin of Laodicea—they are hot or cold—they have not succumbed to inertia and apathy, they often speak too much and too loudly and sometimes stupidly and ignorantly, but they *speak*. It is when the men of good intent are *silent*—as perhaps many of us too often are—that the soul of mankind is in danger."

"Could that be the sin against the Holy Ghost Hank was talking about?"

Upon the bishop's fine, ethereal face a faint wave of color showed. "That is for each man to say for himself," he said, a little sternly. "Back to your question, yes, there are a great many unorthodox churches, or cults, as they're usually called. Perhaps in some cases unjustly. What is known as the metaphysical field, this includes Christian Science, now highly respectable, of course, and the New Thought Movement and a remarkable group known as Unity. Then of course there are—or is—Homoiousianism and the Puseyites and then the Yoga and Vedanta groups—they are not Christian, of course—"

Mellie said, "I don't think they would be appealing to Hank, not that Hank is himself such an orthodox character, I know he regards Billy Graham highly and he watched Jehovah's Witnesses for *hours* on TV—in Yankee Stadium or the Cow Palace—somewhere. I remember too that once he said it was at least worth speculating about as to what might have happened had Calvin and Luther and—is Wesley the other one?—had they stayed *inside* and attempted to clean up City Hall, as it were. Dear Bishop, if he came to you would you advise him against this move? Would you tell him to stay a Christian, if he now believes all that—

Jonah and the whale—but that's in the Old Testament, isn't it?—and he can be president of the board or chief fund-raiser—wouldn't that be a more helpful thing for him to do?"

Her brows drew together as the bishop hesitated.

"I couldn't answer that unless I spoke with him first," he said finally.

"You don't *believe* all this—" Mellie began.

"Probably not," the bishop said. "I have always been rather against visions and voices and lights and such, but I can't quite figure what—it would be a strange thing for a young man such as Hank—to *kid* about such a subject, such an occurrence."

"Then—it's plain psychopathic, isn't it?" Mellie said. "Like those characters who levitate or climb ropes or can be in two places at once."

The bishop ignored this. He said, "I should seriously advise against any seminary admitting him without some thought and conviction that his wish to be a minister is based on something besides a psychic experience of some kind. There would be—a good deal of talk. Such an act by a young man like Hank Gavin would be—noticeable. Probably be considerable talk, and television programs and stories in the sensational press. It would indeed make considerable commotion, I fear, which greatly disturbs the balance of the church in times like these. Then of course if he didn't stick it, as we say, that would further discredit the church. They would say Ah, you heard about young Gavin, he was supposed to have seen Jesus walking on Lake Michigan but he couldn't stick the church, not at any price. This does no one any good. So I could at least advise you to persuade him if you can to allow time to have her perfect work with him."

"I am," Mellie said, "oh—I am. I wish I knew about this letter business though." She stood up, so slim that she seemed taller than she was, and began to draw on her white cotton gloves. To the question on the old gentleman's face, she said, "He gets letters. The address is typed—you remember that it was a capital A out of line and a clipped Q that enabled Lord Peter Whimsey to acquit Harriet Vane of murder? Well, I deduce myself that these letters are addressed on the typewriter on Hank's own desk at the office. It always has a smudged o and no tail on the g. The small g. And they are mailed in Chicago."

"No doubt business papers sent by his secretary?" said the bishop.

"Then why keep them locked up?" Mellie said, and picked up her enormous white bag and hung it over her arm, ready to depart. But instead she stood quite still, looking out over the bishop's garden. "You know this chaplain they had in Korea, Captain Freiberg. How I know it has to do with him I can't tell you."

"I know of him." A pause followed, not a happy pause. "Certainly Captain Freiberg is not orthodox," the bishop said, and Mellie opened her eyes wide. Could this be *spite,* or *envy* or *fear,* in the voice of a bishop? Still—*we are men of like passions with you*—wasn't that in the Bible? Or was it Walt Whitman? The bishop was going on, "I said at the time it was a mistake to allow a recent convert with his mystic views and overdramatic presentation thereof to be with young men subject to the nervous strain of war. As has been said there are no atheists in foxholes, on the other hand does such faith carry over into peace?"

"Peace?" Mellie said. "Actually, it's only been a cold war, hasn't it?"

The bishop said, "Tell your husband to come and see me."

I didn't know until later that, without scruple and also without success, Mellie had tried a hairpin, a bobby pin, and a nail file which broke in an attempt to open the tarnished brass lock. The box where Hank kept what Mellie herself called the Casket Letters was covered with dark blue leather, its gold lines and gold monogram H.A.G. blurred by time.

When she got back from the bishop's that afternoon late she found a call from Hank waiting her. From New York. That meant he wasn't coming home tonight. Returning it, the operator at the Plaza said Mr. Gavin's room didn't answer but she would let him know that Mrs. Gavin was now ready to talk, and would be there the rest of the evening.

Putting the receiver back on the telephone with meticulous care so as not to crash it into a thousand pieces, Mellie Gavin lowered herself down in a catcher's squat and stared at the lower drawer of Hank's desk. Keeping her balance on the balls of her feet, she drew it open. Staring at her were three or four books of press clippings. If she cared to open them they would reveal details of Hank Gavin's career as a halfback and a first baseman. Nothing in it would be later than his graduation, though since then the press had noted a couple of medals he got in Korea and his chairmanship of civic groups and youth activities. In one corner of the drawer were some dog-eared autographed photographs of Chicago Cubs named Phil Cavaretta and Kiki Cuyler and one member of the White Sox named Luke Appling. Holding these down was a torn fencing mask which must once have belonged to Colin Rowe. In the other corner was the blue leather box, resembling those Mellie had always imagined as carrying dispatches to and from the Queen.

Staring at this Mellie allowed her mind to go back to the Casket Letters. In school, Mary Queen of Scots had been her favorite, she had thought her cap the most glamorous headdress she had ever seen, there had never been any mystery about the letters. In them for her, then and now, was the ring of true passion which like the expression of pain or the shadow of death cannot be faked. Mary of Scotland had loved Bothwell and only Bothwell, to the loss of her kingdom and the danger of her immortal soul. A blessing and a privilege not given to all and thus the basis of a great deal of misunderstanding, such as still surrounds the sonnets of Shakespeare.

Quickly, in a totally involuntary action, she put out her hand and held it hard against the leather of the box. At the moment it was the nearest she could come to touching Hank. To pressing the palm of her hand against his cheek or stroking the thick thatch of his hair.

Loneliness took hold of her, it was something she had never known before, it dumfounded her and just for a moment rattled her badly.

Only a few of us feel like this, she thought. Or maybe a lot of us. Who knows? Look at the pictures in the paper of people who kill somebody for love. And the somebody they kill for the love of. You'd never suspect it.

All this time her inner being was being shaken by an earthquake.

She reached behind her onto the low table, got a cigarette from the box, and used the silver lighter, maintaining her position with grace and ease. With the first puff she reiterated to herself that a woman does not read letters addressed to her husband and hidden away under lock and key.

It is dishonorable.

It is unprincipled.

Let us admit this.

Or/and

There are times when a woman is justified in reading anything whatsoever she can get her hands on if it will assist her to save her husband from steps and errors of which the consequences must be fatal.

Or to save her marriage. The happiness of her whole life.

That was not apologia, nor Tweedledum and Tweedledee, not the end justified the means.

I could not love thee, dear, so much, loved I not honor more.

Crap.

Slush. Lovely slush.

Her eyes, wide and dark and stinging, noted the fencing mask.

Colin.

So she was still fighting Colin. In him was represented the most frustrating and infuriating of all human conditions—the tyranny of the weak. The destruction of the strong by the demands of the weak, the unwritten law that the strong must yield to the weak.

At that moment she realized that the small key was *in* the keyhole of the box.

Swaying back on her heels, she put her cigarette down on the edge of the table, sat down on the floor with her legs out in front of her, took the box from the drawer, and placed it on the floor between her knees. As she turned the key her hand was perfectly steady.

The letters within were higgledy-piggledy, no order chronological or otherwise. On a typewriter whose o cut a small round hole in the paper and whose small g lacked a tail, they were addressed to Mr. Henry A. Gavin at the house in which his wife now sat looking at them. This was the typewriter in Hank's private office which he used himself, she had had love letters written on it and sent to London, or Honolulu, or Aspen, Colorado. *It's worse than my right arm missing, beloved, it's all of me, there isn't any me when you're away, just a robot waiting for you to come back and bring him to life again, Your adoring husband.*

The one on top which she picked up first, was bulky, over thirty pages, more like a book than a letter. Maybe Hank was writing a book, who wasn't?

The Epistle of Paul the Apostle—

"What the *hell,*" Mellie Gavin said aloud. Very aloud. The cook could probably hear her down in the kitchen.

Her eyes skipped down frantically and found:

Paul, a servant of Jesus Christ, called to be an apostle. . . . separated unto the gospel. . . . to all that be in Chicago, beloved of God, called to be saints. . . . I am debtor both to the Greeks and to the Barbarians. . . . So much as is in me, I am ready to preach the gospel to you that are at Chicago also. . . .

She got that far.

Then she did a double take.

Chicago?

Looking back she saw the first line, all in capitals, read THE EPISTLE OF PAUL THE APOSTLE TO THE CHICAGOANS. In one swift twist she was on her feet, her toe shoved the box, and the letters scattered on the floor. She went backward to a shelf and took down a magnificent Oxford University Press Bible, the thin pages fluttered and stuck under her icy fingers, in time she found it, fortunately it was the first one.

There it was.

To all that be in Rome.

Rome Rome Rome.

Further, the fourteenth verse, *I am debtor both to the Greeks and the Barbarians, so much as in me is I am ready to preach the gospel to you that are at Rome also.*

Rome! Not *Chicago.*

At the time Paul the Apostle wrote his epistles, Chicago hadn't even been Fort Dearborn yet, there were only tepees along the river banks, if that . . .

She picked up another envelope; this time the letter was only seven pages.

Paul and Captain Freiberg, to all the servants of Jesus Christ which are at Chicago . . . if there be any consolation . . . comfort of love . . . fulfill ye my joy. . . .

Frantically, she located it. This time, it was *Philippi.*

Then shall I see thee again?

Ay, at Philippi.

Why, I will see thee at Philippi then.

But that was Shakespeare, not the Bible. That was Brutus and the ghost, not St. Paul and Timotheus. But certainly it wasn't *Chicago.* Or Captain Freiberg.

This time, she lifted the box, picked up all the letters, put them back, and set the box on the table. She rubbed her hands up and down on her slacks, like a pitcher, and lifting her head saw her face in the beautiful old mirror. "You look like the first man outside of Australia who ever saw a kangaroo," she said grimly. And instead of a laugh found that the tears burned her eyes. A smoldering anger and dismay began in the marrow of her bones. Their marriage had been an odds-on favorite, not a hurdle ahead. From where had this storm come roaring upon their slick happiness? For at the first glimpse of those letters she knew it was a storm.

Hank wasn't kidding! But he could have blown his stack.

At a sound, she swung around and in the doorway the colored maid said, "Mr. Margolis, he thought Mr. Gavin was home."

"Ask him to come up," Mellie said, the maid smiled adoringly and went. *Nobody else can get any,* Vadne had told me once, *Mellie's stay forever.*

While she waited Mellie wondered if a visit from Stu Margolis at this moment might be a fortunate coincidence. Perhaps she could use some other judgment, not fired with anger or cold underneath with terror or edged with resentment like her own. If there was one thing for which Stu Margolis was famous it was cold, clear, swift, unbiased judgment. Instant and unerring decision in a crisis.

As she brought him a bourbon and water, Stu Margolis saw that the skin under Mellie's eyes was faintly blue and her lashes were wet. Not a girl to weep easily, but he saw also that whatever had been strong enough to knock her down, she hadn't stayed, she could get up off the floor, she was on her feet.

"I've got a problem," she said, and in one quick motion held out to him a blue leather box. "Hank left the key in it, would you take a look, Stu? Be prepared to fall flat on your face."

His look at the box, back at her, was quick, penetrating, and he sat down at once in Hank's big chair and opened the lid. A different man, this was, than the amused and amusing gentleman she was used to seeing at parties, or sitting next to at dinner. Here was the man of accustomed authority, consulted by experts from Washington, a pillar of steadiness, respected by his Board so that no decision was ever final without his opinion, whose Achilles heel in the form of his wife was inconceivable but concealed in the market place even from himself.

When he had read three or four of the letters, he put them all back and said, "I assume the rest are all a repetition of the original premise? Well, it's an ingenuous device."

"It seems to me a bit on the mad mad mad mad side," Mellie said.

"This fellow Paul always interested me," Stu Margolis said. "My folks sent me to a denominational college where Bible courses were compulsory. There are more of us about than is sometimes realized. Paul was an anomaly. Seems to have been going along, an aristocrat, leader in his time, knew the corruption of the high priests all right, but at the same time was all for controlling these fishermen and carpenters and hotheads who wanted to fight Rome and were going to get everybody in trouble. Then all of a sudden he did one of the biggest about-faces in history. And became, you might say, the first public relations man for Christianity. No real explanation except that he said he *saw* something— Well, of course, men who *see* things—"

"Are men who see things," Mellie said. "I heard a psychiatrist on Kup's show one night say that if he'd lived today Paul would have been locked up in Elgin or Watusa."

"Every man to his trade," Stu Margolis said and took a large drink from the glass he'd been holding. "Some psychiatrists are inclined to see all men as candidates for psychiatric wards. But Paul—"

"Darling darling sweetie pie," Mellie said, "let us forget Paul for the moment, shall we? What about Hank?"

"Where is he, by the way?" Stu said. "I thought he was due back—"

"As far as I know," Mellie said, "he's at the Plaza in New York. I'm not quite sure where he is. It's one of the—oddities."

"Is he still talking about—going into the ministry or some such tomfoolery?" Stu Margolis said. "I've heard no more recently about his resigning."

"I'm afraid you will," Mellie said.

The man put down his glass, reopened the box, took out one letter, and sat staring at it. "Forgive me, Mellie," he said, "as I said before this is ingenuous, it's a *raw* idea, got a bit of ham in it, but it's a cunning way to try to sell himself. Have to do that before you can sell anybody else. Didn't Hendrik van Loon write a book once where he could summon any figure out of the past to dine with him—you know, Napoleon or Cleopatra or Socrates—this is the same rather childish fantasy, isn't it? As I remember it, Paul's letters—or epistles —weren't written as a *Bible* or even for a book. They were practical instructions, advice, sent to groups he'd converted and left around on his travels or to friends, raising hell with them—of course this business of sending them to *yourself*—I mean actually *doing* it—it's odd to say the least. Dangerous probably. If it went *on*—"

He was smiling at her ruefully, but Mellie saw that his eyes now were cold and very thoughtful.

The first requisite of a great investment counselor was trustworthiness. Stability.

A man who wrote letters to himself might not be stable. Or trustworthy.

Mellie got up quickly and locked the blue leather box and put it back in the drawer. "I thought you might have an idea of what we could do," she said arrogantly. "He's probably experimenting. Men do."

"Don't misunderstand me," Stu Margolis said. "I would do anything for Hank. As a man and—I need him in my business, as we say. If we fight him on it, I think we might push him over. He's a very stubborn guy, I've watched him, he never gives up, he keeps at a thing. Time is on our side, I think, and when it comes right down to it, Hank's got a practical Scotch streak in him. But possibly it would be better not to aggravate him—"

"I may have to aggravate him," Mellie said.

"You have advantages I don't," Stu Margolis said, "and remember you can always call on me—"

The telephone rang.

"It always does, doesn't it?" Mellie said. She picked it up, and listened, and her face changed completely. She said, "Oh Hank—how wonderful . . . no no, of course it won't be too late . . . how could it be? . . . Have you? so have I, lonely as a melon in a cornpatch . . . you come home this minute, you hear me?"

Delicately, she put down the phone. She moved back toward the man in the chair, moved now light and loose, her body flowering and eager. Her eyes were blank with anticipation of delight.

"He got lonesome," she said. "He's going to catch the nine-fifteen plane. Everything is going to be all right, Stu. Don't worry about it."

"All right," Stu Margolis said, "I won't."

The woman I love, he thought.

There it is.

He went out into the long late lovely twilight, toward the woman he loved, and the old suspense came back, there was always the chance that he'd find her still in bed with whomever she'd gone to bed with that afternoon.

Just the same, it was Hank Gavin he was *worrying* about, in spite of his promise to Mellie. This business of a man typing out letters and mailing them to himself, this would have to be watched. After all, Margolis had a responsibility to his clients.

2

Neither Mellie nor Stu Margolis noted a flat compartment inside the lid of the leather box. Thus they missed a letter, part of Hank Gavin's correspondence with Captain Freiberg. Later Hank let me read it and it is before me. Due to his language and his earlier travels in troubled areas, the chaplain was sent to distant posts and he and Hank never found it possible to meet at this time. Often it seemed to Hank that the chaplain's letters were all he had to guide, support, and strengthen him as his fight began and the usual temptations wrapped octopus arms around him.

This time the chaplain had found more and bigger paper, the text was clear, if Mellie had found it she could easily have read as follows:

Dear Hank The difficulty is that nobody <u>reads</u> the New Testament as though it was intended to make <u>sense.</u> Fewmen I've met have been able to read it as living continuity applied to US. Being brought up in an Orthodox Jewish home Ihadn't ever opened it, it was new to me except as literature and quotations. Once in South Africa I knew a real able rigged tough citizen who'd growun up and never heard of Shakespeare. When he met up with the plays he read them as though they'd been written the daybefore,his reaction and what he had to say about them was amazing.He brought Shakespeare out biggerand better, showed me nothing great <u>dates,</u> as they say, except shallow people. Me reading the forbidden book was like any man reading any forbidden book, I got a big kick out of it,but my thought processes weren't wrapped up in other men's opinions nor hogtied with what I was supposed to believe Jesus <u>meantby</u>

what he said. I was a blank white page. It was all so damn simple it took me a wnile to find that men could under<u>stand</u>it okey but they woulen't stand for it, they had to screw it upwith a lot of doctrines and <u>interpretations</u> and <u>do</u>-<u>it</u>-<u>my</u>-<u>way</u>-Or-you'll-go-to-hell, otherwise like the multiplication table which is simple too they would have to <u>use</u> 2x2=4. IfI was in your spot,buddy, I'd have as little to do with all this as you possibly can you'll probably have to go to school and study theology to get in, but don't let them bury you in intellectual sepulchers The only thing you can satisfactorily dissect is a corpse. And of course you can learn a lot of organizational needs and you'll meet a few great men who walk in his steps, and some hungry youngsters.But avoid all you can the books that areonly <u>about</u> something.Some of them sure are allright, but why is their opinion any better or as good as yours if you are seeking an honest man?I've known several gents who wrote abooks about the New Testament and what Jesus <u>meant</u> by cast out <u>devils,</u> they figure he <u>couldn8t</u> possibly have just meant <u>cast</u> <u>out</u> <u>devils</u>and I swear wnile I'm not a vain man you know they're no brighter and less honest and eager than I am. I want to cast out devils. The point is, the BOOK is there. Itself. The Gospel. The Word. What even the greatest and holiest and most gofted scholars and teachers say is just saying something ABOUT it.About and about and about. Down at St. Johns' University they discovered there were a hundred books and all the rest were ABOUT them. There was a probelm some old mathematician that <u>said</u> it about relativity if anybody had bothered to read carefilly. The <u>About</u> books can be great,they're stimulating sometimes ,they keep you from getting bored or having to think when you're lazy and getting bored is something we never admit in religion-so-called but it is one of our dangers,buddy. But the BOOK itself the Book the BOOK the BOOK itself is without fault or flaw unless you begin with the premise that Jesus meant it onlyfor the xxmxyxd limited few who heard his voice. And never intended The Way to do it and the thing to be done to apply to us.NOT Ceasarea only, but Washington and Chicago. The Word is there. I speak not of myself, the Father within t ells mE what to say. The inspired part of me. Sure, you can adjust it, you can use examples from our tixxxx times, and healings we have done, just as mathematicians and scientists can prove Einstein but buddy buddy you better be real sure you know your multiplication table before you start proving infinity by mathematics,hadn8t you? It would have been great if we'd heard him on The Mount, but what's the difference, we know what he said there. I'm going to tell you about a practical experiment I made, probably just as well on this if you t ell no man. When you meet up with theologians and Sxxxxx seminarians, you'll find not many of them have the courage to preach the doctrine of renewal anyhow and up-dating the miracxles is an uncomfortable business to face/ However remember that Christianity today and all its churches are useless, by God, unless they are operated by men,of a certain degree of faith in the works by which Jesus proved and told us to prove his words. Some sense of obedience to his command go and do likewise. Son, it won8t work any other way. Greater works than these shall you do because I have taught you and shown you that I go to the Divine Power for my power and so can and must you. It's the first obligation. You see that? It's important,When you start substituting and being satisfied with the words, all you've got id an adventure like the Illiad or the Odyssey. As a teacher, Jesus was specific about the xxxxxx Works. Prove it or shut up.I believe in our age that's what they long to hear and see, not a lot of double-talk and don't-let-your-preaching-show. Brotheryyou better let it show, is all I believe. Why,buddy, there isn't anything in all history and invention as tremendous and excitint as when he said to the man with the withered hand *Stretch forth your hand* . You think you know what takes guts,son, and I saw you disOlay quite a few that night we took the Pusan outpost. But think a minute.Here he stood right in front of a crowd of people who were out to do him in, the audience was composed pretty solidly of his active *enemies*, high muckamucks bent on ~~discrediting~~ discrediting him *and* above all his *works.* Organinzed in conspiracy to make a monkey of him and show he was a fake and a charlatan. And *he* said Stretch forth your hand! That's putting it on the lind buddy. Stretch forth your hand and I'll do my works so they all see, that's how sure *I* am. That's what faith I have in Our Father. And it was restored whole as the other. Top that. We have to *begin* there. No James Bond .007 or no Colonel Glenn or anybody else had guts like that.Well,anyway, when I read the Book and a whole new world opened up to me I decided to make a trip around and see the places where it all happened. I wanted to see the places Where Paul carried The Word to the Gentiles.And the Greeks and Barbarians.AllJews are imaginzative and I got thinking about the *letters* Paul had sent to little groups in Corinth or Galatia by camel and horseback and ship and caravan.They got to be real to me.Paul had been trained as a tent-maker. Allrich and educated young Jews had to have a trade also,and after his grandfather had disowned him for being a follower in Christ's footsteps, Paul made his living that way. At the end of a hard day's work he prayed and then later he'd write letters.Anyhow, buddy, my advice to you is to copy all the epistles as though they were letters from a friend or a teacher or me,,God help me,if I was wise enough. There are 14 from Paul and then some by James and Peter and James and John. Just sit down and copy them on any old kind of ~~pupxxx~~ paper and mail one to yourself. Every day.Every week. Or just when you feel like it.Open them as though they'd come to you fresh, new, in your dilemma, the way they came to his "beloved sons" Timothy, Titus, Philemon~~xxx~~ That's what I did.I've never told you about my family, have I?You tink Paul's family cut up rough, mine would have had me put in a strait jac ket if they could have thought of a way. Sometimes I got very lonesome, to the Christians I was a Jew and to the Jews I was a traitor.You will find if you really begin to give his flight pattern a try, there are some very lonesome places along the road. So when my letters I'd copied from Paul came along, a couple of times they saved me. After all, what's 1900 yea s or so? He meant them for me,Ike Freiberg,too.Whynot? Iwished to serve his Lord, I wish to know what God is and that his love for me is power for me to use,for Him. If you are wacky enough to try this,God be with you. Open your heart to the Owrd,offer nim yourdesire to walk in his steps and to obey his commandments as he gave them, and if you make out with this one I've got one that's even screwier. Little by little, day by day, in joy and thanksgiving in all circumstances, we may get to where we have the guts and faith to say Stretch forth your hand or your sin or limitation or fear and by the Grace of God it will be whole in God's image.Maybe we will get this renewal off the ground and say to tbe poor,hopeless, ~~benighted~~ benighted , heart-broken sinners and lepers and dead-in-apathy little fellows I will, be thou clean. Works insteadof all this talktalk talk. Yours in Christ. Ike Freiberg. P.S. Of course Paul wrote pne ortwo things for his day, like Jesus talking about sheep, but you can ignore those. Only those:

"When it came to carrying out my chaplain's fundamental preoccupation with the New Testament," Hank Gavin told me, "I'd started with the letters. I don't know just why, somehow they seemed near to me. I could figure Paul, so it seemed all right to have the letters come to me, you know about that. I realized I'd never *read* any of Paul's letters, not all the way through. I knew a quotation here and there—the ones everybody knows—*though I speak with the tongues of men and of angels and have not love, I am become as sounding brass or a tinkling cymbal—avoid profane and vain babblings and oppositions of science falsely so-called—An unknown God whom then ye ignorantly worship him declare I unto you* —but I wouldn't have been sure whether they were from Paul or Shakespeare or Spinoza.

"I figured since I'd never read them on a printed page, if I *didn't* do so now, when I did receive them as letters to me I could *really* make myself believe it. Let's go for broke, Hank old boy, I said to myself. Then I got to thinking about who I could ask to make a copy of all the letters of St. Paul as quoted in the New Testament. This takes a little doing. She certainly couldn't do it where everybody could see her—she'd have to do it in my private office on my typewriter. Nothing else for it—but by that time I wasn't going to let anything turn me back. You know my secretary, Mrs. Amelia Giddings? Remember Edna Mae Oliver—all right that's my Amelia. Her husband in whom I always had trouble believing was killed at Guadalcanal, and let me tell you Mrs. Giddings was efficient, silent, and as discreet as the Washington monument.

"The sweat was standing out on my forehead when I handed it to her, and I thought of giving her some explanation like somebody was writing a *play* or somebody's mother couldn't see very well—but I knew I couldn't fool Mrs. Giddings. All she said was, 'What will I do with them when I've finished?' and I said, 'Oh—just give them to me, please.'

"The day the first one arrived I kept it—Mellie was used to papers being sent home to me by mail—and finally after Mellie went to sleep, I got up and went in by myself and read it.

"Maybe it was nuts. I don't know. I know it was the biggest adventure I ever had. To this day—this day—I don't know whether I revved up my imagination and believed this gimmick or whether it was one of those river-of-time bits I've heard about or whether Paul himself could make time *one*, make his letters forever new to whoever *read* them, that they had been written to that person specially.

"I donknow.

"To me, it was real."

When Hank Gavin told me this we were waiting to see my friend the editor of the B. C. Press about helping to get probation for a kid named Juan Galloway.

"Things can—become real. Mellie and I were in Rome on our honeymoon and without our knowing exactly where we were going, there we were in the catacombs which neither of us had intended to see or were the least bit interested in. Just the same once we *got* there, I remember Mellie saying no one could come down in them without getting all het up about them. It's funny, one of the times when I can make a perfectly clear picture of Mellie, as though Renoir painted it in a frame, is in the *catacombs*. Which is not, I agree, the setting you'd choose for her, would you? She had on one of those little suits she wears, she'd as soon go on the street in her nightgown as in a dress, it was the color of real cream and she had a plain brown scarf knotted around her throat and a topaz lapel pin and earrings I'd given her for Christmas, she loved topaz. She'd bought those kind of high-polish takes-a-bootboy brogues in London and she had on a soft little felt hat she got in Italy pulled down over her right eye—now I'm telling you about it, the reason I remember all these details which I couldn't do about hardly any other time in the world is because she was so *modern*, the experts told me a chic American girl is chic-er than the chic-est Parisienne, and there she was and there the catacombs still were and they didn't seem as—much at odds as you'd suppose. I remember chuckling to myself because I thought if she'd been there she wouldn't have put any little pinch of incense on any altar to some god because the emperor told her to. He'd have his hands full, that's what I thought. Anyway, her Italian was good enough so she got the guide all excited by asking him more questions than he'd heard in years that made sense. History and everything. She'd translate for me, about how the catacombs had been lost for centuries and only found again about four hundred years ago, and then I remember her saying *Imagine, dear husband, there are 750 miles of these goddam rabbit warrens and they lived in them and cooked in them and if this silly guide would go away we could make love just the way they used to, poor things, scared to death all the time.* I remember she stood on her tiptoes and tried to touch the ceilings but even the tips of her white gloves wouldn't reach and she put both palms against the walls, I know she was trying to imagine what it was like to stay down there. I don't think either of us thought about the people who'd been there as—as religious refugees. Not at the time. Nor that the place was literally an Underground."

After the light came into his life, so unexpectedly and conclusively, Hank was able to revisit in memory this underground into which these early Christians fled from persecution. He could picture the groups gathered in those narrow earth-walled passages to hear the rolling thunder of Peter himself, telling them only and always what the Man had taught and what his presence had been to his followers. The Word must never be lost and Peter gave it into their keeping and they into the keeping of others and finally, Hank thought, into mine. It seemed very *odd,* in a way, but that was what his mind said to him.

"While I was running around in circles, trying to find out what to do and how to do it," Hank Gavin said, "I *read.* That sounds simple enough and it was in a way, the chaplain kept writing me to stick to the New Testament. But you can't, not really. You have to read something else sometimes. I used to get up and sneak downstairs without waking Mellie, and read till dawn. I never got much sleep. I had no one to direct me, to tell me what you were supposed to read at a time like that. I felt there must be treasures all around me but I didn't know what they were and I—I didn't get any advice from—anyone. Now I think that was a good thing. I refused a lot of frozen-in mistakes.

"People are swayed and led and helped by writings of their own times. Not always by sacred cows of the past. We're moved by what our contemporaries who live in the same world we do with all the same problems and tempos and trends, speaking in our own idioms, about places and people we know, have made of it. With our own increased knowledge of an unfolding universe. Of course all that is in *de Chardin,* but it took me six months to read his *Phenomenon of Man,* it revolutionized my thinking, but I don't have it in shape yet to talk about it. I understand what he means but I can't *say* it yet. I was a good deal suprised at how many top successful authors have said great things, with faith and aspiration. You always hear so much about all the repetition of filth. What excited me was—they recognize the Word, all right, the truth that never changes from Plotinus to Einstein no matter what they do with it afterward, but some of these writers have the guts to scrape off the barnacles. They tell the same story, but they tell it with—well, let's say with airplanes flying the Atlantic, not Columbus in the *Santa Maria.* With telephones, not letters that took years to get somewhere. The way they reach out—it's an adventure to read them.

"To me, just an ordinary reader, a confused man as I was, some of the books were like—like an amateur astronomer seeing a new star through his little old telescope on the roof."

His eyes had grown luminous again. From the first I had been aware of their power, their ability not only to stir me but to convince me.

He said, "You know a book called *Black Lamb and Grey Falcon?* By a lady named Rebecca West." When I nodded he said, "Well, I'm here to tell you it amazed *me.* Haven't people paid any *attention* to this? Or are prophets still without honor in their own time and country? I had never read anything *like* this—"

"There isn't anything like it," I said. "In the first place she's the greatest living journalist and *writer,* and she has true vision."

He said, "Well, I'd never heard of her, to tell you the truth. You'd be surprised how much a lot of us have never heard of." From his pocket he took the brown wallet, it was stuffed now with pieces of paper, most of which looked as though they'd been torn from paperbacks; they were heavily lined and underlined. He said, "The whole book got me, but here's one thing she said that was important to the—the man I had to become."

He handed me the clipping. I read: *There is that in this universe half inside and half outside our minds, which is wholely adorable; and this it was that men killed when they crucified Jesus Christ. Our shame would be absolute were it not that the crime we intended cannot in fact be committed. It is not possible to kill goodness. There is always more of it, it does not take flight, it perpetually asked us to take what we need from it.* When I looked up he was looking at me, through me, far away and beyond me. Here was one of the times when I was sure he was one of those to whom Peter had handed the Word, that it shall not be lost. "The way I get it Rebecca West thinks a lot of the war and pain and hate and blood in the world comes because about the fourth century we were persuaded to make the crucifixion the center of Jesus' teachings about the way to live. She thinks he taught us that the power of good is always greater than the power of evil, that good can always be triumphant over the evil and cruelty and bestiality that's in all of us. IF we obey the rules he laid down, as you have to follow the rules in the—the science of relativity or flying or writing a symphony. *The basic* commandments—like how you mix paint no matter what picture you want to put on the canvas. She's never humbugged once, not once, into the only sin against the Holy Ghost."

"You're always talking about the sin against the Holy Ghost," I said with some impatience, "but you never tell me what it is. Like Hercule Poirot who won't tell you what anything means until he's solved the whole case."

He kept staring at me. "You can't tell, if you're not sure yourself what it means," Hank said. "In one of his letters, Paul says—you know I don't agree with *all* Paul says. He'd been dazzled by the light, his whole life changed. He had to convince those same Nazarenes that he'd *seen* Jesus and now *he* was their man. Paul let himself be overwhelmed at one point with details and what seemed like sort of minor rules, but whoever chose him on the road to Damascus was right, because he did carry the Light around the world. Did you know Bernard Shaw made a deep study of Paul and Jesus? As a matter of fact he didn't think much of Paul, but he thought Jesus was tops, for all time. I always thought of Shaw as an old man with a beard who wrote the play from which they made *My Fair Lady*."

The crumpled pages he had continued to smooth almost reverently showed sentences marked in red ink. "Shaw says here Jesus was always for joy, he told them all not to be of a *sad countenance*. All the promises would be kept, on condition as laid down. He says Jesus wanted to clear himself and everyone of the inveterate superstition that *suffering* is *gratifying* to God. He fought suffering every inch of the way and batted about .842. He says Jesus advocated counteracting evil by good. Not, he says, by some other hostile evil, such as a God who takes a whole jaw for a tooth and the top of your head for an eye. One thing I wish I could thank Shaw for. I was as ignorant as most people my age are, I guess, about the real man Jesus. Here Shaw says *Gentle Jesus meek and mild is a snivelling modern invention*. I was having trouble with that one. You know how Chicago is about art, they think buying it or going to see it or subsidizing it or hanging it in the bathroom proves something. When Mellie and I were in Europe we saw a lot of it and the fact that Jesus survived what the art of the Middle Ages made of him ought to prove his power. That's a miracle all right. It can't be true, you know. He couldn't possibly have been that skinny, emaciated rack of bones *steeped* in defeat, hopeless as a run-over dog. That man isn't going to rise up again, he's up there for always, a symbol forever of defeated good. I—hated it, even then, before I *knew* him. Mount Hermon isn't such a hell of a mountain, on the other hand the Jesus they have hanging up there couldn't have climbed it. Nor sailed a fishing boat nor *walked* from town to town the way he did. Another thing. He was a carpenter. I went down and watched some of them. You ought to see their wrists and forearms and back muscles. Do you think that meek-mild-puny idea they've tried to sell us could have lifted lumber and slung beams and used an old-fashioned saw? Not ever. Look—*this man* had authority. Spiritual *authority* has power. The centurion said to him I, too, am a man of authority, I say to a soldier go and he goes, speak the word only and my servant shall be healed. He recognized *authority*. *This man* Jesus could take on the lawyers with good will, but he could *cope* with them. You have to be quite a guy to say to the chief priests and top elders the publicans and the harlots go into the kingdom of heaven before *you*. A lot they've written about him and some of what they've preached about him—look what Shaw says, he says, *That such a figure could ever have become the center of the world's attention is too absurd for discussion.* I couldn't see how I could *follow* the man they did set up, or get anyone else to. Remember I mentioned to you the Dali Last Supper. Well, somebody told me I ought to go down to Washington and see it. So I did. There is the Man of Galilee. Dali, who used to paint jokes, must have *seen* or he couldn't have painted him. After the night on the barge, I knew this was an *experience*, that picture. A portrait.

"Right after that I had a real black fall from grace. Thomas Merton says you will never fall out of God's hand—but for a spell there it looked as though I'd never been in it.

"Mellie really took out after me. You have any idea how—*cute* that girl can be? She sure did a snow job on me. She quit saying she wouldn't come with me, she just went off on another tack altogether. She gave me the big I-adore-you routine at which nobody can be any better and assumed I wasn't going. She had *plans*. And she began hypnotizing me into the notion that what God wanted me to do was stay right where I was! I'd be a big feather in His cap. I could raise money and be head of the Men's Club at the church and arrange *missions* for the Young Marrieds and stay in my own *vineyard* where probably whatever this was I believed in had been preparing me. This, she said, she could go along with—not agree with—but go along with and when Mellie is going along with you, you need wax in your ears and bandages on your eyes. She's something. She's so—so *sweet.* It's a side of her you don't see much of but it's about as close to irresistible as you can get. And you have to remember this. You knock over one of those silly little floozies that run around without any tops on their bathing suits and who did you ever lick? Like hitting a cripple. But *Mellie!* It's got to make you feel you're—it gives you a lot of confidence in yourself. I began to think maybe I had blown my roof. She was such fun."

I thought about Mellie for a minute or two and so did he.

"I had a pain in my gizzard," Hank Gavin said, "but I had just about settled for this. I'd begun to see myself as a sort of whirlwind assistant to Jack Knowles. In addition to being vice president of the golf club. Let the Christians eat cake. You know who saved me? This one may surprise you. You said you'd read *Catcher in the Rye*—so many women didn't?"

I said I had, that it had been one of the great moments of my life. I thought at last in Salinger we had a great modern novelist. Hank nodded and said, "He's not just modern, he's a tomorrow writer. Mind if I try to tell you something else he wrote in his book *Zooey?* Zooey's a young TV actor, one of the Glass family, remember? And he's talking to his sister Franny who is having a slight nervous breakdown partly from trying to say what they both called the Jesus Prayer. You know about that? Well—it's just a simple prayer to tune in to the power and presence of the Risen Christ, that's what it actually is. Hold your hat, I can't say it exactly but it meant so much to me—I can't give it the Salinger *magic* maybe—but what Zooey said to his sister was he couldn't figure how she could pray to a Jesus she didn't even understand. He had an idea—this is still Zooey—that like a lot of other people Franny misunderstood *Jesus* entirely, she got him mixed up with all the sticky sentimental people like Heidi's grandfather and maybe even St. Francis—or their own brother Seymour—characters like that all rolled into one. Zooey said that to say the Jesus Prayer, which is actually from a little book Salinger uses such a lot called *The Way of A Pilgrim,* you had to say the prayer Lord Jesus Christ have mercy on me, have love for me to *Jesus,* not anybody who was the least bit different from the way he could be heard or seen if you really read the New Testament. It's odd in a way, Salinger representing as a writer all that's *modern* in *Catcher in the Rye* and everything he wrote—but he calls Jesus not only the most intelligent man in the New Testament but in the whole Bible, he keeps on talking about

Jesus' *mind,* and he goes into the fact that nobody—*nobody* —not David or Solomon or the prophets or anybody—*knew*—knew for sure that the Kingdom of Heaven was put inside us, it's with us, the way they use that expression now—we can get with it, the Kingdom of Heaven, because we've already got it. I may not have the words exactly right but it's right about them that he says we're too goddam stupid and silly and *unimaginative* to look there. Inside us. He keeps saying you have to be aware—to keep asking, as it were—to be sure you're a son of God to know all that stuff. He keeps saying that's the whole *point,* otherwise the whole point of the Jesus Prayer gets lost. You miss it, Salinger says, if you don't understand Jesus as he was. A big mission, the biggest and most important any man ever had, that's what he says Jesus was on. And I remember one word Salinger uses right there—he always found the right word, didn't he?—he says Jesus was an *adept.* Naturally God would pick the right man and he says Jesus *was,* the most loving, never intimidated anybody, never got sentimental, just loving so he was the right man to teach us how to come into our birthright as sons of God. Talking about the tune-in prayer, he says its one aim, the only one it ever has, is to tune you into Christ Consciousness and all its works."

Hank stood entirely still then. I couldn't hear anything, but I thought he could. He said, "It sort of leaves you, what Salinger writes there, thinking of how it would be if we built all those lovely silvery airplanes with all that power and lined 'em all up on a airfield and then nobody ever learned how to fly them. Or all the big shiny cars, and they were left in the garage and nobody ever drove them! You know, the chaplain used to talk a lot about the Jesus Prayer. He said the same thing about Christ Consciousness. He said Jesus could tune in to the full power of the Christ Consciousness, the *knowing* the kingdom of heaven within us, knowing our sonship with Our Father, and the Jesus Prayer is—it's the number of the channel by which we reach it. The chaplain used to say—wait a minute, Salinger says something about it, too—he says there isn't anything *cozy* or—or selfrighteous or—or I think he calls it holier-than-thou about the personage called Jesus who wasn't one of those who set up as what Salinger calls some alibi psychiatrist, or anybody who'd relieve you of all your duties and discipline. No no.

"You see, when I read that—you notice he keeps on underlining that Jesus *knew,* he *knew,* if you read the book you'll notice the underlining that Jesus *knew* and that's when I woke up out of that lovely half-assed *dream* Mellie was arranging for us both. I'm one of the ones who *know.*

Don't ask me why *me*—that I don't know. But when I read those words of Salinger's I did know I had to go and tell all who would listen."

I had to wonder what Jerry Salinger, retired and hidden from the world in his retreat in New England, would think of this, of the *carrying power* of his word about Seymour—the character who led them all. To recall this Jesus as he really is in the New Testament to the men and women of *his* generation.

Hank said, "I remember looking at Mellie when I went up to bed, curled up like a kitten, her curls that she keeps all slicked down in the daytime all around her head on the pillow like a cloud. Her arms were bare and she had them flung out and her hands clasped and I could see a little flat white frill or something, transparent, over her shoulders. I was standing there thinking what a funny bunch of oracles and mahatmas had opened up my path and held me steady on it. A red-bearded Irish atheist like Shaw, the *très moderne* author Jew and genius I've just been quoting from, a Spanish surrealist who depicted Freudian dreams, that brilliant Englishwoman Rebecca West, whose rebellion against convention had once created a *haute monde* scandal but who now was a D.B.E. To say nothing of Fulton Oursler, author of detective stories such as "The Murder of the Clergyman's Mistress," who came through *conversion* to give so many of us a key in his *Greatest Story Ever Told,* today's life story of Jesus, to the reality of the New Testament. . . . to which we must always go in the end."

None of them what we call religious, he pointed out, not *church* religious, not preachers, all worldly-wise gifted people *of our times* who had achieved and possessed everything life has to offer and had come in the end to the feet of Jesus Christ as they *knew* him.

All this he had thought as he stood looking down at Mellie his wife. On an impulse he leaned down and gathered her up and went to sit on the chair by the eastern window. Her eyes opened a little, through the dark lashes she smiled at him, and he began to tell her what had come to him and what it meant. But her eyes closed again and when he tried to awaken her she lay soft and sweet and sleepy against him, making small sweet sounds like a bird half awake in the night, and her fragrance filled his senses. This time he didn't falter. The sweat came out on his brow and on his upper lip and he touched her hair and her lovely curving cheek, but when the dawn came he carried her carefully and put her into bed without awakening her.

When she did open her eyes upon the morning, he had already started on his odyssey, leaving a little note to say that he had to go away on business and would call her that night. And that he loved her beyond anything he had words to tell her with.

"I thought a good deal about it," he said, "now that I knew the time had come for me to find the steps. Like everything else, all his guidance—it was the clear and simple, leave your nets, let the dead bury their dead, leave your father and mother and wife and follow me. But you only had to leave them if they wouldn't come with you.

"I knew Mellie would come with me and I knew it was going to be rough on her. But there just plain wasn't anything I could do about it."

"Suppose she didn't?" I said.

He didn't answer that.

Suppose he doesn't? I had said to Mellie.

Both of them were so sure they didn't think the question worth answering.

3

When Hank Gavin arrived at his own university's divinity school that summer, it was manned only by an assistant dean. Hank had never seen a yogi, but the quiet that surrounded the dean was what he'd imagined it would be like if he did. Within fifteen minutes, Hank had broken his resolve to tell no one at all of the light of presence and power that had come to him on the barge.

"Mellie thought it was the height of bad taste and that I was kidding, and my grandmother was sure I'd gone fey in the good old Scottish way and of course you're a *writer,*" he said. "Nobody would want to hear it, nobody would believe me, I didn't know yet just where I was going and I didn't want to start as a fanatic who saw purple snakes and pink elephants. There's one thing I'd like you to remember. *Money* had been my business. Nothing affects people like *money*. Rich or poor, too much or too little, hot or cold, greedy or spendthrift, no man can handle *money* all the time for all kinds of people without knowing reality. And I knew too that money's best isn't good enough, either. Money can buy lots of things. People who haven't got it think it can buy everything, but I *knew* better. Only the day before I'd seen a full-page picture of the world's richest billionaire in a magazine, there he was, his tight, pinched, terrible *hopeless* face, and I knew he would never believe in anybody's disinterested love or friendship or affection or loyalty again, and this had hurt him so that he was alone forever.

"I thought I was seeking now for a reality that the world of shadows had lost. But you have to get *elected* first so I thought I'd be sensible until I knew what I was going to do.

"Then the brother of a man I'd been in school with told me that this guy was a great teacher, and my pal said sometimes half this man's lectures were in *silence,* and he had told them someday he'd teach a class that was all in silence, then they would *listen*. He said the most important thing he could teach a class in theology was how to *listen*. Prayer should be listening for the answer, he said. Well, I must say that what he *was* spoke louder than anything he could say. Emerson said. This guy's *tenderness* while he sat there in silence flowed out and comforted me. In one of Paul's letters, I think it was the second one he wrote to the Corinthians, he said, *Blessed be the God of all comfort, who comforted us in all our tribulations, that we may be able to comfort them which are in any trouble, by the comfort wherewith we ourselves are comforted of God.* I liked that idea so much I memorized it, up to that time I read the letters I'd never heard anything about God *comforting* us in any trouble we might be in, which we always *are,* and another thing, I knew this man that very minute was comforting me by the comfort wherewith he himself had been comforted of God and that was the first time I met in daily life and action what I was hoping for. Faith and hope and comfort active in our daily troubles and tribulations and guidance.

"We had quite a spell of *silence* and then he said, 'Go ahead, my son. You are to do pastoral work. You must have active church work. This isn't the place for you. We are inclined to prepare teachers and writers, not *pastors*. Seek and *listen.*' I asked him then if I was right to try to enter the ministry and he said, 'Oh yes, you have been called and chosen for this. It is simple enough, but it won't be easy. A former student of mine has a church now in New York. Part of what they call the renewal group. In answer to the hungry, seeking multitudes there are stirrings within the churches but whether they be of Christ or whether they be of the wisdom of men, I don't know. If you seek, you will find.' "

Listening to the comfort Hank Gavin took in reliving that hour was like watching a man conjure up an oasis where he had stopped and been given a cup of water. When he came back from that memory he had been refreshed and consoled again, I felt it myself, the apprehension with which all of us live daily had dissolved in the light of it.

Which was as well for Hank. His visit to New York had been a descent into hell. In the long pause before he began to tell this story, I heard the beat of what I have always called John Brown's drums. As a young reporter, I'd covered a mine disaster, Standing on the brink with the wives, mothers, children, waiting for news from the rescuers below, I had been filled with the beat of drums which was anger against the owners whose greed had refused to make the mines *safe*. The muffled roll of man's inhumanity to man. I had, too, a clear recollection of the first man they brought up alive. Under the grime and blood and sweat-of-pain I'd seen his face bitten to the bone, he was a young man but *youth* had been burned away in that hot hell. Yet as he saw that the light was still there waiting for him, a smile had come and it was the other end of the *hope* that had sustained him in the long black hours while we tried to pray. Hank Gavin's face, I saw, had settled into those same bone-bitten, harsh lines.

The drums were in his voice—*John Brown's body lies a-mouldering in the grave, John Brown's body lies a-moulderin' in the grave—*

It seemed that in New York he had gone to dinner with a young man who'd been with him and Colin in Korea. And, of course, had known the chaplain. His name was McGuinness, naturally they called him Mac. Now he was married to the girl for whose letters he had waited with such passionate longing, they had two little girls, and he'd heard they had a new baby boy. Hank had planned to go and see the dean's student that night but Mac kept saying, "Nancy would like it so much if you'd come." And in Hank's ear the insistence was strange and violent. A vast proportion of Hank Gavin's work with people had been done over the telephone. Soft-sell hard-sell sure-sell—buy—sell—buy—sell—the youngest president of the biggest insurance company or the oldest bootblack or the dogged husband who wanted a few eggs in a basket of stocks and not on his wife's carcass—he had learned to *hear* over the telephone.

In Mac's voice he heard the call of desperation.

A nice apartment, in one of those new glass towers over by the East River. Mac must be doing all right. Nancy in the kind of print dress that could get dinner in the new all-electric kitchen and pass it through the bar-arch and come on around into the dining area and play hostess. Two nice ordinary little blonde girls. All safe and sane and successful.

Hank's first breath came easily. On the second one he almost strangled with the pain and passion and protest.

What was this all about?

What had been done to them?

Who had done it and why had it been done?

In this great rich happy never-had-it-so-good country.

What'll it be, Hank? How about a vodka on the rocks? The little girls proudly—were they too quiet?—bringing in the jellied consommé, in gold-edged cups—the casserole of chicken with rings of green and red peppers making it gay and the big wooden bowl of salad—and they talked about the Mets and the stock market and foreign policy and an old friend from the days in Korea who lived in San Francisco now and had gone into politics.

And all the time they existed in an unreality like a set on the stage right after the curtain has gone up and before the actors make their first entrances.

Nancy went to put the little girls to bed and Hank and Mac went and sat by a picture window looking out on the dark, moving water. Below them the lights of the bridge had the fairyland quality of a big city at night, hiding even a suspicion of the depths of the river, of the city.

"So Colin jumped out a window," Mac said, and his voice now had an edge honed with hate, "No guts, huh? I always had a hunch Colin had no guts."

"No, you didn't," Hank said, "you know better than that. Some men have guts for one thing and some for another." Then in a voice that was not his voice, he said for the first time, "What is it? Can I help?"

Suddenly, he knew.

He *knew*. *How*—how did he know?

"Nancy can't—she tried," Mac said, "she keeps on trying. She's a good girl, Hank, a real good girl. Only she can't get it in her head—such a *little* guy—what'd he ever do to anybody? God or anybody? What'd we ever *do*—she keeps saying that and saying it, that's what makes me sore at Colin jumping out a window—" He got up and went to the window, and Hank followed him, shaken, and put one arm around his shoulder and moved him back, inside himself he said *Let me comfort him—Oh Lord—let me—I don't know how, I am a blundering fool, I don't know how, as much as a mustard seed.*

He did not many mighty works there because of their unbelief.

Who are you kidding? They quit all *that* nonsense years ago. Bernard Shaw says Jesus was ashamed of his miracles, Jesus wished he'd never gotten mixed up in that kind of claptrap. He was so kindhearted he couldn't resist helping them when they *asked* him, the blind, the lame, the leper, the woman taken in adultery, he was a do-gooder, poor old Jesus, he *healed* them. *Immediately the man received his sight*. So? What did that prove? Some kind of *magic,* sure. But suppose *Jesus* was able to heal, and Peter and John at the gate of the Temple called Beautiful, and Paul saving poor Timothy's tormented sinful soul. You, my lad, are a young investment counselor in *Chicago* in the last half of the goddam twentieth century that knows more than any other century in history. Ask anybody.

"They thought—" Mac said, "they finally persuaded Nancy it was better for him, for the *baby,* they could take better care of him at the—the institution, they were geared for it, and then of course there were the girls. Well, they say time cures all things—"

"Is there no chance?" Hank said, and Mac shook his head.

So here it was, Hank thought.

The thing nobody would ever face. The things that went on happening to children.

No no.

Not in this great scientific never-been-such-advances-pretty-soon-we're-going-to-get-to-the-moon country.

Who *needs* God?

If there is a God, why does he let such things happen in the first place?

Somebody had to answer that question.

It was the one people asked most often.

Why does God *let* innocent people get killed and children be born blind and broken? I don't say there isn't a God, I'm an agnostic, but *if* there is a God all I say is why does He let such things happen?

A minister, a pastor, a man Mac and Nancy could send for in bitter despair would have to be able to answer that question.

Nancy came back into the heavy silence.

Oh yes, she said, when Hank asked her, they went to church, they *belonged* to a church. The little girls went to Sunday School, they were learning folk-dancing for a fall festival the church always had. Yes, the young minister was nice, he had come to see Nancy in the hospital, that was before they'd told her about the baby. Well, no, in their grief and terror it hadn't occurred to them to send for him. They looked a little embarrassed when Hank mentioned praying with their minister, and Nancy said hurriedly she didn't think —he was *busy*—they'd read in the paper that he was on a committee of Christians and Jews and—no, they wouldn't have *felt* like asking him. "I'm not criticizing him, understand," Mac said. "I like the guy. I like his sermons, he doesn't keep trying to ram *God* down your throat all the time."

"Like the chaplain used to?" Hank said.

Mac gave him a queer look. "All right, all right," he said, "but the chaplain had God to ram down your throat, didn't he?"

No chance no chance no chance.

That's what Mac had said.

No chance.

Why could not we cast him out?

Because of your unbelief.

Plain words.

Or cast *out* anything.

You want to end up in Mattewan?

My unbelief. I see through a glass darkly. Not knowing what God I pray to. Help thou mine unbelief.

For I—I, Hank Gavin—I *know*.

Yet knowing I still haven't faith as a grain of mustard seed that the power of the Spirit is available, that it acts now.

Except for the hand of a friend, the arm of a Marine Corps pal on his shoulder, he hadn't comforted Mac.

Even the silent little man up at New Haven was just sitting there telling people in silence how to do it. Go forth, go forth he had said to young Hank Gavin. Why the hell didn't he go forth himself?

As for you, Hank Gavin said to himself, you had better go forth to Chicago and crawl into bed with Mellie and show up at your desk for a change, all this is pretty far out, this is. Unless the big man with whom he had a date tomorrow morning, the famed and much-quoted man whose books Hank couldn't read which was probably his fault not the man's, unless he could show him a way, the way, Christ's way across the waters, that was probably exactly what he would do.

He always had difficulty sleeping away from Mellie, he woke in the night and his arms reached for her as for part of himself. That night after his dinner with Mac and Nancy was one of the worst he'd ever known. The next morning as he walked along the stately corridors of the big school devoted to teaching young men and women to become ministers of Christ, his heart was heavy, torn by pain for Mac, by missing Mellie with anxiety, by doubts that attacked like heavy artillery, rumbling and bursting and landing around him.

Needing a shot in the arm, he had come out early to hear services in the school chapel, to sit in the soft light within the paneled walls and look up at the high altar, his soul as open-mouthed as a squawking fledgling in the nest. Church founded on the rock. Feed my lambs. Feed my sheep. Around him were the students and faculty of this institution of divine education, and his eyes turned upon them with curiosity, with pleading, with suspicion, with a pang of envy.

So much younger than he was, most of them.

But—they had decided.

They were the committed men.

They had been called and chosen.

A pattern emerged from that scattered congregation. All races, creeds, colors, habiliment, and the key of it was a bright-eyed intelligence. On his right, a commonplace girl with a sweet face and wide-awake eyes, the light brown hair drawn into a pony tail on top. Beyond her, an impassive yellow face, the slant eyes intently peering through horn-rimmed glasses. A row of boys in a pallid sameness, but bright, a little high-brow, the highest type of postgraduate scholars. On his left, a typical woman don, gray-haired and academic, and a man with sleek white hair and a benevolent, undisturbed smile. As the voices of the robed choir rose in song, light on and in the two or three hundred faces came and went, and Hank Gavin began to feel himself a lost soul. A black sheep? Something was missing between him and them. A most peculiar place for him to be, this was, and he thought with puzzlement and longing of his breakfast on the little table in the bow window of Mellie's sitting room and of Mellie in a copper-colored Chinese housecoat across from him. Of the familiarity and responsibility of his small, important office, the excitement of the constantly ringing telephones, of the changing figures on the Board, of his lunch date with Stu or Al Patton or sometimes Mellie, at Maxim's or the Casino.

What was he doing here amid all these strangers?

The dean had made this appointment for him to talk to the big man, the top guy, the famous leader. "You'd better see him," the quiet man in New Haven had said, "you'll know more then than you do now. Don't forget you're something of a catch, Gavin. Although the laborers may not be so few at this moment, we need power hitters. Go see him."

The faculty member who, in academic gown, spoke the Word from the pulpit that morning was gruff and grave. Certainly, his manner said, it would ill become such as we to get emotional about this. Calmness pervaded all. In fairness, Hank Gavin told himself, what else should there be? Why did he expect anything different? Yet toward the end that calm and superior man in the pulpit said a surprising thing that hooked his attention. Almost absentmindedly he said, "I wish I had the courage to sign my letters *Yours in Christ* as my opposite numbers in the Catholic Church do." And whether it was a small, academic joke, an arrow of sarcasm, a piece of honest envy, Hank Gavin couldn't tell. No one around him appeared to pay it any attention. Yet it was a sincere longing, it was a small candle to light Hank's unsteady soul.

Chatter, laughter, the sound of moving feet on tiled floors filled the corridors and again to Hank it seemed like being back at school. If he went on, this was going to be a weird experience for a top investment counselor, the husband of Melanie Cheyne Gavin, with a golf score in the seventies. Could there be a way around it? Ways around most things, he had found. Or was this a first step in obedience and discipline, like Paul's going alone into the desert? He was thinking now of the corridors of a monastery he had visited in Kentucky because of a true book he had read by Thomas Merton, of the hooded, silent figures of the young monks preparing for a life of service to Christ, moving in and out of prayer and prayer and more prayer at all hours of the twenty-four. Well, that was a different approach and they weren't going to be in the world. Ministering to others in all the noise and turmoil and tumult and shouting and *temptation*. Though probably temptations came at all levels.

Was his doubt now a temptation?

The man he was going to see would be able to guide him in the way he should go. The proper steps and channels, the shortcuts if there were any. This man was a power. His very name was a name of power.

All the chairs in his waiting room were full and a middle-aged secretary with a serene and regal air said, "He hasn't come down yet, you may wait in his inner office, Mr. Gavin," and ushered him through a heavy oak door. She did not switch on any lights for him. The room was dark oak, polished and somber, and the panels absorbed what little light came through the amber windows. Before him, Hank saw an enormous, antique desk. A man sitting behind that desk must be somebody or it would dwarf him. You had to bow in advance to the man who chose to sit in that chair behind that desk.

In a business suit, at that.

Curious, admiring, restless, Hank Gavin moved about a little, no harm in that, he found it difficult to sit still. Mellie had taught him to recognize the grace and value of the silver inkstand, the cup that held pens, the old leather box. This richness Hank enjoyed. So far, he had not been able to find anything in the gospels nor the letters that commanded poverty as a desirable state for the sons of God. That had all come later in the repentance and penance and propitiation of wastrels, of men who had once sold their souls to gold. An earthly paradise might be more difficult to surrender to God, but a state of want and woe hadn't been recommended as a permanent residence for the followers of the Risen Christ.

If it had been a private letter, a personal document on the big desk, even Hank Gavin's curiosity wouldn't have lured him to read it. It was, after all, a printed pamphlet, one of those little magazines the size of news weeklies, he could see heavy black type on white newspaper and the word CHRISTIANITY in the name of it at the top. It lay on one side of the leather-bound blotter and the mail, opened and neatly stacked, on the other.

So much was new to Hank Gavin in this new world.

If they had magazines, maybe he ought to know it.

Nothing warned him, as he stretched out his hand, that his second great moment of crisis was upon him. As he went to sit down in a leather chair under the windows, he told me later that he was thinking about Mellie and remembering that she had written copy for some of the hospital drives and once had been on the press committee in a political campaign.

The front-page article was entitled

MAN, THE UNREGENERATE TRIBALIST

Whathehell! Hank Gavin said to himself and then rebuked himself. This was, he saw, a publication written and edited at the intelligence level of graduate students and their faculty. In their work, for instance on segregation in Harlem, which was, after all, a stone's throw away, it might be important to know that a man was an unregenerate tribalist.

Having read it, he was, however, still bewildered.

Maybe I'm not intellectual enough, he thought. In fact, you are the man in the street, buddy, let's face it and moreover you are and always have been an eager beaver.

Lots of people probably aren't intellectual enough for this. I must get a copy and take it home to Mellie . . . or maybe not. Go on, get with it, maybe it's like television, you're not supposed to like everything.

On page 2, a small headline above the title said

Faithful Steward of the Mysteries of God

See? There you are. This is an official journal of Christian opinion, it says so, so naturally you get to God at least on the second page. And never forget, buddy, that the important vote is the one you haven't got. Maybe it's better not to start right out with God. These people know what they're doing.

In larger type what they were doing was

THE BERGMAN TRILOGY

Berg*man?* Berg*son* he knew, he and Colin had been captivated by Berg*son* in a philosophy course, there was, they felt, a sprightly promise of unexpected good in the Frenchman. But who was this Berg*man?* The article had been written, it said, by a man who "when he isn't to be found at the cinema" taught religion at a well-known college. Why the cinema? Then he found out, for this trilogy, it turned out, consisted of three *films* produced by a Swedish writer-director and come to think of it this was great, a proper and up-to-the-minute idea, keep the readers and churchgoers in touch with that master means of communication and influence, the motion picture. His curiosity came alive and kicking because he and Mellie had gone to see one of them and he, peasant that he was no doubt, had taken Mellie out of there about half-way through. What he had seen didn't quite gibe with *Faithful Steward of the Mysteries of God,* but these folks might be more enlightened than he was.

He began to read:

> . . . I think there is here a fruitful analysis by which to discover certain elements of the unity and integrity of each film and indeed a basis from which to appreciate the kerygmatic achievement. . . .

Kerygmatic?

Come now, Hank Gavin said to himself, you aren't any intellectual giant to be sure, neither are you an illiterate ignatz, you did graduate *cum laude* from Yale and there are a lot of citizens in your shoes. On a table near him, with other books held by bronze bookends, was a small collegiate dictionary.

Kerygmatic wasn't in it.

He went back, carefully, to the Bergman Trilogy.

> . . . Neither do I suppose that my suggestions about the Bible in Bergman comprehend the fullness of his artistic achievement; he can lay the Bible down and he can pick it up. . . .

Make a nice popular song, that would. Lay that Bible down, Babe, lay that Bible down. Or, if you preferred, Pick that Bible up, Babe, pick that Bible up. Put to good Beatle music it might be a little more evangelical than this atmosphere had suggested, but it might be a sort of *West Side Story* from the Book of Ruth instead of *Romeo and Juliet.* Though his own experience had been that above all others teen-agers hoped for dignity and authority from those who claimed spiritual ignition.

No escape now from the rest of this article, though his heart had begun to thud against his rib cage.

> . . . the central figure of *Through a Glass Darkly* is the young woman Karin. It is too glib merely to say that the progress of her mental illness causes her gradually to lose contact with reality and other people. In the film, all the characters suffer isolation and impeded personal relations. Her mental illness reveals only what their more conventional behavior conceals. Furthermore, Karin's "illness" can be said to put her in touch with altogether authentic, if more awful, reality.

Go crazy enough, buddy, and you'll be authentic, anyhow.

Hogwash. His spinning, staggering brain said to him intellectual hogwash. You boys a couple of blocks over there in Harlem, we're not going to tell you we can offer you hope of a happier life, a saner, stronger sense of the reality of good. Hell no. Take a pop of heroin, buddy, and you'll get in touch with more authentic reality.

And away we go, because sure enough, there it was, down on paper.

> . . . She, Karin, is subdued with a hypodermic, and she tells what she has seen in her terror. The door of the closet opened, from which she expected the divine to appear. What emerged, however, was a great spider. Karin described him:
>
> > He came up to me and I saw his face. It was a loathsome, evil face. And he climbed up on me and tried to penetrate me. But I warded him off. And all the time I saw his eyes. They were cold and calm. When he could not enter me, he quickly climbed up on my breast and my face and then onto the wall. . . . *I have seen God.*
>
> That the suffering girl saw as a horror what was in fact meant as an agent of her rescue and rehabilitation is after all what Bergman, with Paul, announces as "see through a glass darkly."

Young Hank Gavin came to his feet, his perfectly cut coat bulged over his shoulder muscles. Yellow lights were flickering in his eyes. He knew that he had never been so profoundly angry in his life. He had a soul and he seemed to be watching it falling behind as he'd seen horses he bet on go back in the stretch.

He was remembering the day Paul's letter—the first one—to the Corinthians had come and he had read for the first time in his life the thirteenth chapter of it. No other day would ever be like that one. Drummond, in his classic sermon that he had read in a little brown-and-gold edition, said Paul's definition of love was the greatest thing in the world, and those words—*through a glass darkly*—those were embedded in its glory. They were part of its immortal beauty. This was what he meant as he said so often in prayer, You know you can't let the darkness out, you have to let the light in. Now this man had smirched and twisted the clear, sweet beauty of Christ with sacrilege and blasphemy, and the hope and the promise was gone from them.

Hank shook with rage and then he was in a mighty silence.

He said to me that the silence was as much a fact as though an orchestra had crashed into "Onward, Christian Soldiers" or "The Star-Spangled Banner," it was the opposite of a great magnificent sound. It was a silence for listening whether he wanted to or not. Then into it came the words of that chapter which had changed his life, which had changed many men's lives, which he had read every day for months.

. . . *Is not easily provoked . . . thinkest no evil . . . rejoiceth not in iniquity but rejoiceth in the truth . . . Love never faileth . . . whether there be prophecies they shall fail . . . knowledge it shall vanish away . . . for then we see through a glass darkly but now face to face. . . .*

You can't have it both ways, the chaplain had told him.

You can't have it both ways, Hank Gavin repeated to himself. You can't have it that *they* have to obey that chapter but now you're mad at them you don't.

Now face to face.

God help me, I don't know what I'm doing. The chaplain said you could always holler for help, *always,* any time anywhere, and the post would be defended by Our Lord himself. Defend me oh God just for today . . .

Still trembling in the marrow of his bones, Hank Gavin sat down again. All this amazed him then, it still amazed him when he told me of it, it was, he said, like an adventure in an international spy story. It felt like that to him, it was a matter of life and death and here he was in the office of this leader and he was reading papers that seemed to him like dark secrets but weren't, only they were another part of the new world. Probably this was none of his business. He was a raw recruit, a man waiting to enlist in something and put on the whole armor of God. These men had been here a long time, they were the *church,* they had power and no one thought of contradicting them. Harlem had been there right next door to them a long time, too, but that wasn't their part of the business. There were ministers in Harlem, weren't there? These people here had a right to use words like kerygmatic if they wanted to and teach them to their students. And if some of them didn't have the guts to sign themselves Yours in Christ they wished they did, and you are supposed to think of them with *love.*

At last he focused again on the magazine in his hand.

Go ahead, see it through, he said to himself, don't judge until you know what it's all about and don't judge *then.* Don't try to sell it short until you've gone over the whole prospectus.

Lastly (*the next paragraph or two said*) there is The Silence.

Okay, *The Silence* was the motion picture he and Mellie had seen. Mellie had thought it was a bore, what they'd seen of it. Anyhow, it was about two women on a train, sisters, and the son of one of them was along, he remembered that much.

> . . . He is an innocent and winsome lad of perhaps eight or nine and we see the film's portraiture of the two women largely from his perspective. With him, we behold the altogether unlovely life of his mother and his aunt. The young mother's nymphomania and the older sister's lesbianism and self-abuse are shown to us with little detail spared. . . .

All right, have a detail of self-abuse and nymphomania and lesbianism how the hell could you see them through the eyes of an eight- or nine-year-old boy unless he recognized them? But of course Bergman, that faithful steward of the mysteries of God, *and* the reviewer who when he wasn't to be found at the cinema taught religion to the mothers of coming generations, who certainly ought to be shown all the details of these things, hadn't taken that into consideration.

> . . . Is there Gospel in *The Silence?* Bergman obliges his audience to see through the eyes of the boy. His obedience and his ingenuous affection toward both women, his boyish and unsentimental compassion make it impossible for us at any time to view the candid portrayal of sexual aberrancy wither with disgust or contempt or condescension; certainly not with prurience. . . . Further the curious troupe of midgets reinforces this point of view. . . .

Midgets?

Why were there always *midgets?*

Well, probably these gentlemen were working around to *unless ye* become as a little child ye shall in no wise enter into seeing lesbianism and nymphomania and aunts and mothers who allow an eight-year-old boy to be involved in sexual aberrancy and horror without disgust or contempt or condescension.

But children saw evil as evil!

They knew the sin against the Holy Ghost.

If you become as a little child you can enter the kingdom of heaven—that's what it *says*—it doesn't say you can view the sin with childish complacency, it doesn't say you can condone it.

I don't want to cast the first stone at anybody, Hank Gavin said to himself. Neither in disgust nor contempt nor condescension.

But I'm not going to be suckered into calling *evil* GOOD. *That's* the sin against the Holy Ghost. Where is the Christ who said suffer the little children to *come unto me* in all this? Neither do I condemn thee, go and sin no more and I give you power to sin no more, I forgive your sins by my grace which destroys them, which is sufficient to melt the thorn and cast out devils. I take up the sword of the Spirit to overcome them. It was Paul—Paul whom this man splattered and smattered—Paul who cried to the worshipers of an Unknown God—Him declare I unto you, and His name is Love.

Who that needed God, who that waited to be saved and served by ministry from and in their fears and sin, who was there who would understand all this subtle and hideous and depressing method of reversal or whatever it was? He remembered something the chaplain had said once in his simplicity, that had served them so well in the midst of war. Never fall into the trap of presenting the evil just to show it's evil. You must show the good, too, and how it can always overcome evil. Fear not, little flock, it is my Father's good pleasure to give you the kingdom. That had been on a night when the snuffies were very cold and very scared and very lonely in the dark. But the chaplain hadn't told them any stories about *spiders*. He had let his light so shine that they believed in the armor of God.

What were these characters getting at?

Ah—here it was;

> In my view, Bergman has portrayed with consummate art the biblical experience of the divine Enemy.

Enemy?

Out in the dark, God, too, was to be their Enemy?

On those dark and bloody nights that so many men have endured and deep down now fear that they may have to endure again, what did men and women and eight- or nine-year-old children need most? The chaplain had one answer for that. Hope. Hope, he said. Hope hope hope and again *hope*. You've got to give them hope, he told the young officers. Maybe it was wise to teach young divinity students that God was the divine Enemy, maybe some deep psychological subtility grinned at you like a wolf to explain this contradiction in terms, like Red Riding Hood's grandmother. This, it came to him, this in his ordinary worldly newly converted eyes was a lot of intellectual crap. *I say it's spinach and I say the hell with it!*

Send some of your young students and priests—*ministers*—to stand on a corner in the hungry, hopeless jungles of Harlem a few blocks away where there are plenty of all the vices and shout to them God is your divine Enemy, come to church, come to pray, we will show you that God comes to you like a spider, we offer you hope in the masquerade of a tarantula. Great fun!

What did they *believe,* these people in this new world?

Here it was, some of it, quoted:

> Martin Luther expounded it:
>
> We seek to be saved and God in order that he may save rather damns. . . . They are damned who flee damnation, for Christ was of all the saints most damned and forsaken. . . . God's favor is so communicated in the form of wrath that it seems farthest when it is at hand. . . . This is the pain of purgatory. . . . I do not know where it is located, but I do know that it can be experienced in this life.

That's not news, buddy.

That you can experience purgatory in this life, that's not news to Colin who ended broken on the pavement, nor to Mac and Nancy whose baby is better off in the institution, nor to Stu Margolis whose wife is an amorous alcoholic, it's not news to them, buddy, that they are in purgatory.

What'd be news to them is how you get out.

Be news to them to understand that the Father saw His own son, who'd had a bellyful of husks, while he was yet a great way off and ran to meet him and put shoes on his poor, tired, bleeding, stumbling feet.

If you could show them it still works, it would be news all right.

Abraham didn't call God Enemy. He called Him Friend.

Moses called Him Lord, Who will open the Red Sea and lead us into the Promised Land when we have no other gods like spiders and golden calves and phallic symbols before Him.

David called Him Shepherd, never giving up on His lost sheep and spreading a table before us in the *presence of our enemies.*

And Jesus called Him *Our Father,* your Father and my Father, the Father within Who will do the same works for you He did for me and we have known and can believe the love He hath for us.

With careful hands, Hank Gavin put down the pamphlet.

For a moment he thought he was going to be sick, as he had been after he'd seen the children splattered against the walls in Korea. Or on the night he'd killed the first little brown man.

Pray, he said to himself, pray yourself.

Be silent.

His human mind refused to be silent. Not it! It knew nothing about *silence*. From the depths came things he thought forgotten and they were odd and peculiar and they marched again to drums. His hands, he found, were wet and sticky and his stomach and his soul were clammy. *The winter falls and we lie like beleaguered stones in the black, cramped ground.* A mess of impotent intellectual pottage has soured our membranes.

Back and forth he found himself walking, trying to see his way. In darkness as black as it had been on the barge. Where was Moses when the light went out? Where do I go from here? Mellie is right, I am hallucinated, I am schizophrenated, whom the gods would destroy they first make mad.

Purgatory!

This is hell . . . descended into hell . . . the third day he came out of the closet as a big black spider . . .

Long afterward, when he was telling me this, Hank Gavin sat still as a statue, as though if he weren't careful the trembling might catch him again. As though he'd slip off the road through that doubt, which is purgatory, into the loss of faith which is hell.

"What came to me then—" he said, "Colin and I took a pipe poetry course in English Lit one year and Colin went off his rocker about Stephen Vincent Benét, he practically held me down and chanted *John Brown's Body* at me. And—it seemed to be Colin's voice again, and whether it could come back to me or just came off the Eustachian tube in my ear like a radio tape I don't know to this day. I don't suppose it matters. Anyhow, it was in Colin's voice and it said:

What do the people say?
Well, you've just read some questions and some answers,
Not all, of course, No man can say that's all.
A man's a humbug if he says that's all.
But look down into your own minds and memories,
And find out what you find and what you'd keep.
It's time you did that and it won't be earlier.
I don't know what each of you will find,

What memory, what token, what tradition.
It may be only half-a-dozen words
Carved on a stone, carved deeper in the heart,
It might be all a life, but look and find it.

Lookandfinditlookandfinditlookandfindit, the drums said now.

But when he looked nothing was carved there at all, it had put that Bible down Babe and not a word remained.

The room grew darker and his empty heart thudded against the wall of his chest in a leap of mad fear.

But it was only a man standing in the doorway, blocking what little refraction of light had come in from the outer offices.

All Hank Gavin could see was that he was big, square, and it would take a truck to move him out of there. Then lights came on, in candle wall brackets, in the desk and table lamps.

This was the man in whose private room Hank Gavin was pacing up and down listening to the voice of a dead man. Easy to recognize him. A face so often pictured in the newspapers, on the covers of magazines, on the TV screen. Plain at once that this was a power of the twentieth-century church and a most ribald and disrespectful and adolescent line scampered through Hank's dizzy brain. . . . If the cardinals can make a Pope it seems like the Giants ought to do something for Willie Mays. Pope John love itself and now this man the other churches had put up so high stood before him.

Lines deep as scars seemed to pin his mouth down at the corners and drag his eyes in a downward slant. So that the whole face was slashed down in terrifying strength. Bitter cold had sucked out the heat and the fine eyes were ideated and commanding and indomitable. A man to bewilder a simple seeker, tongue-tie him, weave webs of inferiority around him.

The man of power came across his own office, nodded to the stranger he found there, it would, Hank thought awestruck, have taken too long to change his expression, it was nailed down too tight. And in consequence he felt his own control slipping, he was pixilated by a sort of freakish fury at himself. What was he *doing* here? He was Hank Gavin, he could sell anything, he wasn't going to be intimidated and whether this major general knew it or not there were plenty of men-in-the-street, plenty of the Common Man, plenty of fellows who'd been at Anzio and Iwo Jima and the Yalu and Viet Nam who thought the church a failure, that it didn't offer them anything, in a lot of places it was just a small piece of social life, a social club, though there were *some* churches that tried. Find me men to carry the truth like a lamp. To tell the glad tidings as the apostles did. Men to move my mountains!

In his best you-ought-to-buy-it-and-put-it-away-in-your-safe-deposit-box voice he said, "Good morning, sir, it's kind of you to see me. By the way, can you tell me what kerygmatic means?" and he made a gesture with a crooked finger toward the pamphlet back in its place on the imposing desk.

The great man crossed and sat down in the chair, and when he spoke his voice was resonant with controlled oratorial power. "The Kerygma," he said, "is the preaching or proclamation of the primitive church, the gospel as presented by the original Nazarenes and the first apostles."

"Not very intellectual gentlemen, were they?" Hank Gavin said in a come-along tone. "But—this man here—this cinema man—he doesn't do that and his big gun Bergman doesn't do it. Far otherwise, if you'll forgive me. Where are the commandments of Jesus in this, sir? Preach good news, glad tidings, heal the sick, raise the dead, cleanse the leper, cast out devils—"

The great man, lifting his eyebrows, was speaking now, rich and deep and baritone.

It didn't matter because young Hank Gavin of Chicago didn't hear him.

All he could hear in the depths and the darkness was some mocking deviltry saying to him You won't find it here, old boy. This is the citadel of intellectual pride and the stronghold of let's-not-allow-ourselves-to-sit-on-cloud-nine-we-are-dealing-not-with-moral-attitudes-but-political-realities-and-God-is-our-divine-Enemy.

He said loudly, "Well, I thank you, sir, it's been kind of you and I appreciate it don't think I don't appreciate it and I'll see you again some time and give that guy who wishes he had the guts to sign himself Yours in Christ my best regards," and then he found himself walking and walking out of that fine stately academic office and down the chattering academic corridors and through a garden and a new housing development and into the streets of Harlem that nobody, *nobody,* would believe who hadn't seen them and who was he, one man, one nobody, one nothing, one hallucinated poop, to try to bring a *lamp* into this dark and terror-stricken world from Africa to Africa?

4

Hank went into a dark, dark bar and found a telephone. He had no change so he bought a beer and drank it thirstily, he picked up the silver and told the bartender's wooden countenance to give everybody a drink.

You gutless bastard! he said to himself.

A few lousy bucks.

The bulb in the booth wasn't working so he was in the dark again. It took a little time because he had to get the number from information and then the long-distance operator told him blithely that he could *dial* and his impatience grew and the angry drumming words piled up and began to mutter and when at last the quiet voice said hello he said, "So I saw him!" without any preliminaries.

A moment of silence did Hank no good, no good at all. His blood began to boil against it. Silence! In this kind of a world, at this time in the history of that world, with spiders sitting down beside little girls and licking their chops and little boys of eight, like the ones he'd seen just now out in the gutters full of urine and offal, little boys who knew sexual aberrancy at firsthand and whose bellies were as empty as his own heart.

What did a man do? One man? Walk with that goddam phony smile or that academic superiority on his face and pretend he didn't see any of it?

Silence. Let him stew in his own silence.

"I take it," the man in New Haven said without expression, "you didn't find what you were looking for?"

Hank's yelp of laughter bounced off the filthy walls of the little phone booth that was like a coffin stood on end. "Find it?" he said, and then he said other things which if the man at the bar could hear would have been familiar to him, there were no highbrow words like kerygmatic, the words Hank used he had learned in Korea, he went back for them, a lot of them anyhow. He really blistered.

"Are you with me?" he said.

The answer came quickly. "Oh no—no, certainly not," Dr. Mathers said.

"Well," Hank Gavin said, "of course you're nice and cozy and safe up there, in your ivy-covered tower."

"I suppose so," the quiet voice said, "but I've never been of the blow-up-the-building-because-it-has-features-I-don't-like school. A good deal of what you're goddamning is the result of exactly what you're now planning to do. Isn't it? Either privately or if you can think of a way publicly. It's been my theory that it takes considerable time and thought and care and work and even art to build any kind of a church from a log cabin to a six-million-dollar cathedral. But any fool can blow it up with ten cents' worth of dynamite unless God stays his hand."

"Some of them ought to be blown up," Hank Gavin said. "What good are they? All right, so I went to see your renewal boy. Renewal and *stirrings,* that's what you said, wasn't it? So they've substituted art galleries for rummage sales and coffee houses for ladies' luncheons and square dances and ball games for Christian Endeavor meetings. *That's* renewal? The whole thing's a farce and somebody has to say so."

You don't really know enough about it, do you? Aren't you making a snap judgment? Where that came from he didn't know, must be crossed wires someplace, he said grimly, "I know all I need to."

Not all. The man who says that's all is a humbug. "And I'm not a humbug, that's one thing I'm not," he said and the quiet voice from New Haven said, "Oh, I'm sure you're not."

Boiling, hot, confused, despairing misery weighted Hank Gavin, he had been so ready to obey the command to leave his nets and follow me, and now the great and glorious hallelujah was heard no more in the land. He began an angry assault to the stinking telephone and the dead cigar butts and burned-out light bulb and the grotesque backs at the bar against those who had failed, those who hadn't loved enough to keep His commandments, those sunk in the morass of their own egotism and vain-glorious self-complacency and had forgotten the works the works the works.

When he had spilled his guts, the phone was silent, that goddam little pause came again, that pretentious little *ham* giving him the moment-of-silence treatment as though he was some drooling under- or postgraduate.

His ear picked up through the pounding, "Ah. So you've found out that the church is loaded with phonies and mercenaries, and, as you say, poops who would starve to death if they tried to make a living selling stocks and bonds. And you already knew there was a lot of terrible pain and emptiness under all the materialism of the men who can make a living selling anything. But you see Our Lord doesn't need you in heaven. He needs you in the burden and heat—and cold—of the day. Picking on a lot of things and people isn't going to do any good that I can see."

"Somebody's got to tell them off," Hank said, "go around letting the church be a bunch of whited sepulchers—"

"Very hard to be sure about a whited sepulcher, isn't it?" the quiet voice said, "and a blanket attack doesn't feed many sheep, do you think? It's *Mark*, isn't it? You've had your nose in the New Testament. Where John, who usually knew better, told the Master they'd seen somebody casting out devils in his name and they forbade the fellow because he hadn't joined their group. Jesus wouldn't have that, of course, he said there couldn't be any man who had done a miracle in his name who'd ever speak evil of him and if he wasn't *against* them then it added up to his being on their side."

"They aren't doing any miracles," Hank said, "they'd crawl under a rug if you suggested such a social error. They even object to moral attitudes in politics—they say deal with *realities*. George Washington, if I remember my history book, said if we didn't have pillars of moral attitudes the whole damn democracy would fall down. And moreover, Jesus threw the moneychangers out of the temple with whips—"

This time, the pause waited and finally the quiet voice said, "Go on."

"Go *on?*" Hank said.

"You remember what comes after that, the rest of the sentence."

"What is this?" Hank said, "a TV game or something?"

"No no," the voice said, ". . . but actually it says he overthrew the tables of those that sold doves and the blind and the lame came to him in that temple and he healed them. I don't suppose one should be surprised that we split the biblical atom, it's easier to throw people out or overturn tables than to heal the lame and the blind, and that's what we've been doing for centuries, isn't it? Like render unto Caesar—that's been as good an alibi as any psychiatrist ever came up with, but actually *that* sentence reads render unto Caesar the things that are Caesar's and unto God the things that are God's. It's very easy to render unto Caesar but unto God takes a bit more *doing*. Remember, many of the promises are conditional."

Morosely, Hank said, "You're goddam talkative this morning. But that is what I'm trying to tell you. These goons—they're academic and useless, they turn a lot of oafs that don't know anything about life loose on the church—they don't *want* works they want words—I met a chap the other night who told me about a friend of his that was the minister of a church and the chaplain of a college for eleven years and then one day he felt the presence of Christ and knew the reality of God and—"

"Only eleven years? What a fortunate young man."

"Oh no," Hank shouted triumphantly, "not on your life! They caught him casting out demons in the name of Christ and they took his church away from him and brought him down to take some courses in *psychiatry*. How do you like those apples?"

"You didn't think any of them—these men over there—were *funny?* In a nice sort of way?"

"Funny!"

"You weren't sorry for them?"

"I'm sorry for the people that are going to get 'em as ministers and jog along without *hope* in the world."

"It didn't occur to you to wash their feet, I suppose?"

Nasal, ugly, Hank's voice said, "Before I'd wash that uncle's feet I'd see myself in hell."

"Well, of course, it's strictly your choice. But you see if that uncle isn't Christ, there isn't any."

This time the long silence was Hank's.

"If Our Father is true and there's a brotherhood in Christ then all the uncles have to be brothers," the voice said gently.

Depression settled down on the young man in the phone booth, it squeezed the young man in the phone booth like an accordion, he bleated out a discord that seemed to say I'm one man—one dumb, ignorant man—but I'm not like *that*—I'm not a hypocrite or a One man—I know, you see, I know, no I don't know what to do—I can't go into the *church*—but I'm just one man, what can one—"

We all start there.

This wasn't the voice from New Haven, was it? Not this time, and yet Hank Gavin resisted it with a blind and senseless fury.

"One man," the quiet *real* voice said, "Lincoln had that problem. He said once somewhere he always wanted to get it all at once. One man. Let's not do anything for anybody because we can't do everything for everybody. There are a thousand steps to take, what's the use of taking *one*. It always begins with one man. Christianity began with one man."

"Well," Hank Gavin yelled and this time he thought he saw heads turn from the bar, "I'm not Jesus Christ, am I?"

"No no, but—were you thinking of doing this on your own? Even Jesus said I can of mine own self do nothing, *the Father within me*—that's what does the work, isn't it?"

The receiver crashed from Hank's hand, it rat-a-tat-tatted

against the thin wall with a hollow sound. Requiem for a dead sanctimonious crumbum, Hank said to himself bitterly and went up and sat at the bar and ordered Scotch and got *whiskey* under any name and began to wipe the sweat from his forehead and in the hollows under his eyes and off the end of his nose.

Hope was ashes.

Hope was one of the three. Love was the greatest but faith and hope were in the money. Nobody stopped to remember that hope was a gift of God, and every good gift and every perfect gift cameth down from but he didn't believe it. Not one cell was cracking with any belief. Might be a good idea to get drunk. Get drunk like a man and a Marine and go down to the Village and see some lesbians in one of their for-tourists hangouts like the Montmartre in Paris. Or go where the gin was two bucks a throw and watch the little teen-age gals, who'd been sold what a great career it was to be a nympho, running around with their poor skinny little butts hanging out proving they didn't draw the color line far otherwise, don't tell them to go and sin no more or show them the glory of God, just cheer them on without condescension. Sure that stuff about the faithful steward of the mysteries of God was prurient. Send half those pallid young men out looking for some, with their Adam's apples pumping up their phallic symbols or was he mixing his metaphors?

He had never desired any woman but Mellie since the first time he saw her. His desire for her was all things, from the gutter to the golden streets.

And she had sense. She had a lot more suffereth long loving kindness than *he* did.

He had better go *home*.

This whiskey was rotgut, it hurt his throat and burned the lining of his duodenum with ulcer warnings. He laid a bill on the bar and went out. Five thousand miles of streets in New York, which mile he was on he didn't know. Here the tenements leaned toward one another like the houses in the old cities of France, and they were veiled in the kind of drizzle which intermittently holds up a ball game. Somebody jostled him, his shoulder came in contact with a wall, then something hit him behind the ear and his arms refused to obey his last command and he descended into a pit deeper and darker than the one digged for Benjamin.

The next thing he knew he was vomiting, with his cheek against a stone pillow, and his coat and tie and shirt and watch and wallet and shoes were all gone.

Violence.

He had been chucking hand grenades and somebody had hit him with a blackjack.

Could ye not watch with me one hour?

To his astonishment his spirits soared. I say the whole earth and all the stars in the sky are for religion's sake. I'll wash their feet. I will wash their feet.

Be quiet, will you?

Listen.

Which *way*, Lord? Which way? What wilt thou have me to do?

5

At about that time I'd gone back to Chicago to gather up, before it got lost or kicked around or people died, some material for a book I knew I'd wanted to write some day, and finding Hank was out of town I'd asked Mellie if she'd care to go to a pop concert with me since they were going to play Mozart's Symphony in C Minor.

Afterward we had come back to her house for a bite to eat. Music always makes me hungry and I remember with satisfaction and delight the sausages and beer we used to have between acts at the opera house in Bayreuth. On the low table in Mellie's sitting room we found cold consommé in china cups bedded in silver bowls of ice and plates of sandwiches, very thin and delectable, and I sat enjoying them in that detached silence which must, in the case of sensitive listeners, follow hearing Mozart.

Mellie was restive, she seemed to be driven relentlessly, her eyes were on the door and her ears on the telephone, and I thought that she wasn't sure that Hank was coming but that she had to expect him. She wore a suit of pearl-colored Italian silk, with a sheath dress and a tight little coat, and around her neck and arms slave bracelets and necklaces in flat mesh gold. Once she took up a sandwich and put it down after taking a moonshaped bite, she kicked off the heel-less gold sandals and then sat down and poured herself a glass of champagne, which was exactly right with her color scheme, and picked up a book that lay face down on the floor and stared at it with distaste.

"What is it?" I said, first because I can never resist my own curiosity about books, and secondly I felt this wasn't just a *book,* it was part of or piece of something that was taking place with her.

"You've heard of a man named de Chardin—Pierre Teilhard de Chardin?" she gave it the French pronunciation and made it sound, somehow, pretentious. I nodded and she began to trace something on the page with the tip of one glowing pink nail. "Hank's underlined a lot of things in this—it's called the Divine Milieu, by the way—how about this? *The sanctification of human endeavor*—no no—wait a minute—wait—here's what I want. Quote. *In spite of the practice of right intentions and the day offered every morning to God, the general run of the faithful simply feel that time spent at the office or the studio, in the fields or in the factory, is time diverted from prayer and adoration. It is impossible not to work, that is taken for granted. But it is impossible, too, to aim at the deep religious life reserved for those who have the leisure to pray or preach all day long. A few moments of the day can be salvaged for God, yes, but the best hours are absorbed, or at any rate, cheapened by material cares. Under the sway of this feeling, large numbers of Christians lead a double or crippled life in practice; they have to step out of their human dress so as to have faith in themselves as Christians—and inferior Christians at that.* . . . End quote." She kept her place and looked up at me, the lovely eyebrows lifted as far as she could get them, and said, "Does *that* make sense to you? Never mind you! Would it make any sense to *my husband?*" But before I could answer she said, "There's another bit—*Try, with God's help, to perceive the connection—even physical and natural—which binds your labor with the building of the Kingdom of Heaven; try to realize that Heaven itself smiles upon you and, through your works, draws you to itself; then, as you leave the church for the noisy streets, you will remain with only one feeling, that of continuing to immerse yourself in God . . . if your work is dull or exhausting take refuge in the inexhaustible interest of progressing in the divine life*—" She put the book back, face down again and stood up and came over in front of me, her hands on her hips. "You think that's the kind of grandiloquent drool a healthy young man ought to be reading?"

"It won't hurt him," I said. "There are those who believe a new world age began in 1960, and there are those who believe de Chardin is one of its major prophets."

At that she gave a little shrug of exasperation. "I suppose he'll outgrow the whole thing," she said, but this time her little theme song didn't sound so confident and when I asked her where Hank was she said, "I'm giving him enough rope," and at that exact moment we heard a key in the lock. Before we could do more than perk up our ears the front door banged and a voice from below shouted "Where are you?" feet hit the stairs in leaps and bounds, and there Hank was coming through the door like it was a hole in the line.

They held each other, with that passion of reunion which is possible only when union exists in the first place. They kissed long, deeply, satisfying a thirst, and there were little sweet touching sounds like the duets of Papageno and Papagena and I thought *how they have been missing each other, minutes have seemed days and days years, they couldn't live without each other, could they?*

They stood back and I saw the scraped skin down one side of his thin face and the swelling, big as an egg, behind his ear, and Mellie saw them at the same moment and said, "What happened? You're hurt, what happened to you?"

"I got slugged," Hank said, and his fingertips explored the bump that through his sandy hair showed dark purple. "In Harlem. *And* rolled."

"Sit *down,*" Mellie said, "I ought not to allow you out by yourself. Be still—I want to look. What were you doing in Harlem?"

"Looking around," Hank said, and the gesture he made was a flourish, a bravado, but nevertheless the thing that caught me was his hands. I have been trained to watch people's hands when I interview them, to watch hands of witnesses on the stand and in the jury box. I was quite sure about Hank's hands. Strong, ordinary, well-kept pass-catching ball-throwing young male American. My exaggeration here may sound ridiculous but I know no other way to say it. They were now other hands—or another man's hands. He had changed—he had been changing—this was complete.

Grinning at Mellie he said, "Along came a spider and sat down beside her—I won't let them frighten you, love. You aren't frightened of spiders, are you?"

Mellie stared into his eyes, she said, "Have you seen a doctor with this?" and when he said No she let out a breath of furious exasperation and went to the phone. We heard her getting the doctor, explaining to him, and all the time Hank was talking to me, with a sort of secret remonstrance. "It's all wrong," he said, "this script is all wrong. This is not the way it is in books, you know that, don't you? It isn't even in very good English. It is neither comedy nor tragedy nor a mixture of both as books about religion are supposed to be, this has too much excitement in it, this is melodrama. And I am the wrong *hero,* I am a commonplace guy off the street I ought to be either more Caspar Milquetoast or more Walter Mitty or more *Seymour* and I got to live long enough to find out how Salinger gets out of *Seymour* having committed suicide but I am no hero, in a gray flannel suit a man cannot be a hero can he?"

"I don't seem to find the apostles were anything special," I said. "That's why they were—they are so important. Why their *Acts* make one of the great books—"

"Peter!" Hank Gavin said, "I mean I am not much worse

than Peter was for a while there. Cutting off people's ears and trying to walk on the water and then denying him thrice—that's me."

Mellie's voice cut across him, she said, "Did you vomit?"

He turned and looked at her, he said, '*Vomit?* Oh yes—come to think of it, darling, I did—" and into the phone Mellie said, "Yes he did—" and then, "Yes—yes—I will—all right—"

He stood just looking at her, unable to move his eyes. I got up to go, he wanted to be alone with her. This was, I saw, a man turning to his wife, *his wife*. This was what a man ought to mean when he said *my wife*. For the first time it seemed to me that I knew what the word *wife* held within itself, a combination of all things to all that made this strong young man. For it was plain that he desired her as a man desires only the woman he truly loves, but also he would be safe in her arms as a child in its mother's, and he could speak to her as to no other friend in the world and yet since he must protect her and care for her it was as though she was his child as well.

Meeting Mellie's smiling eyes as she turned away from the phone I saw how soft and smiling and desirous and mothering and sweet she was, and she said, "You're to go to bed right now. The doctor's coming by to take a look—and I'm going to keep you there for *days* and days—I've had enough of *this*."

As I went down the stairs I thought she had him bound there forever.

Two mornings later when she called me she was laughing, but her laughter wore rue.

"He's gone again," she said.

"Gone?" I said. "Where?"

"I don't know," Mellie said, and I felt a pang of sorrow for her, because she was angry and worried and filled with deep loneliness. "He left at about dawn and there's a note. All it says is 'You can't keep a squirrel on the ground. I'll be back tomorrow—I love you'—What'd you think?"

I said I was sure that whatever it was he was doing he was approaching the end.

"End?" Mellie said. "What end?"

"Of finding whatever he's looking for," I said.

In this, I was right.

A young renewal minister, who was a student of the quiet man in New Haven, had told him about several schools. One in Minnesota and another in Southern California and still another only a short flight away in the South-Midwest.

"I went there first because it was closest," Hank told me when he dropped in to see me soon after he got back. "By that time, if you want to know the truth, I wasn't sure whether I was on my head or my heels. I had no—no light—no *guidance,* I think that's the word. I kept wondering how it could have been so *easy* for the—for men to pick up and pack up and leave everything to follow him. Then of course I knew that some *didn't.* They went back to take care of their dough or do the spring planting.

"So I figured I'd give it one more shot. I wasn't exactly *proud* of the whing-ding I'd pulled in New York. Not the bop on the ear, that could happen to anybody, but the way I'd felt about those uncles that got out that magazine. I knew the story about how *angry* Jesus was with those who were profaning the temple, moneychanging, using it as a market, and I wondered if after he got through giving them *hell* he wanted to get away from the whole pack and start all over. And then—the second half of the story came to me, where it said the lame and the blind came to him *in the temple* and he healed them. So he didn't, as the politicians say, desert the party—he stayed in there and tried to *improve* it and I had to see that his idea of improving anything always was to do some works. Of course naturally the *fourteenth* chapter of First Corinthians follows the thirteenth, which I read every day, so I read that pretty often too and it says If the trumpet gives an uncertain sound, who shall prepare himself to battle, and to myself anyhow I sounded as uncertain as a kid with a Christmas horn. And Mellie looking at me all the time with such a *loving* sort of quizzical look.

"The young renewal minister in New York was a fine fellow, and he was real patient with me, and encouraging actually, but somehow it was like you showed him a man with leprosy and he suggested we give him a manicure. Or the termites had got at a building and it was sinking and he wanted to call in an interior decorator. All the time something kept telling me this wasn't the way I was supposed to go, bolting the party wasn't it. A—a friend of mine had studied a lot about Christian Science because his mother was healed in it, and *he* told me that in the beginning Mrs. Eddy didn't want to start *another* church, as though the Protestants didn't have *enough* already, she hoped—I think what he said was to restore apostolic divine healing to all churches. But they started putting her—her people in jail for curing people without a license or something so she *had* to. I kept noticing Billy Graham didn't start his own church, he just sent those who *felt* they wanted to know about Christ back to their own church or their grandfather's or somebody's.

"The divinity school I went to was down in a little town in a state that seemed to me typically American but of course I'm a Middle Westerner myself, and there wasn't any trouble about me seeing the head man. He was a short, stocky, square man that reminded me of Jim Cagney so he got off to a good start with me. His office was bare and businesslike except that framed on the wall behind him in a—a glare from the windows was a copy of Dali's Last Supper, in a plain wood frame. Artistically, I guess, it was about as out of place and as badly hung as a picture could get, but my head quit aching and my stomach quit jumping and I said to myself God, stick with me, maybe this is the place for me.

"He couldn't—the president of this—have been less like my friend up in New Haven and yet there was something alike about them, it was that alikeness that comes from fighting in the same Army.

"We talked a little about things in general and then he asked me why I was there and what he could do about it. So I told him without going into anything about—about *how* I'd been converted, I just said I *had* been, and that I'd been spending most of my spare time for quite a while studying the New Testament and trying my best to pretend it *was* new which in a manner of speaking of course it *was*, to me anyhow. I'd come to the conclusion, I told him, as Chesterton and Bernard Shaw kept writing, somebody ought to *try* it. The way *Jesus* taught it—not the way about nine thousand guys had interpreted it and then interpreted each other.

"He—started discouraging me right away. He had light blue eyes—his name is Olsen and he had some Swede about him though I thought probably his mother was Irish—and he looked right directly at me and he wasn't very excited about what he saw, he sure didn't come out whooping over my arrival or hanging any leis around my neck.

" 'So what do you want me to do about it?' he said.

" 'Well,' I said, 'don't put yourself out any. I am a Yale man myself but I thought I'd like to go to a quieter school and become a minister.' And then I gave him that pitch about wanting to stay *inside* and serve and not romp out onto the fringes.

" 'You could stay home,' he said.

"My gorge rose on that one, and then I thought about how the Catholic Church screens and screens and all the trouble *Thomas Merton* had, and I started to tell him about the *light* and then something inside me said No, you glib bastard, that's bragging, you're not trying to help or rejoice him, you're showing off that you were called in person, he'd better treat you as somebody pretty special because after all this dump is a small-time operation and you are a big operator, and right then I thought how about a little *humility,* buddy, just a touch, you can't start any earlier.

"I looked at the Last Supper and thought about *Peter,* saying *though I die for it, I'll never walk out on you* and a couple of hours later sitting around the fire saying *Who, me? Never saw the guy before in my life.* So, as simply as I could, I told him I'd heard somebody call the apostle Paul a great salesman and I thought I'd like to help sell the teachings of Jesus Christ, he didn't seem much impressed so—I told him about mailing those letters to myself—and I'm here to tell you that bugged him."

We were in my sitting room at the hotel, and I got a clear picture of what Hank Gavin must have looked like to the head of that school, Hank sitting on a straight, uncomfortable chair, in his carelessly worn and not-too-well-pressed three-hundred-dollar suit, with his pleasant big-toad-in-a-big-puddle to big-toad-in-a-little-puddle air, so *friendly,* I've got an old school tie, of course, but I'm not wearing it because of my *humility* . . .

I said, "What's your definition of humility?"

His eyes came back to me. He said, "What's yours?"

"Not belittling yourself," I said. "Somebody—Huxley, I think, says it's giving God His share of the credit—something like that. Go on—what happened then?"

"He laughed," Hank Gavin said, "I don't know that I've ever gotten a bigger laugh. Then he said last year he'd had a night lieutenant of police through here a short time ago. He's a true Christian. Do you plan to teach? With your Yale degree—

"Then I saw what part of the trouble was and I told him I wanted to be a pastor if I could, that I knew I was getting a late start but—you know, the routine about *people* and *money* and my experience—but I wanted pastoral work in the field and he was still giving me that you'll-have-to-show-me look and I didn't get sore exactly, I really didn't, but I'd been conditioned to think I was quite a catch even at a higher level, but it looked like this little character was working from a different set of values and entrance requirements. I thought well there are always two sides to everything, I've got a right to ask him about the management and equipment and the plant and take a look at the books, before I start buying and selling.

"So I said, 'I wonder if I could ask you a question or two?'

"He drew his forehead into one of those be careful, buddy, frowns and it made him look squarer than ever and he said, 'Go ahead,'

"So I said, 'I know you teach the two commandments that Jesus gave as the greatest—Love God and Love Your Neighbor. What do you do here with the other four?'

"I got a dirty look for that, like a freshman trying to put the prof on the spot, but I thought whathehell, this is what it's all about as far as I'm concerned, so I said, 'Our chaplain out in Korea used to say that most of the churches tried to obey the first one—about preaching the good news to any body who'd *listen!*'

"He just kept on looking at me though I thought his eyes were popping a little. All he said was, 'Go on, explain what you're talking about.'

"Then I thought to myself well I may want to come here as a student but I'm a grown man and I know a lot about people if I do have to keep repeating it, and I have been *called* so I stood on my hind legs, figuratively speaking of course, and I said, 'Well, as our chaplain used to point out there were four more commandments as clear as—as a bugle.' I laid them out, the way the chaplain used to do. One by one.

" 'Preach the good news of the gospel.

" 'Heal the sick.

" 'Cleanse the leper.

" 'Cast out devils.

" 'Freely ye have received, freely give. That makes five. I'll deal with the first four. Why don't they belong under *if ye love me keep my commandments,* just as much as the first two?'

"He just sat there looking at me, his lower lip thrust out the way men do when they don't exactly know what they think. So I said, 'I saw them carved in pink marble on the cornerstone of a big church on one of the big avenues in New York the other day. I stood there,' I told him, 'quite a while and I wondered what would happen if a lunatic or a leper or a man lame from his mother's womb like the one Peter and John faced came in and *asked* somebody to do something about it *immediately.*'

" 'You think this may be the cornerstone that the builders rejected?' the president said, but all of a sudden I felt—impertinent and a goddam *prig* in my ignorance and my silly human best that wasn't good enough so I said, 'I don't know what I think.'

" 'I wish you hadn't brought all this up,' he said.

" 'So do I,' I said. 'I don't know what—what do you think I ought to do sir?'

"He said, 'As to that—I'm not sure we want you here. Now now, wait a minute. I'm not altogether sure you have what is called a vocation for the ministry, which is a different matter from a conversion, no matter how authentic.'

"I said, 'Many are called but few are chosen,' and he said, 'Something like that. Anyway, it's great to be starry-eyed about it but it requires other attributes. I don't know what your *plan* would be if you served as the pastor of a church and I'm not sure you do. How prepared you are for all that is involved with many people at different levels of faith and education and intelligence. We here regard ourselves as—not evangelical but as—shall we say—non-intellectual and perhaps I can say scriptural and spiritual.'

"I said I'd been told that in New York and he looked pleased and much more amiable. He said, carefully, but most sincerely, 'At the same time we have a reasonably definite curriculum and we are denominational to some extent and supported financially by a nationwide church setup, though I must say they never interfere with *me*. But—it's a small school. We've had a certain number of men—older men—who'd spent some years in business or professions, but none of them who'd had the amount of worldy success and living you've known. You're a super-salesman, and how much this would disturb and in what way it would sell our younger, simpler students I don't know.'

"He came around his desk and somehow we found ourselves standing there looking at the Last Supper. At the shining Hand of the Christ lifted—*I if I be lifted up will draw all men unto me*—and I knew this man beside me was a man of God.

"In a—a tight, challenging voice he said, 'I'm not closing any doors, you understand. Go home and think. I agree with you about the other four commandments. We may have abandoned the heart and bowels of the Teaching. But I have not thought what I am prepared to do about them. If I have to give you an answer now, it's No. If you come back after deliberation on both our parts and say you believe you have a true call to the ministry and wish to take your Christian pastoral training here, we can review the matter and I might choose you. If we pray and you're right—we should have a sign.'

"That's where I am now," Hank Gavin said, "waiting for a sign!"

I said, "Except ye see signs, ye will not believe I suppose."

A flashing, tempestuous, irresistible smile that made me say to myself *he can turn it on* lit Hank's face. He said, "What comes after that?"

"After what?" I said.

"What's the rest of it," Hank said, "Jesus said except ye

see signs ye will not believe, the nobleman said Sir, come down ere my child die, and Jesus said unto him Go thy way, thy son liveth."

I had never seen him so pleased with himself.

"It's always like that, isn't it?" he said, "it ends with—thy son liveth."

Then as if somebody had turned a switch, the light went out. He's not going to do it, he's not going to make it, I thought. And I thought of the *many* who had been inspired and filled with *hope* by the words of the Man of Galilee, but when they heard what seemed to them the *hard sayings* had turned back and walked no more with him.

A sign, I thought bitterly, and there shall be no sign given except the sign of the prophet Jonah. And to hell with *him,* I thought, because the resignation in Hank's eyes hurt me. I'll go home and read how Kipling thinks the whale got his throat.

6

Let me make clear that my spectator role at the scene which took place in that small but perfect art gallery which Al Patton had built across the back of his apartment to hold the gems of his modern art collection was entirely accidental, or whether this, too, was *meant,* I don't know. Certainly I had no idea when the tableau composed of Stu Margolis' wife Natalie, well on with her fourth or fifth martini or more, and the not-quite-young actor playing the lead in the Chicago company of a big Broadway hit, revealed itself to us as eyewitnesses that it was to be a turning point. Even now, I'm not sure whether I regarded it then as a *sign following.* The significance is that Hank Gavin did.

The occasion and the background of this were a cocktail party given by Al Patton and his wife Biddy, a tall, plain, witty, and outspoken lady of great popularity whom Al had had the good sense to marry and whom he apparently adored and appreciated more each year. For my own part, the cocktail party is composed of one part vulgarity and nine parts sheer physical discomfort with a dash of lack of imagination twisted over it. I once asked a brilliant young man whose marriage had broken up why he had married this obviously unsuitable girl in the first place and after a moment of solemn consideration he said that at a cocktail party he had suddenly realized there was no place else to go in New York between five and seven or six and eight and looking up found her at his elbow. He had thought, he said, that if he got *married* he could go *home.* Later it turned out his wife, who had been shopping all day, wanted to refresh herself at a cocktail party. As cocktail parties go, the one at the Pattons was outstanding for places to sit down, celebrities, and some really interesting people which in the noise and crowd essential to success at such a gambol was frustrating since even if you could fight your way through to them you couldn't hear anything they said. I had come because I had a sincere affection for Al Patton and I knew his insistence was honestly based on the conviction that I'd be missing something if I stayed away. The occasion for this particular gathering was the departure of a delightful young French couple who had been in charge of the consulate and were now recalled to Paris. It was attended by some thirty or forty more distinguished, squealing, hilarious bon ton and *haute monde* guests than could comfortably fit in the enormous lofty drawing room of the Patton apartment. A couple of guitar players and a bongo drum or two filled in any possible moment of quiet, and as Monsieur le Comte de la Coudray said to me in the passing, he was overwhelmed by the *year* of the champagne.

This will give you as general an idea as you are going to need.

I saw Mellie across the room with her father at her elbow, which surprised me because usually Francis Cheyne didn't go to cocktail parties any more than I did but I assumed he probably knew de la Coudray and his wife and I remember a passing thought that Melanie Cheyne Gavin was able to combine absolute neatness with unutterable *chic,* which seemed to me rather a juggler's feat since so much *chic* nowadays tends to be untidy. We waved, I didn't see Hank, I had a word with a former movie star then appearing in the round nearby, and finally, bruised and battered, found myself in a chair in the corner with the president of a celebrated university explaining to me that it was possible to achieve unity between God and Mammon and between the conservatives and the liberals of the Republican party. Plate and cup balanced on my knee, I had listened to such of this as I could hear before Al Patton loomed, red-faced and uproarious, to insist I must come up and see his new Passmore. He explained that he kept the gallery locked at cocktail parties since a guest, as a prank to enliven the festivities, had sliced the eye out of an early Dali. Boys will be boys, Al said without rancor. But, he said, he was conducting a few select tours and I was one of them. With his square, still-muscular figure he ran interference and we passed close to Mellie who was talking in French exactly like theirs to the guests of honor and was, I saw, creating in them a sort of warm merriment which was her special gift. Shouting commands to *open up,* Al got us to the foot of the steep little staircase—the gallery had been servants' quarters when servants "lived in"—and finding there Hank Gavin and Stu Margolis and Francis Cheyne in a huddle he swept them up and we began together the ascent for which, Al shouted happily, he probably ought to provide ropes and pickaxes. In a way, it was wonderful to see this exuberant sophomoric man, who could fight with unequaled brilliance and skill and dauntless courage in any court against any opponent, so starry-eyed as we approached the treasure which in his case I knew really filled his heart not with pride or exhibitionism but with delight.

He led us almost tiptoe across a little foyer, tried the key, and found the door already unlocked. This caused him only momentary pause and then silently as though entering a holy-of-holies he flung open the door and ushered us in and spotlighted the picture with a dramatic flourish.

At once, the room gave a sense of space, of revealing light, of green-white simplicity.

But the picture that held our eyes in that moment was one with which the most violent Gauguin could not have competed.

In the first shock, the tableau reminded me of a game called *Statues,* which we played when I was a child. Whoever was IT was whirled until dizzy, sent spinning, and obliged to remain in exactly the position and expression, however grotesque, of the moment he stopped.

As we stopped whirling, we were statues just inside that room.

There seems no particular reason to describe the sexscape that met our gaze. Its details are now so familiar that each reader can supply those he prefers. Not that this was *in fragrante delicto,* only in process toward. Five minutes more and who could say? Unfortunately so many women who drink too much are taken amorous, here was Natalie Margolis in the arms of this actor, and the silly alcoholic lust on her face brought to it some suggestion of the decayed youth restored by plastic surgeons. Of the man, we could see only his bending back elegantly tailored, his curly hair streaked with gray, his fashionable heavy-threatening profile.

My reporter's trained senses came out of the trance first. I took a lightning look at the others who had come with me upon this heartbreaking indecency. In that light designed to reveal everything, Stu Margolis' distinguished face was frozen in time just after he had swallowed the gall and wormwood in the hemlock cup of murdered pride. Francis Cheyne was a thin, dark exclamation point put after *I can't believe my own eyes!* and Al Patton had the purple, congested fury of a man who had found a snake in his bed.

My eyes, heart, and attention stopped at Hank.

Still and silent as a statue of Mercury poised to take off on his winged feet when the gun barked, his head was tilted back and he was listening *beyond,* what exactly I meant by this I don't know, except that he was holding his breath, stilling his very blood to hear it. His eyes, blazing and luminous with hope, took in the woman, her husband his friend, and the man who hadn't yet reacted enough to let go of the clinging, fumbling creature in his arms, or perhaps he knew if he did she would fall and that would be like seeing a cripple tripped.

Swiftly my story mind took over, a storyteller never loses touch with his story if he has one, I roughed-in the vital character of the lover. He was probably the only man in those crowded, luxurious, hilarious rooms who wouldn't know what fork to use on what dish. What did a handsome-by-profession ambitious man, who by now had to know he'd never be better than the No. 2 or 3 company of a Broadway hit, do when a member of the Inner Circle made a pass at him *within* the Inner Circle? No actor can be unfamiliar with the reverse aspects of rape, but he had no more understanding of the tribal rules prevailing here and now than if he'd found himself in the pot in a cannibal hut. He'd seen Mrs. Stuart Margolis, a name oft appearing in society-and-about-the-town columns, as he came in. Shod by Delman, coiffed by an artist whose autumn tints were copied from Corot, gowned by Mainbocher, rather on the lines of the Duchess of Windsor whom Mrs. Margolis was told she resembled though of course the duchess was years older, about her neck the status symbol of triple strings of pearls placed there by her husband. When she said, *Let's go up and see Al's new pictures, he locks the gallery but I know where he puts the key,* from this should a vain man run screaming? Flattered, bemused, even before we crashed in he would have been unsure. If he repulsed the blandishments of this lady—and he had tumbled finally to the fact that she was as sozzled as Judy O'Grady—would he be regarded as ill-mannered, would it rob him of all claim to be a man-of-this-most-desirable-world? If he yielded, would it appear presumptuous, a sponge or even a swindler taking advantage of Potiphar's wife with too much four-parts-gin-to-one-of-vermouth under her girdle? Or was the humorous touch required? Always leave them laughing and you'll always get asked back. Perhaps a bit of drawing room comedy, such as he'd done in a summer stock production of *Private Lives?*

Ah, there was the rub.

Rape, rejection, or repertoire, how was he to write his own script? To escape his below-par origins he had become an actor. Someone created a character, wrote dialogue, a director told him what to do. Now, after all this frightful indecision, he was asked to cope with a real scene in real life, and his statue of when-the-husband-found-him-in-the closet couldn't have been surpassed by Bert Lahr. Yet to me it was this poor, phony *other man* which changed everything, for it not only increased the voltage of what people ought not to be allowed to do to each other, for Stu Margolis it made the thing *public* instead of *private.* It subjected him to the peculiar chagrin of a man who sees his wife prefer a man he himself considers beneath competition, a mountebank as far outside as a dancing waiter. So that the whole drama became as public as the bar in Harlem, as disreputable and shabby as the blackjack and the gutter. For the fantastic reason that always applies in such tense moments there went through my head a line from Bobby Burns which I'd had quoted at me, *A Chiel's among ye takin' notes, And faith, he'll prent it* and I knew the heaviness in our hearts was partly because this actor would *talk* as all vain men do.

The scene cracked and dissolved, statues moved and spoke, Stu Margolis, gone death white, swayed forward, and I wondered if we were to see murder done. Al Patton's quick step told me he had felt the alarm also. For it was upon her husband that Natalie, tearing at the pearls around her throat, began to vent venomous self-justification. As a reporter I had learned the hard way that nice women know all the words, so it was not her choice of words that desolated me. It was her *lostness,* out-in-the-hills-away-far-off-from-the-gates-of-gold rang its old hymn tune in my head. Something worse than murder was befalling us, Stu was shriveling, I thought God help us he doesn't want to kill her. Has she at last driven him beyond the point of no return, so that he is bankrupt? An ache knotted my stomach, Stu was a kind man and an honorable, and as the pearls broke and bounded and scattered over the floor I knew there was a jewel of greater price in this woman, who had created such a love in her husband and children that it had survived the devils that had possessed her and I thought what a good life they ought to be living and I knew it was against God's law that they were not, that there had to be *a way*. The Way.

I was still looking at her poor face on which maudlin tears had dripped mascara and streaked pancake when Hank Gavin spoke.

"Natalie," he said.

This was not such a voice as had ever come from Hank Gavin before and it would have melted the heart of his bitterest enemy if he had one.

I tell you the room was now transported, we were isolated in some other world-without-end orbit as boundless as the sea out beyond the dimension we knew. I cannot say it was filled with light for it was not light as we know it, but a radiance of which the air was composed such as is *almost* there in a painting by Renoir or a certain afterglow over tropical seas. In this radiance I knew for the first time that the power of good is greater than the power of evil. At this moment in Al Patton's so-modern art gallery, as I watched Hank Gavin *in a business suit,* holding out his hand to the woman, a storm shook me and I smelled the sea. There is no other smell like a wind filled with sand and sage and sea hot in the sun, and something made me believe this was the way it had smelled beside the Sea of Galilee. In my head, like the electric sign going round in Times Square, words moved, I could see them. *In His Name In His Name In His Name Stretch Forth Your Hand Your Sins Be Forgiven Go And Sin No More Come Forth Come Forth,* dead in sin as you are, *Come Forth.* I knew these words were transmitted to me as Morse code transmits from one instrument to another and I saw by the expression of the face of that pushover for angels, Al Patton, that he was getting a few dots and dashes, too.

Hank's eyes were open, fixed on the disheveled, debauched creature, prayer came from him, and it seemed to me that this was an astounding time and place and occasion for prayer and yet—was it? What were a few centuries between that other time and place and same occasion, the breaking of this particular commandment from the ancient Scriptures was more careless and common, and drunkenness was on the rise and the institutions were filled with its wreckage, and no human best had proved good enough to deal with it as honest medical men and psychiatrists would tell you. Whatever Hank Gavin was doing he might as well try it. Odd that it should be Al Patton, and Francis Cheyne, who'd told of the Air Chief Marshal's angels in the Battle of Britain and me with my angels of Mons who were gathered here, we wouldn't make it any harder because of our unbelief. We weren't *against* him, what had we got to lose? Somehow as Hank Gavin held out his hand he had shifted the actor upstage a little, he was just part of the company.

We all saw what happened.

As people had witnessed the dipping of the Bouhouhorts' child into Bernadette's spring at Lourdes.

We saw that Natalie was changing. My heart was hammering so I thought the others must hear it and I did hear the breath Francis Cheyne drew.

The hand the man stretched forth that day in the temple —all those people had seen it *withered*. A withered hand. You know what is a withered hand! While they stared at it, it was restored whole like the other. The man with the unclean spirit, chained in the tombs, possessed of all the neuroses and complexes and psychopathic terrors, whose name was Legion as whose devils aren't, who pleaded with Jesus and Jesus *cast them out* then and there. He didn't send for a straitjacket, nor call a psychiatric conference nor suggest a padded cell. They found the man clothed and in his right mind when they came to put him in fetters again which was probably in those days the only asylum for the insane they had.

As the countdown began, I tried to keep my thoughts on those things, *greater works shall ye do,* Jesus had said.

Slowly slowly it went on.

This . . . your daughter . . . whom Satan . . . has bound. . . .

Come forth not in Gennesaret but Chicago, not on the shores of Galilee but Lake Michigan, not in A.D. but now now now. It's the same, isn't it?

The foolish drunkenness vanished, the amorous leer faded away, the toads stopped jumping out of her mouth. The face Natalie Margolis began to show forth now I had never seen before, this was the way she would have looked had she grown middle-aged gracefully, in joyful sobriety able to move in the world of her husband's love, this woman would be fun to love and to live with, it was easy to see why they had persisted in loving her and hoping to restore her.

Wasn't that the password to free Dr. Manson in *A Tale of Two Cities—Restored to life?*

Natalie was restored to life, she came out of her wanton befuddlement as though she'd had twelve hours' sleep, as though she woke from a trance, and remembered nothing that had happened in her blackout. Quite simply and naturally she was doing all the things a woman would do after a long trip in a crowded car, adjusting her dress, running her fingers through her hair, smiling at her husband.

The smile brought Stu Margolis to her side, he slipped an arm around her, he was accepting the obliteration, *Carthage must be destroyed,* he was looking at her as man looks at a dawn he wasn't sure was going to happen, if he was aware of Hank Gavin nothing he did showed it. Perfectly naturally he slipped his arm around her and said, "Al, we've loved seeing the pictures, but I think we ought to go now and say goodbye to the de la Coudrays, don't you, Nat?" and she said, "I do indeed," and Al began to roar and rustle, he was muttering words like *miracle* but he wanted to go, too, he escorted them out but just before he went I saw his fingers *bite* into Hank Gavin's shoulder. Swiftly, accurately, without an unnecessary gesture, Francis Cheyne picked up the pearls and dropped them into his pocket to return to

Natalie. Then he stood still, watching Hank. It is not often that we really see anyone we know well, to whose presence we are accustomed. Francis Cheyne was seeing now all the way back as we all do, all the memories and our own opinions that go to make up what we see and what we don't see. He was seeing this new Hank. The tawny-yellow eyes, the furnace-tried face with the cheekbones and beaked nose showing more than they used to. The new expression of the mouth. His own expression didn't change when Hank said more to himself than to us, "My best isn't good enough, but *his* is." Francis Cheyne was listening, he kept on listening when I had to say, "I suppose you regard this as a sign?"

Hank roared with laughter. He said, "Could be, could be! Come on, father-in-law, I want to find my wife." They went out together but even then I did not suspect that Francis Cheyne's presence there that day would be a factor in the days ahead, possibly because I still had no idea how strong and determined and unwavering his daughter could be.

That left the actor and me. Now he reminded me of a fighter in the dressing room when they are trying to bring him around after a knockout. His eyes kept shifting from the door, to the pictures on the pale walls, to the windows going dark, back to me. He said, "Well! Now I've seen everything. I must say—" then he brightened. He said, "Of course I've heard a shock can sober a person up, right away or anyhow in a few minutes. A real shock. Haven't you heard that?"

I said I had.

He said, "Well! That certainly must be the explanation of this, don't you think?"

I said it was certainly a possible explanation. Miracles, I said, were always extremely inconvenient things to have around.

He gave me a startled, sullen look and said, "Well, I don't mind telling you I'm just as glad it all worked out this way. When women get loaded they're a real menace, I don't mind telling you."

"As are also men who talk about them?" I said firmly.

We went out and downstairs together. Everything was exactly the same except the noise had stepped up some. I saw Hank and Mellie over by the big windows and they beckoned but I slipped out into the little hall and rang for the elevator.

Of course the actor's explanation might be the one, but I wanted time to consider several others.

7

The following morning while I was having my second cup of coffee, the phone rang, a voice said, "I'm in the lobby, may I come up?" and I said, "Who is it?" and when she said, "Sweetie, it's Mellie," I figured by the early hour for a call and the icy tones that Hank, his *sign* tucked under his belt, had called for the showdown which Mellie, I hadn't quite understood why, had been avoiding so long.

I was not prepared for the blazing anger under Mellie's for-her careless exterior, under a tailored suit that was a little at random, her small, slim body was taut as a fishing line with a barracuda on the other end, her lipstick had a tiny smear at the corners, she hadn't taken time to subdue the Josephine curls, they were rebellious behind her ears and at her temples.

"You're partly responsible for this lunacy," she said without greeting.

I have long since found that it accomplishes nothing to let the young bully you, so I said, "No, I am not."

"You've encouraged him, you can't deny that," she said.

"I wouldn't think of denying it," I said, "I'm a natural-born encourager."

"You've always been on his side," she said bitterly.

"My darling child," I said, "I have principles of my own. I can't toss them overboard because I'm unusually fond of you."

"You might listen to how it looks from where I sit," she said, picking up a piece of toast, covering it with marmalade, and dropping it untasted. "I do have a side, you know. Not as dramatic or far out as Hank's, of course. I haven't been seeing lights or hearing voices—"

"Mellie!" I said.

Her upward look then was bland, wide-eyed, almost contemptuous. "Do you think it's pleasant for me to see my husband making a fool of himself in public?"

I interrupted her there. "Be fair, be fair," I said. "I saw him at the Pattons when he was far from making a fool of himself. Did Hank tell you about Natalie Margolis?"

"What about her?" Mellie said.

As well as I could, I re-created the scene in Al Patton's picture gallery.

The effect on Mellie was, for me, totally unexpected and shocking.

"Oh God!" she said, hitting her closed fist into the palm of her open hand with a sharp crack, "that's what I mean! Exactly what I mean. If that isn't making a fool of yourself in public it'll do, won't it? I've put up with that poor, witless, spineless *Natalie* for years, I'm sorry for her, what a life! I'll even go along with this idea that alcoholism is a *disease.* But don't expect me to believe in some kind of phony miracle because for once she was *scared* sober, do you? You've heard of that, haven't you? Let's not be ridiculous! Please, please, this is just what I was talking about."

"If you had been there," I said with some heat, "you wouldn't talk like that. You didn't *see* it happen."

"As I just told you," Mellie said, "I'm not given to *seeing* things. What you don't—won't—see, is that if this goes on it will break up my marriage and ruin his career." She kept shoving the coffee pot and all the useless silverware and glasses that come up from room service back and forth until I said, "Stop that and sit down and tell me what has brought this about."

On the extreme edge of an ottoman, she gave me a tight-lipped smile to show that we were still friends, but the hot anger remained though now she had it under control, she began to talk quietly enough.

After the Patton cocktail party, Sybil Rowe and her new beau—*she's a fool,* Mellie said, *he's not a marrying man*—had gathered up a group for dinner, but Hank said he wasn't hungry, he wanted to go home. So they'd *gone* home and had a salad and hot French bread and made light conversation about the party and the people there and neither one of them heard the other. As they left the dining room, Mellie started upstairs and Hank put out a hand and stopped her and turned her into the big drawing room. "I want neutral ground," he said with a warm smile, he was all keyed up, she could tell that, bells ringing and fireworks going off, and she knew that he meant to force the issue and inside she felt herself that the time had come.

Evidently she saw a question on my face for she said impatiently, "I'd been playing a back game. It's always better if things aren't *said,* once you say them they seem bigger and you can't take them back. Things can't ever be the same. I didn't want him to know how far apart we were. Besides, I thought he'd snap out of it. Remember I said to you when I first told you about it, He has to be kidding, doesn't he? Well, I found out he wasn't kidding, but at the same time I thought it was a mistake to take it too seriously. I—I didn't want to jest at wounds that might leave scars all the rest of our lives and Katie kept telling me Least said, soonest mended. I wasn't the only one that thought his was an emotional—upset—binge—I knew men who'd been through a combat war and especially—the ones who were in *Korea* seem to have been hurt somehow worse than usual—and I was willing to believe this was his own particular psychosis or neurosis or whatever they call it. His mental *quirk*—and I detested Colin myself but I knew that was a combat-soldier-college-day friendship and—Hank took it hard and had a sense of guilt about it. So I was willing to keep as quiet as I could and hope he'd get a mixture of method into his madness, I didn't think that was too much to expect or—hope for."

Also, plainly, she had a real horror of *defeating* Hank.

Of course she was sure she would win, anything else never entered her head. And perhaps because of her father, and even of Colin and Sybil, and possibly the memory of David Kenyon crawling at her feet—anyhow she had rejoiced in looking up to Hank Gavin. Way down inside her feminine subconscious was a conviction that a marriage is happy only if the man is the stronger. Though a woman would always continue the fight to be boss or wear the pants she now aped, something in Mellie told her that this was a Pyrrhic victory. In the dark lonely night while Hank was away on his mysterious errands, she had tried to think all this through as honestly as she knew how, her mind was a good one, and to some extent she could see the other fellow's side, which is not possible to most women. She was still convinced that this was an aberration and had been clinging to the one thought, *this, too, shall pass.*

"I wasn't digging my heels in," Mellie said hotly, "so I think the whole church setup is antiquated and a good deal of a bore. I was willing to go along with Hank on it and I told him so. The way Judy did when Sam went mad over duplicate bridge and started haring off to *Italy* and *Mexico* and southeast Abyssinia or wherever to tournaments, Judy learned to play *bridge* though to this day I'm not sure she knows the difference between Blackwell and Blackstone. Anyhow I told Hank—I suggested he could work with the Youth Group and get up some bowling teams out in that black-and-white development center, and I said I'd even join the Young Marrieds with him and go to all the *missions*

—a wife can't speak fairer than that, can she?" Anger flared out of the light gay sky, a jagged menace of lightning. "Until last night, I didn't say right out what I believe, I hoped, I honestly hoped, sweetie, that I'd never have to. If it made him happier to have his little fairy tale I wasn't going to blast it. I didn't want to have to tell him that down underneath like most people I know I'm an atheist, or could be an agnostic, that I couldn't agree with Nietzsche more when he said the two great narcotics are Christianity and alcohol —of our time."

"His version of Christianity," I said, "he knew nothing about it, actually, and I'm not at all sure his Superman theory has done very well. May I remind you that his Ubermensch got the hell kicked out of them by soldiers a good many of whom tried to be Christians?"

After I'd said it I was glad she hadn't heard me, but Nietzsche and his pronouncement have always aroused the devil in me. Mellie's eyes on me were hard and bright and I knew her ears were stopped. She said, "This is my *life,* can't you see that? This is *my* love. *My* marriage. Until last night I thought I could—I thought we wouldn't have to go through—" She had to stop there. When she could speak again, she went back to the night before.

Hank had been right, the drawing room was neutral, not *her* room like the upstairs sitting room. This seemed bigger than usual, impersonal and empty, probably because they seldom used it except when they had guests. They sat down side by side on the big divan that faced the stately fireplace, but Hank didn't like that, he pulled up a small, straight chair and sat so that he could face her, and after a moment he reached out and took both her hands.

"You know I love you, don't you?" he said. "More every day since we got married." When she said she didn't doubt that, he said, "I have to ask you now to listen. I have been —exploring—experimenting—looking around, I wanted to be *sure* of what I have to do before I put it all before you the best I can. In a way it has as much to do with you as it does with me, you're part of it. Let's start with I don't know why I've been called and—now it looks like *chosen* except perhaps the Lord has to use whatever laborers he can reach, and because of the war and the chaplain and—Colin—he reached me. I think too that—all times are more or less alike. We've made great scientific strides but Steinmetz and he was one of the best of them, one of the great scientists, he said himself that unless we learned the truth about prayer in the last half of the twentieth century we'd wish we hadn't learned so much about the atom in the first half. But—any time—time of Moses—time of Noah—time of Richard Yea-and-Nay or Abraham Lincoln, we've always needed fighters. Take Gandhi, so his weapons were fasts and salt marches and spinning wheels and non-resistance, but he was a fighter, a front-line fighter for God all the time. Now I have *seen*—I can speak—"

Apparently he had meant to go on, but Mellie interrupted, keeping her amused overtone, "Look pet," she said, "could we talk a little sense? I'm your wife and I know you better than anyone else does and I know you have one of those glowing optimistic imaginations, but—isn't it just possible you'd had one over your limit that now-famous night on the barge?"

"No," Hank said.

He didn't draw away from her outstretched hands, but he put them back in her own lap, and his face had sharpened. His No was so flat, strong, and uncompromising that it rocked Mellie to her second line of defense or attack, anger began to mount, and she decided to lay it on the line.

In strong, ordinary words, she told him that he must now see where she stood and what she thought.

She had as much right not to believe in God as Hank had to believe in Him, she had a sane, sound right to discount his alleged vision and she did.

She regarded his attitude as superstitious and dangerous.

Without softening it, she gave him the Nietzsche quotation.

Basically, she was a tolerant you-go-your-way-and-I'll-go-mine anti-religious modern thinker. She had, she said, hoped for coexistence, as it were, but he was going too far. Or she was forced to judge that he intended to. She disliked arguments and she didn't intend to wrangle over their difference of religious or non-religious beliefs. What she wanted now that she had been frank was a definite statement of what he was up to.

She didn't get it at once. He sat looking at her, and she noticed how tawny-yellow his eyes were and this disturbed her for she couldn't remember that they had always been like that. With a smile whose sweetness took her breath away, he said, "Beloved—do you remember when we went to Tahiti? The time we went out on the deck of that boat crossing to Fiji—and you were all upset because you couldn't find any of the stars or constellations or the Dipper or anything? And then we realized we'd crossed the equator and this was a new heaven? A different heaven? The stars we'd known weren't there but—there was the Southern Cross?

Remember? And, Mel, when the dawn came we were in our deck chairs and it was a new earth, too. *We'd crossed the equator*. We couldn't change anything. That's the way it is with me, my love—you don't mind if I call you my only love because you are, you know. One and only. You and me. You see—I *know*. I can't make you—I can't tell you—but I can never change back now. I've seen—face to face. You might as well try to convince me there is no such thing as light."

For some reason this had frightened her into a full flood of anger and pain and she said things which now, she told me, she wished she had not. As I listened, I thought this could so easily have been another kind of a girl—another woman entirely. A selfish, self-indulgent, peacock-vain creature of sex and the fleshpots altogether, of driving ambition, of just plain Eve-and-the-apple weakness. But as she sat there, arrogant and elegant as she was, I knew it was at once better and worse, higher and lower, more tragic and dangerous ahead. This was a strong character, a young woman who *believed* a commonly held side of the world's religious controversy, who had been willing to leave the church alone as an instrument for minor respectability and good will but if her hand were forced would, in the end, take a stand against it.

So she had then, suddenly, shifted her ground. She said quietly but insistently, "I think now, my pet, you must tell me exactly what it is you want to do—mean to do. Not in evangelical or visionary terms, in practical outline. I have a right to this now."

He said, "I want to qualify myself so that I may try and see what it would be like to follow *in his steps*. To see whether he meant it when he said Follow me and I will make you fishers of men. We—we need fishers of men, baby. He had twelve disciples and then seventy also and I think I must now be a disciple and I can't be modest or meek about it because the twelve and the seventy started about where I am. I want to see what it would be like to be a minister who believed that Jesus meant what he said as he said it. To be obedient to his teaching, which is simple and careful and direct and definite. I'd like to take his theory that God has *power*, power always available to us, and that the power of God is greater always than any power of evil, and try the experiment of proving this, step by step, according to his instructions and example. The way the mathematicians at Princeton took Einstein's theory of relativity and made the experiments to prove it, the way they proved that we can orbit in outer space at Kennedy. This is what we ought to do now, to try honestly to prove it. Talk isn't much good any more—just talk."

"Don't give me that old bromide about Christianity hasn't been tried and found wanting, it hasn't been tried!" Mellie said. "Nonsense. It's been tried. Joan of Arc tried it and won the Battle of Orleans and then they burned her at the stake—remember?"

"But you do remember she won the Battle of Orleans and saved France," Hank said absently. "It isn't being tried so much—I know I'm one man, the old old objection—one peanut, one grain of sand. Man's got to the place now where he can blow himself off the earth unless he returns to God and to return to God he has to think there is a God and that God can help him and wants to. You have to do more than *say* it. Mellie, all the promises are conditional. Please listen another minute or two. Seek ye first the kingdom of God and all the other things shall be added unto you. There are a lot of them. The TV commercials tell me IF you want to make a cake out of a box of cake mix you have to follow the directions, even *they* don't claim you could have a cake by buying the box and reading the directions. You have to open it and put the mix in a bowl and add water and beat and put it in an oven at such a heat. Well—I saw the chaplain follow the directions, I saw him build his house on the rock, and I saw him make it work. I—I have to try."

Now she was frozen with this same icy rage she'd had when she first came into my rooms. With a little smile she held out her hand, she got up and walked him across to a table that stood endwise in the bow windows, with a lovely Chippendale chair on either side, and she sat down in one and made a little gesture for him to sit in the other.

"Businesslike, isn't it?" she said, tilting the lamp so that it shone on both their tense young faces. "I am about to be businesslike. I must. You propose, then, to do exactly what?"

"I shall have to go to a divinity school, a theological seminary for a while," he said. "I think it can be arranged that if I go for a year I can probably get a post at a church as an assistant rector or pastor and that will be used as part of my training and also to get my degree—"

"I wish you knew what that sounds like to me," Mellie Gavin said.

"Well," Hank said a little impatiently, "I can't be a Trappist on account of you, for one thing, and I don't want to be—I'm not cut out for the contemplative work anyhow. I can't start off with a begging bowl—"

"You might as well," Mellie said. "Now let me show you how this looks to me. Some years ago, you asked me to marry you. Hank Gavin, of the firm of Pulliam, Margolis and Jones. You were then a sane, sound, successful young American businessman making thirty thousand dollars a year and pretty sure to raise it to fifty thousand in a hurry, which I must say you have done. You were a sensational investment counselor trusted by one and all. An important guy in your own hometown and mine. I wasn't only being offered the man I'd fallen in love with but the life I wanted to marry. I could live in a city I love with people I know, with social, philanthropic, and cultural contacts and work such as I could do and felt was worthwhile. I could go on with my riding and you could whittle down your golf score. It couldn't have been nicer.

"Now—if you had come to me and said I am merely an adventurer who wants to explore the Galápagos Islands for turtle eggs, or I am a mining engineer and we will have to live in a tent in the Andes, I could then have made up my mind Yea-or-Nay to that particular deal. On known facts and values. Sure I've known girls who married and went to Saudi Arabia or Moosejaw, Minnesota, or agreed to spend their first three years putting their husbands through law or medical school. That's their privilege.

"But Henry Angus Gavin. you did *not* come to me and say I am a minister, a preacher of the so-called Christian gospel, I am still in a seminary actually and when I get out I will be able to earn, say, six thousand dollars a year *if* I pass my clerical bar or get admitted to practice or whatever they *do.* I will be sent to Chattanooga, Tennessee, or North Platte, Nebraska or Montpelier, Vermont, and we will live in a four-room rectory or whatever and at this point I would have said Thank you, Reverend Henry Angus, but NO. NO! In the first place I wouldn't have fallen in love with you, I'd probably never even have *met* you, and I certainly wouldn't have married you."

His eyes never left her face but they told her nothing at all.

"What actually took place," she said, "was that we made an agreement on conditions as they were and as you presented them to me, didn't we?"

"I seem to remember something about richer or poorer, better or worse."

"Oh sure, and I remember they played the *Lohengrin* wedding march, one has as much to do with it as the other, we aren't expected to *eat* the wedding cake the rest of our lives. And say anybody believed it, there have to be recognizable limits even inside a calculated risk, don't there? Any church, any court, will grant you that *fraud* is outside the limits.

"You have considered that we have no money? Our equity in this house—a few jewels we might pawn—we've just been getting started and Katie wouldn't give us a crust of bread. So you are asking me to start living on your salary—I've done that up to now. But your salary as a minister—I don't think I could. Anyway, I won't. I have been thinking that over."

"Compared to what we have," Hank said painfully, as she paused, "I agree it's not much. I'm asking you to make more sacrifices than I would have to make, I see that. But, Mellie, I know this isn't something that can be arrived at overnight, this—joy and grace. I—think if you'd give it a chance you'd see that we spend our time and energy on things that don't last, that are always shadows, and if we find grace—I can't tell you the wonder that it brings—"

"I'm quite sure you can't," Mellie said. "I've just been reading a book—I want to be fair—called *The Role of the Minister's Wife*, and a very nice little book it is, too. It doesn't say anything about the wife having to believe in God, or *grace*, or anything like that, but it does give quite a look at her problems. The ladies of the parish would detest me, darling."

"No," Hank said, "you always get along better with people than anybody, you know that. In the hospitals, you're always the one they want. I thought of that, too. You put new life into everything you run—like the bowling teams and all. People love you, Mellie. I—sometimes it has surprised me and I don't know exactly why—"

"Because people are contrary," Mellie said, too sweetly, "that's why. At heart they all want somebody to tell 'em what to do."

"If we could help—and heal—and give some faith and hope by prayer to the—despair of our times, if we could show them that there is the love of God for them behind all this chaos they've accepted—"

"You see," Mellie said, "I don't believe it. I do not believe one word of it. So aside from everything else you have no right to ask me to do something that is against all my principles, against every fiber of what I do believe which is that the quicker a man toughens himself up to meet the chaos the better and the devil gets the hindermost. So if you persist in asking me to do this, if you insist on following this will-o'-the-wisp sweetness and light it will damn well be dark and high noon and lead you right spang bang into the divorce court."

The words lay cold, white, menacing on the table between them. Hank went white and still as death, but Mellie let them lie, her eyes narrowing in triumph.

Then she said, "You see this is a breach of contract, don't you? You see it's wholly dishonest and a repudiation of everything you offered me when I married you. We're so—happy—I can't do it—I can't—"

Unexpectedly to them both, she began to cry.

Terribly. Tears streamed down her face and the sobs shook her as a wind shakes flowers in a garden. She got up and stumbled around to him and he shoved back his chair quickly and took her in his arms. Her hands went behind his head and pulled his lips down to hers that were hot and quivering and salt with her tears. She clung to him, trying to force her body into his and her teeth found his lower lip and closed, she seemed trying frantically to *hold* him, to make them one flesh.

"Love me," she said, "I can't bear it. Oh *stop* all this—love me."

He picked her up and carried her upstairs, her sobbing moans in his ears, her hands clutching him in passionate longing. "Don't leave me," she said as he put her down on the bed and again her arms reached for him, "You can't leave me," and this time her lips were soft and sweet and warm beyond a man's dreams of desire.

All night she clung to him, lay close, laughed in fulfillment to remind him of this earthly paradise they shared.

Sometime when the promise of returning day was a faint, dawn light, she woke, startled, and sat up in bed, her hands feeling to find him. The place beside her was empty and she gave a gasp of terror. Then she saw the kneeling figure silhouetted at the window against the coming luminous glow. It was the first time she had ever seen him kneel to pray, and something in the pleading of the bowed head and body started her heart jumping like a caged thing against the cage of her ribs.

He *meant* it.

This was—there was a reality in this.

The beating of her heart almost suffocated her, and her whole body was suffused with *embarrassment*. A man—to get down on his knees like that—in their bedroom—and pray. Then she wanted to scream, to throw the lamp at him, he was far away from her, as he had never been before in their lives. Pull down the pillars around his head! Make him say Who me? I never knew him! But her embarrassment choked her. As though he felt her gaze, heard her throbbing heart and drawn breath, he turned and the brightening dawn caught his face. She saw it gaunt and haggard, from his hour's watch. The temples and the cheekbones were standing out and there were tears or sweat upon his cheeks.

For a moment their eyes met and she was not sure he saw her, he spoke and what she made of the words made no sense. He said, *"It won't be earlier."* That frightened her, but out of the fright came steel to her will, as though she picked up and concentrated all the challenge the world would offer him.

When she woke next, he was standing beside the bed, already dressed.

"You're up early," she said, smiling at him in that one moment of everything-as-usual, this is me waking up to kiss my husband goodbye before he goes to work which is there before memory does its work.

Hank said, "I've got an appointment with Stu at ten."

Mellie got out of bed, pulling her tailored robe of tie silk around her. In a grave new voice she said, "Hank, you aren't going to—"

"I think I must, now," Hank said. "I—won't be going back there and it's only fair."

"Hank," she said again, "I am your wife. I love you. *Don't do this*. Don't do it! I know it's wrong. I don't believe you're asked to go to such *lengths*. Make sense, my darling. Don't do this."

He waited a moment, then he said, "Mellie—I may not be back tonight. After I see Stu I'll go down to—"

Mellie said, "If you go—don't come back."

"You don't mean that," he said and came and kissed her gently, and she said, "You're going to miss me."

He said, "Oh yes—and you'll miss me, too."

When he had gone, after she heard the downstairs door shut, she stood without moving. Then sure triumph began to beat through her mind and body.

He would be back.

Of course he would be back.

That was what she said to me. "He's gone but he'll be back and on any terms. He'll get very tired of waiting for me to come to Phoebeville whatever state it is to live in a dormitory while he goes to *school*."

"Do you really mean if he goes through with this you'd divorce him?" I said. "You'd actually leave him?"

"He left me," Mellie said.

Then her head went back, quite deliberately she picked up the silver coffee pot and threw it through the window. The glass shattered and tinkled and left a gaping star-shaped hole.

"I hope it doesn't hit anybody on the sidewalk," I said.

"They'll think you did it," Mellie said sweetly. "It will ruin your reputation. At your age, Godmama, you should have learned some self-control," and then she had a short, violent fit of sheer hysterics.

"Don't think this means I'll change my mind," she said. "Never. Never never never. It's just that—it's so early in the morning to have your—heart broken."

At that moment, I knew later, Hank Gavin was driving along a crowded freeway which ran south and west toward the divinity school where he now meant to ask the president to enroll him.

After an hour of calm, collected, and careful conversation with Stu Margolis in which he had stated this intention and they had reviewed it, Stu had begged him to take a leave of absence instead of resigning. "No harm done," Stu said, waving his cigar, "if you are as you put it *called,* you can resign at the end of the year as well. If on—closer examination and the discovery of all this rather drastic move entails, you find you can—can serve here as well, then there won't be a lot of red tape to reinstall you."

"You make me sound a bit of a smug prig, pal," Hank Gavin said.

"No no," Stu Margolis said in a swift protest, "no. I pay you the compliment not only of believing you are sincere but in—to some small extent—understanding what you think you're trying to do. We are in—in serious need of *something* —perhaps it's God."

Nothing whatever had been said about yesterday. Stu hadn't mentioned his wife Natalie and Hank thought it might not be tactful to ask how she was. He still wasn't sure whether Stu knew what had happened, but if it lasted—then he would see.

Driving along with the empty, racing trucks, going back after leaving their loads in Chicago's vast marts, a feeling of such overpowering loneliness swept Hank Gavin that he heard himself groan aloud. The agony of it made him grip the wheel until his knuckles showed white. Where am I going? he said to himself. I can't live without Mellie, how can I, it's all very well for you, Lord, to say leave your nets, you never had a wife that was part of your very being. It says you were tempted like as we are—if you *were,* in those days of temptation you went through before you could preach the Sermon on the Mount, help me now. Who is my mother and who are my brethren? You didn't mean your own weren't yours, you meant our hearts must be wide as the sands of the sea to take in all others—

He kept talking to himself to steady himself, to keep himself from turning around and going back, back to Mellie and his job and the eighteenth hole at the Old Elm Country Club. He wondered if *Paul* had sweat it out in those years in the desert, he knew why Peter had said Who me? Never saw the Man in my life!

Pray! he said to himself. You're the one wants to show the world that prayer is answered, that God is to be known and loved and that God is able and willing to make His children to be happy. You are the one who wants to go forth and preach the good news that if we ask the Risen Christ for love every good gift and every perfect gift will come to us. What is it de Chardin says—let me remember—*the apostles of today—Even if I were not a Christian but only a man of science, or only a man of business, I think I would ask myself is not the Christian phenomenon which rises at the heart of the social phenomenon the palpable influence on our world of an other and supreme Someone?* And he was a *great* scientist but he found you, Lord, always you, at the end of all, science showed him that. So did Einstein. So did Colonel Glenn. Out out out—and there you are. Give me grace. Grace to know you, to offer myself to you, bring Mellie to see and know that she is my helpmeet for your service so that we can walk hand in hand in your power and glory. You came not to judge the world but to save the world. Save me now.

When he arrived at his destination in the late afternoon, the short stocky man who was president there looked at him a long moment and said, "So you're back. I take it you've thought it over. You still want to start obeying all those other commandments—cast out devils—cleanse the leper—raise the dead—"

This time Hank Gavin was not to be bullied.

He had paid too high a price.

"I'd like to try," he said, "and somehow I think you'd like to help me."

"I've never been more interested in my life," the little president said and came around to shake hands with him "Wife coming with you?"

"Not just now," Hank Gavin said. "Later, I hope."

So that was where I left them when I went back to California, to lock myself in and finish a book.

Often as I thought about it, and prayed about it, I

couldn't come to any real conviction about what was going to happen or how this deadlock would resolve itself.

Nor, above all things, how Hank Gavin's experiment would work out.

8

The news that their boy, that upstanding, up-and-coming, go-getting, money-making, sports-minded, about-town-business- and Yale man Hank Gavin had left them and some pretty nifty fleshpots to enter training for the *ministry* shook Chicago with incredulity, curiosity, and fever-heat excitement.

Chief among the fleshpots was his wife, Melanie Cheyne Gavin, who had been left behind in their *mansion* without a *penny*.

The blast of this reached me first through Colin Rowe's widow, Sybil.

In California on some political convention, she had dropped by to say hello, bring me messages, etc., etc., etc. Soon I realized she was there to chew over the scandal of the young Gavins, and she did it with that peculiar glee, venom, and pity which we reserve for those to whom we owe more gratitude than we can swallow—as Sybil owed Mellie Gavin.

"Of course you knew about Hank running off to the Protestant equivalent of a Trappist monastery," she said, her bright eyes taking in everything in my loggia-living room, "everyone's furious with him, so phony, doesn't it seem to you? But you have to admire the high-handed way Mellie carries it off, I suppose she thinks she can do better and she'll probably get away with it at that. I sometimes wish I had her *toujours de l'audace,* that sort of *après moi le déluge—*"

"Or *l'état C'est moi,*" I said, "I doubt if you need it."

She fumbled in a big flat pocketbook and brought out some newspaper clippings. "I thought these might amuse you," she said.

"I can read them after you're gone," I said.

The last thing that drifted back to me as Sybil said goodbye was something about Katie Ogilvie Gavin cutting her grandson off with a shilling—

One brilliant and read-by-everybody male columnist had written:

While her husband is away at what I believe is called a theological seminary, before entering the pulpit, our favorite belle, Mellie Cheyne Gavin, is allowing the town's most spectacular bachelor, Bobby Clay, Jr. to act as her escort. In these days of violence in the streets a woman so young and attractive as Mrs. Gavin can't go about alone after dark, can she? Any time Bobby is tied up on one of his previous commitments and Mellie needs a replacement I'm hers for the asking.

From a woman's point of view Maggie Daly remarked in print:

The idea that Hank Gavin is toiling over his hot books down in Phoebeville still rocks Chicago with surprise but meantime his wife, that smashing former debutante sensation Melanie Cheyne, is filling her husbandless days with good works as usual. Just been made head of the Junior League Auxiliary of the Children's Hospital. Of course there are also social activities such as the David Kenyons' elegant party for the Windsors. Now that she's a temporary grass widow, the same line forms to the right and though the favorite of the moment seems to be an adroit and eligible young man, there's an older beau whom Mellie jettisoned when she met Hank Gavin who certainly has a gleam in his eye.

Only the none-too-oblique reference to David Kenyon bothered me. At a dinner where Bobby Clay and I had been the only unattached people, he had seen me home. I found him gay, well-informed, and cheerfully cynical, but I felt rather sure of the reason why he had always been able to resist feminine wiles. A revival of the David Kenyon affair would be different. Hurt, perhaps where she sat feeling herself disillusioned, now more experienced—harder maybe—a little older, this might offer a rich full life of triumph—and of course disaster, but who ever foresees that?

All this I tried to tell Mellie's mother when she phoned me in a state of vague violence. "Call her, darling," she said, "I'm sure Hank will get over this. I mean Al Patton drove down to see him and try and reason with him you know and he says the place is a barracks and the headmaster a perfect ruffian. If Mellie will just be patient—of course if he insists on going on with this—I mean it's quite mad, isn't it?—Mellie will have lots of other chances though as you say she ought to be careful not to make a—not to get into a scandal—still second marriages, don't you think? The oddest thing—

Francis—her father—I can't make out what's gotten into him. For the first time in her life he raised his voice to her the other night, all about *whither thou goest* which Mellie told him wasn't about a wife going after her husband at all, actually, it was a daughter-in-law after her mother-in-law or a mother-in-law—either sounds most *improbable,* don't you feel? Ruth her name was. Anyway, Francis said she was behaving very badly—Melanie, I mean, *not* Ruth—she should go with her husband who had perhaps been called to do a great work—which is all very well for *Francis* but actually doesn't pay the rent, does it darling?"

"Is Mellie in real difficulty about the rent?" I said, for having spent half my life in this predicament I knew well how it can influence decisions and even morality.

"Well, darling, not *yet,*" Vadne said, "but it's all most unsatisfactory. Hank *arranged* everything but of course she can't live on the income and when the capital runs out which it always *does,* doesn't it, I mean if you live on it, no matter how spiritual, Francis—he isn't really in a position to be practical—I wish you'd talk to her."

"About what?" I said.

"For one thing even nowadays it never does a girl any good to get talked about I was saying to Marianne LeMastre only the other day about Biddy—you remember Biddy she's only seventeen—ought not to go up to the lake without a chaperon—but really I'm quite sure if Mellie put some pressure on Hank, things were all so nice weren't they?" After a longer pause than usual, Melanie's mother said, "Or would it be better if you called *Hank?* Get him to come home. The bishop thinks he ought to, he says it seldom works unless they catch them very young—or anyway that was what he *meant*—an older man—"

"I assume the bishop thinks Jesus should have left Matthew in the income tax office," I said.

"But darling," Vadne said, "That was *Jesus.* Al Patton says the president looks like Papa Halas of the Bears—or is it the Cubs? But you wouldn't need to see *him.* And tell Hank I'm sure the bishop would give him a *civilian* job in the church here—"

Whether by coincidence or conspiracy, I also had a call from Al Patton, whom I had expected to be on the side of the angels, which I am sure he *was,* only it turned out he expected the angels to take advantage of Al Patton's wisdom and experience the same way his clients did. He said, "You know I'm all for religion. It's a fine thing. Man's always better with it than without it. On the other hand there's no use a man becoming a religious fanatic."

I said if Hank Gavin was a religious fanatic what this country needed was more religious fanatics and that if St. Francis appeared around here somebody would file a suit to have him declared incompetent and unfit to handle his own dough, and with frost all over it Al said, "This is the twentieth century and no one is talking about *saints*" and I said even the bishop knows that without a few around in any century the church is nothing but a hollow shell. He said, "The boy ought to come home and so I told him."

After some thought, I called Mellie.

Partly out of curiosity, which is the sparkplug of all writers, partly concern. She said she was dressing to go out, she sounded gay and cocky, she rattled on about the horse show in which she had ridden a jumper for Joe Haki. A clear picture of her in the severe black habit, white stock, high hat receiving the blue ribbon came to me. "It was *spiffy*," she said, "and Joe was obnoxious, strutting around like Bathouse John or somebody." The hospital, she said, was planning a new wing, the Kenyons had asked her to go to Phoenix but she rather thought she'd go to Italy and Spain with the Spencers. For the first time her voice broke as she said, "Some place without any memories." Then she said, "Do you hear from him?" I said no, and she said, pleased, and not pleased, "I think he only writes—he doesn't write to anyone but me. But I thought you might know—he writes me every day."

Only one of those letters survived a fit of fury in which Mellie threw them into the fire. The day she knew Hank was flying to Washington to meet the chaplain for an hour. That one she found in a book and while nothing infuriates me as much as letters that have been *burned* and thus destroyed pages of history or a missing piece in a story, I was grateful for it when she gave it to me.

Long and heartfelt rather than intelligent, it was scrawled on sheets of yellow legal note paper with a spluttery pen. It said:

My beloved wife—

I thought I knew how much I love you when we were together. Now we are apart, I've really found out, for I can never believe you aren't there when I wake up in the morning and when I know it at first the day doesn't seem worth living through. Interrupted only by a massive effort on Biblical Literature under a prof named Smithson, I've put in 12 hours on a chart I'm trying to work out. Simple garden-variety chart, if I had crayons I'd use them. How to make this work! The instructions, commandments, all in the same kind of straight navigation chart that shows you how to get from here to Istanbul or Tokyo or Dallas. I came on Peter's wife while I was about it. At first it did what the word wife always does to me, made me think of you. Then I got to thinking about *her*. Peter's wife, I mean. You're always so wonderful about imagining things, remember that winter we read Shakespeare? I wish you'd think about Peter's wife. There's not a clue, we haven't even got a jawbone to reconstruct from. All we know is that she existed and had a mother who lived with them. One night—right after he had preached the Sermon on the Mount, which the New York Times magazine—I found the piece in the library—says is probably the greatest single event in all history—Our Lord went to Peter's house to dinner. It says he saw Peter's wife's mother in bed with a fever or a virus and he touched her hand and the fever left her and she got up and ministered unto them. I don't know whether there were a lot of them packed into that small house or whether his mother-in-law always did the cooking, but when I tried to *be* there, which I have to do, with the big fisherman and his wife and his mother-in-law right after he had healed the centurion's servant, it was somehow—an adventure. Did I ever tell you what a gift you have for turning a simple little thing into an adventure? I've seen you do it so many times—with the nurses at the hospital, or the kids out at the ball park, or a little present for my secretary or going to call on Rudy Bergdorf's mother out at the Edgewater Beach Hotel! It is one of great blessings and more and more priceless because I am unearthing that one of the things the matter with so many is *boredom*. It could even be our most deadly enemy. We put up with all kinds of claptrap and get sold all kinds of tinsel because since we've given up prayer and an inner life which will always keep you from being *bored*, we grasp at any straw to escape its suffocation. Anyhow I kept wishing you were here—when don't I—to help me. Do you remember how Lloyd Douglas described Peter in *The Robe?* And Taylor Caldwell in *Dear and Glorious Physician?* They made me understand what it means when the Holy Spirit takes over a guy who isn't at all what religious people think is the right kind of a guy for the Holy Spirit to take over. So I thought Peter's wife must be the kind of a girl who would marry a man like Peter. Must have a twinkle, must have a sense of humor. Maybe before the night when the Man from

Nazareth came to dinner, she'd said, "Look, Pete, you've got a pretty good business going for you here, good boat, good crew, good customers, why don't you settle down and stick to it for once? You can go to the temple oftener if you want to, but you start running around with people like *Judas Iscariot* that you know is one of that underground gang of Barabbas's, you'll end in jail. You're a fisherman and a good one and we're doing all right, we never had it so good, why do you want to go off somewhere and how do you *know* you should?" But maybe after the young man came to dinner at their house, when Peter was gone, leaving his nets and his boat and her, maybe she and her mother whispered together, "When he just touched my hand right away I felt better—when he spoke my heart burned within me—was there a light around him?—suppose he should be the One sent from God."

Oh Mellie, little love, that's adventure. We can still follow him, don't you see he couldn't have meant it just for the few who saw him in person, that would have been cruel. No no. Come with me Mellie. How can you, of all people, resist it? He'll give us the courage we need. If he tells us to climb a hill we won't notice it's a hill if he is with us. If someone is in terrible trouble we won't have to depend on ourselves when even our best isn't good enough. In his name, we work by his power and only for his glory. Can't you see how exciting it will be? This is the great adventure, far beyond outer space, inner space is the one place you can never be bored or have to keep going around and around, chasing leprechauns and poltergeists. I promise you this, I your adoring husband.

An aspect of tactlessness suggested itself, this stress Hank laid on Peter and his wife and his mother-in-law, since the controversy, if that's not too mild a word, between him and Mellie had to do with Hank's determination to do in the 1960s what Peter had done in A.D. 30-something. Yet I got the impact that it was no use ducking any of it any longer, his one idea was to bring her his way, make her partner to his adventurous future.

I read this letter much later, of course, not at the time when Hank was at the seminary in Phoebeville and Mellie was in Chicago holding onto a way of life she had married, though the man had changed his course. But since it was written by him and read by her at that time I put it in here.

And at that same time, in spite of the barrage shoving me to call Hank, I felt too much reluctance. A man fighting for his spiritual faith had a right to go away into his own desert and there learn what it would be like to join the ranks of the apostles, under the discipline and in obedience to the instruction—the *plea—if ye love me, keep my commandments*. All of them.

Moreover, he knew where I was, I kept reminding myself that you can help the young only if they come to you. Your desire to rush forth into the highways and byways shouting Hey, kids, don't go thataway, I've been *there,* and there are hammerheads and goblins, this has to be controlled, they *want* to see the hammerheads and goblins for *themselves.* If it had been possible to communicate spiritual light and red flags against evil from one generation to another, by now we'd have been some place more worthwhile than the *moon.*

The decision about Hank over which I was pondering was taken out of my hands by a letter from him.

It needed three airmail stamps, so I hoped it would contain some of the whats and hows of his months at the seminary and, since he knew he had my sympathy, maybe some problems he wouldn't admit to the opposition. I felt a good deal of suspense as I unsealed the envelope, out in the patio where I could hear the waves thundering in from the wide Pacific, and drew out some leaves from a ruled notebook, closely covered with bad typewriting.

Dear Godmama-in-law,

I've got some big news for you. Biggest thing that ever happened to me. But first let me tell you if I'd had any idea how tough it was going to be, I'm not sure I'd have tackled it. Maybe the one thing I had to recommend me was that I'm tough and I can see now why sometimes Our Lord picks men who've proved they're tough-fibered, tough in stamina. This is a tough proposition right now—I suppose it always was. I read somewhere the other day that this is no voyage for a frail and timid bark. You have to believe what the Lord said to Gideon, "Have I not sent you?" If I didn't honestly believe that I would have cut my throat.

Several reasons I haven't written before.

I write Mellie every day, for one thing.

Naturally, I've had word from those friends who think I ought to know. All right, I'm jealous, green-eyed with it, ignoble as I know that trait which robbed Othello of his wits to be. Yet mine isn't the most ignoble kind. I'm jealous that she is with others and not with me when I miss and need her so much. That they have her strength and sparkle and truth, though I'm the first to grant she has a right to follow truth as *she* sees it, not as *I* see it. As for the dark hints in the press, they don't know how fastidious my Mellie is. More than that, she has her own code, she says it has nothing to do with God, I know it's there for a man to stake his life on, or most of the time I do. Sometimes at night when I'm so tired my teeth ache—but most of the time I do.

There are times when even that kingdom of heaven *within me* has been lonesome without her. Yet deep down inside me where *I* live, I know I can go on even if I have to do it alone. Or—do I? Yes, because I am never *alone*—or I don't have to be. If I'll listen instead of clacking with my tongue and mind until I'm deaf. Nobody knows what happened in those 40 days when *he* was tempted like as we are, so I think he must understand how I feel, there are so many of us who seek comfort from, that he must understand, don't you think? So—I write her every day and pray either that she will come to me or that I shall be able to go on without her though as of now the mere thought turns my marrow-bones to jelly.

Another factor of the modern bugaboo of not-time-enough is that I'm so anxious to get out of here and into active pastoral work that I've set myself a schedule which the *pres*—a nice gent who feels it necessary to be skeptical about me and thinks he may awaken any morning to find I've flew the coop, but is nevertheless rooting for me—anyhow he says my schedule is impossible.

A lot of things could be skipped. The first thing he suggests is Aramaic, but that's one I wouldn't give up. It was Jesus' own language. Sometimes there is a word or two that shines like a beacon light.

Don't misunderstand me. A lot they teach here which at first glance seems unrelated and pointless is invaluable, indispensable. The boys—they are mostly boys—need it for many and varied reasons. By the way, there is among them—here and at all the schools I visited a sameness of type. Help me, Lord, not to *judge* but I must face facts and recognize present needs. They are all a little *pallid*. However—they have a big job to do, they must have *rank,* as it were, when they go forth to battle for souls of men. I've gotten over some of my hostility. I do see that in an age when you can't get a job running an elevator without a college degree, ministers must not appear as ignoramuses in a world where education is glorified as the answer to all problems. They mustn't present a raw unschooled aspect which makes others think they could have been sold a bill of goods about a myth called Christianity. I'm also increasingly sure that you can't have Christianity without Christ.

I've read a good deal about this. A man named Charles L. Taylor, head of something, makes more sense than anyone else I've found. He wonders if it must always be the "other fellow" knowing and doing, not the minister of Christ. "Who will enter understandingly into the forces and passion that account for the rising nationalism and the emancipation of the nonwhite races? Who will study the exploding population, the urbanization, the results of automation, the feeding of new multitudes, gerontology or the uses of leisure? Are these the business only of the layman? Granted that they all will require technical experts, how can ministers deal creatively with these and many other problems with which they will be confronted? Only if their education has given these ministers such awareness and insight that they are on the way to become lifelong students of the Word of God in these difficult places where men live. Are these Christ's business? Clearly so, and if his, then his ministers'."

Well of course all times are difficult, if anybody thinks times were easy and tranquil in Jerusalem in the days of the Man of Galilee they have another think coming.

Mr. Taylor speaks, too, of the tools to be used, he wants to know if an ill-prepared ministry will be adequate for a modern congregation. Yet as he points out —and I've been thinking a lot about this—it might be easier to organize and impress a thousand people than to save or heal one. Activity at any level sometimes covers a lot of emptiness.

Prepared? For what? Ill-prepared? By whom?

Paul was a highly educated, cultured man. So was Luke. But Peter wasn't. Nor Mark. Times were different —were they really? War and peace and human relations seem much the same. Places? If we knew Thessalonica the way they knew Thessalonica—I betcha it had a South Side and a North Side and all the boys and girls in between.

Godmama, you and I know you can wire a house

with all the knowledge and workmanship and material of the head of the Electricians' Union. You can buy the finest lamps, infrared, diffused, spot, and chandeliers. If you haven't got the electric current much good it will do you. You won't have any *light.* You can have the latest in dishwashers and electric toothbrushes and submarines in the depths of the sea and capsules for the farthest star and if you haven't electric power you ain't going anyplace a-tall. You can have the newest color television set and all the best tubes and biggest screens and if you aren't hooked up to the power you won't see any more than it will do you to know *all* about urbanization and automation and gerontology and population explosions unless you know how to get to God.

The light is the light is the light! And just as Sir James Jeans says all the big boys in the sciences have actually got no farther than the first chapter of Genesis where it says And God said *let there be light* . . .

In a final paragraph I must say for Mr. Taylor he comes to that, too, and that's why I liked him better than most. He says, "Who is able to be a worthy minister of Christ? Nobody, no, not one. But the Lord's command does not return to him empty. It accomplishes that which he purposes and prospers in the thing for which he issued it." This means I must be a doer of the Word not a talker only and it ain't easy.

While I am here I am trying to be obedient to what is required. We must work within the framework set up on the rock of his church where it seems he set it. The pres agrees it's not sensible to waste time, we haven't got too much. Termites are eating away the foundations. We've got to come out of this mushy, fuzzy, flabby thinking, this smirking theory that if we compromise with evil, everything will stay a-okay. If as a man or a nation you get far enough away from God—you are in outer darkness and I don't care whether that's too strong language or not. This wishy-washy milktoast crap isn't getting us anywhere. Boredom is corroding as leprosy is setting in. Yet I know that those who sit in darkness can see a great light if they will turn their faces toward it. I wish I could make them see it. I love 'em all.

Anyhow, the pres and faculty are finally—they weren't at first—impressed by Yale and the courses in comparative religion and philosophy that Colin and I took. I've been through a war as an officer commanding combat troops. I've had 10 years experience in organization and business. As a salesman I have a glimmer of psychology, so I don't have to take Psych 1. Just 2, so I can converse with any of my parishioners (I know, it sounds incredible, doesn't it? Me with parishioners) in that language and while I'm inclined to regard Freud as the anti-Christ of this century maybe he is only Pandora, and I've got to welcome all additional means of communication.

So here I am, even so, a freshman back in school and it's not much like Yale. The old buildings are brick, they stopped watering the ivy because it's destructive, thus they look rather like state institutions for the criminally insane. The new ones resemble what I made with my Erector Sets when I was a kid, except they're glass and why they want so many windows through which to look at this dust bowl I do not know.

As for the folks, they are folks.

I know now, there is no way we are ever going to achieve the brotherhood of man until we begin with the fatherhood of God. I wonder if the Commies know that at the end of his life Karl Marx went to church every Sunday.

There have been days, don't think there haven't, when I've looked at that fellow in the mirror and said to him, Gavin, you smug so-and-so, you look pretty self-righteous to me. Who do you think you are buddy? Then I remember who I am. I am the prodigal son and if you'll reread that bit you'll see that the father wouldn't even listen to the son's self-condemnation and breast-beating, he just welcomed him home. I must discuss that concept of God with my grandmother some day. Do you think it's wrong that for Mellie's sake I kind of hope Katie, instead of supporting a missionary to the Fiji Islands, might consider a little bit of support for a hard-working young minister to the ill-fated and lost right at home?

I remember that of my own self I must admit at once that I can do nothing but that he will always be with me. Then I quit letting any phony inferiority separate me from him.

(I'm coming to my big news in a couple of paragraphs now. I think I'm holding back the way I always did with my *big present* on my birthday.)

But I want to make my point first about false modesty. I go back to Acts. You remember when Paul healed the cripple-from-his-mother's-womb at Lystra and the people *saw* it. So they started yelling that the gods had come down to them in the likeness of men, they brought garlands and oxen to sacrifice to *Paul.* When Paul heard them he—it says this in *Acts*, did you know the whole *Book of Acts* is just that, the acts Peter and John and Paul and Barnabas and other followers of Jesus did in his name after he was gone? I only just realized this —*anyhow* Paul ran among the people crying out to them. We also are men who have the same passions that you do, and preach unto you that you should turn from these vanities unto the living God which made heaven and earth and the sea and all things therein. Well, I faced up to it then, that it is the *living* God and the Holy Spirit that doeth the works, and *not* Hank Gavin, and I got back on the track.

Once I was at the very bottom—*I tell you*—ready to turn back and not follow him any more—I thought I'd settle for being head vestryman and I got a phone call from the chaplain.

He must have extrasensory perception or whatever they call it about me, that guy. When I am going down for the third time, he *knows* it, he stretches out a hand and says all right, buddy, take it easy, you can't walk on the water yet, it seems, but I am not mad at you as long as you're trying, here's my hand, I'll help you into the boat.

The chaplain says my angel tells his angel.

That time, he was in Washington, and he was in a hurry.

When I got through explaining my troubles, he said, "All right, let's keep our seats a minute, I've got a little thinking to do." He was quiet so long the operator cut in and he told her it was *all right*, we were *thinking* which I suppose people almost never do over a telephone, and then he said to me, "Listen carefully. You have now *read* some of the New Testament. I suppose we might say you have studied it. But of course the whole Bible as far as especially the Gospels and Acts are a *life's work*. As you grow, it grows—it's a million different books—deep and deeper the way *you* can read.

"What's going on with you isn't the worst that can happen. It's a bit of arid climbing. It might lead to something great and grand for you.

"Do your best to read the Gospels and the Acts as though you had never read them before in all your life or even—if you can manage it—*ever heard* of them. You told me once that at Yale they really taught you how to read Shakespeare, as though it was all new. They say sometimes an actor like Olivier will make you believe no one ever played him before. As a matter of fact, this is what changed my whole life, buddy. It'll do it for you, too."

After he hung up, I thought about this some myself. When it was the *letters*, I had done it by mailing them to myself—that made them new and real somehow.

To read the Gospels and Acts as though they were *new*, not all chopped up into bits and pieces, well, at first I was sure this took more mental control than I had. Then I thought maybe it *wasn't* mental control—maybe it was imagination and fair play and free-wheeling thinking.

You can see I had to try, can't you?

I started trying to figure the—the new approach. First thing I had to have was a brand new Bible. So I went down to the book store—we only had one in Phoebeville—and wandered in and began looking around at other *books* and then I found the Bibles on a back shelf, a lot of them hidden in boxes. The first one I opened had all those pronunciation marks which I felt would stop a man cold reading it for the first time. He wouldn't have any idea of reading it *out loud* or pronouncing it yet a while—they made the book look different from the ones you *want* to read—then some had such thin paper your hands would make you self-conscious. Took me a while to find one that was just a good book to *read*, it turned out to be very expensive—but this was what I had to have if I was reading it for the first time—I'd never have turned page 2 in those others. I knew that.

My room is small, it had a bed and table and two chairs, and I bought me a desk. I sat down in the most comfortable of the two chairs, which isn't saying much. Then I put every bit of—of strength and anticipation and control I had into making my mind a *blank*. I'd done this before a few times—I did it halfway before exams and later on stock issues and things like that—now I tried to go a long way beyond that. I wanted to drain my mind so there was no—no memory, I guess you'd say it, no preconceived notions, no one else's opinions or conclusions. Each quote and every scene had to go. I wanted to be like the men who took their lives in their hands to *read* it—*for the first time* because all they'd been told was that it was the *Book of Life.*

I knew as well as you do that this is next to impossible, but I did the best I could. After all, the impossible always gets done like landing on the moon. I remembered what I'd been told about Marconi, when he made the wireless work for the first time he was too young and ignorant to know all the reasons why it wouldn't. The older and more famous scientists were working to *overcome* the resistance but Marconi just opened up his mind and found there wasn't any.

I tried to feel there wasn't any resistance to making my mind a blank and reading this book I had in my hand there at my secondhand desk in that funny little room.

The chaplain hadn't mentioned whether to read straight through or to stop if something grabbed me or puzzled me—so I thought the best thing to do was to be natural and do what I would do if this *was* the first time and what that was to be I couldn't possibly know.

It took me 3 days and nights—with a few catnaps—and the funny thing was I didn't get sleepy or tired. Read that way this was a book *really* kept you up all night. I honest-to-God (I didn't mean that as a religious pun) I couldn't wait to find out what happened, Ian Fleming never wrote a greater thriller and suspense story if you just wanted to take it that way and didn't know what happened next. We forget this because we are too familiar with it and we are always hearing bits and pieces and interruptions.

As I read I did what I always do when I read a book the first time—I made some notes—things I wanted to go back and reread—points I didn't understand—things that really got me. I didn't get the tares and the wheat story at all. And I was sore as a scalded cat over the man who could come in at the last minute after I'd borne the burden and the heat of the day and get the same wages. A lot of questions.

What got me really—two things—

The leading character. Jesus Christ himself.

And I came out with my private notion that this was a scientific theory subject to study and confirmed proof.

$E=mc^2$

The formula for the Einstein theory.

So—I didn't have my formula and I still don't have—but it's there somewhere. The power of God plus man's tuning in by prayer equals the kingdom of heaven on earth—within me—I know, that's pretty corny—but I was—and am—trying.

I knew I had all the instructions because it was plain to me now that this man Jesus *was* the greatest teacher who ever lived, whatever else he was. Explicit, at many levels, simple for the child, deep for the scholar.

It quite literally bowled me over. It wasn't a book, it was an experience.

One thing I knew for sure. What I was supposed to do.

I was supposed to chart this out, list all the instructions and explanations and commands, and then go find me a Kitty Hawk somewhere and see if this damn thing would FLY. I wasn't supposed to be responsible for the whole future of aviation. I didn't have to meet all the problems of landing fields and jet engines that would perhaps come in time. I just had to go and in my own way DO what it said and see the results. Why this was so important I didn't—and don't—know yet. The times are in his hands. But I saw my strait and narrow way all right. And all ways that lead anywhere are strait and narrow. Try monkeying with the 2×2 table and see where you get in higher mathematics. Or mix red and purple paint to get blue and see what comes of it.

About this time seeing I hadn't been to class or meals or around, the pres sent for me and—I told him what I'd been doing and I thought he'd laugh at me. He didn't. He said it was quite an idea. The yogis had to go into a trance for full concentration and meditation and how did I do? I said it wasn't supposed to be that kind of concentration—just that I'd never read the book before and that just about the time Judas was selling out I went off for 20 minutes wondering if as far as I was concerned the White Sox would ever be the White Sox without Nellie Fox and deciding it was because he wasn't there they'd lost those 10 straight games to the Yankees, Nellie was the guts of that ball club, he wasn't afraid of anybody—but I found if I didn't get sweaty about it I could always get back to Judas—and one of the things that troubled me, which was why Jesus didn't *heal* him, of his treachery and greed. I'm still *on* that one.

That reminds me, I don't know anybody else to ask or I wouldn't trouble you. Only of course busy people are the only ones who ever *do* anything for you. Could you find out anything about Natalie Margolis? This has a point for me. Nobody has ever mentioned her, not Stu the day I resigned, nor my father-in-law from whom I hear sometimes. Mellie just ignores it. Did it *take*? You know what I mean. Has she—stayed sober?

I don't call Mellie often. Can't afford it for one thing—and hearing her voice wrecks me for two days. Probably just as well she didn't come down here. I wouldn't be doing 19 hours of work a day with her here. When I get an assistant to an assistant or an assistant in a real small church or some one nobody wants—then we can start together.

Two final things came out of my adventure with the Gospels and the Acts.

Not final—except as things that are vital.

I *know*—I *know*—Jesus didn't intend the power of God as a redeeming and helping and healing Presence just for a few followers in a small country in a period of 3 years. I *know* this. If he had, it would have stayed there.

I know that if we end the story of Jesus Christ with the crucifixion, we are lost. But isn't that what we have been doing? Much of this I still have to work out, but I *know* we live in His redeemed world; with the Risen Christ as our companion and comforter whenever we turn to him. That his second coming happens daily, hourly, to each of us. If we begin with a grain of faith in this theory—this idea—this hope—then everyone who comes, whether it's a child or a tormented adult, whether it's a whole churchful of dark, despairing souls or just one in grief or pain, whether it's a nation sitting in darkness or committed to gog or magog I can help them through him. It's my job to make his unseen glory of good into a present reality of daily living.

Pray for me. Temptation hits at all levels, the Achilles heel is always with us.

This is the longest letter I or probably anyone else ever wrote but without letters where would we be? Letters have carried the torch through the centuries, and while I don't expect mine have any historic importance it has helped me to set down my thoughts as clearly as I can so that you might understand. For now, having read the gospels for the first time I am more than ever sure that I want to sign myself

Yours in Christ,

Hank

At the end I was in tears. Sometimes the frustration, the dust, the loneliness—always there are lonely places on this road—came off the page. Mostly they were tears of joy because he was walking this road, the road to Emmaus, and the words of the Christ, who will always walk that road with you if you care to go burned within him. I thought it was an amazing thing to see, and always after some cogitation I sent the letter on to Mellie which of course I had no right to do without Hank's consent, but I was willing to commit this small breach of privacy in the hope that it would move her as it had moved me. If it did, I heard nothing of it, she didn't even acknowledge it. Also, I wrote to Al Patton, asking by-the-way whatever became of Natalie Margolis.

Some months passed while I was submerged in work and unfit for human companionship when I surfaced. At the time I had a family problem of my own and even my beloved goddaughter seemed far away.

Besides, apparently all was status quo.

Then as apparently the laws of drama decree, everything began to burst out all over.

First of all, Hank's grandmother, Katie Ogilvie Gavin, died in her sleep and left a most extraordinary will.

9

Sitting in the heavenly light from the stained-glass windows, watching the frail, ethereal bishop and his surpliced attendants moving through rituals, listening to the majestic music to which Katie was supposedly crossing the bar, I felt she must be satisfied with HER FINAL EXIT. She was still playing to the most exclusive audience in Chicago and to standing room only. Long gone, I felt sure, from the bronze box—what box could hold Katie?—I wondered what she'd find it like to be where she hadn't been able to take it with her. Disconcerting, to say the least.

Afterward when we gathered at the home of her grandson Hank and his wife Melanie, Katie's memory slipped back into her formula *always leave them laughing*. When anyone as old as Katie dies, there is no passionate grief or sense of loss, why should there be? At that age, no one comes first with anyone, and while you can win track meets with enough points for second and third, the cheers are few. Soon people were exchanging Katie witticism, everyone roaring with posthumous appreciation, and agreeing that Chicago wouldn't be the same without her and they didn't come like that any more.

None of us knew that her distinguished once president of the Bar Association lawyer, John Winchester Martin, had her last joke up his sleeve.

Soon I became aware that Mr. Martin was part of the snow job my goddaughter Mellie was putting on for her husband.

Young Hank Gavin's house was at its best, one of the most all-around lovable, elegant, but with places to put up your feet homes for a young married couple ever conceived. Now it wore enough flowers to give your heart and eyes and nose the joy of a summertime garden. Wedgwood bowls of peonies, slim cut crystal vases holding sheafs of aratum lilies, on the dining room table a mirror piled with grapes black, purple, Tokay red and Nile green surrounded by stacks of Royal Worchester plates and family Georgian silver. Polished, shining, yet the rooms were lived in, the chairs to sit in, the maps to see by. These things represented the beauty and comfort which, with taste, money can buy. But no one would think of that; the house had that special charm of things that grow, Mellie's habitation and background as the oakwood of a deer, the sea of a racing yacht, your memory of it would call you back, or hope some day to be able to have one like it.

Curiosity was rife, had to be. Those two had been separated, the word divorce had been spoken, printed. Yet now it was apparent that the voice of the turtle was heard in the land. Mellie was still Mellie, wearing a small, qualified smile, a chic black dress that was mourning yet managed to suggest that her husband was now The Gavin, head of the Clan. Her proper sadness for Katie was hardly able to conceal her joy, and I noticed that her eyes, her feet followed her husband, her hand kept finding his arm, his shoulder, once—a butterfly touch since she disliked exhibitions of affection in public—his cheek. Between them passed their own vocabulary, glances meeting across a crowded room, gestures possible only to lovers.

Hard to associate her, this Mellie with the ill-fated and the lost. Yet young Mrs. Gavin had spent much of her life working with and for the poor, hungry, delinquent, and helpless. Unbidden, I asked myself whether they were any more real to her than the bleeding, blistered feet had been to those of us who knit socks for them to wear at Cemetery Ridge or the Argonne or the Battle of the Bulge. With her kindness and gift with people and willingness to work for them, did she *believe* that they hurt as she was hurt by disappointments, discouragements, and delays? When in nurse's aid uniform, tending with gentle hands, did she feel the same blood bled or that they needed as warm coats in winter or as cool seaside breezes in summer or would die the same death of the same diseases? Of course they had hands, organs, dimensions, senses, affections, passion—*but not like mine!* I didn't know the answers but as I watched her I realized how much I loved my goddaughter and how nice it was to see her happy once more.

So often we had seen the young Gavins as they were now. Though no one could help remarking the change in Hank.

Francis Cheyne, who had spoken harshly to his beloved child because she hadn't followed her husband whithersoever, or so his wife Vadne had told me, spoke to me quietly—he was a quiet man—of this. The Yale accent has not received so wide a press as the Harvard, but it is notable. In it, Mellie's father said, "Does recklessness and rebellion always give dash and swagger as it has to my son-in-law? Or is that impression because he is too thin?"

Just then across the hall I saw Hank talking to Natalie Margolis. It had taken, all right. Frankly middle-aged, she was dressing with style becoming to this, but her eyes were serene, her hands tranquil, I saw she had that kind of sobriety having a glow which comes *only* to those who *know* they have experienced answered prayer. Over her shoulder Hank made the sign of thumb and forefinger in a circle, and I felt that this happening here and now was important. As above all things was the moment at the gate of the temple when the cripple walked and leaped at the word of Jesus' disciples.

Hank could hold onto this answered prayer as the morning star.

It was proof that compassion opened the soul to a love which could continue even to our neighbors.

Vadne first put into words for me the obvious fact that Katie's death was bound to make a difference. A big difference, Mellie's mother said. "After all," she said, sipping champagne with a cream-and-cat expression, "I was fond of Katie but I'm sure she'd be the last to be mealymouthed about such things. She was really rich, it turns out. She had things sewed up in mattresses, hidden in flour sacks, you know what I mean."

I knew. "What do you think will happen now?" I said.

"I rather imagine," Vadne said—we were again in a corner, Vadne's preferred tête-à-tête to group conversation—"that Hank will come home and *behave* himself. I hear—not that John Martin would tell anything—that Katie left a sum earmarked to buy Hank a full partnership. If he's still *obsessed* they could at least live as Mellie has been accustomed to live and find an attractive pulpit. Francis doesn't agree with me. You know Mellie was talking about selling this house—she couldn't keep it up—"

Plainly, it was impossible for her mother to imagine any other kind of life for Melanie; I found it was also difficult for me.

"Practically speaking, darling," Vadne said, holding her glass up to the trim maid for a refill, "Melanie wasn't brought up to wash dishes."

"Lots of us weren't," I said, "but some of us had to learn."

"We *had* to," Vadne agreed. "Melanie doesn't, especially now that Katie—we knew she was rich, of course, but not *really* rich—"

"Mellie's a wonderful cook," I said disagreeably.

"It's not quite the same, is it?" Vadne said. "Showing off

with French dishes and Oriental curries with someone else to prepare and clean up."

"All the packages and cans and frozen foods and TV dinners," I said, "young people get by."

"It's being accustomed to manage everything at once," Vadne said, "and beds to make every day and Mellie thinks an *unmade bed*—"

"As a nurse's aid," I said, "she must have learned to make a bed."

"Oh—once in a while," Vadne said airily, "not every *single* day. The girls dramatize everything especially after we got them those Dior uniforms. Weren't they enchanting? But Mellie wasn't brought up to do her own *work!*"

"The great ladies of the South came to it," I said.

"Yes darling but there'd been a war and don't tell me they *liked* it," Vadne said, "or if a grandmother had left them a fortune—"

I said I saw her point.

There was something wrong with it.

Not for a moment could I believe that really rich or not Hank would give up his goal. He'd been called, whether to the back of an ass's colt or a helicopter, to find out whether it could be made to work by careful obedience, of the quality given any other theory, whether his truth was true or something we'd swallowed from habit and from such respectable sources that the original words and meaning had been obscured.

To me there could be no true reason why a rich young man must be barred from preaching the truth. As a penance for his years of waste and self-indulgence St. Francis had dedicated himself to poverty. But I had to be sure that in his I'm-reading-this-for-the-first-time examination of the Red Letter Testament Hank Gavin had found nothing that made an *ideal* of poverty and want and cold and ugliness and hunger. Jesus had, to be sure, said that it was hard for the rich, who could obtain so many of this world's good things, but he went on to explain in the next sentence that it is they who *trust* in riches who shall find it hard to enter the kingdom of God. Jesus himself had worn a robe that the Roman soldiers found worth a dice game, and when he said the Son of Man had not where to lay his head he was almost certainly speaking politically and theologically. For physically, he had plenty of places, rich and poor, Judaic and Roman, outdoors and in, where those who loved him desired him to lay his head. Moreover he knew and said that in his Father's house were many *mansions,* not just huts, either, nor shacks nor tenements, nor cold bare floors—*mansions.*

I didn't want Hank and Mellie to be poor. I am not a believer in nor advocate of poverty myself, I think it embitters and warps and is as dangerous to a man's soul as riches.

Yet I felt a shaky reluctance at the idea of seeing Hank and Mellie enter the church as *really rich* young people. It diminished them. I recalled not too accurately a story, in *Judges,* I thought, where the Lord said to Gideon that if he depended on manpower, Israel would sooner or later *vaunt* themselves against him, saying it was by their own brains and might they had conquered the Midianites. Gideon must know that this was a triumph which could never last. The billing must read *The Sword of the Lord*—and of Gideon. I couldn't help but feel that if the young Gavins came into the church with Katie's vast fortune behind them, the billing would be Hank and Mellie and Katie Ogilvie's money—and the sword of the Lord and that would never last as we now know.

Earlier, before the funeral, Hank had told me he'd be through school the following week. Two years' work in one, his Yale degree and experience in business, were going to let him finish in the field, serve his interneship as assistant to the pastor of a church in a California beach city. Now, observing the organized temptation Mellie was promoting, watching her spread before him all the kingdoms of the earth and the glory thereof, seeing Stu Margolis discuss with him a challenging management problem as though Hank were already a partner, hearing his shout of laughter as Al Patton told a golf anecdote, I began to doubt whether he could remain as sure of what comes first as a man would have to be to turn his back on all this, and take to a disorganized church in a California beach town, which could well be an anteroom of hell.

Somehow, it wasn't going to be the same if he and Mellie took the golden calf with them and set it up at a villa on Lido Isle with a yacht standing off the Newport Yacht club nearby.

Just then Mellie took my arm and swept me into the downstairs cloak-and-dressing room, it smelled of spices and lemon verbena, she shut the door and said, "Mr. John Winchester Martin is going to read the will in his office tomorrow, do come with me, sweetie."

I said I had to take an early plane to New York. Mellie, staring at herself in the full-length mirror, holding her hand flat on top of her head though whether to hold down her hair or her conspiracy I couldn't tell, her eyes were enormous, she said, "Do you think it's respectful to Katie's memory to go off without hearing her will?" My father had an old-fashioned word—bamboozle. People would try it, he said, and some of them could. Mellie said, "How can you resist the reading of a last will? In this case it's routine, but for some reason, darling, Mr. Martin is making a production of it. He's very distinguished but he is also rather stuffed, isn't he? I can't take Mama, you know how she pops out with things, and right at the moment my father thinks I'm Delilah because I won't buy something you two saw at the Patton party, about Natalie Margolis. We have our own lawyer I think, but I wish you'd rally round. We're to meet in Mr. Martin's office at eleven, then I'll buy your lunch and take you to the airport in time for an afternoon flight."

It bothered me that she was so nervous about this routine matter, so I said all right.

I can tell you that I never got any lunch and missed several afternoon planes.

There is no way to make the reading of a will unique in setting, language, or procedure. A will is a will, and provides its drama by the content thereof. The offices of Martin, Dorander, Isaacs, and Smith were a status symbol, when we were ushered to the innermost sanctum we found it unchanged since Joseph Medill founded the Chicago *Tribune*. Yet I felt even here, surrounded by mahogany and plush of the ages, that Mr. John Winchester Martin was unsettled and as he usually sat like poise on a monument the hairs on the back of my neck began to prickle.

When he double-cleared his throat, readjusting his gold-rimmed spectacles, Mellie glanced at me, but I could only give my head one of those you-know-as-much-as-I-do shakes. We both looked at Hank but he had caught no note of warning. As a matter of fact, around him was an aura of satisfaction, he looked to me as though a layer of wax had been poured over him, though certainly he couldn't have gained weight overnight. Especially a night of reunion with Mellie.

"This will—" Mr. Martin began, and stopped. Nobody stirred until Mellie said, "Do go on, dear Mr. Martin. We are consumed with curiosity. Has Katie made one of those wills that lead to murder? Leaving her money to her cat or a home for unmarried homosexuals?"

Well as he knew the conversational looseness of the nicest modern maidens, Mr. Martin gave her a frown of disapproval and began to read.

I, Katie Ogilvie Gavin, being of sound mind—

No use going into all the legal language the simplest problem employs.

Only once did Mellie interrupt in a silken voice, "*Was* she actually of sound mind, do you think?" to which Mr. Martin replied, "Her doctor who'd been taking care of her for some time was present to certify that she was. A shrewd old woman."

At this moment I do not know whether I heard for the last time Katie's eldritch chuckle or whether it was an inevitable memory reaction.

What it boiled down to was that *I, Katie Ogilvie Gavin,* had left more money than even her grandson knew she possessed to Henry Angus Gavin, said grandson, on the condition that he employ part of it to buy a partnership in his firm and that he be gainfully employed in the business capacity to which it had pleased God to call him according to K.O.G. If, on the other hand, he had so far disregarded the mandate that some are called to one thing and some to another and was a preacher, or an evangelist, he was to be cut off with a shilling, the rest to go to the University of Chicago for historical research and to Northwestern Medical School for further inquiry into neurological diseases and—final flick of the scorpion's tail—foreign missions.

As Mr. Martin's eloquent voice flowed on, Hank Gavin had gone that gray-white which is the color of bitter disappointment.

I knew then that he had counted on this money to bring Mellie his way. A poor minister she might refuse. A rich one must have a decided advantage. All he said was, "You believe this will, which restricts my personal liberty, can be made to stand up in court?"

Mr. Martin removed his glasses and polished them on a linen handkerchief, as though to see this document better, and also the young man who had asked this question. "I do not like conditional wills," he said, "I tried to persuade her—all I did was point up possible weaknesses which she then took steps to overcome. I doubt you can break it. Moreover, you can see you would be opposed by powerful and respected institutions of higher learning and service to mankind. However—she meant well, she was fond of you, y'know."

"I thought so," Hank said grimly, though he still looked lost and bewildered. Plainly, his connection with the power which had called and chosen him had snapped. No emergency prayer upon the very present help in trouble seemed to have occurred to him.

"Need it be so serious?" Mr. Martin said warmly. "She has left you a great deal of money. She felt—and expressed this to me—that this idea of a ministry was an—an immature action and psychologically a reversion, or an overdramatization like the Converters which she ought not to encourage as it would lead in time to disaster. She expressed a strong conviction that these conversions based on—seeing lights—or hearing voices—as she put it, always backslid disastrously in the end. She said she had seen many hit the sawdust trail and they always backslid and she was sure you would, and that therefore she didn't wish you to sacrifice money and opportunity for a passing emotional seizure. Or psychopathic aberration. On her own terms she was a religious woman and faithful churchgoer. Some might say she had laid up treasure where she was sure neither moth nor rust nor inflation nor tides of war nor trends of automation could corrupt. If she finds the financial policy of the kingdom of heaven unsound—who knows? One other matter. Note, in the will she speaks of her jewels, all left to Melanie. Perhaps they are more valuable than you realize. She hadn't, she told me, worn the best of them since before the Second World War. Certainly not the pearls. They are part of the estate, however, in a codicil she points out that they would be unsuitable to the wife of a minister, so in that case they're to be sold and go with the rest of her fortune."

"Quite logical," Mellie said. At that point, I could make nothing of her words, voice, or expression. The hands with which she smoothed the little white gloves on her knee were entirely steady.

Hank stood up then, heaved himself up through heavy waters, on his feet he looked tall and thin, somehow off balance, the ridges above his eyes were stark, he said, "Well, Mr. Martin, I'll let you know."

This was the only time I saw Mr. John Winchester Martin disconcerted—in almost a squeak he said, "Let me know!"

"There's a condition, you said, attached to my inheritance," Hank said.

"But my dear boy—" Mr. Martin said and left it at that. Mellie and I forgot him, we were watching Hank, hardly daring to breathe. In the old habit of the newspaperman who always makes quick reference to the most famous case-in-point, I was saying to myself, Well, it's a lot more than thirty pieces of silver, or is it? As Carol Channing said in *Hello, Dolly!* the difference between no money and a little money is enormous, but the difference between a little money and a lot of money is relative. To young Judas Iscariot, seeing feet of clay on his Master because Jesus wouldn't lend the eloquence of his speech on the Mount to the Judas underground rebellion that meant an attempt to overthrow Rome, thirty pieces of silver may have been more than the fortune Katie had left conditionally to her grandson.

Be sensible. Look at both sides. Here's his wife, his job, a *fortune,* that house, the majority of people would think him mad to hesitate.

But hesitate he did.

My throat began to ache. Quit it, I told myself, don't try to sell the idea that a man ought to turn his back on *money.* A poor man, a man that hasn't anything to lose or look forward to, *he* can join the church. This isn't your temptation, you can't even tell for sure which one of the three temptations it is.

Mellie and I sat absolutely still, waiting for Hank to say yes or no. Her astonishment increased second by second. Hank! Say—yes or no. Don't stand there like that Richard Yea-and-Nay which in the end defeated even his Lion-Heart. Say—Yes, I am one of them, a Galilean, I was with him when they arrested him in the Garden, he called me the Rock on which his teaching must be built, the recognition of the Christ. *Or* say Nay—nay—I never knew him, I'm just mogging along on my way back to my boat, a plain fisherman, it was all a psychopathic aberration and they never last.

All the plush and mahogany of the stately old office couldn't deaden the tensions, even their imperturbable owner showed himself shaken.

"I'll let you know," Hank said again.

From the next room, I wouldn't have been sure who was speaking.

In the middle of Mr. Martin's continued protest, Mellie rose and said in my direction, "We've got to get you to the airport, sweetie, thank you, dear Mr. Martin, I hope Katie's enjoying all this, poor old thing."

No one mentioned lunch, we drove straight to O'Hare and no one spoke all the way. My own mind was squirreling round and round. I was sure both Hank's and Mellie's were, too. In the waiting room we saw on the board that the next flight didn't leave for almost an hour and Mellie and I stood silent while Hank checked my bags. When our eyes met, Mellie lifted one shoulder in a shrug of unknowing.

Outside the day had begun to darken. A misty fog was blowing in and out. It would be a bumpy ride. When Hank came back Mellie said, "There's quite a nice restaurant, my knees have begun to buckle after all that drama, I'd like a drink—or some coffee, frankly." She tucked her hand inside Hank's arm and he gave her a sudden smile of recognition, as though he'd been away. A pretty blonde showed us seats near a window, the coffee came, it was hot and strong and welcome. Without any green felt on the table I was conscious of stakes piled high, all blue chips, the moment of truth spinning and where it came down would change life completely, beyond imagination. Katie had left no middle ground. Take it or leave it, 54-40 or fight.

Without warning, Mellie made a sweeping gesture, the silver and crockery rattled. Both hands shoved back her hair and she came up talking a fiery streak. "No—no—I will not have it! That awful old miser trying to force you—*I'll go my way and you'll go my way*—or I'll cut you off without a shilling. Her pearls! God damn her lousy pearls, who needs them? Hank, my love, tell the University of Chicago what to do with her money. I won't have her bossing you from *beyond the grave*—" Mellie had not noticed staring waitresses, travelers at the next table agape, she couldn't have cared less if she had, she said, "*You* decide, lamb. We can make up our own minds. Maybe *you'll* go *your* way and *I'll* go *my* way but *we'll* call what way it is, no grandmama from her *tomb*. Oh Hank—darling—we've got everything, you and I, can't you see that? We can be so happy. What do we need with this—this extravaganza about *god?*—You stay here with me, lamb."

He gave a shout of laughter, his face showed through it burning haggard and deeply lined, on so young a face such new fresh lines were like scars. But the light was back. His eyes were yellow and luminous with joy through the pain. In that flash, I knew his indecision was over.

"No," he said.

This time, Mellie could in no way mistake the strong, clear, utter finality of that one word. He spoke with authority and not as the scribes and Pharisees. Her breath caught, she put both hands on the table with only the fingertips touching, like someone at a seance awaiting a message, she never took her eyes from his face. But I saw her accept his decision as final, she had too much pride and young dignity to make a useless protest or knock her brains out against that stone wall.

I have always been sure that until that moment she had never once considered the possibility that in the end Hank would refuse to come her way. All her words, works, and thoughts had been based on that conviction. She had never in her whole life been crossed. What evil there was in her bore the name of *self-will*.

Now the choice had been passed to her. She must either make good her threat of divorce or go with him into this inconceivable new life. I could see the lines of her jaw firm and clear. The chips were down. But she wouldn't or couldn't speak, either she hadn't decided what to say or was too breathless to say it.

Hank said strongly, "You kept saying you have to be kidding—I'm telling you now I'm not kidding. No personnel department would have picked me as a salesman for him, but *he did*—and I'm going with him."

Into the vibrant silence, the public address system whirred, from its emptiness came a squawk, people nearby got up hurriedly and gathered their belongings, neither Hank nor Mellie heard or saw any of this, and I thought how things take place in peculiar places, Big Moments are seldom on purpose.

"Two by two," Hank said. "Two by two. You are to come with me!"

"No!" Mellie said, in a bright clear voice.

She started to get up from her chair, fell back, and began to plead, "Oh, Hank—what good would I be? I still do not believe in this myth you call god, I don't feel any need of *religion,* the god they taught me in Sunday School wasn't anyone I'd care to meet myself. Not in a dark alley, anyhow. I am not going to grovel for small favors. Or a remedy for jitters about the cold war or a cancer. I'd rather take a tranquilizer or a sleeping pill. This god your church preaches—"

"Herbert Hoover—" Hank said, and Mellie let out a wild, angry sound, she beat with the palms of her hands on the table, she said, "What the *hell*—how did *Herbert Hoover* get into the act?" and Hank took both her hands in his, grinning at her, "I'm sorry love. Because Hoover was President once, we forget he was also really the greatest *engineering* mind of our country, and once *he* said that Jesus was the greatest teacher—who ever lived. Mellie, Jesus didn't teach anybody to grovel, the God he told about ran out while His beloved son was yet a great way off though He knew that son had been wallowing with the husks and swine, and He wouldn't even listen when the prodigal wanted to beat his breast and tell his sins. That God wanted him to get on with *living* a good life, a happy life, with music. Jesus taught that it was worthwhile to be good, more interesting, merrier, not goody-goody, to stay in tune as you'd obey the law of counterpoint in order to produce the line of melody. That's the God I want to preach—teach about—maybe *prove*—"

"Hank," Mellie said, breathlessly, "people don't want your Jesus! They want fun and games. They think the whole thing's phony, even the Supreme Court says we better forget all about teaching it to the next generations. Sure, people go to church out of habit, they don't want to believe it for fear they'll have to do something about it—"

"They do want to believe," Hank said. "Mellie, every man I *know* wants to find God. God almighty, *you've* seen it all—you've seen how much *emptiness* there is under all the never-had-it-so-good—gotta be *empty* for people to jump out windows and behave the way they are. *You* know all these poor damn people rushing around like the devil himself was after them, afraid to stay in one *place* more than a few minutes for fear he'll catch 'em or be *alone* for fear they'll *think* or quit without turning *on* something—anything. You know the *hate* in some of the big rich families—hell, it's bigger than the poor in your hospitals, they've got more *time* to get their feelings hurt or cheat each other. Why do they have all those smashing parties like the last days of Pompeii or Versailles—all the kids coming out of college, they want a job that's *meaningful*. What the hell they *mean* by that *they* don't know. A world without *God* has to be *meaningless*. We have to give man hope. Hope is the first step. We have to tell him he has a duty to hope for good in his life and then let God make it so, as they say in the Navy."

"You've gone into some hallucination because Colin jumped out of that goddam *window*. Colin was a dementia praecox, a mumpsimus, a schizo," Mellie said furiously.

"Not true," Hank said. "When you see the light, you *know*."

"I never saw any light," Mellie said.

"You can," Hank said, "anybody can in time. And oh Mellie you'd be so wonderful! Think what you could do for the *people*."

Mellie thought, while the clock ticked several seconds, then with a little shrug, she said, "Oh I could do the *church* part, organizing bazaars and raising money and putting on plays. I just have a feeling it'd be better if the minister's wife believed in the god he's preaching, how about it?"

"It would," Hank said, "but we have to start with what we've got. WE have to go forth without shoes if we haven't got any shoes."

There was something formidable in the way he said that.

The light fell directly on his face. He had passed the test of the temptations against Katie and her money and all the power in his own world it would give him. He had *stood*. Angels had come and ministered unto him as far as I was concerned, something had been burned away, he *was* formidable now in a power of his own. *My best isn't good enough but His is.* I found myself thinking of the *goodness* of Alyosha that Dostoevski had made like music. Could this formidable force in young Hank Gavin be *goodness?*

Just then Mellie remembered that I was there, she looked at me and I knew she was touched, stirred, though I do not believe she knew by what. I saw that she had to accept that Hank's love for her was not great enough to stop the momentum that was plunging ahead. She was looking at an obsessive devotion stronger than anything she—or Katie—could offer. A fire of delight flamed in her white, pinched face. She was delighted as all women must be by the fact that her man was stronger than she was. Had proved himself stronger. This is a delight that grows rarer and rarer as men, poor fools, accept the weaker role. Melanie's defeat was plainly a triumph of everything basically feminine within her. A woman will scrabble and scramble, bite and claw, lure and tempt and threaten, weep and nag and belittle with all her might until the last possible moment. She will take jobs and invent for herself some kind of *mystique,* she will cater to his laziness and self-indulgence. For that defeat of herself which is her true victory is worthless unless she has put up her best fight and played her best game not to be dominated. In the end, if she loses, she will rejoice.

"It would be a mistake," she said, and now the seriousness of her thought, purpose, could not be hidden. "I can't do it. I don't think I *can.*"

Her surrender wasn't complete. She had not discovered whether her love for Hank was so much greater than all else that she must give up all she knew, desired, had always had, to follow him. The unknown was a yawning abyss at her feet. She was being a good loser but she had not expected to lose, she had never considered what losing would mean in practical terms, never for a moment contemplated its consequences in time, place, activity, never faced details, gain, and loss. Now the roots of her being were being tugged at, torn up for reasons from outer space. It hurt, she still resisted. I thought, too, that for the first time in her life she was frightened.

This time, the speaker's blast caught Hank's ear. *New York NEW YORK* it squawked at us with the insane insistence of Donald Duck, people scurried, Mellie blinked and said "That's your plane—" and I thought *life goes on* in all its idiotic triviality, *flight 27 for New York now loading at Gate B,* who cared whether I got to New York for dinner with my publisher? Now I wanted to know the curtain of Act II, to see and hear the last scene and the final line.

As we turned down the corridor Mellie burst out, "All very well, but actually what would we *do?* What would I be expected to do? In senior English we read a book called *In His Steps.* Miss Hollines—remember her?—our creative writing teacher said we had to because it had sold more copies than anything but the Bible, twenty million or something fantastic like that, and this wasn't a book that had any advantages like being banned in Boston or attacked as a dirty book, it was nice and clean, a lot cleaner actually than the Bible. A minister, he had a wife and of course her name was Mary, he and some people in his church decided they'd go around all day and whatever came up—damn little did, actually, not what we'd call much in our day and age—anyhow, they'd ask themselves *what would Jesus do* and then do it and this would solve everything." She tilted her head back to look up at her husband as she hung onto his arm, she had cracked the whip of her courage and whatever her fear it stood back for the time being. She said, "You wouldn't be up to anything like that, would you, my lad?"

"It sounds corny," Hank said. "We have to figure out what he *taught* and then see how we can *do* it now—today. There isn't any getting away from it, he taught by their *works* you can tell, and if you keep my rules you can *do* the works. We'd have to *try*—"

"We!" Mellie said in a hoot, then mocking herself she said, "I'd make a frightful ass of myself in a deal like that. One thing. You didn't know I know *all* the hymns. My Cheyne grandfather was an authority. 'Bringing in the Sheaves'—'Throw Out the Lifeline'—'There were Ninety and Nine'—not as rousing as 'Onward, Christian Soldiers'—oh yes and that gloomy little classic 'Lead, Kindly Light'—"

"Gandhi's favorite," Hank said, just as we arrived at Gate B.

"Even I," Melanie said with exaggerated simplicity, "know that *Gandhi* was a Hindu."

"Sure," Hank said, "but the only picture on his ashrama wall was of Jesus Christ. Under it was written He Is Our Peace." He was speaking quietly, as a man will not to disturb a wildcat that is coming closer, "and Gandhi says the Sermon on the Mount had given him comfort and boundless joy. It does, you know, darling. Sheean called his book about Gandhi *Lead Kindly Light*."

"Maybe the hymns would be a bridge for me, to start with," Mellie said, "while I got up committees. Then they wouldn't notice I don't believe in god and never expect to, by god."

She threw the lines away but Hank took a quick step toward her and I fought back my tears.

We both knew they were a covenant.

To cover it and give Mellie time Hank said to me, "You're a Californian—ever hear of Beach City?"

I said I had. One of my foster sons had coached high school football there for a year or two. So I knew it recently as well as from childhood. Time was too short to try to explain Beach City. Mellie looked a swift question and at what she saw gave a shudder. Though really it didn't, then, matter too much to her, any place with Hank, even the depths, she had accepted as better than paradise without him. All right, Beach City could be what the modern world refers to as a challenge.

That was because she didn't know Beach City.

They kissed me and I went down the ramp. It had begun to rain heavily, as I turned a corner it darted through and hit me in the face, so I could pretend it was rain drops I was wiping away. Gallantry is the thing that always—and only—makes it tear drops.

From my small window, I could see them pressed against the wire fence, standing two by two, her head just reaching his shoulder.

I could not get out of my mind what I knew about Beach City.

Its very poor and its very rich. Its young and old—ditto. Once the land on which it stood had been a vast rancho, founded on an original Spanish grant. Little by little, taxes and transportation and industry had forced the family to sell, there was no more cheap labor to make their way of life possible, the old-timers were gone and their descendants scattered. A city of oil and industry and far-flung shipping had grown where once cattle roamed and horses galloped and wheat waved golden and orange trees were green and glossy and fragrant. In a way it was quite as drastic as the disappearance of the plantations of the South. It is called progress now, in California, and I have long since ceased to throw myself upon its rapidly revolving wheel. So I merely thought with present-day intensity of the city's vulgarity and violence. Its oil pumps and stench mingling now forever with the sea. Of all the gaudy, terrible, and adventurous things that go to make up a port, from Marseilles to Said, from Honolulu to Buenos Aires. *Or* Beach City.

Of course there is another side to Beach City. When the South and Middle West and New England heard about the California climate and began the trek west that has made California the most populous state in the union, the old and tired and middle-aged settled in Beach City in droves. Now the various state societies were larger than the counties they came from. The children and grandchildren of the early squatters—so different from those who hit San Francisco in '49—were native sons and more were coming every day.

I was sure the young Gavins knew no more what lay ahead

of them than the Middle Westerners who came by slow freight at the turn of the century.

It was going to be *rough.*

Any rougher than Jerusalem? said I to me. Or Capernaum? Or Ephesus—there was a town, Ephesus, to hear Paul tell it. Or Rome in the days of the catacombs when the deteriorating Romans grasped at any straw—like Christ.

Or France in the days of Joan of Arc?

Or England at the time of Becket?

Maybe Beach City hadn't any idea of what was ahead of it, either.

Maybe Beach City didn't know that it might be a laboratory for a dangerous experiment.

By now, Hank and Mellie had slid out of my small window frame, we were airborne through the heavy blowing curtains of rain and wind. It still sounded fantastic to think of them in Beach City.

After having explored all the mother-knows-best-mama-fixit channels, I was reminded to pray. If I had faith as a *grain* of mustard seed, could I feel in my bones that Hank could do the same job the seventy had done—*even the devils are subject unto us in Your Name?* Could I accept that one man—one grain—one straw—my prayer wasn't very sensible, I could only hope the intent would compensate for the inadequacy. The intent, I told myself, was deep and true.

Me too, Father, I tried to say, let me help his hands as he goes forth, this young disciple of my time and place.

Oh, blessed Lord, give them the morning star.

They're going to need it.

Book THREE

PREFACE

Though I did not hear of it until later, and little enough then, I know now that Hank felt those few words with the chaplain on the docks, when his Navy ship stopped there on its way to the East, were a direct communication from the spiritual power which had taken over Hank Gavin's life out of the blue, as it were.

Chronologically, it belongs a few weeks after the young Gavins arrived in Beach City, California, where following his graduation from theological school Hank had been assigned as associate to Dr. Charles Hastings Ffolliott, pastor of the Church of the Redeemer, who was getting old.

At that moment, Hank found himself in an unexpected trough, just keeping afloat by swimming as hard as he could, which wasn't good enough.

For the first time, he was face to face with his separation from his fellow men. Never again could he be what was meant by *one of the boys*. Nowhere no time. And his fellow men had been the fabric of Hank's existence.

Perhaps it hit him with full force the first time he met Steven J. Retzlaff, head of said church's all-important Building Program, who at the moment would have won any popularity contest in Beach City. As they shook hands in Dr. Ffolliott's shabby study, Hank Gavin saw himself actually as a pastor, a preacher, a *minister,* through the other man's bright, observing eyes. Hank Gavin could not be as other men, he was no longer brothers-under-the-skin with members of the male race.

A chill invaded Hank from the effort, plain through the too man-to-man quality of Retzlaff's approach. He had the cockiness peculiar to many small men. Hank was sure that if he beat him on the golf course Retzlaff would say, "Nice going, padre. We'll have to get you in the next tournament."

And when Retzlaff said, "Come up to the club and have a drink, padre, and a spot of lunch?" Hank's cold midriff told him that his days of come-have-a-drink-and-a-spot-of-lunch, the picturesque days of language over a missed putt, the all-night sessions of cent-a-point bridge, the locker-bar-club rooms, even the vocabularies, the way they said *Jesus Christ,* must be contraries. For Hank Gavin it was a dilemma, at once petty and enormous. He must *be a man* to other men. How escape the horn of priggishness on the one hand, the loss of authority in conciliation and condonement on the other? Had St. Paul, that rich and worldly, luxurious and cultured young Jew, who was also a Roman citizen, found this staring him in the face when he arrived in Athens?

Perhaps one of the blessings of the chaplain was that he had been able to show his manhood under fire, when the guns were booming, in tight places, where he'd been a better man than any of them.

I do not know what the chaplain said to Hank in those brief dawn moments on the dock.

Whatever it was, it gave him his orders and his crest-of-the-wave glory once again.

1

The good Dr. Ffolliott, pastor of the Church of the Redeemer, had given Hank Gavin less than thirty minutes before he made his totally unexpected move.

All of this that I am now going to tell you happened some time prior to Hank's meeting with the chaplain on the docks, but I put that first because it was the leitmotiv, the over-all plan, the inspiration and cornerstone of all that follows.

I found out about Dr. Ffolliott as soon as I got back to my oceanside house a few miles north of Hank and Mellie and found a phone number and a message to call Mrs. Gavin immediately.

Her shriek against my telephone ear gave me a feeling of warm welcome—even need—and when she said "Come and see us at once!" I explained that I was supposed to be working eight hours a day on a book with a time-interest deadline, but admitted to a curiosity as burning as any I'd known in a profession consisting largely of burning curiosity and would it be all right even if I could only stay a couple of hours?

"Come tomorrow if it's only five minutes," Mellie said.

"All right," I said, "where are you?"

"Oh darling," Mellie said, "we're in the *parsonage,* otherwise known as King Tut's Tomb. Do you mind?"

"The parsonage!" I said, "but Hank isn't—"

"Yes, he is, lovey," Mellie said, "and I am his consort. You're not going to believe any of it, but I tell you now Dr. FFFFFfolliott was—is—pixilated. Anyway—hurry. Hank is nearly always in around lunch—"

On my two-hour solitary drive beside the ocean, which was already reclaiming me, making me wonder how I survived away from it, I kept thinking of our last meeting at the airport. I had no idea what the time lapse had done. Nor just how Hank had met being precipitated into ministerial charge of a large, well-attended-on-Sunday, old, respectable, and reasonably representative church in this staggeringly overpopulated, overgrown, overtrafficked, over-advertised section of the United States known as Southern California.

For background purposes only let me insert here that when I settled down there once more at this time, after travels around the globe, though much of it felt and smelled phony, I was amazed by a growing feeling that it was more *American* than other places. *Now,* I mean. More than I had realized. A melting pot, from the Orient, South America, Canada, the other states, and Europe. Center of new life, mushroom growth, far-out concerns, as New York and its environs now settling into *business* above everything, had been when I first went there to work on a New York paper. Southern California was the heart of creative communications, of unusual scientific discovery and manufacture, of incredible ratio of educational facilities especially at the top levels. The land of sunshine, spiritually sometimes dark as the pit of Doohan. If it had smog, this had been typical of most cities in the peak years of the Middle West. If it had fringe crackpot religions, this had been an accusation hurled against New England in its halcyon days of national leadership and transcendentalism. No one could duck the statistics that proved Southern *Cal* the fastest growing place on the globe, and obviously its political importance loomed as the still-fabled and dramatic West led a revolt against the domination so long held by New York.

It was Now—Today—America.

The neighborhood through which I had to drive startled me somewhat. Obviously it had been an exclusive residential district and was now fallen upon evil days. In the windows of most of the once-stately old houses were signs reading variously Rooms for Rent, Dressmaking, Insurance and Income Tax, Dressmaking, Clairvoyant Palmistry and Horoscopes, and Piano Miss Drayman. Some of the lower floors had been turned into shops which were reached by paths leading through dried-up overgrown gardens.

I felt that this was a sort of drab and hopeless place to build a church congregation, life seemed to be moving away from it.

Pulling up in front of the parsonage, I realized that it adjoined the church, but my desire to see Hank and Mellie was so driving that I had then only a fleeting impression of a large, once-handsome, now crummy-looking and neglected building of gray granite, a tall square tower, dark stained-glass windows which I knew to be one of Beach City's nineteenth-cetnury solid and expensive Protestant churches. I only felt that it was decaying inside and out and must be dark as Tophet within.

Then I heard Mellie squeal and saw her in the open door. A brilliant scarlet dress, tightly belted, her hair brushed into a smooth, dark, shining swirl that made it difficult to tell whether it was long or short—and my heart shed one apprehension. This was *Mellie.* Whatever emotions, earthquakes she had lived through or was living *in,* she had survived as herself. Some don't. She was greeting me with jubilation and a sort of incredulity. Not that of a shipwrecked sailor sighting a rescuer, but of a kid shouting come-and-see-what-I've-found!

As she pulled me up the stairs, across the big old porch, through the door I knew that she was undefeated so far.

"Don't look now," she said, waving away the huge hall, the wide straight flight of stairs. "Ignore it. It's like one of those houses in New York where somebody had lived for forty years with all the old newspapers and a relative or two chained in an upstairs closet. Though I must say I don't believe dear Dr. Ffffff had been upstairs since his wife died and we haven't found anything yet."

She held me off so that we faced each other squarely. "You're working too hard again," she said, and when I said, "So are you," she said, "Not *again,* sweetie. This is my first go-around. Nor is it as easy as it looks."

Much too fine drawn, I thought, that faint aura of fatigue, and then I saw that the change was to a hard, ruthless determination. It reminded me of a pioneer woman in a covered wagon halted in Indian country. Once in a picture I'd written about a pioneer woman, I had used some scenes to show that things we now deem essential which were nonexistent to her—clothes, change of underwear, home-or-away hair waves, lotions, creams for the hands, scented soap, powder and paint. But she had *something* that made those things trivial. Here stood Melanie Cheyne Gavin, honed, polished, perfumed, chic by nature, habit, training, and custom, to whom they were personally and nationally important, and she had that same something. That something which had picked up a fallen shotgun, given birth under moving wheels of a covered wagon, conquered a trackless wilderness with wild animals and without water. A *toughness* that would dare the Donner Pass. I thought with leaping heart that American women are really like this, they are not the dripping, self-indulgent, narrow-minded *bores* of the *Feminine Mystique* and *The Group.* Call on 'em and they have it!

Yet I also knew right there that like those women who won the West, Mellie would have to find the journey worthwhile. Believe in its goal. Or she might grab the reins, swing the team around, and head back for Kansas. This she would give a trial—that was where she was now. Give it a trial.

"Come into our oasis," she said. "Our Youth Group helped me paint, which infuriated their mothers, who say that at home they won't pick up their own clothes. Tact—it all takes tact. But then everything does, doesn't it? This is rather nice—though I must say the paint still smells."

The old-fashioned sunporch, which most California houses had possessed before all walls were glass, had been painted a deep adobe cream, the wicker furniture enameled a golden brown, there were venetian blinds now hauled to the top. It seemed to obey the basic law of taking the outdoors in, not moving the indoors out. On one wall hung Mellie's beloved copy of Van Gogh's Skylark, as great a link between heaven and earth as landing on the moon, whatever that means. But all around this small, bright, done-over oasis, as she called it, I felt surrounding us the long dark corridors of Baskerville Hall or the enormous chambers of Castle Rackrent.

There was a flurry of welcome as Hank came in and then Mellie pushed us down onto the couch and said she'd bring lunch out there at once, she set up some little metal tray tables, with wobbly legs, touched Hank's cheek with her hand, in the doorway she paused and with a wave toward them said, "I've made a lovely parody for you, *listen.*" And with hands on hips in the old way she said:

Some can live without poetry, music, and art,
Some live without conscience and some without heart,
We may live without travel, forget to change gears,
But what civilized woman can live without Sears?

She went out, put her head back in the door, "And let them as has never lived without cooks turns up their noses at TV dinners," she said.

"She seems in good shape," I said rather inadequately and Hank, shaking his head a little said, "Yes. It's—peculiar. The mechanics of living in this mausoleum are a main problem."

"Now," I said, "tell me what *happened.* You are, as I understand it, now actually pastor of this church?"

"So I am," Hank said cheerfully.

"How and where and when and why?" I said. "Did anybody know Dr. Ffolliott was going to resign just like that? Weren't you surprised when they gave you the top job? After all, there must have been more—experienced men waiting for promotion. I don't know much about the modus operandi of churchdom—the hierarchy, isn't it?—but it sounded rather like making an interne head of a big hospital. You've only been *converted* a couple of years."

"Well, some of them haven't been converted at all," Hank said with a grin.

"Tell me about it," I said. "From the beginning."

"The first Sunday I was here," Hank said rather carefully, as though it was still not altogether clear in his own mind, "after he'd shaken hands with the last of the congregation he went into his study and I followed him, and there he was sitting in the chair behind the big desk and he had a—a delighted, long-gone—Mellie calls it pixilated expression on his face. Not to be trite about it, he had the old swallowed-the-canary look as plain as plain could be. Did you ever see him? Well, he was a bit overweight, probably eating had been his last pleasure, anyhow he looked at me quite a while, and then he said, 'Wasn't that sermon of mine a lollapalooza? Could you recognize it for my swan song, Dr. Gavin?' "

When young Dr. Gavin said he had not, Dr. Ffolliott snickered—Hank's word for it—and said, "Good. My valedictory, that was, a long farewell to all my greatness. Words words words—I'm fond of them, son. Long ones and short ones. Books and books and books, fat and thin, old and new, I'm fond of them also. Philosophies and systems and schools of and doctrines about existentialism and positivism and epistemological idealism and 28 brands of the best filter Christology—and who cares?"

Hank had taken the seat opposite him, but he had almost at once a feeling that it was to himself that Dr. Ffolliott was saying all that, not to his deputy vicar or curate, even when he looked full at Hank he didn't seem to see him. "They want a new church," he said. "Bah!" at which Hank, who had never heard anyone actually say Bah before, made some gesture which brought the parson's attention back to him. "They want an athletic field and a social hall and an art gallery and a *Good Housekeeping* kitchen. True true this church where you attended this morning is now in no-man's-land as far as Beach City is concerned. The operation here is as anachronistic as the Republican party—and I am a Republican myself so who should know better? Well well, let us agree that only the Catholics are born real estate operators with a vocation and *real estate* is vital to ecclesiastical welfare. When my efficient pre-pre predecessor bought and built here, it was on the charming outskirts of a sleepy California town. Fine houses, gardens, *trees*. Such trees. I wish you could have seen the pepper trees, like green-gold lace embroidered in bright scarlet. A fine show they made but naturally they had to come down, in some way that is not clear to me they impeded progress. A quiet retired neighborhood—residential—proper place for a church. My immediate predecessor told me when I arrived that the building wave might come in this direction—he could not foresee it would be tidal in its proportions. It came and kept right on going, it swept through fields of poppies and lupine and felled the yuccas at the rise of those little foothills and climbed right on up. You haven't yet seen Steven Retzlaff's estates including his own? Of course not. They are on the sides and tops of them. And here we are, God's house as it were, as I said, in a no-man's-land between the city's traffic jams and the green trees of the country club out yonder. We are neither fish, flesh, nor fowl.

"True, they need a new church.

"You will find that the chief thing that occupies their attention these days."

"*I* will find?" Hank Gavin said loudly enough to get the old man's attention.

"Yes yes," Dr. Ffolliott said, "at least I hope it will be you. That's one reason I am resigning to take effect *at once*. Immediately. You see. I have a new job—starting Monday."

His breath, Hank told me, was by that time coming in something that would have been pants if he hadn't controlled it with care. "A job?" he said. "Look—Dr. Ffolliott—you've caught me way off base—"

"I hope I shall do likewise with the bishop," Dr. Ffolliott said, and it was—it had to be—pure mischief in his smile, "I don't think they will hold it open for me. I'm going—never mind, I'll explain that to the bishop—I shall recommend you highly and not as an interim—of which I know he doesn't approve."

"Wouldn't it have been better to wait a bit?" Hank said, "until you could know a little better—"

The old man looked at him then. Full. The mischief went and Hank saw that there were tears on his face. "No no," he said, "no no no. Steve Retzlaff is up to something. I am not strong enough—any more—perhaps I never was. He is taking over my church. You—you have *faith?*"

Hank said, "Yes—yes."

"I had it once," Dr. Ffolliott said, and then rapidly, the pixie beginning to come back. "Ah well—we must all pass on the torch, hand over the baton. Groups—groups, groups—this church today is made up entirely of minority groups. In that it is rather like the world today, isn't it? Youth Groups, Young Married, Choirs, men and women's forums, discussion and liturgy and literature and Fund-Raising and books on Christianity Today and Christianity without Religion and New Terminology— Have you ever heard of a man named Boenhoffer?" Hank said he had but the old man seemed to lose the trend of his thought, and with a bright smile he picked up the telephone and began to dial. "The bishop should be back from service by *now,*" he said, "I shall tell him and then of course follow it by a letter in proper form— Dear dear, I see no reason to—I may be a poetical leftover, a horse-and-buggy has-been who isn't *reaching* people today but I—I do not feel I need bring this up. Do you know the bishop? You will find him a man of business. I wonder if I dialed the correct number? Ah—I forgot one must dial the three code letters first." He began over again, he kept on talking, he said, "Do you like poetry? Remember *For this your mother sweated in the cold, For this you bled upon the bitter tree—Up goes the man of God before the crowd with voice of honey and with eyes of steel—Nobody listens—O Prince of Peace! O Sharon's dewy Rose! The stone the angel rolled away with tears, is back upon your mouth these thousand years.* That's Edna St. Vincent Millay—a *poet* she was. I don't think anybody listens to anybody any more, we're all talking to ourselves. Seventeen minutes—I'm eloquent and poetical—so they can get away to their golf game and have I any better solution to offer them? You take over. You're filled up with *ideals* —maybe they'll listen to you—" The old man was still saying, "No no—they won't *listen*—nobody *listens*—why should they? Do you know how to pray? I've forgotten long long ago if I ever knew."

At that point, there was an answer and the old man's head came up alertly, and after a moment or two he was obviously speaking to the bishop. Naturally, Hank Gavin only heard one side of the conversation, which was enough.

"And good morning to you—your old friend Ffolliott here. I called to tell you that I am offering you my resignation as of now. No no—kindly let me finish—regret me no regrets—I have accepted a job as night clerk at the hotel on the Point—

"But my good sir, I cannot live on my pension you must know that, and I haven't been able to save on my salary— You people expect to get first-class men in this market against all competition, if you mention more money the populace howls that the church always has its hand out, then they despise their minister because he can't be much good if he'll take a salary smaller than a ribbon clerk.

They must look down on you. The food's good at the hotel and I shall have a great deal of time to read."

Here, Hank said, apparently the bishop, miles away in Los Angeles, managed to assert himself both in loud and resonant voice and a measure of episcopal authority—Dr. Ffolliott was silent, placid, but attentive.

"But my dear Bishop," he said at last, "I have no intention of flummoxing you. I have waited until a young man arrived who can quite well assume all my duties here and probably be a better match for our fund-raising chairman and treasurer than I could ever be. You surely know all about young Gavin?"

He listened again, nodding, he made a *he-knows-all-about-you* face at Hank Gavin, which one could assume he did, he said, "But your grace will have to act at once for I shan't be here Monday."

"So," said Hank Gavin, "that was that. It wasn't much good appointing me as an *interim* or *acting* head because things were too unsettled anyway, Dr. Ffolliott's hand on the reins had been loose for a long time, the business of the new church was advancing—"

"But—" I said, "I should have thought they had men more—more experienced?"

"In what?" Hank said.

"Oh—for goodness sake," I said, "it's like anything else. Running a church. Sermons every Sunday. All the things ministers are expected to do."

"Groups," Hank said.

"All right," I said, "groups. And I know you went to Yale and that divinity school—but I read a great deal about intellectual grasp and the philosophy of this and that and meeting the *thinking* of our time—"

"I know," Hank said, "but after all the first thing—the rock—I mean Peter wasn't what you'd call an intellectual phenomenon at a time when in Greece and Rome *and* Jerusalem there were some very bright boys around not to mention Egypt—but—did you ever notice that John the Baptist, poor fellow, *asked* Jesus—'Art thou the Christ?' he said, but Peter didn't ask, he knew, he *said,* 'You are the Christ.' Anyhow, the first thing needed is the rock to build the church on, isn't it? The power and the glory."

"He—the bishop—he might think you're too—all this is pretty far out—"

"Far back, probably," Hank said. "The revolutionary today is the man who insists on fundamentals, isn't he?

Anyhow, I don't expect the bishop had anything to say about it."

"The bishops I've met would have," I said. "Who else?"

"This is the Father's business," Hank said, smiling at me. "I'm not doing it. Neither are they. When I was selling stocks in a company I put management ahead of equipment or real value. Wouldn't it be bungling incompetence for the Holy Spirit to go to all the time and trouble of finding me—the most *unlikely* choice—and then not provide me with a *place?*"

I wish I could convey to you the—the *modesty* with which he said this. Somebody once wrote that God gives the skill but also a man's hand to use it. I felt that Hank knew he was the man's hand in this, but all else of skill and timing and place and occasion was what he called the Father's business. There was also something endearing and engaging in the casual way in which he used the old-fashioned terms from the Book itself, rather than the modern gobbledegook which is, to me, a little like paraphrasing Shakespeare or Keats. This has been done but never importantly.

Mellie came in then, she stood a moment, the tray on her hip, the way I'd seen Italian peasant women carry baskets of grapes. She took a quick look at Hank and said, "He's been telling you about Dr. Ffolliott. Poor lamb, I'll never forget him. They broke his heart, you know."

"His was a frail bark," Hank said unexpectedly.

We sat down to lunch and Hank said, "The bishop accepted his resignation a week later and—I think he realized it had to be done at once and that I had to have authority. So here we are."

Mellie said, "Yes, aren't we?"

"I've made you a lot of trouble," I said.

"You have, indeed," Mellie said. "The trick is, I find, to get everything *ready* at the same time. And I say let them as is without cooks be the ones to decide on whether TV dinners are the greatest invention since the knife or not."

"I hope I'm worth it," I said. "You could save yourself considerable time if you gave up peeling the tomatoes."

"One must dress for dinner even in the jungle," Mellie said.

"One of the things that has disappeared from the world on its march of progress," I said, "is the tomato. You've never eaten big, dark, red, luscious ones ripened in the sun, with a flavor fit for the gods. These bits of pale pink rubber, no taste, picked green and left to struggle to maturity in a freight car's refrigeration—"

"Like so many teen-agers," Mellie said. "Hank, go get

Dr. Ffolliott's *list*. I think godmama ought to see it, especially if she's coming to the church supper. They are having a sort of Welcome to *you* church supper for Hank next Sunday night—you will come, won't you?"

Hank went out and Mellie folded up the table trays, her back was to me, I said, "Mellie—" and she stood perfectly still. "Do you—I can't tell—is it worth it? Is it going to work? Have you come to believe in it?"

She swung around then, she said, "I can't say I believe much in the god who left an old man—such a gentle old man—weeping and—destitute, after he'd done his poor best to serve him all his life. He did, you know. Dr. Fffff—"

"I expect the disciples were tough characters," I said vaguely.

"Hank is tough," Mellie said, with a little laugh, "they will find that out. I—one thing I do believe, Hank has to do whatever it is he has to do. There are some frightening things going on around here. I can see why Noah began to build an ark. I get along very well with the people. They are—people. Except for the *dishes* which it seems to me are always with us—my price about now wouldn't be a mink coat or a diamond bracelet or a town car—just a dishwasher—except for that aspect my work here seems about like what I did in Chicago. I do my best."

Hank came back with the lists and Mellie carried the trays out and came back.

All the lists were set down in Dr. Ffolliott's delicate, educated hand, to me it seems a new Caste of Characters, in this new Act, with its new scenery and location. Opposite each capitalized name he had written a comment, an analysis, now he had felt free to make them for the young man who was stepping into his shoes, they were filled with triumph and satisfaction and an accent of malice, they rattled like parting shots. By the time he wrote these he had dried his tears.

As Hank spread them on the table I realized that some of the names were familiar to me.

The very first one, for instance.

Mrs. Marguerita Vosburgh.

Beside it, in that spidery hand,

> Pillar. Backbone. Would have been quite as satisfactory at the May Company or the Janss Investment Corporation. On terms of pleasant equality with God. Do not call her a gossip. She is vitally in-

terested in her fellow man and serves him with good will and corresponding conversation about him, his affairs and his weaknesses. I beg you to believe she knows everything before it happens and there will be no privacy in your bedroom. A widow with married children and some grandchildren about.

"I went to school with her," I said. "I wonder if any of us ever really change. However, Margie has character. Sterling character, we used to say."

"I'm going to need her," Hank said smiling.

Jack Nestor came next, a name I knew from the papers as a union mogul of savvy and right intention.

Membership on the board of a respectable church is a good card to have in your hand. It is hard to get him to promise to do things but if he does it will get done. According to his lights which he claims are primitive Christianity he is honest and concerned for the welfare of humanity. He asks me to speak at some gathering from time to time. So also does he ask Father McBride and the Rabbi. They both do better than I, but he can become neither so he includes me in. After all, there *are* more Protestants than anything though you would never think so if you arrived from Mars by flying saucer. Probably because we are divided into so many pieces by petty differences. And we have so little sense any more of drama and our public relations are inadequate.

"It's hard to do it in a business suit," Hank said and fell into a fit of laughter. Through my mind slipped *He has sent me to heal the broken-hearted.* I thought it was lovely work if you could do it.

Marvin and Norma Gregory. Heads of the Young Married. Beside these Dr. Ffolliott had written an enormous black question mark. Then, as though in compunction, some light gray scrawls.

I am out of touch with Young Marrieds. Norma, Radcliffe. Marvin, UCLA. They have more Discussion Groups than anybody. Could this be because they have more problems? They also have Outside Speakers and Celebrities, like Divorce Judges, Interior Decorators, TV Panelists and Spaghetti, chop suey and enchilada chefs. They also have cookouts. All admirable and worthy. They are good young folk.

I am a bitter disappointment to them. I cannot even be picturesque in a shabby cassock. Their present project is a Hobby Group.

"Mellie is one of their hobbies now," Hank said.

"Intellectuals-on-the-make," Mellie said, "Norma has problems—she's married to a man with nothing but charm. Like lots of intellectuals, she isn't really very *bright*. Oddly enough I'm fond of her, which surprises me; Radcliffe girls on the whole make me a little seasick. Norma is *kind;* she means well; she always has that spot or two on her sweater that is the badge of Radcliffe, however this appears to make the wharf wives more at ease with her, not that they ever have spots, it simply brings her down so they don't feel inferior."

The Cutlers.

This was long, and carefully constructed, a word or two crossed out and another substituted.

Here we have A Family. Composed of Mr. and Mrs. Art Cutler, and Mr. Cutler's mother. In the most technical sense the younger Mrs. C—whose name is Gertrude—was a Career Girl. She had been secretary to the head of a department store and became a window dresser. All this she gave up to marry Art Cutler and except for or in spite of her children I fear she has sometimes wondered why. She has 4 children of exceptional good looks and she is what I assume is meant by a rebel against the FEMININE MYSTIQUE, which until recently I had supposed to be something riding a broomstick at Halloween. Maybe it is. No, I am now told it is a permanent state of discontent with having to do something in this life which these ladies consider to be unworthy of their gifts. This happens to many of us, most of us know that there will be much in our work, our jobs, whatever they are, which must be endured with forbearance, calmness, compassion for those around us, and what good cheer and good manners we can manage. Gertrude Cutler is actually a very good-natured woman and romps about between times. Right now she has a part-time job at the store doing special windows. She came to me one day dressed to prove that when they call her a sexy number they are correct and told me frankly that if I wanted to prevent murder I had better get her mother-in-law out of their house. She told me her dislike of the elder

name for them, it seems to me. I'd like one that can hit over .300 if possible. Marvin Gregory can't seem to deliver."

"What does your friend say about the Gregorys?" I said.

This was really brief.

> Gregory. Marvin and Norma.
> A charming couple. I cannot think *why* they hardly ever accomplish what they so willingly and enthusiastically set out to do.

"Probably their best isn't good enough," Hank said, and I saw Mellie bite back a word.

"God must send me a top kick," Hank said, and for a moment he closed his eyes.

I couldn't quite get my breath. The lights went up and up, like stage lights that are at first dim and then gradually grow brighter and brighter, only it wasn't outside that I was seeing this, it was inside. *Within.* The kingdom is *within* you. I had looked everywhere else, that was for sure. Hank said, "Where two or three—" and stopped, he made a strange appealing gesture with both hands, palms up, and we were silent for as long as it took to draw three deep breaths.

The only way I know to describe the expression on Mellie's face was as an affectionate exasperation.

Mellie still wasn't going to buy that *her* best wasn't good enough.

We went back to the list and with amazement I caught a name that was indeed familiar to me.

"Archie Paddock!" I said, "Archie Paddock, the publisher of the *Star?* I worked for him years ago. He is a mean, arrogant, terrible, we'd-be-better-off-if-they-dropped-the-bomb-and-let-the-monkeys-start-all-over-again, hard-boiled newspaperman. I love him devotedly. But—he is not a churchgoer.

"No, I expect not," Hank said, "it says here he inherited his place on the board, as it were. His family were churchgoers, it seems. Dr. Ffolliott notes that he has never yet been to a board meeting nor any other church activity. But—" and he quoted—" 'he has always been extremely kind to us in the matter of printing our notices and announcements and he remains a member.' "

"I may have to do something about him," I said rashly, though what or how I didn't know.

There were now two names left.

Olin McAddams.

This one was longer, it needed to be. For here we had two-for-one, there was, it appeared, also Mr. McAddams' wife Bertha. He was president of the board, and yet being sensitive always to handwriting, which I take it reveals both character and the state of mind and health at the time, I felt that over this one Dr. Ffolliott, so unexpectedly definite and decisive in most cases, was of two—maybe three—minds. The old-fashioned spidery hand wavered. If this was prophetic I had no warning of it at the time, and indecision is one of the things we have had to learn to live with in this day and time.

Reputation was big-businessman. Shrewd, sharp, substantial, and I am told far-seeing. Most agreeable to deal with. Seldom outwitted on a deal, financially able, in these days when honesty is a pedestrian virtue and too often synonymous with stupidity I believe him to be honest. Nor do I regard him actually as two-faced. He has the easy quality of adjustment to circumstances and people and if he is all things to all men he considers this—as do many others—an excellence not a fault. He is said to handle customers—he owns a large department store—with bluff, good will, and great adjustability. I like him. As I have perhaps already indicated I have no gift for this new-fangled science(?) called psychiatry and may even entertain a prejudice against it, to an old fogey like me it seems to do more harm than good but so too does aviation and I agree this is here to stay. Though I regard myself as a failure as a minister, *any* minister must come to have some comprehension of human beings. Though we have abrogated so much of our usefulness, we still see many of them in times of stress. Mr. McAddams, leading citizen though he may be, is what we used to call henpecked. True, as I see it, women now openly rule most homes and you will note that most often of a couple the woman is driving the car, but Mr. McAddams' case is exaggerated beyond the usual. This I mention at length because I am inclined to fear that there is something wrong with Bertha McAddams. The surface is ordinary enough. She wears expensive clothes badly. She is a semi-invalid and one sees relatively little of her. Yet she seems to be—shall I try to explain by saying that the good Mr. McAddams seems always to be looking over his shoulder and that when he says he likes to sleep on a matter before giving his answer I have come to feel that what he really means is that he must find out whether Bertha will let him or not. He is, I fear, subservient to this quite inferior female and this is a phenomenon that I have never understood. Men of ability and position, importance in a community, who live in terror of their second- even third-rate ribs. This man is solid, beetle-browed, jutting jaw, yet if your memory goes back to the irreplaceable Edgar Bergen and his Charlie McCarthy you will understand that the Misses hold the Master on her knee and in the end I very much fear manipulates the strings. Again, I have been aware of this but never been able to do anything about it. I, too, have been terrified of Bertha on the rare occasion when I have come face to face with her. A faded, plain little woman, I conjecture that she is consumed by some ruling passion and these people are possessed of the strength of a madman. On the surface you might not see this for some time, so I take this opportunity to warn you that Mrs. McAddams may well be one of your crosses.

"Have you met this extraordinary character?" I said. I spoke to Hank but I was looking at Mellie. Her expression spoke amusement, and yet her eyes were narrowed, wary, knowing. Why wary? Had I ever seen Melanie Cheyne Gavin wary before? Surely not. Perhaps it was because this danger would be to Hank.

"I've met her once," Hank said. "If it hadn't been for this"—his forefinger moved Dr. Ffolliot's memo—"I'd never have given her a second thought. She seems to me one of those ordinary, slightly disagreeable women whom a man must have married in extreme youth and she's taken all the wrong turnings ever since."

Mellie said, "I don't suppose *la dame sans merci* was necessarily always *belle,* was she?"

"Have you found out yet the name of her consuming passion—it sounds rather like possession by devils, the way Dr. Ffolliott put it," I said.

At the same moment Hank said *No* and Mellie said *Yes.*

"But Hank darling," Mellie said, "surely you know. She's a greedy pig. You're the one who must know money is the root of all evil—isn't that in your book?"

"That's not what it says, love," Hank told her. "It says the *love* of money."

"All right, pal," Mellie said, "our Bertha has the root of that matter in her. I wouldn't be surprised if she'd steal the pennies off a blind man's eyes. She's a miser."

"Oh Mellie—" I said, "how in the world can you tell a thing like that if you only met her once?"

"You forget," Mellie said, "I have been raising money since I was fourteen, I know. They have a look in their eyes." She waited, and for the first time I realized that the small line between her winged eyebrows was there to stay. "Maybe she'll come to the church supper and you'll see her then."

"What church supper?" I said.

"You remember—I told you—they're giving a sort of welcome brother evening a week from Sunday for the congregation to meet their new minister in person," Mellie said. "Do come. In the Sunday School."

"And after that," Hank said, "I'm going to call my first board meeting. I can't put it off any longer. It has to be done."

The last name on the list, written out so fully, disclosing so much that perhaps Dr. Ffolliott had never known he knew, was Steven Retzlaff.

Opposite it, was one word and one word only.

Steven Retzlaff . . . Lucifer.

Lucifer?

"He was a fallen angel," I said.

"So he has to be an angel still, doesn't he?" Hank said. "He lost paradise—did Milton say *he* regained it?"

It was a long time since I had read *Paradise Regained*—if ever. I am a spotty poetry reader, and Milton never was a favorite. I couldn't remember much about it except that the hero was Samson—wasn't he?—"—eyeless in Gaza—" but I knew that Lucifer had set himself up with all his rebel angels—but in spite of the greatness of his rhetoric and the riches of his vocabulary Milton to me had none of the splashing color, the snarling trumpets, the human symphony of Shakespeare when *he* gets profound.

Mellie said they didn't have a Milton—not here, of course her father had one—she had brought along Bartlett's *Familiar Quotations.*

Pandemonium, city and proud seat of Lucifer—she read, "I didn't know that," she said. "Pandemonium—not a bad synonym for Beach City." She kept her eyes on the book, quoting bits . . . *justify the ways of God to man—the mind is its own place and in itself can make a heaven of hell, a hell of heaven*—"If," she said, "one can find a way to control the mind—"

"By the same Mind that was in Christ Jesus," Hank said with that simplicity which C. S. Lewis says costs not less than everything.

"Here it is," Mellie said. "Better to reign in hell than serve in heaven."

"That's what *he* thought," Hank said.

"This one," Mellie said, "*our* one, Steven J. Retzlaff, is head of the building program and fund-raising activities. Likewise, I hear, he's City Hall—he'll be at the church supper, count on it. So you will come?"

"I'll come," I said.

Mrs. McAddams kept nagging at me. So that when I got home and telephoned my onetime friend and colleague Archie Paddock in his office at the *Gazette,* to announce my irregular connection with the Church of the Redeemer in his city and to inquire about his, I also asked what he had on Mrs. Olin McAddams whose husband was president of that church's board. In that oddly New England accent which Archie had acquired at Harvard and retained still in California, he said as far as he knew Mrs. McAddams was something of a recluse, enjoyed ill-health, was often referred to as poor dear, such a good woman. This jolted me. In my professional capacity I have known several murderers, a corrupt Cabinet officer, a traitor or two, a homosexual who was beaten to death in jail after he annoyed a child. One of the few *wicked* human beings I'd ever met was a woman who called her icy meanness *good,* and broke her husband and children into a thousand pieces of self-doubt and guilt.

"Keep in touch," Archie said, and I said, "You keep in touch. I want you to take me to the church supper to welcome Dr. and Mrs. Gavin."

"Say that again more slowly," Archie said, "I myself once helped teach you to dictate clearly and accurately over the phone."

"The church supper," I said.

"In a church?" Archie said.

"In the Sunday School," I said.

"I haven't been to a church supper in forty-four years," Archie said, "and I can still smell the meat loaf. Nobody had waked up the flavor and it had an odd odor —I won't go into that."

"I need you there," I said, "and you may not be able

to print anything but unless all my instincts fail me this may be the beginning of a news story that will rock your readers sooner or later."

After a moment, he said, "Ah. The new church!"

"Partly—" I said, "but where is there a better cross-section of saints and sinners, rich and poor, old and young? You're a newspaperman. All this gobbledegook can't be fooling you. We *are* the only hope of the world, America is, the only true idealists of freedom left, we'd better find an *answer* pretty soon."

"Not in the church," Archie said.

"Where else?" I said. "Moreover, you have to go to the board meeting. You are on the board. You may have heard that a nation is in danger when the good people in it *do nothing*."

"I do quite a good deal," Archie Paddock said in his terrible-man city-editor tone.

"Come and see," I said, a little frantically. "At least come and see what young Gavin is all about."

He would, I knew, propelled by devouring curiosity. He would now have to find out why I was making such a bloody fuss about a supper and a board meeting to follow in a church.

"Can ventriloquism be exercised *in absentia?*" I asked.

"Oh yes," Archie said, "control-by-fear is a long-distance weapon."

It had not occurred to Dr. Ffolliott to put down for his successor's benefit several other names which were to be uppermost in the testing of that theory which Hank Gavin was to suggest, then put forth about himself at the board meeting and eventually ask for support of from his entire congregation in his great and controversial sermon at the Church of the Redeemer.

Some of them he may not have known.

Beany Teran, for instance, who played a guitar with magic. Doubtless Deedee Retzlaff, Steven's slim gold-and-white daughter with the voice of a minor angel, probably seemed to the good old doctor too young to be a serious factor.

Nor had he mentioned Lucifer's wife, Gloria. Yet as I walk back in these memories, which are more real to me than many of the things around me this minute, it seems to me that Gloria Retzlaff and her neurotic fears and from-the-psychiatrist's-couch philosophies—*it gives me a hole in my guts,* Gloria said, and she was or tried to be a lady—were as strong a force in the church-laboratory as Bertha McAddams' greed. Obviously, as Mellie saw almost at once, Gloria had fancied herself as an adventuress, but her capture of the super-ambitious young moneyman from the West had turned out far otherwise. If he was going some day to be *governor*, and on his chart he was, his wife must be above reproach.

Perhaps his ignorance of these characters had been a factor in Dr. Ffolliott's self-denominated failure which put Dr. Henry Angus Gavin in the catbird's seat at the Church of the Redeemer in Beach City.

2

When I recall that buffet supper in the Sunday School of the Church of the Redeemer in Beach City, California, I find it was there that the new rector, Hank Gavin, took the first of his steps In His Steps. The capitalization of those letters releases his voice, vaulting that night in the silence, saying "Terminology! I agree we need some new terminology. Everything does—everybody does—all trade talk changes somewhat. We could—you say In His Steps is old-fashioned, but it's fairly simple, could become *our conformity to the prototype which is the Christ*—bigger words—mean the same thing—may be better understood today you think?" At that moment I remember he was talking to Steve Retzlaff, whom old Dr. Ffolliott had called *Lucifer*.

There were more people in the big, bare, badly lighted room than it could hold comfortably. Small tables with gay paper mats and matching napkins had been crowded together and in response to the many reservations called for by those who wanted to meet and welcome their new minister had flowed out into the hall, and onto the paved court of the pergola which would have been charming except just then Beach City was having a spell of the fog which rendered the nearby airport so uncertain. The pergola was of the old-fashioned California-Spanish type covered with wisteria, and lay between the church and the parsonage, both looming dark and mysterious and apparently enormous among leftover trees. Like all rooms not acoustically designed for the female voice, it was noisy as hens disturbed by a coyote. Half-sentences, squeals, laughter came to the top. I knew nobody except the young Gavins, who were the stars of the show, and my old friend Marguerita Vosburgh. I kept getting pinned in corners and then spun out of them and I could only assume that this was a good cross-section of the American people, though I still think beach towns are always a little more violent about everything.

This was the first occasion upon which the church membership met with the new minister and his wife. All eyes were upon them. Curious, avid to make contact, having heard a great deal about his spectacular story, part of them forced themselves forward and greeted him heartily, some held back shyly, no one seemed quite at ease. It was a good many years since I had attended a social function in the church of my fathers and I wasn't quite sure of either the tone or tempo and of course no more were Hank and Mellie Gavin. Mellie of course was entirely herself and quite at home, if I saw a slight indication of boredom no one else could have spotted it, any more than she had ever showed it when she was arranging a children's fashion show to raise money for the hospital or supervising a rehearsal for the cotillion.

Only Archie Paddock, as far as I know, spotted Hank's first move in his great experiment.

Plainly, they were all a little startled when the tall, tanned, oddly young-looking minister said grace. He stood at the head of the head table, made to hold eight by putting two together, watching them with interest, he looked gay, almost debonair, he seemed glad to be there. But he waited. Everybody had gone round the big table loaded with meat loaf and fried chicken and enchiladas and Hank waited until they had all found places, settled down, and put their loaded plates in front of them.

Quiet came as they realized he was the only figure standing and they turned their faces to his smiling regard. A big young man, they saw, too thin, not much more than ordinarily good-looking, nothing unusual about him until for some reason you became aware of his eyes.

The grace he said was, as far as they knew, his own invention.

He said, "Grant, Father, that we may believe above all things in Your active presence here and now. And the Presence of Your Son, the Risen Christ. Grant us the grace to accept Your gift of faith in things we cannot always entirely understand. Grant that in the days to come we may never be of those who say Lord Lord with their lips only and forget to serve You in the hours of our daily life and need. Grant that we do not waste the power You alone can give us to love each other and all our neighbors especially those we do not like or agree with. I thank you, Father, that You have heard me."

Nobody picked up a fork or said a word for quite a spell. For it was quite plain that this man was speaking directly and with a complete conviction that he was heard, it was *reverent,* but they had never before heard anyone who had that *happy* and friendly and taking-it-for-granted way of addressing God, as if there were a God and He was *there.* That was what both *embarrassed* and to some degree, let's face it, terrified them.

Then the buffet began and a buffet is a buffet is a buffet whether the plates are paper or Meissen.

"They look so young," I said to Archie Paddock, who had showed up late and maneuvered us to a table in the corner where we could see a good deal of what was going on. "Hank and Mellie Gavin, I mean."

"To us," Archie said, "from where we sit. Actually as things go now, they're a fine age to run the Senate. The best age, in some ways. Neither too young nor too old."

Watching Mellie, who I could see then clear to me for the first time, "It's as big a job for her as it is for him, isn't it?"

"The Brotherhood of Railroad Engineers keeps a close eye on the wives," Archie said.

"He has a dedication," I said, "he has a call to do what he's doing and he believes the active help of—divine intervention. But she's been yanked out of everything she ever knew, brought to this really raw—you know how different it is—and she hasn't anything but him."

"Oh, I think she has a good deal more than that," Archie said, "strikes me as a young woman of strong character."

"Yes, but—he's been converted and she hasn't," I said. "I don't know how that's going to *work.*"

"Does your young man call it a conversion?"

"I—think so," I said. "Don't you believe in conversion?"

"Nobody can deny the possibility of sudden and—what you might call miraculous conversion, or an experience that adds up to it," Archie said. He was still looking at Mellie, most men I had discovered over years did this. Her hair, that night, was done higher than I'd seen it, a sort of fan on top held by a comb with little prongs of gold that were repeated in the lights of her burnished dark hair. The square neckline of a straight, simple, rather old-fashioned looking dress showed the way her head was set on her shoulders, giving her a look of fearlessness, of courage, as though to say *if you see a thing is right and don't do it you are a sneak and a milksop but nobody is going to tell me what is right, I will make up my own mind about that.*

Still a little absently, Archie said, "She'll be popular with the young people. You know—like trees—churches die at the top. All very *well* to be charitable but you have to send somebody to be charitable. These young people—this kind of a congregation—*typical*—these are the winners, if they settle—for no-God—it can't keep alive on just the lepers, especially if nobody does anything about them. I'm not sure what

I'm talking about but I have a hunch this could be important."

I said, "Is Bertha McAddams, wife of the president of the board, here tonight?"

Archie's attention was on his plate, he was curious about the meat loaf, which smelled definitely unaccented, he said, "I shouldn't think so. Not in the flesh. In a manner of speaking, where Olin McAddams goes, Bertha goes. What made you ask?"

Then I told him about the old rector's list.

Some of them I'd been able to recognize; they were as I had pictured them. Steve Lucifer Retzlaff, for instance. There can be only one Steve Retzlaff to a group, if any. Cannot be two cocks to any one walk for long.

I told Archie that Dr. Ffolliott had called Retzlaff Lucifer, and Archie turned to look at the head table and said, "Lucifer? Could be."

At the head of the table, Hank Gavin had authority. In the ecclesiastical chain of command, this was his church. If Steve Retzlaff had become the power behind the pulpit, it was by now taken for granted, or perhaps nobody had noticed it. Nowadays when it has become the custom to give the presidency of a university to a money-raiser, possibly Retzlaff had counted on running this show and letting old Ffolliott or young Gavin attend to the God part. If he was including Hank Gavin in this pattern it might lead to complications.

I see that I am putting off a description of Steve Retzlaff and I judge this is because I feel you can do it better for yourself. You have to know one of him. The guy who has taken over and gets things done. The all-things-to-all-men technique. The poker player who plays his stack, not his cards. Some are fair, some dark, some fat, and some lean, they all have that air-of-command. I do not know why their tailoring is slightly exaggerated. To an enormous degree but nearly always hidden, a masked battery, they have personal magnetism. They are electable.

Steve Retzlaff was a small-medium size. It was the way he carried himself that made him look taller than he was, the tilt of his head that gave him personality plus on purpose, the fact that even when he was still he was always going someplace that made him look considerably thinner than he was.

All this is a patent exaggeration.

A life-size portrait must always be larger than life or it doesn't *look* life-size.

Steve Retzlaff was a dark, could-get-pudgy, just-off-handsome American Success Story in the flesh.

The funny part of it is I liked him.

Years ago at a dinner in Washington I sat next to Bill Bullitt who had been our ambassador to France when the Germans walked into Poland and I asked him if it hadn't seemed a terrific responsibility, and he said quite naturally: "Oh no, I just thought how lucky we were to have me there."

You had to know that Steve Retzlaff thought the same thing about Beach City and, good bad or unscrupulous, there wasn't anything that he wouldn't do for them. Could anybody ask for more?

I found that Archie, who was editor-publisher of the city's largest and more powerful newspaper and naturally had known him well for years, liked him, too.

"That's not to say I trust him," Archie said. "He's a very useful guy to have around if you don't underestimate him. Are you any more sensible than you used to be about ambition as the motivating force of a large percentage of the human race?"

This was a dig at the time I got my throat cut by a friend after Archie had warned me not to get it between her and the object of her ambitions. I still had trouble believing him while I was mopping up the blood.

"Ambition," Archie said positively, "is the sin by which the angels fell, and that's probably why old double FF called Steve Retzlaff Lucifer. Evidently Steve pushed the old gentleman around and he noticed it. Retzlaff is a born politician. Why we do not all realize that politics and politicians control our destinies, nationally and individually, I can't make out and never have. Standoffish about it. We're getting better, though. What we need is more good young candidates. Just about four years from now, it'll be time for the party to elect a governor from Southern California. Should have been two states—North and South California, as it is they rotate the offices. Steve Retzlaff ought to get the nomination. He never misses a trick. And he will trample anyone down with the pure and undefied conviction that it's his privilege and obligation so to do—anyone but his daughter Deedee."

"Which is his wife?" I said.

"On your young convert's right hand," Archie said with a sardonic grin, "next to her Jack Nestor, labor lieutenant for this district. As usual Gloria's got on too much lipstick. I will make you a bet. Having seen Mellie Gavin close up, Steve will see to it that Gloria doesn't have on too much tomorrow. Gloria is Steve's second wife, if he had it to do over he wouldn't but since a politician is only allowed two chances the best he can do is make her over."

"Striking looking," I said.

"He thought so then," Archie said, "I'm not sure it turned out just the way she expected either, I wouldn't call her an intellectual giant, and he hasn't much time for fun." And for some reason I found myself thinking in a flashback of another marriage that hadn't turned out, Colin and Sybil Rowe of Chicago.

Many people stopped to greet Archie. This helped me to attach the person to Dr. Ffolliott's short and simple annals of their characters. The all-well-lost-for-charm of Marv Gregory couldn't be missed as he said: "It's good to see you at one of our little shindigs, Archie," to which Archie muttered that the event of a new minister seemed to have hooked everybody except Bertha McAddams.

The name created a slight silence for itself. I was to find that it always did. Why? My reportorial sense came to life and even as the charming Mr. Gregory explained Bertha's unfortunate ill-health, supported by his wife's sympathetic murmurs, I had a glimpse of Bertha resembling a picture I had once seen of Hetty Green, the Witch of Wall Street, with her rusty, black, and old reticule scaring even the Morgans and I began to plan how I could get in to *see* Bertha the semi-invalid. Some of these had changed the map of empire quite as much as Cleopatra's nose.

Jack Nestor came by, he and Archie exchanged pointed remarks about places they'd been, elections they'd shared, and bosses they knew in Detroit and Hawaii. Then Archie said, "What'd you think?" which was understandable to Nestor who said, "He's been around more than most ministers, is that good or bad I don't know. What I've heard him say—he seems a little far out—religiously, not politically. I brought him some statistics he asked for yesterday and he said something about Pentecost—he said it happened every day to any man who'd stand still for it. I got a hunch—only a hunch, mind you—that his ideas about a new church and Steve's might not see eye to eye."

"That'd be too bad," Archie said.

"Sure," Jack Nestor said, "but if this—if Gavin means what he says—"

"Whatever it is or was," I said, "he means it. That's what he keeps telling everybody. He says one reason the church is now stagnant, fearful, and frivolous and makes it seem a social error to *show* any works, is because the intellectuals have doubletalked us out of believing Jesus meant what he said and expected us to do likewise."

"Be seeing you," Nestor said, and beat a hasty retreat.

Now I saw that Archie Paddock was looking for the first time with real interest at the big fellow who was eating heartily and apparently enjoying his company. Archie's eyes had snapped to attention, he said, "You used to take Q and A in your head when you worked for me, was that an exact quote? The church is stagnant and fearful and frivolous?" and when I nodded, "Does he expect to say that from his pulpit?" Hurriedly, I said, "I'm sure—he doesn't think we have much time."

After a considering pause, Archie Paddock said, "He will be thrown into the modern equivalent of the lion's den and the fiery furnace."

A blast of opposition shook me. "All right!" I said. "He *expects* all these people to call it foolishness and ignorance but they're not doing so good, are they, and where were they when God said let there be light? Moreover, Daniel *and* Shadrach Meshach and Abed-nego came out unscathed and unbitten as I remember it."

I saw that Archie was shaking with silent laughter, but after a bit of that he said, "The future candidate for governor isn't going to like that kind of unorthodox doctrine," and I said, "Well, do you want Mr. Retzlaff to be governor that bad?" and to this he said, "He's a hometown boy, Beach City probably won't have two chances, I've got to want him."

As nearly as I can remember it was about here that a sudden and unexpected and total silence fell upon the noisy, stuffy, overcrowded room. The kind of silence we used to say meant it was twenty minutes to or twenty minutes past. It held for a couple of seconds, into it came, clear and powerful, a conversation going on between two men. Behind the casual manner of speech, the hear-it-anywhere accent of exchange between two thirty-to-forty-year-old American males, the ordinary much-used words, a tremendous force sounded distantly the double double double beat of the thundering drum.

Chairs shifted to face them. The pergola contingent crowded their chairs into nonexistent spaces. Quite openly, everyone's attention had been caught. They were listening. I saw Mellie's eyebrows lift and for one second her lips tightened in exasperation. On the whole, she was looking encouraging, pleasant, and proud. As a wife should. Mellie started with decided advantages, of course.

The first word that rang was *terminology*.

". . . terminology," Steve Retzlaff's clear, resonant, used-to-speaking tones could be heard in the farthest corner, "I say again a lot of what's wrong is the terminology, it's either *stale* or it's uninteresting. For instance, nobody any more is very much interested in *sheep*."

The young minister's spontaneous roar of laughter released

some titters and guffaws, Hank kept on chuckling a little as he said, "Not only are they not interested, sheep got themselves a bad reputation in our beloved early days of the West. Got to be a dirty word—sheep—sheep men—"

"We still have fishing fleets—boats," Steve Retzlaff said. "Some night Nestor and I will take you out, it's picturesque still, at night. But farming has changed—what with machines and subsidies and science—a good deal in the last two thousand years. We sow now by airplane and helicopter."

"Still you have to sow *seed,*" Hank Gavin said mildly, "and that was created before it was in the ground. Burbank did a lot—but he didn't *create* any seeds. Now Jesus—stop and think about this a minute—" We stopped. Hank had said Jesus as simply as he would have said *Arnie Palmer* if they'd been talking golf scores, it was reverent but it was without strain or change, and all around the tables there was a startled movement, Archie says there wasn't and he is a great editor but I am a better reporter and I know there was, the small shock began to reverberate, in ordinary circumstances of social meeting when a man says *Jesus* it isn't the minister I can tell you, and more often it is pronounced *Gee-sus.* About Hank Gavin, the pastor, using it as just part of a talk with a plate of food in front of him it had a faint air of impropriety though, of course, we do know that some of Jesus' best work was done at dinners and at weddings and such. "Jesus," Hank went on, absorbed, glad to be talking about this, anxious to make himself understood, "used the tools to hand. He spoke of things, people, happenings familiar to the thousands who followed him, waited for him, brought to him those who were lame or blind or possessed of devils. Sheep, farms as he knew them, laborers in the fields, vineyards, wind sand rock storm boats— Some of what he told may as you say be wrong terminology for us now, some are as fresh as they were then—fresh as Shakespeare when you read his best work today. A good writer once told me that the Prodigal Son is among the great short stories of all time. We could bring the adventure of the man who got beat up and the Good Samaritan up to date, sure, have it on a city street and not a cop in sight, or a man thrown out of a car beside an eight-lane freeway, but human nature not changing at all ever it'd be hard to better the basic tale."

"They won't listen to those stale old quotes Sunday after Sunday," Gloria Retzlaff said in a little burst, "I know. It gets tiresome. Even if you're religious, it gets very tiresome. To try to sell it to *new* people—they don't believe blessed are the meek."

A breath of agreement moved, Hank Gavin said, "That

old Uriah Heep, wringing his hands and telling how 'umble he is. Or maybe Dickens' terminology is difficult now too, just as a couple of years from now nobody will be able to follow Kerouac. But you see, meek didn't mean that at all when Jesus used it."

"What did it mean?" Isabel Mayhew said in a warm and applauding voice.

"I found an illustration in a parchment at school," Hank said, "like the drawings we put beside words in the dictionary to help with their definition. Meek was like this—" he made a cup of his hands and held them out straight, and he said, "Jesus used it meaning willing to receive, to accept. The great experience. You hold out your hands and love fills them so full you can use it. For yourself. That's what Jesus was talking about."

We were all caught up in this, I must if possible convey that this was *talk*. Trade talk maybe, but real full dynamic conversation. At every table from every chair the listeners were taking part in it. Gert Cutler, who looked as though she should have on a short skirt and come in carrying a trayful of drinks from the bar, her husband animated out of the sullenness generated by being the bone of contention between two women, Isabel Mayhew in a strange, bitter admiration and Norma Gregory drinking at the fount of wisdom in all sincerity. This was—could be—a feast of reason and a flow of soul, communication from one to another such as above all things solaces man's loneliness, at least we were injecting a few raisins of personal expression into the tasteless dough of canned entertainment and debate which surfeits and brainwashes us until we believe Dr. Kildare is a more important doctor than Schweitzer.

"If you're going to make any impression," Steve Retzlaff said, nodding with emphasis, "you need new parables, anecdotes, illustrations."

"I've been trying out a few on my wife," Hank Gavin said, they all turned to where Mellie was seated, beside her a girl pretty enough to survive the long straight blonde hair whom I found out later was Deedee Retzlaff. Young Mrs. Gavin waggled one finger at him, a faint smile touched her lips and disappeared. It was enough but it wasn't riches by any means. Hank said: "At Notre Dame, Knute Rockne said no defense even if perfectly conceived and executed can stop a good football play perfectly executed."

Steve Retzlaff made a little face, he said, "Grant sports as the common denominator of our language, how do you apply it as terminology in modern Christianity? I may tell you I rather dislike the man-to-man type of thing myself."

Hank said, "Jesus told ordinary stories so amazing in their psychological diagnosis and so unusual in style that they've lasted in all their power and glory two thousand years if you'd care to reread them." He got to his feet. One side of this horrible room had a blackboard set into the whitewashed wall. Some Bible verses had been written there—Luke 2:46, that was Jesus at twelve both hearing and asking questions of the elders in the temple, and Daniel 6—good old Daniel in with the lions. Hank picked up the chalk, took a clean spot, and began with the little crosses and circles familiar to anyone who has followed football at all, and with these standard figures began to diagram a play.

"Let's say it's a touchdown go for broke," he said. "Here's your defensive team. Waiting. They have to. Sometimes a good defensive team can spot a play in a second, sometimes a good defensive captain guesses the play the quarterback will call in that situation. But they can never be sure. The element of surprise is with the offense. The defense has to try to be ready for half a dozen different variations of a play that can come off the same formation. The offense *knows.* An enormous advantage. If every man on the offensive team does immediately, exactly, and perfectly what he is supposed to do on that play, if every offensive player takes his man or fulfills his assignments, no defense can stop it. Steve, you remember a game when Bobby Layne with a fair team beat the best defensive team of all time, the 1956 Cleveland Browns, some silly score like 56 to 12—his men were up and nobody made any mistakes."

Steve Retzlaff had risen too, he had drifted over to stand watching our man at the blackboard, from where I sat it seemed to me the man with the purse strings looked thoughtful. He said, "Again, padre, what use can you put that to in this particular year of Our Lord?"

"Christ has given us the perfect play," Hank Gavin said simply, "and the power to execute it. It's all there. Take a piece of chalk and a blackboard and the New Testament and get your plays out of the Sermon on the Mount and if you call that corny, corn too is the staff of life, I say. Probably the story of the lost sheep is a little on the corny side, too. No defense of Lucifer or the devil or isms or orgasms can stop us for we will do the *works.*"

Side by side, they came back, both grinning, both taut and intent. I saw that Hank was a little taller, the strange thing was that Hank moved—I don't know how to explain this—as though there was no floor. All right, just the same, he did. I had noticed this a few times before, in a business suit in a Sunday School smelling of meat loaf and fog he had that—

that grace and spring of Nureyev. *Did he always have it?* I asked Mellie once, later, and she started to say *Godmama darling, be sensible,* but instead she gave me a cold stare and lifted one shoulder half an inch.

The actual conversation about terminology was started by Steve Retzlaff. He said that so much of religious terminology was old-fashioned, stale, had been quoted into meaninglessness, wasn't understood by many people who hadn't, he said, actually read the Bible any more than they had actually *read* Shakespeare.

"I agree we need some new terminology. There are old ones that still apply—remember Jeremiah saying something about My people have committed two evils; they have forsaken me, the fountain of living waters, and hewed them out cisterns, broken cisterns that can hold no water. New York would understand that. No one even began to begin to try to stop Hurricane Betsy or any of her sisters, did they? We can't always do it—but we might *begin.* We'd better begin." Hank said, "Help me out. Suggest something you would call *old* —and perhaps not responsive for people today."

"In His Steps," Steve Retzlaff said, not kidding, but the way he spoke it sounded as though he understood it less than hieroglyphics in an Egyptian tomb.

"In His Steps," Hank said, "of course what it means is to try to follow his example as a way of life. Well—how about *conformity to the prototype which is Christ?* Bigger words—mean the same thing—might be better understood today you think?"

"All right," Steve Retzlaff said. "What about *heaven and hell?"*

"Cosmos and chaos," Hank said, "isn't that what we call them now? The cosmos of harmony and order by the One Who runs the universe and never lets the sea spill no matter what we do. And chaos, a universe which says No God, and is making cold war and hate around the globe. Now now—see here—that's where we make our mistake. We don't go on the offense for the Risen Christ—and we fight among ourselves all the time, scarcely a spot anywhere, at home, in school and traffic, among allies, even among our own different interpretations of the Christianity we believe where there aren't rows going on—so the play won't work."

"I am the Light of the World," Marguerita Vosburgh said, "I hear some disputatious remarks about that."

"But that's the easiest," Hank Gavin said. "Sir James Jeans, not a churchman nor a minister, an eminent mathematician and astronomer of the Royal Society says all they, as scientists, have learned, all their concepts as of now, have simply reduced the universe to *light*. Potential and existent. So—he says this, he wrote it, it's not mine, it's his—he says therefore science now knows that the whole story of creation can be told with perfect accuracy and completeness in six words from the first chapter of the Bible—God said Let there be light. Who else? And Pierre Teilhard de Chardin says science shows us now that the history of evolution is up to the Risen Christ, which is another way of saying that Biblical cliché *As in Adam all die even so in Christ shall all be made alive.*"

He made it sound simple.

We felt it deep. For a moment it seemed rather wonderful to be just talking like this.

"Here's one you'll have trouble with, padre," Steve said, triumphantly. "How about the strait and narrow way I heard so much about—and we still do? Nobody likes the strait and narrow. We all resent it—at least I know I do. Life is short and I'd like a little fun myself."

"Fun—sure—" Hank Gavin said, "the old word is joy. But Steve, my friend, you'll have trouble if you try anything but the strait and narrow. Try driving home some other way, you'll land in jail or the morgue. Try telephoning to New York or flying to Bangkok or building a new bridge—they'll all have to be done on the strait and narrow."

"Mechanics—" Gloria Retzlaff said in a high, breathless way.

"Oversimplification," Steve Retzlaff said.

"I know," Hank said, "and a lot of people think foolishness and ignorance are synonyms for simplification and we're all so afraid of losing face, more than of anything else in the world, that we never get to the joy of it—the joy—in simple truth is where you find the angels of His Presence and—"

"There again—" Steve began. They were both back in their seats, and for a moment little ripples and rustles of talk began around the room, expressions of their own, questions, opinions, up and down. Steve sent his next words above it, flagged it down, got them back, he said, "Now *angels*—honest, padre, that word's worse than sheep—"

Angels, I thought, not again!

"Wait a minute," Hank Gavin said. "We must be careful not to let the effort to speak in rational, modern, or intellectual terms lapse into a dilution of spiritual insight that can be found only in revealed truth. A parable, a tale to be told, an anecdote or illustration to make a point, these change. Words are bridges from one of us to the other. But in the beginning was the Word, that's the big bridge from God to us, and angels come across it sometimes bringing messages, thank God—"

"You wait a minute, padre," Steve said, chuckling, "I'm a sentimental man myself as my daughter Deedee will tell you. I like her sentimental songs—she knows that. Angels on —oh, Easter cards, and she has some charming little white statuettes of angels, sort of like kewpie dolls, and in the cemeteries that are some in white marble—but surely you can't mean you believe in *angels* with wings, who—who exist."

For the first time, Steve Retzlaff had drawn his voice as a weapon. A stiletto.

I was swept back into one of those moments . . . this I've seen and heard already, I've been here before. Or of double vision such as an alcoholic has. Things keep repeating themselves. Across the room, I saw Mellie had her hand up, fingers outspread like a fan, over the fan her eyes were enormous and very bright, we were both in two rooms, two times, with two sets of people at once. She was covering her anger more carefully, more charmingly from these strangers, in Hank's new position, than she had bothered to do, needed to do, on that long ago Sunday morning after church at the country club in Chicago. She knew what Hank was going to say as well as I did and in spite of her father's angels that had helped fly the planes in the Battle of Britain so that so many could owe so much to so few she not only didn't believe it, she thought it was childish and in slightly bad taste.

"I have to accept and try to find out, don't I?" Hank said. "We've spent considerably more time on flying saucers of late than on our good or bad angels. But there was an angel who came to Jacob at Peniel, wasn't there? An angel named Gabriel spoke to Zacharias in the temple, as a messenger to tell him that his wife Elizabeth would bear a son to go before and prepare the way for Our Lord. An angel explained things to Joseph so he wouldn't put Mary his wife away when he found she was pregnant and of course it was an angel who announced to Mary that she was blessed among women—"

"We are Protestants," Marguerita Vosburgh said, in a chill key.

"I know," Hank said, "we all know that. But—don't you think we protested the abuse and corruption of the way certain Christians then in power were running our church? We weren't protesting the truth of the New Testament, were we?"

"There's a great deal of Oriental imagery in all that," Mrs. V. said. "You're not really saying—implying—that you yourself believe in them with wings and are going to expect us to?"

"I'm not sure," Hank said, in a troubled way, "I'd like to think I have a good angel that will come to me when I need help. And I need help! They came to help Jesus often—and John—all the early Christians. It's as difficult for us to be sure about them as it would have been if you'd told Peter we'd have submarines that would go under the Sea of Galilee. Or Ambrose that we'd fly through the air with the greatest of ease. Look at what they did to Galileo, now we seem in a way to be in reverse. Everybody'll believe anything about science or intellectual gobbledegook—but if you say Holy Ghost they lock you up or throw you out of divinity school. I don't know whether they have wings or not, Mrs. Vosburgh. I can't see that it makes a lot of difference myself."

"Perhaps not," Marguerita Vosburgh said. Dubious perhaps but no longer icy. A faintly maternal interrogation was in the long look she gave Hank.

That was because—most of us felt it. Or some of us. Didn't we?

Whatever it was! *Is.*

Darshan.

What is darshan?

A blessing. A benediction. Darshan happens. The Presence of the Holy Spirit. When it is evil—that feeling—we call it magnetism—hypnotism—possession by the devil. When it is good it can be called by its Indian name of darshan. Gandhi, who so loved Jesus Christ, had it for millions who could neither see nor hear him. A channel—a pervading *blessing.*

Hope—that was what it brought.

It brought hope as a candle brings light.

Harshly, Hank was saying . . . "Good things come to us—happen to us—get into our minds—somebody called angels God's thoughts passing to man—or reaching man. On wings or not, I don't know. None of this is more unusual than orbiting or flying to the moon—my wife's godmother knows the most wonderful story about the angels of *Mons*—"

This, Mellie wasn't going to have.

She was up and around several tables, her arm went around her husband. With a sort of brilliant arpeggio, she took us into another movement altogether, she said, "Hank darling, we *adore* you, it's been such fun, but we've got years and years ahead of us, we don't have to come to grips with this theory about angels tonight. The ice cream is melting, the coffee is perking until I firmly believe it can stand alone—I saw some apple strudel over there—"

Hank held the authority, the darshan, for a moment—not noticing—then he gave a laugh like a small thunderclap. I had never heard him laugh like that, I thought we're *intensifying*—

"The apple strudel with ice cream," Hank said, and Mellie put one hand against his cheek and then went, smiling enchantingly, to get it.

A buffet is a buffet is a buffet as I said before, last time it had been Call-Me-Jack the rector who had broken up the play about angels. This time it was—*and how deliberately*—Mellie. Moving in, as what wife doesn't, thinking in terms of trying to check her husband's costly indiscretions. Employing her social know-how to take him out of this foolishness and ignorance. At fast tempo the arpeggio led into gaiety, into everybody *chattering* at once, milling around the tables where the desserts were spread, coming back with plates and cups of coffee—no one could go back to angels nor wanted to.

Except Archie.

In a voice I hadn't heard him use since the day FDR died, he said, "I knew a man who was at Mons. I knew him well. In England, in the second war. I never met anybody tougher even here during the dock strike. He told me the angels rolled back the Germans at Mons. He saw them, he said so. He believed it. I hadn't thought of that in twenty years."

He sat absolutely still, watching Hank move from table to table, getting acquainted, stopping to talk, sitting down for a moment beside Mrs. Mayhew and her son Bobbie.

"That's a bad one," Archie said, "he was probably born on the fence and his mother's pushed him over—that boy. What'd you think an angel can do about that? And Isabel would rather be married to a minister than anything else on earth—she's a real cozy gal, too. Good—but she makes up a lot of rules as she goes along. How's your convert with that temptation?"

"It's a sort of freshman one—isn't it?" I said. "I don't think I'd ever worry about Hank and another woman. You see—this *is* a real love story, this is, this is Romeo and Juliet if they had lived to grow up and marry, everybody says it wouldn't have lasted but if it *did*—they are in love, the Gavins are. That's where real danger comes from for a man like Hank. Not from without. Only from within. The only woman who could destroy Hank is his wife."

"I can see that she *could,*" Archie said, his eyes on Mellie as she bent over to put the apple strudel in front of Hank, "but why would she?"

"She wouldn't mean to," I said, "except that—*she* hasn't been converted, you know."

"I see," Archie said.

We also saw Steve Retzlaff talking to Mr. McAddams, and in a few moments the president of the board got up and rapped on a glass and made a little good-night speech, filled with folksy language and good nature and enthusiasm. He was sure they were all as delighted as he was to welcome their new young pastor. To see and hear how eager he was to get on with the new church, with this kind of teamwork they might even be *in* the new church by this time next year. Certainly the new church was the most important thing for all of them, not just as a status symbol but as a symbol of a new start in what they might accomplish. Why, now he felt they had practically begun *digging*.

As the laugh subsided, Hank thanked him. He said, "Where were you planning to build this new church?"

Mr. McAddams, with an assist from Steve Retzlaff, told him.

Hank listened and said nothing.

The leave-taking, the crowding toward the doors, began. It halted abruptly, in surprise, when Hank said, "Just a minute—" and held up his hands, "After this manner therefore—" he said quietly and spoke for them that prayer which must have been inspired since in a few lines it covers every human need. They were to find this a precedent, a *custom,* it was impossible to meet with their new eager minister without a prayer, even if it was one small tenth of a second of pause, of eyes closed, of one word or two.

"I have a feeling," Archie said to me, "that before this is over we're all going to have to choose up sides."

For a moment, in the pergola, I found Mellie beside me, under the dripping, shrouded trees, wisps of fluffy powder-puffy fog drifting between and around us. Her hand on my arm felt hot.

"My husband turns out to be a young man who strikes matches so he can look and see if there is any gasoline," she said, very low.

"He—he has some plan," I said.

"I know, I know," Mellie said. "I wish I knew what I am doing. First it's the things you actually do—you make your mistakes there. Then you think them, you get them into your head, and some day they get into your guts and then you're in trouble."

"I should say it's the other way around," I said.

Mellie shook her head, she said, "You are a pet, you know. I simply couldn't have stood the angels of Mons again, in front of all those strangers."

3

Within a few weeks of coming to Beach City, Mellie Cheyne Gavin was living at all levels the life of the wife of a minister. This, she found, is not only something you do, it is something you are. Twenty-four hours a day, not only a demanding job but an *image*. And no woman born had ever had less to do with image-making than Mellie Cheyne.

Inevitably, in spite of her smooth poise and enormous self-confidence, she felt as though she had made a parachute jump and landed in another country where strange people spoke a different language and had other customs. "Nor," she said to me at that time, "did I jump voluntarily, lovey. You must agree that I was *pushed*."

My fumbling words to Archie at the buffet welcome that she had taken on this mad enterprise and fantastic experiment without either the call or the faith which sustained her husband were truer than I knew.

For my icy apprehension grew as to whether Mellie could stick it or not and what it would do to Hank if she couldn't. I saw that the outcome wasn't dependent upon washing dishes, the depressing, unmanageable antique-in-a-horrid-way parsonage, the chill fact that now very often for the first time in her life there were things she wanted and simply couldn't afford.

Many *firsts* showed up in this parish which was now Hank Gavin's.

Most of them might have happened to a girl who married a soldier and found herself in Alaska, or the lady of a diplomatic mission to the Far East, or those early brides who rode in covered wagons, or even just marriages or job transfers from a farm to a factory, from a small town to a vast metropolis, from a college campus to Cape Kennedy.

Those did not necessarily nor usually involve *division*.

True, Mellie detested Beach City and who could blame her? This crude raw town had the power, the gaucherie, the restless, often reckless drive of a new American city. Originally, it had not of course been Beach City, it had had a Spanish name, a small quiet little town for the ranches and orange groves and leisurely ocean trade, for those looking for its famed CLIMATE, in winter. Like New England and the South, such towns had been overrun by the coming of some industry, like La Pueblo de Reine de Los Angeles, people came pushing and Santa Juana awoke to the sound of the oil derricks in its quiet hills and the traffic jam at its docks to find itself Beach City. The people who came were looking for jobs, for a quick buck, for a possible oil well of their own and soon shoved out the older residents, as urban growth usually does. The people who would have been of Mellie Cheyne's world had moved. One by one, then in toto, they had built homes at nearby Balboa or on the Lido Isle or Newport Bay, praying these would last their time before Progress transformed them. Marguerita Vosburgh was one of the few old-timers who had stayed put. She was a rich widow, she cared little for Society, and she had decided to die in the house in which she had been born, brought up, and married.

Much that had been Mellie Cheyne Gavin's whole life had been swept out of her present life *entirely*. Not only family, friends, home, and Society which she had ornamented and whose round of work and play had been her own, but these were times to try a woman's soul in petty ways as well as those too huge and vital for mortal tongue or pen to scribe.

Dishes to wash, on the one hand.

To the best of her considerable ability and steely young horsewoman-swimmer strength, Mellie coped with the *daily* housework. She found as a-many of us have that it takes a different set of muscles.

Never never never again dispute that the modern tiny little kitchen is progress beyond the wildest dreams of womankind, she said. Those lovely big roomy kitchens, she said, people used to say that. Only a *pedometer,* she said, would make anybody *believe* the number of miles per day. From the screen porch to the stove to the storage pantry to the china closet to the wash tubs to the dining room, upstairs and downstairs and in my chamber—fifty miles a day. The *house,* I mean, *and* especially the kitchen, the big roomy kitchen with lots of cupboards and shelves!

This, I found, was not what she minded.

And to tell the truth, it was the kitchen and its poltergeists that brought her together with a good many of the women of the church who had either thought her standoffish or thought they ought to be standoffish themselves. In omnipresent neighborliness which never dies and the same good will my grandmother had known when she rode the Methodist circuit in the last century, they would come to her aid, and Mellie, who long ago discovered that the shortcut to integration and unity and to using other people is to let them do something for you, cheered loudly as they came. Naturally, it was easier for Gloria Retzlaff, who made the best marriage, and Gert Cutler, with her one and only extraordinary talent for reconstruction and decoration, and Isabel Mayhew, owner of Cordon Bleu cook books, and Norma Gregory, who felt guilty if she *wasn't,* to make friends, to be at ease with, Mellie Cheyne Gavin's inescapable elegance in the kitchen where they were obviously her superiors in knowledge and know-how than in the parlor where they weren't. To sit over a cup of tea or coffee at two ends of a kitchen table would probably prevent some of the alleged feminine mystique epidemic. Gert Cutler, who in her secret heart always was a little on edge with what she still called a *lady,* had found the minister's lady cursing like a walking delegate, wearing a priceless gilt scarf tied around her head for a dust cap and too large rubber gloves on her hands totally unable to defrost the goddam man-eating Frigidaire. This Gert had done as swiftly and slickly as in a TV commercial. In fact, she'd accepted the soft drinks necessarily served in the rectory by saying, TV commercial-wise, "Come alive, you're in the Pepsi generation—here's looking at you!" and then, over cigarettes, had offered to redecorate and refurnish this dark hole of Calcutta.

That night Mellie said to Hank, "What the hell is a prayer cell?"

She had come out into his office-study-library where he had been seeing people all evening—he was drawing them, he was making them believe that he was always there, Dr. Ff had always been vague and distraught if they interrupted his evening hours—to get him to come to bed. "Now with that seven o'clock prayer service every morning whether anybody comes or not and lots of them don't," she told me, "I have to see he gets some sleep."

If either of them were actively aware of the contrast between this big room with its morris chairs and huge desks and tables and the exquisite house in Chicago, they didn't show it. Hank didn't really think of this actively any more. Mellie had forced herself not to notice it the way one can grow accustomed to the cast on a broken arm.

"What made you ask that?" Hank said a little absently.

"Gert Cutler is going to transform the kitchen," Mellie said. "She said it reminded her of the catacombs you'd told them about and what a nice place it would be for a prayer cell meeting—make you feel like an early Christian."

"It's just a small idea," Hank said. "Our opposition which is trying to make do with man-god instead of God made Man, has some fair technical devices. Cells, for instance. I like small, known-only-to-each-other prayer groups, that meet often, the way the disciples did. To ask and seek and sort of—pray together. It reminds them to pray. I thought the Cutlers had a fair start—three of them—and three outsiders—"

"They oughtn't to be living together at all," Mellie said. "Any psychiatrist would tell you that."

"Not if I saw him first he wouldn't," Hank said.

She stared at him for a moment, then she said nothing. At least he had, so far, been noncommittal and discreet, he hadn't joined battle with anybody about his own sharp rejection of Freud, Adler, and Horney, to put forth his support of Jung and Frankl and their concept that Love being the supreme energy the only answer to anything they uncovered lay in God.

Gloria Retzlaff had a psychiatrist. She had been going to him for years. It was, as Mellie knew only too well, one of her chief topics of conversation.

"I don't think it would do anybody any good to run away from this," Hank said slowly, "any of the Cutlers, I mean."

"If there isn't a murder," Mellie said, looking black, *"which* I will do my best to prevent. Does Gert say she believes in Operation Prayer Cell?"

They had this in common, still, Hank thought. People. People people people. Mellie could talk to them and they talked to her. His eyes on her then must have been full to the brim of his heart's longing.

"She's faced that she hates the—the children's grandmother so much she'd like to feed her rat poison," Hank said, "and she's willing to try anything because she says Art Cutler—and maybe the kids too, though they love her best—would hold it against her forever if she booted Grandma out."

"Gert's a hulk of emotional superstitious female flesh," Mellie said kindly. "She *so* does her best. Don't we all?"

"A prayer cell won't hurt her," Hank said, "but one thing is needful. It's inside the house now. Watch it work—"

Nothing more was said about the prayer cell.

Neither of them were trying to convert the other. They were trying to play what seemed to them fair.

Once on a visit I found on Mellie's table, set up in the bow window of her bedroom, some books on *What a Minister's Wife Should Know, The Role of the Minister's Wife, How to Succeed as a Minister's Wife without Really Trying,* or titles to that general effect. They explained all about the duties, Mellie said, and the social activities, the bazaars, the music, the protection of the minister's time when he is writing his sermon, the dealing with silly women who wish to spend time alone with him, the ambitious who want to run more things than they should be allowed to, what they serve at buffet suppers. None of them, Mellie said with triumphant glee, say a goddam word to speak of about her spiritual life or whether she is supposed to help anybody in that field or pray with or for them or believe one goddam word her husband says or think it's a lot of mythological hogwash. "However," she said, "I couldn't have a prayer cell in the catacombs without calling it the whited sepulcher, could I?"

On another plane, dishes had brought her to a pleasant, surface, well-mannered intimacy with Isabel Mayhew. Mrs. Mayhew, it turned out, was a *collector,* something that Dr. Ffolliott had overlooked. Smiling sweetly, Mellie said nothing was as inborn as collecting. Either you were or you weren't. If not, it was as definitely missing as being tone deaf or having no card sense. If so, you *collected* something, anything, everything. In the beginning, Mrs. Mayhew had collected teacups. She had inherited some her grandmother had received when engagement teas brought out dozens of them, all different. To these she had added for years, when she went to New York she spent time on Third Avenue and certain dealers, when a stray teacup arrived in Worcester or Crown Derby or Sevres showed up, notified Mrs. Mayhew, and of course in San Francisco it was possible to find *treasures* in Gump's or Chinatown. Now she had them in glass cabinets—they were really lovely—Mrs. Gavin and the rector must come to dinner soon and see them.

"I hope Bobbie's wife will care about them some day," she said to Mellie. She came by in the morning, to see if there was anything Dr. Gavin wanted her to do for him; she always came to the parsonage first. It was part of the role of a minister's wife to see, without offending her in any way, that she never got any farther. "Now that Bobbie's seeing a good deal of Deedee Retzlaff," Bobbie Mayhew's mother said, "I'm hopeful. She's such a darling and so well brought up and I'm sure she'd know better than to wash them with detergents. When Bobbie came in last night and told me he'd been out with her again—I didn't ask him, I never do, but he nearly always stops by my room if my light is on and we have a *visit*—I had a feeling that—he was quite *stirred* —which I wasn't sure about before."

To this there had been nothing Mellie Gavin could say.

She knew Bobbie hadn't been out with Deedee—Deedee had been at a rehearsal at the high school.

"She's my brownie," Mellie said to me about Deedee on one of my visits, and I remember with what gay affection she put her arm around the girl's slim shoulders. "You must have read about the Brownie who used to come and do the work while you were asleep and all you had to do was leave them a saucer of milk? That's my Deedee!" They laughed together and I thought that Mellie *could* have a daughter as old as Deedee, I thought I had never seen her show so much affection for anyone and that Deedee must have fitted somehow, very specially, into some of Mellie's nostalgia, her loneliness for all the things she had known. "Now," Mellie said, "go play something nice and quiet—like Chopin, or Grieg, or even a tinkle of Debussy." The girl went to the enormous concert grand in the corner of the old drawing room, and Mellie said, "I've got some ideas about our church music," and then to me, "It's good to have you here. I'd like to just sit for maybe fifteen minutes—shall we? She has a nice touch, doesn't she?"

The music of a small étude by Chopin soothed the room, soothed us, made me feel better, more at home. Shabby and unused as the big parlor was, there was a certain dignity to it and I saw Mellie loosen up under it.

She took a couple of sheets of paper from the pocket of her coat-blouse and handed it to me. She said, "I found these—scribbled—on the telephone pad."

In Hank's bold pointed handwriting I read *even though when they ask you give them a diamond as big as the Ritz, the biggest diamond in the world, it's still a STONE, it's not bread, they cannot eat it, they will go hungry away.*

"It's a good line," I said.

"What does it mean?" Mellie said.

"You remember what they were talking about the other night," I said, "he and Retzlaff. Terminology—I suppose Hank's—working on that—he thinks they'll understand that about the diamond better than just a stone—If he asks for bread, will he give him a diamond and if he does—*I* don't know!"

"Try the next one," Mellie said, lighting a cigarette as the music drifted into a lilting little Spanish song I seemed to remember from somewhere—Deedee didn't play very well but somehow it came off the paper, it moved you. She was playing now to herself and happy in it.

The next one said *The church everywhere is in retreat. In withdrawal. In compromise.*

"Fighting words," I said.

"True, however," Mellie said. "Do you know what the final heresy is?"

I told a lie then. I knew what Hank thought it was. And it was to come up later—the final heresy of an earthly paradise always built on sand. But I had some inner hunch that right here and now I didn't want to seem to understand things about Hank that Mellie either didn't or wouldn't.

It wasn't dishwashing that was trying Mellie's soul. It was that she was outside Hank's real life.

What he scribbled on the pad beside the telephone, what absorbed his thought day and night, was his inner self. She was now no part of that. They were living together in great love, passionate love for each other, and yet they were living in different worlds. His wife was taking part only in the outer action, an adequate comparison is difficult, as though she were married to a man whose life was composing music, therefore self-centered as only the dedicated musician can be, and she did not like music. A thankless task, without unity. Those women who married soldiers and went to Alaska, or perhaps followed their husbands to oil jobs in Saudi Arabia or saw their men vanish for months into the space program or atomic projects—they had *unity,* they were separated by miles, by time, by circumstances, but they were at *one* in sympathy and acceptance. Mellie had only her love for Hank to sustain her in her sacrifice, they could have been in a tent in the middle of the Sahara, in a small unseaworthy boat in a storm at sea, she wouldn't have cared, if they were one, united, speaking heart to heart as they used to do. They spoke different languages, when they talked to each other there were many times when the languages had no word in common at all. Her love was so great that sometimes she found herself in the chill of a wintry night alone, unable to get into that other sphere though she could see him in it. If she could again feel that sense of oneness, beyond what most people ever achieved, which they had had before this—this—*obsession* took hold of him. She was a fighter. She would have fought anyone—anything—for him. But she did not know how, she was afraid to fight *him,* if she won she might destroy the very thing for which she fought.

She did not talk to me directly at this time, but I knew her so well I could ESP her inner feelings sometimes, and I felt that she had stopped shadow-boxing. If she could be a tiger in defense of her love, I think she knew now that she was fighting Christ the Tiger, as T. S. Eliot called him. And *then* she had to stop and remind herself that she didn't *believe* in Christ the tiger or Christ the anything else!

You would have let me go, she remembered, you would

have left me that time. *You* would have left *me* flat to follow in these footsteps I don't even believe are there. Left me forever. I couldn't. I couldn't have left you. But you would have—you think you have the morning star so I come second. I *know* this. And I can't see the morning star.

Finally she said, "Do you know what he's up to about this board meeting? You know he's been waiting to call his first board meeting—and he's up to something, but I don't know what."

"No more do I," I said truthfully.

"Neither does Lucifer," Mellie said, lighting another cigarette. "Gloria has been trying to pump me. A minister's wife must never be pumpable, it says so, not quite in those words but that's what it says. Nevertheless it's just as well I don't know."

"Are you going to the meeting—when is it?" I said.

"Next Monday night," Mellie said, "and no. I'm not a member of the board, ducky." She got up and came quite close to me, seeking companionship, and I put my arms around her knees and felt that they were not quite steady. "Don't pay any attention to me," she said, "I'm not like this except at odd moments of which this seems to be one. Most of the time I am doing my job. I am a top job minister's wife. They adore me, on the whole. It's that *Chopin*—he always makes me make a fool of myself, that'll be all, Dee."

The phone rang just as Deedee got up and Mellie went out into the hall to answer it and Deedee watched her. Her voice came back, "No no—that's kind of you Isabel, yes I expect he will go early, he always does, but you won't need to come for me, you see I'm not on the board—I think it's better for a wife not to be on boards, don't you? Thank you just the same, my love."

To Deedee she said, "Off you go—" and the girl ran out taking the Chopin melody with her and I thought for a moment about *Chopin* and how he spoke to us being dead so many years and wondered if he could *hear* it, if he was connected with it still.

"Who is on the board?" I said.

"Come out in my lovely new kitchen and I'll tell you," Mellie said. "I have to start TV dinners—Hank has no idea any more what he's eating."

Moving about, she named them.

Mr. Olin McAddams, husband of Bertha.

Mr. Steven Retzlaff.

Archie Paddock.

Mrs. Marguerita Vosburgh.

Mr. John Joseph Nestor.

Mrs. Isabel Mayhew.

Mr. and Mrs. Marvin Gregory.

"A strong board," I said.

"How right you are," Mellie said, closing her eyes, but whether to shut out the board or the TV dinners I couldn't tell. "And all Lucifer's."

"Oh, no," I said, "don't believe that. Not Archie—at least I don't think so."

"He's never been to a meeting yet," Mellie said.

"He'll be at this one," I said grimly. "Hank is persuasive."

"I think it's about the new church," Mellie said. "He was giving it back to God in his morning prayers, that much I do know."

4

Meeting Meeting Meeting.

Board Meeting Board Meeting Board Meeting.

The history of our times can be told in terms of meetings, he's in a meeting, he had to go to a meeting, this is the day of our board, financial, up-the-down-staircase, stockholders', non-stockholders' Monday Tuesday Wednesday Thursday Friday Saturday meeting, he has a meeting this afternoon, he has a committee meeting a subcommittee meeting this morning let's have a meeting tonight yes he's here but he's at a meeting sometimes people have been known to spend 82 per cent of their business, working, professional lives in meetings.

Nobody knows yet whether this is good or bad.

After he had been in office, as it were, for a time that seemed short to some and long to others, dotted by only prayer cell and small committee meetings about minor points in routine, the new young rector had called his first board meeting.

To start with, it seemed ordinary, run-of-the-mill, with only a little more zing and speed than old Ffolliott had permitted.

Reporting on it to me, Archie Paddock said that at first he had decided that I had lost my nose for news entirely. As it progressed, he concluded that I had merely reverted to my early days as a sob sister, so-called. "You always were a sentimentalist," he said defensively over the phone.

When upon my insistence he came to report in person, while by no means a convert, he admitted that he had come as far as to be of two minds about Hank Gavin and his bomb.

The first half hour was taken up with the usual personal polite chit-chat, the next with routine moves.

Then Gavin himself brought them to the real issue.

"On mention of the new church, and I must say Gavin

was courteous about it," Archie told me as we sat in the loggia which at my beach house is really the living room. "Steve Retzlaff took over." He told me the story of that board meeting as he saw it. I will tell it now as a narrative. Archie Paddock was a sound editor with that trained memory for words and faces which is beaten into any good reporter, and the objective and impersonal fairness required of a publisher-editor for all his readers if he fulfills his true function of the most necessary of all the four freedoms. But I must leave out repetition of circumstances with which the reader is already familiar, though the board was not, and I can also now add some sidelights, opinions, and emphases which I got later from Hank, from my old schoolmate, Marguerita Vosburgh, and, quite a while thereafter, from Jack Nestor.

At the time Steve Retzlaff got the ball, there appeared to be under his expert hand an amiable and accustomed unity among all those present. Above all, even on the part of Norma Gregory and Mrs. Mayhew, a habitual smiling willingness to allow the able and energetic Mr. Retzlaff to go ahead with his well-advanced plans. Nobody had any reason to disagree with them, nobody else wanted nor had the ability to take over, and if some of this was serving the ends of Steve Retzlaff's ambitions they were all in accord with same as worthy and advantageous to the whole..

The only difference between this meeting and many others in the big, wood-paneled, book-lined, badly lighted library where such meetings took place didn't seem to change anything. Not in the beginning. Of course they were aware of the substitution of the tall, skinny young figure with the shock of sandy hair for the fat old gentleman with his white poll who used to sit in that seat, across from the chairman, Mr. Olin McAddams. They took cognizance of the ease with which the new pastor sat there, two or three of them felt rather than saw that behind his gravity was a sort of joy-is-an-inside-job smile. Steve and Archie Paddock and Marv Gregory knew that the well-worn, dark-gray suit had been made by a tailor far from Beach City and that his yellow-silver-black tie bore a famed name. The conclusion was that it was nice to have somebody around who was so—good-looking?—so at ease—someone they could be proud of. He would look well anywhere. In the swimming pool. On the playing fields with the youth group. In the new church.

They had rather liked opening with his quiet prayer for guidance and light. Why not? After all, this *was* a Christian board meeting.

The first thing he said when they got down to the real

business of the meeting was: "You feel that a new church is imperative?"

Oddly, he asked this not of the head of the building program, but of Mrs. Vosburgh, and this was all right, she was an elderly woman, she had social standing, a well-known name. Never taken by surprise, Mrs. Vosburgh said emphatically, "This address is bad—you know, it's not at all attractive to new people moving to Beach City. It's a run-down neighborhood, you know. Dr. Ffolliott at one time drew a lot of people to hear him on Sunday, he had quite a reputation for oratory, but we've had a steady loss of membership—and none coming in."

The new minister looked around the table. It was then, Marguerita told me, she noticed his eyes. As they passed from Steve Retzlaff's dark, intelligent countenance to Mr. McAddams' middle-aged muddled but shrewd, to Jack Nestor, sharp and ready for anything, as a labor leader in Beach City would have to be, Marguerita had a—a strange impression that there was—not light exactly—that they saw more—she couldn't explain it—but *something.*

Something in this familiar shabby old room, this routine-I-have-to-go-to-that-board-meeting, that could not be entirely explained by a mere change in their pastor. A new vitality, a feeling of extraordinary importance, as though this was actually *part of* the mainstream, not a bit of still water. To her own surprise, she connected this *somehow* with the slight argument—discussion—about *angels* at the buffet supper. When she was a little girl her mother, who had been a remarkable woman and *accomplished* far beyond what these present-day highly educated young females had any idea of, had always spoken of little Marguerita's guardian angel—and there might be something in this give-me-a-child-for-the-first-seven-years because, though she hadn't thought of it nor admitted it for some half-century, she still—just as a bit of superstition, probably—asked for help sometimes. And in her nightly Bible reading she had come upon the *angel* who smote off Peter's chains in prison—in *Acts.*

"You all feel the same way about this?" Hank Gavin said, and then they all—including my pal Archie Paddock—got the impact of his voice. *I could see it hit old McAddams,* Archie said, and Steve Retzlaff sat up at full attention.

Hearty satisfaction was what that voice gave old McAddams. This youngster would not be eloquent—eloquence was out of style. No no—he had style of his own, he wouldn't quote so many *poets* of whom most people had never heard in spite of so many more going to college, but he would have more communication, as a speaker at the Rotary Club luncheons, high school graduations, local TV panels, radio, and meetings of all kinds, he'd be a knockout. His eyes met Jack Nestor's and they confirmed an opinion they'd been in the process of forming. This was exactly what the church needed. On the button, their nod said.

"The vote on our need for a new church as soon as possible is unanimous, Dr. Gavin," Jack Nestor said.

A momentary pause and then Hank Gavin said with a chuckle, "Forgive me—this *doctor* business. I am a doctor of divinity, when you've been plain Mr. Gavin all your life, it's a trifle surprising. Of course it's proper. For I am your priest."

That word, in the slightly harsh, memorable, strongly masculine voice, was heard by them all, echoed, seemed to go on tolling in the quietness that fell upon the room.

Priest?

Surely not.

Many words, some of them not understood, had been used here by Dr. Ffolliott's threatening reactionary predecessor who had arrived in a predominantly Catholic community loaded for bear and ready to resist all things suggested by the word *priest*. Priests were part of what had started the initial separation of Christianity, which had gone on separating into so many pieces that sometimes it was difficult to believe they were all supposed to be about the same thing.

Into the startled void, the new man's words surged quietly, as he began to tell them for the first time a little of his own story, in order to convince them that he was convinced that he had been *called* to serve them. There is no need for me to repeat it here. But a few things are necessary, either new to us or because on them his all-important board began to judge him—and judge of him.

He was, Marguerita said, halfway through his opening sentence before anyone realized it was a sort of paraphrase of a quotation—the way he said it, it just seemed a man talking. "The spirit of the Lord is upon me, because he has anointed me to speak the gospel to the poor, confused, unhappy people, to preach to them deliverance of the captives and recovering of sight to their *blindness*, to set at liberty those that have been bruised and beaten by life, to tell them that this day—today—*now*—all years are acceptable years—to come and see the power of Our Lord relevant to observable human needs whatever they may be."

Of course he had twisted it some, they felt embarrassment, surprise, and question, and a first unconscious stiffening resistance.

Steve Retzlaff gave it a tolerant attention, tinged with slight exasperation at the delay. It was strictly church talk, and as such came up from time to time, but he had hoped to get home early and get a night's sleep. Loving your neighbor was a good idea, sometimes impossible, if you didn't look out for yourself first who was going to and then you could get things done for your neighbor. He was a patient man, when necessary, but he'd expected better sense from a fellow with Gavin's background, still probably all preachers had to give out with their pitch from time to time and this was the man's first board meeting. Not that he, Steve Retzlaff, wasn't for *the church*. In its place it had a good influence. As plans for his future shaped up and he began carefully, unobtrusively, building a personal political organization, he knew exactly where the church fitted in, neatly as a piece in a mosaic. Where the personality and drive and style—he had class—of this new man could and would be used legitimately. Religion was an effective thing, if a man knew how to use it and did not go too far. The Rotary went for it in a big way at their meetings. Most of the service organizations opened with prayer. A respectable, no doubt beneficial procedure.

"—I was a businessman myself," Hank Gavin was saying, smiling at the realtor, the industrialist, the labor leader, the publisher, the CPA—Marv Gregory—"like the men who were his followers—the fisherman, the doctor, the tax collector, the tentmaker, the financier. The Twelve. Then the Other Seventy also, of whom we are the uninterrupted, time-space continuum moving in the direct order of the stream of Light. And that's why a prof I had at Yale in comparative religions told us that *the* most important moment in Christianity was when Peter and John met the lame man at the gate and healed him. I didn't get it then, but when I tried to pretend I'd never read the New Testament and started all over—I knew. Third chapter of Acts. It's quite a story."

Again, Archie said, he somehow managed to get them—though Steve Retzlaff looked slightly annoyed and McAddams was on edge because he always told Bertha just what time he'd be home, but this boy—not boy of course, except to Archie all men under forty were boys—made it something new, quite a story, *not* a repeated-until-it-makes-no-sense-and-what-has-it-to-do-with-us bit of jargon. Something which, as he said, made clear *the relevance of true religion to observable human needs*—Archie liked that line, it became one of his favorite quotes.

"Of course you're way ahead of me on this one," Hank said, "but I'd—if you don't mind—like to start off with it in our first meeting as—sort of a platform. Remember, this was *after* the crucifixion and the resurrection, this all deals with the forty days when he came back, *now* the Risen Christ and wrapped it all up for them. This was *after*. Well, there was a certain cripple, born that way, who was carried up every day to the front of the church, and when he saw Peter, the big fisherman, and young John going in he asked them for alms. I sort of see Peter shaking his head and saying I haven't any gold, or even any small silver, but I'll give you what I do have. In the name of Jesus Christ of Nazareth, rise up and walk! And it says Peter took him by the hand and lifted him *up*, and I like it that it says they all went into the church together and the lame man went with them *leaping*. Everybody *saw him* and they'd known he was a cripple for years. Of course a crowd gathered, so Peter said to them: 'Don't think we did this under our own power, making this man walk and leap.' Then he told them that it was the way the Christ had taught them—the Power of God who loves us does this for him, so that his heart will know that there is a God who loves him."

Hank stopped then and took a long breath.

Nobody interrupted. Their faces were turned to him.

"You can imagine how this rocked the high priests," he said. "They had a meeting, and they said, 'What good did it do to crucify this man if his followers can do the same *works*. That's the whole point. There have been others who could heal but nobody else ever taught his followers how to do it. Maybe we've only made things worse.' And they had because here *we are*—you and I—and he still teaches us by his words—and his presence—how to lift up those who are crippled in life. None of it would have been worth a hoot, would it, if it only worked when a man named Jesus of Nazareth was there in person? No no—we are the continuum of Peter at the gate of the temple, we know that."

As he got to this, I remember that Archie Paddock stopped and was a long time lighting another cigar.

We could hear the waves crashing on the beach, a high tide was running, and the waves shook the house and sometimes the spray splashed on the glass and ran down in foamy rivulets. A few houses down, someone had turned on a huge searchlight, which made a path across the sand and showed a panel of breakers, rising and coming down again like a waterfall of silver and gold and turquoise. The dark sheen beyond was restless under the stars and the sound of the wind had a threat in it. It might have been any beach anywhere, a time-continuum, a storm rising on the shores of Galilee, Paul's ship sailing close by Crete against a tempestuous wind called Euroclydon and running under an island called Clauda. I thought I had better go back and read *Acts* and I knew that Archie had done it already.

After his cigar was really puffing he said, "Does this kind of talk strike you as slightly mad? A little fanatical?—tell me the truth now and never mind about being a godmother."

"No, it doesn't," I said, "you ought to know we can't jump at any such conclusion after the things you and I have seen happen that we were quite sure were mad. What I want to know is how the others took it."

"For a couple of minutes, we were mesmerized," Archie said, and gave me an annoyed grimace that I knew was meant to be a grin. "He put a lot of sound dramatic value in it. The stockbrokers I've known in my time were salesmen all right but not—anyhow none of us had figured on this guy being so—so dramatically persuasive. I suppose we should have—that's part of being a top salesman. Today everything is salesmanship. Hammers in your head, sponges in your sinus, and gremlins in your stomach and your bathtub in a Roman forum."

"Hank has precedence," I said, "Jesus and Paul and St. Francis and John Wesley and George Fox—"

What came next at the meeting was Hank turning directly to Steve Retzlaff and saying, "I'm in accord with you about the need for a new church. I'd like to be brought up to date on your plans."

Gavin wasn't the only top salesman at the meeting, and Steve Retzlaff had come prepared to put this through *tonight*. Now that the doddering, meaningless delay caused by old Ffolliott from sheer inertia was out of the way they could start. Retzlaff had a man who was willing to gamble on urban renewal and was sure that in twenty-five years building would be solid from San Francisco to San Diego and every foot within reach in Beach City worth triple its value. The man would buy this present property. Also he had brought pictures of the site he'd selected for the new buildings. Lovely, low, rolling fields, at the base of the little foothills that were becoming the town's best residential section. A few clumps of live oaks, a picturesque row of eucalyptus, even one pepper tree, probably been there in the time of the mission fathers, and a small winding road. To look at it, it was hard to believe it was only twenty minutes by car from downtown Beach City. With this went an architectural drawing of a very tall, thin church with a high, steeply pitched roof, two walls of glass, and above all a tall, thin cross. On one side was a patio, leading, Retzlaff told them, to a recreational building with offices and a bookstore and a library and rooms for lectures, luncheons, get-togethers, and meetings. Could be used for any educational or even civic purposes. On the other side, one of the fields had been converted by bright crayons into a swimming pool, a sports field, a play yard for smaller children, beyond that open playrooms with tables and blackboards opening into a room that could be used for dances and had a bar—soft drink of course. Behind all a large space had been left, marked off as a parking lot of impressive dimensions.

After Hank had looked at them for some time he passed them on without speaking, they went round the circle to the delighted gasps of Norma and Marv Gregory, Mrs. Vosburgh's "This is splendid," to Jack Nestor's startled "Oh Boy!" According to Archie Paddock, it was a setup hard to beat.

"With the sale of this property here and what we have in the Building Fund," Steve Retzlaff said, "we can buy that land, once we own it we'll have no trouble getting financing to build. Some time ago when there was talk of a subdivision out there I took an option for us at a good price."

A murmur of approval went around.

"As you all know," Retzlaff went on, "for some time now it's been necessary to get a permit to build a church anywhere. I can tell you, property values go down in the neighborhood so they tell you. However, I don't think we'll have any difficulty getting a building permit from the City Council. Mike Aguirre the president is a friend of mine and I've talked to most of the residents out there. They won't make any objections."

So things were rolling along nicely, why not? Could anything be more forward-looking, advantageous, prestige-making, and convenient than the actions of the head of their building program? If he had an eye on his own future, surely a candidate had to have a church and to see photographs of him, his wife, and their lovely young daughter entering his place of worship in this most attractive setting couldn't do Beach City any harm. Fine citizen, good family man, successful in business Steve Retzlaff had become. He and the new young minister would make quite a team, with Retzlaff, who had so much more experience, calling the plays.

No wonder approval was unanimous.

Or was it?

Though he didn't move, their eyes turned to their priest—no no, not *priest,* minister—and found only the shape of his smile left. His jaw, the falcon nose were noticeable, when he spoke there was fire, though he began on a low key. He said, "So far from their daily lives, their businesses, the places they go to lunch, from shopping and parking and going to the movies and City Hall—is that a good idea?"

After a moment of bewildered silence, Olin McAddams answered comfortably, "Well, now, Dr. Gavin, they don't exactly shop or go to business on Sunday, do they?"

"Were you figuring to build a one-day-a-week church?" Hank said, and bent forward to face his chairman. "The six other days, twenty-four hours each. What about them? Six days of temptation, fear, indecision, unrest, boredom, phobias, tired nerves, greed, lust, growing social diseases once more, sick, worn-out bodies, fighting traffic, political strife, news, hating the job and the boss and the in-laws and the bill collectors and each other, wanting things we can't have, not wanting things we've got, envying your neighbor, unruly children, too many children or not enough, clashes of interests and personalities and war and catastrophe screaming and drumming at us from every front page and transistor and TV. Christ promised he would be with us. I ask you this—shouldn't his priest hold open the door of his house where his brothers can come in out of that every day to pray?"

Again the pause. Mrs. Vosburgh said, "A good many will use a bookshop, a library, playgrounds, every day. We plan to have a program of activities, book reviews, morning musicales, meetings, so that there will be something to do each day." Looking around, she got nods from most of the board. "I'm afraid I don't know quite what people you're talking about, Dr. Gavin."

"I'd like you to," Hank said simply. "I was remembering about a night in Korea—it was raining and in Korea rain sticks to you. We weren't sure where we were or where we were going or where the enemy was and the snuffies were wet and cold and hungry and miserable and all of a sudden our chaplain shouted Either the church is *here* or it isn't anywhere. Either I can bring you God's love to warm and feed and comfort you here and now or it doesn't exist. And—Mrs. Vosburgh—he did. He prayed and we *were* warmed and fed and comforted though nothing outside had changed any. Those are the people I'm talking about—most of us never forgot that night. I'd like our church to be like that."

As usual, he was on his feet. Easy to visualize him that night in the rain, a big, skinny young Marine officer in Korea, helping his men to listen.

Yet the board was resistant and troubled.

What *was* this?

He went right on, "A church, a place of prayer should be handy," he said, "where a man can stop when he's worried

—a place where he can stop when he's afraid he's too worried about the first of the month bills to make a good pitch to his next customer or client. Or a woman stop to pray when she feels she's going to fly into a thousand pieces, instead of going into a bar for a drink, or a drugstore for pills. A place you could barge into with your anger, or sneak into with your guilt, drunk or sober, or to take a nap the way I saw a woman once in St. Patrick's Cathedral, an old bedraggled drunken woman asleep in her Father's house, or to have a good cry or to yell for help, Come and Save me, you promised. I'd like it to be *handy*, otherwise the impulse to turn to him can go, and I'd like them to find there what the apostles found on the Day of Pentecost."

The strong young hand, dangerous now, a hand that had held a gun and fired it, reached to pick up the beautiful serene drawing, the picture of peaceful places, swaying trees, hills on which homes presented untroubled fronts. He stared at them grimly, thin-lipped, jaw jutting a little. He said, "Wouldn't it be *loverly?* Maybe some day we could have them both."

A stir went round the room. Tension eased a little.

"This one—" he laid down the drawing, "would be easy and convenient for some of a Sunday. Room to park. If you overslept you could still get to church and come parading down the aisle after the first hymn, which isn't to say you'd have time to prepare yourself for the glory of the service, to get quiet inside so you might hear the Word. You could get to it in a quick drive so going to church didn't take too much time even on Sunday. Christ spoke everywhere—anywhere—to everybody." His voice broke—he looked at them with pleading—he steadied himself and about-faced and spoke to Jack Nestor, "Your people could never come from the West Side, could they, or from those neighborhoods down near the harbor?"

"Well—" Nestor said, "a few of us have moved nearer—and of course there are—some churches down there—"

Not taking all this too seriously, his tone packed with sincerity and tolerance, Steve Retzlaff came in loud and clear. He said, "Look, padre, when you've been with us here a little longer, you'll realize that we—this particular church—aren't exactly either a workingman's chapel nor a businessman's auxiliary—"

Quick, hard, hard-hitting, Hank said, "I'm not blaming you, but I was called to preach the good news to every poor creature and every rich creature I could get to listen. You see, I *know* the good news, I have to spread it. In the marketplace where the world spends so much of its time, to the trouble spots, I have been sent—I read in a New York paper once where the critic said a new musical was lousy because they always had to stop the show every time anybody wanted to sing a song or do a dance. Walter Kerr, the critic, claimed a good musical should be all in one piece. *I tell you I know* that is also the way of Christian life. We mustn't stop our daily lives and sing a hymn or dance before the Lord or just find an hour on Sunday that God is on the field or serve Him only when we feel like it. We are the redeemed. We can walk by His grace with the Risen Christ—*hope* is what the world is crying for—we can hold out hope—a *great*—even a little hope—hope downtown where they can get at it when things knock them hopeless—"

With full social ease and urbanity, Steve Retzlaff laughed. There couldn't have been anything more cordial or well-intentioned or sympathetic with a man who'd let a fanatical enthusiasm run away with him—than that laugh. He said, "Padre, we've all heard about how a new broom sweeps clean and I expect you feel like you're a new broom round here but I'm afraid we'd be opposed to your sweeping out plans we feel are right and have spent a lot of time on. We'd oppose any radical changes about building our church, which is what we're all here to talk about. If you'll give yourself time to get better acquainted with conditions here, you'll come to see it our way."

"Nobody's got that kind of time," Hank Gavin said. "You are members of this, a Christian church. Do you or do you not believe Jesus meant what he said?"

Still carefully, Steve Retzlaff said, "At the time he said it, I'm sure he did. Isn't it now a matter of interpretation and adjustment? Things have changed."

"Outside, maybe," Hank said. "Inside everything's changed nothing's different, everything's different nothing's changed."

"He said," Steve went on, "cleanse the leper. Medically, we've wiped out leprosy. You won't find any to cleanse in Beach City."

"That doesn't leave us without things to cleanse," Hank said, "and I am not talking reform, I'm talking cleansing. Venereal disease is way way up again due to promiscuity and ignorance. Corruption is taken for granted. Morals on college campuses condone behavior that's dangerous. About the way Jesus found things in Jerusalem or Paul in Ephesus. We've been told what to do about it."

His temper slipping, Steve Retzlaff said, "Oh come now—let's make sense. I realize a minister must do a certain amount of preaching. You can't mean to claim you intended to do these things."

"I intend to try," Hank said. "One man. One man can make a difference and every man must try. If they decide to shoot me, it's going to be for *trying*. You had better accept that."

"You don't expect the rest of us, those of us who have to raise the money and build the church and run it," Steve Retzlaff said, almost matching his tone but not quite, "to go along with anything so extreme?"

"I intend to have his words carved on the cornerstone of my church," Hank said. *"Go forth into all the world, heal the sick, cleanse the leper, cast out devils, raise the dead, freely ye have received freely give*—if I put that up there deep in marble and don't try to do it, the Better Business ought to get after me for fraud—"

This gave them a chance to laugh, the laugh was louder than the joke, if it was a joke, merited.

Some of their eyes, Archie said, were serious, thoughtful, fastened on this young fanatic, wondering, disturbed. The interesting thing was that none had stopped listening.

Nor shall my sword sleep in my hand.

For the first time, Archie told me, he and at least two others, Nestor and Marguerita, *saw* the sword flash in his hand.

It made them very thoughtful.

But now Steve Retzlaff took over again.

He had himself well in hand once more. Opposition stimulated rather than discouraged him and the shock of hearing pulpit talk at such voltage in a routine board business meeting had passed. In all ways and at all points, he was a shrewd, experienced, able politician, used to getting his own way and with tried methods of doing it. Accustomed, in Beach City, to deal with weird types such as channel swimmers, oil millionaires who were sometimes Indians, crackpot political parties, fringe religions, and swamis with ashrams up in the hills, he was not easily knocked off balance by the unusual. Most crackpots were speedsters, in-and-outers, not consistent.

Steve's conscience was clear, what he did had to be right because he knew more about Beach City than anyone. He had been able to get old man Ffolliott out of his daze long enough to get a building fund started. Now, if necessary, he would deal sternly with this overenthusiastic young *zealot* to avoid an unholy mishmash. This vague Utopian experiment which Gavin seemed to have in mind would produce a veritable Tower of Babel, as you might say. If he remembered correctly his name-saint, as they called it, Stephen had had to be dealt with severely by Paul, though the exact circumstances eluded him. He had never admired his name-saint particularly, a man ought to be able to keep from getting stoned. This young man who now occupied the pulpit of the Church of the Redeemer didn't seem to take into consideration any of the important things.

Some of them—oddly enough these things popped back into Steve Retzlaff's mind, where from he couldn't imagine, his thoughts sort of spun in and out, real estate values, for instance, and then he thought that probably there had been some questions of real estate values between the Jews and the Romans. *Freeways,* absolutely vital to the growth of Southern California, try as you would they were traffic-jammed before you got them built—well, the Romans were great for road-building, too. And come right up to today, of course a man probably couldn't understand those obscure books by highbrows but he should be able to talk about them and drop the names of the famous intellectual theologians who wrote them. And trips to the moon were just trips to the farthest-out point, every age had its farthest-out point, like the Indies Columbus started out to find, or Egypt when Mary and Joseph fled there with their child, well, we'd used up the earth we thought so now we had to have some fun so we'd try for the moon. Nor did this young fellow Gavin take into full consideration the television, the population explosion, homosexuality, though St. Paul had run into plenty of that in Athens, it being one of the reasons the glory that was Greece went out.

If Steve was building castles-in-the-air—he had some things on his side, they did need to be more up-to-date about everything than old double Ff had been, but obviously this young idealist couldn't be allowed to take over parts of the church operation that were not any of his business. Time to show him that they weren't prepared to go along with any idea that Jesus meant his sermons to be guides to a seven-day-a-week way of life, everybody was very happy in a social sing-along-with-Mitch way of spending Sunday morning and a first-class organization for old and Young Marrieds and Youth and if Gavin thought differently he would have to be brought into line.

The other day somebody—who was it?—had told him about a student at one of the big theological schools—father had been a famous minister—he wasn't clear about names or details, hadn't paid much attention, anyhow they'd refused to give the young man a position when he graduated because he insisted the Day of Pentecost returned for each of us when we were ready for it—when we asked for it— Well, when the time came for looking at the record, as it would, Steve Retzlaff could not afford to have membership in any crackpot outfit that spoke with tongues on *his*. What kind of tongues had they spoken with? Now of course even a second language was worth five to ten thousand dollars a year to a young man. And all this was in his mind, spinning around in it, when he pulled himself together and said softly, incisively, "I don't think any of us here are prepared to rush into anything so drastic."

McAddams stirred and he let him take over, Mac was smarter than some people gave him credit for. McAddams said, "Dr. Gavin, I think it would help us if you'd explain exactly what you have in mind in a—a practical way."

"All right," Hank said. "A church downtown. Where we'd get the drop-in trade. Mrs. Vosburgh spoke of the fact that our membership wasn't increasing, it was growing less and less. We're talking to ourselves. I'd like to be where we could say *Come and See* to troubled souls that hadn't thought of religion as having anything to *do* with their problems. You're a realtor, Steve—you know how necessary a good location is, where people can see what you have to offer. I'd like to —to spread a table in the presence of their enemies and show them God's love—you know that *moment* when you actually *know* God loves you—is the most wonderful thing of all—nothing like it ever happens to anybody. True happiness—"

Mrs. Vosburgh spoke first, she said, "All this is most unexpected, Dr. Gavin. A downtown church is something I think none of us ever considered. There'd be no room for the things we need to pull the young people to us—as I've often said before, a swimming *pool* instead of a *pool* hall—"

"Rome tried swimming pools," Hank said, and gave her a merry smile, "I've always thought I'd like to try—*stretch forth your hand and it was restored whole like the other*. You have to admit that took more guts, right there in church in front of all his enemies, than Babe Ruth pointing at the center-field fence when they were booing him—and they both got home runs— *Come and See,* that's what Jesus' whole life said, wasn't it?"

In a come-come-you-don't-really-need-another-drink voice Marv Gregory said, "I'd like to go along with you, my friend, but I must say a great deal of what you say seems to me a little fantastic—and fanatical."

"It always does," Hank said, and without preamble he said to his chairman, "Mr. McAddams, you own those two big lots on the corner of Pacific Coast Highway and Rio del Rey, don't you?"

In a thoroughly startled answer Mr. McAddams said, "My wife does."

"She's a member of this church?" Hank said.

But Steve Retzlaff, with his good red American real-estate-is-the-biggest-industry-in-the-United-States blood actually boiling now, still managed to say with open astonishment, "You're not talking about building a church *there*? The City Council wouldn't let you, for one thing."

"The church used always to be the *center* of the city—town—*the green—the square*—" Hank said. "It was the *center*."

"That was before they had to get a Zone Variance," Steve Retzlaff said, shaking his head. "You'd never be able to get one for anything as—let me say offbeat as this. A Zone Variance—changing the zone regulations as to what can or cannot be built in given areas—it's a serious part of urban renewal and development. Besides, who could afford to put a church on a corner that's worth, let's face it, some millions of dollars. You used to be an investment counselor yourself, padre—"

"One of the best," Hank said.

"Would you advise a client to invest in a no-income *church* on that *corner*?" Steve said.

"Now I would," Hank said. "Lay not up for yourselves treasures where atom bombs and changing governments can wreck them. And old age. Sometimes the many things you buy with income, you are not able to enjoy later on. I had a grandmother once who—anyhow—I advise all of you who are now my spiritual clients to invest in the honor of God."

"I try to be a God-fearing, churchgoing man, myself," Jack Nestor said, "but I don't follow you, Dr. Gavin. We have to learn to live in a world the way it is—"

"I promise you we don't," Hank Gavin said, "any more than Debs did, or Gompers or John L. Lewis or Walter Reuther. Mr. McAddams, is your wife a happy woman?"

Foursquare, padded, kind shrewd and limited, Olin McAddams went a bougainvillea purple, the blaze in his eyes was frightened and pitiful, his best would never be good enough to make his wife happy.

"Very *personal*—" McAddams began and Hank said, "No no—I just meant I thought we could make her happy, that's all. You see I know that in the end it would make her happy if she sold those lots to her church—or maybe gave them to us. Thank God the church has its hand out so you can put something in it and not let all God's supply go for moth and rust—I'd like to tell her for sure that there isn't anything she could buy with the money that would be as much eternal joy as giving us a rock to build on."

"I expect she'd just like to—to keep it," Mr. McAddams said.

"I had a grandmother once named Katie—" Hank began.

Mr. McAddams did not seem to hear the interruption, he said, "In fact she'd think I was crazy, plain *crazy,* if I so much as mentioned—"

"My wife thinks that about me too from time to time," Hank said, and then without pause, "let us pray."

Here I must put in what Hank told me of that moment, it was a special one for him, one he never forgot.

By that time he was shaking inside, he felt cold sweat dripping down between his shoulder blades, he was aware that he had met in Steve Retzlaff a foreman worthy of God's steel. That didn't trouble him so much as the potent sense that they didn't want to hear any of this, he was hammered by the certainty that a board convinced by human eloquence alone is of the same ferocious hostile *leave-us-be* opinion still. The climb ahead made them dizzy—they didn't want to try.

So that when he said, "Let us pray," it was a desperation move for himself.

He said aloud, "Father, where two or three get together in Your name, You have promised You will be with us. I claim this promise."

For a moment he could hear them breathing, in the circle of chairs set around the library, could see the color of their clothes, the varied expressions on their faces.

Then he could neither see nor hear them, inside him gradually was a sound as of a mighty rushing wind in Darkness, Unknowing Darkness, he shut his eyes and it began to be light.

To himself he said with a great shout You are here. You are actually here. You are not words words words—You are not things things things nor even prayer which leads us to You, to the open door that You have never allowed to be closed to us. You are not an idea or an intellectual concept difficult to figure out nor a magic formula nor a dread destiny which we must propitiate. You are the Christ who walked the roads as we do, You are the Holy Spirit that descended on the apostles. You are *here*.

Aloud, after a pause, he said, "He will give you the morning star."

They opened their eyes and saw him standing there, a tall,

thin young man. His eyes were full of some expression that was new to them. Like *light*.

"If you will go back to your first love," he said, "He will give you the morning star."

Nobody moved.

After a while McAddams said, "I always like to sleep on a thing."

"We have been, for quite a while," Hank said, and Mrs. Vosburgh rose, smoothing her skirts. She said, "A remarkable weekday sermon, if I may put it that way. Most unexpected." She admitted to me afterward that she was hot with annoyance. *Whippersnapper* came into her mind. Of course Jesus had been only thirty when he began his ministry but that was different. All this, she thought, was in the worst possible taste. In church, as elsewhere, one had a right to choose one's company. "I will think about it of course," she said, "but I warn you I don't think I'd care to make so radical a move."

The meeting broke up then, they all got up and moved doorward, they made some vague pleasant remarks about how *interesting* it had been, they said nice things personally and Jack Nestor held onto his hand and Norma Gregory was smiling and he was aware that Archie was thoughtful. And to each of them the minister said, "God bless and guide you."

Until only Hank and Steve Retzlaff were left.

Steve said, "I wish I knew what you're up to."

"Don't worry about it," Hank said, unsmiling. "Before too long I'm going to tell the whole congregation."

"You can understand it all seems a bit overzealous to me," Steve said, "and if you'll forgive me, I think you have to watch it that it doesn't get a little *hammy*."

"All right," Hank said hotly, "I'll really ham it up for you. *Let us unflinchingly join the vanguard of those who are ready to risk the climb to the summit. En Avant*. That's a quote from a man I hope you'll get to know, Teilhard de Chardin. Come on, Steve, you're a forward guy. Let's start the climb to the summit."

Steve Retzlaff shook his head, and he was smiling now. "That's your business, padre, I see that. I'm a man who likes to move pretty carefully—"

"Make me good but not just yet," Hank said, "make me loving but not to people who get in my way. Make me a Christian in name only. Give me the earthly paradise I'm earning and I haven't time to look to see whether it's built on sand or not."

"Beach City's built on sand," Steve Retzlaff said, "some of it. Seems to be doing all right."

"You think so?" Hank said.

"Well," Steve said, "we're doing our best anyhow. Look, Gavin, even if you could convince the board about this church switch, which you can't, you could never get a Zone Variance to build downtown."

"I'm not sure exactly what a Zone Variance is," Hank said.

"You must have run into it when some new company wanted to build a factory," Steve said, "it's a real estate law here. Certain zones are restricted. You can't cross over. To break the zone restriction you have to get a permit from the City Council, and they won't give it if any of the property owners in that zone come in and register an objection. In this case, it would be impossible."

"It says with God all things are possible," Hank said.

"Come now," Steve Retzlaff said, "you don't really think God is going into the real estate business, do you?"

"He often has," Hank said.

"I have a feeling, padre," Steve Retzlaff said jovially, "you might as well join us now. In the end we're going to do this my way."

"Oh no," Hank said, "I think you'll find we are going to do it His way."

"How did it go?" Mellie said.

Some of her own family heirlooms had come to perch, temporarily it seemed, in the big dark bedroom, and new slipcovers hid the old upholstery of the enormous davenport and two armchairs, in the window. *I bought them in one piece and fitted them on,* Mellie had told me, *aren't they incredible? Awful, but clean.* She was propped against pillows in the big, old brass bed, she had on a jade green, much worn Chinese coat and a paperback in one hand and a cigarette in the other.

She looked expensive, simple, tough, well-designed, and executed.

Hank said, "You don't look like a minister's wife."

"Who said how they are supposed to look?" Mellie said. "Queen Elizabeth the First thought married clergy were absurd and would never work, maybe she said something." She held up her face for his kiss.

He sat down on the bed and put his head on her shoulder. She managed to let the book slip and snub out the cigarette while he said, "Mellie—I promised them the morning star."

He felt the quick jump of her breath. Some of the excitement that was always her reaction to life whether she agreed with it or not came through to him. She said, "Oh well—why not? If this man you think is so extraordinary really is, he'll get the morning star out of hock so you can give it to them. As for me, I've got a very early date tomorrow to hear Deedee Retzlaff try out in church before she goes to school. I've had a bright idea—we should change soloists—offer them something new—maybe every other Sunday. So get on with it, love. How did you do with Deedee's old man this evening? I have a feeling he is at his brightest and best at meetings."

"Over the long view—" Hank began and Mellie laughed, she said, "He's used to getting what he wants and he wants his wee lamb to be a soloist in his church—"

"My church," Hank said violently, anger gunned him to his feet and he stared down at her, eyes blazing.

"That you'll have to settle between you," Mellie said, "I don't think his wife likes him any too well, either. I wonder why. Anyhow, let's be diplomatic and get as much of our way as we can. We'd better take them to dinner one night soon. I impress hell out of her."

"What about Deedee?" Hank said. "You're—very fond of her, aren't you?"

"Yes," Mellie said, "yes. How do we ever know *why* we are fond of people—anyhow, Deedee has that angelic type of puss which keeps the average high school or college boy from trying it out in the back seat, SO when somebody gives her the full treatment she hasn't worked out any *de*-fense and she's in bed before she knows the play has started. Like Desdemona, a fair maid whose papa doted on her too. Don't worry about it—I'll take care of it."

"I'm glad I love you so much," Hank said. "It makes me know how much other people love you in spite of your not being exactly a lovable type."

"Quit stalling," Mellie said. "What happened with the board?"

Walking up and down, he told her. Slowly, she got out of bed, pulling the little green coat about her, and went to sit on the edge of one of the chairs, never taking her eyes from his face.

"They must think you're mad," she said, when he had finished. "I'm not at all sure myself. Hank—you ought to know better—this isn't the way to do it—so fast—"

"Not fast enough," Hank said. "We wait much longer all we'll be able to do is build the Ark. Mellie—we have to begin to see—we're all bogged down—we're using the very things we pride ourselves on in this age of what we call enlightenment for more material things—and none of—no decent proportion—of money or manpower or effort is exploring for spiritual energy or the power of faith or growth in love. What else can end wars? Is this intellectual compromise with evil getting us anywhere? Let me try to make *you* see, Mellie? If you saw—"

He took a deep breath and began quietly, "The chaplain used to say the troops said their prayers in the morning and the rest of the day went back to everyday life. They thought he had time to live in Christ, that was his job, they had to get on with the war. If they wanted to be Christians they had to stop, like a bad musical stops for songs and dances. So time was empty of God—had to be. But if you once make the connection with the Light of Christ it—it's quite all right to use the Light for ironing or reading or illumination or cooking—you don't have to go around turning it on every minute. You *are* in Christ. If the Risen Christ is here with us—you can work—and play—and live—don't you see at all?"

Mellie put both hands up and shoved back her hair. Her eyes were very bright and very hard. She told me that she knew they were hard, behind them her mind hardened against such talk, she had begun to fight as a swimmer fights a tidal wave.

"No," she said, in a hard high voice. "No. I don't really know what you're trying to do."

"As you leave the church for the noisy streets," Hank said, and forgot that he was quoting, "as you leave the church every day you will remain with only one feeling, that of continuing immersion in God's love. Mellie we must—be humanized at all levels—we must keep the unity—"

"You talked like this to the board?" Mellie said.

"No," Hank said. "No I didn't. I was chicken. I tried to be tactful. I told them the church was in retreat from life—"

Her anger subsided into a tortured, tearing, terrible lack of *understanding*. All this was beyond her. His words were ordinary words but he was using them differently. "You were the one who objected—who objects to intellectualism," she said, "and this man—this one who wrote *The Phenomenon of Man* which doesn't make sense unless you have a Ph.D. in science—he's worse—he's made up a vocabulary of his *own*—"

"Break it down," Hank said, "he's a scientist and the great modern philosopher, break him down and it always makes *sense*. Spiritual sense. Scientific sense. Ecumenical sense. This is the language of science and philosophy, not some obscure half-baked psychiatric and intellectual flapdoodle. He says—Teilhard says—exactly what Jesus said about the glory of Nature and the great destiny of evolving man—Christ in me the hope of glory is what he says. Whatever you do, do it to the glory of God whether eating or drinking or working and that is unceasing prayer— Mellie if you love, you do not stop being in love and loving because you have to go to work—or are separated—you are still *in love*—"

She did not know what to say.

Strength—there was a strength here—yet it seemed to her her heart was breaking for him.

Not peace but a sword—where had she heard that?

Yet the Bible called Jesus the Prince of Peace.

A lot of peace Hank seemed to be headed for!

This man if he had ever lived at all, which she did not believe, anyhow he'd been dead two thousand years, men who were dead two thousand years should stay dead that probably was the point he was supposed never to have stayed dead at all but that had to be as silly as Cinderella's slipper—maybe his peace came after the sword—

The whole thing was confusion worse confounded.

She held out her arms, she wanted to forget all this for a while anyhow—and so should Hank.

When she woke up the next morning Hank was gone to this early morning prayer service for men on their way to work to which no men on their way to work had time to come. Naturally.

On the window seat was his Bible, open as always now to ACTS.

For a while, they had forgotten—then they began to talk again and for two hours she had tried to make him see that a church downtown was nonsense. She thought she'd won. This one, she said to him, you have to lose. If you go too far they'll call in the bishop. At which Hank had laughed and said, "Steve Retzlaff will never appeal to the bishop, he thinks he's head of everything *including* the church."

She thought she had made some headway and now here they were back in Acts again.

Peter in prison and an angel coming to get him out!

Here they were back with angels.

She threw the book and said a word of which she was instantly ashamed though it had expressed exactly what she meant.

"How did I get into this?" she said aloud to herself. "How did I get into a life where somebody reads the *Bible*—the Book of the Acts of the Apostles—bearded old gents that have been DEAD as long as King Tut, they looked like the ones that run the fishing boats up at Santa Barbara—and that no-good bully St. Paul—they'd lock him up if they caught him now! How did I come to be living in Beach City and doing my own work with a man reading a book by some old paleontologist who was a member of the order of the Black Pope—and never having any fun or new clothes—what kind of a life is this?"

However, she thought, I will now surge over into the church and see how I do there as a minister's wife before I sally out into the noisy streets to buy detergent and some frozen macaroni and a can of soup.

"I wish," she said to herself, "I was going out to buy some new *clothes*. I mean CLOTHES. Not something to cover me."

But, she thought darkly, "If Hank would make sense about this church deal—we could make a passable kind of life here for a while, until we can maybe get back to Chicago—if he doesn't start this mad mad mad mad WAR—I mean looking for trouble."

Next time I saw her, she looked thoughtful and dark. She said, "I don't know—" and showed all her very white teeth in a cat-like smile, "whether my marriage can exist half-slave and half-free. Or any marriage. Or which half is which I will be damned if I know—you'll pardon me for saying damned, won't you? All I can say now is continue—we continue—but I don't like it."

5

The early-morning, before-school date to hear Deedee Retzlaff sing in the church was also the time when Mellie first saw and heard the boy of whom, almost to the end, Steve Retzlaff kept saying *How did she ever get to know such a boy? A boy like that!*

Marguerita Vosburgh, who, being on the board of the Hollywood Bowl was naturally the church's music committee chairman and who was also present, wondered about that too. Otherwise her contribution was negative, especially in the matter of the "Pop Folk Mass."

My house lay halfway between Beach City and Santa Barbara where Mellie was going to spend a day with Al Patton, his wife and Sybil Rowe, who all had come out from Chicago for some sunshine. Mellie stopped by in midmorning and as she tossed her fur-lined coat on a chair I said, "Do you mind much?" and she said, "Mind?" and I said, "About clothes." She laughed and went over to the window and said, "The Pacific is a different blue altogether, isn't it? I mean from the lake or the Mediterranean. Yes—in a way I mind a great deal. It was part of my life, wasn't it? Being the best-dressed in your league gets to be part of your time and thought. My ego enjoyed it. I have now needled my ego into rising up and saying You can wear clothes better than anybody. Even though you're *thirty* the way you wear them nobody will ever know where you got them, at Sears or at Rexall Drug. And there's one thing about good clothes, if you can manage the initial investment. They look as elegant as the day you bought them—especially Chanel." I thought this was true when, sitting straight and at ease, she informed me that the suit she had on—in seal-brown with a honey-colored shirt—was a Chanel she had bought in Paris "on my honeymoon, sweetie," she said. Her profile against the white sand and coming-on-winter blue sea was a travel poster Get on the next plane and come on down to Florida or Puerto Rico or Acapulco, or some place, only don't stay home! It seemed out of line that *Mellie* wasn't going any farther than Santa Barbara.

"I'm worried about my father," she said, without turning. "Mama's letters are vague—have you heard anything? That's one reason I'm going up today to see Al Patton, he'd know." I'd always known that Mellie had an affection for her father that Vadne had never inspired. Fathers and daughters are sometimes more devoted than any other combination; I remembered that Archie had said the only person in the world Steve Retzlaff really adored was his daughter. I said I hadn't heard anything disturbing about Francis Cheyne—and of course Al Patton would know.

She bent to light a cigarette and I said: "You smoke too much," to which she said, "Dearly beloved, leave me one minor vice? I'm so frozen with virtue that I can see the psychiatrist's toothy smile looming and he recommending that what I need to get rid of this hole in my guts—a psychiatric term, lamb—is a spot of murder. Of course the minister of *my* church says you shouldn't need a psychiatrist—he says we were told to *cast out* devils whatever their names were. He wasn't talking about *my* devils—they were Gloria Retzlaff's. Poor Deedee."

"Tell me about the Retzlaff girl," I said.

"Well, lovey, this is a sticky bit, because it puts me—and Hank—in the middle where Steve Retzlaff is concerned.

"Our church had a soloist who'd been there back in the good old days before processed cheese, moreover a basso profundo who didn't know there had been any church music written since Handel. I got an idea that we ought to have different soloists—one a month, say—or even every other Sunday—and I thought the biggest swing to follow old Asleep-in-the-Deep would be Deedee.

"Even getting up at *dawn,* I was—filled with optimism, it was one of those mornings that make you forgive California everything. Nobody can phony that one, or phony it up and ruin it either. California has to have something right, and I could feel from my toes up that this was it. Bright winter sun *warming* things, glittering blue and gold, and that smell of sand and sea and sagebrush no place else has, I admit it.

"The light came through into the church—you know those glass windows we have? Remember the one of Jesus looking like a rogue's gallery shot of a refugee from a concentration camp in technicolor? Even that was all lit up until it looked like the one in the cathedral at Assisi.

"Deedee and I were on time, but Mrs. Vosburgh, who was supposed to bring the organist, hadn't showed up, and when she did she was sans organist. He'd goofed on the day. So

Mrs. V. said, 'I daresay you can give us some ideas without an accompaniment,' and Deedee went on up to the platform. When she walks, Deedee gives her behind an attractive little wiggle, I'm sure by instinct, but I could tell by the way Mrs. V. folded her lips that she thought it was on purpose. Standing there by the pulpit, scared to death, her hair hanging straight like a nun's coif, I admit she still looked somewhat as though she ought to be in a high-class discotheque or on the 'Tonight Show'—and I know Mrs. V. went to school with you but so did a lot of other people and look where some of them are. She didn't *want* Deedee. Of course she *talks* big about youth, but I could tell she thought it was sacrilegious for anyone under ninety to sing the solos! And it came over me that I wasn't going to have my *Deedee* do anything so goddam gruesome as sing in that dim church without any *music*. I was young once myself."

I have total recall of Mellie's face as it was that minute, angry, thoughtful, perplexed. Yet it had a tenderness that had never been there before. Not that she'd lacked it, but it hadn't been awakened, Hank always had the full flood of it, but she hadn't released it to anybody else except perhaps, I was to find, her father—and perhaps to me a little. I treasured this. However, I knew as I watched Mellie that what young Mrs. Gavin had had in Chicago for those she served was *noblesse oblige,* tolerant understanding, even perhaps too much what-do-I-care-really *indulgence,* and now I saw real tenderness glowing in her for a girl who might have been her kid sister.

"Mrs. V. didn't like it," she said, "but I figure as the minister's wife I have to get something besides dishes and the Book of Acts, so I said I'd changed my mind, we'd wait until our dear chairman could come up with an accompanist, otherwise it wouldn't be fair.

"At that, to my amazement, Deedee began to say something, very fast in double-talk, and her face all of a sudden was rosy as—as the *dawn.* I looked where she was looking and for the first time I saw a boy in the last row—*pew*—I hadn't noticed him and neither had Mrs. V. Deedee called out something that sounded like *Beany?* and turned out later to *be* Beany and the boy got up. I couldn't tell whether he was short or tall but he had a lot of black patent-leather hair, and an olive skin and, I found this out afterward—*green* eyes."

"I know," I said. "A green-eyed Mexican. You spell it TROUBLE."

"Trouble?" Mellie said, and gave an exasperated sigh,

"We've already got volcanos smoldering all around us. Why is Beany trouble?"

"You're not a Californian," I said. "If he has any Mex in him, her father'd drive him off with a shotgun, like a rabid coyote. *Go on.*"

"When Deedee waved, he stood up. He had on a white pullover and a sports coat and his face was blank as a blackjack dealer's at Vegas. He came halfway down the aisle and stared at Deedee as though he'd never seen her before and she said, 'Where's your guitar?' and I tell you now Mrs. V. grunted as though she'd been hit in the stomach by Jimmy Brown. If they heard her they didn't pay any attention, and Deedee said, 'Well go get it, stupid.' The way she said it—you can always tell by their voices, don't you think? they can't help it—I knew that *whatever* she'd done or might do it was to please him and not because she—he went out and came back with a guitar, I do not know much about guitars but this looked exactly like the one Segovia played at Carnegie Hall. Deedee kept looking at him but she spoke to me, 'Of course it's not an *organ* but we've—he's been helping me to *practice*—"

"Do you have the Joan Baez records? There's a new one—something called I think 'Bachianas Brasileiras'—it's almost classical—lovey, I give you my word when Beany began to play a prelude it sounded like an *organ*. Then in a small true voice–almost a coloratura, that *kind* of a voice, she began the Sibelius. You know—from 'Finlandia'—the one that begins *Be still, my soul, and hear him*. It was—I have to tell you all I could think of was a bird singing by a rushing stream. I couldn't breathe.

"When she finished that one, he said—or his *guitar* said—or something. 'How about the "Pop Folk Mass"—sweetie, have you ever heard the "Pop Folk Mass?"' " Mellie opened her eyes very wide and took a deep breath as though she'd been underwater too long. "Well—I'd never heard the 'Pop Folk Mass' nor had Mrs. V. and it was something like Hiroshima as far as she was concerned, so I said No, no, kiddies, let's have something a little more legitimate and *moving*, if you know what I mean and then—they did the Lord's Prayer. Whose music—that I don't know—could be their own. On the first two words *Our Father* it was pitched so low you could only hear it with your red corpuscles, it began to pick up with *Thy Will Be Done* and when it got to *Forgive us our debts as we forgive* you could hear it across estuaries and deltas like an Indian war drum and on the *deliver us from evil for thine is the kingdom and the power and the*

GLORY, they belted it so I had to look to see if the *roof* was still there.

"If you heard that every morning, you wouldn't get it out of your head without ceasing, like one of those singing commercials, *Schaefer is the one beer to have when you're having more than one hallowed be thy name thy kingdom come—*"

Mellie got up as though she'd been yanked, she looked at me solemnly, for her, and it took a long time for her to light a cigarette. She said, "All right all right all right I say—that's all it is, just another *commercial*."

"They sell, I suppose," I said, "and—few things have lasted two thousand years."

"It seems longer," Mellie said.

"What happened after that?" I said.

She glanced at her watch and said, "If I'm going to get to Santa Barbara for lunch—that reminds me, you know how Al Patton is about angels, a youngster brought in a design for a window of the angel rolling back the stone from Christ's tomb, do you think Al would like to endow it for our new church if we ever get one? I must ask him. However—at the *Amen* even your old school buddy was all choked up, and when I told Deedee she could begin to sing every other Sunday she began to cry because Daddy would be so pleased, he wanted her to be a singer, did I think she had enough talent? I said talent wasn't everything, sometimes a woman went through life able to believe that because she had a little talent she also had the stamina, and stick-to-itiveness, and ruthlessness, and up-and-coming-on-four-hours'-sleep, and don't-know-when-you're-licked championship heart that it also takes. So she became a feminine mystique and makes a lot of people miserable for years when the truth is she was lucky not to get her nose rubbed in failure on the first go-round. You know—like Gertie Cutler. The one who keeps promising to murder her mother-in-law—and she might at that. Look at the people who do, after she becomes a feminine mystique—" Mellie broke off and sat for a moment looking out to sea.

I let it ride and at last she said, "I am trying to figure out whether I really understand all this about feminine mystique. I have arrived at the conclusion that I don't. Do you understand what is a feminine mystique, lamb?"

"It isn't *a* feminine mystique," I said, "it's *the* feminine mystique. I believe it to be the doctrine or theory that woman's highest destiny is as a wife, mother, homemaker, and keeper of the sacred grail of mankind. The doctrine that was created as helpmate for man, mother of the universe, and that the arts and graces of homemaking and housewifery require more brains, stamina, genius, beauty, and wit than any other profession known to the world. I'd like to endow some chairs of the Art of Homemaking and give a degree to the Housewife-Bachelor of the Art of Homemaking and Housewifery. Now the uproar seems to be that a lot of rather frightened and silly young women, whose number as far as I've been able to explore is dangerously exaggerated, and some who've been made to feel that it's a social faux pas or an admission of inferiority to be *happy* with their lot as homemakers, of whom I've found more, have decided to rebel. All this is beneath their talents, they should come down and be equals with men. Go out and sell something or beat typewriters or anyhow have a *career*—though those with careers are certainly looking for husbands with all their might and main—I think the difficulty comes perhaps when they continue to look down on their jobs after they're married—they still rebel—it gives them an excuse for neglecting the work which all jobs involve—"

"I know," Mellie said, "so Gert Cutler isn't *a* feminine mystique, she is a rebel against *the* feminine mystique—Gert keeps telling about the big *career* she gave up to marry Art. If she has some ability and brains she's lazy, she's self-centered, she's a sucker for all mass hypnosis, but she's good-natured, and her kids adore her, she's never grown up so they're all about the same age. Her mother-in-law thinks it's less demeaning to *make* a bed than to have an *unmade one* around the house. Without her, they'd live in a pigpen and eat out of cans and the kids would wear unmatched socks and dirty drawers to school and Art, a tidy, mediocre soul, would sicken and die. On the other hand, mama-in-law is tactless, I don't think she loves her enemy, she's got a sort of supercilious superiority that's *asking* for murder, and she can't help resenting the hell out of it that worthy as she is, Art and the kids still love Gertie best.

"The funny part of this tale is that they're all well-meaning, pretty good, kind-hearted ordinary *people*. Neighbors. I can see all their points and they all mean well, the poor bastards. Most people do. There is no malice—not really—in any of them and—yet they're going to work themselves up to some kind of *catastrophe* if they don't get some help. Or just a stew of unhappiness!"

I said, "Isn't that what Hank's talking about?"

She didn't answer. I watched her put on her coat and draw on her driving gloves. I said, "So what became of Steve's daughter and the green-eyed Mexican?"

"He's as American as you are," Mellie said sharply. "A little far-out maybe, his eyes when he plays—Mrs. V. said he went into a *trance*—but he's not a *Beatle* or an *Animal* exactly."

"The Retzlaffs are apt to regard him as being in a totally different strata," I said.

"We call this a democracy, don't we?" Mellie said.

"Oh yes," I said, "but when it comes to whom our daughters marry—we don't expect it to include our daughters marrying anyone but white men."

We walked out to her car, between the delicately pointed gray-green leaves of the oleanders and the adobe wall over which a bougainvillea had flung cascades of unbelievable scarlet.

With one hand on the gate Mellie said, "What shall I *do?* Probably her parents don't know of the existence of this romantic guitar player—and he is romantic, sweetie. Bobbie Mayhew and our Deedee are using each other for cover-up and here I am in the middle. Steve—our chief money-raiser—and you know raising money is a gift like playing the violin—for Hank and I know he's planning to see that this new young pastor from the effete Middle West either goes his way or gets out of it. The girl's only sixteen. And Beany—his real name by the way is Bernardo—is no older. Suppose Steve Retzlaff found out I'd known—or suspected—seen them together—I mean if anything happened—and I hadn't warned him? That might give him a weapon against Hank. I know Hank talks all this what-would-Jesus-do. On the other hand I'm sure the parent'll foul it up, Steve and Gloria, they'll drive these kids to some such foolishness in the tomb like Romeo and Juliet. Remember the Capulets and the Montagues? *We* think things change so much, I say nothing's different, is it? There are still *people,* aren't there?"

She watched me, more disturbed than I had ever seen her.

"How sure are you?" I said. "About these young people?"

"Oh, I'm sure," Mellie said, glumly. "I'm sure. Have I any *right*—?"

I said, "Why don't you talk to the girl herself first? You're not parents or teachers, that's a help. You look even younger than you are, you could talk to her—"

"*Talk!*" Mellie said, and after a couple of long breaths, she said, "It's an idea. Your green-eyed Mexican doesn't look to me the patient type. I've only heard him play hymns, but even so there's a reckless beat—no no, not reckless exactly—about as much self-control I'd say as Hurricane Gladys."

Her voice shattered, and I was suddenly aware that she was shaking with anger. I had always known the violence of her temper, but she did have self-control, I'd only seen flashes of fury, under this flash there was a new, desperate, driving note. She said, "Do you know what *Hank* is doing about all this so far? The Cutlers and the Zone Variation and the goddam new church? *Praying.* Yes he is. And that's all he's doing. I can tell you it's extremely peculiar to live with somebody who prays about *things*—real things, I mean—and expects something to—to happen. He can't help it, I know that much now. Do you know what he said to me? I woke up at some frantic hour, like three o'clock in the morning, and he was sitting by the window. I want you to understand one thing. He doesn't look any *different.* No halos. He doesn't burst into song like he says Peter did in prison. So *I* said, 'What now?' He turned around and gave me a big smile and *he said he was praying to transcend the limitations his reason was trying to impose on him.* Does that make sense to you? You know where he got it? From a book about Picasso. *Picasso* is supposed to have said it."

She seemed to be thinking this over and so was I.

He is praying to transcend the limitations his reason is trying to impose on him.

Like George Washington at Valley Forge.

Or Benjamin Franklin flying his little kite.

Like Einstein or Schweitzer or Mahatma Gandhi or John XXIII or Julian Huxley or Edison or Colonel Glenn.

Are reasonable men any good at transcending?

"You know what Hank is planning to do?" Mellie said. "On the Sunday before *Christmas* he is going to preach some kind of *sermon.* I take it the church is apt to come tumbling down around his ears. Christmas! How corny can you get?"

"We're a corny race," I said. "The biggest-selling record the world has ever known is Crosby singing *White Christmas.*"

She got into the car and slammed the door. "Can you believe all that about the virgin birth?" she said in high disdain.

"It doesn't seem too difficult to me," I said, "we're being led into believing more and more every day. I don't see why we shy away from believing things in the spiritual field that transcend reason—we believe them everywhere else."

"They go ahead and prove those," Mellie said.

"Isn't that what Hank's talking about?" I said.

She hurled her freshly lit cigarette in an arc over my head, the sparks flew like pinwheels, at our beach we are careful of sparks, she watched me find it and put it out, she said, "You're all mad. Who said if there had been a lunatic asylum in the suburbs of Jerusalem they'd have shut Jesus up in it immediately after his conversation with Satan in the wilderness?"

"A rather inferior contemporary of Freud's said it, if anyone can be inferior to Freud," I said. "This one was a specialist in the criminally insane, you know specialists always see their own specialty."

Mellie said, "How did *I* get into all this?" She gave me an unexpected and enchanting smile. "Ho hum!" she said, "it's true I'm worried about my father and I would like to see some home folks who speak my language, but actually I'm escaping for a few minutes. For now—I've had it." As the car began to move, she put her head out the window and said, "That's a good idea. I'll talk to Miss Deedee Desdemona Retzlaff the sooner the better. Poor baby. Like so many of these terribly smart men her papa is too egotistical to see her as anything but an extension of himself. One of those *How-could-she-do-this-to-me-guys*."

I watched her drive away down our dusty little back road and wheel into the mainstream of traffic going north to Santa Barbara. I then went into my house and looked up the Sunday before Christmas on my Peanuts calendar and in the space allotted for engagement wrote down

Hank's Sermon.

I was sure that no matter what happened I wanted to be there if I possibly could.

6

About one thing, Mellie had been wrong.

True, Hank was praying about the ordeals, trials, human tumults, church differences and discords and the thousand natural shocks that flesh is heir to which faced him as minister of the Church of the Redeemer, he was quite sure that without God's active help he had no more chance of solving them than man had of solving those around the world.

But that most decidedly was not all he was doing.

When I asked him about it, Hank said he had walked around talking to people, in the downtown area, not exactly trying to influence them but perhaps to make some friends. Also, his training was to understand what he was up against.

That this had been the method of the early apostles he did not say. But I believe that it was at this time that he began to follow *in their steps,* not only in those of their Master.

He had discovered the Book of Acts about the same way Columbus discovered America. He fell into it, was absorbed by it in an advance as practical and workable as that which Einstein made on his theory of relativity when he went to Princeton.

"*Acts* gets lost, if you know what I mean," he told me once. "Very peculiar, but there it is. Between the glory of the gospels, all about Jesus and what he said and did and all the great stories that just reach out and grab you, *and* the poetry and intimacy of the letters—the epistles—even if Peter wasn't a—he didn't quite often, but when he did he said a mouthful and there we have it, *letters* from the Big Fisherman, why, that's the way all historians and biographers and historical novelists put a man and an era together—*anyhow,* in there somewhere ACTS seems to have sort of gotten *lost.* On a TV show the other day—a game who—five—five real intelligent people, educated people didn't know what the *fifth* book of the New Testament is, bless them. Yet there we are —you and me—the man in the street, the woman next door. At that moment in time they'd heard it from him, they'd followed him, been taught, seen it all—and then he was *gone.* They had to find out how to go forth and do likewise all the things he'd told them to do. So here we are—we have the gospels, which is a record of all *they* saw and heard, and the letters all about them and what happened, but we have in ACTS a full report of how they did it for the first time. This is the blueprint—the flight plan—the record of the first great experiment—the log book—all identical, all marking the trail. This is where what Jesus did in the forty days when he was the *Risen* Christ—and the coming at Pentecost of the Holy Spirit which could—should—happen to us all—and Peter in prison—and Paul spreading the Word—"

So Hank went down into the town of Beach City, the business district, to find out what to do about building a church, just as Barnabas and Peter and Paul and eventually Augustine and Ambrose and the Pilgrims in New England and the bishop and Father Valiant in Willa Cather's *Death Comes for the Archbishop* had done.

Had I been inventing a novel, I might have done differently here. If I hadn't been bound by facts. I might have thought up something more like other novelists of today (and very fine novelists some of them are). I might more easily have gone South, as in the fashion of the moment, or West, or Jewish, as that brilliant and moving school does. Or black-and-white. Certainly among the *losers* somewhere, for it has not of late been popular to write much about the winners, who after all control the destiny of the losers as well as of themselves. I would have preferred a pigsty or a resort hotel or a rarefied boy's school or even just one man's touching moving inner experience.

Real estate is much more difficult to glamorize or gutterize. A Zone Variance? A Meeting of the City Council in the New City Hall? This isn't the type of story I've covered, though eventually it led to murder as all human stories do, since each man kills the thing he loves.

If I hadn't been bound by the facts of Hank Gavin's experiment *in their steps,* I'd have imagined something more fictional.

And that would have been too bad, for *nothing* I was to find covers more tragedy, comedy, history, pastoral, pastoral-comical, historical-pastoral, tragical-pastoral, tragical-comical-historical-pastoral scenes individable than real estate.

Retroactively, in a way I find it strange that it was Steve Retzlaff who opened up to me not only that real estate is the biggest business or industry in the United States but also more part of the American mores, the melting-pot bloodstream, the shared experience than anything else.

No one breathes outside it. Think for a minute and you will see that this is so.

Real estate is a roof over your head, the earth beneath your feet. Urban renewal. The farm vote. Big cities that have by their enormous population mass vote taken control of our elections. Little towns that in microcosm show more plainly all the struggles and defeats and victories of human beings. The family, on which civilization has always been founded. At every level, here is the pathetic frantic glorious magnificent evolving destiny of man. The poor trying to make a home in one inhuman lousy too-cold-hot room in a slum tenement and eking out the rent. The semi-rich and well-to-do in some inhuman nerve-racking soulless insomniac skyscraper apartment house with paper-thin walls and the terrifying automatic elevators and haunted hallways where the first-of-the-month rent is sometimes a more backbreaking abject funk and seems to come oftener. Many are still filled with man's oldest urge to win one square foot of their own, they are driven to buy it in some impersonal cooperative with the Jones' glass bowl and more people *jump* from those than from tenements. But that's not all Zimmerman of Harvard calls this apartment house living the Atomistic Age.

That's not all the story—nor maybe the most vital part.

The goal of everyone, everyone of us, every man and woman, is to *own* a home. These are the laurels to the winner in life. This is the ideal—a man's home is his castle, put your roots down in some good real estate, whether it's in a restricted residential or a housing development, flat bottom or Bel Air. Whether it's $13,000 or $33,950, whether it's FHA or VA or you have a friend at Chase Manhattan or the Home Loan Association.

But if you know the young people today you know they call all this mortgages for the masses. They call it that because they're too bright not to know that a home has become a luxury few people can afford. I'll never be able to own my own home—they tell you this. They agree that they have a friend somewhere that'll make it possible—and then, they say, you have sewers and sidewalks, bonds and taxes, upkeep from the lousy buildings—and the mortgage going on while the plumbing in our Age of Plumbing falls apart and the plumber charges you portal to portal by the hour.

Housing—housing—housing—that's real estate.

Years ago a great colored preacher in Chicago said to me, Give me housing for my people and racial integration will be accomplished without bloodshed. Housing is real estate.

Winners. Losers. All are touched by real estate.

Nor does the terrible restlessness of the homeless begin

and end in the classical majesty of *Grapes of Wrath* nor the itinerant dairy worker or the rich-rich traveler. Look at the yearly migrations in the big cities. One couple I know. At staggering expenses which leave them in financial hot water of bank loans for the rest of the twelve months, moves every October with weeks of inconvenience, discomfort, remodeling, remaking curtains, resetting carpets, rehanging pictures, from one apartment to another so much alike you cannot tell the difference nor can they. The moves from country to city, to suburbia, to little farms, moves East West North South, yet as they march you can hear America singing "Home Sweet Home."

There is the climbing divorce rate coupled with the population explosion that makes two houses grow where one grew before, so that building cannot always keep up.

And there is the need for a few acres on which to build a *factory,* the guy in Dayton or Detroit or Salinas or Sioux Falls who wants to start making something—wants to put down his roots in American private industry.

That's real estate, too.

All that Steve Retzlaff told me one day when he came to try to get me to help persuade Hank Gavin to give up this crackpot notion of a downtown church—and he told it with a sudden passion that was moving, endearing, though it did not move me to interfere in Hank's Father's business as Hank saw it.

It did, however, show me that Hank wanting a new house for God in a place where His children could come home more easily and often was a top-flight, laborite, miserly-husband-wifeical, romantical, political-industrial, political-businessical, comical-historical-tragical-pastoral individable scene of and in real estate.

The conspiracy, the double-triple cross about the lots at Pacific Coast Highway and Rio del Rey was *real estate* all right, at Bertha McAddams' most Herodias-Salome, Judith and Delilah best. Interwoven close as tapestry with the romance of Deedee Retzlaff and the boy named Beany Teran, who lived in a neighborhood of which Deedee's father said over and over, *How could she ever get to know a boy who came from there in the first place?* A boy whose parents couldn't buy a better home for him and his dozens of brothers and sisters than that shack on the waterfront, while Deedee lived in the most delightfully rich and artistic house in the most fashionable new section, The Oaks Park.

Everything winners and losers interwoven with each other and with warp of real estate and the woof of the spiritual growth and future safety of Beach City.

Steve, without meaning to, had convinced Hank that he'd better go forth and explore this stumbling block called a Zone Variance.

Hank had been first, of course, to a young lawyer, a real estate specialist who had all the varied legal technicalities of Commercial, Downtown, and R-4 Zones, Building Permits and initial presentations to the Planning Commission at his fingertips. That was Hank Gavin of Chicago operating—a very talented and know-how guy. But Hank Gavin-with-a-mission wanted to talk the highways and byways among all the people. Their church—it was to be their church. The lawyer said, "You realize, among other things, there's trouble brewing with the Negroes, it's bound to come. You build this church where you're talking about and you'll be right on the edge of it. You might even be in the middle." "So?" Hank Gavin said, and when the young lawyer shrugged Hank had those peculiar crawling drops of sweat which came when he wondered whether he'd sounded smug, glib, self-righteous, those doubts which still besieged Hank Gavin-of-Chicago. Doggedly, he went on, "The church that shuts its doors to any man or woman or child of any color is not Christian," he said. "The church that shuts its doors is not Christian. The church was born in the middle of trouble, wasn't it?" "Now that you bring it up," the lawyer said, "I seem to remember that it was. Plenty of trouble. Well, you're asking for it."

His pilgrimage around and about Beach City came to me in a series of what in the theater they used to call blackouts. From Jack Nestor, from Archie, and as I've said once at least from Steve Retzlaff.

The new City Hall was an imposing building ten stories high on a busy corner. There was a small park around it, with neatly clipped hedges, and at this time of year tall stiff bright red poinsettias grew spindly and splashing against the glazed white walls.

In 211, a large corner room lined with filing cabinets and bisected by a wide counter of green plastic, the clerk said, "Zone Variance? Sure—that's us."

He was the new civil servant, shoddy-smart in dress, and naturally contemptuous of anybody who had to ask him a question, revealing thereby that they knew less than he did. He felt that he was underpaid for his superior knowledge and could not persuade himself that he should also give away any courtesy. Yet deep in his blue eyes it was somehow plain to Hank Gavin that there were a good many questions he would have liked answers to himself.

"What'd you want to know about?" the clerk said.

"I'm a newcomer here," Hank said, "I may want to invest some capital. I've heard about your zoning laws."

"What'd you think it would be like without them!" the young clerk said. "They have them in every city in California, buddy."

In a way, Hank Gavin was glad to be reminded of the chaplain, who had called them all *buddy.*

He tried then to see this boy as the chaplain had seen them.

"Are yours different?" Hank said. "I'm not familiar with them at all. Tell me about them. Do you have some kind of zone map?"

"What'd you take me for?" the clerk said, he dove into recesses under the counter, he came up with a map and spread it out so that the squares and diagonals and even cut-puzzle bits in green and yellow and blue and red and pink showed plainly. His finger lit first on a big 4—he said, "They just rezoned that one for apartment houses and buildings up to eight stories. Somebody made a pile out of that all right all right if you knew about the rezoning ahead of time you could have cleaned up. Here we are—Zone 1—" He took out a pencil and made two small dots, "we're standing right in the middle of it. This is the business district and I'd like to own a couple of square feet of Zone 1, I don't mind telling you." And in his ordinary young voice he began the California hymn of real estate to which every resident has his own calypso verses— My folks once owned the corner of Slauson and Main, my folks owned five acres at Franklin and Vermont, grandfather and grandmother had a house between 11th and 12th on Grand Avenue where the Title Insurance Building is now (that is my own topical calypso version and true it is), and the newcomers add their improvisation on IF they bought when they came ten years ago, or five, or even ONE. "If," the young clerk said, "my folks had bought the house we lived in—hell, there was *oil* under it—" He began to laugh uproariously, and when Hank laughed sympathetically he was friendlier, few of us can resist anyone we can make laugh, he said, "What do you want to know?"

"I understand Number 1 is zoned against churches," Hank said, as casually as though he'd said if you swing at the ball and don't hit it they call it a strike.

"Churches?" the young clerk said. "Are you kidding? At that, there's an old one down on Frontier Street yet—but it's Catholic. They pulled down a couple—seems to me I heard there was a Methodist—or Baptist—or Presbyterian what's

the difference I don't know—at 22nd and American Avenue when they put up the City Hall—and another one—somewhere—"

"Do you have to pull them down if they're in the wrong zone?" Hank said.

"They don't have to," the young man said, "but you can see for yourself. Either they get left in a sump hole, or the property gets so valuable they can't afford to keep it. When you got a boom on they have to have places for business downtown—progress shoves them out I guess—"

"Christian churches used to have a bad time in the early days, too," Hank said at the conversational level, "some very interesting stories about that. When Paul got the Philippians they were having services down under a bridge over the River Gangitis which probably was about as dry as the Los Angeles."

The young clerk was looking at him suspiciously, he said, "You're not serious are you about—about church *zoning*—you're not looking around *here*—"

"Well," Hank said, "to tell you the truth I am, I'm a minister of one of the Beach City churches—and I got to thinking that all of California in a way was pioneered by churches, the missions were a day apart, weren't they?"

"That was quite a while back, buddy," the young clerk said, "we got a real estate boom on now."

"You think we're happier," Hank said.

"Well for godsake it took 'em a day to *walk* from—I donknow—San Gabriel to Los Angeles I guess and now I could do it in about 6½ minutes. I guess it took 'em weeks—months—from Los Angeles to Frisco and now I can drive it in 6½ hours."

"If there was a church around here would you go into it, sometimes?" Hank said.

"Me?" the boy said. "Not me. I quit kidding myself when I had my first girl. Sorry, buddy—I didn't mean to—"

"I know exactly what you mean," Hank said. "Tell me a little more about the zoning laws. How could they stop me if I—if I just decided to build a church around here like on—well, let's say Pacific Coast Highway? Could they put me in prison like Peter? Just how does it work? How do they enforce it?"

"Enforce it!" the clerk said and hooted loudly. "Look, buddy, to begin with you gotta get a *permit*. You gotta apply to the Board of Public Works and get a *permit*. Understand? A *building* permit. Nobody'd sell you any lumber or you couldn't get a member of any union to go ahead without a permit and every few minutes like they say you have to have an *inspection* and they won't go ahead and put in the plumbing if you haven't had the building inspector inspect your foundations—and even in a church you got to have plumbing. You'd be standing at a standstill. You got to have a permit and inspections and you won't get a building permit if it's against the zoning restrictions on account of it's zoning restrictions that make real estate valuable. I took a course in real estate at City College my freshman year. You want to build something against the restrictions you have to go to the City Council and unless you have got political influence you are like wiggy, you are like *wrong*. I wouldn't fly this one if I were you."

"Suppose I told you you could trust the love of God," Hank said, and he had adjusted his voice, his tone, his tempo to the young clerk's. "What would you say?"

"I would say you are wiggy," the young clerk said. "With all due respect, you got that, haven't you, but I will have to say you are *wiggy*."

"Who do you trust?" Hank said, very quietly.

"Look," the young man said and for the first time threw a glance over his shoulder at the big busy typing filing moving about the room behind him, "this is your job, you have got a cush job and I do not blame you at all. I am not against anything like religion, I know some at City College who were—I just say let them go their way and leave me go my way, like it says in the song. But if you will take a little *advice*—maybe you are in an ivory tower or something—if I could give you a little advice, I would say you better go see a good real estate firm. Like, say, the Retzlaff firm. They are sharp people. I—I was trying to get a job in a real estate firm like Retzlaff myself, that's where the money can be if you're smart—a real estate man when you got a boom going like in Southern California, until he can get to be a multimillionaire and a philanthropist he has got to be *sharp*. Retzlaff has made his pile all right and he is as honest as a real estate man *can* be."

"You've been very kind," Hank said, "and I thank you. Just make me one promise. If I get a church downtown promise me you'll come in some day and see what's going on."

"That's as safe as saying when black gets to be white," the clerk said.

"No," Hank said, "no—"

The young man watched him go.

To himself he said He ought to have a keeper he ought before he starts going around investing any capital—somebody will sell him *Disneyland.* He goes around trusting in the love of God, that'll be the day.

The biggest drugstore in town was kitty-corner from City Hall.

No need to describe it. There is one on some corner of every hamlet, village, town, and city large or small in America, all as alike as the pyramids. Come down to it, they are as typical and identifying to the U.S.A. as the pyramids to Egypt, though unfortunately not being as well built they may not last for history to see.

One of the young ladies, starched from white apron to bleached triple-decker and hair-do, recognized Hank Gavin, she had been to whatever his church was called with a boy friend who had a friend named Beany Teran whose girl friend, one of the Upper Crust from The Oaks, sang solos there. She had liked the way the man talked, and meant to go back, but so far she hadn't really had a Sunday when she didn't have a date and she had dropped Beany Teran's pal because he didn't so much as *ask,* so now she passed the word around that the tall young man in the real elegant sports coat and white shirt was the preacher and they all watched him as he moved between shelves loaded with deodorants and tables piled with cosmetics and screens hung with seventeen varieties of beach hats, some as big as tents and others just small bright rubber caps.

Not bad, the girls said.

"Besides being a minister," said the girl who had been to his church, "he is also married and I don't think it is as easy for them to get a divorce. His wife is a knockout, my friend pointed her out to me, she dresses as good as Liz Taylor used to before she got so fat."

"What's she care?" somebody said. "She's got it made."

"Personally," another girl said, "I think Richard Burton is a catastrophe myself. I mean put him beside *Elvis*—"

"She could be his *mother,*" the girl who had been to church said, "and anyhow she's not his type."

All the time they were watching the tall lanky young minister looking around, they watched him go to the rear of the store, where behind a neat obscure counter stood an elderly man, in a starched gray smock-coat. He was small and ferocious-looking, with very heavy glasses and a fringe of curly going-gray hair.

"He must have a prescription," one of the girls said and somebody else said, "Well, they're human too, aren't they? He looks *human* to me," and then they lost interest because a couple of boys in sweaters came in and sat down at the soda fountain and the girl whose boy friend knew Beany Teran turned upon them an icy indifference which she had actually read somewhere was more provocative than the old wiggle-your-ass and show-your-tits technique.

Men behind counters, Hank was thinking.

Everywhere, men behind counters and desks and gas pumps. But it is easier than street corners. No use kidding myself, I was not cut out for a street corner campaigner, I don't see how they do it. On the other hand, *Paul* did. He was first-class at it—*Ye men of Athens—Athens,* of all places. Jesus, too. Just walking along, and they followed him and he stopped at corners and told them things that changed their whole lives. The winners as well as the losers—though of course the losers followed quicker though he never indicated that he had come *only* for them. Hank was sure that God was the God of the rich man and that Jesus had never turned away from the young man who had been born with a gold spoon in his mouth. Hank kept telling himself that. The prodigal son obviously came of a very rich family with fatted calves and gold rings and bands and best robes.

To the ferocious little man behind *this* counter, Hank said, "My name is Gavin, I'm a newcomer—"

"Mine's Hirschberger," the little man said, and his eyes looked enormous and very dark and deep through thick gold-rimmed glasses, "Moe Hirschberger. Dr. Ffolliott told me about you. From the looks of you I'm not going to get as much business from you as I did from him."

"My health," Hank said gravely, "is at the moment the best thing about me."

"Some have one thing and some have another," Moe Hirschberger said, "and you can call it health as far as Ffolliott was concerned, but I call it nerves. He was frustrated and lonesome. I'm not talking now about psychosomatic ailments—nerves are something to torment a man as definitely as arthritis which probably comes partly from nerves like asthma. I have a good many tranquilizer customers and they hurt, too. What's your first name—or do you prefer doctor?"

"My first name's Hank," the young minister said, "and I don't hear it often any more."

Hirschberger peered at him through the thick glasses and Hank thought suddenly of a character in the Wizard of Oz book—or one of them anyhow—the Woggle Bug! He could almost hear Katie's voice reading about the Woggle Bug. That was the thing now that he remembered best about Katie, her reading to him, and that must be good because he used to think mostly about the trick she'd played on him though he had forgiven her, partly he had to admit because it had backfired and partly too because it had tipped the scales in Mellie's decision in his favor.

"Tranquillity is quite a word, isn't it?" Hank said.

"It's only in the Bible once," Hirschberger said triumphantly, " 'Thy kingdom shall be sure unto thee after that thou shalt have known that heaven rules. Wherefore, O King, let my counsel be acceptable unto thee and break off thy sins by righteousness and thine iniquity by showing mercy; if it then may be the lengthening of thy tranquillity.' "

"King Nebuchadnezzar," Hank said, "that must be in *Daniel.*"

"The Old Testament," Hirschberger said.

"That was what Jesus meant when he said *Search the Scriptures,*" Hank said.

"Few remember that," Hirschberger said.

"How long have you been a pharmacist?" Hank asked him.

"Thirty-six years," Hirschberger said. "Got my license in New York, then I was in the Navy, I was a medical orderly in the boat when the Fifth Marines landed at Iwo. When I landed back in San Pedro I decided to stay."

"Drugs have made stupendous strides in your lifetime," Hank said.

"I sell forty times more tranquilizers," Hirschberger said. "They always think everything is new, after all what is a tranquilizer but a grown-up pacifier and some doctors say give it to baby and some say not. The Chinese have been smoking opium as a tranquilizer for six thousand years, it's no more habit- or dependency-forming, if you want to put it that way. We feed everybody all these things but I keep figuring about this generation of brittle ballplayers. When I was young in New York Mel Ott played every day and never got hurt, Ole Meal Ticket Carl Hubbell pitched in rotation without somebody else having to pitch the last four innings all the time, Mickey Cochrane kept on stealing bases like Ty Cobb had done without breaking any legs, can you imagine McGraw or Connie Mack not showing up for an Opening Day because they had a nervous stomach? Or Tris Speaker staying home with a sore throat? Nowadays nobody fields a team every day—there's always somebody in a hospital for something. A minor matter. But I wonder. Now they have a baseball commercial where they *worry*. I looked it up in the dictionary, just for fun, and to worry is to fret and torment yourself, feel uneasy and anxious and suffer fearful thoughts. Worry worry worry. That's an ideal? And in that commercial we're supposed to try, anyhow, to imitate a dog. What's on your mind, Dr. Gavin?"

"I came in to see the boss, the owner—" Hank said.

"He's a chain," Hirschberger said, "up in Los Angeles. We have a fine manager, name of Ellis, fair and reasonable and smart. He's up in Oakland at a divisional manager's meeting. Unless you just want to get acquainted, I can prognosticate what he'll say to anything."

Hank looked at him for quite a long time.

Something passed between them, Hank told me, he didn't think either of them could put a name to it but he was sure they'd never get it disentangled again.

"You're a Jew," Hank said, "yours is a great heritage. The law of life and of One God came by your prophets. Tell me something. Can man do it without God?"

"Of course not," Hirschberger said. "Riches lead to the next step—power. They all want to rule the world. So they try to ignore God, because man cannot rule God's world. He can't rule it without God either, but he keeps kidding himself that he can, he keeps trying."

He peered through his glasses, his eyes were piercing and a little malicious, he said, "There's a question I've wanted to ask for years but it wasn't any use with old Ffolliott or any of those other sectarian boogle. Can I ask you?"

"Maybe I can't answer it," Hank said, "but you have a right to ask it."

"Whatever gave you people the idea you could build a church that would work and stay alive spiritually on a negative?" Hirschberger said and Hank began, "I don't—" but the little man exploded right through that, he said, "A negative is a *negative*, you know what a negative is, don't you? A protest is a negative, isn't it? A protester is a negative, isn't he? The pro-test-ant church came into being on a negative, like a man campaigning for office telling you how crooked and corrupt and inefficient his opponent has been. That doesn't elect candidates. Before long, he has to tell them what *he's* going to do about it. Speaking as a Jew, all that's a negative. Why don't you start offering them an affirmative church? It was the *works* of Jesus and his apostles—they ought to have crucified Peter, too, and they nearly did, you know—that gave him his authority—that and his own faith that he was the Son of God."

"All right, I'll try to answer that one," Hank said, "a lot of us are trying to—accentuate the positive. I know a Methodist in Houston and a Baptist in the slums of Jersey City and a man in a little white church on an island down in Florida—"

"Why have they got him on an island in Florida?" Hirschberger said. "Read Einstein, who was a Jew—he'll show you the evolution of what he calls cosmic religious feeling from the Psalms to Schopenhauer."

Unexpectedly, the dark, thin, wizened face changed. He took off his glasses to wipe them on the skirt of the gray linen smock. Without the heavy lens his eyes were visionary and surprisingly beautiful. He said, "Something's up, young Hank, something's abroad, we're stirring in our long sleep. I'm not an intellectual giant though many of my race are philosophical thinkers of the first water, I'm a pharmacist in a drugstore built on sand, but I have antennae, we all have, we've had to develop them to survive. Something vast and new, as when Moses came down from the mountain, evolution is *converging,* the glory of man is beginning to force up a little green shoot through all the crap and crud of what's called reality. You know why the people are using tranquilizers. They've got awake enough to be scared. Not of war, cold or hot, nor atom bombs nor starvation nor black-and-white civil war, do you know what they're scared of?"

"Oh yes," Hank said, "don't you?"

"Of course I do," Hirschberger said testily. "Way down inside they know they're only about two jumps from where Noah was when he had to begin to build the Ark. You come over to my place some night and I'll show you a lot that's not even in the Old Testament."

"Convergence—*convergence,"* Hank said. *"You* read de Chardin too! This something stirring could be the Ecumenical Age you know—the whole church. A man like de Chardin doesn't belong to anybody—he belongs to *everybody,* scientists and philosophers, Christians and Jews, Catholics and Protestants—he could be the blast-off, the breakthrough—"

"The time, the place, and the man," the pharmacist said, "I am taking part in this conversation but just the same I do not believe it is taking place at all. Unless I have a tape recording of this conversation taking place here in this drugstore I'll never believe it when I get home tonight. If I try to tell it to my wife she will not believe it either and she is a Christian. Now what was it you wanted to see the boss about?"

"Would he oppose me if I said I thought our new church ought to be downtown?" Hank said.

"Downtown!" Hirschberger said.

"Say on Rio del Rey—or the highway—" Hank said.

Hirschberger shut his eyes, he opened them and looked at all four corners of the big humming store, he said, "Oppose? No. He is a good man but he is always a very smart cookie, he has to be. No opposition. No church downtown."

"Why?" Hank Gavin said. "Why?"

Two or three women were waiting now, stirring, whispering, patient-impatient. "Be patient," Hirschberger said to one of them who was beginning a mutter, he took her prescription and held it gingerly, he said to Hank, "Not just Mr. Ellis. He is a good man and very polite and careful. He is a successful man. He has what it takes to be successful in business, stay out of the middle if you can. That's why with Mr. Ellis no opposition can still equal no church downtown.

"You try to build an *ark* in downtown Beach City where even our customers run around mostly buying cosmetics and deodorants and birth-control-sleeping pills, tranquilizers, hypnotics, LSDs, and whatnot, I tell you my fine Christian friend eventually they will get rid of you somehow. They would have to. You are in direct competition. You are offering the kingdom of heaven built on a rock as competition to the final heresy of earthly paradise which is built on sand. Not on a wooden cross, not even on a cross of gold now, just the same, friend Christian, eventually they will crucify you."

At a loud gasp from the woman whose prescription he held, he began making wheezes like an organ that couldn't get started, he said, "A figure of speech, madam, the merest figure of speech. We are having what amounts to a political discussion, it always did. Remain as tranquil as you can until I fill this." He disappeared behind the frosted glass partition, his head popped out of that box, he said, "A cross of plastic and hand cream and floor wax. Isn't it your theory that on the third day your boy Jesus rose again, so what do you care?"

The bars, grills, smaller restaurants, honky-tonks, and diners.

The bowling alley.

The paperback bookshop.

The barber shop.

The two movie houses known in the trade as ashcans, as well as the big ones. The ashcans which ran foreign and/or dirty and cheap pictures, the pictures in the lobby more pornographic than the dirty post cards in Paris, only so sly and secret.

He made the rounds and his pilgrimage brought out one big surprise.

The old Cracker Barrel League was still in existence.

They didn't whittle any more, they were too busy, but they wanted to gab just the same.

At the bowling alley he found a big Texan, a friend of Nestor. With a broad grin on a broad face his outer aspect was of imperturbable good nature, yet about him was a slight threat of violence. Start something and Tex was your man! They talked about bowling, Hank Gavin said he was no good but the few times he'd tried it he liked it. The new sports arena for the California Angels, which was within driving distance, that'd give the town a boast, not as big as Disneyland, of course, but it'd kick values up some. Plainly, watchfully, Tex was disposed to be friendly. He liked talking to a new, young, healthy, sports-minded minister, and he wanted Dr. Gavin to know that he ran a good, clean, honest bowling alley. "You're welcome any time, Doc," he said, "and your young people are safe here, send 'em in. They won't get into any trouble in my place. Jack Nestor'll tell you, bar a little scrap now and then, I run a real good orderly place, I like to keep it that way, and I'm big enough to handle it," and he gave a big-enough-sized roar of laughter. No need for Tex to say he thought it'd be better if they didn't talk religion here in the bowling alley. Who wanted to? Besides, people got hot under the collar about the doggonest things, worse than politics.

A slight depression began to settle on Hank Gavin.

Not just because the big man Tex had been reluctant to talk religion or churches, which had been plain to see. Commercially, he might figure a nearby church with games and dances and buffet suppers could be unfair entertainment competition with a certain class of his customers. And Tex had certainly been polite. It was a certain wariness, a kind of *hollow* good-fellowship that made a vacuum around him.

Our commercial interests had always been very strong, whether in war or peace.

His insides began to hurt some.

The barber shop, a few doors down, was more of the same only brighter and slicker. Here, as Hank knew, they ran a small book in the back. Numbers—and the horses at Agua Caliente—and the ball games, foot and baseball. As everybody said you couldn't stop gambling, nobody ever had, or would, and Nick the Greek was as honest as you could expect a barber who ran a small book in the back room to be and he always sent a fine Christmas present to the boys at the big Naval Hospital and also provided them weekly with a card on the football pools.

Nothing really *wrong* here.

Quite a lot of snappy conversation. A little too *bright*, maybe. Everybody very busy, busy and bright, as though teacher had just come in unexpectedly.

The girl was what bothered Hank.

Her pink uniform was, to all intents and purposes, as good as a topless bathing suit and she was undoubtedly a girl who could wear a topless bathing suit if any girl could. She was sitting on a low stool giving a manicure to a man in one of the chairs when Hank Gavin came in and she looked up and when their eyes met hers were without any—any expression of any kind, any light, almost as though she were blind. Or had looked too long on things no girl should look on at all. A dreadful swift little panorama went through Hank's mind, this was the girl whom all the boys had known about in the sixth grade, this was the girl who'd worn lipstick at eleven and gone on dates at twelve and ended up at thirteen in a motel with an old man who was a traveling salesman for contraceptives or brought heroin across the border from the factories of Mexico.

Slowly, slowly, the soul-less eyes lit, and hatred flamed at him, so that he almost cried out, so that he wanted with such desperation as he had never known to lift his hands and say Go and sin no more and be able to *make it stick*. She was so tired of sin. She couldn't taste it any more. But he knew that if he made a move she would be as sure of his motives as Sadie Thompson had been of Rev. Davidson. *Pigs,* she would say, *all* men are *pigs*.

Some day—some day when he got his church not far from here—he would come back, or Mellie would, and little by little, if they were close—here—they could do *something*. They might persuade her to come and see.

So this was what the psychiatrists meant by a hole in your guts.

The guy who runs the ashcan, Jack Nestor had told him, used to be a card-carrying Commie, he might be still. He's a professional have-not. Either way, he's still a stinker, Nestor said. Here, Hank found active hostility.

Nothing—nothing—not in this incarnation—was going to make this padded, perverted man *hear*. He was far out, all right, far out from the gates of gold, as the old hymn had it, but if you showed him gates of gold he wouldn't enter.

The dust of his bitter unbelief settled all over Hank Gavin.

Shake the dust off your feet. This was one of his instructions, given the first Seventy. Don't carry the depression, the downheartedness, around with you. None of the *dis-for-death* words, discouragement, disappointment, discredit, dismay, *dis*pair. Don't let this separate the two interwoven strands of your faith, inner and outer, the two commandments, love God and love your neighbor.

Pray, Hank told himself, pray as you have never prayed

before. And as he prayed, he walked and he talked, as he had never talked before.

Continuing his pilgrimage, he found that some—a few —many—most of?—the men responded at least with vigor. With interest, if not agreement. Amazing how eager they were, how they came back with experiences of their own while they talked together of shoes and ships and sealing wax, of Fregosi's batting average, immortality, the real estate values, the chances of the San Diego Chargers, and psychic phenomena—all of them knew a poltergeist or a ghost or two, or somebody they knew did. They displayed a *hunger* that began to turn loose the healing fountains of joy inside Hank Gavin, where the hole in the guts had been. This was the hunger he had been sure existed, had counted on. Feed my—no no, Steve Retzlaff had been right about nobody being interested in *sheep* to speak of—feed the hungry, they were hungry. He didn't mention the downtown church again. And they centered a few questions upon things that had troubled them, they didn't venture far, they approached like children ready to scamper away, away—but venture they did. Reminiscences of their childhood, of how and when and why they'd lost their faith, or allowed it to become sour or static or seen it just drift away.

The small, sardonic, round-shouldered bartender in the Last Oasis had *used* the word hungry openly. He, he said, also knew something about thirst. He didn't think the church on the whole was giving him any competition for the exhilaration of the souls of men. Not enough, he said ironically.

"A bartender hears it all sooner or later," he said in a dry, impersonal voice. "Sooner or later he hears everything. You'd be surprised how often they start hollering for God about the time they get maudlin—about the time I won't serve them any more. I'll make you a bet, Mr. Gavin, that I haven't ever had a crying drunk in here that he wasn't weeping over not having any God any more. I will make you a bet on that, Mr. Gavin. I'm not a full believer in the *vino veritas*, but when it lets down the restraints and—and good manners, and *pride*, like it does, don't I know, then they keep saying God help me God help me *please* God help me—"

"That's prayer," Hank Gavin said.

"Is it?" the bartender said, sardonically. "Well, I once heard it said that there was more prayer said in the emergency hospital than in any church, and a bar can give some of those a good run for their money. They can come in here looking for something to make life happier or more—so they can stand it." He glanced around, things were very quiet, he said, "I can tell you some stories. Late at night, even when they're not drunk, we have some talk in here. Oh—they're hungry, all right, like you say. They're hungry and they're thirsty, I hope you won't think it's—blasphemous, but drink is—drinking is when they're looking for—"

"Would you," Hank said, was impelled to say, slowly, carefully, "could it possibly be that was what is meant—what he was trying to answer when Jesus said he that cometh to me shall never hunger and he that believeth in me shall never never thirst—he said that after he'd fed five thousand—"

"Yes—" the bartender said without any expression at all, "well—maybe. Anyhow, it's a cinch they aren't—they don't know about that or—nobody is doing it now around here anyhow." He stood still, silent, one eye on the assistant who was stirring a martini in a big glass. Then he said, "When I was a kid, I was scared practically witless by the Stations of the Cross that they had in a church where I lived. There's all kinds of churches—this was an old-fashioned one maybe, and the priest was bent on hell and eternal damnation and damn little else. I got a cockeyed idea—I must have been six, or seven maybe, that if I was *good,* if I was good enough, like he'd been, that's what they'd do to me. I been on my guard about that ever since." He gave the tall, quiet, young minister a sardonic grin and said, "Have a beer, Mr. Gavin?" He came back with it and said, "That was all I knew ever happened to him. And all his hair-shirt and suffering and being cold and miserable to please—whoever it *is.* Denying any—any happiness so men come in here looking for it—where's the good or the happiness in any of that? Hell, I could get hung by myself."

"It's not true," Hank said, "it's not true. That stops short. It stops short of all the glory. Maybe when I—I build my new church you'd come—if it's convenient—and help me set up some—Stations of the Resurrection. We could take the things some of them out of the book of the Acts of the Apostles *after* the Cross. There could be a station of their finding the tomb empty except for the angel who told them He is risen. Then Mary seeing him in the garden. His appearing to all the disciples gathered in the Upper Room. Maybe the fourth Station could be his glorious kindness and humor in showing poor doubting Thomas his hands and feet and the hole in his guts. The road to Emmaus—the most wonderful walk ever taken—we could show him walking along with the two men and speaking words that made their hearts burn with happiness. Then the meeting on the shore of Galilee, he had a fire built and he remembered they'd be hungry for their breakfast, he fed them. Then the last one where he left them for good, moved out of their *sight,* though he promised he would be with them always, as the youngsters say *like right here and now.*" Hank took a long breath, his whole face was lit with exhilaration. "No—maybe the end should be the day of Pentecost when the Holy Spirit came as he had promised it would, as it can—well, to show it can always come forever to those who gather together in his name—there were some very odd *characters* there on that occasion—"

He took up the beer and drank it almost at a gulp. "I talk a lot," he said.

The bartender kept right on staring at him with a bright, lively, beady dark eye. "You going to talk like that in church?" he said.

With a broad smile, Hank said, "Come and see."

"Well," the bartender said, with the immemorial gesture of polishing the mahogany in front of him, "well—they're *hungry* all right! Who's going to tell 'em on the level how to—who's going to say what you need or how you can find it? Myself I don't know that."

"If the fields are white to harvest—" Hank said, almost as though he were thinking out loud.

"Could be," the bartender said.

"If they are," Hank said, "we might get sent laborers—"

"That will be the day!" the bartender said, "not that a lot of them don't *labor.* Only—I donknow—you got to think a laborer knows *how.* How about that?"

"Yes," Hank said, "*laborers*—"

The bartender went to serve a customer and Hank Gavin went out into the street, the noisy street, trying to remain conscious of walking with the One Companion. He will go with me, he told himself, as he walked the road to Emmaus. Why not? What's to stop him?

And in the face of the forces of diminishment and despair, grant that I may believe ardently and above all things in your active presence, Lord, everywhere I have been, everywhere I go.

How can anyone tell when you will reach out a finger and lay it on a man's heart, or speak to a publican and sinner as you spoke to that smug and reckless and spendthrift young man-about-town, that bored and boring playboy, who through the angel of your presence became St. Francis of Assisi?

Again he was aware of the dilemma of the very leader that the bartender wanted.

The horns of that dilemma always faced a pastor, a preacher.

That grim sardonic intelligent bartender would detest him if he was *hearty*. A good-fellow, man-to-man approach.

Nor would he care to be preached to or at in his own bar.

The voice of the Jew wheezed at him from his audio memory.

"The authority of Jesus came from faith and works."

Authority.

That was the answer to the dilemma.

From faith and works.

Get on with it, Gavin, he said to himself.

7

Some time went by before Mellie found the right moment to speak to Deedee Retzlaff. For this, she was to blame herself bitterly, though I don't think myself it would have made any difference. It was already too late. Her feeling that she didn't want to force anything, all must come about naturally, young things scare easy even the bad guys, made her wait, jockeying for the right time and place to unfold.

Somehow it didn't then, and she was very busy.

Before it did, per Mellie's suggestion the young Gavins took Steve and Gloria Retzlaff to dinner at Beach City's only plush IN restaurant, on the point across the Bay from where the good Dr. Ffolliott was blissfully serving as a night clerk, despite his bishop's ire.

That evening the sunset was spectacular, which Mellie found gratifying. When people didn't know each other well, scenery or weather—especially anything like a blizzard or heat wave, hurricane or spectacular sunset—was valuable. When the four of them sat down by the curving glass wall, the sky was deeply, darkly blue, over it had been flung a robe of royal purple decorated in fire red, polished gold, and peacock blue, it was reflected in the sea so perfectly that it was hard to tell where the real ended and the mirrored beauty began. Yet within seconds, for there is no twilight in California, the sun had fled on its way to China and the rim of the horizon was violet, it wore unbelievable jade green ornaments and a chiffon the color of a climbing California rose. Then immediately it was dark. They could see a necklace of lights, ruby and emerald and topaz, stop go wait, worn around the line of the bay.

All this lasted them through cocktails. Then the men began talking golf, and Mellie admiring the chic of Gloria's black brocade dinner suit. Amid the easy, jolly talk that followed—for Steve Retzlaff was a man with a fund of anecdotes, of interests, of tall tales and pleasant gossip told with gusto and expectation of laughter and applause—only a few things had struck Mellie as significant.

In time, the talk had to touch Deedee.

On the Sunday before she had sung *In a Garden*, and Mellie repeated the kind of things people had said of it. However, it seemed Deedee had been mistaken. Her father didn't want her to have a career, any career, singing was to be a social asset, a way to fill time, after she married. She could sing to her babies, he said. Be nice if she kept up her singing, which most women didn't do. Idle hands, he added, with all these modern inventions women might have too much time on their hands. Idle *heads*, Mellie said, were more dangerous, and this Steve received as a bit of scintillating wit.

Gloria said, "She's much too young to think of marrying of course, only a baby really, but an only child is older don't you think, she's been with us so much, I don't say it's serious but I think she and Bobbie Mayhew—they start going steady so young now—"

"You'd like that?" Mellie said. "I thought him spoiled as a bad apple."

"They're not going steady yet," Steve Retzlaff said, "I'll make the decision about when Deedee goes steady. But Bobbie's—it's a good family, he needed a father, I'm inclined to prefer a boy who knows the score. Now that he's at Stanford, I expect he'll settle down."

When Mellie told me this I said that looking back over a husband, two brothers, and several sons who went to Stanford I could observe no such effects, and Mellie said, "What bothered me, they thought the boy came down at Thanksgiving especially to see Deedee. He didn't."

Watching both the girl's father and mother, she threw out the name of Beany Teran. The Christmas carols were getting a little flat—perhaps Beany Teran, who played the guitar beyond the ordinary, could accompany Deedee in a group of them. Youth was mad about guitars. Deedee's parents nodded. Either they'd never heard the name or it was without significance. A boy who went to the same school. Who played the guitar.

Then Hank, casually, without overture or preamble, said, "I've been getting some information and reactions about that matter of a Zone Variance. I had an idea I might bring it up at the first City Council meeting in January."

He succeeded in surprising Steve Retzlaff, it was a principle with him he always said to be ready for anything. This time he wasn't ready for Hank Gavin.

Steve Retzlaff showed no surprise. Impossible of course that he hadn't heard about Dr. Gavin's tour of the city. In a tone of friendliness and concern, he said, "I'm afraid you didn't get anywhere."

"I got some information I needed," Hank said.

"I thought I'd talked you out of that notion, padre," Steve said.

"You couldn't have thought that," Hank said with a big smile, "it wasn't a notion."

There, to Mellie's surprise, he left it. He didn't press or explain nor try to persuade Steve. He took the reaction and went on to football without showing any disappointment, and the rest of the evening was fun.

In bed later, Mellie asked him about that. Hank's voice in the dark was first amused, then a little wistful. "I saw it was too soon. I have to wait until after my sermon. The Lord may soften him up for me some then. I can't get over how *sorry* I feel for the guy."

"If I felt sorry for Steve Retzlaff I would go out and cut my throat," Mellie said.

When Hank spoke again, he startled her into turning on the lamp on the bedside table. He said, "What was all that about Beany Teran?"

"Do you know him?" she said.

"I've met him," Hank said. "His mother's a waitress part of the time in a joint down on the waterfront. The man of the house is a sailor but not always the same one. There are half a dozen kids in the family younger than Beany. What was on your mind my love?"

"Oh—" Mellie said, "I'm sure he has talent and you know me about people with talent, I think they're important."

"Nestor thinks he has too," Hank said, and Mellie found herself amazed at how much young Dr. Gavin knew about his parish in so short a time. He was doing a good deal of the youth work himself; they had seen through Marv Gregory's charm in a hell of a hurry.

"Even Marguerita thinks we should use this boy as much as we can," she said.

That was all, she decided, she was going to tell him. If Hank went *pious* on these children, they wouldn't like it, Deedee was bright enough, Beany was a guitar player, they'd see through that, too. To them, all this commitment of Hank's would be—what? old hat, inartistic, unscientific, unintelligent. Expecting God to take a hand in your personal affairs.

In the dark again, the "Pop Folk Mass" began to go through her head, it kept on and on until she went to sleep, was still there when she woke up to find Hank gone, as usual. Her first reaction still was that he'd had an early golf date at the club, then she remembered where they were and realized he'd gone to the prayer service he held for men on their way to work—business or otherwise.

She had never asked him how many came.

Either way, she didn't want to hear.

Also there was about this time a luncheon at the Virginia Club where, Archie told me, there were four people around the table. "It is odd," I said, "how much of the world's business and pleasures take place around a table," and Archie said, "Nothing new. Roman banquets—and King Arthur had one celebrated ever since." After a little pause he said, "There was also the Last Supper." Again he waited, then he said, "You want to hear about the one the four of us had the other day? Your young friend Gavin, Olin McAddams and I? He'd asked me—the preacher—to come along and my curiosity got me there."

"You and Hank and McAddams is only three," I said.

"Ah ha!" Archie said, "Bertha McAddams was there, too. Not in the *flesh*, but her presence had better be taken into consideration just the same."

Young Gavin's air of authority had surprised Archie. It was, he told me, something new, he thought. "He talked to McAddams as one having authority," and realizing he had slipped into a quote he finished it, "and not as the scribes and Pharisees."

"You've forgotten Hank's background," I said mildly.

"My good woman," the publisher said, "I have known a lot of bond salesmen or investment counselors or whatever you call them, and most of them were a good deal like the scribes and Pharisees. This young fellow has authority without being objectionable. I assume you know where he thinks he gets it."

A momentary picture of Hank sitting or kneeling at the window in the early dawn with light—*light*—on his face recalled to me a line he'd spoken to Mellie that I thought was worth repeating: "He's praying for strength to transcend the limitations his reason is trying to impose on him," I said. "Picasso said that and he likes it."

"Picasso?" Archie Paddock yelped, and I felt sure that while as a publisher he attempted to remain objective, he was a Rembrandt man himself. "You mean he wants to doll up his religion in some style like Picasso?"

"No, Archie," I said, "but even you and I must agree that as far as painting goes Picasso changed the face of the earth because he refused to abide by the limitations of reason. I think Hank is setting out to prove a—a convergence between the world and man *and* the Holy Spirit that would certainly change life itself and to do it he must be enabled to go beyond everything there is in the world and of course God has to be the *impulse*—the initial impulse—for that."

"I donknow," Archie said, "I don't know. One thing I can tell you, you never saw a neater trick than the one he pulled yesterday even with Bertha hovering over McAddams' head in ectoplasm. Young Gavin got a verbal agreement out of him. *If* he can get a Zone Variance to build a church there, McAddams will sell him that corner on Pacific Coast Highway at a reasonable figure. Of course a reasonable figure might have considerable variance of its *own* and probably the old boy didn't tell Bertha about this when he got home because he's so sure with Steve Retzlaff in there Gavin can never get a building permit. Does it occur to you that Gavin chose to fight this one on Steve Retzlaff's own grounds?"

"He says he's sorry for Retzlaff," I said, and Archie grunted violently. "He says Steve could be a wonderful man but he's been caught up by the last heresy—"

"Which is?" Archie said.

"I've told you and told you," I said, "the last heresy is the earthly paradise unconnected with God."

"I must say this will be a modern miracle of some kind," Archie said, "maybe that's what he's after. McAddams is a superstitious gent. He covers himself on all fronts if he can. He used to play in our poker game from time to time and he always went home to put on his lucky shirt."

"What kind of a poker player is he?" I said.

"Optimistic," Archie said. "Well—as in all things—time will tell."

As far as Deedee was concerned, young Mrs. Gavin did have three things in her favor. She wasn't a parent. She came from some place other than Beach City. She talked to Deedee as though she was another human being.

The truth was, the girl found Mellie Cheyne Gavin breath-taking. Not only because Mellie wore a skirt and shirt and sweater with more style than anyone Deedee had ever seen. From the beginning, she felt a complete trust, Mellie was somebody to be trusted, not to betray you on the grounds that you were only somebody *young*, it was possible to have a friendship with her which was usually *im*possible because it was based on confidence.

Like an older sister.

By chance, they met in the Cutlers' house. Norma Gregory, who was in charge of the Christmas Bazaar at the church, wanted Mellie's help in needling Gert Cutler into more speed with decorations and costumes. Gert had such a splashing, free-wheeling sense of color, who cared whether anything lasted or not? She'd asked Gloria Retzlaff to come too, for a little informal meeting, and when Gloria arrived she had Deedee with her. "She wants to talk to Norma about the costumes for the carols," Deedee's mother said.

All very familiar, this was, to Mellie.

A TV commercial changing its background only.

The Cutlers' house was the essence of order. Mellie felt her heart skip a beat when she saw the four children. They began with a square, blond fullback aged two, and ranged up to a girl imp with Titian hair and freckles. "They're—beautiful," Mellie said to their grandmother and she said, "Aren't they really? I don't think it's just because—only Randy (the fullback's name it turned out was Randy) hasn't had any nap and he gets tired and cross—" into which Gert cut in the key of resentment that was rotting away all harmony, "—put a big lug like Randy down for a *nap* he ought to be out selling papers," and Randy rushed at her with shouts of glee.

The green lightning struck you could see it, then Gert said, "Run out and play, all of you, we want to talk," and, completely expressionless, the grandmother said, "Go down to the light before you cross the boulevard if you're going to the park—" and Gert, raucously, objectionably good-natured, said, "Oh for gosh sake, ma, they go every day, they're not half-wits, myself I think overprotecting them can be more—can be worse in the end, I believe you ought not to overprotect kids, toughen 'em up early, is what I say," and her mother-in-law said, "I hope that will be a consolation to you if one of them gets hit by a truck."

The sheer brutality of it struck silence and then Norma Gregory blurted out the first thing that came into her head, she said, "And how's your prayer cell doing?"

Mellie thought she had never seen anyone turn such an all-over *hurting* blush-scarlet in her life as Gert Cutler did at that moment. It hurt me, Mellie said. And she saw the older woman put her hands under the chair, gripping the edges. Gert spoke a fraction of a second first, she said, "Now you kids listen to me—you be careful crossing the street, you hear me? I don't want one of you to get hit with a truck—" and her mother-in-law said, "Oh Gert—I know I'm too *fussy*—older people are—"

Mellie Cheyne Gavin took over then. Women were all alike. She could well remember hospital committees, children's fashion shows, political planning groups, with scenes, tears, tantrums, arguments, she'd always known how to deal with this, she still knew. But—in a way—she decided thoughtfully this had been taken out of her hands at the Cutlers' they had come out of it by themselves as it were, and from then on Gert was in high spirits and her mother-in-law was natural—or almost natural—with her.

As they shut the door Gloria Retzlaff said, "Well—that was the most bearable time I've ever spent there—you know I always felt sure that some day sooner or later Gert *would* —however, come along, Deedee."

Mellie said, "I'm thirsty. I was afraid to ask for anything. Gert would have given us beer in a can while mama-in-law was making tea and cinnamon toast. What I need is a big foamy chocolate shake. Lend me Deedee, will you, Gloria? I expect she knows where to get the best one."

The drive-in was a circular building of glass, around it parking spaces where girls in orange leotards and green ballet skirts were carrying trays. "This is beyond me," Mellie said, "Hank says I spill things. Let's go inside, is that all right?" and Deedee said, "Oh, we always go inside. They have music."

Inside it was shocking pink and sky blue, it had a circular counter in the middle, behind which men and boys in white coats moved with the speed and grace of ballet dancers, the booths in the windows were done in blue and pink leather.

This was the center—a center anyway—for the high school social life.

California, Mellie thought. They still have this glorious illusion about their weather. All these fogs—they don't consider them at all. Nor the heat waves.

She sat watching Deedee begin to stir her saucer of vanilla and chocolate ice cream into a beige soup. Like a kid. A young awkwardness. For all that air of aplomb, her hands were as young as a baby's bottom. Now they were restless, they could be tender, sensitive, warm, or cool. An amateur, Mellie thought unexpectedly. What a word to float into her stream of consciousness. Still, it is true, she is an amateur, they all are, they've been thrown into a world that allows them to play professionally. Don't worry, honey, the nice rattlesnake won't bite you. Black headlines. 500 Pregnant Girls in City Schools. Slum children! No no—they weren't—and if the girls at the top—the winners, Hank called them—had almost as large a percentage, what did it make the losers think?

Heal at the top too, Hank said. Then you have leaders.

I escaped, Mellie thought. I played at being a pro. Dear God, surely I was older than this? I knew more? Did I? Really?

The young voice which always had music in it was saying

—Gert is a ball of fire, when she comes to help us she keeps everybody in stitches, I mean in a way she's lucky to have her mother-in-law there, isn't she, I mean some women with lots of kids, or girls with real little ones, you wouldn't believe, no sheets on the beds, I mean they have washing machines but they never get around to putting the sheets in it, and the dishes not washed, sometimes for weeks and the smell—they could, I guess, but some of them don't. I think it's kind of goofy that people in the same family can't get along when it's so much better after all Gert can trust her mother-in-law with the children, it's not like some baby-sitters you know that—why is it, Mrs. Gavin?

"If I am going to be a big sister to you," Mrs. Gavin said, "you may begin calling me Mellie. I don't really know. Nowadays different generations seem to find it more difficult than ever to—to communicate and compromise, they all want to have their own way, the old and the middle-aged and the young," and she wondered if one of the houses where the dishes weren't washed sometimes for weeks was Beany Teran's. Had Deedee ever been to Beany's house?

"Like my father," Deedee said, breathlessly, pulling her shoulders up to her ears. "My father's a duck, I do love him, he thinks he's boss of all he surveys. Big shot—poor lamb. Everything with him is a big deal. I'm a big deal. My singing is a big deal. Everything I do has to be a bigger deal than anybody and maybe I'm not. How is he so sure he knows what's good for me so much better than I do? He's so—inconsistent. For weeks he forgets I'm alive—he'd slay me if he heard me say that, he forgets so completely he doesn't even know he's forgotten. Then some night he's out on the porch practically with a shotgun when I come home, he's roaring and going on about locking everybody up—and he loves me better than anybody in the world—big deal!"

Mildly, Mellie said, "He's used to running a city, a county, a state some day. Naturally he thinks he can run his own daughter."

Just possibly he's met his match in his church this time. No no—he had that well in hand. As to Deedee—his daughter—pretty soon now she wouldn't be able not to mention Beany. If she's in love with him. One of the sure signs, *talking about him somehow,* they couldn't help it.

"You remember the boy who plays my accompaniments on the guitar?" Deedee said. "He's made some wonderful arrangements of some of the carols—I thought we might get the choir—or a quartet—and I'd do a solo—"

"Yes," Mellie said. "Has your father met Beany?"

"No," Deedee said, "that's one reason—we'd have to practice late—"

"You can practice in the Sunday School auditorium," Mellie said. "Look, lovey, you're in love with him, and since you're in love with him—you'll have to agree that I can trust you."

First a quick smile of denial, a head shake, a quick sound of negative. Her hands betrayed her. A spoon jumped off the table as her hands came down on it. A wave of color up to the tousled hairline, Mellie could see the young breasts shake as the heart struggled to rejoice at talking about him, being that near him, remembering, trying to stay self-possessed, to conceal, yet yearning—yearning—to reveal, to make it more real by telling someone about it, someone you loved and *trusted.*

Oh God, Mellie said in a manner of speaking to a god in whom she did not believe. Poor *baby.*

"He's so wonderful," Deedee said, "you don't know, you can't imagine, he's so wonderful, he's not like any other boy—"

"No," Mellie said, "of course not." And to herself, they never are, *he* never is, when it's happening to you and after a while he really isn't, not like anyone else in the world, like Hank. "You—you don't think your father has any idea about this at all?"

"You know what my father would do?" Deedee said. She retrieved the spoon and wiped it and began to stir again, round and round, keeping her eyes on the whirl of beige. "He'd run him out of town. He could just as well kill anybody when he's mad my mother always said, she's wrong, she doesn't know him the way I do. He wouldn't kill him, he's too *cagey* my father is, he'd run him out of town and Beany—he's had so much to put up with, you can't imagine—he's never had a chance—he couldn't stand any more, he couldn't *bear* it, you can understand that, can't you?"

"All right," Mellie said, "we won't let anything more happen to him."

And Deedee looked up at her with—it is true, Mellie thought, it can be, it's not just a phrase—her heart is in her eyes.

Through a soft late afternoon, through the peaceful fields where the sun gleamed on live oaks and gilded small hills, they drove out to the so-new Retzlaff house. Gloria's car was in the drive. Deedee got out of Mellie's and came around to the driver's side. When she put her arms around Mellie's neck they were trembling, her lips pecking at Mellie's cheek were hot as though she couldn't hold back the tears much longer.

Mellie Gavin said, "If you need a friend, baby, I'm available. I am the minister's wife now, but I used to live in the world and I know quite a lot about it. If you're ever in a jam you can count on it that I'll do my best to help you. That all right?"

"Oh—" Deedee said. "Oh yes. It's just—Mellie, I can't let them hurt Beany any more, nobody ever thinks about Beany, and he's so—so—"

"Vulnerable," Mellie said.

With a gulp that was a laugh swallowing a sob or a sob drowning a laugh, the girl said, "Oh—you do know. You do know—I will—oh thank you darling—"

She stood waving bravely, confidently, while Mellie drove away.

She believed in me, Mellie told me.

Much good that did her.

8

Just before Hank came by to invite me personally to his Sunday-before-Christmas sermon, which was to become so famous locally, it occurred to me to ask Archie Paddock how things were going and what he thought Hank Gavin was accomplishing.

This gave Archie time to think. He had the editorial rather than the reportorial mind, he was never one for snap judgments.

"This is a new version of the sawdust trail," he told me finally. "I get the impression he's trying to plant seeds and set an example, it gives you a strong sense of his integrity. But I get an impression he's going all the way. His premise that we're not operating fairly in giving the theories of Christianity a trial flight like—say—Gemini 5—has some foundation in fact."

"What are you doing?" I said.

"I am a hard-bitten skeptic," Archie said, "I am from Missouri—he will have to show me. I—I'm willing. He has some ideas I haven't ever heard before."

"Where do you—and the others—hear them now?" I said.

Archie said, "Oh—he has a couple of small classes going."

With some reluctance Archie said, "Yes, a man has to see what's going on. I've got a hunch that in the next two-three years—odd things will be."

"What particular ideas do you mean?" I said.

"Take the second coming," Archie said. "Plainly some people—and some of the disciples, thought it meant the return of Jesus just as he supposedly ascended. Young Gavin asked me point-blank the other day if it would do any good if a figure called Jesus in white robes was supposed to have come floating down out of the sky over the Merchandise Mart in Chicago, or on a Kansas prairie or walking on a river in Mississippi. Would anybody believe it? I said I didn't think so. Unless they had enough notice so TV could set up real coverage such a rumor would probably give all Christianity a black eye if somebody tried it. So I asked him what he thought the second coming was and he said the arrival of the Holy Spirit in our hearts, the still, small voice, the actual experience of the Christ—he could be right."

"Who else is in your class?" I said and he said, "I think Gavin is sort of not saying much about any of this. He's been going around talking to a good many people, too."

"What'd they think?" I said.

"I'm not sure," Archie said, "I'm not at all sure."

I asked Hank point-blank who was actively in his work and he said, "Watch it and see if you can spot anybody."

"I hope one of them is Steve Retzlaff," I said.

"So do I," Hank said and grinned at me.

Then he invited me to the sermon on the Sunday before Christmas.

The way he said it made me feel this was the takeoff. So I said, "I'll come of course. What are you going to—is there some special thing? Some *point* to it?"

"I hope so," Hank said. "I guess the—basis of it is that no man can break his own bondage, whatever it is. No men can overcome the world's anguish. No man without some help can love his neighbor."

Hank was thoughtful for a moment, then he said, "Ask not what you can do for your church. Ask what your church can do for you. How would that be?"

"You're going to say that to your congregation and mean it?" I said.

"Or would it better to say *demand*—" Hank said, "ask not what you can do for your church, *demand* what your church can do—no no, ask what your church can do for you is right. *Demand* that your church keep the promises."

He looked at me hopefully and the close-up made him frown.

All the fears had swamped me. I felt them freezing my countenance into a distortion of fear and disbelief and protest. Even I—trying to be so full of hope, so wistfully wanting to believe—cried out within myself like a doubting Thomas—don't go to war for any cause whatsoever. Don't come out of your nice dark safe cave. Don't try to orbit in God's universe in a spiritual capsule. Don't quit a good job, no matter if the boss is cheating. Don't climb out on a limb for anybody. Don't be a rebel or a revolutionary. Take it easy. The longest way round is the shortest way home. Keep the noiseless tenor of your ways, boy. Be a middle-of-the-road mind and never show a tooth. Make sense, safety first, produce only theological miracles of obscuratism. Don't stand up before your nice well-dressed successful congregation and promise them the morning star—don't *do* that, *don't* point at the center-field fence and say a home run right over *there*.

All this Hank must have read on my poor unhappy face.

He said, "They stoned Stephen. I've thought about him a lot. Here was a young fellow with so much faith the disciples chose him to be one of their number. With that faith in the power of the Christ, he did miracles. But he wasn't satisfied with that. He started demanding that the temple perform against the works as Abraham and Moses and Daniel and Gideon and Elijah and David had done. And, in their own time, the prophet Jesus of Nazareth. This got the elders and high priests in an uproar because if there is one thing the elders do not like it is for young men to go around demanding what the Church can do for them in the way of works. They brought Stephen before the Council and said this is blasphemy against our 1001 rules. When he spoke some of them admitted later that he had the face of an *angel*—they used that very word, Godmama—who wanted to believe in angels? But he called the Council and all a few things too—stiff-necked, uncircumcised in heart and ears—there's a phrase for you—and he said that as usual the writers and the theologians and the big brass resisted the simplicity of the Holy Spirit, he asked them point-blank if there had ever been a prophet or teacher who demanded action that they didn't persecute him and it says they *gnashed their teeth* at him—I bet you—so the scribes and the elders and the intellectuals and the theologians stopped their ears again, it says, and they ran at him with one accord and stoned him, but he saw the glory of the Lord, and he kept looking up at the second coming which was sent to him then, to help him, and he kept saying Don't blame them. Lord, they do their best."

"Why didn't the Lord save Stephen if he was there in a—a second coming?" I said.

"Stephen had to take it," Hank said, "from time to time, people do. He didn't mind. In the end, losing this life brought him the second coming. Besides, you see, Paul was there. Saul they still called him then. Saul-Paul had consented to them stoning Stephen to death."

"I don't follow any of that," I said.

"That's what broke Saul's heart wide open, circumcised it so that he could hear with his heart when Jesus came and spoke to him on the road to Damascus and he became Paul."

"Hank," I said loudly, hurriedly, "I have to tell you I think you are going too far."

"Too far?" he said, in a sharp hard disappointment.

"Much too far," I said, unhappily. "How can you live up to—to all these promises?"

"They aren't my promises," Hank said in the same hard,

hot harsh, way. "They are the promises of Christ, of Christianity, of every other faith the world has known. Now is the greatest time since Jesus—now there is a possibility that we cannot only fuse our inner and outer lives in the Christ ideal but maybe even fuse *that* ideal into the great non-Christian religions, maybe our evolution in science leads us to God—who can refuse orders in times like these?"

"They aren't ready," I said. "People aren't ready for such far-out talk—"

"Who's going to get them ready?" he said sternly, and it stopped me cold. "The hearts of good men need to be called, too. Don't you see since I know of the Redemption I have to tell them? We said it as children—in the old childish game of hide-and-go-seek—*ready or not here I come.*"

"Does Mellie know what you mean to say?" I said. "This—ask not what you can do for your church, ask what your church can do for you. Will she be there?"

"Paul was there," Hank said in pain. "Mellie's going to have to listen sometime."

Once he had said to me that the hardest thing in the world is for one human being to shine into another human being the glow that burns within himself. Even when he knows this is the true light.

Paul-Saul was there when Stephen was stoned, his heart broke open and let in the light he saw on the Road to Damascus.

I thought then that Hank was somehow again, and again and again, waiting for the truth—for the history of truth—to repeat itself. Somewhere sometime, as he'd just said, in the days to come he believed Mellie's heart must be broken open so that the light which shone out of his own heart could enter it.

Without this, the end must be tragedy.

Whether it could happen to her on this Sunday, I don't think he knew.

9

Here I would like to have a TV camera with a zoom lens. I must do the best I can with my typewriter and your imagination.

As I entered the church that morning, astounded by the suspense and excitement I felt, I assumed that Hank Gavin in the pulpit would be my major interest. Immediately, I knew the real importance to him, to my true story, had to be his effect on this vital audience. This was not, it turned out, a dwindling congregation. Curiosity, gossip, Archie's newspaper coverage had brought out every member of the church and there were a good many new faces, if parking hadn't been such a problem the old place might have been jammed. As it was, only a few vacant seats remained. And paramountcy lay in the result, the verdict, the ability to get their votes, as it had with Paul in Athens or Peter in Rome.

They were too civilized, too apathetic to stone him. If he advocated a commitment to the *works* of the founder of the Christian teachings, as obligations he had laid on all his followers for all time to come, there would have to be decisions. Whether the scribes and elders, the all-powerful Young, the wits and omnipresent wise guys, the satisfied and sophisticated, the winners and losers, the hungry thirsty sincere eager and lonely, the pundits and panjandrums who sat in this church this morning would listen and agree to try to walk in his steps to *see* whether it would work, or, turning away, follow no more after him—who could say, and this was as much a matter of life and death to Hank as it had been to Stephen whom they did stone.

A morning of drizzle. The vaulted nave of the dilapidated old church was not only gloomy, the gray glare had turned the garish windows into fair illustrations for Dante's *Inferno*. Six or seven hundred people, gathered to hear this sermon which their new young minister had announced as the most important of their lives, were restless and depressed by the weather. Under the Sunday-go-to-meeting clothes and manner, there they sat, citizens of the greatest power on earth, a few were consciously glad to be alive, and many were not. God was a far-off event unconnected with the meaninglessness of existence which boiled around them, pressuring their lives out of shape.

My reportorial desire to be an unbiased observer had kept me from calling Mellie. Alone, I found a seat on a bench under a window, from which I could see Hank on my left, the congregation in front and to the right. What occurred on the program before Hank began to speak must have matched the weather—it made no impression on me.

I was centered on him.

Too finely trained now. The sun of mountains, deserts, beaches, had bleached his thick pelt of straw. Wind and sea had coarsened and tanned his skin. Carpenter, sailor, fisherman, mountain-climber, farmer, shepherd, scholar, long-distance walker—the first Christian and his band *must*, at that, have looked more like this young American than the art which has so long led us astray. Hank was good casting for a first-class pro quarterback than whom nobody has more poise, authority, and scrap, and this was the big game coming up. To me, he gave out with the combined confidence and humility of an astronaut in condition for an ordeal.

My training to find a word for everybody came up with the word *challenge* for Hank. He is going to challenge them, I thought. He is not going to apologize for Christ. He won't let them ask all the questions. As God once remarked to Job, Gird up now your loins like a man, for I will demand of thee and answer thou me. Where were *you*, when *I* laid the foundations of the earth and *fastened* them, or when the morning stars I had lighted sang together? Who created this universe which now you boast of invading for a few orbits, on which allow me to congratulate you, who laid the laws of aerodynamics and arranged the winds and clouds whereby to guide your flights?

Spiritual muscle here, the sportswriter in me said, as I watched young Gavin.

A quick traveling shot of those to whom he was about to speak. *People*. Whom Mellie loved, in her way. All sizes, shapes, and colors. Good bad tense indifferent with and without faith. Here and there the camera picked out a face. Small, mean, show me—half-asleep over a stomachful of sausages and waffles—sweet, undisturbed by thought—tormented by yearnings, hopelessness, defiant, I'll-get-by-don't-worry-about-me faces.

Olin McAddams' face. The woman in the interior-decorated hat must be Bertha his wife. This was a peculiarly naked face, I thought. Money-in-the-bank written sharp and deep. Steve Retzlaff, now also wearing a tie striped yellow black and silver, Gloria's mink draped next to his shoulder. Was the word for Steve amused, alert, or tolerant? My friend Marguerita, rakish toque piled on white hair, out of a sense of fair play she had come to hear what Hank Gavin had to say about the church of Jesus Christ. Her integrity heartened me. I mustn't have a side as a reporter, still I was glad somebody was being fair to the side I didn't have.

The thing that began to bug me was whether they could *listen.* My suspicion that the world was overcommunicating until sound sound sound had stuffed their ears with wax, listening hours on end to overdone dramatizations and underdone opinion without time to think what any of it meant, made me fear they were out on their feet, reacting, if at all, from habit and built-in long ago prejudices and convictions and rebellions.

The swift lens jolted me. On the bench opposite mine, near the door, sat Beany Teran. His coat of many colors was too small for him, I'd never seen him wear a tie before, I felt sure this was the first time he ever attended a Protestant service. Unexpectedly, I saw that his appeal was in the fashion of the moment, dark, thin, small, untidy, defiant and hollow-eyed, he had the audacious double-dare of the mongrel pup barking at the world. I understood instantly what Deedee had meant when she'd said to Mellie: *We can't let anything more happen to Beany, he couldn't bear it.* Brash, brave, the underdogs now are more vulnerable than ever. Yet I had discovered that Beany was making a straight B average, he'd written an outstanding paper on Shakespeare as more modern than Baldwin or Albee (and somewhat better) because Shakespeare had written *Othello.* His eyes never moved from Deedee, in white with a little cape like wings. Her ashen hair seemed lank, as though the drizzle had touched it, she put up her fingers and turned in the ends. She was smaller, younger, than I had thought of her while Mellie was telling me of their talk.

Where was Mellie?

Frantically, the lens sought her here there everywhere.

Paul whom Stephen so loved had been there when Stephen spoke fearlessly to the mobs. I was confused about *Mellie*—she was Hank's best friend, who happened to be his wife, it was only fair that she should hear him, yet suppose she could, like Paul, join his enemies?

All this jumbled painfully in my head while Deedee sang Christ is born in Beach City, or maybe she said Bethlehem, what was the difference, Beach City must likewise be Bethlehem as Salinger kept saying the Fat Lady must be Christ—

Then Hank stood up quickly, eagerly, and walked forward. I thought that he had kept his style, yet for a moment there was a young awkwardness, whatever he was going to do or say I saw he would have to come up *above* his youth and natural modesty. Just as he moved into the pulpit, the shifting humming throat-clearing, settling-*down* was interrupted. All eyes turned away from him to see Mellie coming in. Short-jacketed suit of woolly ivory material, chunky gold pin in the lapel, long dangling gold earrings touching the sable throw. Why *dangling* gold earrings on Sunday in church? I couldn't remember I'd ever seen her wear dangling earrings before. Around her head only a scarf of golden gauze. More very pale tangerine lipstick than usual.

Another woman walked beside her.

Sybil Rowe.

Hot temper leaped in me. Damn and blast, insufferably rude as it was to be late, and I knew Mellie was never rude except on purpose, it was worse to have brought Colin's widow. Today of all days. Mellie knew how Sybil felt about Hank. She'd told all Chicago Hank's conversion was nothing but a desire to show off. Or else he was cracked. What was she here for? To heckle? An unbeliever, to jeer? As Mellie's smile and appealing hand made people shove to give them seats, I was sure Hank must have seen them come in, he must have recognized the deliberateness of the entrance. Nothing was giving him any help, that was for sure.

He opened cold.

> I am a fanatic.
>
> Bear with me. I believe that the only thing that can save this magnificent world is more fanatics for Christ. In our day, we have shortened fanatics to *fans*. That's where it comes from—fans. Dodger fans, Cleveland Brown, rock and roll and roll, Picasso, op art, Beatle, discotheque, gold, bird-watching fans. I'm not corny enough to suggest a fan club for Jesus Christ, but originally a *fan*atic was a man of panting, wild-eyed zeal, a zealot, way out yonder, with banners, in spiritual matters. John the Baptist was a fanatic, the saints and holy ones and Puritans and Pilgrims, they're fanatics.
>
> I have been sent to tell you that you must become fanatics for Christ.

His audience stirred uneasily, like sleepers whose accustomed repose has been pierced by a sharp unfamiliar sound. *I am a fanatic*. The young man had said that with cold precision.

I have been sent to you. A little—a little odd, sort of eerie, wasn't it? *To tell you that you must become fans of Jesus Christ*—relaxation could hardly be comfortable with this kind of talk going on—he had shaken them up a bit—no question about that.

They were listening as best they could, hundreds of upturned faces fixed on Hank Gavin, a man I had once known, still knew, knew no longer. Impelled, my eyes moved to Mellie. Blank. Blanker than anybody. Then what was like a bolt of lightning-white lit her, even by that I couldn't read how she was responding to the man who was her husband.

In Christianity, stripped of its subsequent additions, subtractions, and divisions, Christianity, as Jesus taught it, is the cure for all the social ills of humanity.

Who said that?

A hundred guesses—you wouldn't come up with it. Einstein. Albert Einstein. $E=mc^2$. He said it. If we are going to take the Christ out of the Christ teachings we shall have to go to hell before we find it again. In this age, we have to choose between Cosmos and Chaos. If we try—experiment—try the Cosmos of Christ to which we have come, if we follow its compelling, loving teaching as the mathematicians followed $E=mc^2$, I promise you that we can find the kingdom of heaven which is within us all, around us as well. Do you know anyone else, anything else, that's making you as good an offer as that? Isn't it sensible to *try* it as Jesus taught it? I am here today to ask you to agree with me to try to follow the steps as Jesus taught them. The steps of the men who first tried his teachings, made them work so they spread around the globe.

To *you.*

Not to the angel of God's Presence in the church of Sardis or Laodicea. Unto the angel of the church of Beach City, California. In Beach City, you will be told that you never had it so good ever before. You know this isn't true. If we've got an earthly paradise, why are we so apprehensive, so fearful? Why do even advertisments speak language we'll understand best by shrieking hour after hour OOOOOH DO WE WORRY? Why do all statistics show a level of the moral side so low it has to make the most worldly of us cringe if we stop to take a good honest look at it? Has man more joy, is he more at peace? Does he feel the strong glory of progress as he climbs toward truth? Is he closer to God's love for him, happier in his home, more at one with his family, loving his neighbor more, resting sometimes in contentment of the soul, accepting with more enthusiasm the challenge all man can find in life?

Are we so worried about what we have to get and grab that we have lost sight of how blessed it is to give?

What do we *have* to give? To share?

I tell you now that the moment when we must sweep the moneychangers out of *control* of the temple has come.

Are you ready for it?

If not, why not?

A steel click. I heard a steel click. Across the room the cash register in Mrs. McAddams' skull was clicking *this could cost us.* This young man had mentioned the word *money*. This brought Big Bertha out of the momentary mass hypnosis of Hank's compelling, loving, pleading voice.

One other I saw, in the purple-green-red florescence. Sybil Rowe had been hit by that *what do we have to give*? That struck home and she was white as a candle.

He gave them no time to recover.

Civilizations perish in the heart. Not in the head. No no no no. In the heart. For lack of love they perish.

No government—

No college education—

No intellectual plunderbund—

No hierocracy of priests and ecclesiastics—

No financial establishment—

No military might—

No first-to-the-moon science supremacy—

No up-the-down social class—

No integration march—

No business—

No labor union—

No political party—

No rich-rich—

No poor-poor—

None of them can give you love.

Only Christ. He destroys hate.

You cannot have the brotherhood of man without the fatherhood of God. That's love.

Brothers have the same father. That's the law of love.

They do the will of their father together. In love. Then comes peace on earth and good will among men. *Then* —no other time.

Are you ready for that?

You have to be ready to gain the brotherhood of man by doing the will of your Father which is *in* heaven.

I want to tell you! Sunday Christianity has been wiped from Steve Retzlaff. He had heard things he never expected to hear in church. No political party. No business. No up-the-down social class. If he was to reign in Beach City and California he must defy these things which his ears could hardly believe. If he was to remain Steve Lucifer Retzlaff it might be necessary to throw stones.

One look at Mellie and in aching panic I began to pray wildly, don't let it be Mellie. Paul watched them stone Stephen *whom he loved*. Don't let it be Mellie, she is the only one who can stone Hank, and *kill* him.

To the trumpet call: Your will be done, not mine, yours, Steve had begun to shout back in his heart as he thought. You sanctimonious bastard. You smug holier-than-thou drop-out. You—up there in the pulpit bigod. I'm the big shot in this town, I'm respected, sensible. As moral as a man can be now in business and politics—Christian. I am a moral man, bigod. My will is going to be done around here because God helps those who help themselves. I am a smart man, smart enough to know what's best for my town, my daughter, my church by god, and where are *you* going to get the dough to build a church, just tell me that, you psalm-singing *ham?* Don't you come into my bailiwick and start trying to push *me* around, that's all.

Mellie had always wanted her will to be done. Mellie was a *Leo;* her horoscope would tell you she was an absolute angel herself, easy to get along with, as long as she had her own way all the time, which was best for everybody.

Love is now all we have left to hope in. Love is all we can give. We must get love. How? Where? From whom?

Sometimes I feel we aren't as wicked, evil, bad, hard-boiled, slack, psychopathic, or hating as we brag about being. We just don't want to admit that we are lost. Forlorn fellows, lost children of Our Father, lovelorn for our brother Christ. Under the very best of the gaudy, glossy, glittering, bigger and better, ain't-we-got-fun surface, with all the evils dramatized and witticized, do you feel that hours and hands and hearts ache with *loneliness?* We run out, we stay in the midst of the crowd's ignoble strife not to have fun in its company but to shun ourselves, not to be alone with ourselves. The fault that we have missed real growth, true happiness, and the kingdom which is our home—where is the fault, whose is it? First of all—the church.

We are that church. You and I. Not a pile of stones, a membership, a social circle, a board, a preacher. The home-away-from-home that Christ gives us. *Where two or three are gathered together in my name there am I, in the midst of them.* As he is here, now, in this church, you know that, don't you? Oh—we don't much like *churches,* we can pray just as well at home, better amid the beauties of Nature. In pain, trouble, terror, confusion—*can we?* Then is a time you need fellowship. To serve others, perhaps. You may need a priest to help you back into God's loving care. To teach you how to pray. I remind you that Jesus Christ felt it was the Way—to have a church, he told Peter so. But the church must give and we cannot give what we have not got. If the church has not the power of love to give, we are lost. We are phony, lip-service Christians, we are highly educated intellectual brain-washed Christians who are walking away from him who is Love, getting colder and colder, trying to cast out devils by Freud. Not by God. Even if Freud can name all the seven devils and their seven million little batsard offspring, can he cast them out? Or are you supposed to go on living happily ever after with them because now you can call them by their nicknames? Can anybody but Christ say in the irresistible voice of love *Go and sin no more,* I destroy evil, I don't make a house cat out of it? I restore to you the years which the locusts have eaten, free now of that guilt which you hug to yourselves thinking that if you are sorry for all these absurdities and itches this will be enough. No no. The Risen Christ alone can give you the power to sin and be guilty no more, and here we come to the crucial point for the church. We dare not say come and see the Risen Christ in yourself, in all life around you; we dare not say come and see what his love will do for you, unless we ourselves know he will be here. Yet if he is not here, not Risen and therefore still ours, *if* the Cross either on Calvary or in our churches or our own lives is the end, the final word, then we are of all men most miserable and have been sold a bill of goods. Who wants a forever dead god forever nailed upon a tree? No no no, you can't sell that to the world today, and you should not be able to. For it's not true. The cross isn't the end. It never was. We can walk with the Risen Christ, we can make the stations of the Resurrection—what's a couple of thousand years?

We know all about that now.

The church from top to bottom, you and I and its top brass, we need to meet the Master face to face.

We're homesick.

No other homesickness is like that for the kingdom of heaven which is our *home*. This is the sickness of which our generation has been called sick sick sick.

To believe and know the love God has for us.

That he is *real*.

That he is, and that he loves us. I cannot say it too often. You must listen so he can tell you so. He is waiting on you. He will see you when you are yet a great way off; he will run to meet you as soon as you take your first stumbling wavering step back to him as he is—as he really *is*.

I offer you that moment. I promise you that moment. There is no other like it.

I—I have been blessed beyond anything I deserve or could ever deserve. I have seen him face to face, on the water not of Gennesareth but Lake Michigan.

I can say to you come and see. Come and *see*. And I do say it.

Come and see.

Turning up the volume, speeding up the tempo, this had become action. Not a sermon, an experience. *Come and see.*

As a man thinketh in his heart so must he do and act. Something was going on. Eyes slid sideways, quick-glancing to escape, to consider, to reject, to adore, to wonder. The angel of the church of Beach City? What a thing! In their hearts a pulse beat, could there be an angel, there might be an angel, what unmitigated rot there couldn't be an angel that was a lot of talk, a presence—presence—no no, could not be any kind—in the church—this church—that had been for people in places named Laodicea or Pergamos or Thyatira, not Beach City, this had to be way back when people weren't really people but wore *costumes*, togas and robes and armor. Not now this grizzly, gray, foggy morning, *Sunday* morning, in ordinary street clothes, with Christmas shopping to do tomorrow.

One man can make a difference.

You are that man.

About that, Pope John knew—how he knew. But he was not a reasonable man. Would a reasonable man have called an Ecumenical Council? To try to set going the Christianity which Einstein says will cure all the social ills of humanity *if* we do it as Christ taught it.

Pope John was a Catholic—he told you.

Einstein was a Jew—he told you.

Gandhi was the Mahatma—and he told you.

Now I, a Protestant, tell you too.

Oh—don't you know who you are?

Such warmth, such reaching out, I wanted to cry. Their *brother*, that's what Hank Gavin was—was being—was offering.

Then for the first time I realized they were staring at him, with hostility, struck with the incredible fact that they were listening to a young man they knew, in coat and trousers like their own, shirts done at the same laundry or at home with the same detergents, the thatch of thick straw hair cut by the same barber, who used the same eyewash and the same soap and the same not-greasy kid stuff and the same super gasoline from the same pump. Is not this the stockbroker from Chicago? Hadn't his grandmother been rich-rich? Didn't they know his wife sitting there with long dangling gold earrings? They saw him often coming down the *street*, any street, with that walk of an athlete and a Marine, grace in the control so you looked twice maybe, that was all.

You spoke to him not exactly as to each other because he was a preacher—but you shook hands, he had a friendly way of holding out his hand—and when he talked you started figuring which one of the Middle Western state societies he could belong to. Not familiar—but friendly. Sense of humor, too. Told a couple of baseball stories at the Elks banquet. Told a funny one and a tear-jerker about the kids in Korea. Now he was up there talking about God, a *real* God. He said you were homesick for the kingdom of heaven, he was saying God is here come down to it was a very embarrassing and sort of frightening thing to say in church on Sunday morning, wasn't it, this man they knew saying to them, *Be fanatics—there's an angel in your church in Beach City*—saying to them, *I have seen God—Christ—an angel—something face to face on Lake Michigan—actually I promise you the Second Coming—I promise you!*

What *was* all this?

Yet I realized with a blast that shook me loose from—from the limits my reporter's observation was trying to impose on me that *if* they *took* this, if they believed it from him, if he got to them, this had to be the light of a new life for them. The remarkable, earthshaking proposition was—if he, just one of them, like them, the young man from Chicago who now got his hair cut in Beach City, *if he could, they could*. And he said he not only could, he had. That was why Peter and Paul and Luke the beloved physician had led the world to understand Christ, and set off the full evolution of man up to Christ. Why *Peter* the fisherman was the rock on which Christianity was built. Why Paul's letters spoke to our hearts. All these things had happened to-men-like-as-you-are, we are, and when *they* said I have seen the Christ—I know that Jesus Christ is the son of God I have seen him and he has called me his brother—the men followed them.

So Hank was *pleading* with them—

Don't you know who you are?

In the beginning, he picked up twelve, as he went around towns, beaches, countrysides, a young man burned brown by the hot sun of Israel so like our own, a young man sturdy, gracefully strong, a carpenter from a place nobody ever spoke well of—Nazareth. Starting in a very small way, the Nazarene had twelve in his band. They were to be with him on the Mount, and when he put his first feed-the-hungry operation into practice. When he raised Jairus' daughter from the dead, and stopped the smug, self-righteous snoopers, who'd been taking a peek, from throwing stones at a prostitute they knew themselves. Then he began to get calls from all over the country, asking him to come and teach and heal. He couldn't go to all of them, so from those who'd been following him, heard his words, seen his works, he selected *seventy,* and sent them to become teachers and healers for those who asked. To the seventy, he promised they'd have the same power to do the same works. And sure enough, they came back to report on their field trips, they said the devils of power-grown-corrupt, hates, anxieties, depressions, worries, false pride, money-hunger, greed, neuroses, fears, lusts, pain, human and domestic relations, feuds, poverty, no housing, lack of love, unkindness, resentment, envy that embittered lives—all these had actually been subject to their dominion *in his name.* They had been able to cast them out, to overcome them. They would still leave tribulations, Jesus told them, but to those who had overcome in his name it was given to have their names written in heaven on the family tree of God—and *this* was what was important. All the works were steps to heaven.

I will tell you who you are.

There is no break in the continuum. How could there be? Why should there be? Your names are written in heaven, too. You are in time and space and the universe the continuum of the seventy and of those who called for them. There is no change in the promise that as you make your life one with him, your business one with his, your play part of the joy of this creation when all the stars sang together, the power to overcome the world as evil will be given you.

It is yours already. If you care to learn how to use it.

To ask for it.

Have you asked for it?

You must.

In the cosmos of God's orderly universe, you *are* the other seventy also—and those who asked the seventy to come and heal them and teach them.

You are.

Christ said so. Now all the science we know confirms it. Let me ask you something that I spent a lot of time on myself. Who was authorized and where and when and how and by whom to say the Master-Teacher, the God-made-man, didn't mean what he said? Or meant it only for his personal followers? Or only at the time he was walking beside the Jordan and the multitudes were casting their sick and despairing and poor at his feet? Who was given the right to monkey around with the instructions he gave the twelve, the seventy, all he spoke to? Who? To reinterpret what's so clear it can't need interpretation any more than Lincoln's Gettysburg Address. The first impulse to understand him comes from God. You have it. It is your life. I am the Life, he told them and tells you. If you are seeking him with all your heart you will meet him somewhere on the road to Damascus, or San Diego, or Saigon, or Washington or Biloxi or Miami or Buenos Aires. Though you know you're as loaded with hate and resentment as Paul was, when you meet the Risen Christ he will speak to you. He will say: Why are you persecuting me with all this foolishness? From there on—oh yes—yes yes yes—there will be tribulations. The road is uphill a lot of the way. But you will never never never walk alone again. Nor walk without love. There are tigers—but life can never be meaningless again. Find him on the road—I am the Way, he tells you, and nothing else will ever matter, as tough as it can get.

Gradually, the church was filled with light.

Yes yes yes it was. I was there. I saw it.

It wasn't that the rain had stopped, the drizzle lifted, the sun come out. They hadn't. No one can explain it away with that, for outside I could see the smog and fog and sunless sky and little rivulets running off the leaves of the trees. Inside, the church was filled with light as pure and glowing as a thousand thousand candles. Don't you understand that this is why I have to write this story? I wasn't in the Upper Room. I didn't swim ashore that morning when he had lighted a fire and gave them bread beside the Sea of Galilee. I wasn't with the disciples on the day of Pentecost. I have never known an angel personally. I wasn't on the barge on Lake Michigan.

But I was in the church in Beach City, California, that Sunday.

In the pause I tried to tell myself rationally that I had been moved to my utmost depths several times before. By Heifetz playing the Brahms Second with Toscanini conducting. By seeing Dali's Last Supper on the wall of the National Gallery in Washington. By Olivier praying on the stage in a play called *Becket*. By reading *The Phenomenon of Man* by de Chardin, by seeing the cathedral at Cologne. This now, I told myself, was just another great performance in art. I knew it wasn't.

If you could have been there.

Darshan. Blessing. The angel of the *Presence,* the pure majesty of the *real,* coming through the Mahatma to millions.

Even with my viscera, the linings of my arteries, the cells of my brains and the songs of my soul knowing the darshan was Hank's, I resisted violently, immediately. They would not accept that *Hank Gavin* with whom I'd sat at the Drake in Chicago drinking *beer*, or any other young American, could convey darshan to me. These average American citizens, sitting there knowing so well what to expect from the pastor —they would revolt as much as I did—at such necromancy and rune. This approach had to be a sort of Zen Buddhism or esoteric cultism or Billy Graham evangelism or *something*.

Or would they?

What *about* that extraordinary tale in the second chapter of the Book of Acts when there was a sound as of a mighty rushing wind filling the house where his disciples were sitting, just as we were sitting here, and they were filled with the Holy Ghost so that they knew how to speak the word to every man in a way his heart could feel, at the level of his consciousness, in the terms of his plain meaning. What a thing that must have been. There is a time, place, password for some kind of conversion for every human being. Has to be. Some people call a thing abominable trash that others call high mysticism. Simple truth to some sounds like Mother Goose rhymes. But there is somewhere a key word that opens each heart, each heart has a word and a language that is comprehensible and this is what happened in the second chapter of Acts—this was revealed to the disciples, just after Jesus left them, and they were so gloriously happy and so filled with joy that the crowd decided they were drunk. Naturally. Probably what they would think today.

Now, as though his sense of timing was controlled and his words came to him straight and true, Hank began punching. He seemed now to be taking what he said very seriously. But not himself saying it. All self-consciousness had been done away with.

We call ourselves Christians.

Follow me carefully now.

We have arrived at the practice point.

The Sermon on the Mount has been called by non-religious experts and non-religious historians the single greatest event in recorded history.

We have the Sermon on the Mount. We have *all* his teachings as given to his disciples over three years.

In Acts, we have the practice point arrived at and carefully set forth. It says so—the *Acts* of the Apostles—acts—what they did—how they put into practice what Jesus had taught and demonstrated for them.

That was their moment, after Jesus had gone.

This is our moment, too. This is *our* moment to begin our Acts.

His moment, too, Hank's moment, I felt it then I know it now, for here he set the stage for that split in his church, that real estate and political triple cross, that desertion in his own home. Here it began and went on up the final moment when at last he was to be called upon to practice what he preached and to prove what he said by his works in a way I have never been able to forget for one moment.

Archie wrapped up that moment in church that morning when he said to me, *He went for broke with a flourish, I'll say that for him.*

He wouldn't seem to let go of the practice point. He kept saying it.

We have arrived, as everyone, everything does and must, at the practice point.

We sail the boat or admit it's not seaworthy. We take off and jet through space or admit the plane won't fly. We write music an orchestra can play or quit calling ourselves composers. We shall do the works we chisel into our marble cornerstone OR admit our pretense of following their acts is as empty, false, and untimely as the rites of Diana of the Ephesians or the hawk-headed sun god of the Egyptians.

Let us begin.

What do we do first? We ask for grace to deal with the cowardice that keeps us from speaking up for him in whom we say we believe. With the measure of laziness, evasion, the little lusts of the ego, the big lusts of desire to rule.

We begin to weave together now the two commandments he has told us are the great ones—love God, love your neighbor. Here we stand, we have only to ask to love God and our neighbor and mean it and we shall be helped to do it. Yet we are afraid not to be like what we think our neighbor is like. Our neighbor is afraid not to be like what he *thinks* we are like. None of us are like that. If we ask God to open our eyes that we may see, we shall know that none of us are like that at all. We love honor more, hunger more for love, respect decency and courage more, our hearts are lonelier for peace and good than we are willing to let our neighbor know.

Why is this?

We must be doing something wrong.

..*Where* do we begin to practice Christianity, that great way of life that will cure all ills? Everywhere. At home, in church, at work, abroad—everywhere. On our knees, where life as we've been living it has knocked most of us. No man can break his own bondage with only human help. Pray the loving Father to come and help us, loose us, knock down the walls, set us free.

How do we begin? In joy, in anticipation, in prayer we begin to study the teachings of Jesus—as he gave them —that's the key. Christianity as Jesus taught it.

What shall we do to be saved from all ills?

Take care about using that old-fashioned terminology—I've been warned about that. Like two and two is four, if you mix yellow and blue you will get green, you have to put gasoline in your car or it won't run. No matter how I try to put it in today's language which changes hourly anyhow, there it is—we need to be saved.

Look unto me and be saved, he said. Do you? How often? Every day? When you add up the unpaid bills, the overdue installments, colds, rotten things you've done, the state of the world? Watch this. In a letter the Apostle Paul wrote to me—yes yes to me, to you, sent first to that juvenile delinquent Timothy whom he called his son but always intended for us—in that letter he spoke of *The Living God, who gives us richly all things to enjoy*. Oh boy oh boy oh boy as the kids say! Is that something. The *living* God. *Richly*—no skimping, no poverty-stricken hunger and thirst. All things to enjoy—not runny noses and cancers and heartbreaks all the time—that's not His will, the *living* God who saves you and gives you richly all things to enjoy if you turn to Him and obey the simple rules as you would if you wanted to fly to the moon.

What Paul was doing in that letter was trying to convince Timothy that there *was* a living God, who would give him things to enjoy richly, more richly than anything he could get going into town and getting drunk and wallowing around with the homos and the harlots, being brought home belligerent and disorderly and suffering what would appear to have been some real bad hangovers. *I am hard-pressed,* Timothy would say then, between his groans. But in time Paul cast out that devil and Timothy became a great Christian. Well—we can say that again and again can't we—we are hard-pressed. But thank God, Paul had come face to face with the Risen Christ, therefore Paul *knew* that man's hunger and loneliness, his drunkenness and whoring and pill-taking and cheating for a buck were then as now only the measure of his despair over a world without God. That if a man looks to Him, God will find him, he will find God.

Come and see that happen again.

Come and see.

There's joy for you, rich joy. Work, denial, a rough voyage maybe—but joy all the way.

Seek Him first—all the rest will take care of itself. Accept this moment that His will for you is joy, not sadness nor depression nor even melancholy, certainly not meaninglessness. Why should He create so beautiful and magnificent a world and make it meaningless? It is only meaningless when you turn from Him—when you leave the creator out of His own universe. His will for you is peace, not even a cold war. Health not pain. Common sense not neurotic *non*sense, riches not poverty, work not idleness, truth not lies. Since all that is His will for you Christ will give you the power to make it so. The climb will be tough sometimes, but not as tough as what you've got now going downhill. You have to know it's always easier and safer going uphill with the power pulling than going downhill with nothing but brakes. Try and see what will happen if you will begin tomorrow to read the thirteenth chapter of Paul's first letter to us, the one he sent via the Corinthians, read it until it is injected into your blood stream, reaches your heart, your mind, if you open your soul to it, it has power of its own, it will change your life and maybe the whole world.

There are simple things to remind you of God's ever-presence. Work out your own. A couple that—that meant a great deal to me when I was first *trying* this experiment—they still do. When I started my car I tried to remember to say that he steers the turn of my wheels to follow his steps to the resurrection and ascension just as he led the feet of seventy also on their mission. Whenever I touched money I tried to identify it with the coin Jesus found in the fish's mouth to pay their taxes—you'll feel a little silly at first—like if the phone rings and you say Christ give me the answer—but it won't hurt you to feel a little silly, will it?

Don't mouth these things of a Sunday.

Live by them.

This is the promise I am going to ask of you. Live by the things Jesus told us to do.

Will you do it? Will you try it?

Find one moment—I had trouble with this for a long time, I still do sometimes—I'm inclined to be a busy fellow, aren't we all?—to put him first, to find a moment, an hour, to be silent in solitude. If you never stop talking, how can you hear his answers? If you met him face-to-face—what would you have to say to him that's so important? Wouldn't you rather listen to him? Prayer—meditation—it's an *audience*, not an audition. He knows all your questions, your troubles, your problems, he can answer them without your going into all the gruesome details. But you'll have to learn to listen, or your tongue will keep you deaf.

Find the things he told his followers, his friends, his students, his disciples. On the Mount. At the table when he went to Peter's for dinner and had to heal Peter's mother-in-law of the flu or they wouldn't have had any dinner—evidently mothers-in-law were welcome to live in and cook for the family in those days—anyhow, *find* the things before and after the crucifixion which you personally need most. Do a little work, research this a little. As you'd go over your golf game to see what was wrong before your lesson with a pro, as you'd dig in a political campaign for facts and figures. It's all there.

When you hear the answers you will find your life beginning to interweave inside and outside in unity.

Man is blessed with the liberty to choose between two opposing factors, between action and inaction, between good and evil, between God and the devil. Surely our immediate situation requires an endeavor by every man to raise himself above ordinary standards to a higher degree of achievement in God. As Americans we should trust in God's help, to know his teachings and to live in his way. This is the time of decision. J. Edgar Hoover said that.

In this church, this is the time of decision. My call, my orders are to put it to you frankly.

If we are not now going forward to practice, we are anachronism. We are intellectual clowns and collectors of dead images. We are meaningless in a world struggling with the meaningless. We are *not* churches of Christ's ministry which move together in faith and works. And remember this—*the letter killeth.* It doesn't just get you all squirreled up and meaningless. If you have *only* the letter, if you are settling for the *letter,* no matter how brilliant, how educated, how sincere—it will *kill* you. Unless we are going to learn how to put his teachings into action it would be better to take the cold, selfish courage of those who say *There is no god but man.*

There is evil in this world. What is its origin? Why do the innocent have cancer? Why are children slaughtered by bombs? I don't know, no man has known nor does know. But we dare not let the commandments of Christ get bogged down in a sea of man's unanswerable questions. Put into practice the simple things we do understand. Little by little, if we ask, the light will reveal what we need to know. We shan't solve it by griping about it while we sit around pampering ourselves. Did Einstein know all the answers when he propounded the theory of relativity? No no no no—ceaseless hours of work, experimentation, discipline, delving at the Institute were necessary to prove it, to make it work. How many scales before the sonatas of Beethoven?

Practice practice practice.

You do not need to lead a double life. The work we do, the air we breathe, the food we eat, the beauty we look at, the clean things we laugh at, the games we play or see, in them all he is present. *Know this.* Acknowledge it. He will not withdraw from your pen or salesbook, your workshop, your telephone, the piledriver you operate or the prescription you write or—if you are a woman—from your daily tasks in his name and by his power and for his glory. Why should he? Is there some place where God is not? Put him there, and see the transformation of all things.

Unless you want to try to be Christians, it is wrong to keep on saying you are Christians. Moreover, it is dangerous. The lie smothers you in self-complacency and inertia. I challenge you—you my children to whom I have been sent, who have been selected for me—go and find out whether you are Christians in faith and want to go on to do the works. Be honest. Find out whether you desire to walk in his steps.

Let us not pretend any longer.

I ask you now.

I want your promise as members of my church that you will try with me—as a body—as each one of you individually—try with me this untried experiment of practicing Christianity as Jesus taught it.

If you do not wish to walk in their steps it would be better to walk out of my church now. Hypocrisy is fatal.

I could feel the breath they drew sear my lungs. The jumps of their hearts in anger, amazement, accusation, the shock of their incredulity and wonder leaped in mine.

His voice changed as the movements of a symphony can change.

A mistake is just an error in judgment, it is to continue in it once you have been told of it that crumbles your existence. One way or the other clear the ground on which you stand. Go on about the materialism of the world, openly selecting it. Or come and wait for the coming of the Holy Spirit.

Choose. Choose now.

You cannot fall out of God's hand. God will not let you, but this is the time of decision, the shortest way, the most glorious moment—this moment—every moment.

Ask not what you can do for your church.

Ask what your church can do for you.

Come unto me, Christ said, and I will give you love and strength to do what is given you to do. Come to my church and *demand* that it fulfill the Christian promises, do the works. This we must do. We must ask these things of our church, of its pastor and members, the church which is the mystical body of Christ—as are all Christian churches or else what in *hell* are they?

If you make this promise, we will here in the Church of the Redeemer and the redeemed *see* the greater works.

We will *do* the greater works—greater works ye shall do!

I promise you.

I *promise you,* in God's name, in Christ's name, I promise you.

Let us begin.

No sound at all came as the tall young man stood there, bending down to them, reaching out his arms to them, offering them his hands as though they were full of—as though they were a cup filled with the water of life. Of *blessings,* to feed them.

He seemed to shine upon them.

Let us pray, he said.

I do not know how long the silence lasted before he raised his hands and said, "God will go with you. He will never leave you nor forsake you and you must not forsake Him. He will bless you—He *loves* you."

Dizzily the camera began to swing. No dissolves, fade-ins, fade-outs, set-ups. Shifting, milling, the crowd was never still. Some moved slowly in a sedate line, as they were accustomed to leave church on a Sunday morning. Some stopped in groups, large and small, under windows, at the end of pews, in the aisles. Their faces were *more*—more everything. In depths. More solemn, angry, uncertain, superior, insulted, scared, yearning, dark or light, questioning, defiant, what-the-hell-is-this—they were shaken as I had not seen people shaken before. Some were stolid about it, some high, some jittery. Low talk, whispers, suddenly raised voices, speech trying to be ordinary as it usually was in this emptying of the church each Sunday. Some of them—a few—many?—I'm not sure any more—were trying to touch the hem of Hank's business suit.

Flashing brief close-ups.

Bertha tight-lipped as Madame Defarge. Steve Retzlaff was smiling, when I covered fights we said when a fighter smiles it means he is really hurt.

With impact of actual shock, I became aware that the fear shaking me was because two people were missing.

Mellie wasn't there.

I hadn't seen her go, but she was there no longer.

The boy who played the guitar. The end of the bench where Beany had been was vacant now.

This terrified me. Of all those under this roof who had heard the words spoken to the angel of the church of Beach City, California, those two ought to be there still. Must be. Or catastrophe like the swollen dragon would breathe fire against that angel.

I could see Deedee, her small face pinched like a child's with earache, her feet stumbling, her hands reaching to touch Hank's sleeve as she followed him down the few steps into the aisle.

I couldn't believe my eyes.

A woman had knelt for this blessing, her face was wet with tears and her sobbing could be heard by all. The woman was Sybil Rowe. Widow of the man for whom Hank's best hadn't been good enough. She had come in with Mellie.

I must find Mellie.

One thing Mellie did not fully understand.

Maybe Steve Retzlaff didn't consider it either.

Hank had seen the light face to face.

10

I found myself motionless in a side aisle, while people shoved and moved sidewise by me. I couldn't take my eyes off Hank Gavin's face. Impossible that he was actually *thinner*. Yet I knew that automobile drivers lost as much as ten pounds during a race. This man's cheekbones seemed more prominent, his temples were hollow, and his eyes, luminous and yellow with light, shone deep in their sockets.

The crowd was scattering, I found Archie Paddock beside me, without thinking I said aloud, "But he looks—tortured. As though he'd been through an ordeal—an extremity—"

"I shouldn't be surprised," Archie Paddock said, and the way he said it made me turn to look at him. He was regarding Hank Gavin, as Hank made his way to the side door, with compassion.

"I thought it was the most moving—whatever it was—I ever heard," I said.

"Yes," Archie said.

"Then *why*—" I said.

"Use your head," Archie said. "You're not that stupid."

"Please, Archie," I said, "I'm *in* this myself—somehow—"

"Probably no man, even man and also God-in-man, is ever satisfied—it's a big job. And if—if the Holy Ghost was with him, probably it's tough to come *back*—could be? More than that, now he's thrown down the gauntlet as it were. The issue is joined. He has committed himself to that to which men no longer commit themselves—look around you."

Later I came to know what some of these people were thinking. Gert Cutler, saying to herself He means my mother-in-law, I would have to quit hating her guts, the mealymouthed *picky* look-down-her-long-nose old bitch. All of a sudden I'm supposed to *love* her—oh Krisst! And then, she told me, to her astonishment the word she'd used though she was trying to get *over* using it she really was, began to say itself. Differently. I wonder. Gert said, if that's why we keep on using it and using it as a cuss word people who don't hardly know about Jesus say gee-*zuss!* because way down underneath we would like to pray to him—anyhow it said itself differently to me—instead of Krisst like I'd been trying to say, I said—Oh, *Christ* help me—help me to love her—she does love the kids.

With an intensity he had thought he'd never feel again about anything, McAddams was getting ready to make a promise, of course *if* this young crusader could get a building permit if he could I'll give him—I'll sell him that lot to build his church on cheap—

Like a tackle who'd been supposed to blitz the opposing quarterback but saw him get the ball away, Steve Retzlaff was a mask over frustration. A cool careful calculating mask. He didn't seem to notice his daughter, who had come up beside him and was so white I thought she might faint. After all, she was *his* daughter. She had to be all right. His eyes were moving around, estimating the situation, and somehow I knew he knew Mellie wasn't there, but he didn't notice the absence of Beany Teran, why would he? He had never heard of Beany Teran in all his life and no inner gong warned him that he was going to—before long.

There were in that moving scattering crowd good Christians, men and women who knew, many of them, what Jesus Christ had taught, knew already what would be required of them if they promised to follow in his steps, some of them thought they already were but in that *light* that the young minister had thrown upon them they knew better now. There were people who came to church who hadn't *opened* the book of Jesus' teachings in weeks—years—never—they didn't have time, for one thing. There were, somewhat to my surprise, a good many young people besides Deedee Retzlaff and Beany Teran—most of them looked interested and skeptical and yet somehow pleased. The how-to generation, curious, alert, being challenged with something to *do*. A few of the middle-aged still looked like underdone puddings, if they'd heard at all they had already forgotten, they were used to rhetoric on television, it went in one ear and out the other without pausing to make any impression on the brain.

Difficult to tell.

Anything could come of this. Or nothing. Or could it?

"He's for it now," Archie Paddock was saying, "don't you see what he's done? He's not only put himself out on the limb which Christianity has been carefully avoiding, with a few rare exceptions, for a good many centuries. By brilliant maneuvers, its leaders have managed to get by without practicing what they preach or teaching what the Teacher taught. At last they've got people to forget all that greater-works-than-these-shall-ye-do business. Now he's asked the ordinary men to pick up the cross again and go forth with signs following.

"Take a good look at Marvin Gregory over there. See that dear dear my-poor-friend-eats-with-his-knife expression of mercy and distaste. As a member of the board our charming friend will be on the phone to the bishop before nightfall. Now the bishop, who is a friend of mine, is a dynamic, honest, hard-working executive, who'd have done well as head of Sears or president of a bank, in this state he is second to none in his efforts to help the governor and the legislature pass bills for the improvement of education and housing. I like the guy. You don't think such an able organizer as Bishop Parelli is going to let himself or any of his officials climb out there, do you? *In his steps!* Heal the sick, take the play away from the psychiatrists by casting out the devils, forget all the alibis, the day of Pentecost has come again, hey hey! As I said before, use your head, woman."

"But you liked what Hank said, I saw you," I told him.

"The bishop isn't going to," Archie said sternly. "I don't have to do anything about it, he does. And he's trying his level artless honorable best to keep Christianity within the intellectual grasp and what he regards as the good, common American horse sense."

"We're not like that at all," I said. "Americans will believe anything, they love to believe the improbable, the impossible—that's why we have done all the things—"

"Right," Archie said. We had come out into the front courtyard and he spoke quietly, "but I say to you again, we are all from Missouri and you will have to show us—sooner or later!"

"But that's exactly what Hank wants to do," I said in great excitement. "That's what he means—"

"The bishop knows how out of practice they are," Archie said, just the same he gave me a look I hadn't seen from him since thirty years before, across a city desk, now here we were once more. Archie and I, working as a team.

"He's committed himself to miracles," Archie said triumphantly. He was on Hank's side. Hank was his kind of guy, like Glenn and McDivitt and White, and Washington crossing the Delaware and all the Marines who ever landed in Korea or anywhere else. Also, knowing the bishop, he knew Hank was an underdog, and as a rule underdogs make the best stories.

"The works Jesus told us to do aren't miracles—" I began. I was thinking, disconnectedly, of blind Bartemeius, the son of the widow at Nain, the manic-depressive chained in the tombs, poverty-stricken multitudes, people who couldn't pay their taxes, bitter, godless, unhappy rebels—and stilling the storms at sea—accidents—wars—would greater works than these be miracles? Hank said no, this was what being a Christian meant, these were the added things we'd been promised if we followed the redeemer, the Risen Christ.

"The bishop," Archie was saying, "considers miracles just one more thing for the public not to believe in, in the last half of the twentieth century."

"What can the bishop do?" I said.

"Oh—transfer him to walk a beat in the fog belt," Archie said.

"If Beach City isn't the fog belt—" I said.

"No no," Archie said, "Chicago—any big city—where he'd get lost, that'd do it. Well, keep in touch." And he was gone.

I started to walk over a couple of blocks to where I'd parked my car. I had invited people for lunch—late lunch—at my house, and on the following day I had to go to San Francisco for a meeting and I had planned to come back by way of Carmel to visit my dearest friends, who lived there. We'd set this date far ahead so some others might join us for a sort of reunion.

Now I didn't want to go away.

Once during the war a submarine commander told me of selecting a chief, and of how he'd explained to the man that millions were invested in the sub itself, the need for it just then was grave, also the lives of a trained crew—all these, he said, would be in the man's hands, and the man gave him a grin and said, "And then of course there's me myself too, sir, isn't there?"

Now there was me myself, too, in this true story of *one man*. I could judge somewhat of others, what they might be thinking, by myself. Am I willing even to *will* to be made whole? What do *I* have to do? Give up? Think?

Moreover, I had loved my goddaughter more and more as I had watched her try to live up to the strange bounce her marriage had taken. Where was she? What was she doing? Why had she left the church?

I could no more have passed the parsonage than the elephant's child with his 'satiable curiosity could have resisted going to the great gray-green-greasy Limpopo River to see what the crocodile had for dinner.

On the porch I met the old rector. In terror, in *hope*. Why, the poor man hadn't even had hope, much less faith. Turning away from the door, he said, "I don't think I'd better go in. Are you—aware of the courage—of course he doesn't know yet, who should know if I don't—a brave man—will you—

there probably won't be anything I can do but tell him if there is—*anything*—some of us are called you know and don't choose."

As soon as I went in I knew why he hadn't.

Hank and Mellie must be in the deep dark cave way back at the end of the bisecting hall which was the kitchen. Through the half-open door, their voices came like radio when the instrument isn't working very well.

Dishonorable, I eavesdropped as best I could, assuring myself I must stay and see that no one else came in to overhear this.

"—don't you see what you've done?" Mellie's lovely voice wasn't lovely now, it was shrill, meant to pierce, hot and cold with anger, fear, distaste, it had a note I'd heard before and couldn't identify. "Don't you see what you've done?" she cried again.

Hank said sternly, "—pull yourself together—"

I lost the rest and then Mellie shouted at him, "Don't you tell me what to do, you fool. I can't make out whether you're a fool—or a ham. Do you know yourself?"

She moved into my line of vision, standing by the old kitchen table where the telephone still stood. Her face was pinched out of shape, her eyes were bright dark slits. I am sure there isn't anyone she resembled less than Paul's grandfather, that fierce old man who had cursed Paul for worshipping a false messiah. That was it! Mellie was cursing her husband. "The blood ran cold and the skin crawled," Henrietta Buckmaster tells us in her great definitive novel about St. Paul, "as the old man summoned up the ancient curses one by one and cast them as stones in the rite of stoning at his grandson."

Cursed be!

I was shaking now, violently. This was more than I had expected, I did not see yet why Mellie should *curse* her husband, angry and frightened and sickened as she had been.

With steady hands, she took up her big engagement pad, her notebooks, the telephone rang and she ignored it, she began to read off the pages and then to tear them into small pieces and fling them at Hank—like stones, she was using them as stones.

"Old lady Delancy," she read, and tore the sheet as she said, "she has an inoperable cancer, I take her broth. Go heal her, you phony bastard. Why don't you? Here's Deedee Retzlaff—cast out her devils, my fine-feathered friend—comfort her poor sick burning young body and give her peace—and oh yes here's our Ladies' Guild, nasty, sharp-tongued, boring old women but they do the best they can—can you purify them of their hates and resentments—and here's Beany Teran's mother, who's a whore and a starving, overworked, overdriven female—what's your promise to her? Can you help her?"

"—can *try*—with God's help—" Hank said.

He wasn't giving an inch, but the suffering in his voice as the stones hit was terrible to me.

God's help!" Mellie said. "Do you think I am going to be part of this rascally fraud? Do you think I'M going on in this unscrupulous knavery of holding out *hope*—again and again and again—and seeing them break their hearts once more? I could maybe put up with you making a fool of yourself, but I won't condone this *swindle*—this religious trickery that's been exposed over and over—and sell these poor dopes a bill of goods—"

Hank broke in then. He said, "You see what happens to them without God—a world without God? Lack of faith, lack of hope—I have to try to give it back to them, don't you see that? You saw what he did for Natalie Margolis! I *know*. I have to try to show them the joy of life with God in their hearts—he has said I will deliver you—are you *willing* to be made whole—"

"You needn't preach me another sermon, pal," Mellie said, "I heard all your promises this morning—I've had it."

"Mellie—" he said, "Mellie, you know me. You know better than to believe I would—" pleading now, as he had not pleaded in his church.

Steps came on the porch, the doorbell rang loudly, I said, "I'll answer it—it's only me, Mellie—" there was a back stairs from the kitchen in that old house and I heard Mellie running up them and Hank came out to where I was in the hall. His face was haggard with pain and I said quickly, "Hank—it was great—it was just great—Archie thought so too—" and he said, "I don't *know*. I don't reach her—I thought I'd reach her—but I didn't—"

As he swung open the big front door, in came Olin McAddams. Dazed was still the word for the chairman of the board of the church in Beach City. Lord I believe, help thou mine unbelief, he didn't notice me, he said, "Well, young man—" and could go no farther.

The smile Hank gave him was singularly sweet and seemed to cover the pain as light covers darkness. He said, "Come on in," but Olin McAddams said, "No no—must get home—the nurse is giving Bertha a massage, she came to hear you, it always wears her out, she's not strong, you know

—I just wanted to tell you, talking of promises, young fellow, you get a *permit* to build a *church* on it, and I'll sell you that lot at a fair price—you have my promise for that."

If ever I saw a man uplifted, it was that heavy-set square-jawed hen-pecked man McAddams. *I if I be lifted up will draw all men unto me.* This experience had happened to McAddams and he was still a little dazed.

Again the doorbell. This time, I went. A bent old man said he was a Western Union messenger boy and I saw the heavy ring of dark ink around the number on the familiar yellow envelope. Francis—Francis Cheyne—Mellie's father, who had told us the story of the Air Chief Marshal and the angels who helped fly the planes for the Few in the Battle of Britain. I took it upstairs. Mellie was walking back and forth and she looked at me as though she'd never seen me before. I said, "This is bad news, do you want me to open it?"

"I can consume my own bad news," she said, and took the telegram.

"Mellie—my child—" I said and she cried out, "Don't! Don't you see I'm being chewed into little pieces?" Reading the wire, she went even whiter and ran downstairs, do sleep-walkers run? If so, that's the way they look. She held out the yellow paper and said, "My father is dying. He may be dead already. Go ahead, little tin Jesus, raise him—Francis Cheyne Lazarus, come forth—"

Hank took a deep breath. He said, "I don't think Francis would like that, do you? I'm sure he'd have to—to give his consent to death, they aren't meeting for the first time, you know. I don't think the Lazarus adventure is for everybody. And it doesn't always mean physical death—at least I don't think it does. Lots of us are *dead* in a good many other ways. They can be delivered out of despair and uselessness and failure and self-condemnation and boredom and fear—"

"Well," Mellie said, and her hands tore the paper into squares, into smaller squares, *tearing,* "that's one more explanation signifying nothing."

I couldn't bear it. Once years before I had seen young Melanie Cheyne in riding breeches and polished boots judging beagles at a dog show, she was looking at us like that now and faulting us all the way. This curse Rebecca West, in *The New Meaning of Treason,* calls the sin which travesties legitimate hate, because it is felt for those we love and it has to be gall and wormwood. I knew Mellie loved this man but hate had her in its teeth.

I said, "Oh—stop it—stop it—" and Mellie without looking at me said, "Will you call Mama and tell her I'll catch the first plane?"

"I am not signifying *nothing*," Hank Gavin said. "Our best isn't good enough, you know that."

"You're a *fool*. It's better than lies about a god who isn't there," Mellie said. "A lot of the time my best takes care of the sick and feeds the poor."

"—as far as it goes," Hank said. "But there's always the time, the big time of the heart—when it isn't good enough—"

As though on cue, Sybil Rowe appeared in the doorway from the sunporch. This place, I thought, has as much privacy as the United Nations. I realized Sybil had been out there all the time, and I saw that she was a different woman. Her eyes on Mellie were full of love and there was a print of joy on her lips, but what she said was, "You're the fool, you know that, don't you, darling? I'll drive you to the airport."

I waited for Hank to say something more as they went out of the room but he didn't. After a moment he gave me an exhausted, lopsided grin and said, "Hoist by my own petard. My best won't be good enough with Mellie. He'll have to do it. By the way, Godmama, I've wondered, whatthehell was a petard?"

"Some kind of an explosive engine to blow up gates and walls," I said.

"It would be," Hank said, and closed his eyes.

That night Sybil Rowe arrived at my house. "I can't live there alone with Hank in the parsonage," she said, "even if I was really his sister-in-law. That's all Retzlaff's gang would need. Can I stay with you a couple of days till I find a place?"

"Yes," I said. "Are you going to stay in Beach City?"

"Until after the bloody Council meeting I am," she said. "And I *mean* bloody."

"Is Mellie coming back?" I said.

"I—she said she couldn't plan anything until they knew about her father," Sybil said. "But—all right—I don't think she means to. Come back."

When she got to Chicago, Mellie found Francis holding his own. Naturally, even though he ordered her to return to her husband, she didn't think she could leave her mother. Vadne didn't think so either, nor did a lot of other people in Chicago who had always been crazy about Melanie Cheyne Gavin and now were eaten up with curiosity about her and Hank Gavin and Beach City.

Anyway, Mellie didn't come back, even in the period when they said her father was out of danger.

In the end it was Sybil Rowe who told her what had happened to Hank.

"Have it your own way," Colin's widow said, "but if I'd had a chance to do it over again I'd come on home."

Of course this was after the Council meeting.

11

During the time between Mellie's departure and the date of this Council meeting at which Dr. Gavin's appeal for a permit allowing him to build a church downtown on the corner of Pacific Coast Highway and Avenue 22 would be voted on, this Zone Variance was to become a *cause célèbre.*

Beach City was extraordinarily egocentric as most small cities are, and soon its total population saw this coming attraction as a sort of tournament, a battle in the arena as modern as steel sculpture done with a pneumatic drill or an all-glass hotel where you have to keep the venetian blinds shut all the time.

Just why the citizenry of Beach City had gotten into the act was hard to tell, it is often impossible to figure out why one campaign, cause, or personality catches full attention and another equally important does not. Everybody in a place like Beach City has to be interested in *downtown.* They go there. Also, these were local big shots and local news still takes precedence over national and international in most areas. Archie Paddock saw to it that everybody was aware of young Hank Gavin, who had played football for Yale and fought with the Marines in Korea. It is often difficult to dramatize the good, but Archie did a real fine job on Hank Gavin. Also Hank continued his pilgrimages among the bars and bowling alleys and barber shops. By the Monday thereafter, that preradio war drum *word-of-mouth* had carried news of Hank Gavin's sermon and the promises about *in his steps* which he had asked and given, and there was a good deal of back fence debate going on. Thus he was shortly invited to speak at service club luncheons and various meetings where he won applause and acclaim, though whether this amounted to agreement nobody could tell. It turned out, too, that he was a natural on local TV and radio shows and panels which frequently supersede the network shows in the hearts and minds of the townfolk. But of course Steve Retzlaff was their boy, he'd put Beach City on the map, some day he would be governor and anyone could add up what that would mean to all of them in *dollars* and *cents,* coming from ship-building contracts, more freeways, some marinas, and patronage. And there was something all-sublime in the smiling good will, pleasant apologies, and this-hurts-me-more-than-it-does-you with which Steve Retzlaff told the young minister and others that he had to think a downtown church all wrong, the allure with which he made a satisfactory case for the advantages of a site way out near the foothills.

Not much doubt that Archie Paddock and the *Gazette* were for Gavin and this new, unusual, and—far-out—idea of a downtown church.

Which, I may tell you, had involved Archie in a shooting war with his advertisers, but Archie of course never allowed his advertisers to dictate to him—that way lies extinction for any paper—so he went on valiantly.

However, so did his advertisers. A good many of them kept saying they did not *want* a church downtown. Surely they didn't have to tell him that there were things in their windows which passing a church might damper the customer's desire to buy. Time might even be wasted going into the church. Women came downtown to *shop* and should be allowed to get on with it, not stop to pray. Also there were bars, grills, honky-tonks, and dance halls, movie theaters showing pictures whose scripts had been written originally on the walls of men's lavatories—a church hanging around the corner wasn't going to do them any good, was it?

In answer to this last Archie Paddock, as much to his surprise as theirs, henceforth refused to allow dirty ashcan movie theaters to buy an inch of space in his paper.

"Anybody'd think I'd taken the pledge," he said to me, "but you know I can't let those punks push me around."

"Did you take the pledge?" I said.

"It's not a bad idea," Archie said.

The heat was on this one in Beach City.

Hardly anybody was neutral.

As came to pass in Iconium the multitude of the city was divided. Part held against and part with the apostles.

Inside the church it was the same.

Meantime, Marvin Gregory and I don't know who else had most certainly called the bishop.

Steve Retzlaff kept on insisting good-naturedly that things were well in hand and would come out to their satisfaction given a little time.

The board as well as the congregation were choosing up sides.

Debates sprang up all over Beach City, sometimes in the

most unlikely places and were often, Archie said, heated and prolonged.

Hot partisans lined up, preliminary skirmishes took place. Also there were *rumors* after Hank Gavin's sermon. "Don't let anybody tell you people aren't interested in God," Archie said, and printed an editorial to prove that this nation under God always had been. "What they're not on the whole interested in any more is old ladies' rows about Him among the *clergy*. They'd better get with it." The rumors stated and denied, supported and rejected tales about things that took place among the converted. Odd things. A boy in the Long Beach Naval Hospital whose X-rays had altered after his mother attended a prayer cell with Dr. Gavin. And then there was Art Cutler. Everybody knew Art Cutler, he'd gone to high school and City College, he was a real nice guy, last man you'd expect to come up with any poltergeists or black magic. Of course the whole town had known about his mother and his wife. Beach City isn't all that big but what with everybody liking Art—he was captain of a bowling team, too—and his mother'd taught school there and *Gert*—Gert was a loudmouth and a lot of fun at a bowling tournament. Only somebody over ninety or under two didn't know that Gert had said some day she was going to kill her mother-in-law and you read things in the papers sometimes. Now Art looking kind of stunned and a little scared said—*things* were different. *I don't mean just they're trying to behave like Christians,* he said to some of the boys on his bowling team one night over a can of beer, *something's happened to them. I mean now I don't mind telling you they—they hated each other's guts and it got—well, you know, two women like that—and now, I can hardly believe it myself sometimes.* And one of the boys said, *Well, if those two are getting along it's gotta be a miracle, what I mean.* But to this Art Cutler wasn't inclined to agree. He said probably underneath they'd always respected each other—of course it had all seemed very *easy* all of a sudden. *Like,* he said, *a light being turned on in the house. Easy as that.*

Then there had been *something* at a meeting of Jack Nestor's Longshoremen's Union.

Nobody knew exactly what, not even the wives, it was all hush-hush—but it had settled *something.*

Jack Nestor, everybody said, was one of the ones who'd accepted the promise, and made it.

Of all people. Let's not kid ourselves.

So as the meeting drew near, intensity of interest mounted.

If young Gavin could get a Zone Variance permit out of that City Council with good old Mike Aguirre as its president, Mike Aguirre who when he opened his mouth played a Steve Retzlaff record as they'd known for years, then you'd have to give him full marks for *something-or-other*.

If he couldn't, *and he couldn't,* that meant this young fellow didn't know what he was talking about, he'd overplayed his hand, it would teach him something, and show that Steve Retzlaff, a cagey, smooth operator if ever there was one, was still in the catbird's seat. From then on, he'd use Gavin as a lieutenant. Perhaps putting it that way was oversimplification, but it's close enough.

Religion, like everything else in this world today, they felt, ought to work. Just how, they weren't prepared to say. But it ought to *work*. Most IBM computers and jet planes and electric can openers worked.

As Archie Paddock had foreseen, right in here the bishop showed up. Well-briefed from all points of view.

"He came to remove our young friend from the Church of the Redeemer and send him back to the minors," Archie said.

"If Beach City isn't the minors—" I said.

"It isn't," Archie said, "it's up-and-coming to beat all hell."

"Can he?" I said.

"Remove him?" Archie said. "Oh sure, he's the boss."

Suddenly this seemed to me the worst thing of all. The *end*. Like cutting off John the Baptist's head. "Is he going to?" I said.

This was on the telephone late one night after Archie got home. Both of us had been trained to give and take important news by phone, that was part of our business. I waited for Archie to come up with a lead, but this time Archie was going to be brief and chronological, to begin at the beginning which he knew as well as I did is no place for most stories to begin.

"This afternoon," he said, "I looked up and there he was coming in my office looking exactly like a bishop. Usually he calls me and makes a date for lunch or something but this time he'd had an emergency call so he just came up, he has a high regard for the Beach City *Gazette,* I'm glad to say. Now the bishop is no intellectual sword-swallower. Other end of the stick entirely. His platform is that the church is big business and it takes able administrators to run it and he's one.

"First thing he said was, 'What's going on here, Archie?' and then I got two things. He was real worried, which I'd never seen him before, and he was of two minds, he hadn't decided what to do. I figured he wanted my testimony, we've worked together before and he knows I'm a hard-headed cold-blooded newspaper publisher and don't stampede easy, also that I'm a darn good judge of evidence. A thing most people know nothing about."

By that time, listening to him, I was in a cold sweat. "Archie," I said, "if you don't tell me—" but he plowed right over me.

"I had a hunch he'd heard from our Mr. McAddams along about dawn, Mac who hasn't a gut to his name was getting cold feet, he'd noticed all of a sudden that religion was poking its nose into *business* and that *if* Hank Gavin came out of that meeting with a building permit his board chairman could well be stuck with a promise of his own. Bertha would as soon slit his throat. And I thought probably Gregory had called Steve Retzlaff, also he'd heard about the minister's wife taking off—"

"She'll be *back,*" I said.

"You sure about that?" Archie said, "I hear different. I hear she's having a fine time back in the old hometown and she's gone for good.

"So the bishop sat down and began to tell me—he needed to talk to somebody, they all do from the death house up—and he said he walked into his young pastor's office, expecting to find an emotionally disturbed feller. He'd heard from some of the women, too, your friend Marguerita Vosburgh for one. He said the women were mostly on his side—young Gavin's—and I thought I'd quote a bit of Scripture at him so I reminded him woman has been last at the cross and first at the tomb and they'd shaved the heads of the collaborationist women in France because they knew a nation was safe only as long as her women were good, and not a minute longer—look at Cleopatra and Rome and Greece. The bishop stared at me and then decided not to debate that side issue.

"Now here's a funny thing." Archie's telephone voice was more expressive than face-to-face, and I sat up straighter for what was coming. "The bishop said when he went into that office there in the church and saw this young feller sitting behind this great huge old desk with his straw-colored hair cut almost butch and his face tanned as a lifeguard, he couldn't for the life of him remember how the feller *got* there. It came to him clear that this was Henry Gavin, who'd been allowed to graduate from a kind of second-rate divinity school off the track somewhere because he had a Phi Beta Kappa or something from Yale and had been a success in business, and then he'd been sent out to Beach City as an associate to serve a few years of interneship so he'd know *this* business of running a church. It came over the bishop, and if you'd heard him you would have known he was *really* astonished, that nobody would make a young man like that pastor of a church in a growing rough-tough *port* like Beach City especially when there was all this about a new building going on. They might let him sub pro tem for a bit while they called up a seasoned quarterback, but to turn over the team to him in midseason—the bishop was sure he hadn't and yet he knew he had and he said with his friendly smile—this is a sincere man, you know, and while I don't set as much store by sincerity as the end-all virtue having seen a good many people sincere about the wrong things, it has to be there, doesn't it? Sincerity, I mean. So the bishop said, 'I must be growing absent-minded.' But that didn't satisfy me, nor him either.

"When he sat down opposite Hank, the bishop didn't waste any time. Right out, he said he thought that before a young minister made such an unorthodox sermon as he was given to understand had been delivered in the Church of the Redeemer and *certainly* before he went against the older, more experienced, and influential men on his own board about a radical change in the location of an expensive new church, it would have been proper to consult his superiors.

"One word, the bishop told me, impressed itself on Hank Gavin. 'Unorthodox,' he said, 'you call it unorthodox? With respect, sir, I don't think so. I had a letter from my chaplain and he said it was the first truly Christian sermon since Harry Emerson Fosdick.' Now it seemed the bishop knew about this chaplain, he was a firebrand and stirrer-upper, so he decided to ignore that. He said he thought it better to abide by the rules, to play within the rules, these had been set up for the benefit of the majority, but Gavin busted in then and said, 'Whose rules?' and that teed the bishop off and he said he didn't intend to argue these matters. But he realized right then that something drastic would have to be done because it was plain that young Gavin, who was far from being 'emotionally disturbed' like some of these pentecostal boys, wasn't about to abjure, backtrack, repudiate, or eat humble pie or crow. Not a tractable fellow, the bishop said. However, he tried another tack. After all, these fiery young idealists were cropping up here and there, much more so than usual now he came to look at it—they didn't want to lose the good men, the church needed able young men desperately, young men of the caliber of Hank Gavin for the matter of that—so they had to be *handled*. Looking back, the bishop had wondered—but the look back was too far for him to see himself very distinctly—so he had merely gone on to point out in a fine, firm, friendly fashion that times being what they were the church couldn't afford mumbo-jumbo or black magic or sleight-of-hand. He said the church must keep its feet on the ground and then young Gavin gave him a big grin, and the bishop admitted it was a *moving*, an appealing, expression and Hank said, 'Well, sir, if there's a rule for keeping our feet on the ground Jesus should not have walked on the water, should he?' "

Archie's chuckles came over the wire and I began to feel better. But there was always mischief in Paddock, even at his age, and it might *not* mean that Hank was safe.

"I want to tell you," Archie went on when the chuckles had subsided, "the bishop was shocked. Anybody making a pun, a joke about *Jesus*—that was against the rules for sure. So he told Hank with grave and heavy authority that one thing the church didn't want was any so-called miracles. He told Hank—he called him a young zealot about then—that people could look right straight at miracles and simply not believe them. And suspect the church of fraud. Then Hank said how would the bishop know about that? Then, bigod, he quoted *Burke*, who said all Protestantism, even the most cold and passive, is a sort of *dissent*, so oughtn't we to encourage some heartwarming affirmative *works?* He was, Hank here told the bishop, talking about the practice point of Christianity. It had come, like the Wright brothers at Kitty Hawk. Either it would fly or it wouldn't. If it didn't, they would be left with egg on their faces but they had to *try*, or just *be* a dissent. He said that all he meant in his sermon was that *if* we tried to *live* according to the teachings of Jesus and got them fixed within our souls, hearts, minds, the result would show in our lives. Those would be the *works* Jesus had laid on all of us as Christians.

"The bishop stopped about then, and asked me if I'd heard the sermon and I said I had. He was going to ask me what I thought of it and decided against it, because he knew as well as I did that if you call a hostile witness you are bound by his testimony."

"Archie," I said, "did you—"

"Never mind about that now," Archie said. "So Hank told him that they were having classes to study the way Jesus had outlined for them—to prepare themselves to be at one with God, and the young man said it might take a little time but if people did see that following in his steps as near as might be brought about joy and hope and resolution and magnanimity and good will and brotherhood—they'd believe it all right.

"The bishop said that all this kind of talk, against all

common sense, based on nothing but emotion, usually brought about a good deal of disrespect for the church and—here was where for the first time I began to see that the bishop who had been sure he was going to transfer this young man to a town nineteen miles south of the North Pole was on the horns of a dilemma. For Hank got up and began to walk up and down and he said in a voice that broke all to pieces, 'They showed a good deal of disrespect for Jesus when they crucified him, I suppose we have to take our chances.'

"As I've told you, the bishop is a good man—and he said there was quite a silence, it lasted somehow until the younger man went back and sat down in his chair and he said he supposed the bishop knew Tolstoi's story about the three hermits. The bishop didn't—and I must say neither did I. Do you?"

I said I didn't, so Archie Paddock told it to me the way, it seemed, Hank Gavin told it to the bishop that day while they sat on opposite sides of that big desk in the book-lined shadowy office-library in the Church of the Redeemer.

"Once upon a time," Hank said, smiling warmly at his superior, "a high and mighty dignitary of the church was sailing about from sea to sea to visit some of his churches and followers and on a fine sunny day his ship put in at a very small harbor of a very small atoll where, the crew informed him, they occasionally stopped to leave food for three hermits who were the only inhabitants. Sure enough there they were standing on the sand to greet His Reverence, their long white beards and their white tunics blowing in the breeze, looking exactly as hermits should look, and their delight in seeing him was gratifying. For, they explained, they had come out to this solitary archipelago long long ago, in order to enter into pure contemplation, and to say the prayers for those in the world who through lack of faith or time or wit might have failed in this communion with Our Lord, but during these many years they had forgotten a good deal of the doctrine taught by the church and were most anxious to refresh themselves at the fount of His Reverence's wisdom. So the good doctor spoke with them for several hours, reviving their memories of the letter and liturgy, the creeds and tenets necessary to salvation, and instructed them so that they could repeat the Credo once more. Feeling that he had done a fine day's work, the Reverend returned to his ship and sailed away. At dawn—for he was ever an early riser—His Reverence was sitting in his deck chair in the bow of the vessel repeating his office when in the clear light and against the bright horizon he saw a strange—an unbelievable—sight. After trying for some time to identify a boat or a canoe or a kayak or even a raft, the Reverend sent for the captain and they stared through the binoculars and soon had to admit the impossible, for the hermits were running lightly upon the surface of the sea. So there seemed nothing else for the captain and the Reverend to do but lean over the rail as the hermits, beards blowing gaily in the breeze, hove to below it. Great joy was shining upon their morning faces, and the one in the middle cried out, 'Dear and reverend friend, we crave your forgiveness for following you and troubling you with our difficulty. But none of us can remember what comes after *the third day he rose again from the dead,* and since we must know this in order to be saved—' "

"The bishop," Archie said, "was frank about it. He said he felt that in all his life he had never been offered so poignant and delicate and respectful an insult. He hadn't even been aware that young Gavin, pastor of the Church of the Redeemer, was reading this from a letter—which the bishop then assumed was the one from his chaplain. But at that exact moment the bishop made up his mind to start proceedings on an emergency basis to transfer Dr. Gavin to a proper *Seminary* where he could complete his knowledge of how to be saved within the *rules* laid down by the church *or* better still perhaps to return him to a minor position in or near Chicago where, like every other man, he would be without honor in his own country and in the traffic jams of a large city soon lost sight of and belittled into the necessary insignificance of common sense.

"Then—it seemed to him—the young man had read his thoughts.

"Gavin looked up and their eyes met."

I knew.

I could see the light blazing there. Shining forth with the only thing we have left to help us—*love.*

After he had mentioned this—this loving look which in itself seemed to say *Oh no—I wouldn't do that if I were you*—the bishop was silent, Archie said. The silence was longer than usual between people. The bishop broke it finally by saying that Hank Gavin hadn't been satisfied with this much-discussed sermon himself.

"He'd told the bishop," Archie repeated, "that he'd meant to be shorter and funnier. But he was afraid of being *hearty,* the on-my-way-to-church-this-morning type of thing. But he told the bishop not to worry because in the end he'd been able to some degree anyhow to get himself out of the way. To let the Word speak *through* him, which he figured from his letters was St. Paul's way. Well, when the bishop got to this point, he had to ask me right out what I thought of the sermon."

"What did you tell him," I said, shifting the receiver to my other ear.

"I let him have it," Archie said with satisfaction. "I told him it was the plain, unvarnished, unadulterated, uncompromising-with-the-congregation truth. I said, And what's more, I said, you boys will either begin to practice what you preach, at all levels of society—the rich need it as much as the poor, you know—they are the ones who can do a lot of things that need changing—or you will be destroyed like all other anachronisms have to be in time. You cannot go on dissecting with the knife of intellect because the only thing you can dissect successfully is a corpse."

"That's good old newspaperese," I said. "What about transferring Hank to nine miles north of Spokane?"

"I told him," Archie went on, "about a dispatch that came over my desk and it said a clergyman had told the student body of a girl's college that he wanted them to understand that sex was fun, lots of fun, anywhere any time, there shouldn't *be* rules about it. I said as far as I'd been in life, which was quite a piece, there had to be rules about everything or nobody could have any freedom. Only *needs,* I said, can grow outside altogether. I said the church it seemed to me should move in to help stop this debauch of our young in soul and body and not encourage it by phony compromises. I said I'd had another story about the dean of a girl's college who had taken off all check-in and check-out orders and if they spent the week-end in motels, what of it? so I tried to interview her but she said No this was final. I said something ought to be done, and the bishop said Easier said than done, I agree. I said I'm with Hank Gavin, *show* 'em something better! But you just admitted you'd given up the works—so-called miracles—some time back, didn't you? *Then* I asked him what he meant to do about disciplining Hank and I was about to say that I'd take a dim view *in print* of our losing him, but I thought *that* wasn't being very Christian so I just asked politely to *see.* The bishop wanted to know how much chance the young man had of getting this building permit for this ridiculous idea of a church downtown, and I said it was a hundred to one shot he couldn't. Mr. Steven J. Retzlaff will take care of that, I said. So the bishop said, 'Gavin has asked for it, the challenge is his, isn't it.' So then he said why not wait and see how that comes out—he said in fact that he would wait and see."

Thus adding one more vital decision to the Council meeting.

Several days later I got another call from Archie. Necessary to warn me, he said, that whether or not Hank could keep any of *his* promises, the rumor around town was that McAddams had already broken *his*. "You ought to get the word to Gavin," Archie said, "I suppose Mac couldn't handle it. Of course that piece of ground is community property—you know all about the community property law in this state. He couldn't sell it to anybody without Bertha's signature."

"No," I said, "but neither could she sell it without his."

"He's giving away too much weight," Archie said, "and of course he has to figure he's safe when he makes that promise. As I told the bishop, it's a long shot. Mac thought it was sure enough so that he was quite safe in making a bet on it. He could make a big gesture of generosity, because you notice he made it conditional. IF you get a permit, he told Hank Gavin. Now my information is that Bertha has given Steve Retzlaff an option on that corner for a couple of million bucks. You got to say for young Gavin, he moved in on a big game, but I guess he was used to them. You can see that Bertha is real sure there won't be any permit, but I tell you now, even if there should be, Bertha's husband Olin McAddams chairman of the board will fold."

"Archie," I said, "you've never really told me whether or not *you* decided to—"

"All right, all right," he yelled at me, "a man has to have some honor left, even if it is a hundred to one shot."

I asked Sybil Rowe, whom I found to be still staying with me, though she was gone most of the day, pinch-hitting for Mellie as near as I could find out, to tell Hank about this alleged option.

When she came back that evening she said she'd told him, and he only laughed. He said he didn't believe it, there was always a lot of this kind of talk beforehand whenever a big deal was on.

"False optimism will get him nowhere," I said gloomily, "what does he want to build a church down there for anyway?"

"They called it false optimism and worse when St. Paul thought he could convert the Gentiles," Sybil said. She also said, when I asked her, that Mellie had not answered her last letter. As far as she knew, Mellie had been out—or so her mother said—when Hank called her.

12

When Archie and I got to the Council chamber on the night of the hearing, Hank Gavin wasn't there.

"Oughtn't he to be?" I said nervously to Archie.

"May be building up an entrance," Archie said.

Just the same, I wasn't happy. He ought to be here, come down to it so should Mellie. A wife belonged at her husband's side in a big moment. Strange indeed that as this one approached the only member of that gay young married foursome present was Sybil Rowe. As we drove over, Sybil had said quietly, "If Hank had known in time, my Colin would still be here." Well, obviously, it was too late for Colin, but *Mellie*—I didn't tell her nor had I told Hank that I'd telephoned Chicago several times. Vaguely, her mother always said that Mellie was out. "Now that her father's a little better," Vadne said, "the child's having a ball, poor dear, and she surely deserved it." Nor did Mellie return my calls, a discourtesy I regarded with extreme disfavor. Hank hadn't told me that he'd made an overnight flight to Chicago, leaving Inglewood at five, he was back for his early on-your-way-to-business prayer group. He came back alone. Later I knew that he'd pleaded with his wife, and Mellie had danced glittering rings around him, evasive, witty, and hard as nails.

The place for the opening meeting of the Council was a small auditorium in the New City Hall, a glass-and-gleam skyscraper courtesy of Steve Retzlaff, with more where that came from, it seemed to say. Seats for the members were in a sort of jury box, there was a press table where Archie Paddock and I found seats. Inside the rail was a row of chairs for participating parties, though on the democratic theory that citizens had an interest in all matters affecting living conditions in their town and a right to be heard on them, anyone in the audience could rise and demand the floor. Word of mouth and Archie's paper had kept Beach City fully aware of Dr. Henry Gavin's petition for a Zone Variance which would enable him to build a church smang-bang in the middle of the business district and of the battle likely to ensue. A crowd jammed the benches, tapered off into the corridors, and gave it something of the air of big court cases I had covered.

I kept my eye on the wide door for Hank's appearance. My instinct told me he ought to be in, it had been right too often for me to ignore it now. The phantom figure of Bertha McAddams, not there in person, haunted me at every turn, and her husband in the front row looked more comfortable than a man usually can when he is carrying water on both shoulders. The entire board of the Church of the Redeemer was there and a good many of its members.

As the Council box filled, Archie named them for me with brief comments.

Aguirre, president for sixteen years and Steve Retzlaff's political right hand.

A small, wiry man with melon lips and protruding eyes, Jack Nestor's mouthpiece.

Doing-his-duty-like-a-man, a very tall, *very* thin gentleman who ran a high-class bookshop.

General Shields, retired, who couldn't spend all his time on street corners haranguing against General Eisenhower for selling us to the Russians in Berlin.

Housewife Adeline Defoe, proud of this office and of that title, inclined to clichés which, Archie said, made good headlines.

One Juan Portola, dark, slightly greasy, with a bay window. A merchant, owner of a music-TV-radio store.

And Janice Windermere, former high school principal, placid in the conviction that when everyone had a college education all our troubles would be over. Now she had her finger in many pies, but aside from matters of education Archie said she was tone-deaf. Like many teachers she found it difficult to listen. She sat next to Marguerita Vosburgh, who had been a member of the Council for twenty years.

A cross section like most city councils.

In their hands was the fate of Hank Gavin, of what he was trying to do with this downtown church idea.

Steve Retzlaff noted Hank's absence at once. As he and Gloria came in he stopped, put a hand on Archie's shoulder, and said, "Where's our young crusader?" before he took his own seat. Gloria hovered a moment, anxious for talk I thought, and I asked about Deedee as an opener. Deedee's mother looked—puzzled?—a little anxious. Her eyes blinked several times before she said, "I don't *know*. She isn't very *well*. Her father's so upset. He's trying to get her to a doctor, you know unless you see it you haven't any idea how he idolizes that girl! He breaks all up, when anything's wrong with her, *no sense* at all. Now all she does is start to cry and say, 'Oh Daddy please quit nagging me can't you? I'm fine.' Do you know when Mrs. Gavin is coming back? Dee keeps asking about her. Saying—she says Mrs. Gavin promised to do something for her—or *something*—"

Her best, no doubt, I thought bitterly. I said to Gloria that Mrs. Gavin's father was still too ill for Mellie to leave, and with that look of anxious puzzlement Gloria obeyed her husband's signal and went to sit beside him.

For seconds, while Archie rose to see if he could see anybody coming, I thought about Deedee, who was Mellie's *job*. She'd taken it on, hadn't she? Promise to come and talk to *me* any time, she'd said to the girl. How could she abandon her? A montage of Mellie having a ball in Chicago, a sable cape whose collar flared to frame her smooth dark head, filled me with such rage that I wished I could get my hands on her, preferably with a baseball bat in them. Leaving this child to Steve Retzlaff, stuffed with pride as a goose with grass, sitting there so *smug, no sense* as his wife said between his pride and that idolatry that only fathers have for only daughters.

Archie was shaking his head, looking a little worried, and I said, "How can Retzlaff be so *sure?*" and Archie, re-examining the Council, said, "He's got the votes. Except for Aguirre, who's got to be on somebody's payroll, there are well-intentioned people. They've simply been air-conditioned and auto-suggested into a conviction that Papa Knows Best. For Bigger and Better Beach City with your property and business increasing in value every day vote with Reztlaff's man Aguirre. Hurrah hurrah hurrah."

A formidable setup. If there was evil in what they were about to do they didn't know it. It looked good. Therein lay its danger.

"We've got some strong people," I said, "Marguerita Vosburgh—"

"Who know the Vosburghs used to own Beach City?" Archie said. "They don't now."

"The power of labor—" I began, and Archie shrugged.

He said, "The big boy in Detroit may not think this is an issue Nestor ought to mix up in. Stay out of religion. It's an axiom."

"There's you, Archie," I said.

He only said, "Besides, we're not organized and believe me Steve is. We've got two shaky votes, one of them is Mrs. Vosburgh and I'm not even sure of her. The other is the general's and he's gaga."

What followed is difficult to explain. I can only report it as I saw it to the best of my ability.

In practiced delivery, President Aguirre read Hank's petition.

An expectant pause. Aguirre let it roll, then he said, "This is signed by Dr. Henry Gavin. Is he present? Does he wish to address the Council in its behalf before we vote on it?"

No answer. My hands were wet. I knew this was the time to *pray,* but I couldn't think of anything. Where could Hank *be?* The oldest of maternal anxieties got me over the liver. Hurt in an automobile accident. Somebody slugged him. Ought to be here and he was dying in some emergency ward—Oh *God!*

After waiting a proper time, Steve Retzlaff was on his feet, exhibiting ease, poise, good will, as nice a big-brother image as you'd care to see. What he said in opposition was sensible, fair, covered all points. He spoke of his regret at having to oppose the rector, who hadn't been in Beach City long. In time, Steve said with a rueful smile, Dr. Gavin would come to see that the scheme to build a church downtown, put forward here, was ill-advised, couldn't be made to fit into the futurama of Beach City, which soon was to be one of the biggest cities in the biggest state in America. Everyone in this Council knew how long and carefully their plans had been laid, worked out, how they took every factor into consideration—the place to erect a church of which Beach City could be proud—by which it could benefit—

Hank Gavin walked through the door.

My first thought was where in the world has he been? This wasn't an *entrance.* Far otherwise. Here the business suit seemed the proper garb all right, only Hank looked as though he had slept or gone swimming in it. A *rumpled* business suit in which indeed Hank Gavin, after blowing a big sale, might have come rushing in *late* to one of Mellie's small elegant dinners to find the guests already assembled, to make hurried apologies and ask if they'd mind waiting while he showered—been a rough day!

No one else in that packed City Hall had ever seen this Hank Gavin, and he gave me a shock which mounted as he bowed to the president, hurriedly thanked Steve Retzlaff for yielding the floor, and began without prayers or preamble to make a pitch which was as big a letdown as watching Mickey Mantle strike out with the bases loaded.

His opening remarks I couldn't even *hear.* I felt Archie's eyes on me but I refused to look at him. I had troubles of my own.

No grain of salt can help much to make you believe what followed.

Let's just wrap it up by saying this was a lousy speech by a bad candidate who didn't know what he was talking about and apparently couldn't have cared less.

A few things *I* heard him say I can remember in broken dialogue . . . a story about a *cartoon* he'd seen . . . *salesman in a toy store showing a woman a big box filled with blocks, tin rails, little engines, nails, erector pieces, wheels, dolls, and a propeller or two. To her he says Madam this toy is designed to hasten the child's adjustment to the world around him, no matter how carefully he puts it together, it won't work*— What this had to do with anything—oh yes, I remember—something about *no matter how carefully you put Beach City together without God it won't work.*

It laid an egg. It didn't even get a giggle.

That's all *I* heard.

I got scattered reports of things he'd said—

Like—*I am their Father, says God, Our Father who art in heaven. My son told them often enough that I was their father.* He put me in a position where I am their Father, he who is a father *is above all a father, especially their father.* He told them so and I will have to keep his promises to them because my son loves them so and when they pray to me in His Name I will bring them my darling Hope my darling daughter Hope—

That's as best as Gloria Retzlaff could remember what she'd heard, she wants to know what-in-the-world, and I said that My son told them often enough that I was their father especially their father came from a poem by an early Frenchman named Péguy and she had some of the rest sort of jumbled or Hank had jumbled it but my darling Hope part of it was in the first poem in Péguy's book called *God Speaks,* the one where Péguy says a man should sleep and let God look after his universe during the night or he is unfaithful to Hope. But *I* didn't hear Hank quote any of it and I know it by heart.

One thing I have as evidence.

In his story *printed* the next morning in the Beach City *Gazette*—a copy is in front of me as I write—Archie Paddock had quoted extensively from Senator Fry's speech to the United Nations in Allen Drury's novel *A Shade of Difference,* beginning with *How does mankind stand in this awful hour?* and ending *Let us love one another, it is all we have left.* This was a book Hank had never read. And I beg you to believe that he didn't say one word of it, not one word. Yet two people besides the hard-boiled newspaper editor quoted it to me: *Love is all we have left.*

And that night, walking the floor until late hours, Sybil Rowe cried out, ". . . that was what Colin kept saying, something about the Fat Lady is Christ or there isn't any. You know what a *thing* he had about J. D. Salinger—he said Salinger was the only man talking about Christ in *his* language—that was—what Hank—said—something about *Seymour* telling Zooey to shine his shoes and Zooey said not for those morons and Seymour said then shine them for the Fat Lady across the street—the Fat Lady is Christ, buddy—I never did understand it—"

At the end of his presentation Hank Gavin looked to me ready to drop with fatigue. He said quite simply, "I don't want to let you make a mistake. You can't afford to overlook this opportunity to—well, to give God a corner in your city—anyhow, if you do, on the cornerstone I'll cut in—cut in real deep—heal the sick, cast out devils—raise the dead—cleanse the lepers—raise the dead—"

More or less everybody heard that.

It carried no conviction. Meant—what?

Then he looked at them, sort of—helplessly— *I* thought—all of them were a lot older than he was—and he smiled and turned around. There was no vacant seat and when someone offered to give him one Hank Gavin shook his head and went and stood with his left shoulder against the smooth white plaster wall at the very back of the auditorium.

For some unit of time, nothing at all took place.

Don't fight City Hall.

How right they were! We'd just tried it and produced a floperoo of dismal folly. Instead of an inspired young leader laborer Hank Gavin had been as ineffectual as a one-eyed jack.

The first move came from the president, Aguirre. His eyes on Steve Retzlaff, he asked if anyone had anything further to say on this matter. I thought I saw Steve give him an imperceptible negation, Aguirre made a slight gesture to Juan Portola, who then heaved himself to his feet and with a huge flap of his arms said, "Enough talk of this, no doubt. Let us now have the voting, yes? Since I am a working man it is not that we remain here all night, no?"

A grunt came from Archie, he began to write on a wad of copy paper, I could read his lead, *By unanimous vote, the City Council tonight rejected the bid of Dr. Henry Gavin for a Zone Variance . . .* and I hissed at him, "Not unanimous. We've got two votes, don't say unanimous." Somehow I couldn't bear it for Hank not to get *one vote.*

The man who ran the bookshop stood up, he said, "I am an atheist as Spinoza was before me. But I rather approve Dr. Gavin's hearty challenge to us. Though he has bravely rejected the testimony of his eyes which show him humanity as a collection of guzzling, lecherous, dishonest, and silly little mammals, lifted out of the mire only from time to time by *art*, nevertheless I think it's a bit of a sporting proposition to give God one more chance to keep his promises. As Dr. Gavin stated it, it seems to me rather in the spirit of American fair play to let him have this remarkable church in our town. I therefore at this point vote AYE—give him a Zone Variance!"

Archie said, "It can't be that he thinks he'll sell more Red Letter New Testaments—" but he shut up because Portola, still standing, said with a shrug that rippled his belly, "If the bomb she should fall, is no need to take chances, no? If God might so be angry with Beach City which who can tell —I am voting now yes, and I hope it will be remembered, yes."

The elegant academic syllables of Miss Windermere cut in. "As I understand, Dr. Gavin, if this church is built downtown, we are more or less committed to do our share to support it and offer its facilities which are somewhat educational after all to the man in the street. It's always been a question in my mind—how we can expect so much for so little effort in this field. I have a feeling Dr. Gavin may be right. We—the great middle class actually—it is possible we need to study more regularly—to accept some help. At any rate, I say yes, we have given building permits to some very *odd* people, occasionally over my protest—I don't feel inclined therefore to refuse a *church*."

Maybe nobody but Marguerita remembered that the Vosburghs had once owned Beach City, nevertheless a slight hint of something of the kind must have reached them as she stood up. She didn't *fuss* with anything, her hair or her tweed skirts or her face, and her voice had to be a delight to everybody. She said, "I admit that this seems to me a slightly fantastic idea and that as a member of the board of this church, which you know I am, I voted against it. On thinking it over and after listening to Dr. Gavin, we who are old must try to be fair. For I must also admit that there's a vague possibility that the whole church to which I belong has grown a bit stuffy and infirm and stagnant with the passage of time as old things often do, unless they associate with the young. Let us—perhaps we should—give the young a chance to try out some new ideas. They can scarcely do worse than we are."

Whether Mrs. V. had given him the final impetus I can't say. However, as she sat down Jack Nestor's man was on his feet, beaming affirmatively but before he could vote Steve Retzlaff came forward, easy as ever, smiling gently. He said,

"Since you've been persuaded by my comrade and pastor Dr. Gavin—those of you who've voted—may I suggest that the Council make the vote unanimous?"

While they were making it unanimous and official I heard Archie Paddock beside me saying in a low voice, "Why, that Retzlaff is a smarter son-of-a-bitch than I have given him credit for. That is as smart a call as I ever heard a man make. If you can't lick 'em join 'em—get a foot in both camps—"

To myself I was saying, this is only the surface. This Steve Retzlaff is a man who has another gun. He has a second gun and he was so amiable they didn't search him.

Olin McAddams was painful to behold. This, I thought, is a man who stepped forth confidently on a piece of ordinary well-kept green lawn he knew well and felt it begin to move with the shimmy and sucking sound of quicksand beneath his shackled feet.

Enthusiasm was reasonably rife.

I said to Archie, "Where did Hank go?" But Archie hadn't seen him leave the wall against which he'd been leaning.

Just the same as we stood there and looked at each other it exploded upon us that *this* which we had just witnessed was what everybody had said would be a *miracle. Don't fight City Hall.* A victory over City Hall meant that we'd just seen a hundred to one shot win going away. Let us wait and see what happens about this building permit, the bishop had said smugly. Well, he certainly couldn't send Hank Gavin to Flubdub North Wisconsin or to teach English in a proper seminary if he'd waited to watch tonight in Beach City.

"This is pretty remarkable, isn't it?" I said.

"Oh sure," Archie said, "except of course we'll now start trying to figure that there isn't anything remarkable about it, it would have come out that way *anyhow*. We'll all get *intelligent* with explanations for fear they'd expect more of the same. Actually, the doctor's diagnosis was wrong, a catering service took care of feeding the five thousand actually, or the storm on the Sea of Galilee was actually one of those quick thunder-showers.

"What's real and—to me, at least, goddam overpowering—as a sales pitch, as a presentation for a petition, I have never heard anything worse. It wouldn't have persuaded a child of six, who was for it anyhow. Have you?"

"No," I said, "I never have. It was dreadful."

All of a sudden I had a terrible feeling about that *boy*—to me, he was a boy, going home to that big, dark, lonesome place with no one to help him celebrate his first big triumph. It all needed talking over, part of the fun even of a miracle would be talking it over with someone you loved. Then he could explain how lousy he'd been, he could try to figure out why he'd goofed off the way he had and yet here, fine and warm and compelling was what everyone had said would be no less than a miracle if he brought it off.

A major victory and he had a right to celebrate.

But—talking it over, admitting how lousy he'd been—his cause for joy would go far beyond that. He'd made a bad speech, *nevertheless* against great odds what he had, he believed, been given him to do had been performed. Never before had Hank Gavin been given such proof that *Not I but the Father within me, he doeth the works,* as the Master had said, and in this case if he Hank Gavin hadn't and somebody else *had*—this was *the works.* Proof that even when he fouled up as all humans must do, even when I would have lost your cause, you did it—you performed it—

But there wasn't anybody there to talk it over with.

Mellie ought to be there, not doing the Matozo in Chicago.

Somebody ought to tell her so.

I had a firm conviction that it wouldn't be me this time.

Hank must do it himself. He would. Or would he? It wasn't until later that I knew the return home after the Council meeting had been worse for Hank than I'd dreamed.

To him, his own failure seemed to render him unworthy of his call.

He sat that night in his empty parsonage in inner darkness.

Backsliding, my Methodist grandfather used to call it.

Juliana of Norwich called it the only hell there is—loss of faith.

By whoever's conclusions, it is hell.

As usual, the enthusiasm, the impact of their magnanimous gesture in giving God a Zone Variance and allowing Him a right to move into their neighborhood, began to wear off, as Archie had foretold. On second thought, they told themselves, they must consider what this meant to their own interests. People began reminding each other of the practical side of things. After all, Steve Retzlaff had been against it to begin with, he was a shrewd hombre, he'd only given in so as not to be rude to a minister. Minister of his own church, at that.

I had been right about Steve Retzlaff, however. He had another gun.

13

Just as I walked in the door one evening, the phone rang and Mellie said, "How are things out there, sweetie?"

Driving in Southern California is irritating, I may have *sounded* irritated as I said, "Out here? As far as I know, things are fine," for there was a pause before Mellie said, "You're angry with me, aren't you?" and I said, "No. I don't admire you as much as I once did, but I try not to judge."

Again this little pause, Mellie laughed and said, "None of us can know everything, can we? When Hank called me last night he—I felt something was wrong."

"Possibly he misses you," I said. "It must make his work harder. You walked off the job, didn't you?"

"Do you ever stop to think *I* wasn't called to that job!" she said.

"In my opinion," I said, "you were called to take care of Hank."

"Even when I believe he is deceiving people with these *promises*—all this *come unto me*—look unto me and be ye healed promises aren't kept, can't be kept," Mellie said.

"Who are you to judge that?" I said. "His load right now—"

"Plenty of lovely ladies to give him a hand," Mellie said lightly. "Her mother-in-law wasn't always wrong about where Gert Cutler was some afternoons—and Isabel Mayhew has one of those feminine souls who edge up on a young minister by asking him to help her save hers—"

"With his wife off having a ball—" I began.

"Not altogether," Mellie said, "my father—"

"How is he?" I said.

"He won't get—any better, we know that now," Mellie said. "Some days up, some down, but it's just a question of time. We've brought him home, the doctors say it doesn't make any difference, and he wanted to come so much. The only real trouble, he can't bear mama around him. Of course he hardly ever speaks a civil word to me, either, and he's reverted to his Air Force vocabulary, but at least I keep him a little interested in life. We have good nurses and

I'm a very good nurse myself, remember? Speaking of which —I'd better get back—night, lovey, I'll call you again."

And she hung up.

Just at first, she told me all this long later but it belongs here, just at first, Chicago had seemed strange to her when she got back there. The people she knew moved about so constantly, rushing restlessly from Phoenix to Paris, from Madrid to Mexico, from Aspen to Athens, to Honolulu to Hong Kong, that she felt she was in the middle of a kaleidoscope, which was rather *fun* after Beach City, only it filled her with a desire to join them, to be up and away with them.

Strangest of all was her own position.

"Once upon a time," she said, "right there I had been Melanie Cheyne—*heigh-ho*. Being the belle of the ball—forgive me—was an exhilarating experience. You remember a gent named David Kenyon? Girls, you know, really don't *know* anything. How could I possibly have known how David Kenyon's wife was feeling? I give you my word, I never thought about her at all. All girls are self-centered little animals—I was thinking about *me*.

"Then I fell in love. From what I've seen, this doesn't happen to everybody. Many aren't—lucky, they don't wait, they never find the right *one*, maybe they aren't capable of it—Godmama, do you remember what it was like when you found out you were out-of-this-world in love, every time the phone rang heaven was at the other end? You woke with a leaping heart, *he* was in the same world. Do you remember?"

"Yes," I said.

"Can it happen more than once?" Mellie said.

"Not—that way," I said, "but there are other ways."

"Oh—" Mellie said, "companionship, affection, community of interests—I may have to settle for that but don't tell me it's *love*. I had all the luck. He wasn't already married, or some other race or color, or too poor to support me in the style which was all I knew. He was my guy—and everything about him was right and I loved him and he loved me and there I was, *young Mrs. Gavin*. With an elegant little house, elegant little dinners—"

"An earthly paradise," I said.

"Anything wrong with that?" Mellie said.

"Only, St. Paul says, it doesn't *last*," I said.

"All right—mine didn't last," Mellie said, "but it wasn't my fault. Somebody dropped a bomb."

"They are—dropping them," I said, "or threatening to—"

"I did my best," Mellie said, "you know what the real

bomb was? I didn't come first with Hank any more. God came first."

Her status in Chicago was indeterminate, she was neither maid wife nor widow at the moment, but she was still Melanie Cheyne Gavin and more whatever it was that had always entranced them than ever. Her real problem was that though she was, as she'd said, an inspired nurse and had been from the day she put on her first Dior-designed nurse's aid uniform, her father didn't *want* her. Vadne, who was feeling shatteringly bored, neglected, overlooked, and unwanted, was delighted to have her daughter there. Nobody had been asking Vadne Cheyne, an extra middle-aged woman, anywhere evenings, even the casino at lunchtime was depressing, so *many* widows, richer, more important, still shoved to the fringe. And now that he had so little time left, her husband didn't bother to conceal from her that he meant to waste none of it on her.

Just the same his first words to his daughter, when she walked into the bedroom that had been made to look as much like it was in a hospital as possible, were *shouted,* and he said, "You go back to your husband!"

"You need me—" Mellie began.

"What if I do?" Francis Cheyne said. She was shocked by the thin, pinched face, but the eyes were alive and very blue, and though when he *shouted*—you could tell he had—it came out as a shrill whisper, it was clear and understandable. "And he said to another, Follow me. That one said Lord, I've got to go and bury my father first and Jesus said to him, Let the dead bury their dead, you go and preach the kingdom of God. That's in *Luke*. Too much time spent on the dead, *they're all right*. Go preach the kingdom of God as the *answer* to the poor bastards left alive."

"Lamb, you're not ready to be buried by a long ways," Mellie said.

"Yes I am," Francis Cheyne said. "You're not going to make my deathbed an excuse for not following your husband when he follows Christ. I won't have that."

At first she had felt he was too ill, too weak, too old, to argue with. To her surprise, he spent a good deal of time reading the Bible, and this annoyed her more than she was willing to admit. Something *new*—or was it? A rather quiet figure, moving in and out, little to say, her mother had piped the tune to which they danced. In that world where he could neither keep nor make money, Francis Cheyne had been, except for his war years, a pleasant, aristocratic failure—and in it money failures pipe no tunes.

Soon, in spite of her resolve, he forced her into heated battles. She had forgotten that once upon a time he must have been a *fighter*. That he took Hank's side somehow added fuel to the flame of anger that was growing in her. Nobody except *everybody* practically in the known world seemed to agree with her.

"Why does my husband have to be such an extremist?" she said to him one day. "It's a free country, isn't it?"

"It was founded to give men freedom to worship in their own way," her father said.

"That's what I mean," Mellie said, perched on a chair beside his bed, "I have as much right not to believe in God as Hank does to believe. My freedom is not to worship something I know doesn't exist. How about that?"

With hands that were always tender and strong, she rearranged the pillows, lifted him to rest against them. She put one finger first against his cheek, then rested it on the Twenty-third Psalm that lay open on his knees, and making it sound lighthearted and affectionate she said, "'. . . my cup runneth over—sure I shall dwell in the house of the Lord forever—' and I'm sure David had a large staff of composers and ghost-writers."

"Bah!" her father said. "If you found out tomorrow Beethoven hired someone to write the Fifth Symphony, would it sound any different? Probably were several *Isaiahs* and God alone knows who wrote the gospels but who else needs to? When I was young there was a lot of windy controversy about who wrote Shakespeare's plays. Would *Othello* stop being a great play if Bacon wrote it, or the court jester for that matter? And yes, I do believe the Twenty-third Psalm and you'd be less of a fool if you did too."

"You and Hank can't solve everything by calling people who disagree with you fools," she said, "that's one of the things about religion—"

"Balls!" her father said. "Most ministers are so busy bringing God up-to-date—trying to make him in their *image*—time isn't any different on an electric clock, is it? Last time I ever went to church the man in the goddam pulpit was explaining Jesus healed the man with the withered hand by *hypnosis*—what the bloody hell's the good of *that?* You've just got one less man with a withered hand! Sure, that's fine—but that's not going to bring us *salvation*—"

"Oh, darling—" Mellie said. "Not salvation."

On her way out to dinners, she always stopped to tell him good night, once when she kissed the top of his head she said, "I was just thinking—you and mama used to come in, when I was little, and kiss me good night when you were going out. You were so handsome in your white tie—"

"I won't go!" he said, and began to shake with terror, "I will not go, you hear me? I don't have to go any more." He gave her a queer conspiratorial look, he said, "I've found out why they always bothered me so, ever since I came back from the war. They aren't *all there.*" He fought for breath, and got at last enough to go on, "If a man is without a *brain,* we say he isn't *all there.* Right? I say if he's without a soul, he isn't *all there* either. You can't substitute some bullshit about a man's subconscious for the *soul* God gave him—"

Mellie said to me that the words sounded so brave. He looked so small, smaller every day. He was so obviously dying. The nurses, most of them old friends from Passavant who no longer did private duty but had come to help Melanie out, said Mr. Cheyne was in his right mind—most of the time. Of course, they said, the blood wasn't reaching the brain the way it ought to. And any day—any night—sometimes these cases lingered but sometimes—in a *second*—

"He wants you," the night nurse said, waking her rather late, "he—keeps telling me to—to keep your mother out. I haven't sent for the doctor. There isn't anything he could do I haven't done. Tonight your father thought he was back flying—waiting for orders—"

The moment she came in he began to speak, the gasping breath was louder, more difficult, Mellie looked at the nurse, who shrugged, and then in a clear tone of command, Francis Cheyne said, "It came to me that you don't understand why Hank is so important. Listen to me. He knows about God the Father. Prop me up, damn it!" They shifted him, with care, he kept talking all the time, "God had to go outside the church to find someone simple enough and with *guts* enough—not hog-tied and silenced—not an *organization* man—to begin to *follow* the teachings of Christ. There are a lot of young men—on TV the other day—half the football squad were headed for the seminary! What's the good of that if they teach them—if they teach them the Holy Ghost is a figure of speech and not the presence of God? These young men—if Hank *makes* it—it'll get around! Somebody young'll notice. God the Father almighty. You know why sometimes it seems the world is going crazier than usual? You want to know why?"

A color of warmth had come back, in the hollow caverns of his skull his eyes were small, very bright gleams. "They're *orphans,*" he said. "We've got a whole goddam world of nothing but orphans. All the rich poor white black pimps and panderers, pundits and peepots, the poor pitiful poops, they're all orphans. *They haven't got any father.*" He gave out a cackle that was unmistakably laughter. "You know how hard it is to make orphans behave." His breath failed again and the nurse moved forward, a hypodermic in her hand, but he waved her back. "Man takes too bloody long to die, the way I'm doing, he has time to add up what he's seen and heard—you're a highly educated female, Descartes was a French philosopher, he applied the logic of mathematics to analyzing the universe, he said It is not possible that I should have in myself the idea of God if God did not veritably exist."

He was triumphant, he was exhausted, this time the nurse used the hypo and Melanie kept to herself her answer, which was that it is not possible that she should be so sure in herself that there was no God if there was one!

"I'm doing all right as I am," she said.

"Wait till you come to die," he said. "Once that door of death stands open—"

"I won't be scared into anything," Mellie said.

"You better be scared of having a damaged priest on your hands," her father said malevolently, "I want to see that man who buys pictures—the one that believes in angels —I can't remember things very well any more—what's his name?"

"Al Patton," Melanie said.

"If you say so," Francis Cheyne said, "I've got a new one for him."

Of course Melanie Cheyne Gavin had always been IN. She was simply *back*.

This was her world, her way of life, her own people. Changes she found, at first they seemed unimportant and minor. Her pleasure was intense and fresh and in the beginning she could not understand how she had stayed away so long. The changes were minor, unimportant, as seasonal changes in a garden from winter to spring to summer to fall and round again.

At the Saddle and Cycle Club at the moment the small fry wore denim slacks with holes in them, sweaters frayed, faded, and shapeless, scuffed shoes and sandals in the new reverse snobbishness. True, the teenagers, the young mothers who sat on the terrace or swam or played tennis had settled for ugly duckling hair, lank or teased, arranged to give the acme of disorder and downgrading, they had adopted the beatnik long black stockings and sloppy sacks, reaching perhaps for some common denominator of feminine fair play.

Yet at the public rinks the skating costumes were to *behold,* displaying everything but taste.

Mellie did not remember in her pre-during-and-post debut years so much talk of poverty—now they all talked poverty-stricken desperation. The girls who were to have private debut balls as well as the cotillion were always griping about being broke—*and I mean broke to the wide.* Their clothes allowances which were Scrooge miserly—literally *miserly,* my love—to begin with were all spent. *I can't even go to the movies. Thank God for the parties—they're free! Or I'd be home in bed trying to keep warm by nine every night. Literally it makes me easy prey to anyone with a buck in cash.*

Simple, in a way, these children. Raised that way, not to know how rich they were to be. Like little Princess Victoria, Mellie said, who had to have it explained to her that now she was *Queen.* Few of them had any idea that the great solid family fortunes of industry, of mercantile empires were behind them. It was almost, Mellie thought, coming back to it from Beach City, California, as though they were superstitious about it.

A complex, fascinating social structure, where when The Dance—that anonymously exclusive club in Lake Forest—gave one of its bashes, you got the same old corned beef hash and creamed chicken but the Meyer Davis orchestra had been imported from New York. More even than the South now could or dared, the Middle West was trying to keep steady the traditions of their forefathers, those which New York had utterly abandoned to conglomerate titles from Europe and the glitter of art. In New York, where a small group of non-society ladies now ruled the fashion world, editors, columnists, public relations geniuses, were really the *grande dames* and arbiters of what had once been Society.

On the night of the biggest private debut ball of the season when the daughter of the Medills was to star, it seemed to young Mrs. Gavin, arriving with Stu Margolis and his wife, that for all the breathtaking gorgeousness of this hand-picked lot of the Young, Natalie Margolis was the most beautiful woman in the room. Mellie's eyes, considering Natalie thoughtfully, decided that none of the babes could compare. How old *was* Natalie? Must be in her forties—late forties—surely. There was a depth to her glow, or is this sheer imagination on my part, Mellie thought, because I remember now what I didn't believe then and still don't.

Probably we will include the Methuselah kick in our *message* before we're through, Come to church and learn how to be young and beautiful at 969 years of age. But there were also Helen of Troy and Ninon de l'Enclos who'd never been famous for sanctimonious methods. Anyhow, as Hank so often began his sentences, one thing was for sure. Mrs. Stuart Margolis was sober and had been ever since that day in Al Patton's picture gallery though as far as she, Mellie Cheyne Gavin was concerned, she figured that after Stu caught her practically *in flagrante delicto* he had scared her into sobriety or else. The iron hand of Polly Medill and the invitation lists so backbreakingly compiled had arranged it so that there were 2½ young men to every girl. The gowns—Saralie Travers' and all the others—were aglimmer and aglow, they had come from Paris, from Oleg Cassini, from far and near, they were so-near-bridal yet so virginal, they were the Eve of St. Agnes, then why did their wearers look so sad? For sad they did look and sad they did dance and sad and sorrowful it seemed to Mellie they did fling their arms aloft in the Watusi and let them fall in Ophelia's own gesture of despair.

Were they lovelier than Mellie Cheyne had been on such a night—how many years ago was it?—no no. Because even so short a time ago as *that* they had been merry, enchanted, happy. They had not twisted in pain and fear and desire—they had danced and pranced and jumped and thumped and bumped and stepped and leaped with excessive good will and expectation. They had been *gleeful.*

All, Mellie saw, was magnificence.

Even the elevator to the ballroom, used only for Miss Travers' guests, was hung in scarlet chiffon and orange and pink ribbons and bits of mirrors that glittered and showed young Mrs. Gavin figures of her own golden gleaming self small as through the wrong end of binoculars. The stately ballroom of the Blackstones had been transformed by a decorator imported from New York and too expensive for any but the storied names of Detroit, Chicago, Dallas, and even Boston. Tonight, this well-known scene of so many social triumphs was hung in tiger cloth, exactly resembling the skins themselves, it had now the look of the jungle, it even smelled like the jungle, black wicker monkeys hung from the fixtures and saluted their descendants who capered below them and the faces seemed to reflect from each other that simian sadness which even in his most frantic antics the bandar-log never loses.

Oh—the manners were there—the ingrained, beautiful manners, the easy air, the automatic language that ran around the world.

The *air.*

They don't have to prove anything, Melanie Gavin thought, that's why. No mountains to climb, no rivers to swim, under all the changes, the doing away with class distinctions and color lines and even rich and poor, it was still there, the *noblesse oblige*.

Then why were they so sad?

She asked it finally of one of the debutante's young men who had come to dance with the most famous of Chicago's all-time debutantes—Mellie Cheyne. He was a good-looking youth with a mouth a little too sensitive.

"It's the biggest bash of the season, isn't it?" he said, grinning at her amiably. He was perhaps a little tight—not enough to matter. None of them were.

Without intention Melanie heard herself say, "But why are they all so *sad* and sorrowful?"

His fingers bit into her back in a quick *shut* of surprise. The pleasant smile went away, he looked a little bored, like the newspaper pictures of the young jewel thief called Murf the Surf. He said, "Oh—I expect it's the death wish. All this generation has to have it, don't you think?"

"The death wish!" Mellie said in utter astonishment.

"Oh yes, I should say so, rather," the young man said, "shouldn't you? I should say most of our generation are a bit bored with the whole mess, at least a good many of them. Except for skiing perhaps."

"How old are you?" Mellie said, leaning back a little in his arms so that she could see his face.

"I don't think it's a matter of how *old* you are, exactly, is it?" he said. "My father, for instance, is forty-eight, I believe—somewhere around there. He's as naïve as a six-day-old garter snake. Even his charities are naïve. At least few of us are naïve."

Someone cut in then—she was being cut in on a good deal—she was being quite a belle considering all things—and found now that she was dancing with David Kenyon, who still wore his white tie and tails better than anyone else in the jungle.

"Darling David!" she said and paid him the courtesy of trying to smile as though she could actually remember that once she had found heaven in his arms, or a reasonable facsimile thereof.

"I wouldn't have thought it possible that you could grow more beautiful," he said, and she recognized the words but not the music. His voice was—*flat*. This was David—he was only a few years older—how long had he been—what was it?—what was the matter with this attractive, handsome, sleek, intellectual man of power and prestige and place? The tales had reached her, of course. But *lots* of men, rich and terribly busy men, went to psychiatrists, didn't they? Even say a man had had a collapse, it didn't necessarily mean that there was anything *wrong* with him.

What was *wrong* in this paradise?

Psychologically, what had motivated turning the stately old ballroom into a jungle smelling of panther piss? For it did! It damn well did! Psychologically why did these favorites of the gods fling their arms up in what should be gestures of joy and let them fall leadenly, coming down so that they brought the heads and shoulders along with them?

The death wish!

What pretentious show-off juvenility!

Yet she had just danced with a young man who spoke quite familiarly, casually, of the death wish and now she was in the arms of a man who had once been her lover and he was a *mummy*. Why was he a mummy? Where was the goddam *snake* who'd sold them some doctrine of despair and boredom—David Kenyon was *mummified* with *boredom*.

They were all so—so *tired*. Their arms were tired, their eyes were tired. All of them knew, now, *all* about good and evil, and it was boring not to be able even to tell the difference any more. This was a sort of spiritual me-too-ism! Nowhere in that stuffy, dark, monkey-ridden jungle all hung about with tiger skins and fever trees, nowhere was there innocence.

No one any more was allowed to *start* with innocence.

Not only Lolita.

Nothing ever grew any more in the soft spring air of innocence and that seemed rather sad.

Nothing *ripened*. Face it, Mellie said to herself, and she could feel the nausea of hope sickening her. Like tomatoes. What was that godmama was always telling, bringing it up over and over as an illustration, that bit about tomatoes? She was right. Where in this great rich progressive city, in this great richest country in the world with its advances in science, where could you now get a ripe tomato to eat? Mellie Cheyne remembered she had liked them better than ice cream which was too sticky-sweet and she had a moment of total recall of times when they used to go out to the farm, she was learning to ride—about seven or eight maybe—and after she'd done her jumps they would *pick* tomatoes, dark, luscious, *red* sun-*ripened* tomatoes, warm from the golden rays, they tasted divine. Love apples—hadn't they been called that in the beginning? Well, if you thought anybody was ever going to get any kind of love apples ripe any more—no no, as godmama said, they picked 'em green now, and shipped them in cold cold cars, so that in this big rich jungle room where the supper had cost a fortune, in those enormous silver bowls filled with the most expensive salads in all Chicago, were little round pieces of pale pink synthetic rubber with no taste of any kind and called, By God, tomatoes.

Nothing was allowed to grow, to ripen naturally, everything was forced. These poor little rich kids and the poor little poor kids that came into the children's hospital would never know what a tomato tasted like. Not a real tomato. Her heart leaped and almost burst, she felt so sorry for them. ALL of them. The *rich* couldn't buy a ripe tomato any more than the poor.

The flavor had gone out of it.

Deedee—little Deedee Retzlaff out in Beach City, her father was the town's big shot, could anybody now ever teach her the difference? That was the horror, they didn't know they were being robbed of growing things.

Wasn't even any forbidden fruit any more. *Nohow*. Frozen, canned, picked green.

Poor babes in the woods, satiated at six.

Take little Deedee for example, out in Beach City. She was afraid of her father, but fear of hell itself never had worked, not really. Raise hell one night and ignore her for the next thirty. His name and reputation, not love for her or concern for her soul if he knew she had one.

How did Deedee who sang in the church in Beach City, California and had a boy friend who was a bit beatle-*ish* with his *ge*-tar, how did she get into this exclusive, expensive ball in Chicago given for the bored, lank-haired young daughter of the Medill millions who knew some weird things about *her* father too—such as his drinking and the girls in New York.

"My ears picked it up as though I'd put a record on a hi-fi set," Mellie was to tell me, "of that conversation in the drive-in, that day after we left the Cutlers in their simmering hate. *He'd run him out of town, my father would, he could just as well kill somebody when he's mad but he's too cagey, he'd run him out of town and Beany can't stand any more, he couldn't bear any more, you can understand that can't you?*—Deedee, the so-young melodious sweetness—then *me If you need a friend, Deedee, I'm always available, please believe that, if you're ever in a jam I'll do my best to help you*—and then Deedee, taking my promises seriously, believing I'd do my best for her—*Oh thank you, it's just I can't—they mustn't hurt Beany, nobody ever thinks of him and he's so*—I said *Vulnerable?* and Deedee said

Oh yes oh yes, so vulnerable, he couldn't stand it, he's very sensitive—and I said *Promise me you'll let me know if I can help* and Deedee said *Oh I will—I promise*— How do you like that? Beany couldn't stand any more—is that what they call the death wish? That's got hold of these young orphans of our goddam storm? That's what I thought. I found myself thinking *You're* so sure *Jesus* wouldn't keep his promises, you don't keep yours either, I'd have two thousand miles to go before I sleep to keep mine, and all the time we were dancing around pretending we were bubbles in a champagne glass and David Kenyon said, 'Nothing is changed, Mellie, or ever will be—' and I heard the words. I wanted to say nothing but *us*, you and me, we're changed but just then I knew what was the matter with me.

"Hank wasn't there.

"Nothing would ever be real fun without Hank. And he'd found another *kind* of fun.

"But—that wasn't it.

"Hank wasn't anywhere. If David Kenyon was just a good embalming job right where I'd left him, my husband didn't exist at all any more, and *that* it seemed to me was a dirty trick. Out in Beach City there was a—*Changeling*. Yes there was, lovey. Tall, he looked taller, and much much too thin, who always looked as though he'd just gotten up from his knees. He had, too. I realized that and I was furious. He was always trying to make himself—worthier?—for the *message*—"

Over and over it she went.

Hank wasn't there, in the midst of all this superb gaiety, this biggest bash of this or any other season, hearing this *music* that popped blues into your blood stream, drinking the most vintage champagne that it might flow up like a fountain into your brain, this having FUN bash. And she Mellie Cheyne Gavin, she loved it. So this was *the world*. She wanted to love it, who wouldn't? All over the country, even in Beach City, people were trying to duplicate this, weren't they? To have fun, weren't they? Out in foggy bottom somewhere was a man who had stolen Hank's name, he might be *anywhere*, at a death bed, a rape couch, a double cross at the City Hall, writing a letter to his Follow-me chaplain.

You aren't the man I married.

That was what she tried to *send* to him across the distance.

Did this take place in every marriage? A little maybe. Not like this.

The music changed, a second Pop Blues orchestra came

in to spell the other, this new music turned them, twisted them, she looked at David Kenyon and could not believe she had ever seen his head beside hers on a pillow, he looked like a cartoon of that richest tormentedest man in the world, J. Paul Getty, but her own fine young body, at its glorious peak now, began to *twist,* the music entered as the sound of savage drums had entered in the jungles, she was twisting like a snake and she was in deadly fear because she couldn't seem to stop, she wasn't the girl Hank Gavin married either, this defiant, rebellious, love-the-world-and-the-things-that-are-in-the-world woman displaying her body in twists before this old *goat,* if Hank saw her now in her golden skin he might mistake her for a cheap dancer doing a heterosexual shimmy in a *dive.* If Hank was here—look around, look with clear eyes for one flashing second, look at that woman over there who ought to be keeping her beginning-to-get-old body in some dignity, not shaking the flapping upper arms, wiggling the sagging breasts and protruding stomach, flaunting her silly old ass as though anybody wanted it, unless she was lucky enough to have a man she'd married who hadn't noticed that she wasn't the girl he'd married—

Oh poor thing poor thing poor thing.

Under the mask she looks so *tired.*

How could a daughter get anything but a death wish if she watched her?

Poor things.

All of them. The brightest one—so that was why! They knew.

They get so tired of sinning.

They can't keep it up forever, calling it good, calling it *fun.* The whole world is so tired of sinning it has the death wish to blow itself up sometimes. All the starved orphans, all the middle-aged and old whose hope is sick, sick hope breeds a death wish.

How did Deedee get in here along with the heiress to the Travers money?

I have promises to keep and miles to go before I sleep.

In the dark, in spite of anything I can do, the telephone sounded as it always does, harbinger of doom.

Father, give me strength! I'm probably going to need it.

Mellie! Why Mellie *at this hour?*

Had her father gone out with the tide? I could hear a tide outside but it was coming in, pounding in, surging and crashing on the sand like the Götterdämmerung. I'd worked late, I'd only been asleep an hour or so, it took me a minute to know I was home, to see by the light I'd switched on the picture of Mellie in her wedding gown on my dressing table.

"What is it?" I said. "It's four in the morning there. Where are you?"

"I'm at the Travers coming-out ball," I couldn't tell whether it was a sob or a giggle that shook the phone, "and, babes, what bash this is."

"How is your father?" I said.

"Dying," Mellie said, "slowly, surely, bravely."

"Mellie," I said, "are you tight?"

"Being slightly intoxicated on the *very* best champagne cannot in fairness be called *tight,*" Mellie said, "I am Cinderella, I have on a golden gown and glass slippers and the men are mad for me, so they tell me. Is Hank all right, Godmama?"

"I—think so," I said. "I haven't seen him, I've been busy."

Where are the other nine? How had that gotten loose in my head? Were not ten healed? Didn't any but one stranger come back to thank him? None of the congregation, the regulars? I didn't know about the others, but I knew how much he'd done for me and right away here I was, very busy, oh *very* busy, so I was saying to Mellie I haven't seen him, I've been very *busy*. Well, one in ten had been noted as a fair average if you asked them to acknowledge the *works* of Jesus Christ and make them your way of life. I, for one, had been too busy too busy to give him the only thanks that matter—*be there when I need you.* Maybe he hadn't but I didn't know that, I'd been too busy to find out.

"Why I called," Mellie said, "is Deedee all right?" and then she told me what I have written earlier about the memory record that played *back* while she was dancing with David Kenyon once more.

"I haven't seen any of them," I said, "I've been working. Sybil saw them the other night, Deedee and that guitar player —I don't remember his name."

"Beany," Mellie said over the two thousand miles, hardly more than a whisper filled with—pain, anger, defiance? "Nobody thinks of him."

"Sybil saw them dancing out at one of those places on the pier," I said slowly, "I think she said he was hoping to get a job with the band—or he knew somebody—they were dancing and having a high time, she said."

"How is Sybil?" came from far far away.

"She gets things done for whatever her cause is," I said. "She's a right hand to Hank."

"Did she say Deedee looked happy?" Mellie said.

"Hilarious, I think she said," I told her.

"Hilarious isn't the word for Deedee," Mellie said.

"No," I said, "Mellie, what is all this about Deedee Retzlaff?"

"Is she pregnant?" Mellie shouted at me.

"Oh, for goodness sake," I said, "of course she's not pregnant! If there's one thing most of the young guitar-playing set must know it's how not to get pregnant, or there'd be even more unmarried mothers. Let's not be melodramatic."

"I have to go home," Mellie said, "Papa doesn't want me, but he needs me. I always knew he didn't like mama but I had no idea how much."

Naturally, I couldn't go back to sleep which is one thing people who call you in the middle of the night never think of. The surf was quieter, the drums of the waves came in a long, rhythmic roll. I wrapped a sweater around me and went to sit in the open window, watching the white crests break and race up the sands and then go slowly back. In order, under a law. *Who shut up the sea with doors when it brake forth, and said Hitherto shalt thou come and no further and here shall thy proud waves be stayed?*

Thinking about Hank, I decided to call him even if it waked him. But there was no answer. And that disturbed me.

Of the rest of that night in Chicago, I was to know while I still sat there and saw the sun rise in unbelievable rose and copper glory.

Mellie Cheyne called to tell me that her father was dead.

Whatever he had intended to tell Al Patton, that patron of angels, it had been too late. Al and Mellie had arrived at Francis Cheyne's door together and by then his breath was too shallow, too weak to hold up many words. The nurse held up a hand which halted them on the threshold but somehow Francis Cheyne found strength to lift one finger and beckon them in.

This man had not been equipped for all types of fighting, ruthlessness, ambition, the ability to sell himself that there was *any* end to justify *any* means. Once in the night when he was delirious he had said to Mellie *I dropped the atomic bomb* and wept bitterly and long. Foolishness, Mellie said, but it showed the way his mind worked.

His last fight, that early morning, was to die well. He said to Al Patton, "To face the open door of death—so long—" his breath came in gasps with times when Mellie was sure it would never come again and then he said, "I—admit—to great curiosity—soon now—I shall know—some of the answers—"

Mellie heard footsteps outside the door, and the sound of low sobs, and she said, "That's mama—Papa *darling*—could you?—" and he nodded—but she saw the great beads of sweat that slid down his cheeks and stood on his forehead and she was quite sure, afterward, that it had been too late for him to see Vadne as she knelt beside him.

For when he sat up—upright—he was looking over their heads, way over, out through the open door, and whatever he *saw—whatever* he saw—Al Patton was sure it was the angel Gabriel come to meet him, for Francis Cheyne died at dawn *young* and smiling.

"I wish I could have talked to him after that," Mellie said, "it seems so unfair. If there is anything. Would it hurt God any if there is one to let us—oh I know, I know, the future has to be hidden but it's a system I don't understand myself. Even Al Patton—but like everybody else he believes what he wants to believe, he believes now *he* himself saw a glimmer of—of the angel's wings—a flash of them—Pretty soon he'll be telling everybody he saw the flash of the angel's sword and the gleam of the angel's wings—"

For a few weeks after that I heard nothing.

Mellie, of course, made no explanation, her mother needed her and she had taken on a big job at the hospital, as a sort of memorial to her father. One phone call from Archie Paddock told me that beyond doubt the McAddamses had sold that corner to the Retzlaff Realty Company for a preposterous figure and though Hank Gavin had said he would soon call a board meeting no date had been set. "He's slowed down considerable," Archie said and then he took off for a publishers' meeting in New York and a speech to be made at an advertising convention in Minneapolis and everyone else seemed to be busy now, about their own affairs, after all a church, their church, downtown or out of town, was a side issue more or less, they had their own first-of-the-month bills and payments and fun and games to look after. As near as I could gather—I myself was working long, tight, exhausting hours about then myself and I'd had a problem in my own family—the group around the young minister who'd taken the pledge were still with him, they were quiet about it, "Good thing I guess," Archie said to me just before he took off. "Probably wished he hadn't gone quite so far or been quite so definite. Might be wiser just to—to promise them *hope*—not miracles." And I said, "But—" and went no farther. I wasn't sure myself. Just the same deep down inside me I knew that without the full *audacity* of his faith, this would all blow over, this would be just another bright better-than-most young clergyman.

I wondered if Jesus might have carried somewhere a crest on which was blazed *tourjours de l'audace.*

Between my concern and my desire not to interfere, my uncertainty about all things at this time, I was out of touch with Hank. I kept telling myself you could never help people until they came to you, especially the young, that Hank knew where I was and how much—how *ready* I was if he needed me.

But after Mellie's father died I did call him to ask if he was going back for the funeral. He said he wasn't. "Francis will understand," he said. I said, "But—Mellie and Vadne need you," and after a moment he said, "No," and let it go at that. I said, "Come and see me sometime, Hank?" and he said, "When I can—not yet, pray for me."

One thing I did.

Through our city desk I checked the Defense Department as to where a communication would reach the chaplain. A number, some letters, of course, he might be in the Congo or the Aleutians or Saigon. My cable said simply that I thought Hank might have need of him or of word from him.

14

"She just barged in on me," Mellie said.

Her story of Sybil's trip to Chicago came to me a long time later, but as I said at the beginning of this story I shall put things in their chronological order as much as possible.

This was a scene between two young women. Without any lead-in at all.

They faced each other steadily, reflected in a wall of full-length mirrors. My own picture is of Sybil done in sculpture, tall, dark, straight, fiber and sinew molded on over strong heavy bones. Of Melanie by a painter, possibly Renoir, for she wore something slim and flowing in his silvery flower-like colors and her face was forever feminine, flowing too, from one color, one emotion, to another.

Sybil had called from the airport, and when Mellie looked at her face she knew this was no social-between-planes-drop-in call, though of course Sybil wouldn't have done that at seven-thirty in the morning, she'd known that. She said, "Take off your coat," and went to a low table between two old-fashioned bow windows and plugged in an electric coffee pot.

"I flew back to see you," Sybil said, and her voice came from vocal chords so tight it squeaked through shrill and tense.

Mellie's hands were suddenly still like birds who'd heard a distant shot, she said, "Is anything wrong with Hank?" and Sybil said, "I came to tell you about it." Mellie's hand moved again, bringing the little tray with its silver pitcher and bowl from under the napkin, shifting the cups and spoons, she said, "Well, come and sit down, babe, I gather this will take too long to play it standing."

They sat down in the low upholstered chairs, a glance—one only—showed the once-famous gardens of the old, stone, turreted Cheyne mansion in Lake Forest, now a tangle of shrubs, of overgrown lawns, of heavy trees. Long ago, Francis Cheyne had sold off all the land he owned along the lakefront, that was part of what they'd lived on. He'd kept only the acre of house grounds and the old house itself, to this he had clung with the obsessive stubborness of men who are weak in their adjustment to their times, and when he and Vadne could no longer maintain the Chicago apartment they had moved back to his boyhood home and he had died in the bed in which he was born. Now, fortunately, it would sell for enough to keep his widow in some style, lunch at the casino, bridge at a tenth of a cent, new gowns for the cotillion and the opening of the Opera, her season seats at the Symphony, her membership in the Contemporary Club.

"I'm not going to say any of the things I used to think about you," Sybil said harshly, "I'm not much of a Christian yet, but I try to follow—"

"Darling Sybil," Mellie said, pouring the coffee with hands that were far from steady, "I know that patience is a Christian virtue, but I do not pretend to be even a church-on-Sunday Christian and I—is Hank—*what is it?*"

"You—you can't feel what I've come to—to talk to you about—about Hank," Sybil said, "unless you know what Hank did for me, and know that I have a *right*—a privilege—to come. You'll just have to accept that."

Back and back Mellie's head tipped, until she was staring at the ceiling, her hands crossed above her breast, and then she said, "There isn't anything I can do about it, is there? I think you might tell me one thing—is it—serious, about Hank?"

"It's a matter of life and death," Sybil said and gave a strange off-key bray of laughter, "and I am a gal who has a right to talk about matters of life and death, you'll grant me that, won't you? Not that Hank is ever going to jump out any windows—but you see, Mellie, what you have to know now is that I pushed Colin out that window as surely as though I'd done it with my two hands. That's why I never even tried to marry again. I did have decency enough not to let a man marry a murderess without knowing it."

"You're too hard on yourself, I imagine," Mellie said, "I've come to the place where I think a lot of us do the best we can. More of us than we take into consideration. All of us are pretty free at handing out blame. We yip and yelp and dish out what everybody's done as long as it isn't us. I'm inclined to believe that a large percentage of us do the best we can and when we know better we'll do better." Sybil said a short un-Christian word, though there is quite a lot about bowels in the Bible, though often it was used for the seat of pity and mercy. "Darling Sybil," Mellie said, "I don't think so—not really. You did the best you could at the time for Colin."

"No," Sybil said, "I didn't and you know I didn't. I did

my best for me. If it hadn't been for me, Colin might have been alive and a fine—a *fine*—and happy—composer or musician or—something." The knuckles of her hands lying on her lap, she hadn't so much as picked up her coffee cup, were white knobs, she shut her eyes and it came to Mellie that she was *praying*. "In my heart, in my insides," Sybil said, "I knew I not only wasn't doing my best, I wasn't willing to get my own bloated carcass out of the way of Colin's divine circuit. I—I let myself, I made myself believe that I was good for him. That I was—making a man out of him. And then one day he chose death. He didn't die—you must always remember that. He chose death to get away from me, to get rid of me. To escape from me."

Things came into Mellie's throat, but before the fever heat of Sybil's white intensity she couldn't get them out. Who was it Sybil reminded her of now? What was it held her captive under that consuming fire? It eluded her. Somebody she had always read about with terror. Suddenly she knew. *Rosa Dartle*. In *David Copperfield*, Rosa Dartle in her furious determination.

"You didn't know Colin left a letter for me, did you?" Sybil said.

Startled, Mellie said, "Hank thought he didn't, it always surprised him."

"I found it—afterward," Sybil said.

She began to cry, softly, soundlessly.

In the quietness, Mellie got up and went to find a big chiffon handkerchief and gave it to her.

Whatever this was, she now knew, achingly, they had to see it through—both of them.

"A little flat book," Sybil said, "I found it between a volume of Keats and a kid copy of *Treasure Island*. A little black book. So worn the—the back part was broken and it came open at a page that was marked and underlined and had—things written in the margins."

The name of the book, she said, was *The Great Divorce*, by the same man who'd written that book called *The Screwtape Letters*, which Sybil said she had never understood exactly. Hank and Colin thought it was the *greatest*, they rolled on the floor and read bits aloud to each other, but she couldn't understand how a religious book—or anyhow a spiritual book, they called it—could be that *funny*. Colin explained that was why it was the greatest. *The Great Divorce* wasn't funny. Such a story as it told consisted of the adventures of a busload of people who came from what *they* thought was earth but which turned out to have been hell all the time, the way they lived in it, and the journey was to the gates and outer glories of heaven. To the gardens and woods and streams and lakes that lay at the foot of the majestic mountains of light where God dwells. As soon as they got off the bus the humans were, in a manner of speaking, ghosts, and most of them were met by some of the bright people, or angels with golden wings, who had been sent to guide them to the Father.

Not all of them, it turned out, were willing to go.

What Sybil called Colin's *suicide note* began on page 84, marked by a big star in Colin's green ink and some jottings he'd made in the margin. A female ghost was talking to one of the bright women and there were the words Colin had scored and scorched . . . the ghost . . . talking . . .

> **You have always thought Robert could do no wrong . . . you haven't the faintest conception of what I went through with dear Robert. The ingratitude! It was I who made a man of him! No but listen. He was pottering along on six hundred a year when I married him and mark my word he'd have been in that position to the day of his death if it hadn't been for me. It was I who had to drive him every step of the way. He hadn't a spark of ambition. It was like trying to lift a sack of coal. I had positively to nag him to take on extra work, though it was really the beginning of everything for him. . . . . I used to spend simply *hours* arranging flowers to make that poky little house look nice and instead of thanking me what do you think he said? Said he wished I wouldn't fill up the desk with them when he wanted to use it: and there was a perfectly frightful fuss one evening because I spilled one of the vases over some papers of his. It was all nonsense really because they weren't anything to do with his work. He had some silly idea of *writing* in those days . . . as if he could. I cured him of that in the end. The trouble I went to entertaining. . . . Then he got the new job. A step up. But what do you think? He said Well now for God's sake let's have a little peace . . . . well, I got him into the new house at last. . . . Yes I know, it was a little more than we could really afford at the moment, but all sorts of things were opening up to him . . . no more of his sort of friends, thank you. Naturally I had to dress well. . . . As I used to say to him Robert you're simply letting yourself go to seed. . . . I forced him to take exercise. . . . Even, when things became desperate, I encouraged him to take up his writing again, it couldn't do any harm then. How could I help it if he did have a nervous breakdown . . . my . . .**

Who asked you

HaHa!

Poor

OH god!

I jumped out a window

Mellie put the little book down, carefully closed. In a swift gesture, Sybil's hand reached for it, she held it a moment, tenderly, yes yes, Mellie thought tenderly, and for the first time, she smiled.

"Then I knew," Sybil Rowe said. "You see, in his own way, he did leave a suicide note. One only I could read. Maybe he knew it would be better if I didn't find it until a little later."

As it was, when she did find it, and read it, and with each printed impersonal sentence tied it to something that had been part of their lives—hers and Colin's—like the time she'd upset a vase of splashing spectacular chrysanthemums —which he especially disliked, on the piano and the water had run over a sheet of music he was composing and blurred it. *Surely you can remember a few notes like that,* she had said to him.

"There is something else," Sybil said, and took a deep breath, and picked up her coffee cup and drank it all in one desperate, thirsty gulp.

Very simple, this one was.

Easier in a way to understand.

Hidden away among some old music, some old papers, college books, sweaters—really *hidden*—she had found one manuscript.

In green ink across the cover was written
Leave Me Alone with My Song

"I—never could play very well," Sybil said, "but you know how it was, we all had to take *piano* when we were little. That day—that day—" she couldn't go on, and Mellie said, "Sybil—*don't*—what's the use—"

Sybil steadied herself. She said, "No. You have to—hear the *words*. Don't you see that you have to hear the words? Just don't look at me."

Mellie looked out the window where she could see the tops of trees, swaying so gracefully in the winds off the lake. And after a long moment Sybil said, "I told you the title is *Leave Me Alone with My Song*—" and then she began to sing in a husky, not always true voice, and Mellie was sure sometimes she went off whatever melody there was completely—not that it matters.

When there's meaning in the music,
And music in the words,
A song can set the heart at rest
It need not even be the best
Of songs.
As long as it belongs to you alone.

A song is all you need, boy,
The rest is for the birds,
But all the birds have songs of their own
From the highest and mightiest, holiest bird

To the shiest and grubbiest lowliest bird
Each has his own inner song
And that's why I know it's all wrong
That I'm walking away from the song
That is mine—

Oh god oh god oh god, Mellie thought, I can't stand this. This is too goddam awful, this is. I am not going to start going all heartbroken and weepy over *Sybil Rowe* at this late date and that bastard Colin he was a selfish no-good bum and he started all this trouble come right down to it—I wish she'd *stop*—

When she did, Mellie said in a cool, clear monotone, "Well, that's not what I'd call a lyric that's going to make Steve Sondheim turn green with jealousy, is it? I mean it's fairly lousy and also a little on the sentimental side, isn't it—"

"A song is all you need, boy the rest is for the birds—" Sybil said. "Don't you see that was for *me* . . ."

"Come off it, pet," Mellie said, "it's a maudlin bit of Gay Nineties tear-jerking—"

". . . and that's why I know it's all wrong that I'm walking away from my song . . ." Sybil said as though Mellie hadn't spoken, "you can see, Mellie, why I say it was—it was the same as a *letter*—you have to admit that it says why he—jumped out that window and I—I was the one—"

Mellie said a short pithy word for which her mother would assuredly have washed out her mouth *with soap* if she could, and then she got up and made a move toward the other woman. I must try to comfort her, she told herself, this is real to her, she loved the louse, and finally put a hand on her shoulder, a gentle, compassionate, warm hand, and said, "You did your best, honey child, I was always sure of that. And it's over and done with a long time ago."

"You think so?" Sybil said, not moving under the friendly hand. "It is now and always will be still—God heals it. That day I took the—the song written out like that in green ink when he was sitting there all by himself—with me out doing things to make him a big shot in something he didn't *want* —*leave me alone with my song*. I never knew much about music and I didn't try to learn—the song kept haunting me, I wasn't sure whether it was really the song or Colin—telling me the truth at last. It might haunt me—and never anybody else." Her throat closed up again, her hands opened in a gesture and Mellie filled her cup, this time she drank it thirstily with a sort of my-kingdom-for-a-cup-of-coffee, she said, "You remember Alan Lerner? The *My Fair Lady* man? I'd met him when he came out to give us a hand and made an appearance at that charity ball—remember? So I went to New York and saw him. After he'd run through that song, he said, 'Where is this young man? It's—a little raw—but he has a touch of real talent. We must do something about it.' He thought better of it than you do. So—right then—I did my first mad scene, I began to scream and I said No no it's too late, I pushed him out a window. I want to tell you that Lerner was furious. He thought it was a hoax or that I was some kind of nut—maybe I was coming close about then."

Plain to see, Mellie told me, you couldn't help seeing then as she had never seen when Sybil and Colin were together, that he had been her *world*. The breath of her nostrils, the beat of her heart, she had worked for him, all she did had been done for him, right or wrong she had believed in the time and the place and her way for Colin and that, Mellie thought, is tragedy, isn't it?

"All the gag lines," Sybil said, and you could tell it was so bitter she was tasting it, "they don't become gag lines unless they're true. Each man kills the thing he loves. I did it by killing his soul, his songs, I got him and his songs to where he said *I'd rather be dead.* More people do that to each other —Colin used to say they beat Mozart to death, the one right-from-the-hand-of-God musician of them all. They beat him to death with their greed and their belittling—and Chopin, that man-woman drained him of life and probably all he wanted was to be left alone with his songs—how do we know?"

"Oh come now," Mellie said, "Colin wasn't any Mozart. Let's be reasonable. He wasn't Chopin, either. Make sense, Syb."

"No—probably not," Sybil said, "but when you've hushed somebody's song forever it can seem to you it was as big to *him* as maybe Mozart's were to *him*—we never think—*relative*—" She gave Mellie a smile at last, she's so much *older,* Mellie thought, but her eyes are younger now. I like her better. "All right," Sybil said, "I'm all right. This is where Hank comes in and why I had to tell it to you, all of it. I was always jealous of Hank. He had—Colin had an authentic love for Hank, you know that, don't you? Their friendship—we smudge a lot of things these days with our dirty thoughts but nothing could smudge that. I knew Hank had to blame me—and Colin's death broke his heart. So I went out to California and I told Hank the whole thing. I showed him the book and played him the song, and gave him the Lerner quotes and then right there in his study in the church I went *insane. Bats.* I have always had a lot of self-control, restraint, hold myself in, I always could—I went *insane,* it wasn't like a dam breaking, this was a volcano you were sure was extinct erupting all over the place.

"And I screamed at Hank, I shouted at him, I said, *I can't endure this, it's not to be endured, nobody can be expected to endure things like this,* and in my bag I had a vial full of those green-and-pink pills and I thought if it hurts just one hairbreadth more I will go in the can and take them *all,* there isn't any place to jump from—but it will be the same. And nothing Hank can say can stop me. I can't endure this.

"Mellie, I wonder if—in a way I was too close to Colin to hear his song, and I wonder if you are too close to Hank to see—a prophet is without honor in his own household or whatever—I wonder if you know what it is like when the Spirit takes over? It's odd—it's not—these are things that are too—too naïve or simple or *something*—all the prayer I knew much about was fine and flourishing but it was like flipping a light switch but the electric current hadn't been turned on! Nothing came of it. That day when he spoke to me I knew Hank believed that God was within *blessing distance* for real. To help in anything. A God who loved me, and I was out where I didn't think anybody could love a murderess like me including God. Up to then I hadn't thought that God could or would *do* anything, I wasn't mad at anybody about it and I thought there were a lot of good people in churches and out, some with moral responsibility even, trying to help each other. Doing their best. But—Hank spoke of things no man knows with authority as though he *did* know. He spoke about the kingdom of heaven as though he'd *been* there. He spoke about Christ as though Christ had been *here,* as though he Hank had followed him from Chicago to Beach City and down to the waterfront and—*seen* him, just as Peter and Andrew his brother had in Galilee. He spoke *about God*—not a God afar off, nor tamed and molded and brought to fit modern *thinking.* Mellie, do you know the things Hank is doing? With us keeping the pledge, too, simple people trying to do what Jesus taught? I *talked* to the doctor at the naval hospital. A very game guy, with guts. He said he wouldn't go back on his diagnosis by god and how could he anyhow, because there were the *X-rays,* and he *showed* them to me, Mellie, and he said We do some very fine patchwork and we cure when we can but we can't *heal,* and he blew his nose like a whale. Hate isn't any easier to heal than cancer. Real hate and you know that was real hate in the Cutlers' house. Same kind of hate that's loose in the Congo or in political parties or assassins. Hate worse than in any black-white slum.

"I recognized it, because Colin hated me before I murdered him. No no—it was because he was afraid he was *going* to hate me—you see?

"After I'd done the mad scene from Lucia and Ophelia—and made my confession on my knees—Hank didn't like that but then he saw that I felt more comfortable there, then he bent over and spoke to me and—I never intended to try to tell this to anybody, it's—peculiar talking to you when we've known each other so—so differently—but you will see why I have to. He bent over and spoke to me about forgiveness and this was like the coming of the Holy Ghost and it was *real* because it was *beyond* anything we could think about to *make up,* don't you see that?"

Mellie made a quick compulsive gesture and then put her hands over her eyes. Against the lids—in her mind's eyes?—this scene had come into being. Sybil Rowe wasn't just talking. Now she was projecting an old movie. The church study background was muzzy and brown and blurred, the way it *was,* and there was this dark woman screaming with pain and remorse and self-condemnation, *insane,* and then Mellie could see her on her knees in the old old position of the Magdalen, the bowed head, and the tall young man his face alight with compassion and joy. Joy? Oh yes of course. *My best wasn't good enough for Colin.* But it was going to be good enough for this woman who was his wife because new Hank knew *I live yet not I, Christ liveth in me.*

Where was I all this time? Mellie thought.

Out doing my best, I was, she said to herself.

"In a way," Sybil said, "the wonderful part came after that. He said God had already forgiven me, now I must forgive myself, and I mustn't try to pray *yet.*" She got to her feet and began to pace back and forth, she was driving and driven, "Hank said, 'I don't want any remorse out of you, Sybil. I don't want you to yield any more to this *guilt* business. Guilt—remorse—they are the devil's prize weapons among the good. I don't want you to confess any of this to anybody else or go digging around about why you were such a fiend-in-human-form.'

"Comfort began to come over me—as though I were being warmed after I was almost frozen to death. I'll always remember *the word* Hank spoke to me. 'Remorse,' he said, like Bishop Sheen only more so, 'Remorse is deep and painful regret for wrongdoing. It's a biting back—the biting back of a sin we've done until it mangles us and reduces us to blobs of bloody helpless guilt. It's no good. It has death in it—*mors*—but no God. But repentance—ah, that's another thing. Repentance is to change your mind with regard to a past action, in consequence of dissatisfaction with its results. It's to feel such *sorrow*—not guilt, sorrow—such sorrow for a sin or fault that it makes us change our lives for the better, to think again—repense—to find a new way to live, to move forward in the way he has left for us.'

"Did you ever see Billy Graham operate with a Bible? I went once, and it's an extension of his arm, his own hand, not a *book*. Hank made me listen while he read about the woman taken in the very act and I said Well, that's one thing I never was, and he said What does it matter *what* act, unkindness is the worst, or hate, driving your husband to suicide as you say you did, or planning your own self-destruction the way you were—or judging others without mercy or putting a bright face on evil—all Jesus said was *Go and sin no more*. Five simple words of one syllable each, would you think we could foul up on them so badly for centuries? He didn't say anything about digging into the human mind to find out *why* sin got the best of you, or groveling, or smashing your head on your guilt. Just *Go*. Go back to your life, pick up your redeemed life for I have forgiven you, the devil is cast out by your repentance, go bringing kindness with you, go and tell the good news that there *is* a place to go, no man is expected to break his own bondage all alone, *I* will be with him.

"Mellie—you remember how he and—and Colin used to talk about the Bears and the Cubs and their teams and the *plays* and the draft choices and all that? Hank talks about —about Go-and-sin-no-more the same way—as though it was —a daily part of your life.

"I couldn't believe I'd never actually *read* the Prodigal Son, I just knew some half-baked quotes from it. The fatted calf and filling his belly with the husks and bring forth the best robe. *You know*. Hank lit up like he'd just won the championship when he *read* it to me. He said, 'Now watch this, Syb. After the son had wasted the substance of himself on riotous living and got *tired* of it, he began to wonder if he had a place to go—like home, maybe. He began to be fed up with worries and hangovers and betrayals and boredom and he couldn't find any new ways to sin, all the edge was gone, he was going in deeper and deeper without any real pleasure any more, and now I want you to remember every day of your life what happened to him then. He decided to try to find a new way of life. And just as soon as he so much as turned his head and took one step, the father ran to meet him, to welcome him, to tell him he had some place to go, to turn the light on the path so he could see his way. This story, the greatest story of all the stories ever told by the greatest story-teller of all time, with the greatest character, the father, in it—I think sometimes this was Jesus' priceless gift to us. He gave us a better likeness of God, more enduring than bronze or marble, *close to us.* Notice when the son wanted to do the big beating-the-breast remorse number, *I am no more worthy to be called your son, give me a job as a hired man,* the father didn't even *answer* him. He ignored this *guilt* self-indulgence. Not a word, not a single sentence. The father didn't say Well now, boy, it's true you've been raising hell all over several countries and dragging our name in the dirt and you're a failure and you haven't got a dime in spite of the good start I gave you. You're a disgrace. But maybe we can figure out some way if we put our intellects to work on this. We better figure out first what was *wrong* with you. You'd better sit down, this is apt to take some time, anywhere from a year to five years, once a week at least. Contemplate your sins, mistakes, every feeling especially bad or indifferent, you've ever had since you could *remember* and every dream you've had and what gave them all to you. That should explain why you stayed away so long. No no no no. Nothing like that happened, the father put his arms around his son in love, he was so happy all he could do was try to think of ways to welcome him *home*—so that he'd know how much the father loved him, and that there was music and dancing and happiness and beauty *at home,* it was a great place to be, and he could wear the best robe and not sackcloth and find *joy* not hell. A lot of people are kept from going home by the unlovely character of those who claim to live in the kingdom with their father. But Jesus says the father put a gold ring on his finger and *rejoiced*—the same way the shepherd did when he found his silly old lost sheep, all bedraggled and matted and hungry and unhappy that he hadn't had sense enough not to get lost.'

"Then Hank said, 'The teaching always tells us what to do. Always. Go out and put your talents to work for him as best you can, he's reached out to comfort you. He loves you—say that to yourself. He loves me, I don't see how he can, I don't love myself, but I know, I believe, God does. Go make friends with Gert Cutler. Go raise money for my poor children. Go *organize* some prayer cells for my youth groups. But—Sybil, don't stop there. Too many people stop there. Don't misunderstand me—I'm all for it. I believe in love-for-our-neighbors expressed in loving kindness, in giving them a cup of cold water, in *sharing* our cloak to keep them warm. Don't get me wrong about that. But—that's not enough. If you stop there, some day—comes the day—always comes, it always comes, when they will ask you for something you haven't got. The way Colin asked you and me. There are the *two* commandments—and love God comes first—it has to. Give that a little time, too. Look—every day open the New Testament. Spend some time with it as though it *meant* something. Get inside the fifteenth chapter of the gospel according to the dear and glorious physician Luke. Read the story of the son who came home. Not just once over lightly, not just for size. Every day. It peels off like an onion, a new skin. Then pretty soon your best will be transformed by his best and what they ask for you'll have to give.' "

For the time being, Mellie said, Sybil seemed to have forgotten her.

A light was in her eyes. A reflection of the light she had seen in Hank's. She looked so much *older*. Lines were marked now, deeply carved lines that had changed the whole contour of her face, more like Jeremiah than Jesus or John. Perhaps Paul had looked like that, stern and angry, before he fought his way to the thirteenth chapter of First Corinthians.

Except for the *light*. How did *Sybil Rowe,* of all people, get the light?

For the first time, a sort of despair took over Melanie Gavin.

"Because they could believe and I couldn't," Mellie told me, "I'd never wanted to believe, I thought my not believing all this was gay and superior and à la mode and so *honest*. All this artlessness, and simplicity and *lights,* very bad form. I was being *honest* with myself. I lived in a real world, not a mythical kingdom. But I'd been exposed to some persuasive words, things I'd seen came back, and there sat that two-fisted social climber *Sybil Rowe* looking practically pentecostal. When I saw that Sybil's eyes were shining and she believed she'd been actively forgiven, *for real,* a green jealousy seeped through me. *My father*. He'd seen an angel. The nurse said when the moment came a good many of them had hallucinations, 'Or something,' she said. *I* hadn't seen anything except the light on papa's face when *he* saw the angel Gabriel. I sat there staring at Sybil—and you know, sweetie pie, she was quite right, she *had* driven her husband to I'd-rather-be-dead, *now* she read the fifteenth chapter of *Luke* every day. I felt all my muscles, mental and physical, tighten up, I thought if Hank wants me back or wants to try converting me again, let him come himself, he ought to know better than to send *la belle Sybil*. I will not agree that forgiveness came to her like grace, for free, after what she'd done—nor that some boy in the naval hospital—that's *fantasy*."

All this, she said, was so bitter to her she could taste the gall and wormwood. It's a strong stomach that has no turning, she said to herself, and lit a cigarette and shook the match out in a flaming circle. She offered the box to Sybil and said airily, "Or have you given up this minor vice, too?"

Sybil managed a ragged grin. She said, "Vice? Not unless it's an indulgence stronger than you are," and they smoked together in silence. A minute—an hour— *I* don't know, Mellie said, let her come to me, I decided, she said she had to tell me all this about herself and Colin, it's her move.

Sybil said, "Mellie, when are you coming back?"

One hand lay quietly in the other, palms up. Her eyes appealed. In the hall beyond her door, Mellie heard the telephone ring, her mother's too-eager answer, cars were beginning to hum and roar on the highway, beyond the rusting iron gate in the wall that surrounded the old Cheyne place there were shouts of children on their way to school.

"Am I coming back?" Mellie Gavin said.

"Mellie—" Sybil said.

"Oh for Christ's sake!" Mellie said, and came out of her chair in a leap of anger and stood over the other woman. "Stop saying *Mellie—Mellie*—why should I go back? I gave it a try. I wasn't cut out for a preacher's wife. Do I have any rights? Wives aren't slaves any more. I'm not against your being converted. Good for you! But I haven't—"

"Do you know much about Steve Retzlaff?" Sybil said.

Unexpected, utterly disconnected from her thinking, the name exploded and Mellie sat down and stared at Sybil. "What's he got to do with it?" she said.

Her head bent, eyes on the cigarette as she put it out carefully, Sybil said, "This isn't just a church-real-estate-money-Beach City fight," she said. "This is Armageddon. Everywhere. In Beach City—what do you think of Steve Retzlaff?"

"The average very successful American male, isn't he?" Mellie said. "Going places. Why not? Comes to church, raises money, respected citizen, you and I have known a good many of him."

"He's worse," Sybil said. "If you want to see a well-constructed up-to-the-minute whited sepulcher, take a look at him. Oh sure, he does things for people. As long as he gets plenty of credit whether that drags someone else's pride in the dust or not. As long as everybody says *Look* at what Steve Retzlaff did for the Boy Scouts or poor old Joe Doakes who used to work for him and took to drink, Steve got him into AA, *isn't Steve wonderful?* He sits at night contemplating his brilliant achievements and counting votes like a miser with his gold. Steve Retzlaff is a *vote-counter*. He can't remember any ladder, if there was one, he got rid of it long ago. He's forgotten, he hasn't looked inside his whited sepulcher in so many years he doesn't know what's in there, he's made everybody else forget, too. We're all moving so fast, we're all so busy, the polished exterior is all anybody sees any more."

"For a blessed-are-the-merciful Christian, aren't you a little harsh?" Mellie said.

Sybil Rowe didn't hear her, she was intent on Beach City, California. She said absently, "You have to call a whited sepulcher a whited sepulcher, don't you? You do know Gloria, his wife, isn't Deedee's mother, don't you?"

This time, Mellie's dark eyes opened wide, some of the fresh color faded a little. "Godmama," she said to me, "Deedee's name—and I was *in* it. I don't know why—yes I do. You can fall in love with a girl to be your little sister; falling in love isn't just boy-meets-girl, man-woman, I had felt that way about Deedee, something about her face, her voice when she sang, the way she looked at *that boy*—now she had *no mother."*

Through her mind, backed by a symphony orchestra with music by Handel, went *For I have promises to keep and miles to go before I sleep.*

If anything went wrong with Deedee.

Never again would she sleep in peace.

Shoving back the smooth, shining, dark hair, until it was wind-blown curls, she said, "No. I didn't know. How did you find that out?"

Actually, Gloria Retzlaff had told her. On the building committee together, doing a lot of church work, club work, Gloria seemed lonesome. While Sybil never had Mellie's charm, her easy, arrogant warmth in handling people, there was about Mrs. Rowe a certain firm executive competence which the weaker brothers and sisters, Chicago to California, found dependable and comforting. Before and after a committee meeting, Gloria had confided to Sybil that she'd heard some gossip about Deedee and a *Mexican* boy. "You know how Steve is about that girl," she said, figuratively wringing her hands, "partly, he wants her for the governor's daughter—coming out of church where they attended Sunday services—you wouldn't remember Governor Earl Warren and his daughters, specially Honey Bear. Was that something! But—Steve idolizes Deedee, he really does, when he has time. The only thing he really—and now—oh Sybil," it was a *wail,* Sybil said, "I don't know whether to *tell* him—it might be different if I were her own mother!"

Bang!

Of course some stepmothers were better than real ones, they tried harder, they weren't so resentful of all that had to be done for children—but it was Gloria herself who'd said *if I were her own mother.*

"Whatever became of her?" Mellie said.

"Steve got rid of her all right," Sybil said, without expression.

"You mean they found the body under the cement?" Mellie said.

This flippancy Sybil Rowe ignored. "She took off with somebody else," she said, "and Steve got a divorce *in New York.* This was when he worked there for a while. That may be one reason he's so cranky about Deedee and boys, when he notices. He thinks she might take after her mother. When Deedee was about two, he came to Beach City, everybody thought he was a widower. You will be surprised to find how many things people take for granted about Steve Retzlaff. Of course it's one of the great modern business gifts, making everybody take everything for granted, then finding all of a sudden you have pollution. He stayed single a year or so. There was a girl—named Hetty—*very* bright about money. She was a telephone operator, on the switchboard of somewhere important, the way I get it she *overheard* something and they did very well. Gave him a start. And she moved over to the new Retzlaff Company."

With one hand, Mellie made a gesture to stop Sybil, then decided to say nothing. Sybil had obviously been checking on Steve Retzlaff and Mellie already knew that Sybil Rowe was a trained, experienced, able checker, as a woman must be who had collected and dispensed as much private charity as Sybil had done for years in Chicago. One of Sybil's gifts was that a hint led her to the proper line for investigation.

"When Steve met Gloria, he decided she'd be a political asset," Sybil said. "She came of a good family, she'd been around enough so she had the common touch, she was good with women, she could learn fast, so he married her and got rid of the Witch of Wall Street. He got her a job in Miami. Ever afterward, if anything even faintly fishy came up about those get-rich-quick days, Steve could shake his head and remain gallantly silent. Except for the time when he felt it smart to say, 'I wouldn't say this to anyone but *you,* I feel you have a right to know. Sometimes now I have a feeling that Hetty might not have been altogether scrupulous. She justified things as smart business which you and I might not have felt came inside the rules. That's why I had to let her go, in spite of all she had in her favor—she was smart and hard-working, you know that. But you can see I had to get rid of her.' Maybe he never even told himself that Steven J. Retzlaff was afraid of her, and that he couldn't bear to have anyone around who might get some credit—or expect some credit—for helping him rise. He still can't. Not anything. Not anybody."

"Hank know all this?" Mellie said.

"He knows it," Sybil said.

"Why doesn't he do something about it?" Mellie said.

"He is," Sybil said, "he's praying for him. Mellie—Hank has *faith* in prayer. You can't talk him out of it. If you pray honestly—or try to pray—it connects you with the divine circuit of God's *grace*. Steve has to be *saved*. Not just licked."

"This man tries to stop what Hank wants to do—" Mellie said.

"Hank laughs at me," Sybil said. "He says Look at the way Peter betrayed Jesus, yet in the end it was to Peter Jesus said Feed my lambs. Neither pray I for these alone but for them also which shall believe on me through their word. Hank says that means *him*. He says look at the way Thomas doubted him, but he didn't get sore about it, he was quite willing to give Thomas proof since that's as far as Thomas *was*. He says for him Steve Retzlaff has to be what Jesus meant when he said Feed my sheep. Or take up your cross and follow me. He says maybe Steve Retzlaff is one of his crosses."

Hank says Hank says Hank says!

She could hear him.

All she said was, "Could you be prejudiced about Retzlaff? Darling Sybil, I do remember in the campaigns you couldn't see any good in an opponent."

Very quietly Sybil said, "Steve Retzlaff believes his besetting sins are good. Part of our age, like jet engines. Make a fine *good man* image of yourself, the *end* you want justifies *any* means. Corrupt practice is good business, in government or out. His goodness is as phony as an electric eel, he can squirm around any principle, he was all set to use this bright boy in the church just as he'd used poor old what's-his-name. Then he found out this Johnny-come-lately from Chicago wasn't a tool to his hand, he saw him run the end against the City Council, that scared him, so he really smeared Hank with a trap play, the Brand O'McAddamses acting as tackles ahead of Retzlaff. Now he not only knows he can't handle young Dr. Gavin, he knows that anything that does come off Gavin will get part of the credit, and as I've told you before Steve Retzlaff is never going to share credit with anyone. So he must now get rid of Gavin. You know anything about his mother?"

"Retzlaff's?" Mellie said. "Oh Sybil. Do stop. Don't try to tell me he's cruel to his poor old mother. He wouldn't dare."

"You're right," Sybil said, "he's just wonderful to his mother. It's just that he got rid of *her,* too. At great expense. Nice old biddy, a bit raucous, his father died when Steve was five, mother worked eighteen hours a day as a dressmaker (the Dickens touch, isn't it?) to put him through school *and* college, and sometimes she's so proud of him she brags about it, or comes out with something she thinks is *funny* about it. People who met her thought she might have had something to do with his *success,* a little of what I am I owe to my sainted mother, but Steve Retzlaff wouldn't even go for that. You know that smooth way he has, I'm-helping-the-lame-dog-over-the-stile *patronizing* way, well, once the old lady took a cruise to South America and she's never been off a cruise ship since."

"A likely story!" Mellie said.

"Can you think of a better way?" Sybil said. "You can live on a cruise ship the year round, you know. And so *smart.* You go down and look at a travel folder or meet a cruise ship some day—see all those poor homeless old girls, all dressed up with too many places to go when as far as they're concerned if anybody *wanted* them or they could find anything to *do,* if they didn't feel a nuisance and a burden to their fresh punk middle-aged kids there would be no place like home. Spending their lives sailing round and round and round, playing bingo, watching other people's children swim, meeting other homeless well-to-do widows. And of course all the time everybody saying Steve Retzlaff's so good to his mother, she's one of those compulsive travelers you know, show her a suitcase and off she goes, of course we'd like her home with us part of the time but she has to see *India* before she dies or go back to Bangkok—Deedee told me she cried and cried the last time she left for Japan. And Steve looks as though she'd deserted *him* but he wouldn't say No to his mother." Sybil took a long breath, she said, "That got rid of her, didn't it?"

Deedee's voice saying *he'd be mad enough to kill Beany but he's too cagey for that, he'd run him out of town.* Was that a synonym for *get rid of him?*

The door opened and Vadne came in. Sybil told me that she didn't look old or sick, just disconnected. Nor did she show any surprise at seeing Sybil Rowe. Often in the past young Mrs. Rowe had come in of a morning to discuss plans with young Mrs. Gavin. In her hand, Vadne had a book with a shiny blue jacket. She said, "Whitaker Chambers—wasn't he the man who convicted Alger Hiss? Francis admired him. Francis was reading this—he *marked* it—*a civilization which is at a toppling height*—does that make sense to you girls?"

"It might," Mellie said.

"His marking them it's as though they were his last words to me," Vadne said, "he never had a chance to say anything—" and she went out.

"I always thought she was the important one," Sybil said, they sat in silence for a minute, then Sybil said, "It's a—coincidence, isn't it? Toppling height and leave me alone with my song—Colin's last words. What about toppling heights—I read the other day that when more women in a nation didn't believe in God than did—*then* it would topple. Do you believe that?"

"If so," Mellie said, and smiled at her, "you and I cancel out each other's vote, don't we?" When Sybil didn't answer, she said, sweetly, "You're doing what Colin would want you to do, if he—knows about it. Helping Hank. And even if this is a life-and-death struggle, Hank can call on impressive reinforcements. St. Michael and all his angels and such. Hank is on God's side so he knows God is on his side."

Obviously, Sybil was having trouble with her voice. Finally she said, "All that about Colin—what I found in the book, and the song, and my knowing I'd murdered him and what Hank did for me, I told you so you'd give me the right to speak. I've always been a little in awe of you, Mellie, though you've always been very kind to me. Now I want you to say I have a *right* because of what—of all that—to speak to you."

"Go ahead," Mellie said, sitting carved out of pearwood.

"I'm breaking a confidence," Sybil said, her voice creaking under the words, "Hank has lost his faith. He says either God has forsaken him or it was all a lot of malarkey, or his imagination, or the chaplain selling him a bill of goods so that when Colin died he grabbed at anything. The dark night of the soul, Hank calls it. He looks—I can't tell you how he looks, Mellie. He says if it goes on, he has to give up the church; it would be hypocrisy to go on, blasphemy, he calls it, to preach faith and the presence of the Holy Spirit when he—hasn't any. They'd all hear the sounding brass and tinkling cymbals."

Lines wrote themselves on Mellie's forehead, bracketed her mouth, her face had gone so white the bones showed through, but she did not move nor make a sound.

"If you could have heard the music Colin wrote to his song," Sybil said, "I suppose music was the way God spoke to Colin—but *Hank—*"

Mellie moved violently, her face and eyes blazed into life. Triumph waved from her like a banner. *"Hank—"* she said.

"Oh Mellie," Sybil cried, *"Hank's alive.* Hank's *alive."*

Book FOUR

1

I suspect Mellie didn't let her husband know she was returning to Beach City on that wet, wild, windy evening so he'd have no time to put a better face on all that Sybil had flown to Chicago to tell her.

Her call to me came next morning. "Can you come over?" she said, "I ought to be there, and I've got a decision to make."

"Where's Hank?" I said.

"At a seaman's breakfast, he promised a long time ago," she said.

"Is something wrong with Hank?" I said.

"I'm—afraid so," Melanie said, it was more than a phrase, she *was* afraid, "but I think I've found a way out," she said, "I'd like to hear how it sounds to you, Godmama."

The parsonage was a whirl of activity. Mellie met me in a scarf of oriental orange tied so tightly it covered her hair and left plain to see the tense lines on her lovely forehead, the dark, dry, blue circles of a sleepless night under her eyes. "You'd suppose the Marine Corps taught Hank to police things," she said, giving me a hug, "but you'd be wrong. I never can *think* straight in a mess."

From the hall, I saw Deedee Retzlaff policing the high-ceilinged old-fashioned dining room. The usual worn slacks, a pullover sweat shirt so much too big for her that there was no chance for me to see an answer to Mellie's first-fear question *is she pregnant?* As you grow older they look so *young,* the thought made my heart stand still. I thought I saw on her tender young mouth the print of pain and fear *endured* by children who have been ill too long. Probably Steve Retzlaff loved her most, the one possession he could love without endangering his gay, charming, bland, and unscrupulous vanity, a complement to it—She's my flesh and blood, and she's the loveliest. I wondered if in the midst of his preoccupation with success he'd had time to note his little girl grown up into a woman's troubles. The noisy vacuum she was pushing shut off, I heard the girl humming a small, sad, sweet song in rock 'n' roll tempo, her eyes meeting mine were very guarded, I felt *oh dear* I hope Melanie can deal with this. For once my alleged nose for news gave me no warning of catastrophe ahead.

From the floor above I heard thumps, Mellie said, "Gert Cutler on the job. Can she make beds, I donknow, anything, even Gert, is better than an unmade one. Come out in the sunporch where we can be alone I hope."

Through the back window I saw Beany Teran wielding a bamboo garden rake. Against a bright red sweater his Mexican ancestry was conspicuous, showy, I tried to judge whether he was a descendant of early Mexican-Californians with a drop of Indian, who'd been here when this was the Dominquez Ranchero, a Spanish grant, doing a few hours' work, taking long siestas in the sun, having a whole steer barbecued for them on feast days, cheering cock fights, and from time to time fighting duellos or stabbing in the back with thin knives as sharp as razors and as bloody deadly. Or whether one generation back his people had come across the border down Mexico way a few miles as wetbacks. The boy was more cock-a-doodle-do than I'd been aware. His guitar wasn't essential for rhythm, vibrations came from himself; he moved as all Mexicans do, like a cat, his hair was black as a tomcat's, yet his young young *young* face had the vulnerability, the supersensitivity, the I-love-beauty of a Murillo St. Sebastian I'd seen somewhere in Spain. Watching while Mellie was talking on the telephone, I felt I hadn't given Beany enough attention as a member of this cast. This boy and girl had music in common, all musicians are a bit mad, today all young people are pervaded by music, it moves their lives, floods their emotions as never before in history. As an opponent for Steve Retzlaff this slim boy with his deer-dark eyes was manifestly ridiculous, on the other hand one bullet can bring down a President. Mexican blood is often senseless white-hot and hair-trigger.

Coming back, Mellie said, "Gloria Retzlaff has something on her mind. She wants to see me. Also, Gloria says I must see Bertha McAddams, who *Gloria* says is a snob and became a miser because she thought she could buy her way into society. Ha! This Gloria has a notion that she might listen to me about this goddam lot she's given Retzlaff an option to buy so he can build an office skyscraper—even if I got her in the Social Register it wouldn't change anything. Nothing changes a miser. You know, I rather like Gloria, no brains but sound instincts, she says they missed me."

"They love you," I said, discovering it, "so does Hank."

She gave me a strange look and began to talk.

I have reconstructed here what took place from the time Mellie walked into the house that night partly from what she told me, partly from Hank's answers later, partly from what I knew of the story and characters involved. Listening to Mellie was difficult, telephones ringing, visitors appearing unexpectedly, our consciousness of others in the house. Some of what I now tell you is guesswork, but of the kind a football coach uses when he has seen all the film of previous games. I have cut the film somewhat to eliminate interruptions, to highlight action, avoid awkwardness, clarify thought. I have edited the sound tape to get rid of repetition to which we are all prone. Therefore what I have put together from here on comes out a *tour de force* of truth.

Dusk had fallen upon the turrets of the old house, which as she looked at it from the sidewalk seemed to Mellie impossible. Simply *impossible*. Flying up above the world so high all that Sybil had told her grew in unbearable suspense. No light showed, she couldn't bear it if Hank wasn't there, she ran up the steps, the door crashed open at the push of her palms, in a panic she called loudly, "Hank! Where are you? Hank? It's *me*."

From the kitchen he answered *"Hello?* Who is it?" he was in the doorway, perfectly still. Burned browner, darker, his hair a crest of bleached silver, he was an explorer seeing rescue arrive in a long, snowed-in winter. Younger? Older? A lost-boy look was at odds with the bones of his gaunt face, but it was there. "If you keep on loving the guy," Mellie said, "he never loses that for you, does he" and it was the first time as she told it that she cried.

Whatever it was, Sybil had been right. Life and death. Moment of truth. What, how, where do we go from here?

He was *alive*. Nothing is irrevocable but *death*.

Driving through her emotions like trucks with snow tires, solidly, two things hit Hank Gavin's wife. In this obscure church, this garish *stew* of a town, this state becoming the melting pot for all the other states, in this magnificent country upon which this eighteenth of the recorded civilizations must rest for its possible survival, it was possible that one man, any one man, an ordinary man like Hank Gavin, with an idea whose time had come might be important, the grain of sand on the scales of destiny. How had Hank come by that part of himself which had sent him forth to *here* and *now*, certainly not out of his own flesh and blood and intelligence or feeling? Circumstances which control most men and their movements had not been responsible for this. If he had *lost* something as of today, must there have been something to lose? Was this determination to try to obey the teaching of Christ an idea whose time had come at last in terrible simplicity to a world and time smothered in complications?

Sure as death and taxes, enough of this got into Mellie's head so that she knew this time she could never put it all back into kilter under the system nor by the rules she had used heretofore.

I'm hearing a different drum went through her head, too fast for her to think where it came from, what it meant. A man might be out of step because he was hearing a different drum? With one hesitating step, a rush like Niagara, she was in his arms. His fingers bit into her shoulders, lifting her with machine force, they kissed in pain and rapture and confoundment.

"We were beyond depths where we'd been before," Mellie said, "it was schizoid, while we kissed like *starved* things, my mind was off in a clear series of memories complete, plain, in every detail—quite mad, darling—*little* things I'd seen and heard while I lived as his wife in this place of his ministry in which *I did not believe. Do not believe!* His chuckle with a—a *something,* melting the too—too solid vanity of a silly, dangerous *female,* his hands so kind on a discouraged man's shoulders they literally raised him to *hope,* his voice quieting a child *screaming* with an earache—my mind, lovey, squirreling around, nothing having anything to do with anything else, curious facts of history—all this, remember, took a few *seconds*—Queen Elizabeth the First in such a tizzy about *married priests* in the church her father had left her. She was against it. Wrong—wrong—but we are wrong not to face what it asks of a woman to be married to a priest. I came dragging my heels in utter ignorance, I still—she has to be a saint, to become a greater servant of God than he is, she gives him up, she will never be *first* in her husband's love. A man can neglect his wife for business, for art—when a man gives himself to God, he doesn't belong to his wife any more and if he is a dedicated priest he never will. At the same instant that this hit me full, I saw that now if he had lost his faith I could sneak up on his blind side, take him back, I could defeat God—or this hallucination about God."

When he let her go, she put her head down on his breast and wept.

He was *alive.*

He could be hers again. She had another chance.

Sitting side by side on the couch, she thought they were like any married couple who had been apart, disagreed, applied different philosophies to life. Perhaps they were. Only more so, much more so, at the very extremes of more so. This she realized when she heard a groan of mortal anguish smothered quickly. Turning to look at him squarely, in spite of the radiance of the lamp, the flush of the surprise at seeing her, the joy of crushing her hands between his so he'd be sure she was there, it came to her that if she'd just seen him knowing nothing at all her first thought would have been that he was *wounded.*

"Hank—" she said, "oh, my dear, what is it?"

He tried his best for the tone and dialogue, the words and music, that had been their custom, habit, way of life. His lips smiled and he shook his head at her ruefully. "Don't worry, love," he said, "I suppose the thing that a man suffers from most is making a fool of himself. When I think what I've put you through, selling the house, bringing you away from everything, and now—Mellie, whatever it was, it's—I can't imagine what I thought I was doing—who I thought I was—how I dared—I might as well have gone around telling everybody I was Ulysses S. Grant or Einstein or Hemingway—or Babe Ruth. Mellie, I can't pray any more."

He waited for her to speak.

She said nothing.

For the first time in her life she had nothing to say.

Up to that moment, Melanie Cheyne Gavin had been, as young people are, quite sure of herself. She had come directly from the brow of Minerva or Jove or whoever it was, and even when Hank threw their lives into all this fantastic and unfamiliar pattern, refusing Katie's money, giving up his job, coming to this *dreadful* place, she had come along because she couldn't live without him, but with her own philosophy and standards unaltered and unalterable. Being *right*. As far as she could, she had relieved suffering and given a cup of cold water at the point of impact. Not in the name of a mythological figure of shocking unattractiveness such as she had seen hanging on a cross in Florence and looking as though he'd died of malnutrition and ringworm, but at least in the name of *noblesse oblige*. A feudal friendliness. Man's *humanity*—not inhumanity—to man.

Her theory about Hank when she hadn't been able to conquer him and the Holy Ghost has been the oldest one of all. Give a man enough rope to hang himself.

Did people who said that have any idea what they were talking about?

Yet each man kills the thing he loves—some do it with a flattering word, some with a rope of hemp—here, lovey, have a bit of hemp—to dance to flutes to dance to lutes is delicate and rare when Love and Life are fair and our best is good enough for anybody but it is not sweet with nimble feet to dance upon the air because someone you trusted has just handed you enough rope to hang yourself!

Now she was looking at the hanged.

Out of this macabre, morbid moment she fought her way.

She said, "What you need, dear love, is something to *eat*, some nice chicken broth like Mrs. Glass fixed for Franny and Zooey, remember?" and while she got a steak out of the freezer, averting her eyes from the sink, the floor, the screen porch, she chattered with the bright technique of a girl who has always been a success at any dinner party even between two men she never saw before and couldn't care less. All the time her mind kept operating on two frequencies. Why did the word pilgrimage keep coming up? Her father—that was why—reading *Pilgrim's Progress* and John Buchan aloud to her—

The name of the slough was Despond.

A castle called Doubting—wasn't there a castle called Doubting?

Keep away from the light that never was on land or sea that was on her father's face when at last he looked through the open door of death. From Stu Margolis' wife and what she was doing for women alcoholics—for the time being don't commit yourself or him to anything! Wait till you've eaten a good hot meal and had a night's sleep. Let him talk if he wants to.

About there, Mellie got up and walked over to the

window of the sunporch and pressed her forehead against the pane.

Beyond her I could see that Deedee had gone out to talk to the boy in the bright red sweater.

Girl meets boy.

Here we go again. Round and round again.

Recently in London I had seen the world's greatest actor, Olivier, play Othello, been overpowered by the timeliness and timelessness of this absolutist integrated color scheme of marriage, heard in spoken lines the trumpets of foresight hindsight eversight into man's soul . . . *would ever run from her guardage to the sooty bosom of such a thing as thou. . . . For if such actions may have passage free, bond-slaves shall our statesmen be* . . . and then the pathos of the conquering hero the Moor, no darker than one of our own Mexicans, it may be . . . *when I did speak of some distressful stroke that my youth suffered, she loved me for the dangers I had passed and I loved her that she did pity them* . . . I had always thought that silly handkerchief, the forked tongue of Iago too frail as cause and motive for the brutal murder of a beloved wife, but now I saw a thousand throbs of menace . . . *when she is sated with his body, she will find the error of her choice, she must have change, she must.* And I wondered how many other boys had let themselves be swept away and in that frenzy tried to arouse so young and delicate a girl as Deedee. Or had his guitar spoken for him as Othello's tales of war and blood and death had hypnotized the small golden Venetian child Desdemona? Now again I saw East Side West Side all around the town of Beach City, California, everything changes and nothing is different, everything's different but nothing is changed, no slowing down of pounding blood or life forces, the peace of this world is always impossible unless men keep the peace of God. The honor of women is uncertain unless women keep the honor of God. Then the toppling heights must come tumbling down and at last somebody will ask to open tne whited sepulcher and find even that empty of all but words.

"Does her father know yet?" I said.

Mellie glanced at me over her shoulder and then out the window as though she hadn't noticed the boy and girl. "I don't think so," she said.

"You'd know if he did," I said.

"I'm going to talk to Gloria," Mellie said, and came back to sit down on the couch, feet tucked under her Buddha fashion.

"Is the child pregnant?" I said.

Under the lovely skin, the muscles of Mellie's face tightened, she gave me that little cat grin and said, "Have you given up your conviction that the teen-age guitar-playing set knows how to avoid what Kipling once called the Almost Inevitable Consequences? For a lady who's seen as much of the world as you have, you have some very old-fashioned notions, Godmama darling."

"If it's old-fashioned to think it's criminal to fail to warn those young creatures that there *are* consequences—I plead guilty," I said.

Lying requires skill. Mellie had neither the flair for it nor any experience in it—I was fairly sure now that she had lied to me by implication if not in so many words.

She went on smoothly enough with the story I assumed was leading up to her moment of decision, to consider which I had been summoned.

While Hank watched her unpack, after a dinner he'd eaten ravenously, he told her about his visit to the bishop who was in charge of that district where the Church of the Redeemer was situated and who was, you may remember, a friend of Archie Paddock. As his ecclesiastical boss, Hank Gavin felt he ought to know about the wreckage of faith which had befallen one of his men.

The bishop, it turned out, was a bird watcher, and Hank, arriving early, found him binoculars in hand, watching a flight of heavy-bomber pelicans far inland. It was Hank's impression that this surprised the bishop more than his young pastor's confession and request to be relieved of his duties. Kind, concerned, he admitted the younger man's suffering and offered fatherly consolation, but it was to him a twice-told tale. Everybody lost that first fine careless rapture. Rather, the bishop said, like a cherry orchard whose fragrant blossoms must fall leaving the poor tree with a few little green bumps. Only so could the fruit come. This parable comforted Hank for obviously the bishop had used it often, so it might be true that his descent into hell was not unique. Moreover, said the bishop, this dark night was more to be expected from the *type* of emotional conversion which had brought Hank Gavin into the fold. Also, he added crisply, it was why the church was reluctant to accept such pentecostal and evangelical experiences as a *safe* and *sane* foundation for a life of ministry. Recently, he said, there had been a good deal of this preoccupation with the pentecostal experience, they'd had a veritable wave of it in the seminaries, young people insisting they'd been visited by the Holy Ghost and going about *speaking* in tongues. Within himself Hank thought bitterly don't they *want* any help from the Holy Ghost—the Presence of the Holy Spirit? His thoughts darted here and there, in this cold wasteland where a man is neither living nor dead. He was trying to find some contact with the saint who had walked the road to Damascus, to remember some of his *words,* and as though he had read Hank's mind—or was this again routine?—the bishop said, "You must remember, my son, that after the road to Damascus Paul went away into the desert for years to—as it were—consolidate his revelation and that all his life because of its nature, perhaps, he was distrusted by many of the apostles at Jerusalem."

"He hadn't seen Christ crucified," Hank said, "he had only seen him risen. Do you ever wonder—" but he could not *remember* what he had felt so strongly about the Risen Christ and so under the stern eyes of the bishop he was silent. *Neither living nor dead.*

"The only way I can describe it," he said to me once, "have you ever had your wind knocked out? No, of course not, but you've seen it on the football field. It was exactly like that. I was alive, my brain was in operational order on ordinary matters. My eyes and ears functioned. But I couldn't move at all, I was helpless, and I was afraid this would last forever. Somewhere inside me I was fighting to breathe in what once had been life to me—God's Presence. But I couldn't and I was sure I never could again. I wasn't even sure there was such a thing."

As to the future, the bishop had said in a kindly but firm and businesslike way, it would be well to wait upon events. And meantime not to make nor to demand any startling promises. Times had changed. Hank had moved too fast, it would now be essential to revert to the wisdom of the tortoise. Their main objective must be consideration for his congregation. For the good name and dependability and responsibility of the church. Nothing must be done or said to shake the more solid if less spectacular faith of the members and to do this it was *imperative* that they should know nothing at all about this lack of faith on the part of their pastor. He put his hand on Hank's shoulder and said quietly, "Many of us have these experiences, my son. That is why so many books have been written about the dark night of the soul and why it has been said that the only hell is loss of faith. You have preached Follow the teaching of Christ in all ways. The cross you must carry now, is to *carry on* without letting them suspect your burden. You must not add apostasy to your—mistake in offering them more than you could perform. You see that?"

He had then outlined the practical plan which he, the

bishop, proposed to enforce. Hank Gavin would remain as pastor of the Church of the Redeemer at Beach City, taking up his appointed rounds, continuing his work as usual, as best he could, until the bishop felt that the time was ripe to transfer him elsewhere. Until he could make plausible arrangements, possibly for him to teach for a period, with his degrees he would doubtless be most welcome in one of the smaller divinity schools or even, considering his services to them, at Yale itself. For a time, at least, it seemed to the bishop that this would be better than keeping him in the field. Soon he would be absorbed by the wide machinery, the executive branches, and intellectual levels of the church and his—should they call it zealotry—the failure of this experiment would soon be forgotten.

Hank did not answer him.

He could not.

April is the cruelest month in the wasteland because spring does not come round that year, it seems.

Doggedly he knew that he had breathed in power insensibly, who breathed it now no more, but he could not remember what it had been *like* any more than the men in the wasteland can remember the color or the smell of lilacs in the spring.

He said, as quietly as the bishop himself, "Will the light ever come back?" and did not wait for the answer since he was sure now that the light had been an illusion, an hallucination, *you have to be kidding, don't you?* an aberration, somebody had slipped a marijuana cigarette into his pack by mistake, champagne and vodka had crossed into a potion like that mixed by Dr. Jekyll. It wasn't that he had lost the light, *there had been no light!*

"My dear son," the bishop had said, "the church itself is old and reasonably wise. We've come to know what we can do, what we can't, what people will accept, and what they won't. We belong to the civilization of our times, we've adjusted to it. Better not to promise more than we can deliver, we found that out a long time ago. Once these promises are flung about we're open to fraud, to uncontrolled fanaticism, in danger from the charlatan who claims pentecostal fires and miracles by divine grace. The Catholic Church, which has had even longer experience than we, waited *a long time* before accepting miracles at Lourdes and agreeing that a little girl named Bernadette had indeed seen the Blessed Virgin and therefore must be a saint. You said something, my son?"

Hank's throat was too dry, his tongue swollen too much, he couldn't speak. He had meant to say that if *Bernadette* had waited there wouldn't have been any miracles for them to worry about. And then the moment of hope went sick and gray, he didn't believe anything about Bernadette any more than he believed Cinderella and her glass slipper.

Myths, the simple-minded children of this world went on believing generation after generation, and he must not *stay in Beach City to perpetuate myths.*

"Great things are attained from great hazards," the bishop said. "A philosopher said that. But we find it sounder policy in the long run to calculate the risk and see if it's worth taking . . . whether we're prepared to hazard the church's whole position on such a throw."

Through Hank's empty brain went four words, to a muffled drum.

Came Christ the tiger.

He thought they were from the wasteland, too. But he could not be sure and they made no sense and if he spoke them aloud to the bishop the probability was that he'd include him among the frauds and the charlatans and the slightly demented pentecostal whirling dervishes or the sects or the fringe cults or the spiritualist seances and he would shortly be an uncalculated risk.

Besides, what did they mean—those words?

Came Christ the tiger.

The bishop said, "You understand what we must do to protect others, don't you, Hank? I know Steve Retzlaff has been talking of resigning from your congregation and that is an occupational hazard of itself which we in the ministry have to face. One might, I daresay, call it a mild form of ecclesiastical blackmail. But I really shouldn't like to lose a man as important as Retzlaff; he's very active—and generous. But mainly, you understand, I don't want to cause an open —disappointment. I don't think we need pull the rug out from under them all, do you?"

"No," Hank said.

"Then we'll play it by ear for a bit," the bishop said.

All this Hank told Mellie, brokenly, disconnectedly, trying to get back to their accustomed indirect lightness, to find a witty word, a note of laughter, while she put away her straight dark little suits, hung up the flamboyant little wash dresses, got into an old bathrobe.

The room began to fill with her perfume.

His love was frantic. She did not like the desperation, the escape mechanism of it. "In the morning I thought they might come around with the scarlet letter they sewed on Hester Prynne's bosom," she said, "after the Reverend whatever-his-name-was had worked his will with her. Strangely enough, lovey, while he had his faith and—light—it was quite all right, no sin about it, all right and splendid. Does that seem odd?"

I said it didn't, though why it didn't was too long and involved to explain, except that if you have learned to depend on prayer, when you can't you don't know *what* to do.

"He went to sleep as though I'd hit him with a blackjack," Mellie said, feeling her way now, "and I knew I couldn't sleep so I went downstairs. The house felt so dark and drear—so *empty,* I kept going upstairs to be sure there were still beads of sweat on his forehead.

"I can't say I thought the bishop had been all that helpful, but of course bishops have to combine art and industry, as it were, it's an executive job as well as a spiritual one, he probably thought if Hank couldn't pray it wouldn't be gentlemanly to suggest it, but I thought—he might have liked to know someone else was praying *for* him. However, the bishop's been at this a lot longer than I have. I figured out that the church as it now stands has continued to exist by a brilliant policy of compromise—and there I was.

"I kept walking back and forth in the sunporch and the hall and upstairs and downstairs and I thought about Sybil. For her, there had been no compromise in it. Now here she was prancing along singing a song all by herself.

"You know, Godmama, I have always been hostile to these—*extremes* of Hank's. I mean he was about his religion like a kid who takes a *dare.* You know what I mean? I am all for *de l'audace, encore de l'audace, toujours de l'audace* myself, even if it was Danton who had it as his motto in the French Revolution. On the other hand I used to wish he wasn't so *definite,* it always seemed to me *absurd* this heal the sick, cast out devils, cleanse the lepers, raise the dead—it was one of the things I was angry about, he said the thing they needed most was *hope* and he wanted to give it to them but I daresay so did Danton and all they got was *Napoleon.* In the end. I was willing—*I am willing*—to agree that Jesus Christ was a Teacher divinely inspired but—as the bishop said—all teachings must come to belong to the civilization of their times."

"No," I said, but—fortunately probably—she didn't hear me.

"My mind began to work and—I want you to know that I'm now willing to come part of the way. In Chicago, I found nothing would ever be any good to me without Hank. No wealth. No travels. No David Kenyons. No nothing, as the kids say. Music doesn't sound the same, lovey, and pictures don't look the same—I know why they are bored. And it's really strange—the thing that brought it all into focus for the compromise that would be perfect was the *picture* of Hank standing there in the door and his hair looked *silver*. I know it's tow-bleached-white, you can see plenty of it down on the beach. But it was—good theater for Hank, if you know what I mean. Isn't it *true* that the Christian Church used beauty and music and color and ritual—*the theater*—candles like hands praying—the vestments—so I didn't see anything wrong with realizing that his hair was the pale white of eternity as someone said, and it changed him, I knew it had probably been bleached by the sun, but it looked as though it had turned white with a night of suffering. All right is there anything wrong in saying it looked like a halo?

"I saw what it was going to mean if Hank gave up the church—and I knew because I know him, he hasn't got a half measure in his future planning and never did have—I saw several things. When Hank Gavin gave up Grandmama Katie's fortune which would have made him a very rich young man, he *did* give all his goods to feed the poor—universities and education is the salvation of the masses they tell us—he did give it all up to follow Christ as he understood him. Simply, exactly. Katie being dead, he let her bury herself. He left a smashing job and bypassed the golden calf completely. Everybody thought he was *mad,* including me. You remember, I thought he had to be kidding. Still, this was in the image of Schweitzer, and hadn't one of the Mellons galloped off to some island to found something, it was sort of in the tradition of *Profiles in Courage*. Everybody thought he was nuts, but they respected him. As though a good quarterback refused satchels full of gold to go to medical school. But if he went back! I could hear it. As you know, no one had been more successful, popular, or *healthy* than Hank Gavin, he hadn't been stricken or become a dope addict or lived hungry in a slum, there wasn't any reason for him to come to Jesus, he was their own man, top of the tree, so it made them *think*. There was Al Patton's kick-off breakfast, remember? And the legend of Mrs. Margolis now in the process of canonization, to give it up after all that hurrah and come back with his tail between his legs—oh, they'd welcome him, say: Got some sense finally, did you? All surrounded by an aura of the ridiculous. Nothing is more limp than a deflated balloon. The girl who against all family opposition gives up everything to enter a convent shares the vocation of many saints. If she takes off her habit and veil, isn't there a bright edge of contempt? Of course there is. How are you going to trust people who do not know their own minds? A man who wanted to search for a *meaning* to life, who claimed he couldn't put up with the hopelessness behind our glittering façade without giving God a fair chance to prove that union with Him is possible and gives hope—if he quits he's going to be an embarrassment to ordinary rough-shod unpsychopathic citizens. A man having put his hand to the *plow* and looking back might as well trip over a banana peel—I looked that up at 4 A.M., it's in *Luke*—not the part about the banana peel—I just saw that as the way Hank would re-enter Chicago.

"In a flash, my pet, I knew what to do. I know what to do.

"Or—I did. Goddam it!"

Confidence in her ability to keep as many balls in the air at once as the juggler of Notre Dame came up in Melanie like a fountain.

A way. *The* way. *Her* way.

Hank was still struggling, doggedly determined not to let them down. Bent on carrying out his plans for their church, his experiment *in his steps,* keeping his *wild* promises. Yet well aware that if he stayed in Beach City he must try to conceal his so-sore loss behind what was—to him—a dishonest front. His wife wasn't going to stand by and watch him yield inch by inch to Steven J. Retzlaff's local machine, glossed over by a phony display of goodfellowship. If she—Melanie Cheyne Gavin—handled Steven J. they could make a deal in the best traditions of secret diplomacy. She'd go into how much her mother needed her. The settling of her father's estate. Her charities and interests which she'd taken back to some extent during the time she'd been forced to be at home again. If Mr. Retzlaff would help her to play this right, Hank Gavin could be recalled to serve the church in Chicago where he *belonged*. For all his love of Beach City, his promises, she would say, if there was no protest from the membership nor the board, and surely Mr. Steven J. Retzlaff could take care of *that,* she—the minister's wife—would see to it that he appreciated the *necessity* for returning to the place where she was so badly needed and where, as far as his work, his call, was concerned he could do the most good.

It meant some careful and expert manipulation but she was sure she could manage it—and after all this would enable Mr. S. J. Retzlaff to accomplish once more what he had done so often and so well in the past—*get rid of* someone who might get in his way—who *was* getting in his way.

There it was. A simple uncomplicated answer.

Best for everybody.

An answer now, possibly for the rest of their lives.

For as far as the Chicago end was concerned, Mellie saw *her* way—*the* way—quite clearly.

In any business, the assets of the young Gavins in these circumstances would be recognized. The bishop was old, frail, his hand no longer sure. The new young man who'd dropped the brick at Al Patton's angel breakfast wasn't up to it. A peculiar town, Chicago. Able for years to turn their strong square backs on ferocious political corruption unequaled in any other city, they were able to likewise admire most a man of incorruptible honor honesty and integrity and accept from him leadership in business under the guise often of humor. Their great fortunes and families held together and survived death, taxes, insanity, mild and not-so-mild, with the rugged quality that made the settling of the *Middle* West more important if not as spectacular as that of the Far West, though the man who grew the wheat wasn't as romantic as the one who roped the cattle.

They were on the whole at once amazingly naïve and likewise sophisticated. Nobody *too* religious would suit them, on the other hand they didn't like a minister to be too worldly, either. Not withdrawn from their way of life but *sincere* about God, no mysticism, whatever that might amount to, but no modern intellectual run-around either. The Board of Trade in those commodities upon which man's life depended had been the center of their lives and culture long before the Stock Exchange arrived in their midst. They didn't want a preacher to talk too much about the Holy Ghost, who was not their favorite member of the Trinity, but neither did they want him telling dirty stories in order to be one of the boys.

If you said Hank and Melanie Cheyne Gavin to them, it would be like switching on a jet engine. She and Hank could get Al Patton to be head of the board, a job he'd refused for years, Mrs. Gavin would put Mrs. Margolis at the head of women's slum and vice clearance and unmarried mothers, bring Sybil Rowe back to take over female finance and fund-raising, and remain herself in charge of hospitals and child welfare. Hank could play golf again at the Onwentsia and this would be good for the church, too, it would teach them as it were to recognize God's golf handicap, and Hank would soon be popular and powerful as a figure in the city. He could be Hank again, with a mission.

This *experiment,* this trial-by-terror, this alpha-and-omega or whatever it was unto the angel of the church of Beach City California hadn't *worked.* That was why he had lost his faith. Steve Retzlaff and Bertha had proved to him that it didn't work and he'd taken it hard, he had descended into hell as the saying went. It couldn't be done here in this exile where there was no music, no theater, no social life as they'd known it. But she was sure that back in Chicago, back in his own environment he'd get back his faith, he'd be reconciled to the premise that it was *better to go to church as it was than not to go at all*. This was what had been keeping the churches full for the past years, ever since the war. Maybe you didn't get much but you got something.

"Put up with me, darling," Mellie said, smiling a little, "*little* things can be so important and change the destiny of any man or woman—and it was his—his silver hair that made me see this as possible. As right. Isn't that silly? But it did. And you'll remember it was Kennedy's *hair* they kept talking about that kept him so youthful, so the spirit of youth. It was the thing after he was gone that everyone referred to. Molly Kazan's divine poem—I memorized it—*his thatch of brown hair looked as though it had grown extra thick the way our wood animals in Connecticut grow extra fur for winter*—and a reporter on our own Chicago *Daily News*—Peter Lisagor—who when he wrote about Kennedy couldn't believe this had happened to the young man with the wheat-colored hair—and some big Indian leader from Bombay who spoke *first* of the *boyish* shock of hair. Somehow Hank's silver hair would show the people in Chicago how he had changed, how he—it was the silver crown for a *minister*. Do you know what I mean? This would be good theater—right casting. He wouldn't be *just* the same Hank Gavin who'd been the top investment man in town. In a way, it was the deciding factor when I was sure this—this compromise was right. For *us*."

The interruption which startled us both was Deedee, when she came in she looked as though she'd just crawled out of Juliet's tomb, but when Mellie smiled at her and said, "How's my girl?" she came to life, she said, "Could I make Beany a sandwich—he's so hungry—" and Mellie said, "Bring him in—and you're welcome to anything you can find." Deedee dropped a kiss on the top of her head and went out. Mellie said, "You see how much good we can do in Chicago, don't you?"

Unexpectedly, my whole being followed hers. I wanted Hank to be sensible and I felt somehow that he would. I wanted him to be led by Mellie's love of people, and theirs of her. To give up this leave-your-nets *experimentum crucis*, this *extreme* venture. Look at the power of the intellectuals in the church today. At the agnosticism and atheism and don't-give-a-damn-one-way-or-the-other outside it, especially among the young who hadn't been taught anything except that for some reason they couldn't understand they were running things with no one to say them nay. None of them had ever been taught that the greatest story ever told had anything to do with them and their poor silly ferocious unhappy youth.

I didn't want Hank Gavin to go any farther with his claim of answered prayer in everyday life. The fight ahead would be life-and-death, it always had been.

If Hank had lost his faith in that light of which he had once told me, what would there be to fight for—or with? Could he settle for an intellectual concept, a meek-and-mild pleasantness, for a return to the letter where there might be no fervor but would be a *reasonable* chance to serve in a foreseeable way? The pressure of the school, of realism, so-called, would flatten anybody unless *faith* was there, active, poignant, strong enough to move mountains and *moving* them in the combat. Just recently, I had found that when I went to swim in the ocean I could still ride a wave in, or go under it, I could no longer handle the violent backwash of the undertow. Best not to go out too far. Considering Mellie's cool and satisfactory affection for people, her ease in making things the fashion when she was the reigning debutante, her expert way of handling disturbed characters—the incident of the girl in the shocking pink dress at the cotillion came back to me—considering Hank's popularity and personality, as a team I could see them, the verve, the *style,* the *noblesse oblige* approach, the lack of any fatal puritanism, a word the devil had made do a lot of his work of late. I wanted these children to have all worldly goods. Why choose the rough when they could have it so smooth? Within Hank's call, they could do so much for so many. *The poor ye have always with you.*

"Why did you say first you *knew* what you were going to do and then you didn't?" I said.

Mellie tightened the scarf around her head, her eyes narrowed. Without a word, she went out. Voices murmured from the kitchen as I heard her feet run upstairs. Deedee and Beany passed the back window, heads close enough for whispering, I heard the purr of Deedee's sports car.

When she came back, a book was in Mellie's hand, she held it open, peering down at it. A worn book, dog-eared, underlined, notations scrawled in the margins. "I wish books would leave me alone," she said bitterly, "out of your memory, or your subconscious—they're worse than television, they are. They make your thinking. Papa and *Pilgrim's Progress,* Hank and the New Testament, Colin and Keats. Once upon a time Dante and Milton Browning Kipling—when you were young it was Edna St. Vincent Millay, wasn't it?"

"My candle burns at both ends it will not last the night,

but ah, my foes, and oh, my friends it gives a lovely light—" I quoted, "Yes, it had an effect on us. She was a true poet, you know. Yes, she was—is—part of my thinking, as Shakepeare is of all the world that speaks English."

"My day in school was the beeg T. S. Eliot explosion," Mellie said, "bad as the Beatles, that was. We didn't understand it much, but we absorbed it and squealed and we had an English teacher who drove us to it. In the preface here it says T. S. Eliot exerted the strongest influence on the thinking and conduct of *times*, and got the Nobel Prize for the power and authority of his contribution to literature. I was trying to find what he said about the *Hanged Man* and whether somebody gave him enough rope to do it with. Isn't there something about a *Hanged God*, too?"

"That's Frazer," I said, *"The Golden Bough."*

"Is it!" Mellie said. "I dug this book out to find what Eliot means by *Came Christ the Tiger*. Hank quoted that, you know. I didn't know whether that meant Christ was a Good Guy or a Bad Guy. Here it is—in the juvenescence—apparently I looked that up, a note says it means reaching the age of youth, going up to it or slipping back into it—*In the juvenescence of the year came Christ the tiger*—in a poem called *Gerontium* of which I must admit I can make neither head nor tail. But I kept thinking if Eliot was alive now he'd pick up that commercial Put Christ the tiger in your tank, he and Whitman both liked to use modern symbols, better than so much about sheep which we don't really care for, let the church put Christ the tiger in your tank and get to heaven faster—very sound imagery and rather like Jesus and *fishing*. Do you think the church has a tiger?"

I said nothing. I was watching the actual physical change taking place in her face.

"Once I asked our dear teacher if anyone ever called Eliot *Tom* instead of T.S.—here sweetie, I want to read you something—"

I could see the printed lines on the page quite clearly as she spoke them. Low, entirely without emphasis.

"Thus your fathers were made
Fellow citizens of the saints, of the household of God,
being built upon the foundation
Of apostles and prophets, Christ Jesus Himself the
chief cornerstone.
But you, have you built well, that you now sit helpless
in a ruined house?"

She juggled the book, her eyes closed, she repeated the last words with a drumbeat in them—"sit helpless in a ruined house—" and she said, "Is that true? Is it true? Don't answer —listen—

"You, have you built well, have you forgotten the cornerstone?
Talking of the right relations of men, but not the relations of men to God.
'Our citizenship is in Heaven'; yes, built that is the model and type of your citizenship upon earth."

For a moment she stumbled, her face had gone white and still—she said, "—it explains here why we haven't found the Holy Grail and then—

"Remember the faith that took men from home
At the call of a wandering preacher.
Our age is an age of moderate virtue
And of moderate vice
When men will not lay down the Cross
Because they will never assume it.
Yet nothing is impossible, nothing,
To men of faith and conviction.
Let us therefore make perfect our will.
O God, help us."

A cry. O God, help us, was a cry. The book fell, Mellie shoved it aside with her toe. I heard a car stop, feet coming up the walk, if Mellie heard it she paid no attention. She said, "If we went back to Chicago would Hank sit helpless in a ruined house? I will not—" she snatched up the book, frantically riffled the pages, she found the lines and spoke them in italics, changing one word, "This is the way the Hank ends, this is the way the Hank ends, this is the way the Hank ends, not with a bang but a whimper." The door moved, very low she said, "I will not—if the bang blows us to *hell*—" A woman's voice called, the door stood still, I heard Hank speak and then the woman, asking a question, Mellie still ignored it. She said, "I'm not going to let all those people get hurt. They believe what he told them; joy is the carrot and hope is the light— I didn't start this goddam bang but I'm not going to let it end with a whimper."

Hank came in with Gloria Retzlaff, who was so glad to see Mellie she began to cry. Together they went upstairs, Hank watched them go.

Nothing I could do. You cannot give what you have not got. I wasn't sure which end of the tiger I had hold of. All I wanted was to go home and think about all this. So home I went.

2

On the sunporch, Hank and Sybil, who'd come in together.

In Mellie's bedroom. Two women facing each other in the big window seat, facing the crisis moving in on Gloria's stepdaughter.

At my beach house, where I found the chaplain's letter waiting for me.

Simultaneously, these scenes at three different levels.

Hank's hello to Sybil was vague, he didn't know of her trip to Chicago, nor her part in Mellie's return.

His mind and body were in turbulence, he was still re-experiencing the prayer breakfast and his session afterward with Steve Retzlaff, going over and over it, over and over.

Jack Nestor, who was president of the union, had arranged that prayer breakfast. Of these, President Lyndon Johnson had said that they were becoming again a practice in our times and that such assemblies, for moments of strengthening prayers, were one of the oldest public traditions of our national life.

"Be kind of like your morning prayer meetings," Jack Nestor had said cheerfully when he asked Dr. Gavin to speak.

There, with several hundred men in work clothes gathered around long tables, Hank Gavin had known for the first time the agony of trying to feed the multitudes from empty hands, shame and guilt had filled him as poignantly as the power of pain might have done.

Standing there tall, tanned, his manner automatically as easy as it had been at fund-raising or civic breakfasts in the Chicago days, he had gotten by. *Just!* As far at least as the men were concerned. Most of them were ex-servicemen, they knew he'd been in Korea, carefully—almost wistfully—he'd read to them what General Harold K. Johnson, Chief of Staff of the United States Army, had said at a presidential breakfast on the value of prayer in moments of danger. *Fourteen years ago on a lonely road just southeast of Pyongyang, a road that was deserted except for a small handful of American defenders, a lonely commander was deeply troubled by the threat to the men that he was charged with safeguarding. Could he do the job that was his to do and still give his men a fighting chance to survive? And out of the still of the night, as if from some great distance, came God's voice saying, "Be strong, have no fear, I am with you." And in the years that have since passed by, I continue to turn to God, both in my infrequent hours of accomplishment, to thank him, and in my frequent hours of tribulation to seek his help. In short I am here because I believe. I am sure that you are here because you believe.*

So he, Hank Gavin, hadn't had to say *I* am here because *I* believe, he'd been able to let the Chief of Staff say it instead.

If there was any place he knew he could sound as though he put his heart into, it was a lonely road somewhere southeast of Pyongyang, where he could still hear the chaplain shouting, "When *he* joined the two men on the road to Emmaus, remember it was after *he had risen.* Nothing should make you doubt he can still join you on this lonely road somewhere southeast of Pyongyang." Hank's heart had stood still then, perhaps that was where it had really begun, the wonder had now ended. He had thought *suppose it should be true.* Suppose you could walk a road with the Risen Christ!

At the breakfast he had meant to go on, to speak about answered prayer from which came daily strength for daily needs, he was too long getting his breath and from the floor a question hit him about prayer cells. A deep rough voice said: "My wife's taken up with what she says you call a prayer cell. What the—what is a prayer cell, I don't get it." And Hank had said easily enough, "Where two or three are gathered together in his name, he promised to be there in the midst of them—like on the road near Pyongyang. A prayer cell is a small group, meeting in unity of purpose in his name—once a week—every day—in your neighborhood. Here—for instance, you could have one for ten minutes just before you go to work—two—six of you—remember, *no talk.* Don't turn it into a bull session or a debating society. *Pray.* Come together in hope, stay together in prayer, silent or spoken as you like, part in new faith. It *works.* That's all I can tell you about it."

The words should have choked him.

Hypocrite!

I am here because I believe. *Pray.*

Liar!

He'd waited, hoped, pleaded then. No moment of light

came. No sound of an answer. All he had was a hole in his gut.

And he was sure he hadn't given any man there a ray of hope, a pulse of strength, a mustard seed of faith. The very thing he'd been crusading against, lip-service, glib quotations, trade talk, patter and personality, that's what he'd given and that occupied a pleasant breakfast hour—he might as well be Soupy Sales—and perhaps this happened to *all men* of his, perhaps *right here* was where they turned back and followed no more in his steps, settled for *the letter*—spoken glibly as he'd spoken it.

Finding Steve Retzlaff beside him as they walked out through the crowd, Hank said, "Is your deal with Mrs. McAddams complete?" and knew that he had led with his chin. If there were any more mistakes around, probably he'd make them.

"We can work this out if we sit down together," Steve said, forthright, charming.

Not speaking, Hank stared at him. This was a man like the men he'd always known. To some extent, he was—he was *the* young American businessman. He—it came to Hank Gavin that in a way he liked—he could like—Steve Retzlaff. They'd have gotten along all right.

"We intend the same thing," Steve said.

"No, we do not," Hank said with such force that Jack Nestor turned to look at them. "All right—it's your move, I'm willing to talk it over."

The small waterfront cafe was clean, empty, the proprietor said *Morning Mr. Retzlaff,* from their back booth they could hear the juke box already playing, a Second World War tune that reminded Hank instantly of Colin. It's that kind of day, Hank thought. *Don't sit under the apple tree with anyone else but me, oh oh oh*—a gay tune, it timed him to say lightly he hoped, "If we're supposed to be on the same team, I thought it dirty pool of you to offer that poor old lady we both know to be a miser thirty pieces of silver to break their promise to me and let you option that lot so you can build bigger buildings thereon."

Steve smiled. He looked surprised, superior, and amiable. "Hey padre," he said, "thirty pieces of silver—that's a bit rough—isn't it? You knew Olin had spoken out of turn. He can't deliver without her and he can't deliver her. When I decided to let that Zone Variance go through the City Council—"

"You mustn't say things like that, buddy," Hank said, "if we're going to try to work things out together we must tell each other the truth. Neither one of us had a thing to do with that going through, that was God's answer to prayer. Second, under no circumstances am I going to let you run my church."

"It's not your church," Steve Retzlaff said, too quietly.

A wave of despair, discouragement, black-hearted remorse, chill loneness swept over Hank Gavin and he could feel drops of sweat between his shoulder blades. Do unto others —he could at least hold onto that, even if you didn't believe there was a God, you could hold onto trying to do that—not just to nice old ladies, or the men he'd spoken to that morning who were part of a vast historical change, but to young, self-satisfied leaders, the executives of the new society. Preach the gospel to every creature, it said, the vaingloriously know-it-all, thirty-pieces-of-silver embryonic ulcers, ambition-the-sin-by-which-the-angels-fell, teen-age daughters, dull marriages, these are being persuaded by the Enemy whatever you want to call him or it, they were all under attack, but these were the votes Christ hadn't got and he wanted them, needed them if the world was to be changed back, brought back to power under God. For the first time in this ignominious purple pit, this last ditch, into which he had fallen he knew why if there *was* a God he might choose a guy like Hank Gavin on a barge in the middle of Lake Michigan; he would figure that a guy like Hank Gavin could speak to these kind of people, people like Steve Retzlaff and even Olin McAddams, speak their language, *reach* them —and Hank Gavin could see why without them the battle might be lost—the modern Armageddon.

Maybe Retzlaff had sensed his weakness, for now he was saying forcefully, some of the threat showing, ". . . you must admit I have never attempted to deceive you. I think you're off the beam about where to build this church and a number of other things. I've told you this from the beginning. As I say, it's not *your* church. Not altogether. I have an interest in it, too. Long before you showed up, I'd been giving it a good deal of time—*and* money, in my own way I got a lot out of it, too; it's our church as much as it is yours. I don't like this high-falutin' program of yours—and neither do some of the others. We're not angels, we're just ordinary average pretty good guys, trying to do the best we can for ourselves and our kids and—we're community-minded. This is my town—our town—and you come in out of the blue with a lot of way-out ideas about the *Holy Ghost* and *In His Steps* and want to take over my real estate deals—"

"I wanted you to make one for Our Lord," Hank said, and wondered bitterly, *bitterly,* if it always had to sound like that, pompous and priggish, and like that record out of the British show *Beyond the Fringe—my brother Esau is an hairy man but I am a smooth man*—and knew forever and beyond any doubt that it always sounded like hollow drums and untuned guitars and tinkling cymbals and fake political orators unless it was *real,* unless it had love, unless it was alight with faith and merry with hope. *Real* love and faith and hope.

". . . and don't get the idea I'm not in favor of presidential prayer breakfasts," Steve said, pressing his advantage a little bit, "good thing for the country. Keeps up our morale. And our morals. What I'm not in favor of is mixing religion and business, or politics and religion—I don't think the bishop is either, is he?"

Oh oh oh—don't sit under the apple tree with anyone else but me—the juke box filled the pause while Hank Gavin tried to control a tidal wave of anger such as he hadn't known since the poor dark little battlefields of Korea. When it ebbed he found himself flung up on the shore like a piece of flotsam or jetsam or seaweed. *Hopeless.* Was he supposed to go on with this when he himself was *hopeless?* What did people *do* in trouble when they couldn't pray? How did they live their *days* with no one to turn to for help? What rope held for them in perilous moments on the climb?

He said, "The Man I've promised to follow, if God gives me the strength, didn't stay out of *anything.*"

"And look what they—" Steve began and Hank cut him off with real violence. "*You* look," he said, "he didn't have to let them do that, you know. He accepted the full attack in the war between good and evil, he went into every battle, he never ducked anything, the way you agree to do when you enlist in any war. He won. Remember that, will you? *He won.* Maybe he lost a battle or two—but he came down from the cross—and he won the war. Or we wouldn't be sitting here talking about him. There are chances we have to take—"

"Times have changed," Steve Retzlaff said almost soberly, "I don't think any of us really took that seriously—that *in his steps*—it's a fine idea, I agree, and it's all right for you—that's your business. But in *my* business I feel I'm using the talents he gave me to the best of my ability, and he told us to do *that,* too. I think the best way for us to work together is—with all due respect, padre—for each of us to tend to his own business."

Their eyes met.

"It won't work that way," Hank Gavin said, "I can't deal with you as treasurer in God's house and of his congregation of which I am *minister* and pretend I don't know what you're doing to defeat me about McAddams' corner of Pacific Coast Highway and 22nd Avenue which I don't think is *Christian.* I can't separate the Christian life from the everyday life—they've got to converge—convergence is our only hope—don't you see that?"

He dried up. How much was he supposed to say when he had to struggle to say any of it, when he was only *talking* a good fight, when he was fighting in a whited sepulcher where the air was bad so he couldn't get a good solid breath that didn't stink?

Steve Retzlaff got up, he said, "Doesn't look like we're going to converge on this, does it? My first resignation was a gesture, so you'd have a free hand. This time I'll put it on paper as soon as I get back to my office—and this time it's on the level."

Staring at Steve Retzlaff's back going out through the dark empty bar, Hank Gavin's mind raced to his first day in his first—and it might well be his last—church. *Unto the angel of the church in Beach City I know thy works that thou art neither hot nor cold*—that's the way Steve Retzlaff wants to keep it—and I'm not going to be able to do anything about it—*I know how thou hast tried them that say they are apostles and have found them liars* and the biggest liar and fake and son-of-a-bitch in the bunch is Hank Gavin, you yourself, buddy boy—*Repent and do thy first works* —oh God if I only could. I can of mine own self do nothing and that's all I've got now is mine own self my piddling puny *smart* self—*Or I will come quickly and remove thy candlestick out of his place*—don't bother, if I can't get out of this I'll remove myself—I have all Job's boils, I *am* one of Job's boils, that's what I am—I ache all over—

He was still aching all over when it seemed to him without any intermission that he could remember there he was in the sunporch of the parsonage, Sybil was talking—*Sybil*— and apparently from what she was saying he had confided to her some of the things he'd been thinking—for all he knew he had told her he was one of Job's boils, she was saying ". . . it makes *me* remember that afternoon in the Yale Bowl when Colin kept saying what's *wrong* with him for God's sake, and it turned out you'd played the whole last quarter with a broken *toe*."

"Boola Boola," Hank said, focusing on her as she sat on the end of the couch, "big stuff, rah rah Gavin."

"Don't be childish," Sybil said, "I don't say I'd be as good as Retzlaff, but I've always been treasurer and fund-raiser of everything I've been in, I've made a few friends around here, if it's any good to you I could carry on for a bit, if you want to accept his resignation."

"Who told you anything about his resignation?" Hank said.

"You just did," Sybil said.

"I might just as well throw you into a cement mixer," Hank said. "What does it prove if I have to accept Steve's resignation? Where does that get us? All right, it's blackmail and maybe I ought to call it. Either way, I lose, he's licked me. Would that be loving my neighbor—even if he is my *enemy*—pray for them that despitefully use you and persecute you—they need it most—I mean if we're on the level with this—don't you see this is where loving your enemy comes in?"

"I find it difficult to love Steve Retzlaff," Sybil said.

"All right—let's stick with our line—if you only love those you'd love anyhow—what thanks have you then? Anybody can do that," Hank said.

"Hank," Sybil said, "you're not going to quit, are you?"

"I—can't stand much of this," Hank said and began to pace up and down, "I can't stand lying to the Holy Spirit. I can't stand this—ham performance I'm giving. How low do you get, acting a part, deceiving these good, decent people? It's like robbing a kid's bank—pretending I'm carrying a light when I'm darker than they are. I think I better quit trying to be a hero and tell the coach I've got a busted leg. I'm a flat failure."

"At the time of the crucifixion a lot of people thought the whole thing was a failure," Sybil said uncertainly, "and—a good many times *since* it's looked that way. Only it never—it never *is*—Hank, you don't know how it would shake them. Our faith—it's not even faith yet, it's mostly just hope—Gert'll feed her mother-in-law ground glass or vice versa and there's Jack Nestor going to have his first lil' ole prayer cell. Maybe—you know St. Teresa—I forget which one—I read something about her saying *dry* prayer is the most acceptable—dry prayer when you don't believe, she means, and she says it works. If you keep on even with dry prayer—of course, too, you have to figure that you can *take* Steve Retzlaff any time you want to. He isn't in your class as an operator. I saw you in Chicago."

In a sharp clear whisper Hank Gavin said, "It's not good enough. Beat up as I am, I know that one when I see it. They offered it all to him. *Your own people,* Pilate told him. The board of directors of your own church, they delivered you to me, Pilate kept saying, *I* haven't accused you of anything, he probably said take my advice young fellow, stop throwing out the moneychangers, or arguing with their lawyers, or exposing the important Pharisees, or hollering right out in church to a man with the withered hand—*stretch it forth*—you behave yourself, Pilate probably wanted to say, you're young, you got time, you do the way men better-educated, more sensible, much more experienced tell you to and you'll be a full-time rabbi, and that's not a bad job, buddy. *Recant*—they told Joan of Arc, say you never heard any *voices* or saw any lights—and she had *moments* when she wasn't sure— Of course Jesus wouldn't agree, he wouldn't back down and be humble to the world at God's expense—they kept on tempting him—be *reasonable,* boy—no *miracles*—and—" Hank Gavin took a long deep shuddering breath, he said, "It *says* he—he himself was tempted like as we are—and they kept on tempting him throughout his whole life, not just in the wilderness. Make up some act to show off what a big shot you are with God, jolly them along, dazzle them with your footwork—you've got a lot on the ball just on your own. Of course, pretty soon, the angels wouldn't come any more—they offered him all the kingdoms of the world if he'd play it their way, and Jesus said—he said Look, friend Satan, if my kingdom was of this world, then we'd fight you and you or anybody else couldn't perhaps deliver me anywhere. What good is it to do it that way *again?* It's been done so many times. Peter woke up in the garden and saw Judas and the cops, Judas had squealed and so the cops decided they had enough evidence to make the pinch—the big fisherman always had been a fighter, so he ups and cuts off a cop's ear. Jesus said, Simon—it's no good. They'll get you in the end. Sooner or later somebody will get a bigger bomb, or more nuclear weapons or a death ray or something. We must win by the power and presence of God, we must discover the kingdom within us, we must stick to the way of God's will, or my teaching will die again and again and again.

"Sybil—I've lost the faith that makes it work—I'm not even sure—anyhow, I've got to leave it that if there is a God He can remove a little mountain like Steve Retzlaff and if I did it on my own I already know my best isn't good enough, don't I? So what good would that do? Have I got to cut Steve Retzlaff's ear off and then try to heal it? Am I supposed to betray what I—I did believe—"

"As far as Steve Retzlaff goes—" Sybil said, and Hank cried out, "You don't understand. He's my boy. He's the man I was sent to get. Don't you *see* that? He's the symbol of all that Christ wants—"

"You still sound like a minister of Christ to me," Sybil said.

"Don't I!" Hank said, "talk talk talk is a habit. Christ! Houdini used to get out of a coffin, too. I'm not even sure there ever was a Jesus Christ—that he ever *lived*."

"That's what Schweitzer thinks, actually," Sybil said with interest, "I read in one of those wonderful Bible issues of *Life*—I think it was a quote from one of Dr. Schweitzer's books—and he said something—He comes to us as one unknown without a name . . . as in the past he came to those men beside the sea who didn't know him either—and when he comes to us he will speak the same way maybe even the —the same words, he'll say Come, follow me. Those who try to help do the things that have to be done in our time —to them he will reveal himself—and if we walk with him and obey his commands we can learn in our own hearts— that's the only place—*Who He Is*—and I think he said—in that same book—it wouldn't matter actually whether he ever lived or not. I liked that."

They were both very quiet. From upstairs, a laugh drifted down to them.

"But Hank—" Sybil said shyly, "you—*saw* him."

"People see pink elephants," Hank said brutally, "Colin's death gave me a bad time. The *cum* mal de mer on that goddam coal barge. *Cum* eyes—I never could see in the dark, *cum* insomnia—I don't know any more what the hell. I feel like a horse trapped in a fire."

"You look a little that way," Sybil said, "but I'm no pushover, pal. You had something when you—when I— when I knelt down that morning. Maybe it's—you are—we all are sort of where we were and what we were when God found us. I find I've got a lot to learn—there are a good many things missing like as you just said loving Steve Retzlaff—and having humility—"

"Humility," Hank yelled at her, "intellectual superiority and humility—alibis for getting licked. Read your New Testament and see how many times Christ came like a tiger. The lamb of peace is supposed to be an *end* product, not a way of life, and *he* won it by fighting like a tiger a lot of the time. Not groveling. Nor ducking issues. Nor staying out of things." He put his hands over his face and stood perfectly still for what seemed a long time to Sybil. He said, "Do you know what it's like to have known and then not to know, not even to know whether you ever did know or not?"

"I don't see how you can lose it, if you *knew*," Sybil said.

"Well—you can," Hank said harshly.

Sybil just sat there, hunched on the end of the couch,

saying nothing, her face pinched with sympathy. Maybe Mellie should leave him *alone*. With *his* song, whatever it was. Maybe I should have left Mellie in Chicago.

A soft light came through the wide, old-fashioned bow windows. Distantly, there was a sound that might be the gentle roar of breakers at low tide or the hum of midmorning traffic on the Pacific Coast Highway going to San Diego. Aware every instant of Hank's voice downstairs, Mellie tried to concentrate—Gloria Retzlaff always said a thing a good many times, in a good many ways, it had taken some time to get her to Deedee, though that was what she'd come to talk about.

"I've never known really what to do about Deedee," Gloria said, "not from the first. I'd never had anything to do with children and—not being my own—she was only three, you know, and she didn't remember her mother and at first we couldn't make up our minds, but in a place like Beach City somebody was sure to tell her. We—of course her father—when she was *little,* he always made so much of her, she didn't know there was anybody else in the world and that suited him, too, if you know what I mean. If—if she was like the teen-agers you read about, wild and sort of crazy and smoking things and drinking—it might be easier to understand. But except for the clothes they wear and her hair—though I do think that *lank* cut they wear is becoming to Dee—you could certainly take her for a lady and of course some of the nicest girls do dress that way, I saw some in *Harper's Bazaar*. Until I caught her lying right out about the Mayhew boy, I never had any real trouble with her. Not really. You know her school grades are good—nothing spectacular but she doesn't want to go to Stanford anyway, she isn't—*delinquent* about things at all."

"Most of the ones who get in real trouble aren't," Mellie said. "Does Deedee love her father?"

"Yes—yes," Gloria said, "yes—she does. They—love each other. As I saw when she was *little*—you know how a father is about a cute little girl, well, Steve was. And he spoiled her and she thought it was—he was the world. I—wouldn't say this to anybody but you, Mellie, but since then—while she's been growing up—he's away so much. Business—Sacramento—Washington—he expects me to know where Deedee is every minute and what she does every hour of the day. And she walks around me like smoke. I can't keep up with her, she never tells me anything she doesn't have to and I—I haven't any *authority*. So she does what she pleases, they all do, don't they? All I know do. Her father comes home and they're together and everything is rosy, she butters him up and he brings her things and they—they laugh a lot—and if I say a word about anything that happened while he was away, even when he asks me, then it's always *me*. It's because I don't understand her. Then some night if he *is* home and she's fifteen minutes late on a date, when she comes running up the steps there he is—once he'd even called the police—and they had a row—but she cries and—I don't know what I'm supposed to do. If I were her own mother—but so many aren't—"

Busy lighting a cigarette, Mellie said offhand, "You know about this boy?"

"I don't know what to do," Gloria said again, almost in tears, "Steve would only make it worse. For all she looks the way she does when she sings in church, the truth is, Mellie, she's just as stubborn as he is. I thought—I hoped it would *blow over*—if we let it alone I mean—"

Mellie said, "I take it you're sure Steve would object?"

"He'd kill him," Gloria said. "The boy's a Mexican."

"Deedee says her father's too cagey for murder," Mellie said, "she says he'd just run Beany out of town."

"You can't tell one thing about what Steve would do when it comes to Deedee," Gloria said. "You can't—it's impossible to tell—Steve's a lot more emotional than people give him credit for. In some ways I know him better than Deedee does—and where *she's* concerned—what he'd be capable of if—like any father—I don't know myself. I—she's the only thing in the world he really loves, she's an extension of himself—she's part of him, I'm an awful disappointment to him in some ways, you know. He'd have liked a wife like you, Mellie."

"Who wouldn't?" Mellie said, and gave that little three-cornered Gumbie cat grin and then got up and went to the closet, what she took out was a light woolly cloud of green and gold that turned into a sweater, she put it around her shoulders and said, "This California weather, you don't know whether to dress for Palm Springs or Aspen. Come on, ducky, there are a couple of things I need to know before I talk to Deedee. Or a little later *somebody* will talk to her father."

"You think so?" Gloria said doubtfully, busy in the mirror with her lipstick. "You don't know what he's like when he's hurt, sometimes a volcano but usually cold as ice. If we could do something without his having to know."

The voices from downstairs had ceased. Mellie said absently, "We might. If you won't go around looking like you'd swallowed Elvis Presley."

"I'll do my best," said Gloria, between a gulp and a giggle.

Mellie winced a little, then she said brightly, "No woman can do more," and they went downstairs.

For the third scene, the lights went up on the wide lanai of my own house. Outside the sun had burned off the morning fog and the day was blue and gold beyond compare.

On the big low table, I found the letter. My efforts to reach the chaplain had finally succeeded. Not until later did I know that if there had been a postmark, it would have been *Guam*.

A short letter, actually, hurried, full of mistakes, it began explaining that he was on active service but he would write to Hank, and always he would pray for him.

I read quickly, the first time.

. . . no no, I expect Hank's methods must continue to be spectacular-few of the great Christians have accomplished much except by the spectacular. . . . My friend, responsibility witnout power is quite as bad as power without responsibility. Dyou recall the ,way The Establishment ofits day behaved about Lazsrus? Read it. It's in John some of the friends of the family who'd been in the house actually when Lazarus died , they saw him dead and they saw him buried. When Jesus got there, they went with him and Lazarus' sister Mary to the 4-day-old grave. When they saw Lazarus come forth after Jesus thanked the Father ahead of time you notice, some of them believed in Jesus. Others, the practical, common-s ense,unspectacular ones were disturbed. Quite sincerely they hollered fraud and fakery. Finally, the high priest had to call a committee meeting. What to do? If they let this young fellew from Nazareth go on performing these so-called miracles people would begin to believe maybe he was the Messiah, which some of the perfectly honest men on the committee just didn't believe he was.Moreever let's not forget they all lived in a Roman province and the Romans didn't like any gods to perform miracles but their own.So they ~~xfxlxxx~~

felt better one Nazarene carpenter die, than a whole people be ground out under the iron hell of Rome. Best bet-take Jesus into captivity themselves, put him quietly to death, or turn him over to the Romans who would not like his calling himself king of even so mythical a kingdom as <u>heaven.</u> So they began collecting evidence, laying plans. Young Jesus was off somewhere in the country or the wilderness teaching his disciples it would be their duty and privilege to continue to do his mighty works forever in his name and by his power, and nobody thought he'd come back to town for the Passover, if he did, that'd be the time to get him. 6 days before the feast, Jesus came back to Bethany.Now follow this. <u>Lazarus</u> was with the guests at the table, he was there and saw his sister Mary anount Jesus' feet, he ate the supper his sister Martha cooked and served and a crwod gathered. Not only to see Jesus. No no. With their own eyes they wanted to behold <u>Lazarus</u> whom the Nazarene had raised from the dead. And there he was, just like anybody else, having conquered the last enemy, you see that? When the <u>committee</u> in Jerusalem got this report they decided they would also have to put Lazarus to death for just by sitting there, alive and one of the family, eating his supper, many were leaving the no-works church and following Jesus. Now watch this. That's why sometimes Jesus had to say Tell no man, to those he healed and saved from all their psychiatric debils, to pritect them from being eliminated somehow or other as living proofs of the works of Jesus the Christ. Whether or not they got Lasazrus we don't know-sometimes the one healed got his way rejoicing and they forget about him.But the man who can heal the sick and raise the dead, you can see, naturally, those who have a form of godliness <u>without</u> power don't want men around who have a form of godliness <u>with</u>

power. Sometimes very good men qr e afraid of that. Nxx You see that? It's the crucial point. Follow me. Sincere, well-meaning, kindly men rationalize themselves into a right to get rid of miracle-workers as mischief-makers. They must do this otherwise the people will demand to know why they aren't doing the works. So they will find any grounds use any mean, in the old days the cross, the stake, the rack-now they do it by ridicule, oastracism, social declasse blackball, organization, calumny, anathema, banishment, exile, dishonorable discharge, much more crual eliniation.
Tell Hank if he does not want to raise Lazarus, he probably is pretty safe. No one will come looking for either of them. On the other hand, if he does want to, he will have to survive hell,but if he is strong enough he may be one of those who has the form of godliness with power and he may well bring back the kingdom of heaven on earth so we can see it. This is the way it works. There are no exceptions. I can promise you, his friend, that he will never fall out of God's hands , but somebody might persuade him to jump. Pray as I shall that angels may guard him from yielding to this temptation.

I read it the second time, slowly, carefully, and found I was crying. Because I could hear again that note of hope played on the harp which has only one string.

It is the only harp hope has.

3

When Mellie had finished, I said as distinctly as I knew how, "No. I won't. I won't have anything to do with it and neither should you."

For the first time in our lives I felt we were violently at odds. I have seen the circle go round and round and come out at the same place too many times to get hysterical about straight dirty hair instead of clean curly hair, the Twist as compared to the Grizzly Bear of the old Barbary Coast, Vietnam instead of Korea or the Philippines or Vera Cruz or the shores of Tripoli, homosexuality in place of syphilis as a Social Disease, and I now know that as birth control gains medical and social recognition we have bigger and bigger families (look around you) and certainly more pregnant unmarried girls and unwed mothers.

Basic principles are something else again.

The word *abortion* brings me to stand firmly on one of mine and I was stunned to find that Mellie took it as licit if necessary.

I didn't think the late hour, Mellie's unexpected arrival, her it-seemed-to-me air of arrogance amounting almost to bravado had anything to do with it. When I said, "It won't do any good to discuss it, Mellie," it was not that I thought she might persuade me but that I didn't like the pace and texture of her talk, it seemed to me that she was too exhausted and keyed up to stop.

I was in bed and she was standing over me, wrapped in a worn-thin polo coat, and she went on talking, light and high, "Darling godmother, please listen. I can't believe you're morally committed in a case like this. They're in love. First love, sweetie. Remember? They'd get married if they could —it'd be absolutely impossible for them even to get a *license* at their age without their parents' consent—especially Steve Retzlaff's daughter—but this isn't just some teenage back-seat horror. Give them a little *time*. She's a doll— did you know she's a marvelous cook? It's her hobby. I— that Beany, I'm the only one who knows him, you don't know him, her father doesn't know him—"

"What about Hank?" I said.

She stared at me, she waited long enough to light a cigarette and put the match carefully in my bedside ashtray. She said, "I'm afraid this is beyond prayer, I think we have to *do* something. This a remarkable boy! If you could see what he comes from—*fantastic*. They live in a—a shack, his mother is the fattest woman I've ever seen, dark and beautiful, she ought to have flowers in her hair, and there are thirty or forty children all the same *size,* I beg you to believe me, and all *colors. All* colors. His mother has the same kind of white white teeth Beany has—he was baptized Bernardo, by the way—he's the oldest, there doesn't seem to be any father. I'm given to understand he disappeared some time back—they get relief checks and the church and what Beany makes—and sweetie, Beany has *talent*. Of course everybody nowadays has talent, we're shot full of it, they need help sometimes to wrap it up, this boy is *awful good*."

"I don't doubt it," I said, "I can't quite see what it has to do with the fact that this girl, who is what—sixteen?—fifteen?—is pregnant and you want me to go with you while she has an abortion. Plain words for plain facts. This I cannot do, Mellie."

"These girls," Mellie said, and shut her hands in pain, "they don't know anything. The poor little *urchins* are turned loose and exposed at all times when they are quite defenseless to every known form of aphrodisiac that ever came out of Aphrodisia. Movies, TV, records, books—my god the *books*—picture magazines—darling, I once counted thirty-seven pictures of nude white women in provocative poses hung on the newsstands in the main waiting room of the Union Station in *Washington,* D.C. and the very next day a seventeen-year-old Negro boy was arrested for attempted rape behind the lockers—imagine his amazement, I'm sure he'd thought it was *advertised* there—"

"Stop it," I said, "you're rattled—I never heard you rattled before—"

"I am not rattled," Mellie said, clearly, "I am fighting for these children. I am not going to let them be a disaster. They want to get *married,* as soon as they can. Some day, they'll have children, some day he may be a fine artist too, he's got the temperament for it. Why should they pay such a price for a mistake? Look at all the people running around climbing in and out of beds! *I* didn't pay, did I? No—why? I was like the old woman in the shoe who didn't have so many children, *she knew what to do*. So did I. Deedee didn't, she'll be paying for her innocence, her purity, her poor jumpy fool of a stepmother, her swashbuckling bully of a father, eaten up with ambition the poor bastard, *you're* such a big follow-thou-me Christian these days, are you going to cast the first stone at this child who got *caught* in the act?"

"Adding abortion won't solve it," I said. "You have no right—you must talk to her mother—or her father—she's a *minor,* Mellie. This is dangerous medically—and legally—

"That's the first time you ever tried to scare me out of anything," Mellie said and did not bother to hide her contempt.

Holding stubbornly to my principles in this matter, I let her go though I was most unhappy. I hadn't talked her out of it any more than she had talked me into it.

Yet, in the end, I went, as you will see.

Next morning I had a call from Archie. Steve Retzlaff had sent him a copy of his resignation as treasurer and chairman of the building committee of the Church of the Redeemer. Well, I thought to myself, he can't resign from being Deedee's father, that's for sure.

"He wants me to use it," Archie said, "I'm not going to. Hank says he hasn't accepted it. What's wrong with Hank Gavin?"

Cautiously I said, "He thinks he's a charlatan, who's counterfeiting a spiritual power he once had and has now lost."

"Doubt is the Christian's bitterest enemy," Archie said, "Hank is probably now at the place where most of his colleagues stand pat. Has he lost it?"

"What?" I said irritably. I hadn't gone back to sleep after Mellie left, my day's work would be shot, I wished I wasn't involved in all this. Hank thinking he was now a charlatan and Mellie wanting me to go with her to a house on a side street in Redondo, it wasn't at all what I had expected, though I realized, thinking it over, that there had been a good deal of *violence* in the original stories in the New Testament. "What has who lost?"

Patiently Archie said, "*Has* Hank lost his faith?"

Looking back, I find that what is here written about Hank Gavin's loss of his own consciousness of divine grace as present and knowable may not be as clear as it needs to be. I have found it difficult (as apparently writers do since so few have attempted it) to put down spiritual struggles of our relationship to Christ in the here-now continuum as inevitable, recurring, habitual things of pitch and moment and immediacy, but every-day-in-every-way things to be talked of and thought about, as close as whether Mantle would be back next year or Humphrey should have been sent to Churchill's funeral. Spinoza, of whom Renan once said that in him came the truest vision ever had of God, fought the church on relationship to the Christ and says that in Christ alone can we be led to love, to justice, to brotherhood in our lives. Spinoza was a mystic, in Holland in the seventeenth century. To call Hank Gavin in a business suit a mystic is to run head on into semantic distortions. Spinoza himself was a lens grinder, Jacob Boehme was a shoemaker, Bergson was a schoolteacher, Schweitzer was a doctor in *Africa,* Abraham Lincoln was a politician, but today the word *mystic* has got all balled up with fuzziness, occultism, the wrong kind of mediums, and lowered lights and voices. Looking it up in the dictionary, I find that a mystic is one who holds the doctrine of immediate spiritual intuition, or a direct intimate union of the soul with the Divine through love and contemplation, and has himself had proof of this. It is immeasurably difficult to put down mystic experience at a union breakfast, over a telephone, with juke boxes playing don't sit under the apple tree, with zoning permits on one hand and abortionists possible on the other. Yet I knew that Hank Gavin had believed simply and entirely with the Apostle John who a long long time ago, but as near as yesterday or tomorrow, had written in a letter to some friends and fellow strugglers and followers that they had all *known* the love that God has to them. This is the most wonderful thing that can happen to a human being, and John's flowing robes, the long hair, the ancient cities, even the camels, the long-ago-and-far-away—those give the necessary *unreality* and *distance* to make us in some small measure accept that they might have been realities. We are not asked to look it right in the face at this moment as we plug in the coffee pot or start the car. Hank Gavin had known this love for real. Had insisted that we didn't need the flowing robes. None of the long-ago-and-far-away, he said, the right here and now. His whole glory had been his promise that in the time-space continuum it always worked. I knew we had arrived now at a place in his experiment where that definite, definitive, racial, national I-am-from-any-state-in-the-Union-you-will-have-to-show-me of the American mind and heart, perhaps our most consistent characteristic in the long run, would come up fighting. I felt that what stood between us and our believing in the story of Jesus Christ as part of our lives was the fact that habitually and uniformly we had abandoned action, we were not where the action was, we were putting forth words without works.

Hank Gavin had promised to show them works. It seemed to me monumental and dangerous—but that was what he was all about.

I could see that this so-called loss of faith was the most

important thing which had happened, the most vital dramatically and as far as *proof* was to be offered. If faith without works is dead, I greatly feared the reverse might also be true. Without faith, if a man said *Talitha cumi*—it seemed probable that the damsel would *not arise* as she had done when glowing faith spoke the words.

While my own activities, and one of the usual minor family crises which I am, unfortunately, never able to ignore, had kept me from Beach City for a few days, my mind did not cease to occupy itself as I drove or walked with what might be going on there.

All this came rushing back to me as Archie put his question at the other end of the line. I didn't need to rethink what Jack Nestor had told me as part of my answer, for the moment I remembered it at all, its full weight was there. I think I must tell it here. In some ways, it led to the final incredible moment of truth now approaching like an express train. From the day of Melanie's return, I had been waiting for some disaster, but I did not expect the issues to take the tragic form they did.

Jack Nestor's tale restored me somewhat at the time and influenced my answer to Archie, which in turn influenced what Archie did later on.

Stopping by on his way into Los Angeles to ask me details about a young man I'd sent to him about a job, Jack Nestor brought up Hank's talk at the prayer breakfast. He spoke carefully, if I felt from time to time that there was a feeling of disappointment, that the men's reaction had been no different than it was to any entertaining speaker, this was lost in Nestor's praise.

"He doesn't look like a man that'd be a preacher, does he?" Jack Nestor said, "he seems more like a man who knows himself what he's talking about. You might not believe it, but the thing I'm up against most, the thing we know, too, is back of most of our strike trouble—the men get *depressed*. Sometimes I have it myself—*depression*. Not just feeling kind of blue, a man expects that what with one thing and another. This—you might call it the *black-and*-blues—or the *grays*. They've got the—maybe nothing's-going-to-go-anywhere-from-here grays. Kind of maggoty I call it. One of my best men said to me the other day there isn't much *hope* around any more. We've come a long way and they're grateful, but—it hasn't—it didn't *do* maybe all they'd been keyed up to. They got what they were after, more than they expected or asked for, and now it's kind of gray, I know there must be better words for this but I haven't got 'em. I would say we have more depression than ever before and the psychiatrists—we're loaded with psychiatrists in the company, and they're real sincere men—it don't seem to matter any more what you believe as long as you're *sincere,* but they don't lift it any that I can see, and it's that depression that leads to the drinking and gambling and whoring around—if you'll pardon me, myself I never thought it was normal or healthy for a man to spend too much time whoring, not a *man,* and the heroin which is something new—we used to hit an occasional opium pipe with the Chinese but that's not so bad—this depression they get is like an impenetrable fog, like the one we had last November, when the planes and the ships didn't move for four days—and pretty soon you get the idea they aren't *ever* going to."

"We're such good people," I said, "I sometimes wonder why we're such suckers for the images evil tries to put over on us."

"We're optimists," Jack Nestor said, "and I guess enthusiastic optimists at that. And that's where young Gavin comes in. He doesn't mince any words, he doesn't. He looks you right in the eye and says Turn to God and ask in Christ's name and understand why and study what you have to do—and I promise you will get hope and help."

"The men were—pleased at the breakfast?" I said cautiously.

"They sure were," the head of the union said.

"I think Hank felt—that perhaps he hadn't been—he didn't think he was as—he wasn't quite satisfied," I said, "or I got that impression."

"He's probably harder to satisfy than we are," Jack Nestor said, "he was just right. Have you ever heard him tell the story of the prodigal son like it was somebody he knew very well indeed and it was God's *truth* and the same could happen to you?"

"No—" I said, "I don't think so. Did he tell it at the prayer breakfast?"

"Not then," Jack Nestor said, and I could see that he had carried over all the power and the glory of the promises, that they had *held.* "No—it was at one of our—well, a small gathering—I got to tell you this though I won't mention any names not that you'd know him if I did. This is a dilly. I've been depressed a little because to admit to you the truth we have been having some trouble with the drug traffic down on the docks, we got a lot of ships coming and going. Coming in like from Hong Kong and it's no wonder they'll sell you shoes and pajamas with your monogram on them and tweed suits cheaper than dirt! So I naturally keep an eye out and there is one fellow, maybe you won't believe this but he was in the Navy at the time of Hiroshima, we'll call him Walt, he's tough and he uses his fists more than is necessary, but he has a good heart and he has the Navy Cross but he won't wear it, you know why? Get a load of this. He says everybody in the Navy knew the Japs were ready to surrender when we dropped the bomb, he says if it had been Roosevelt, who was Navy himself and the Navy could get his ear, we would not have done this without telling the Japs we could, and knowing this they better surrender. Which we never did! This guy, he says if FDR had been alive we would have ended it without the bomb and he says he has never had any hope for humanity since the *best* the *best* nation on earth could do was drop a bomb on innocent women and children. He said to me what about it I said to him You have a wife and two boys in high school, good boys, you are hurting them and he said They will have to take their chances. Of course his wife is no good, she's one of those women who thinks she's too good to do the job God intended her to do first, she's a *whiner*. The psychiatrist the company's got didn't make a dent. If you'll pardon me but it will show you the *state* this Walt was in, he calls this *top* man we've got, he calls him a pissychiatrist. He says he already *knew* all he told him but *what* was he going to do about it? Walt said to me, I am just as good a goddam godless bastard as he is, so now what?

"I couldn't get to this big lug at all, but I'd done him a favor or two, so one night I asked him would he come to a small men's group, no speeches, just Dr. Gavin answered questions—more like a *class*, Gavin calls it. Walt gave me a big No, then afterward he came around and said What have I got to lose, you want me to go hear this preacher, I go. That's the first time I saw Walt crack, when Hank Gavin told the story of the prodigal son, how the father *ran out* to meet him, afterward Walt said those weren't tears he was wiping away but they were, he wanted to go see the man, he said, so I called and asked Hank and he said send him along. Walt told me he spilled his guts to Hank, *not*, he said, about what he did when he was young or dreamed or had done, but what he wanted to be and do, did he have any hope? He had his bellyful, he told the man, of husks, and he was perishing with hunger for some *hope*, so were most of the men he knew which was why they started strikes sometimes. Well—I don't know myself what—they *prayed*, I know that. They got an answer, too. I have seen too many of them trying to kick this stuff, sometimes they die. This man, this *Walt*, I tell you, like it says in the Book, he was *born again*. This is not some little thing, not that I guess anything is little, it is all relative, this is not a Sunday sermon or a Saturday night mission, or a youth meeting—and maybe if it takes in his wife who like I said *whines* every dish she washes, and the two kids, are they little things? We are—this is *following,* isn't it? Like the man in our church told us."

I had to call Hank to tell him about this. I thought it would help. There was a long silence, then at last he said, "Yes. Oh yes. That was—a while back, wasn't it?"

"Jack Nestor thought you did a fine job at the prayer breakfast," I said, and heard him laugh before he said, "He's still seeing me through rose-colored glasses. But if next time he sends a guy to me—I'm glad he wasn't disappointed anyhow."

As I said, while it has taken time for me to tell you this, I remembered it as one does in a few seconds, and I said loudly, heartily to Archie on the other end of the phone, "I don't believe he's lost it. His faith. I think it's obscured. I think—yes, he's sitting in the dark, but *with it,* if you know what I mean."

"Paul had a rough time with his from time to time," Archie said, "I have been reading the New Testament as we agreed to do. This is a very surprising book. You ever hear the story about a famous prof in a big college and in some mathematical problems they were trying to find an answer—a *formula*—they'd been working on it for *years.* One day when the professor just got through explaining and writing on the blackboard that nobody could find this one, a freshman held up his hand and said he could and he did and when the professor was amazed the freshman showed him where it was in a book and always had been. *Books about!* Books and books and books—the publishers send 'em to me by the thousands. *About* the New Testament. You settle down and read and read it like we agreed to do—Paul said for instance, For the good that I would, I do not, but the evil that I would not that I do—which is encouraging. If *Paul* had to find the way and he did for he says then O wretched man that *I* am! Who shall deliver me from the body of this death of my faith? I thank God I know, Jesus Christ Our Lord, a real power. And Paul was persuaded that *nothing* could separate him from the deliverance power of Christ. I tell you if any of the boys in the city room or Maisie on the switchboard hear me talking like this they will send for the paddy wagon! But we ought to talk like this to each other. Look, what's going on with this girl of Steve Retzlaff's? Deedee—that her name? The one who sings in our church sometimes. Tell Mellie Gavin to be a little careful—

she's a very high-handed gal, our Miss Mellie. And this is a small town."

"What are you talking about?" I said.

"Don't you know?" Archie said.

Difficult for me to lie to editors, but I did. "No I don't," I said.

"No abortionist is safe," Archie said and hung up with a crash.

That is why, I suppose, I went with Mellie and Deedee, the next day.

If safety was a factor, I had to—I couldn't let Mellie go alone.

Actually there was nothing sinister about the house, a square brown-shingle two-story box on a respectable middle-bracket street. I knew it was my imagination going full blast. Once when I was working on a New York paper we had exposed an abortion factory, so-called, down on 18th Street, all the horrors came back to me as I sat in the car after Mellie and Deedee had gone in. A nurse in a sterile white uniform opened the door and, peering out, I saw the small black and gold sign which said Dr. So-and-So, Eye Ear Nose and Throat. Specialists! All the blinds were up, a bright pink oleander tree was reflected in the big plate glass window, the smaller ones were wide open. On the drive over we had talked only about radio programs, of how they made the great music always available to those who, like Beany, couldn't afford the expensive stereo equipment and the big records, so I had no idea how long they would be and tried to get myself impersonal and efficient as a newspaperwoman should be. I prayed, too, as best I could.

In a short time I heard laughter. *Laughter?* In consternation I opened my eyes, probably they had gone *mad* as people did in those strange houses so featured in mystery fiction. I saw Mellie in her cream tweed suit, very high-handed as Archie had said, and Deedee clinging to her arm, with them a round-faced tubby young man in a white coat. He was smiling pleasantly. It can't be *over,* I thought, it can't take only *that* long, such a thing as this.

About that at least I was right.

This had been a preliminary visit.

Five hundred dollars in cash Mellie had handed to the tubby young man and I thought that soon he would be rich, for another car pulled up just behind us, and then he could return to his oath and devote the rest of his life to the poor and their children. That's what *he* thought. He thought he was safe, whether Archie did or not.

When they got back in the car and Mellie pulled away I found that Deedee had been told what to do and to come back the following morning at seven-thirty.

Mellie was driving with one hand, her arm around the girl's shoulder. I thought this is all wrong. I hate it, I suppose sometimes it *is* a choice of evils, I'm so sorry about it, I must love them all—and a burst of love was vouchsafed me even for Mellie with whom I was still angry.

We dropped Deedee at the school where she was to meet Beany for a rehearsal, she wasn't to tell him anything—about anything. Nothing at all. "You do know it's better that way," Mellie said. And Deedee, whose face seemed to me to be smaller, said uncertainly, "I won't tell him till it's—all over. You know—Beany can be—he has some cock-eyed ideas if you ask me. He's crazy about all those little brothers and sisters of his—I won't tell him."

Mellie said, "You'll come and spend tonight with us—that's the best. I'll call your mother."

"Oh please—" Deedee said.

I dreaded going back the next morning.

That I need not have worried about.

None of us went back the next morning.

4

Beany moved onstage to entrance music.

The set was a Big Office, custom-built to pattern, wall-to-wall carpeting, brocaded drapes, overstuffed chairs, a huge mahogany desk, and behind it Steve Retzlaff in a blue business suit with a striped tie.

Pop blues vibrations of his guitar lingered around Beany, he moved in the rock 'n' roll strata of his generation. His clothes, winkle picker boots, tight black pants, a checkered shirt, jerkin with pearl buttons made him stand out like a harlequin against the luxury-respectability of the Retzlaff Enterprises.

First time we've *seen* Beany.

First time the spotlight has stayed focused.

First time for everything, Deedee's father had spotted Beany through the tall wire fence around the school grounds, identified the boy to pick him on the sidewalk saying Get in, I want a little talk with you, he had not looked at him as they drove into downtown Beach City, he'd stared straight ahead through the windshield. Who told Steve Retzlaff, I do not know. I suspect Marvin Gregory, of the Youth Group, his wife Norma is of the sweetness-and-light type who sits on a pink cloud saying brightly *all-is-love* with no conception of the terrible truth of that statement or the dirty riverbeds it must stir up. Her husband had played both ends on the church building controversy, I feared he would curry favor with a future governor rather than a slightly crackpot minister. A careful man at all times, Steve Retzlaff's preliminary work was careful, grew carefuller as minute by minute he got frozen in an ice-hell of suffering. He'd seen everything, the shack, the fat woman with the many children of many colors, the combo in which Beany played the guitar for school dances, the teachers who were uncertain about Beany Teran, never been in any real trouble, they agreed he would come to some outsize end, a million records for Phil Spector or death in a back-alley gang fight.

No comfort now in his first real look at Beany Teran. Slight, 5 foot 7 or 8, Steve estimated, not much taller than

Deedee, 130–140 pounds no more, long black hair, dark skin. Harder to believe his eyes than the unbelievable story had led him to expect. Using his own eyes, Deedee's father missed the appeal of the green eyes and pure suffering and sensuality of the young mouth. *I did beguile her of her tears when I did speak of some distressful stroke that my youth suffered.* All Steve Retzlaff's eyes saw was what Desdemona's father's had seen when he faced The Moor—*to fall in love with what she feared to look on.*

His amazement and anger grew when after a moment the boy gave him back look for look, without a blink.

In the beginning, Beany had been afraid. On the sidewalk, in the car. He was always afraid in the beginning of everything. Now in this big expensive successful room, his love had flowed through his cold veins, he felt again Deedee clinging to him, to *him,* not to this strange man, to *him,* saying *Don't let them don't let them* and he grew ten feet tall with pride.

It didn't need the big framed picture of Deedee, much younger, on the desk, Deedee in white with a ribbon holding back her long straight hair. Nothing could prevent her *being there,* as real as *they* were, Deedee as she was in reality, still with the cloud of childish long lank hair held back by a pixie band. Up to there, they saw the same thing. Teen-age girl 5 feet 6, 112 pounds, pale pink lipstick, fur-collared suede jacket, low-slung fly-front jeans, shoulder bag swinging free. Inconceivable after that how each saw something different. On the same guitar can be played rock-a-bye-baby-on-the-tree-top *and* be my booh-oom-bay-ay vah-ump-nooby-poon-fang-ooh-oo-h, -ayub-bay-ay-bee-beh-ungghbeh-ungggh. Or the wedding march from *Lohengrin* or the Dead March from *Saul,* or "As I Walk in the Garden Alone" or "Don't Sit under the Apple Tree."

For them, it was dreadful to be there together shut in by four walls with Deedee.

Such things ought not to happen to people in this rich golden age.

Dreadful.

Tough enough for a father on his daughter's wedding night with a boy he liked. Men know men. A father's imagination had to recoil, as had Brabantio's years ago in Venice, from the very possibility that his lily-child had made the beast with two backs with this dark outcast. That way led to the Unwritten Law of the old West, justifiable homicide, with his big strong hands he could see to it that this Mexican half-breed couldn't even *remember* anything about Deedee Tetzlaff to tell in the alleys of Sonoratown. But—

he got control of himself—to do that would be to expose himself and Deedee who was an extension of himself. To brand her. Cheapen her value forever. Make her the butt of horrid sympathy and snickering dirty jokes, snide ridicule —*A black ram has tupped Retzlaff's white ewe lamb*— ridicule ridicule ridicule, the only weapon left from which a man's reputation never recovers.

He must go carefully. Cagily.

The boy watched him. He had music in his soul, he'd been born with the gift to offset the things he didn't have. He loved Deedee, he had meant well by her, her kindness, her consent when he was in so much need of kindness, their passion had been an overflow of kindness for each other. *I did beguile her of her tears when I did speak of some distressful stroke that my youth suffered*—the thing the man behind the desk, who called himself a Christian, had missed. The clinging thin arms, the soft surprised lips, the smiles burning away the tears as sun burns away fog. She was his, he was not prepared to live without her, ever.

Unafraid, he recognized the formidable power before him, facing him.

Always in the back of his head he had sensed, today on the sidewalk in front of the school he had known this man had on his side the law, the church, the town, the school itself, the bank and the business, big business, this man who could claim Deedee. He was her father. Everything was against him, this the boy knew, except Deedee.

Now if they succeeded in this that they were planning— they might scare and soil Deedee's love.

They might take her away and he'd never be able to get her back.

Oh—right now—right here—he could finish off this old man who was bigger than he was, but size didn't count.

His flesh was soft.

A knife would slide through it like butter.

Forty per cent of the boys in his high school owned guns or carried knives. Why not? They might need them. They were not sure of much any more.

What good would that do him—to slide a knife into Deedee's father?

Deedee wouldn't be his any more even with this cretin out of the way, this grown man, it was unbelievable that an animal like this had the right and the power to destroy *them,* to stop your music because it wasn't their music, but what good would it do him? Deedee wouldn't be his, they would put him in a room with glass walls and turn on the gas so he couldn't breathe any more, throw him a pill like he was a seal or something.

He must go quietly. He must have only one thought. He mustn't make anything worse for Deedee. It would be worse for Deedee if she didn't have him, because she loved him.

We have to live with it, he told himself.

Or do we?

I am not going to live without her. I am not.

The man's voice, careful, polite said, "Sit down," and Beany said "Thanks, I'd rather stand up."

She couldn't live without me, either.

To his surprise he saw now that the man's face had a smile on it over its wooden no-expression, he remembered that Deedee had said *He's cagey, he's primitive, but he's cagey. Be careful, sweetheart.* And Beany had said to her *Fine-fine-fine-love-baby, I'll be careful.*

Speaking reasonably, persuasively, the first quiet make-'em-listen sales pitch, the man who was Deedee's father was explaining it all. They came from different worlds, they had different backgrounds, religions, customs. You must see that? he said. He wanted Deedee to have a chance to see—to see more of the world. He said he had thought of sending her to an Eastern college, a western girl ought to have some idea of other parts of the country but now, if she really had a voice and was interested, they might send her to Switzerland for a bit for languages and then to a conservatory—Paris, Rome—and Beany began to go the color of frozen custard under the dark of his skin. He wanted to shout, to say Deedee's got a nice little voice no different than lots of girls, she'll never amount to anything without me, me behind her, I can mix it, I could teach her, I'm the one, we're something together without me she's a nothing.

The man said, "These boy-and-girl—romances—in high school—they can't *last*—"

"I want to marry her," Beany said and it was absurd and magnificent, it was a pitiful and insane bravado. "She wants to marry me, too, you know."

Steve Retzlaff got out of his chair. He stood with his hands palms down on the desk, looking down at a reflection of himself in the polished wood. I look all right, he thought. *Fathers from thence trust not your daughters' minds by what you see them act.* So they had talked about *marriage*, this boy had dared, Deedee—and suddenly unexpectedly he thought of Deedee's mother, so long ago, he thought that up to now he had never seen one thing of her mother in Deedee, but now he must remember.

It gave him a real fright which he had to meet with a desperate courage.

His laugh was almost natural. He said, "You're too young, you must see that. Can you support her?"

"I—yes," Beany said, with a big chord under it. "Yes!"

Now the hate rays began to fill the room so that they were both having trouble breathing.

But the man had gotten into stride. Too young—a separation of a year or two couldn't do any harm if—if they really—if they were meant to marry. As an older man, as Deedee's father, they would have to wait. He would insist on that, enforce it. Bang bang bang bang. Shooting from a hip now—over the boy's head. This big, cold, old man with power. All the things he was controlling his lips not to say as they went smoothly on in trite ironclad words were in his eyes.

The boy almost broke first. He moved to the desk and his fingers began to drum on the table. Drum-and-drum-and-drum. He closed his eyes and took a long breath and held it. He always held his breath like that when he was playing. He held it clear through until he finished that roll, that phase, that series of beats, as long as he held his breath like that when he played his guitar the telephone wouldn't ring, the cops wouldn't come, the landlord wouldn't be there after the rent, the teachers wouldn't say silly things, they wouldn't be able to take Deedee away, if he held on.

"Look—" he said. Words hammered in his throat —*soggy* —you're soggy—you're larded—you're old—but he hammered them back, he spoke softly, his voice was soft, it was always a little broken, not exactly an accent, a matter of timing and timber that wasn't Anglo-Saxon, he said, "Lll-ll—look, look, have you—does Deedee know, I'd like to tell you I would—some day I will—what did she say? Don't you see that she has to have something to *say* she had a life—I want to tell you."

He couldn't.

It was the man who let it rip, let it rant and roar in one silly sentence. He said, "Why the hell don't you get your hair cut, you *pachuco*—" Plainly he—he wanted to be sick, he vomited the old insulting-to-Mexican word *pachuco*—

"For the same reason you *do*," Beany said, and his teeth flashed white, against his copper-dark face. He said, "I wouldn't want to look like you, would I?" and he said to himself, I might as well, he said, "Because I got some Mexican blood and I play the guitar and I am young I do not exist? I do not add up to a bonafide human being, is that it? The way I wear my hair, I am not a bonafide human being. You got a world spinning around like crazy so maybe it will spin off its axis like for good, with no Big Daddy God in it any more, you don't stop to find out anything about me, maybe I am like a young Gershwin like he was at my age, or like a young kid named Irving Berlin when he was a little Jewish singing *waiter*, or did you stop to look at a picture of Mozart like when he was twelve years old, they kicked him around and in a way they crucified him, too, but you wouldn't know any of that, you are *larded*, you know that your brain is larded, you can't see nor hear—"

His voice had gone that odd, teen-age world-weary.

Even the best ot them. The survivors, the strong ones, often their voices have that world-weary music, children in a world where their adults do not believe in God, nor try to, where nobody tells them what the rules are in a way that makes any sense they belittle the rules. Where it's the adults who ought to have their mouths washed out with soap and their brains with Lysol. In that world-weary voice to sort of Stephen Foster music the boy said, "Your world you make it, who needs you to make a world for him? You made a world like for animals. Who needs a world like for animals? You're a condemning man. We're trying to make a world of our own, maybe with Mozart music how do you know you can't hear with that lard in your ears can you? You got nothing to say about our world we want to build but—you don't like my hair cut. I don't like yours, it's foolish and silly and clumsy like you are, afraid you will get bald you chop it off, so you are like a *skull*." The boy's hands went up as though he was trying to lift a guitar over his head, both hands, holding up something, "We may be having a culture all our own, it's *unbelievable* you are so condemning on one side and the other you are so like you do not know what is going on all you can say is why don't I cut my hair or wear my pants different anybody knows your pants are clumsy and like *laughable* and have been for years. You can't move right, if you have to do anything you have to go home and get your other pants like ski pants or shorts or golf—who needs you? You say we have not, Deedee and I" —he stopped there for his first breath, he was running his sentences together without any stops at all—"got anything in common that is a lie. We have got music in common and our world might turn out better some people like Beethoven had a *terrible* world but they made new ones for everybody—"

Struck dumb, held motionless, now Steve Retzlaff broke loose, came roaring from behind his desk like a charging rhinoceros. The boy stood his ground, but he could not stand the pain, he began to cry.

Oh—men cry. Men weep. I have seen them. In the death house, once. On receiving the *we regret to inform you* telegram, seen them weeping on their knees and making promises they never even tried to keep. At injustice and defeat. This boy wept at his own helplessness.

Hate rays were thick orange, sulphur blue, blood red, his head flung back the boy's long hair danced on his collar, he cried high and thin: "You are a decayed old man. Do not try to take her away from me I won't let you I warn you—*I warn you.* I will not let you take her away from me."

Each word a small chunk of ice, Steve Retzlaff said, "If you will not play ball with me I'll have to do it the hard way.

"In twenty-four hours you'll be south of the border where you belong, where you can't try to rape any more white girls, we've had enough of that around here. You won't be able to get back even by the wetback route this time. And if you do, I'll put you where you won't have a name you'll just have a number until everybody's forgotten you ever lived. You understand me?"

Beany put his hands crosswise over his face, one from his forehead to his chin, one from temple to temple covering his eyes. His flesh seemed to have come away from his bones and be shaking by itself.

In the elevator. In the street, walking wildly, whispering to himself—*this old man can do these things.*

Somewhere in the snow, she will be alone without me to keep her warm. She won't even be able to sing to keep her warm.

If they took her away all those miles, kept her for months—he would never get her back. It would be the end. To such as us—he thought—such as us are *helpless.*

A way out a way out there must *be—not to such as me.* If the old man sent him across the border what chance would a Beany Teran have?

Deedee would be left alone.

We can't live without each other!

Today when she had told him—oh, she hadn't meant to tell him, how could you keep anything from each other in such love? One minute she had been his his his, they had been like one like music chords, then she had begun to cry he felt her tears on his bare shoulder and then she told him, not meaning to, what they had planned to do the next morning. No one had thought how terrible, how repugnant this was to Beany Teran with all his little bastard brothers and sisters. He had made her *swear* they wouldn't do it, no matter what—her beloved Mellie or anybody—she had *sworn* to him.

But now that he had spent that time in her father's office—any minute now, sooner or later, any second, that larded old man that hideous old man with his threats like—like whips, like bastinados, he would find out he had to find out any minute—then oh god what would he do to Deedee? *I won't even be there she's mine and I won't be there*—

The two things whipsawed him dizzy and almost senseless and his temperament—oh he had the *temperament* for a great success in *music*—shook in the earthquake of them.

To let her go tomorrow morning at seven-thirty. No. No. She must keep her promise—

Or to *not* let her go, and any minute—any minute—

There had to be a way out—another way—a third way—didn't there?

Picking up the phone, Steve Retzlaff dialed. Hearing Gloria's voice he said, "Where's Dee?" and when Gloria said "I don't know—" he yelled at her, "You don't *know?*" and Gloria hurried, "Oh Steve for goodness sake wait a minute, I mean exactly, she's somewhere with *Mellie Gavin,* they ought to be here pretty soon to pick up Deedee's things, Mellie wants her to stay the night."

This time Steve Retzlaff gave a pause, he said, "You're sure about this? It's not just Deedee saying she's going to spend the night with Mrs. Gavin?"

Gloria said, "What *is* the matter with you, Steve? Yes, I'm sure. I talked to Mellie myself; she called and asked me herself, they're coming by for Deedee's things. Is anything wrong? You sound upset."

"As long as you're sure she's with Mrs. Gavin," her husband said.

The next number he dialed didn't go through any switchboard.

He said, "How are you Chief? Good. Got time to drop by this afternoon? Oh—any time. After five—say five-thirty or so? Good."

5

Only Mellie could have persuaded me to stay all night at the parsonage. I kept saying "I'll meet you *there* in the morning," to which Mellie said, "You mustn't let yourself get into the rut of having to sleep in your own bed. That special quote from your pal Bill Mizner you come up with—*even the cops are with you when you're right, friends have to be with you when you're wrong.* Remember that one? I don't think I'm wrong, but I do smell trouble. Do come—you've been neglecting Hank shamefully."

As I gave in and agreed to be back by nine o'clock, it came over me that Mellie knew a great deal about people. Right now she probably knew more about this boy, Beany Teran—which was why she smelled trouble—than his own mother and though she didn't put it in those words she understood about Steve Retzlaff.

Agreed I have come to prefer sleeping in my own bed, there was a sharp reason I wished to be in it that night and not in Mellie's guest room next door to young Deedee Retzlaff who had an engagement at seven-thirty the next morning and would doubtless be restless. This Youth Tragedy was coming to a climax and I wanted no part of it. About youth, my sense of guilt was enormous and I didn't want to take this one on. I have found growing old extremely pleasant and profitable, I like to be useful and I am convinced myself that no civilized country can continue under the use-and-throw-away pattern of which the Youth Cult is the leading factor. But either this is a prelude to something or it is indeed without meaning and we have dared to slam shut the door into immortality so that the noise you hear is often the children of our day beating themselves to pieces against it. And the noise noise noise in which the young now live, the noise to which they are conditioned must keep them from hearing anything within. At last, at moments, I can hear faintly—faintly—those words of Love which John heard in Patmos and they promise such beauty that I want to wait in silence *sometimes.* I want to listen as well as I can, especially in times of crisis. Nothing is more difficult to find now than silence. My sympathy with youth kept me awake in my own bed often enough, their pitiful plight in having been handed this terrible burden of running things before they have the strength or even a little of the wisdom which experience sometimes brings. You will note that nearly always their revolts are to ask for more discipline and better teachers for they have begun to suspect that the human *spirit* will defy all natural laws but that it is fatal to defy them unless it is the *spirit*.

Sleeping next door to Deedee on that particular night gave me what she would have called the wobbles.

Although all the lights were on full in the hall and sunporch there was no one in the front of the house when I got back to the Vicarage just before nine. I set down my overnight bag and went through to the library. Opening the door I saw Hank on his feet making wide and emphatic gestures and Mellie curled up in a corner of the davenport, itself as big as a trailer, which made her look small and exquisite. I had walked in on a husband-and-wife parley and before I could move out of it I caught, as though hung on the walls of the cavernous book-lined room, bright pictures from my memory. Hank and Mellie Gavin at the country club breakfast where Francis Cheyne had told us the story of the angels who flew in the Battle of Britain. The airport gate where Mellie had surrendered and agreed to come here to Beach City. Hank preaching his Follow Me sermon. These came, I'm sure, because I was startled by these two entirely different people. People change by the day hour and minute. No change I'd ever seen before seemed to me so far-reaching, so deep, so real. In his mirror, shaving of a morning, Hank must see a face that had been in battle for many days and yet it was without any of the brittle eat-drink-and-be-merry unhappiness we meet around us. With no makeup at all, her hair dragged tight back, Mellie had—how shall I say what I felt then?—at once settled for something new and retained much of the old.

Hank said, "Don't go, Godmama," and Mellie said, "we're only going round and round, we shan't get any forwarder," and she gave the little cat grin which is her sign-off, she got up and said, "If we stay here in Beach City much longer they can dig us up like they did Tutankhamen, nobody'll know what I'm supposed to represent," and as we went along the hall she said "Deedee ought to be back," and I said "Where is she?" and Mellie said, low, "A drive with the boy friend, he came by, and it is a night for lovers young or old isn't it?" With adverse surprise I said, "Aren't you taking this rather lightly?" and she gave a small shrug and said, "No, not really. I didn't know what else to *do*. She was quite frantic about him. She's so afraid somebody is going to hurt him; right now she thinks she can't live without him. I'm doing my best to play this one by ear. If I said no, she might go anyhow and I'd lose the confidence between us. They promised to be in by the good old curfew hour of nine. Don't worry, sweetie."

I thought the faint worry shadow was in her eyes, not mine.

Hank hadn't heard any of this, as we came into the oasis of light and color Mellie had created, he said, "We can't make up our minds."

"About what?" I said.

"Anything," Hank said, and added in a burst of forced good cheer, "except that we've carried our marriage to the other side of hell, which I suppose everybody has to. It looks unassailable now, doesn't it, love?"

"I'm a very exceptional woman," Mellie said smugly.

"It's my conclusion," Hank said, "that the circle is ever traveled anew and the only way out of a rut is up or down."

"And which is which we *don't* know," Mellie said.

What I feel is necessary to understand those hours, what came later that night, I have put into my own words. When two people are as close as the young Gavins, they use a language sometimes hard for others to comprehend—they do not finish sentences, they have names for things which offer no identification to anybody else, they exchange jokes which are Congolese and phrases which are jargon.

Hank began it by prowling up and down the room, always in the gloaming that room was, and when Mellie suggested he stop he said "I feel like a scruffy wolf, my stomach is going up and down and so is my mind."

"It's an advantage if you know it," Mellie said.

"Do you see that I have *promised* them things and now I don't think I can deliver?" Hank said.

"Do you think that will matter much?" Mellie said.

He stopped in front of her then and she felt, she told me, there was a damper on his usual extraordinary aliveness. She confirmed his attraction which was masculine but had at the moment nothing to do with sex. *A man.* But a man at this moment in grave distress. He said, "It's the whole business. That's what I thought I was sent to do."

"Big brave words," Mellie said, "I've never been sure just what you think you mean by them."

His stare was belligerent. Finally, he said, "They mean

you have been sent to keep the promises or it's like that movie about Jesus that is a series of beautiful pictures and couldn't ever have anything to do with our lives. I opened my mouth and said the Risen Christ is happening to you now. Let's go. You heard me! I was going out among the multitudes—Stu Margolis' wife who's slopping up gin all day and Mrs. Vosburgh's varicose veins that she's too proud to admit make her life a misery and Olin McAddams' soul that's shriveling up like a pea—I said I was going to do something about all this—"

"You're trying all the time," Mellie said. "Trying's the key word."

"No it isn't," Hank said, "or maybe it is at first. Comes a time when you either *do* it, or you get to hell out, or you degenerate into a middle-aged fat-assed prig which I jolly well could."

While he talked he was studying her, almost hanging on to her, this time it would seem he knew that she had to become the other half of himself and his mission *if* it turned out he had one, or it'd dry up and blow away. She'd won so much love from his people. More than he had. She understood people a damn sight better than he did. Responsibility was the highest form of humanism, it was a string you could never let go of, Mellie was where other people were concerned a responsible human being. If he didn't have the Light then Mellie was far out and up above him. This quality of responsibility was the true feminine mystique, wasn't it? A special quality of *woman*, her divine responsibility for all the really important things. He burst out suddenly, loudly, "Have you been too unhappy here, my dear love?"

Mellie gave him a slow smile, a slow answer. Her eyes were shut and she was seeing her other life, what up until this exact moment she would have called her real life and to which she had always—and still was—determined to return. To Melanie Cheyne Gavin it seemed that from the day she came to California she had lived two lives, and not alone because of her still incredible change of circumstances. Rather because Chicago was Chicago and Beach City was Beach City. The Middle West was the Middle West and California was California.

Her eyes were hot, dark, she gave Hank a ferocious glance, she said "Not unhappy. You're here. I miss a lot. I loved my way of life in Chicago. People there care about so many things they seem to ignore here. Hell—I don't like housework, I wish I'd been taught to do it well, I thought I'd loathe it to a point of maybe not being able to do it or stand it. I've found out if you have any *sense,* you can make do with it. We're trying to be as honest as people can—aren't we?—" his grunt made her laugh, the dark cloud over him seemed to lift a little, she went on—"I want you to know that you must not let anything about that influence you. A wife's first business is her husband's business. If this is your business—I'll manage."

He started to speak, but she uncurled herself and sat on the edge of the davenport, holding up her palm to stop him.

"Wait a minute, I want to get some things straight," she said. "You say religions like trees, like nations, die at the top. Oh—*actually* the roots begin to quit functioning because nobody has watered them, they have not had enough water, or fertilizer, nobody's cut away the dead wood or the tangles where one branch is strangling another. But they *show* they're dying at the top, that's how you can tell, that's where the warning comes. Right? I understand all this. So—begin at the top. Chicago is a top. It's a center of the heart of the United States and as goes the responsibility of the United States so goes this twenty-second civilization of which we have record. Am I still on the right track?"

"Yes," Hank said, "except to save the whole thing we—"

"Don't interrupt, kindly," Mellie said. "This is over my head, I'm out of my depths, if you interrupt I'll get so mixed up I won't be able to say it at all. Now. Philanthropy, which I've tried to practice all my life, the welfare state, the war on poverty, seeing children get medical care, educational betterment—as I see it and I think you do too, this is our best, our responsibility, but it's not the roots—it's the top. Now you and I know how to read the warning at the top in Chicago—and we'd know how to give a hand at digging around the roots and maybe dumping a few wheelbarrows full of manure—we'd start at the top there. We ought to go there."

For a moment or two he seemed trying to answer her, struggling to answer her. Then he gave up, and began to walk back and forth and out into the hall and back in again.

Oh yes. This would be wonderful, this would be easy, this would be smooth, especially now. *With what he had,* at this very minute, he could go back to Chicago and give out with all that was left—what Mellie had described—philanthropy, the best of humanism. Empty at the top already. But he could serve. *Well.* Successfully, as many better men than he were content to do.

Almost inarticulately, he began to roar some kind of answer, "No," he said, "no no. No. It's got to be in Beach City—don't you see it's got to be in Beach City? If I'm ever going to find him again—I'm not going to find him in Chicago."

Almost visibly, racking him physically, he put that temptation behind him.

He said, "It was here. To these people."

He seemed to be counting them over to himself.

Jack Nestor and the man named Walt.

The bartender.

A guy who'd stood by in the pinches like Archie Paddock.

The upturned faces that morning he'd preached the sermon, telling them all—the promises will be kept. Come and see.

The City Council. Even though he had struck out looking, something had reached them, they'd given him what everybody said to be a miracle.

To Mellie, he cried out, "These are the people I made the promises to. Right here in this town I kicked up all that uproar about that goddam Zone Variance. Here on Pacific Coast Highway I was going to build them a new church where they could always find God. I challenged a man named Steve Retzlaff—"

With real anger, Mellie said, "He's my idea of a complete wart."

"Even if he was, which he isn't," Hank said, "He's my wart. I chose him. Mellie—" he broke off, his eyes shut and he shook his head.

Every man is afraid to speak to anyone else about his inner life in plain, simple terms. Every man is afraid to say in simple plain terms that he has an inner life. After all this time, beginning way back in Chicago, Hank couldn't speak of his inner life to Mellie, his beloved, his best friend and severest critic to use an old gag, not in plain simple terms. How could he say out loud to Mellie the inner torment and sorrow that was upon him, how could he say out loud My God, my God, why has thou forsaken me? *Old terminology*. My God, why have You forsaken me? Get with it, boy, that'll sound phony, you know nothing phony ever gets by Mellie, he knew he wasn't phony, but he could so easily be ridiculous—there echoed in him that first *You have to be kidding* of Mellie's. You have to be *kidding*.

Carefully, he said, "Mellie—I'm lost. Listen to me a minute. I thought I saw our life, our way of life, it seemed plain to me. Then—I got to that moment—you know there was a day when the disciples, the apostles—they had to face it, he was *gone*. The man they loved and who'd loved them, who'd been with them—he was gone. He's gone from me, too. I'm trying to find him again. When I look at Steve

Retzlaff and know I haven't got anything to fight him with —no sword—no nothing—"

"I wish it didn't have to be Steve Retzlaff," Mellie said, and for the first time in her life sheer panic made her blood run cold.

Where was Deedee?

She shouldn't have let her *go*—

"I wish so too," Hank said, "but it can't. This one—we have to finish this one. I don't know much any more but I know it has to be Steve—"

"Don't let it bother you too much," Mellie said, "If there's one gent I can take care of, it's good old S. J. Retzlaff."

As soon as I sat down in the sunporch I noticed that Mellie's attention raced to the windows every few minutes. Once she went and opened the door and peered up and down the street. There was nothing to see under the light from the lamp on the corner and right there Millie told me later, began a difficulty with her breathing.

For some reason, I thought of the chaplain. I didn't know why I hadn't told Hank about his letter. I expect it was because I felt he would have every right to think I'd been meddling. The chaplain was his own special voice. But I found myself saying lamely that I'd had a letter and that he was praying for us all and had sent Hank a message, though I assumed Hank had, by this time, heard direct. If so, he didn't mention it. He asked me to repeat the message and I said, "Tell Hank—I think this was it—if he doesn't want to raise Lazarus he might as well go back to Chicago."

"Did he mention how you raise Lazarus—" Hank began with terrible bitterness, "by your faith, it says. If you haven't got as much as a grain of mustard seed, did he say how you are supposed to raise Lazarus?"

"It was something about thanking the Father *before* it happened," I said. "He had particularly pointed out that Jesus had thanked the Father and said he knew the Father always heard him *before* he told Lazarus to—to come forth."

Hank made a sound like a groan and the sweat broke out all over his face.

Mellie hadn't heard the groan. She was furious with Steve Retzlaff and now to this was added the chaplain, that mythical offstage figure who had become to her the bane of this existence into which he had somehow lured Hank. She was edgy anyhow, she was tense with apprehension, a flame was lit in her eyes, in her cheeks, she was talking—*talking*— in a higher voice than usual, she was saying ". . . about raising Lazarus and the other young man, the one from Nain whose mother was a widow—I can't remember the name exactly, but I've seen people at the *hospital* when I was a nurse's aid nobody could tell, and that's the truth—you know how shock or an internal wound can cause paralysis. We had a man once, quite young, they brought him into Passavant in a comatose condition. The doctors called it an nth degree of cadaveric shock I think they said, but that was afterward. I mean when they brought him in he had no blood pressure at all, no breath, cold and clammy—they had quite a consultation in all directions before they could be sure whether he was dead or not . . . and of course, everybody knows people have been buried alive by mistake—"

She ran down.

Silence came, in it I heard that the wind had risen, as it did most nights this time of year.

Hank said, "The chaplain understood about combat. Nobody understands about combat unless they've been in it. The chaplain understood combat. So did Colin."

Under her breath, Mellie said, "Colin, goddam him. So this is now combat. It's going to be a fight. That's why my husband now wants Colin. Came Christ the tiger."

To herself she was saying all right, Hank's alive, and I have to let him have his battle hymn of the republic, but not alone, not alone by God.

She said, "All right. What is it you want?"

"Pretty plain, isn't it?" Hank said, "I can't turn back and follow no more after him now. I—whatever's there I have got to go forward, haven't I?"

Mellie said, "If that's the way you feel about it—and away we go."

A shriek of the wind died down and left the sound of a car, coming into the street, hesitating, stopping before the parsonage.

Mellie gave a gasp of relief and ran to the window.

It had to be Deedee and Beany.

Not until they got out of the car, big as it was, did she realize that it was Steve Retzlaff and his wife Gloria.

6

At that moment, I began the strange experience of double-vision-emotion, a part of the makeup of every newspaperman and/or writer. I was in deep sympathy, at one, with all that I saw must transpire here, now. In the familiar drum beat my heart announced the coming together of all the elements and characters of my own story and I was filled for those I loved with terror and compassion. At the same time with a callousness that never ceases to dumfound me I was spectator-reporter, noting with professional care every detail, photographically, recording every word on my built-in tape recorder, peering with interest and curiosity at reactions, expressions, suspense and suffering, hope and fear of this scene as I had of a courtroom where we waited for a life-and-death jury and the defendant, the ghost of the murdered, the families, lawyers, witnesses, were the cast.

As Steve and Gloria Retzlaff came up the front steps in the wildly moving lamp-lit windy night I saw that she had bundled herself into a coat, held tight around her, but Steve had stopped for nothing, he still wore a sort of smoking jacket in wine-red, pan-velvet and he was talking *talking* so loudly that sound came to us, though no words.

I looked first at Hank, standing perfectly still, his jaw set, the sun-bleached hair making that theatrical halo of which Mellie had spoken and a quotation came to me *whole*, nothing is so good to have by you to replace your own panicked thinking in crisis or heartbreak, in fiery ordeal as great words and records of shining deeds and songs of glory, as Anne Morrow Lindberg has said. *The big courage is the cold-blooded kind, the kind that never lets go even when you're feeling empty inside and your blood's thin and there's no kind of fun or profit to be had, and the trouble's not over in an hour or two but you know is going to last for months and years. One of the men in the war was speaking about that kind, he called it fortitude, and fortitude is the biggest thing a man can have, just to go on enduring when there seems no guts nor heart left in you.*

The head man, for that was Hank's old friend, the apostle Paul, who'd once written him so many letters to Chicago. In one to Ephesus, where he had all that trouble with the silversmiths, who were certainly trying to do him in, Paul had said *that ye may be able to withstand in the evil day and having done all to stand . . .* and as he began to spread the Word around the known world he had told the citizens of Rome I am persuaded that neither death nor powers nor things present nor things to come nor heights nor depths *nor any other* creature shall be able to separate us from the love of God which is in Christ Jesus our Lord . . . which seems to indicate he'd been in the forefront of the battle between good and evil.

Fortitude.

He had it, Paul did. Hank had it, too.

I thought this with some reassurance as I saw that Mellie had on her fighting face which meant she was appalled and nervous behind it, knowing that Beany and Deedee were due back any minute. This, I said to myself, is going to be very unpleasant, for Steve Retzlaff striding through the door looked to me a totally unscrupulous and insanely enraged character and his wife had obviously been weeping until her eyes were swollen and her makeup was smeared, so that it gave the effect of a clown.

A little later I decided that unpleasant was the understatement of the whole story.

On entering Gloria gave that squeak which presumably fulfills social obligations, Steve ignored this flummery, his opening line was classical, he said, "Where's Deedee?"

Hank glanced at his wife and his eyebrows went up. For this was Mellie Cheyne, debutante glamor star of the cotillion, this was young Mrs. Gavin who bullied the rich into donating millions to her causes and she presented to Steve Retzlaff what I call Ceezee-Guest's-Cover-of-*Time* look.

It was also, I realized, the carefree expression of a top pro gambler sitting behind a four-card flush on which, against amateur competition, he had just bet his last chip.

A warning came up in my throat. *Dear darling blessed child, Mellie my pet, Steve Retzlaff is not an amateur, many other things but not that.*

Even so, I saw Mellie's friendly slightly amused insolence stop him for a moment, and Mellie got a little more time by going to kiss Gloria. To my knowledge she had never done this before, she was not a promiscuous *oh-darling* cheek-kisser. This time she did and then she held Gloria off and said, "My dear, you've been crying." And she gave

Gloria's husband the brilliance of that little three-cornered cat smile and said, "Stevie, have you been beating your wife again?"

Actually, it was easy even before I had firsthand knowledge, to put together that scene in the Retzlaff mansion on top of its charming little hill which was the forerunner of their arrival at the Gavin parsonage.

No chance at dinner, served by the colored maid, to say anything. Afterward, Gloria as usual went upstairs to what unfortunately she called her boudoir. Instead of going to his downstairs library-office-den, this time her husband followed her.

What's all this about Deedee?" Steve said. "Why is she staying all night with Mellie Gavin?"

Already sitting behind a card table on which she was attempting to put together a numbered mosiac of a basket of fruit, Gloria kept her eyes on it while she gave as convincing a burst of exasperation as she could manage. "Oh Steve!" she said. "There are times when you are too absurd about that girl. She's not ten years old, you know. I ask you—where is a girl supposed to be safer than at the *parsonage* of her own church with the minister's wife as a chaperone? I ask you. And you think Mellie Gavin is the greatest—"

"We're going to have to see about that," Steve said, "I knew he was some sort of—give him the best of it, visionary or something—but I thought she was as sound as a woman can be. Now I'm beginning to wonder about both of them." He picked up a piece of lemon-yellow tile and fitted it into a pomegranate, it didn't belong there, he left it anyhow and Gloria shot him a look of real annoyance. He said, "Come to think of it in any practical sense, a man who'd give up the job he had in Chicago and come out here for the money we pay him—it occurs to me there may have been something wrong back there. I've got an idea I may stop over and talk to Margolis next time I go to Chicago. Gavin has a lot of pretty dangerous theories and now I'm coming to the place where I'd like to ask a few questions about his wife, too." They both seemed to be intent on the small, bright-colored tiles, not looking at each other. Steve broke out hotly, "All right—let's have it—why should Deedee go and stay *all night* there? Or anywhere, for that matter. I don't like it, I tell you."

Is all your family within? Here is her father's house!

"She's got as good a home of her own as a girl could want," Steve Retzlaff said, and got up restlessly, "a hi-fi, a TV, a beautiful bedroom, why should she want to spend the night somewhere else?"

"Girls do," Gloria said, poking at a dozen tiles one after the other, "I can remember when I was a kid in high school, either I was calling up my folks to ask if I could stay all night with Lizzie—she was my best friend—or Lizzie was calling up to see if she could spend the night with me. It—they think it's an adventure—"

"Adventure," Steve said, not liking the word, "they'll be better off without any adventure at that age."

"Oh nothing bad," Gloria said, "you know yourself Deedee has what we used to call a crush on Mellie Gavin and I can't say I blame her and if she can learn to speak like Mellie does and grows up with *style*—Deedee needs that, you know, Mrs. Gavin has it and no use kidding myself I don't have—not *style* so that you put on anything—"

"I know all that," Steve said, "but why tonight specially?"

Sans witchcraft—to run from her guardage to what she feared to look on!

"What *is* the matter with you?" Gloria said.

How could she know nor would he tell her of the boy with the blue-black hair and the dark-dark-ivory skin, who had said I warn you, don't try to take her away from me, and ever since he had spun like a ballet dancer on one toe, and run out, he and his words had haunted Steve Retzlaff as no man had been haunted since Hamlet.

Now Gloria, as she stirred and matched and picked up and put down, was sure her husband had found out something, her hands began to shake, if he finds out I knew and didn't tell him he could just as well kill me, she thought and said loudly, "Steve, you are making a lot out of absolutely nothing. Deedee is a good, sweet girl, if you don't drive her by too much opposition. Of course I admit it's hard now when the poor little things never have any real—I mean when they're allowed to date when they're practically still in rompers—how can you read their minds or know what they're thinking? Just the same—"

Fathers from hence trust not your daughters' minds by what you see them act. As long ago as that, Brabantio had cried out to the Duke: "Who would have a daughter?"

"What is it you want Steve, for goodness sake," his wife said.

"I want to find my daughter," Steve said, "I want to see her."

How could he cry out of this—savage hunch—this apprehension—cry out like Desdemona's father *O thou foul thief, where hast thou stowed my daughter? Judge me the world, thou hast practiced on her delicate youth*— Why had she chosen tonight of all nights to spend away from home? Who could be trusted with her delicate youth with a boy like that prowling around? A woman like Mellie Gavin—a worldly woman—he must know where his daughter was or he'd suffocate. Yet if he went to the Gavins—Deedee would hate it, and he could see that amused expression on Mellie Gavin's face.

"I really think you're out of your mind about her sometimes," Gloria was saying and he shouted at her, "If she'd had a mother—"

Gloria upset the table as she stood up in one quick move. Through her teeth in a whisper that hissed and squeaked she said: "You gave her the mother she had, I didn't. It's not my fault you married a woman'd rather be a whore than stay married to you—oh, I'm sorry Steve, I'm sorry. God forgive me—only you pick on me and I do try to do my best for Deedee–a teen-age stepdaughter isn't so easy to know—"

"Take it easy," Steve said wearily, "it's just—tonight I'm sort of on edge. Mellie Gavin's all right, only how do I know with all this premarital relations in high society, I've heard about, I don't like it. I just wish *tonight*—"

Are the doors locked?

Gloria had begun to cry, softly, this was the first time they had ever really talked about Deedee as though she was *theirs*, when they had *time*—Steve never had *time* it always seemed to Gloria—to go over things the way parents used to—she said, "I suppose we could go and get her."

Steve gave her a quick smile. "That's a bright idea!" he said.

"Oh—" Gloria said, retreating from it, "we couldn't. What in the world could you say to Mellie Gavin—I mean to *explain* it."

"Get a coat," Steve said, "I can't see why they'd object to our dropping by when our daughter's there. They can understand how a father feels."

"You love her more than anything, don't you?" Gloria said.

"Yes," Steve Retzlaff said, stooping absently to set the card table right side up, he was a man who liked things *tidy*. "Yes—a man loves his daughter more—no I—I don't mean more than his wife, Gloria, but it's different. It's—you don't have anything to do with it, and it all starts when she's a *little girl*—that's what the difference is. She gets bigger but she's still—this sounds like sentimental crap but it's true—she's still always in a way your little girl—"

In the car driving down the lovely winding slopes under the sycamores and live oaks toward the lights of the town and the tall moving shapes of the oil wells, the wind began to talk and drive and scream at them, wind always affected Steve Retzlaff, Gloria knew that, though he would never never admit it. His temper began to answer to its lash and scream, he muttered, he remembered, *are the doors locked?* a fine thing for other people to keep a man's daughter at night and how did they know the danger that threatened her. *Often did beguile her of her tears when I did speak of some distressful stroke my youth suffered—and I loved her that she did pity them—*

"Like a stray cur dog," Steve Retzlaff said, "from the time she was a little thing, I remember one damned drowned female *cat*—she always brought them home."

"Yes, I remember," Gloria said, "I remember that, too."

"A mangy *cur,*" Steve Retzlaff said. "She'd pity him if he howled–"

So that when they walked up the porch steps through the high dark hall into the sunporch of the parsonage, his voice was angry again and Gloria's eyes were wet. And Mellie said, "You've been crying. Steve boy, have you been beating your wife?"

"Is that supposed to be funny?" Steve said, and Mellie quickly put a hand on his arm and said, "No no—you took us by surprise, and I never saw Gloria cry before."

Gloria tried a small laugh. "I think Steve's ulcers have been kicking up a little," she said, "they're sort of his receiving set for this ESP they talk so much about. He says that's just plain *hunches*—anyhow, he had a hard day and that makes his ulcers kick up and he was cross because Deedee wasn't there when he got home."

Steve had recovered himself now, he had full recuperative powers as all leaders must have. Now he was Steve Retzlaff and this was his town. He was cockahoop, smiling, showing all his teeth, he spoke to Hank ignoring Mellie, "I'm sure you can understand, padre, a man likes his girl waiting for him when he comes home at the end of the day."

"Even if it's very seldom," Gloria said with a giggle.

Steve ignored her, too, he said, "You haven't any children of your own—" and Hank cut in, with pleasant authority, "I wouldn't say that," he said, "Mellie had a whole hospital of them in Chicago and they loved her very much. My mother, who died when I was quite small, told me—it's one of the few things about her I remember—that God had to make childless fathers and mothers to take care of the motherless and fatherless kids."

Mellie said, "I've heard my godmama say that."

"Well, now," Steve said, "Deedee isn't exactly fatherless. As I said before, where is she?"

"Probably gone to bed," Gloria said, and I could see Mellie toy with that gambit for a moment and discard it as worthless.

Quietly, Hank said, "Where is she, my love?" and only then did Mellie face him, smiling. The lights in the sunporch were a dark shaded gold, as flattering as footlights, there were no curtains, no blinds, and the shadows from the big eucalyptus trees came rushing in and out, and Mellie was somehow spotlighted, she took a big gold hairpin out of her hair, inspected it, tightened the knot piled high atop her head and stuck it back in, she said, "I know where she is, my love my love, but I am not going to tell you."

Steve Retzlaff said nothing, his expression didn't change, except that his eyes grew hot as you see the wall heater begin to glow when the electricity is turned on. He watched them, waiting. Coiled waiting, I thought.

"Point of honor," Mellie said, with everything she had behind it, she said "I'm sorry, Steve. As I say, this is a point of honor. Deedee trusts me." The corners of her mouth went up, she looked full at Steve, "I am the only person in the world she does trust."

The solar plexus blow knocked Steve speechless for a moment, then he said, "What am I supposed to do at this so-called *point?* I am her father. I came here to see her. Where is she?"

Mellie's laugh was warm, beautiful, confident. She said, "She promised to be back by nine." One finger with a pale pink polished nail pointed at the grandfather clock in the hall. Its hands stood at 10 minutes to nine. "She's always kept her promises to me. Wait at least until nine o'clock before you do anything foolish—please?"

The pause fell chill again. Then Steve Retzlaff nodded.

The minutes, nine more of them, began to go slowly like camels in the sand, weighted with apprehension.

Mellie sat down on the ottoman of Gloria's chair, she kept both feet on the floor, so I knew the clock was ticking painfully inside of her. Moving toward the appointments she had with Steve Retzlaff's daughter, one in eight minutes and five seconds, one at seven-thirty the next morning. She expected Deedee back on the stroke of nine, if she *wasn't* back it would spell disaster, yet her whole mind had to concentrate on *willing* them to *see* the Retzlaff car so that Beany wouldn't come in.

Thinking at some level of all the wise and foolish, tortured and careless, worried and anxious fathers and mothers who had watched, were watching, clocks around the world I saw part of Steve Retzlaff smashing against windows, listening until his ears seemed to grow, seeing cars flash by on the avenue, one two three turn into quiet streets and pass on by. His ulcers, receiving stations for this thing called ESP, were sending out painful signals. The other part of him came back to see his wife in a light that was kind, he could remember why he'd married her. She and Mellie Gavin had fallen into one of those low-voiced tête-à-têtes two women can conduct anywhere under any circumstances. His feeling scrambled, to all intents and purposes he found himself alone with the tall young minister, he was still determined to get rid of the fellow but he *might* be a Man-of-God, better go carefully until Deedee was home safe. He felt anger against them all. I am *suffering,* he thought in surprise, and nobody cares.

In this he found he was wrong. Hank Gavin said automatically, "She cannot fall out of God's hands, Steve," and dry or not, it was a prayer. Then he said with what could only be loving kindness, "Do you mind if while we wait I explain why I haven't accepted your resignation? As Kipling and Ecclesiastes tell us, there is no discharge in this war."

"I'm not taking on any war with the church," Steve Retzlaff said.

"Nor am I," Hank said, "I joined it. I just think it needs the shot in the arm that some—*works* would give it."

"That's not my department," Steve said stiffly.

"It has to be mine," Hank Gavin said, with extraordinary and moving sincerity. "Wouldn't you like to *see* the angel of God's presence in—our church? I can't agree to let you leave, Steve. Jesus Christ didn't leave the church. According to Scriptures, he went on to the very end, speaking *in* the synagogues, teaching *in* the Temple. He drove the moneychangers *out,* he stayed *in.* All he wanted was to get rid of them. So the temple—the church—could be what it must be—Our Father's House."

"Maybe that's all true," Steve Retzlaff said, moving to the window and back, "I can't see what it has to do with us."

"It *is* us," Hank said. "The church has to be us."

I was held by this, I was aware of Mellie's growing tension.

It was like a countdown now.

Just as in the courtroom, waiting for the life-or-death verdict to come in, I kept all the main figures under my eyes, yet my imagination *had* to go into the locked jury room trying to see—to estimate—what the old Sour Dough Mountains farmer was doing, what the pretty young woman in the flowered blouse would say, whether or not the artist with a beard had followed the evidence—how many votes had they taken? How did it stand now? How much longer would it be before they reached a verdict? So my imagination, which Napoleon said rules the world, Emerson said is the health of every man's soul, and White calls the gateway to reality, was reaching out to the boy and girl wherever they were. Painting with an impressionist's brush the best I could do.

The murmurs of Mellie and Gloria—

Phrases of Hank's, of Steve Retzlaff's—hunger, oppression, crime, you can tell the ideals of a nation by its advertisements, one of them said that, war and peace—new ways new ways always searching for new ways—the way of Christ is the newest way–

Tick tock tick tock the clock carried on its countdown.

All faded into an unreal background.

The children *the children*—come out come out wherever you are—

Compact tight little sports car. Deedee's fifteenth birthday present. You can get a driver's permit at fifteen in California. Parked where young things always park, high on the cliffs. Trees and seas whispering a song, perhaps the same that ofttimes hath charmed magic casements, opening on the foam of perilous seas, in faery lands forlorn. The casements of that tight little car opened on perilous seas now. Seas named we-can't-live-without-each-other. A man was transforming the world, hiding the perils, but the song never stopped its forlorn beat. Their passion was a clear hot flame, clear with innocence and hot with desire and golden with first love but now it shone forlornly—

Too old to be children, too young to be man and woman, that was what made their faery land so forlorn. You'll lose that lovin' feelin' strummed and vibrated in them played by *fear*, fear of the adult world around them that had grown up and now knew nothing.

In broken words they had talked about tomorrow morning.

He clutched her.

A wild cat was after them. They pulled the leaves up over them, a mountain lion was prowling.

The moonlight came in at their magic casements but they had their eyes shut now.

By tomorrow morning at seven-thirty there might be fog. Often as soon as the moon set, the fog entered on its little cat feet. They clung together—if you have had a child waking up in the dark pursued by a bad dream you know how they cling, nothing clings like a child. This I knew, I knew it then, I felt it in the marrow of my bones and in my news nose.

They came home, oh yes they did, they came home *first*.

Deedee, remembering, looked at the clock on the dashboard, it said five minutes to nine. She said, "We have got to go! I promised Mrs. Gavin I'd be back by nine or she wouldn't have let me come at all—"

"Let you!" Beany said furiously. "Who are they to *let* you—" he couldn't sustain his defiance. He knew who they were and well he knew and they could tell his love to come and go and *when*. He had known this since he was three. Long ago, Deedee had said to Mellie Gavin, "He's so vulnerable—he's so helpless—he's so *vulnerable*—" now he was clutching her again, saying, "You can't live without me, don't let them take you away from me, baby."

"I won't," she said, "I won't." He knew she meant it. But she was so small. How could she make it so? She was like his littlest brother Mark. Mark was two and a half, he wasn't afraid of anything yet, he stuck out his chin and defied *anything* but he was always too small.

A car turned into our street.

The clock whirred to announce its coming tintinnabulation.

Just as in the house the first stroke sounded, in the car Deedee moved closer to Beany and said with a gasp of terror, "That's my father's car—" and Beany jammed his foot on the floor board, they shot by and around the corner on two wheels, though now they had no place to go but on and on over the cliffs. They thought, felt, to the beat of music, they did not know silence, you'll lose that lovin' feelin' you're going to lose that lovin' feelin' that decayed old man covered with lard is going to take it away from you, the music strummed, the music had always taken Beany over, it pounded in his blood stream and the blood stream went to his brain the music strummed you're going to lose that lovin' feelin' and swelled on into *Leibestode,* to him one great love song into another great love song and Beany cried out—"Deedee—*love*—oh god Deedee—"

As he heard that car gunned recklessly, Hank broke off, he stared at the windows where the shadows grew darker and darker and the trees whirled in a macabre dance, swinging and swaying. He held the room and those in it still by main force or it would have begun to roll with the trees, he said, "This is *combat*. We fight not against flesh and blood but against the powers of evil. I have overcome them, Jesus said, to those who *overcome* I will give all things. *Combat,* don't you see, so that our eyes can begin to see and our ears to hear what is always here, about us now. I had a friend once that was always shoulder to shoulder with me in combat. I need a friend now. This is a fight, you're a fighter, a power guy. Retzlaff, if we could try this experiment of the *power* of good coming into the world, if we could get a little something going, it would give people hope. There's no use giving them everything else if they haven't got hope. Don't you see what I'm trying to do is like a seed, young men now everywhere, hungry, thirsty, they want action in Christ—if you and I—"

He was talking against time.

The clock began to strike.

1 2 3

You've never had it so good. Yet it's bustin' out all over, evil is.

4 5 6

Heavy dull bongs.

Only four more bongs to go and it would be too late.

I knew, don't ask me how, I knew Romeo and Juliet had been in that car that gunned by so recklessly even though that's the way all teen-agers drive now. What can happen in seconds—I knew that, too, in seconds a plane can crash, an assassination can destroy Camelot, a suicide pact, adultery—they are all a matter of *seconds*–

7 8 9

The strokes squeezed my heart. You never had it so good but those strokes squeezed my heart not my head, and I thought it began to drip. 7 8 9 drops dripping inside me and we all never had it so good but what do you do now?

On the last stroke Steve Retzlaff said savagely, "Now goddamitohell I said I'd wait until nine and it's nine by your clock. I am going to call somebody to find my daughter." Gloria's cry sounded like the first one coming out of the anesthetic and Mellie said, clear and cold, "We must give it a moment or two of grace." The grace of God? There but for the grace of God go we all sometime somehow without grace where do we all go? "You're too angry to think straight, Steve," Mellie said. "Going to the police will start a lot of talk," and Steve said, "The police don't talk about Steve Retzlaff's affairs. You refuse to see she can come to worse harm with that *pachuco*—" and Mellie said in a shrill whisper that still held generations of authority, "You leave this girl to me. You men!"

But Steve took a step toward the telephone beside the clock in the hall, he said *getoutofmyway* and moved her aside and Hank, his hands on Steve's shoulders, swung him back. He said, "You will call nobody until we have prayed. You hear me? I may not be a very good follower in his steps, but I know one thing, we are going to pray on our troubles whether we think we can or not. Always. Now. *First*. Then you can call the cops and the Marines and the militia if you want to, but not until we have looked to Him concerning His children—"

Frenzy persisted, for a moment it was frenzy contained by silence.

Then Hank began a few fumbling words . . . "Your promise—a man came to You and said my son is off his head—he's a bad boy—he falls into the fire, You cast out those devils—a man came to You and said my only child is dead, Mary came to You and said If You had been here my brother Lazarus would not have died—You healed them all—Oh Christ risen, Christ ever present, open our eyes, our ears, come as You promised—"

In the most shocking sound I have ever heard in my life, Steve Retzlaff began to laugh, the high horrid laughter of scorn.

"Jesus!" he said, "I must be out of my goddam mind standing here listening to this goddam mumbo-jumbo—"

Once again a car sounded in our street. The beat of the engines was slow and muffled. It was it was. This time it stopped. The beat of feet on the sidewalk, coming up the steps, crossing the porch, was heavy and uncertain. Dum dum de dum, dumdedumdedumdedum. Dum dum de dum dumdedumdedumdedum and we're hanging Danny Deever in the morning.

Hank opened the door.

The best he could, Beany was carrying her. Heavy for him. Too heavy.

Young love lies sleeping, I thought stupidly.

Fluid, I saw what had been, you can know of it only what I can tell you, it was in color, the colors ran together as it slid out of the past with the speed of light.

Last minute, he had hit the brakes madly. Wheels spun, the car leaped and swung sideways to the edge, he had braked automatically from inside his head where it had flashed to him *suppose it kills me behind the wheel and only smashes her* once on the highway he'd seen a car smash where some were killed and some weren't, he could hear those who weren't screaming, *suppose she lay there crying out* and he dead, helpless beside her. It had been then the brakes screamed. He said *Deedee, love, will you go with me?* Whether she heard him or not she had sealed that pact with her *understanding* smile, he's so *vulnerable,* of course she would have to go with him anywhere. The thin sharp knife, boy's knife, teen-age weapon, Mexican-Indian weapon, all the Mexican boys at school and some others had knives, even the girls carried them in their built-up tangled hair, the thin sharp little knife was like an ancestral extension of his *hand.* His hand went through her heart, he *left* it there, of course he left it, it bound them together still, she gave a small sigh and leaned against him, *rag doll,* Oh—*Deedee, come back come back*—what had he done what had he done oh godwhat-hadhedone—a regret so sharp and terrible that it almost of itself accomplished what he would now do to fulfill the pact, with that same small knife, but a boy who had just killed the thing he loves isn't thinking very straight is he? The colors were blurring, the blue was a *cop.* He hated cops, even Mark hated cops, they would be the first ones there, they always were, they'd drag her out of his dead arms and turn her over to see if she was dead. They were so stupid they wouldn't know they'd put their hands on her—no no he had to take her home. *I have to take her home I have to take her back*—then he could unsheathe the knife and—go after her, *some day I'll find her, wait for me Dee I'll be right back I'm going to take you home* a boy who has just killed the thing he loves doesn't think very straight he is like a little crazy or so it seems to me and he thought he had to bring her home.

To her friend.

To Mellie.

So—he brought her home.

She didn't breathe. Nothing breathed. No heart beat. No clock ticked. One hand hung limp over the boy's arm. A small hand with short stubby fingers. A strand of her hair was caught on a button of his blazer. Her face was turned from us, crushed into his shoulder. I couldn't get my eyes away from the stain on her white sweater. Here was a color I knew all right. The spot was small around the knife, it had seeped *inside,* only a little on the sweater, now it was still, a *still* spot of rust red. Mellie turned terribly clear perfectly aware not-deceived eyes on me. Never ducked anything. Never let herself off anything. We thought Deedee was dead; we would not admit it. We couldn't. We just could not. But knew she was dead.

The boy walked up to Mellie, he offered her young love sleeping in his arms, and we knew why he had come back.

He couldn't bear to leave her alone.

Even now, he couldn't bear to leave her.

Nobody moved first, everybody moved together. Too fast, the projectionist had gone mad, the screen was off vertical, off horizontal, off contrast, jumping drunkenly, through the maze a clear picture would come with terrifying unexpectedness and then the snow and staggers would be back.

Mellie took the girl from Beany. Mellie's face was as white and pinched as the girl's only it was for a flash what she would be as an old old woman who had done her best. Between us, we put the girl on the couch, it shook me that she was so light, so *little*, her bones weighed nothing at all.

Steve Retzlaff turned to stone watched us, he stared down at her, when he moved it was not toward her, a snarl, not human, a jet engine winding up to take off, *I think she is the only thing he ever loved,* his takeoff rolled toward Beany and at the same instant Gloria began to scream at the top of her lungs: "Get a doctor. We must get a doctor. Oh god a doctor, a doctor" and ran wildly to the telephone, her hands were uncontrollable, she couldn't dial any number, she kept dialing and dialing anyhow and screaming into the phone for a doctor.

This is the whole world, I thought. This will hit us all, us here, many others. Dully, dumbly, I thought what does it *matter* if Steve kills this one boy? Steve's going to kill him, well, if he doesn't the boy will go out and kill himself, he has to—that boy, he has killed the thing he loves, we all do, in such mean, pinching, unkind cruel little ways, belittling them to death sometimes. They had a pact, he and Deedee, so he must.

But we killed her, whichever way the pact is now completed. We will have killed him, too, children above all others cannot live without God because they remember, let Steve do it for him, I wouldn't mind seeing Steve Retzlaff dancing with nimble feet upon the air at the end of a rope, that's how much Christian I was right then. What the black bloody blasted hell does it matter whether Beany Teran goes out as soon as he can tear himself loose from looking his last upon Juliet's tomb and puts that thin boy's knife into his own heart or cuts his throat with it or whether Steve Retzlaff strangles him and throws him on a dust heap like a dead Mexican chicken? What do we care, really? Everybody will read about it and say Tut-tut what bad kids and continue to deny them a God who can do anything about it.

I know now what was in Hank's mind in that second that was less than the breath we tried to draw into collapsed lungs. He was thinking there is too much death. Everywhere. In Vietnam north and Mississippi south and Harlem east and Hollywood west, on front pages on television on stage and screen and magazines, everywhere all the time we are never immortal *now*. Talk of death. The death wish. The wrong *kind* of death. This death they talked and wrote about was not not not the open door to another life, another incarnation, a heaven or even a hell. This death was the other kind, without immortality at all. This was no river to cross with trumpets already sounding on the other side and the joy of Our Lord waiting on the other bank. *To know me is life eternal.* No no. This death was a victory over life. This grave had a sting. Maybe we were so bored and hurt with a life without God that we didn't *want* life to be eternal, we'd *had* it, so we dieted and drank and doped and danced and were merry oh so merry in groups from Darien, Connecticut to Beach City, California as our feet went down to drab death, tomorrow we would die and that would be the end of *us* chickens. Yet all the time inside we knew this was cockeyed. Once in a while somebody in person, in song or story, took off into the wild blue yonder and our hearts went with them and that wasn't to get to the moon or walk in space, it was a taste of eternity.

As Steve lunged, Hank was between him and the boy. I hadn't seen Hank Gavin move like that in a long time, he threw a block that would have stopped anybody but a madman, the mad have mad strength, this madman came on again to commit murder, it took more than one to subdue a madman, and the boy just stood there with his hands down. He didn't run, he waited for his fate, never moving his eyes from the quiet body on the couch, he was chained to her by that unswerving look.

Out of nowhere, in a split second, I had that queer sense that comes sometimes when you know a friend has come into the room or a plane or train though you haven't yet seen him. Colin was there. *Colin?* The silly little tune of *Joan of Arc* came up to me–*Joan of Arc we are calling you*—two of them at least there were two of them to subdue Steve Retzlaff bent on murder, they were in combat together again to hold this madman. Who had seen his daughter dead—*mine only child*. Or maybe she wasn't dead. *Comatose.* To the tune of *Joan of Arc, comatose* whistled in my dizzy brain. *Comatose condition. Cadaveric shock.* They'd given Juliet a potion which looked like death but wasn't, they'd burned Joan of Arc at the stake but her *heart* wouldn't burn, they found it. Could it be that the little girl Deedee was paralyzed with shock? Be a reporter. Make sense. But Mellie would never leave me this out. She said *The girl was dead.* She said: Do you take me for an amateur? I was in hospitals too long. Sometimes you can't tell, but sometimes you *can.* This time—she was dead. Kids have to have a reason to go on living.

That was afterward.

With difficulty, Hank had halted Steve's panting, crimson-faced, deadly charge. Maybe Colin *had* come, maybe he had brought angels to help them. I know this is poppycock, I said so to myself. Let's keep this intelligent, I said to myself, let's keep it sane and reasonable and intellectually possible for the boys. Let's not have *angels* again.

I knew what Mellie was thinking, we were all so tuned in you could not miss what people were thinking, Mellie was thinking bitterly *I am so afraid of looking a fool, I go and am a fool. One of those bright fools who used to believe that human progress is possible by the human best alone.*

Face to face with Steve Retzlaff, holding him by his upper arms, Hank said, "Listen to me. You must not—I cannot do anything—we cannot do anything unless you forgive them. You hear me? We must repent. Repent for what we have done to His children. We cannot do anything until you *ask* for love with which to forgive him. Steve—ask. *Ask!* You can't do it alone. Ask love to give you the grace to forgive. Continue you in his love, the love that is life cannot enter here and now unless you forgive him for what you drove him to do. Judge not! Oh Christ, here present, give our hearts the love with which You have forgiven us."

He was gasping for breath as though he had run ten miles.

Mellie stood looking down at the small still figure.

My work, the torment of her said, *my work this is.* I'm to blame. She seemed stripped of everything, by torment, by grief, by failure. I saw her hands go to her throat, but she couldn't free her voice, only her face spoke bright and terrible with a final bitterness. Mirror, mirror on the wall is this the same face with which Hank looked upon Colin—will he recognize the expression—slowly slowly she turned it to him, she said, "Hank—" and there came from her a sound of lostness. She had no place to go, *I have said there is no god, if only I could believe in a God who could help me now,* her voice came through at last and she said, "The *promises—I* hated it because—the *promises,* Hank—you said—"

He had turned to her, their eyes met, everything else stood still. We had forgotten ourselves.

"You promised me," Mellie said. It was a please but it was still a challenge, the challenge of her whole truth and life, she said, "Kept promises are the cornerstone—" it sounded far away, she could lift one finger and then she was able to reach out both shaking hands to him.

"Please?" Mellie said, "Oh—*please.*"

Hank smiled at her.

A voice cried out. Soon I knew it was my own, shouting for joy.

The light was back. The light was back in Hank's eyes.

The invisible light becoming visible in that room.

I do not ever hope to see it again. I do not need to, I saw it then and I knew where it came from.

None of us would ever be the same again.

We knew there was hope. We knew if we got to the moon we wouldn't put its light out. We'd heard the cry Choose ye! and we'd chosen love.

None of us would ever be the same again.

Hank was saying— "my marks and scars I carry with me to bear witness that I am fighting your fight, oh Christ who is risen—Steve—come now and fight it with me."

Mellie's fingers bit into my arms, there were marks and scars there the next morning and I followed her eyes and saw Steve Retzlaff on his knees as though slowly, slowly the great weight of the light had brought him there. On his knees, his head bowed, a great groan came from him—and then Hank walked, the way he always walked, to the couch.

What happened then I did not see for my eyes were blinded and I was on my knees.

Whether he spoke or not I cannot say. We all heard a different thing again. Each of us. This is the truth, believe it. I heard *Come forth,* and Mellie heard *Talitha Cumi* though she did not know what it meant, had never seen the words nor heard of them before. I had to show them to her the next day in the fifth chapter of Mark. Steve heard Jesus Christ have mercy on us Jesus Christ have mercy on us and Gloria heard nothing at all and Beany heard only music which he had never dreamed of before.

Into the still beyond anything we had known, the stillness of the first morning, in the still small voice of hope, Deedee said, "Where are you, love?" and held out her arms.

Tell no man.

Often he said that. The wisdom of the serpent. He advised it. Their eyes were opened to see what had always been there and straitly Jesus charged them saying See No Man Know It. Not always, though. Sometimes. If they see a cripple or a drunkard or a schizophreniac healed at the gate of a church on Broadway they will call it a fraud. If I, the Prince of Peace, came again in my glory they would name it a fake. We must work the works of him that sent us while it is yet day and when it has been done *it has been done,* sometimes it is wisdom to move quietly in that grace. Let them see if they have eyes to see. More and more will they be moved quietly into hope and faith which bear much fruit. Sometimes, he said speak the word to every creature, tell what things you have seen, how that the sick are healed, the dead are raised, the devils cast out, the winds and waves are still, sometimes he said even if they stone or crucify you, speak of the works, tell the good news.

Maybe from Tecumseh Oklahoma to Poland Springs Maine, from Minneapolis Minnesota to Tempe Arizona, from Albany Oregon to Key West Florida there are those who are doing the works, putting the power of the Risen Christ back into Christianity. They don't know which command fits these times. As things are today, they are afraid to bear witness. So they hide behind Tell No Man.

Sometimes he said that.
Tell No Man.
But I have.

Let us begin.